The Critics Hail Charles Ingrid's
PATTERNS OF CHAOS Novels:

D0612634

**Books by Charles Ingrid
in DAW Omnibus Editions**

THE PATTERNS OF CHAOS

THE SAND WARS

THE PATTERNS OF CHAOS

OF CHAOS

Volume Two

The Downfall Matrix

Soulfire

CHARLES INGRID

DAW BOOKS, INC.

DONALD A. WOLLHEIM, FOUNDER

375 Hudson Street, New York, NY 10014

ELIZABETH R. WOLLHEIM
SHEILA E. GILBERT
PUBLISHERS

www.dawbooks.com

First Paperback Printing, February 2002
1 2 3 4 5 6 7 8 9

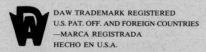

DAW TRADEMARK REGISTERED
U.S. PAT. OFF. AND FOREIGN COUNTRIES
—MARCA REGISTRADA
HECHO EN U.S.A.

PRINTED IN THE U.S.A.

Dedicated to Meyer Elkin,
with thanks for the years
of readership and support.

And to Maureen,
for reading over my shoulder and giving
encouragement on a daily basis.

The Downfall
Matrix

Chapter 1

The humankind was easy to spot amid the flow of Choyan. His smaller, clumsy body walked sticklike in the parade of flesh. His hair had a singular forelock instead of a lush mane intertwined upon a proud crown of horns. Even had he been on his home planet, the young man could never have achieved the agility of a Choyan. Wrought as he was, he had not the structure for it. The priest watched him keenly from the moment Rand caught his eye. Though, Chirek reflected, even if he had not caught sight of the humankind, he could hardly have missed Palaton striding along beside Rand. The *tezarian* arrogance that set him apart from the other Choyan came naturally, fueled by his skills as a pilot and his flawlessly melded strength and grace.

Tezars were the pride of the Choyan people. Without them, the stars could not be crossed safely, and the fabric of the race's existence would be woven far differently. They might all even be little more than meat scraps in some stew brewed by the always voracious Abdreliks. The great purplish amphibians traveled the stars hunting for fodder as much as for enlightenment. And then there were the quill-cloaked Ronin, much stealthier, no less predatory. Chirek signed himself in blessing against such enemies.

Without the *tezars,* the Choyan would live at the mercy of others. So the outlaw priest forgave Palaton if he moved in an aura of arrogance and ability. Without such as he, Cho could not exist in the firmament of stars and worlds as it did. With them, they were not fodder, but leaders, pilots for all space goers, and even the Abdreliks and Ronin reluctantly gave way.

Yes, the sheer presence of the emperor's heir would have

attracted Chirek's gaze, and then, his strange, alien shadow would have been noticed as well.

The other watcher stirred at Chirek's second elbow.

"Do you see him?" Chirek queried.

"I have him. It will be difficult to get to him."

"Your operatives must," the priest said, his dual voices vibrating with intensity. His own horn crown ached abominably with worry. Palaton and his alien companion had not been so open and unguarded since the abrupt beginning and end of the Two Day War. "We might not have this opportunity for a long time."

The Choyan at his side, a thickly bodied, yet short and scrawny-horned commons, one of the God-blind who had no talent of the sort the stately Palaton possessed, made a sound deep in his throat and then spat, wetly, upon the street.

The priest looked heatedly at his accomplice. "Why do you wait? We lose all opportunity if you hesitate—or doubt."

Sullenly, Miska answered, "No one wants to touch him. He's off-world."

The priest swore, words that nearly singed the air in their secret observation post. "He brings the Change, not the plague. Do you think he would be allowed to walk about freely if he carried disease?"

Miska glared back with narrowed eyes. "It is your hope, priest, not ours. Change was never prophesied from such as *that*. We were always catechized that it would come from within Cho. Not from an alien." With a drop of one shoulder, he put his mouth to the broadcaster and thumbed open a com line. "Move in." Bowing his brittle-horned head slightly to Chirek, the commons retreated and went to follow his operatives.

Chirek watched him evaporate smoothly into the crowds thronging the streets below. Even if he had wished to, it would have been nearly impossible to follow Miska's passage. The Choya was nothing if not competent at his art.

Although it should have, that thought did not engender the outlaw priest's confidence. Miska belonged to Qativar, and Qativar he did not trust. Qativar ranked high in Cho's only permitted religion, undersecretary to the aged and esteemed Rindalan. Yet he risked all to participate in Chirek's underground sect. He professed belief in the Bringer of Change and was fluent in what his fellow churchmen would have called heresy.

There was more about Qativar's duality which worried Chirek. The Choya had risen through the rankings far quicker than any could have predicted, to stand at Rindalan's right hand. Rindalan's near fatal beating at the hands of rioters seemed more than accidental to Chirek. What was the elder doing among rioters with no escort other than Qativar, and why had Qativar failed to protect him? Had he been led into a trap? And if so, what were Qativar's motives? Such an act surely had not been done to further Chirek's movement.

Chirek had no proof, no foundation for his suspicions, and Qativar was one of the mainstays of Chirek's movement, but an uneasy one. It was part of Qativar's value that he held a high post and could move almost at will, and that Rindalan had given him an extremely long leash, as well as much authority. But Chirek knew that Qativar hadn't been on a long leash that riotous night; he had been at Rindalan's elbow, and the elder one had fallen to an ignominious fate. He still lay in a coma, almost as if dead and in state, fighting for his life with every breath.

Chirek blinked. He found shadows in every corner, he thought to himself, and moved restlessly within his own post of concealment. But those with little or no *bahdur* talent in the world of Cho found themselves treated as second-class citizens by the ruling Houses and their House-holdings, and though his own fervent religious beliefs kept Chirek looking forward to a day when *bahdur* would flame among them all, he had learned to be circumspect. Only the Bringer could metamorphose the Choyan he served. He was not the first underground priest among the commons, and chances were that he would not be the last. But if he were, oh, if only he were. *That* he would give his life for.

In that regard, the high House-born Rindalan and the lowly street Chirek were not so different. Each had faith engraved deeply in his bones. Rindalan, unlike many High Priests of the various Houses, had always served the people. Perhaps there was the answer to Chirek's unasked question as to why Rindalan had walked among the rioters, trying to heal a rift which would ultimately bring their ene-

mies down upon them. For that commonality, instead of
their differences, Chirek mourned Rindalan's approaching
death.

A shout arose. The parade below moved with its own
deliberation, a victory march toward the war memorial constructed especially to commemorate the deadly quick Two
Day War. Still smarting from the riots, Choyan had been
ready to strike at Choyan, and the Abdreliks had dared to
attack, risking the very fiber of the space which contained
them all. The war had been so quick that most of them
scarcely knew it had happened, coming on the heels of the
weeks of civil unrest and rioting. Yet once the smoke had
cleared, all on Cho knew how close they had come to the
brink.

Hoping finally to conquer their enemy, the Abdreliks had
broken—no—shattered, the Compact which held all the
worlds to an uneasy truce. They had found renegade pilots
willing to bring in their warships, and they had come ready
to strike at the very heart of the Choyan empire, their
single planet, Cho. Yet the Compact had failed to punish
the aggressors while they returned to a shaky balance.

From the ashes of rebellion, Palaton had risen to drive
the Abdreliks back. He had struck when they were most
vulnerable, decelerating out of Chaos, still unsure of their
bearings, and if he had not turned them back then, the
Abdreliks would have been unstoppable. The massive, rapacious amphibians must have been drooling down their
tusks, contemplating war on Cho. Chirek shuddered at
the idea.

His people had thought themselves inviolate. Only the
Choyan *tezars* could efficiently pilot through Chaos, and
surely none of their own would bring warships in. Yet a
handful had, because of conflicting loyalties, and that
brought to mind other troubling problems. *How had they
known?* How had the Abdreliks known that at that very
moment Cho had threatened—and still seemed all too
likely—to come apart at its seams?

The priest watched the serpentine march draw close to
the memorial. If Rand were to be approached with impu-
nity at all, now was the time. He searched the crowds for
Miska and his operatives, gave up looking for them, and
searched instead for his own. His trust in Qativar being

incomplete, he had made other provisions. The girl was not hard to spot, her luxurious sable mane done up in ribbons of celebration. She wore a blue which fairly vibrated with intensity. She would be unmistakable, once viewed.

Which is why Dorea wore what she did. Having interacted with Rand, she had the ability to become as invisible, as dull and drab as any of the commons, disappearing into anonymity. Shed the ribbons, the robes, and she blended into the very dirt washed up along the curbs.

Chirek found himself leaning on the railing of the observation post, his muscles tightening into cords with tension. He made himself take a step back, reaching for sighting glasses. He forced a deep breath downward. It would happen, or not. It was ridiculous to hope for a metamorphosis which his brotherhood had waited centuries for, to hope it would happen here and now. And even if it did not happen, that would not mean that Rand was not the Being of Change which his religion had prophesied centuries ago. It meant only that the circumstances had been altered. It meant that whatever way the catalyst performed had not yet been found, stabilized, or understood. Perhaps it took more than a mere touch.

Chirek knew that it would be difficult to preach what hummed upon his lips, what fairly burst to come out of him, without the proof he sought to obtain that day. Even that proof would not be enough. He would have to find a way to draw Rand out himself, to coax him from behind Palaton's awesome and protective shadow, and show him what the humankind had no idea he could do. He would have to persuade Rand to move among them and work his miracles. And even then, there would be many who would not, could not, believe. The humankind was an alien, after all. Who could have imagined that an alien would fulfill the prophecies?

Yet there was a fervency upon the priest he could not contain. He needed no further proof for himself. Rand could do what Chirek suspected. He, himself, had been transformed by the presence and touch of the humankind.

It would be foolish for him to reveal himself now, but there were times when the newly found *bahdur* sang its way through his veins so loudly that he felt others must know as well. Chirek veiled himself for the moment, hoping that the time when he could give hope as well as succor and nurturing were near. Miska did not know, nor did Qativar. No one, not even Malahki, who did carry a faint thrilling of *bahdur* himself, knew or suspected what had happened within Chirek.

A bolt of blue drew near the knot in the procession. Then, like lightning, it struck.

Rand felt his muscles tighten as he attempted to keep up with Palaton. His braces off, bones newly regenerated, sinews rehabilitated through exercise, he still felt awkward as a toddler unused to walking. Palaton slowed and turned, looking down at him. "I am too quick," the Choya said, his voices rumbling with amusement.

"And I'm too slow." Rand could feel the breath in his chest, raw, as though he'd been running. He pushed his dark hair off his forehead. He needed a haircut, but had not found a barber who would do what he wished. The Choyan prized their luxurious manes. Men had lower foreheads and he preferred to be able to see out of his eyes.

Almost unconsciously, he scanned the crowd, feeling the electricity of their excitement as Palaton moved among them. His stolen *bahdur* rippled inside him. He shrugged away from it guiltily, the power which by rights had belonged to Palaton and would one day again be the pilot's, if only they could find a way to restore it. Rand had no right to it and scarcely knew how to use it, but it ran deep in him, like a river of unknown strength and wealth, and there were times when he could not ignore the tides of its movement.

Now was such a time. It made him achingly aware of the throngs which swelled forward to see them. He could feel the heat of their emotions, and underneath it, a peaking of hatred as well. That enmity was directed at him, alien, ugly, a plague-carrier, a weakling who depended upon his powers to trespass here, a stranger who did not belong here. The xenophobia branded his perceptions. Rand turned as if he could see it. He stumbled on a bit of uneven pavement. Palaton swept out an arm to catch him, steadying Rand. As he did so, the *bahdur* answered to him as well, thrilling into him, for Rand felt it go, like a flashflood into a dry riverbed, whose soil sucked it up eagerly even as it was threatened with destruction by a flow which it could not longer conduit.

Palaton gasped audibly as he felt the flood. He looked down, large amber eyes brilliant with the touch of his forbidden power. The touch lasted but a split second, and in that moment, Rand felt all that was courageous and bereft in his friend. His throat shut with the swell of passion and longing from the pilot for the heritage which had been stripped from him.

Rand's lips parted in involuntary apology, but the words never came. There was a shout. Then a scream. Footsteps pounded on the street. Choyan bodies swung in movement, and then Rand could feel the *bahdur* leaping in him, a flood tide. *Trouble.* He wrapped his hands around Palaton's arm, pulling him away from the rush of danger. A wall of three Choyan surged at them. He could not see if they carried weapons. There was no time to get Palaton clear.

Palaton had been alerted as well, his horned crown tilting toward the source of trouble, much as an elk stag would move to a challenge, but Rand's weight threw him off-balance. Rand could feel the other's body shift with his, abruptly. His mind swirled. All he could think of was to push free. The Choyan charging them stumbled to an abrupt halt, as if hitting a wall, and then rebounded, sprawling to the street. The three found themselves with Jorana and her security guards at their throats. The Choya'i snarled as she called for them to halt.

Rand staggered back into the hands of another Choya'i, her brilliant cerulean robes swirling about both of them, while Palaton fought to regain his balance.

"They're unarmed," Palaton snapped, annoyed at Rand's reaction and collecting himself. He shrugged away.

Bahdur still in flood tide, Rand found himself alone with the Choya'i. There was a bridging between him and her for a second, sparking through them. It shocked through him, leaping. Rand fought to retain his senses. As he gasped, the *bahdur* guttered away. His mind darkened for a moment as he lost it. And the Choya'i, barely as tall as he was, leaned forward, smiling, hazel eyes with more than just a tint of mellow green in their depths, murmuring her own apology for bumping him. She turned and left with a swirl of blue more vibrant than the Choyan sky, leaving Rand to stare after her.

Jorana stood over the prisoners. Palaton looked between her and Rand, seemed to realize that he had left Rand standing alone, and reached out for him. His nostrils flared. Rand knew instinctively that the pilot could smell the afterburn of the *bahdur* he'd just expended.

"I'm sorry," he began, but Palaton shut him off with a flick of his hand.

"Later. Are you all right?"

"Yes." He looked down at the prisoners who were being efficiently trussed by a handful of Jorana's guards. "No one shot."

"No," the *tezar* answered briefly, "they are Godblind. They haven't the *bahdur* to know where to strike most effectively."

Rand flexed his neck in an attempt to ease tight muscles. Vital organs were vital organs, he thought. He ought to explain that to Palaton some day. The most skilled assassins in the galaxies, the Ronin, did not rely on *bahdur* to tell them where to strike. These three did not have to, either.

Jorana snapped orders about where to take the detainees and counted off four of the guards to do so. Then she pivoted around, her eyes searching out both of them.

"Everyone still standing?" she asked. Her voices showed strain despite their lightness of tone.

"We're fine." Palaton waved his hand, dismissing the problem.

Her expression opened slightly with relief. "We're almost there," she said.

Palaton nodded. Rand could feel the connection between the two of them, the sense that ran much more deeply than the few words they shared, and acute loneliness nibbled at him. There was no one like him on all of Cho, nor was there likely to be. The only Choyan who collaborated outside their race did so in space, or on Compact worlds such as Sorrow. The Choyan who did not travel off-world were a narrow-minded xenophobic race.

Rand tried not to think of the implications of spending his life alone, bound to Palaton, unable to ever leave him.

After a few more moments of confusion, the procession began again.

Miska and his operatives had failed, but Chirek could not contain himself, for he'd seen the Choya'i move in swiftly, using the failure of the first three for an opening. Rand had literally stumbled into her arms. The contact between the two of them could not have been more powerful, under the circumstances. The priest's heart felt as though it drummed in his throat.

After the procession moved by, he climbed down awkwardly from the post, heading to the rendezvous he and the Choya'i had previously chosen. Head down, crown-throbbing now with joy instead of apprehension, he hurried to the bistro. Success was within his grasp, hope within all their grasps, *change* on the very eve of being.

He took his seat and ordered a pale, daffodil-colored wine, the best the house had to offer, and two glasses, and sat. The table and chairs overlooked the debris of the parade route. A breeze stirred the afternoon.

The dewy chill of the wine carafe had long evaporated when Chirek finally stood. He looked out over the streets as they began to fill again, the memorial rites finishing, Choyan going back to their daily routines. He did not know what to think. She either was not coming, or could not come.

The Choya'i had disappeared.

Chapter 2

Qativar watched the three Choyan being marched off. Wrapped in the robes of the office of High Prelate for the ceremonies, there was little he could do but wonder at their motives. He thought he had seen Miska among the throng before the attack, and the sighting was enough to pique his curiosity. He would give the invocation, then murmur that he ought to return to the infirm elder's side and leave. He knew Jorana would question the three as soon as she returned to the palace—and he knew that she would not return until the ceremonies had finished and her charges were safely on palace grounds again. If he hurried, he'd have time.

There was a glint off the war memorial he found disturbing. He squinted against the glare, then smoothed the lines on his face. Never must he appear bored or unhappy. Never must he broadcast his real intentions or feelings toward the throne. Never must he give any impression that he was other than he appeared to be, some religious hidebound fool, determined to live and die in the harness of servitude to the God-in-all.

He lifted his chin to watch the humankind being helped awkwardly onto the podium, his stride something more than a child's, but the step still a little tall for him. There was nothing in his stare, he knew, that would reveal the extreme distaste he felt upon looking at the creature. And, indeed, he told himself, he might find a use for the alien yet. Already it had had some effect on the love the commons had for the *tezar* Palaton. The innate xenophobia of the planetbound Choyan might be manipulated to an even greater advantage. Wheels within wheels, he thought, and turned to take his place as the ceremonies commenced. Returning to his earlier strategy, he made a graceful departure as soon as he could.

Once within the palace, he shed his robes in the temporary rooms assigned to him. Qativar did not take the time to sit and check his monitors. He did a quickscreen analysis and then went to the hidden inner corridors of the palace, corridors only the priests knew, though there were undoubtedly corridors only the emperor himself knew about and could use.

Smiling to himself, Qativar stepped into the narrow, dusty confines. Wouldn't Panshinea and the heir be confounded to find out that their own keep was not as safe and impenetrable as they hoped? To discover that their own priesthood had, through the centuries, wormholed its way throughout the stone walls. These secret ways could not be used without *bahdur* to screen the user, but what was a priest without *bahdur*? A real priest, not one of the sniffling conveyors of pap like Chirek and his brethren.

He found the corridor he needed, leading to the old subterranean holding cells. Once upon a time, the priesthood, to rein in the emperors, must have found it necessary to make this way downward. It was more than convenient to have it now. The stone moved reluctantly to let him into the cell area. Qativar looked up quickly, saw that he was beyond the monitoring system, and allowed himself a smile. He put a hand in his vest, found a vial there, and palmed it.

The three prisoners looked up as he entered, wary, commons, eyes wide and nostrils slightly flared as if they could see and smell the *bahdur* which fueled him. They withdrew behind the prison barrier, sullen, uncooperative.

Qativar let a pleasant expression flow over his face. "I'm here to help," he said. "Father Chirek sent me."

The one closest to him relaxed, dropped his hand, and approached, saying, "When are you getting us out of here?"

"Soon." He rolled the vial in his fingers. How much to use? How much would free their tongues—and how much would kill them? He was still working on that. Qativar made a decision. It mattered little one way or the other. "They have *bahdur*," he said. "You won't be able to stand against it. You know it."

They looked at him apprehensively. He flashed the vial in their faces. "I have something which will protect you. They will not be able to force you into betrayal."

The three looked among themselves, and then shrugged. "We'll take that chance."

"And destroy everything you've worked for? No. Don't let it come to that. Push the water canister here. Split it amongst you, three ways." Qativar waggled fingers at the carafe.

They seemed hesitant, until the youngest said, "I'll try it. I don't want them with their fingers in *my* brains." He wore a scarf defiantly woven in amongst the scallops of his horns. He toed the canister through the barrier.

It set off no alarms. Qativar emptied the vial into it, swished it around, and pushed it back. They drank, deeply, and he waited. The first two dropped, even as the third finished his portion. He stood, scared, as they toppled.

"What the—"

"Pay no attention. It's temporary. Look at me. Listen to me." Qativar approached the barrier, pressing its matrix as close as he dared without interrupting the beams. "Who hired you? And why?"

"I—" Confusion supplanted the defiant expression. The Choya put his hand up, childlike, entangling his fingers in his colorful scarf. "What did you say?"

Qativar fought to keep the impatience out of his voices. He was running out of time. Jorana, ever efficient Jorana, would be here soon. "Who hired you?"

"I . . . can't tell you. It wouldn't be. . . ." His thin voices trailed off. He looked at the floor, at his cellmates. "What's wrong with them?" He began to breathe roughly. "What's wrong with them!"

"They're dead, and so will you be unless you answer me."

The Choya looked at him, brown eyes the color of newly loamed earth wide and frightened. "I can't—" He choked. "I look for the Bringer of Change—" His knees buckled. He began to topple like an old felled tree, instead of the green young sapling he was, and writhed to death on the floor of the cell, still mouthing prophecies of the underground sect.

Qativar made a tsking noise through his teeth. He turned away and found the passageway, squeezing into its narrow tunnel once more. He thought he heard the grind of machinery as the lift brought someone down to the level, and the emergence of bootsteps upon the flooring as he disappeared.

Unsettled, Palaton could not relax. Without his natural powers, he'd felt naked under attack. More than naked, and it did not help that he'd felt Rand react in their defense.

"What happened out there?" He roamed the study, the room small and secured, encased within the massive Choyan palace which had become their stronghold.

Rand felt drained. He could not stand, but he did not want to sit and look up at the much taller alien, so he leaned a hip on a marble sculpture in the corner. Its coolness insinuated itself through the fabric of his clothes. Rand shook his head. "I don't know."

Palaton swung toward him, anger washing over his features. "How could you not know? I felt it," and he thumped his chest, "and I feel nothing anymore, I'm like stone in here."

"It's like adrenaline," Rand told him. "You were threatened, I reacted."

"And spilled *bahdur* like water," the pilot threw back at him, his dual voices rich with accusation. "Anyone out there might have felt it."

It was not that the Choyan were not used to feeling *bahdur* in its many paranormal forms, for they were gifted with it, they valued it—but Rand knew what Palaton feared was that they would realize it had come from Rand, and not from himself. If his fellows knew that he was barren of the powers which had made him not only a *tezar*, but a great one, and the heir to the throne, he would be stripped of everything at a time when Cho could little afford to be without leadership. He kept Rand with him, because the young man could not help but project the aura of the *bahdur* and anyone who knew Palaton knew the flavor of his abilities. The assumption that it came from the pilot would naturally follow.

Rand spread his hands. "It uses me. I had no way of channeling the flow—you felt the strength of it. For a moment there, I thought you were taking it back, that we'd accomplished a transfer."

The Choya looked at him levelly. "So did I," he said. He cleared his throat. "But we didn't, and so what remains for me is to find a way to train you to use what you have. I can't afford any more incidents." Palaton leaned on a chair back, his strong fingers gripping the carved wood.

Gathon rapped on the doors and leaned in. "Your private appointment is here."

Palaton drew himself up. "Ah. Send her in."

Gathon hesitated, looking at Rand, but the pilot added, "He can stay."

The minister nodded gravely and bowed out. He moved with the stiff grace of the aged. His presence had scarcely left the doorway when Vihtirne of Sky swept in, her handsome young aide close behind. Both were typical of Skies, flashy, dark hair, luxurious manes which hung nearly, to their waists, although Asten had his topknot shaved, to give him a stand-up fringe of thick, bushy hair. She had black eyes, his smoldered dark brown, and both wore deep, rich blue clothes which accentuated their coloring. Rand could not judge Choyan age. He knew they lived nearly a hundred and eighty years, but he did guess that Vihtirne, although still in her prime, had edged into middle age. She did not have Jorana's sharp-edged prettiness.

She shot Rand a look of keen disapproval. "I was led to believe this was private business," she said, taking the chair Asten held out to her. He took up a stance behind her, frowning slightly. She spoke Trade out of a desire to humiliate Rand, he thought.

"It is." Palaton answered smoothly in Trade, and now the conversation would be continued in that, but it wasn't necessary. With *bahdur,* Rand understood Choyan although he couldn't read much of it.

"You sent for me," Vihtirne said, her tone implying that she came because she wanted to, not because he exerted any undue force.

"It's been brought to the attention of the throne that your House has been quietly going through the courts, attempting to take back your water recyling patent."

"The House developed it. We have a right to earnings from the procedure. It was stolen from an incompetent old fool—"

"It was given over to public domain." Palaton twisted slightly to pick up a paper from his desk. "There isn't a county that doesn't depend on your system. Although the courts have been unable to stop your petitioning, the throne can. I've been instructed to tell you, Vihtirne, that the patent will not be recovered by your House. It stays as it is, for the common good."

Her delicate, translucent skin, accented by the implanted jewelry many Choyan favored, flushed heavily. "You have no right."

"Emperor Panshinea has every right. I'm merely enacting his wishes. As for your other petition," and Palaton looked down at the paper in his hand. "Colonization is rejected out of hand."

Vihtirne kicked herself out of her chair. "You won't be in the seat of the heir long, Palaton. You or Panshinea."

"I take it the spirit of conciliation offered from the House of Sky after the Two Day War was either false or has worn thin."

"You can take it that as soon as Nedar returns, you will have a rival for the throne."

That clearly took Palaton aback, as it did Rand Vihtirne could not help but notice it. "Oh, yes," she gloated. "He didn't die on Arizar. He returned to Cho, to me, to heal. I know that colonization can succeed off-world, and I know that our Houses need those opportunities. So deny them now if you wish. There will come a future when you can't. Nedar is in the ascendant. And when he has the evidence he needs of your treachery on Arizar, there won't be any Choyan, not even the Godless, who support you." With that, she wheeled in a flourish of blue silk and left, Asten following in her wake.

Palaton's face closed as though he attempted to settle himself.

Rand said, "If she knows about Arizar, Nedar *must* still be alive."

"He has to be. But where is he now? Who hides him? If Vihtirne still had him, she'd have brought him here herself." Palaton looked at him. "I should rejoice that a fellow *tezar* returns, but I can't find it in me."

"If there was ever bad *bahdur,* he has it."

"The power is pure. It's the user," Palaton murmured.

Rand contemplated the near slavery condition of the

many born without power, and what the threat of losing it altogether might mean. "There can't be many Choyan who misuse their *bahdur*."

Palaton's gaze faltered. He looked away. "No," he answered briefly. "They aren't given a chance to. A child who can't be trained is terminated. But there are temptations later."

Palaton pushed away from the chair he'd been leaning on. "We love our families. It's a difficult thing to face. None of us conceive our children lightly. The legacy of *bahdur,* the soulfire, is not an easy burden."

"I know," Rand commented. He closed an eye and massaged it gently. "You have a monopoly."

"One that gives us power, and one which my people are no longer certain they want to bear. Or can continue to bear, even if they desire to."

"What happens," Rand asked, "when there are no more *tezars*?"

"I hope to God," Palaton answered slowly, "it never comes to that." He changed his tone. "If Nedar intends to challenge me, you had better learn to deal with the burden as well." He got up briskly and went to the comset panel.

"What are you doing?"

"The best way for you to learn is the way I did—baptism by fire."

Hathord of Blue Ridge settled into his late afternoon routine uneasily. His waist had thickened a bit more than he was used to, coming out of a hard winter. The summer heat hadn't yet melted it away, and he made a mental note to join the cadets in their fitness runs. He realized that the other instructors as well as *tezars* and cadets looked up to him, that he had passed a milestone and become a fixture, young as he'd been when he'd first accepted the post. He had worked hard to maintain Blue Ridge's reputation and he was proud of it.

But there were other, personal concerns on his mind. He stood to lose it all if the authorities came to question him about the stolen fighter which had shot down the imperial transport. He should never have given the plane to Nedar, and he didn't know for certain that was what Nedar had intended—but it had been weeks now with no word. Commonly accepted as the first strike of the Two Day War, Hat thought privately it had been Nedar's own personal blow at Palaton. It seemed inevitable it would be traced back to him as well.

Nedar had tried to convince him that the only Houses which ought to exist on Cho were those of the pilots. They were the strength upon which all else leaned, the bond which kept their civilization alive. To forsake the House which had given his genetic heritage, to cleave to a new brotherhood, to attempt what the outlaw colonies on Arizar had tired—Hat had been left chewing on that. Now Nedar had not returned and he wondered even more if the pilot had been found by his enemies and destroyed.

He could not believe that of Palaton. He'd been through Blue Ridge with both of them, he knew the stuff they were made of. Arrogant and powerful, Nedar had always been alone except for Hat's friendship. Palaton had been quiet at first, before growing into strength, maturity, and leadership which he did not always feel comfortable with. Nedar gloried in conflict and adulation. Palaton—well, who knew what Palaton thought now. He was the heir to the emperor, and breathing that rarified air might have done what all the years of piloting had never done.

Hathord had hidden Nedar. He had given him the weapon which had struck the first blow. How long would it take for someone to divine that the fighter had not been stolen as reported. What could he do to save himself and Blue Ridge?

As if his thoughts had materialized the Choya, the view screen lit up with an incoming call and he found himself looking at Palaton.

"Hat! It's good that I've got you on the first call. I thought you might be out at the plateau."

He found a funny feeling inside his chest which almost prevented him from answering. He bowed awkwardly from his chair, saying, "Heir Palaton."

"Don't give me that." The other eyed him sternly through the monitor. "You were there at my first crash."

"Aye," agreed Hathord. "And you were at mine." He relaxed a little then, at the thought. Raw, eager recruits, dying to fly. Some of them *had* died flying. Had Palaton called to soften the blow? How much was he forfeit?

"I need a favor," said Palaton.

A favor for a lifetime of service? Hat sat silently. Was Palaton asking for confession, so that whatever might transpire would be easier for both of them? He shifted, thinking, unable to decide what to do. Finally, he repeated, "A favor?"

"Yes. I need something from you that only Blue Ridge can give me."

The truth, Hat thought furiously. He wanted the truth. He sat frozen before the view screen, afraid to look it full in the face, afraid that Palaton would read his mind even across the transmission. Stars were notorious for that. "What do you want me to do?" he asked, his voice barely audible.

"Bundle up my old flight suits and helmets and send them out. Throw in that old depo helmet, too."

"The deprivation helmet?" Hat repeated, with a surprised stutter. What possible use would Palaton have for his old gear? He did not pilot now in his role as heir.

"I'm getting rusty, Hat. I need to get back to basics, just like the old days, you, me, and Nedar."

Hat found himself blinking rapidly. "All . . . all right. As soon as I can get to them."

"Good. And Jorana sends word that as soon as the crash investigation is concluded, you'll be copied in. I understand the fighter was from Blue Ridge."

"Yes. But all my cadets are accounted for."

"It could have been anyone who'd washed out," the other countered. Palaton's warmth faded slightly. "The Two Day War took a high toll," he said. "Too high."

War usually did. Hathord agreed with his old friend. The screen went dark. He sat in stunned silence. He should have felt relieved, but he did not.

Perhaps Nedar was right. If so, Palaton had become devious beyond Hat's understanding. Fear crystallized in his chest, like a snowflake gathering others until it balled into a chunk of ice, and he could not breathe. All he wanted to do was teach. What would they leave him with when they were done with him?

Hat pushed away from his console. His chin dropped to his chest and he let out a sob of fear and worry.

Palaton watched the dead screen. He let out a sigh, then looked at Rand. "He knows nothing, thank the God-in-all. Hat could never tell a lie. But this means we'll have to watch our backs. Wherever Nedar is, he's nursing a long-time hatred, and now he has the strength of his House behind him."

Chapter 3

It was good to view the bubbling mud ponds and brooks of home again, even if it was only a view, and the hot, musky odor could not be drunk down or the soothing mud slathered over one's body, GNask thought. The sight alone was almost the balm he needed. It had been long since he'd visited home, and even though he looked at it now because of the president's summons, it was pleasurable.

He watched the president enter. Frnark called himself by this title because of the Compact. It behooved him to do so, but no Abdrelik would ever make the mistake of assuming his rule was a democracy. His bulk was as magnificent as ever, lean and fighting trim, and his color was good. His battle scars crisscrossed him, scars few but GNask and the president Frnark had battled to replace had ever seen. Though he was aging, the Abdrelik did not show it except in the yellowing of his tusks. The *tursh* of his line rode his shoulder. If any weakness existed, it was there it could be seen. The sluglike symbiont looked shriveled and it kept its pseudopod antenna closed in, hugging the warmth of its partner's skin.

GNask did not let his gaze linger, knowing the president's sharp eyesight would catch his every movement and expression. He might someday inherit the president's beautiful mud garden, along with the power and politics of the position, but he was in no hurry. He intended to be fit and the only candidate, and Frnark to be clearly on the wane, before engaging in the battle of succession.

The president settled himself in a clear spring, the water surging about his body in bubbling agitation. When he looked into the screen, his eyes were dark. GNask concealed the shiver which ran down his spine. The feeling of homesickness fled, pushed aside by a healthy dose of fear for this one who ruled.

"You were hasty, GNask."

He bunched his muscles to avoid moving restlessly. Reprimanded, again. He thought this topic was done. The Two Day War had been an opportunity which he had seized. For that he had been both praised and reviled in the same breath by his ruler. That was past. Why dwell on it? Unless, of course, Frnark had learned of the two prisoners he held as spoils of that war, the human girl and the *tezar*. It had been three scant weeks. The *tezar* was now close to breaking, and the girl, while his, had to be reminded that she had always been his. The days had gone by slowly and leisurely. Almost enjoyably.

But if Frnark knew— He got his answer in the president's next statement.

"We have been asked to strip your line of its *turshes*."

GNask's gut went cold. It felt as though he had swallowed a chunk of ice that stabbed, where it lay resting. An Abdrelik was nothing without his *tursh*, introduced at nesting, carried throughout his life except for military personnel, who often went a year or so without their symbiont. It did not matter with the military, where aggressiveness was encouraged.

But an Abdrelik without his *tursh* was a mindless carnivore. No destiny, no thought, no glory.

He felt nausea rising in his cavernous throat. Yet the trap which he thought had caught him might not be the one which had been sprung. He would not incriminate himself.

"Excellency?"

The president lay a thick arm on the mineral spring surface, played his fingers through the water. "I refused, of course. But," and he looked up at GNask again, his gaze piercing even through the transmission screens. "You are warned. Do you understand?"

Did he really? GNask thought of all the implications of the president bringing this to his attention. A serious warning, then, balanced by a vote of confidence in the refusal and then . . . what?

Encouragement to continue to play it on the edge, regardless of the consequences? Pleasure in his protege's boldness? What could he read into this conference, a personal warning?

The president looked impatient. GNask bowed his head. "I do, Your Excellency. And I think you for your wisdom."

"As you should." Thick yet supple and powerful fingers rippled through the water again. "I have word that we may be successful in tracking the Choyan who fled Arizar. Your information could yet be invaluable." He sucked his tusks. "You failed there as well, yet there is always success in your failures. Choyan living beyond the reach of Panshinea, renegade, can be very useful to us. I may ask you to take action again, action which may not be viewed well in the eyes of our fellows, but which will prove both necessary and fruitful."

His ass was on the line, GNask thought, and the Nest preserve him if he refused or failed again. The president had him by the throat, and both knew it. He inclined his head. "Ask, and I will serve," he answered.

He had no choice, but it did not matter. To be asked to hunt Choyan was his pleasure. He thrived on it. He would not have refused if the choice had been given.

Earthlab XVI chugged through deep space in a steady flight, sheltering behind planets of little or no interest to any of the multitude of alien races which made up the Compact. Its occupants worked without interruption, eating, sleeping to a schedule of their own making, beyond the laws of man and nature. As the freighter engines droned, corridors dark in downtime, a researcher looked at his screens again, at the spikes of chemical profile, and then at his hard copies, and his lips tightened with satisfaction. Brushing a hand through some of the most advanced lab equipment available, he put in a call to his client.

The visage which answered the private line had a handsome face in spite of its nearly five decades, the dark hair receding, the eyes still fresh and measuring. Maren felt pride that he'd done a good job for this man, who'd certainly done what he could for Earth. The client had even sacrificed his own daughter, though it was Dr. Maren's job to make it possible to retrieve her.

"Ambassador," said Dr. Maren. "We've got positive results."

John Taylor Thomas showed no sign of emotion at all for a few heartbeats. Then the import of the message grew in his expression. "What?" he asked, his voice shaking.

"We've got positive results. The blood samples are coming back clean. There is some risk, because there is no way for me to test with a live subject, but I've got a drug here which will wipe out any imprinting the Abdreliks have done to your daughter. Now all we have to do is get her back."

"My God." The monitor camera tilted wildly as Thomas collapsed into a chair. "Are you certain?"

"Yes. There's no doubt about it. I may have to vary the dosage, but we can handle that." Maren felt himself grinning. "John, we've done it!"

"No," the ambassador denied wearily. "You've done it. How long can you wait?"

"The antidote is stable. I don't know what the shelf life will be, for certain, but I would guess years if we have to." Maren's grin faded, to be replaced by a frown. "Will it be that hard for you to get her back?"

Thomas looked away from the monitor, thinking. "The Abdreliks," he said, "don't give back anything they've ever taken. Impossible may be a better word for it."

Chapter 4

Inside the massive arched chamber of the Charolon gallery, Rand felt quite alone. He waited, suited, his head masked against sight and sound, uncomfortable inside the padded sensory deprivation helmet. Made to fit the munificent skull of a Choyan, the helmet had been badly remade to match his. The lack of a dual brain pan and of the thick, scalloping horns which adorned most Choyans made the adaptation difficult. Inside the helmet, he could smell the sweat of the others who'd worn the instrument, thick, spicy, musky, totally alien to him. He wondered whether if Palaton were to don the helmet, the smell would be as sharp and clear to him. The scent lingered pungently, worn into the leather over the years, the brow and scalp sweat of hopeful pilots. And perhaps more than a touch of fear was in the chemistry as well.

He could imagine the distress of those blinded, muted and deafened inside the gear. And to be taught to fly this way . . . his heart did a quick-step beat. To be launched in a thrust glider, to search out winds and thermals by *bahdur*, to live or die by that ability, the very thought dried the inside of his mouth to cotton. At least here, he knew what he had to face. Palaton had set him down in a closed, quiet room of the palace, placed three elegantly sculptured candles around the room, and then given him the helmet and told him to put it on.

The tiny speaker inside the helmet activated with a buzz. "Find the candles I've lit," Palaton said gently. His voices blended so that it was difficult for Rand to discern one pitch from the other. "Show me where and tell me how many."

Sitting in bleak isolation, how could he know? But he knew what Palaton wanted him to do: channel the *bahdur* and read the heat and the very essence of the flaming candles.

Rand sat. The helmet strap under his chin dug into his skin. He thought of a hooded hawk, and found it difficult to breathe. He sucked in a lungful. The acrid smell of smoke bit at him. He could tell that much, he thought. Something had been lit somewhere. But where? Frustration began to knot in his chest. The *bahdur* lay coiled inside him, stubbornly unavailable. Its ribbon of energy, like a river of brilliance, ran elsewhere, out of reach of both his mind and his physical body. Yet Palaton had told him that, in a Choya, intuition was either reliable or it did not exist at all. It might manifest itself in different ways, according to its scope, or the House which had passed the talent down, but it was always there. Always tappable. Always within a single thought. Always, for a pilot, until the day that neuropathy began, the disease that haunted the *tezars* of Cho, cutting short their careers as well as their *bahdur*. It raged through their very nerve fibers, shredding them, numbing them into nerve death after years of incredible pain, leaving them shorn of that which had always been theirs. And more than their health, the neuropathy took away their ability to pilot the stars. No *tezar* escaped this ultimate fate. Upon Cho, fewer and fewer Choyan with the talent to become pilots could be found, and fewer and fewer Choyan could brave the disease long enough to have the fruitful careers needed to offset their dwindling numbers. It was a vicious and secret circle which Rand had come to learn about by accident, and which the Choyan might have to go to war to keep the other races of the Compact from learning.

Palaton had been suffering from the onslaught of that disease when he had bonded with Rand, for a renegade faction of Choyan colonized on Arizar had discovered that the powers could be lent out, for a short period of time, and when given to a humankind, renewed, rejuvenated, cleansed of the pathology of the disease.

Choyan did not colonize. The differences between one world and the next, no matter how subtle, affected their genetic makeup. It made their talents erratic and subject to mutations which they could not control and would not accept. Cho was a closed society and meant to stay that way, balanced upon a double-edged sword of stagnation and careful resource management. Their world suffered from their continued occupation of it, and so did they, but they had decided centuries ago that they had no other choice.

The House of Flame had taught them that. Among the very first Householdings in the almost forgotten history of their past, its sons and daughters all had *bahdur,* but not all understood or could control what they had. Healing talents, for example, were a knife edge away from the ability to murder. And worse, within the House of Flame, there were Choyan who could seize possession of unprotected minds and exercise influence far beyond the touch of *bahdur.* This was an abomination the other Houses could not endure, and they had fallen upon the Flames and destroyed them.

Palaton told him that the remaining Houses of Star, Sky, and Earth then obliterated the Flames from their history and their people. But a few had remained, in hiding, and eventually, he supposed, it was they who'd fled the planet and gone to Arizar. How they had discovered the ability of bonding humankind to Choyan, Rand and Palaton had never discovered, but they had lost no time in siphoning off frantic pilots. Using their rejuvenated talents and loyalty, the displaced renegades concentrated on building a society of their own. Rand had been drawn from Earth, hoping to win favors for his family and his planet, viewed as a citizen from a backwater world. The recruiting done secretly, his family hadn't known they were dealing with outlaws who never intended to fulfill their promises of aid and influence. As for himself, he'd never had any choice. The stars had been offered. He'd had to follow.

Palaton had been coaxed to the experiment, unaware of the association and the implications. They had begun their bonding in desperation, and then lost all, and nearly each other, when the renegades fled or were driven away, taking their secrets with them. Arizar's Choyan colony was annihilated, first by the enemy, then by the surviving Choyan who wanted to leave no traces. They fled, and Rand and Palaton were abandoned.

Now he had the power which Palaton so desperately needed to rule Cho and to fly again, and he had no way of giving it back or of taming it himself. Not that he wanted to give it back if it made a pilot out of him as well, but never did he wish to deprive Palaton.

It became patently clear to him that, if he could not "view" three candlesticks, he could never sense the patterns among Chaos that were necessary to piloting.

He could sense Palaton's growing impatience, if nothing else. But even without visibly seeing the Choya, the bond between them, the power which had passed from one to the other, linked them together. Sometimes that linkage could be incredibly strong. Other times, as quiet and normal and unobtrusive as taking a breath. Still other times, not detectable unless reached for. Rand could sense Palaton's emotion now, brusque, curt, *impatient,* mirroring his own frustration.

How could anybody learn to pilot in one of these helmets!

Feeling balky, Rand got to his feet. At least, on his feet, he could think. "I can't feel anything," he said. The helmet muffled his words, but he knew Palaton would hear, because the Choya had, if nothing else, an extremely keen sense of hearing. The horned crown acted as an auditory sounding board and more than offset the lack of ears.

"Try. Think of it as listening. Listen with your mind for the heat, the burning, the whisper of the candle as it consumes the air about it."

It was dark inside the helmet, so dark that all he could see was his own spidery web of veins inside his eyelids, a tracery against the velvet. He kept his eyes open, blinking, as though he would be given sight by the *bahdur* at any moment. He had utilized it that way not long ago, before its usage during the Two Day War had burned out the optical nerve blocking drugs in his system, given him by the same Choyan who had given him Palaton's power. A humankind with *bahdur,* they'd taught, would go berserk unless his senses were damped down by medications. The initial dosage had all but blinded him, yet the *bahdur,* unasked for, had restored a kind of overvision to him. Then, when the Abdreliks had attacked and he had had to pilot for Palaton, the *bahdur* had burned out the last of the medications. He hadn't even noticed it at the time.

So he was living proof that holding the Choyan power did not necessarily make one insane, although if Palaton kept designing little tests like this one for him, it might.

Rand took a step, knocked his kneecap sharply against the edge of a table, and halted in sudden pain. The injury flared, like a Roman candle firework, growing more and more intense until—Rand jabbed his hand out. "There," he said. "There's one."

The heat of the flame grazed the underside of his palm as he pointed.

"Yes," answered Palaton dryly. "Although I'm not sure how we can qualify that one. You're supposed to find it with *bahdur,* not an awkward position of your anatomy."

"It doesn't matter," Rand said forcefully, for now he was into it, this alien game of Blindman's Bluff, and his senses were telling him, hot, hotter, no, colder, no, there, and there, and—it reared in front of him, crimson against the obsidian curtain of the helmet and he paused confidently. "There's the second one."

"And the third?" asked Palaton, the frost in his voices clear even over the primitive speaker in the helmet.

Rand swiveled on heel. He cast about. Coolness met him. "Only two," he declared. He put his hands up and jerked the helmet off.

Two candles burning in the room met his eyes.

Palaton lounged against the massive wooden panel doors at the far end of the room, the comset in his hands.

"I can do it."

An eyebrow raised elegantly on the Choya's strong face. "The veriest child among us could do that, unless he were as God-blind as a stone." He straightened and set down two more candlesticks.

"Sit down," he commanded. "And do it again."

Qativar sat and tried to maintain an air of passivity and resignation as he watched the rise and fall of the elder Choya's chest beneath · thin, white sheets. The room hummed with monitors and smelled of the disinfectant used for a sickbed confinement. He shifted, lifting his chin from time to time, as though his collar rankled at his neck. He did not wear the robes of his office of Prelate, uncomfortable in them more for their lack of style than for any imagined hypocrisy. The sole badge of his office was the collar-stole fastened around his neck and on his shoulders, and even that was abbreviated to what Rindalan would normally have been wearing. But Rindy was lying there in a coma, unreachable by friend and foe alike.

Old fool, Qativar thought, and tried not to show his thoughts through a tightening of the cords in his throat or a twitching in his jaw. *Either die or give up. You harm me greatly by lingering.*

Or perhaps Rindalan knew exactly what he did by lingering, Qativar added to himself. Such perversity was the hallmark of the High Prelate of the House of Star, counselor as well as minister to the emperor himself, Panshinea. Old, shrewd, and powerful, Rindalan alive had circumvented many of Qativar's ambitions. In his current state, he still did the Choya no good. *Die, old fool, die!*

Qativar sat back in his chair, eyeing the monitors. The activity in this wing of the palace was limited, muted, all attention directed toward any fluctuation in Rindalan's condition. If only he could have the comatose priest removed to a hospital where the everyday hustle and bustle might hide a great many developments. Yes, within the hospital routine, a number of things could go very wrong, almost without notice, until it was too late.

He would use the *ruhl* again if he could, transformed by his experiments into a chemical weapon the like of which his world had never seen or suspected. Used by the Choyan only in small doses as an aphrodisiac, highly toxic, he had diluted and altered it, combining it with another drug, until he had what he desired, a drug which would be a great equalizer, blocking psychic powers in all Choyan, and only he could provide an antidote which would restore it.

But traces of *ruhl* would show in the extensive monitoring now being performed, and he dared not apply it again. He would risk no link between the prisoners downstairs and a death here. If Rindalan were up and about, his body would burn through it quickly, but his comatose state would let telltale traces remain. Now Qativar had no choice but to sit patiently, biding his time, giving the public impression of support and grieving while privately he seethed over the disadvantage of Rindalan's injuries. Despite the image of loyalty he knew he projected, he would not be there at all, except that he had hopes Rindalan might speak again, rave, lost in the fever of his injuries, and either confirm or loose more secrets.

It had been days and days since that first, fevered moment when Rindalan had tried to rally, had mistaken him for Palaton, pulled him down close and whispered the secret of the heir's heritage. Had Rindy known what he'd known, or had he feverishly dreamed it? Dare Qativar act on the ravings of a dying old Choya? And, for that matter, dare he not?

Qativar licked lips growing dry. He got up, strode to the waiting table by Rindalan's bedside, poured himself a glass of water and drank, all the while watching the patient. Beneath the pristine white sheets, his body was tubed and wired, healing mixtures flowing in, mending fixtures in a framework of steadiness. But Rindalan showed no awareness of his position. He did not shift when the bed was rotated on its gyro-base, to avoid bed sores and blood clots and other dangers. He showed no sign of waking from the great unconsciousness into which he'd sunk.

But neither did he seem to weaken further.

Qativar let the empty glass drop down to the waiting table. Did he relive his days? Journey back to the moment when he had tested a young child for his *bahdur,* discover the Flame in his veins, and agreed to both nurture that child and hide his heritage? Did Rindalan even now look upon young Palaton, of the Householding of Volan, son of Tresa, the father fortunately unknown and deceased? Many had thought privately that Volan had gotten a son off his own daughter, in an attempt to preserve the somewhat dwindling powers of his Household. They had never questioned that Tresa might have crossed the line, besmirched her genetic heritage, an act nearly unknown now among the Households. They could not afford to water down their powers by consorting with the God-blind, no matter how lust pulled at them.

Or had Rindalan merely imagined such scandal in his damaged brain?

Qativar looked down, and then laid gentle fingers on the comatose Prelate's shoulder. The *bahdur* for which Rindalan was so famous lay pooled, smoldering, banked, a reservoir of almost unheard of strength. Only *tezars* such as Palaton or the lost Nedar, Palaton's schoolmate rival, or the emperor himself, erratic as his own *bahdur* had become, could match the power of Rindalan.

Yet what did the old fool use it for except to seek God and improve the sight of those who had lesser abilities than his own?

Qativar swallowed down the bile rising in his throat in protest against such a waste of ability. He snatched his hand back. Rindalan would not rouse in time, if ever, and the window of opportunity for Qativar to act upon the knowledge given him would pass. If indeed, it were not already too late, considering the approval Palaton currently held as heir-designate to the throne of Cho. He would have to strike now. Panshinea would destroy himself, but Qativar could not say the same for the heir. That, he would have to engineer.

Qativar forced a soothing smile, said a blessing over his Prelate's still form, and left the apartments. A nurse watched him go, nothing but mild curiosity in his eyes, and noted the time, though the automatic monitors in Rindalan's makeshift hospital room would have done the same. He went back to charting the quantitative analysis of his patient's latest blood work.

A large, boned hand crept out from under the sheets, tugged on them fretfully, and then stilled, as though a creature of independent will, into a tangled nest of the sheet corners bunched on Rindy's chest. Rindy moved his head from side to side. "Palaton?" he whispered. His eyelids fluttered as if the coma which claimed him might be shattered as he roused. But then the moment calmed, and the old Choya relaxed back into his pillow.

"Qativar," said Jorana, as she paced the security offices of the palace, "sits vigil by Rindalan's side, and I can prove nothing, but I *know* he led Rindy into the riots and disaster."

Gathon listened with his head tilted, one hand propping him up, as though his horns had grown too heavy for him, as indeed the office he occupied within the palace might have. In his emperor's absence, he effectively ran the government of Cho, though Palaton's role had become more and more influential. He had found the heir competent and integral to the Choyan future, and he did not look forward to Panshinea's return from the Halls of the Compact, though he knew it was inevitable. Involved in his own problems with succession, he had not thought particularly of Rindalan's. The High Prelate had not slowed down or become infirm, although he did have a mild heart arrhythmia which necessitated medication on a regular basis. But now, with Rindy on his deathbed, the affairs of the ministry for the House stared Gathon in the face. He did not share Jorana's dislike for Qativar.

"Jorana," he said mildly, as her pacing ceased for a moment. "Has it occurred to you that this fixation upon Qativar might be an unconscious diversion from what really bothers you?"

The head of security looked at him. She was still beautiful, if not the entirely fresh and young Choya'i he remembered her as when she'd first joined the palace guard. Her horn crown was thick and flared, not shaved as fashion currently decreed among the aristocratic set. Her masses of bronze hair were clipped back by gold and silver pins matching the faint imprinted tracings of jewelry on her face. She was the first generation of her line to be Housed, having shown enough *bahdur* in her testing to be brought in and adopted from among the God-blind. Like many in a similar situation, she worked hard, overachieved, and had a remarkably thin skin about her abilities. She did not want to go back, he knew. Never back.

She had been passionate over Palaton before the young pilot had been exiled after angering Panshinea, and since his return, had stood in the shadows, waiting, watching, hoping for more, Gathon thought, than an occasional sexual alliance. The discomfiting bond between Palaton and the humankind kept her apart from him, yet another abyss she would have to find a way to cross and had not.

She put her fingers into her mane and ruffled it vigorously. "And what, Gathon, would you do?"

"You're wasting energy trying to prove a crime might exist where evidence shows that Rindalan went willingly, no, even led Qativar, into the riots. He thought he could help, but they pulled him down. We simply cannot prove anything beyond what Qativar and other witnesses have told us, and our security monitors recorded. Let it go, Jorana."

Her expression soured slightly. "Or is that Panshinea speaking?"

Gathon lifted his chin from his handrest and straightened. "It is true I spoke to the emperor this morning. But while he governs our planet, he does not rule my mind. You asked what I would do. I told you."

The corner of her mouth quirked. "Temper thinning, Gathon?"

"Like my hair, yes. I don't like Rindalan lying incapacitated any more than you do, and worse—" he glanced upward, as though he could see upstairs to where the high priest lay, "—the longer he stays that way, the more I fear he will never recover."

"Rindy is no quitter."

"Which only proves to me that if his body dies, I shall doubtless be haunted by his tough old spirit as long as I live." Gathon sighed gustily. "And what about you, Jorana. Are you a quitter?"

Her eyes softened. "I cannot tame Palaton. He will either look at me one day and see what I offer, or—or he will always be blind."

"The humankind does not help."

"No. Palaton takes his guardianship of Rand very seriously, yet he does not suggest that we Choyan extend our patronage to all of Earth. I can't pretend to understand the bond between them. If, as the Abdreliks suggest, there has been Choyan contact with Earth beyond the perimeters of Compact edicts, the boy would be better off at Sorrow, giving testimony." Jorana shrugged. "Perhaps Palaton is correct. The fewer who know Choyan business, the better. The Abdreliks need little excuse to renegotiate representation in the Compact. Yet I cannot help but feel that Rand is in far greater danger here than he would be in the midst of that galactic stewpot. Witness the three we have cooling their heels right now. Although I can't prove an assassination attempt." With an uneasy toss of her head, she began to pace again. "Our three prisoners committed suicide two days ago."

"What? Why was I not informed?"

Jorana bit her lip, not slowing in her pace. "Palaton doesn't even know yet. I've been waiting for the autopsies and toxicological results. Nothing shows. I don't even know *how* they did it, let alone why."

The prime minister fiercely showed his teeth for a moment. "The way is easy enough. Martyrs to embarrass the throne. Hiding their death will not help, Jorana, once the facts are known."

"I know," she repeated. "It seemed the best course at the time. The communicators were hounding the gates, clamoring for interviews and statements. Now they've gone on to other news."

"You'll have to inform Palaton, and I'll take on Panshinea."

She nodded, lost in thought.

Gathon stood, straightening his uniform of office. "With your leave, Jorana, I'll not stay to see you wear a path in good marble floors."

A momentary grin flashed across her lovely face. "I've kept you too long as it is." She gave a fleeting salute as the official left.

With Gathon gone, she came to a halt again in front of the bank of monitors, searching each of the view screens intently. Her *bahdur* had stood her well throughout her career. It did not give her the love she wanted, but it had given her power, and influence for those she'd left behind her.

And now it gave her warnings, dire warnings, about the fate awaiting Palaton and Rand, and she could do nothing to stop it.

Chapter 5

"Dead?" Palaton rocked in the formfitting desk chair, which had been built for a generation of emperors, neck rest sculpted to take some of the weight of the horn crowns. The pilot did not use the neck rest now, he sat forward in his chair as though attempting to defy gravity. Rand sat in another chair, one actually built for juvenile Choyan, content to remain in Palaton's shadow, knowing that if it were not for his stolen power, he would be confined to apartments in another section of the vast wings of the palace. He listened intently to the conversation.

"What do you mean, they're dead?"

Jorana perched on the edge of the desk. She wore the lean cut jacket and trousers of her office's uniform, though occasionally she would wear a mid-calf skirt instead of pants. Either way, she displayed a figure which Rand had come to appreciate as stunning for a Choya'i. She reached out and rubbed her forehead between her brows as if soothing a headache. "What didn't you understand?" she countered. "They're dead. We found them so in the detention center the first night. Suicide. We've only been able to identify one so far. His name was Miska, minor street muscle among the commons, of no importance to anyone save himself. The others will eventually be ID'd through work rolls. The autopsies and toxicological results were inconclusive. And, at this point, with only a light interrogation on record, we cannot surmise their intentions when they came at you during the procession."

"And they had no weapons."

"None found."

"So it would be difficult to assume they had assassination in mind."

Jorana gave Palaton a look of mild amusement. "It is

possible to kill with the bare hands. Perhaps one of them thought to strangle you."

Palaton made a face, deflecting her levity. "Jorana, they didn't commit suicide over the detention center's food. You know that, and I know that. If they did not intend to kill us, then why the attack?"

She shrugged. "Our best assumption is that they intended a demonstration of some kind and were thwarted. And whoever hired them does not brook failure. They could not return when released. Or perhaps martyrdom was the goal of both the attack and suicide."

Jorana swung a booted foot. "But we can't prove what they intended. My suggestion is that we leak word that the detainees have been sent to a labor camp, and 'lose' them. Their employer will know differently. I doubt if any of the communicators will track down the story. If they do, there are a number of illnesses in labor camps which our three could have fallen prey to."

"Cover-up," said Rand.

Both Choya looked to him as if they'd forgotten his presence. Jorana's eyes widened a bit with humor. "This is not done on Earth?"

"Only too often."

"Hmmm. Well, it's not agreeable here, but it seems the most expedient way to work at the moment. If we had not had the God-blind riots or the Two Day War, we would not try to manipulate the public confidence. As it is, this is a matter which we don't want worried over in the streets."

"You wouldn't have to worry about the streets," Rand said, "if you gave them what they wanted. Palaton promised to be their voice, but I don't see anyone giving them representation in Congress."

"These things take time," the pilot said, even as Jorana's eyebrow rose in shock. He looked at her. "It's not unthinkable, Jorana."

"They're God-blind. They can't see what we—" She broke off abruptly, turning from Rand. She added, more quietly, "They don't have the sensibilities we do."

"I agree. They have their place, as we have ours." He looked at Rand. "And that's why I can't rush things. Reform like you suggest and Malahki presses for can't happen overnight."

"It's not reform. It's justice. And you're trying to sweep it aside like those bodies."

Jorana ignored Rand's last comment, and said, "We have to act before word gets out that they're dead."

Palaton rocked in his chair again. He tapped his desk. "Do what you have to," he said. "But I want to know who they were. And, being God-blind, if they have any connection with Choyan that I should know about."

Her glance went back to his face. "Malahki?" she asked gently.

"I should hope not. But I promised Malahki that I would be a voice for the commons. I will not let these three deaths go unnoticed. Manufacture your lies, if you have to, as a cover for the rest of the investigation," he finished.

Jorana slid off the corner of the desk. "Then perhaps we should notify Malahki of our intentions. That would avoid any question of a cover-up later."

He nodded.

The security officer paused en route to the door. She glanced at Rand. "Does that meet with your approval?" she asked.

He could feel his face grow warm. He shifted his feet, intently aware that his world had a very poor rating with most Choyan. "I suppose," he answered slowly, "that you have no choice."

"Oh, we have many choices," she answered gently. "But this appears to be the best of them." She left the office, closing the door quietly behind her.

Palaton did not speak until her presence had cleared. Rand was keenly aware of a lingering aura. It struck him that the Choyan, those with *bahdur,* at least, must view the world entirely differently from others. What would it be like to investigate a crime scene, with the essence of the perpetrator's self hanging over it, far more distinctive than fingerprints or physical evidence? And yet, Rand thought, mere presence did not mean guilt.

And the presence of *bahdur* did not mean a perfect world, either. Rand had begun to notice more and more systems of engineering and architecture which had been dependent upon a people with the psychic power to run them and respond to them, and it was clear that such systems no longer functioned the way they used to. *Bahdur* itself seemed to be faltering, weakening with the civilization which depended upon it.

"Our power weakens," Palaton said, eerily echoing his thoughts. Rand looked over, his attention captured. "Yet I think it's to our credit that, even at its height, we did not invade another's mind to determine guilt or innocence or to possess him." He lay back in the chair now, letting the head-rest take some of the weight off his neck and shoulders.

"So there's no way you could have known the motives of those three."

"Not unless they told us, consciously or subconsciously." The absence of the delicate chain facial jewelry which most Choyan placed just under the layer of their translucent skin made Palaton's face even more striking. There was charac-ter there which did not depend on the etchings of gold, silver, or ebony to trace it. "We may yet learn—or we may not."

The deprivation helmet sat within Palaton's reach. He put a hand out and snagged it. "I'd like to take you to Blue Ridge," he said suddenly.

"To the flight school? I can't be ready."

Palaton's mouth curved slightly. "No, you're not ready. My concern today is to see for myself why the flight schools are having difficulty enrolling and graduating candidates. These reports give me numbers and statistics, but it's not the same. Blue Ridge, Salt Towers, and the Commons are all less than half full. With the rapid attrition rate we're experiencing now, and the expanding needs of the Com-pact, we can't possibly provide enough pilots. The Abdrel-iks and the Ivrians have already raised the question that we are limiting our supply to increase our fees. They de-mand that the *tezarian* drive be furnished to those qualified outside of Cho to use it."

"Won't they need you here?"

"Gathon runs most of the government for Panshinea's purposes. But the emperor isn't a pilot, has never been. I am. Or was. If I can help anywhere, it's there. And, I'd like to take you with me."

Rand hesitated. Then he asked slowly. "Won't they know? All of them *tezars*, or potential pilots. Won't they be able to tell you've lost it?"

His friend did not meet his eyes, but looked across the

office as if he were scouting the horizon of the future. Then he shook his head. "I don't think so. Most of the younger candidates will be so frantic about mastering their techniques and passing the first phases of training, they won't see beyond the end of their nose. The seniors are too busy preparing for graduation. As for my old friend Hat—I'm not sure. If Jorana can't tell, or Rindy or Gathon . . . it may be that I still have a faint residue, an aura of *bahdur* which remains. Or perhaps you shield me without knowing it, which—"

"—is why you can't go without me," Rand finished wryly. "Jorana won't be pleased we're going. She doesn't like to handle security that far away from Charolon."

"She's already discussed it with me. She and Gathon are uneasy, but the pilot situation needs to be assessed and remedied, if there is a remedy, as soon as possible."

It looked as if Rand would be visiting the famed flight school. The thought pleased him, even if it was not to further his training. "When do we leave?"

"In a day or two. I have another matter to take care of first. My grandfather's Householding is being torn down by the new owners. I've been asked if I wished to come and salvage my mother's memorial. I said that I would appreciate it. Rufeen is flying me out later today." Palaton's voices had dropped into a tone of contemplation. His eyes met Rand's, and they were very bright. "I won't need you with me for that. I'd rather go alone."

Rand could feel the intensity of the Choya's emotion. His own throat lumped in sympathy and all he could do to reply was nod his understanding. He said, by way of an answer, "I'd like to stay and sit with Rindy for a while. If Qativar's not there, I mean. Just in case he wakes a little."

Palaton responded, "I think he'd like that. There is a part of me that wants to believe he'll wake and wonder why all of us aren't sitting there, waiting for him."

Ambassador John Taylor Thomas stretched his lean figure and looked morosely out the picture window of his ambassadorial offices. He reflected that, like himself, the view from those windows had changed greatly during his years of service, though more accurately, it had been the offices themselves which had changed. Though he had not succeeded in getting his home planet removed from Class Zed status, they were close, very close, and that reclassification would open up a panorama of options. He had worked hard to get where he was, elected originally on a techno-eco cleanup slate, and remaining where he was by sheer dint of will and some fancy footwork.

Then, luckily for him, the World Council had decided that the ambassadorial post should no longer be based upon election and reelection. It was changed to one of appointment, lifetime appointment unless voluntarily resigned or gross misconduct and violation of the code of ethics was discovered. So he had his breathing room, finally, and could concentrate on achieving his objectives, most of which were altruistic and based on the welfare of his home planet, and only a few of which were strictly for his own welfare and that of his family. Not that he had a family left after twenty years on Sorrow. His daughter who had been missing for nearly four years was presumed dead, but he knew who had taken her then and who had her now. First the Choyan, and now the Abdreliks. At least when the Choyan had her, he could recognize her. Now. . . .

Alexa's life was not a sacrifice he was prepared to make. He would get her back, even if it meant his lifetime of work. He would get Alexa back, not as the twisted, dark creature of Abdrelik appetite and cunning his allies had changed her into, but as the human she was meant to be. And he would do it no matter what it took.

"Ambassador Thomas?"

"Yes, Jean," he said aloud, responding to the soft voice of his computer secretary, live personnel having gone. He continued staring out the window, over the crystallized lake which fronted the shore of the island which comprised the Halls of the Compact. From the tower level, he could not see the lake well, or the canals and streams which flowed throughout the artifacts of a barren city discovered in that state by the races which eventually founded these Halls. Its people, he knew well, were frozen in the crystal waters, frozen in a time which they could not identify, by a method they could not duplicate or free them from, for a reason they could only guess had been a horrible act of war.

He had never met a being in the Compact who questioned why this planet was called Sorrow, or why the Halls had been placed here, amidst the constant reminders of the consequences of conflict.

"Your appointment is here," the computer informed him.

John had been waiting, but he had not dared hope. The emperor of the Choyan had come to him for reasons he would not disclose. When Panshinea had first contacted him, Thomas had not known how to react. The Choyan emperor had been forced to give up several of the influential posts he'd held within the Halls of the Compact, but Panshinea was and always would be a force to reckon with. What did he want from an ambassador from a Class Zed planet?

On the other hand, because of his wary alliance with the Abdreliks, John had risen, as Panshinea would be well aware. If there were an underground of influence, an understrata to the obvious layers controlled by the other races, John Taylor Thomas had been quietly but convincingly moving to the fore of its leadership. He turned at the sound of the Choya entering.

Panshinea was as tall, elegant, and powerful a Choya as the ambassador had ever been privileged to meet. He was just edging out of his prime, but the proud head of hair was still full, brilliant red-gold, not carrot red, but a dark copper. His eyes were jade green, sparkling and electric. He loved to quote Shakespeare. John had listened to him play the *lindar* once, a floor-sitting, full keyboard version of the instrument, and he could have rivaled any pianist in Terran history. But Panshinea possessed a very shrewd and devious mind, and John knew he would do well not to forget that.

He bowed deeply as the emperor said, "It was good of you to see me, Ambassador, with such little notice."

"I'm privileged. Would you sit?"

He had arranged chairs neutrally before the scenic window. Panshinea took the larger of the two, the one with a slightly skewed view of the snow peaked mountains in the distance. The Choya waited until he approached the remaining chair, then quietly requested, "Please turn off your recorders. I want no log kept of our conversation."

"It would be irregular, Your Highness. And you might be carrying equipment of your own. . . ."

Panshinea looked at him. Nostrils flared slightly under

the high, roman nose, as if the other took offense, and
stifled it. "I give you my word," the Choya said shortly,
"that I do not do such a thing."

Thomas seated himself. He did not want to cut short the
recordings, but he weighed the advantages of doing so and
said aloud, "Jean, shut down the log."

The computer intoned, "Doing so," after which Panshinea visibly relaxed.

John commented, "You want it known that you were
seen coming here, but you do not want it known what we
spoke about."

"Your security system should prevent unwanted retrieval
of any logs."

"No system," the ambassador said ironically, "is that
secure."

"Then my little eccentricity does not seem such a waste."
Panshinea made a regal gesture with one hand.

"Perhaps," agreed Thomas.

Panshinea turned to look out the window. His jawline
had long ago lost its chiseled appearance. A comfortable
sag now replaced it, but that and an occasional gray strand
in the luxuriant mane were the only signs of age Thomas
could see. He realized he did not know the life span of
a Choya.

"You have done well for your world," Panshinea
remarked.

"I've tried. I do as well as I can without a full complement of pilots, and without treaty recognition and the basic
rights of a fully classified planet. I expect to do better when
Earth is reclassified."

Without looking back, Panshinea said, "When, not if.
You are an optimistic race."

"I think, in this case, optimism has little to do with it.
We can offer the worlds of the Compact a great deal."

"As they can offer you."

"That goes without saying." The ambassador inclined his
head slightly.

Panshinea moved his hand impatiently upon his knee. "I
have not," he said to the picture window, "been able to
confirm that factions of my people have violated Compact
sanctions by dealing with your people."

"I have evidence if you do not."

The emperor's head turned sharply to him. "I have evidence," he said. "Simply not enough."

John froze.

The vibrant green eyes continued to regard him. "I have no doubt that some of my race have done as egregious evil as we've been charged with, but it is important for me to tell you, privately, that this was a faction none of us had been aware of—one we thought had expired several hundred years ago, and which, hopefully, will not rear its ugly head again."

John scarcely dare breathe at all. What was this ruler telling him in confidence? That they had renegades somewhere in the galaxies, and had not even known? No wonder the emperor wanted his words off-record. He wet lips gone suddenly dry. "Go on," he said.

"I've come to ask you to drop your charges against Cho. In response to that, we're prepared to back your move for reclassification. Our backing, as well as what you've obtained from the Abdreliks, ought to be enough to put you through the vote." One of Panshinea's brows danced upward. "It is rare when you will find the two of us in the same voting block, though it does not quite make history."

John rolled the information around in his head. The emperor did not guarantee him a successful vote, but once Earth had rescinded the charges they'd made, they could not be reinstated unless founded on new evidence. He'd have difficulty putting Cho back in the same position.

Yet this was as close to a lock on a vote as he could get. He would be a fool to turn it down. John scratched a nail thoughtfully along the edge of his chin. "There's more," he said, "that you want from us."

Surprise dawned in the Choyan eyes watching him. Panshinea straightened a bit in his chair. This little exchange was going to carry portent and prices beyond what he'd been told on the surface. Panshinea steepled his fingers. He looked over the tips at John Taylor Thomas. "What makes you think you have anything else we could want?"

"You stole our children once," the ambassador said confidently. "I should imagine you'd like to do it again."

Chapter 6

"What you suggest is an affront. And it would hardly make sense to ask you to rescind your charges, then provide you with new evidence to reinstate your case." Panshinea countered, "I would remind you who you are dealing with."

John Taylor Thomas took his thoughts back a little, reexamining them in his mind, combed through them with years of service as a diplomat, and concluded that, no, he could not be wrong. The Choya wanted something more from him, and though the taking and subverting of Earth children was the core of the breach which had eventually taken Panshinea down, this still must be the key to why the emperor sat with him now. "I beg your pardon," he said smoothly. "You misunderstand me. Or, rather, I have misstated myself. From what I know of Choyan history, very few aliens have ever been allowed dirtside. Your knowledge of us as a people must be limited to your dealings with us here on Sorrow, or on a contract basis. In trying to resolve the charges which face Cho, you must be regretfully short of information. Of what value or interest could our children have been to your renegades? Why would such a breach have been committed? Understanding the motives will ultimately help you refute the charges."

The spark in Panshinea's eyes dimmed a bit. "Your apology is accepted, Ambassador," he remarked. "Yet you still offend. Like the Ivrians, you must always suspect a good deed."

"Asking us to rescind charges which, according to my research, can be proven, is not performing a good deed. Emperor Panshinea, you, of all whom I must deal with, must understand how precarious our situation is on Earth. We have limited resources which must be maintained, cleansed, renewed, if possible. Our colonies are limited. You, as I understand it, maintain no colonies at all. We both walk on a sword's edge."

Panshinea's face remained impassive, but the eyes showed fire again. "Our situations are hardly the same. We are not fledglings who soiled our nest before discovering we could not fly. However," and he stirred in the big wingback chair, "your suggestion that we could become further acquainted with you is not unwarranted, nor should you think that we do not share a certain sympathy with your struggles. Reclassification requires that your world show a common interest, a united front, and a spirit of cooperation so that any and all aid given you be available to any citizen, not just a prevailing government or warlord, or scattered on fickle winds. I know that you've worked exceedingly hard, Ambassador, to provide us with a benevolent view of your world, perhaps too hard. Those of us in the Compact do not believe that Earth does not have garbage. We only hope that you use gutters, drains, and proper sewage treating systems to deal with it as best you can." Panshinea gave a bittersweet smile. "We all have garbage."

John answered slowly, "Yet by asking me to drop the charges, you're asking me to violate a confidence that my people have placed in me. They expected that I would demand fair and equal treatment for them. You're asking that I ignore a heinous wrong."

Panshinea chose not to meet his eyes this time and instead surveyed the panoramic view. "I can't dispute that. We've sifted through the remains left on Arizar, and there is little there, but we do have evidence of a crematorium. The majority of the ash within tests for humankind DNA. That your people lived, and died, on Arizar is indisputable. Who brought them there and how or why they died remains unanswered."

John's daughter knew. She had survived Arizar after infiltrating the colony, but she had never given her father the answers he sought. She had reserved her information for the Abdreliks who'd imprinted her. He had sacrificed her for the knowledge, and lost all. Restlessly, he rose from his chair. "I had a daughter taken to Arizar," he said.

Panshinea's attention shot back to him. "You what?"

"My daughter was taken to Arizar. So you see, Your Highness, I have complete confidence in our case. If you wish me to drop it, I will need a great deal of convincing."

The emperor of Cho sat back in stunned silence.

The message from the streets of Charolon came by stealth to the imperial palace until it reached her hand. Jorana took it from a slot cleverly cut into the flagstones of the courtyard garden wall after seeing the green shoot of a grass blade hanging there, a flag that the mailbox was full. She removed the stone only after quietly securing the area and making certain that she could not be observed. For a moment, head bowed, she stood with the missive clasped in her hand, unread. Then she opened it.

Malahki sent for her. She felt a quiver of uneasiness at the summoning and yet could not refuse it. The former luminary of the community of Danbe was now one of the heads of the God-blind, his community numbering in the millions, and yet the two of them had a much more intimate relationship. He had fostered her and made sure she'd been brought forward for the Choosing, so her talents of *bahdur* could be recognized and trained for the future. His treatment of her had come, she knew now, not only out of a wellspring of generosity, but from the need for future influence. She had paid for that fostering, and would continue to pay for it, many times over.

She left the palace quietly, in the fog of the late summer's morning. She could feel autumn toying with the summer season in her bones, as well as in the gray mist which enveloped her. By the time she'd reached the far side of the city, the haze had burned away, and the streets already radiated the heat of the day as she dismounted the jet sled.

She wore a grubby maintenance worker's uniform, and had her hair braided back, woven with a dull scarf to hide its luxuriant color, and felt that was disguise enough. Anyone who knew her well enough to identify her by her facial jewelry was someone she would have to remove permanently. She didn't think she would face that problem on this side of Charolon. Not many of the Housed would be doing business here this soon after the riots.

Buildings lay collapsed, charred, and still reeking of their fiery destruction as workers took them apart, salvaging what they could and hauling off what they couldn't. Breaking open the fragile shell of what had once been a city seemed to leak out the true substance, the odoriferous secret, of the oppression of the commons side of their society. Jorana kept her nose from wrinkling. She spoke a word and passed the palm of her hand over the jet sled's security lock and left it in the parking arena. She could see Malahki waiting for her, seated by a bistro's window.

As luminary, or mayor, of Danbe, he'd lost one of the causes of his life when the river valley community had been shut down and forced to relocate by the Resource Board. Relocation was a way of life they all faced, but each Choya or Choya'i seemed to face it in his or her own way. Malahki had worked so hard to keep the river clean, the community prospering, that it had been a shock when the Relocation had been announced. But Jorana had been with Panshinea then, and she knew the reports had also been correct. Several hundred years of occupation could not be kept from the water, the soils. It had been time, and past time, for Relocation.

Still, the inevitable might have been staved off for another generation if Malahki had not also been working against the interests of the throne. He had held back two generations of children from the regional Choosings, save for one or two to avoid suspicion, and herself, because he had groomed her to become Housed. Holding back those candidates had not denied them *bahdur,* only the Housed training of it, and now, within the ranks of the God-blind, there were those who were not talentless but who had chosen to use their talents for the benefit of their movement.

And, worst of all, Malahki had been conducting experiments with genetic materials, manipulating Choyan DNA, and the laboratory waste which had been found had brought about his ultimate downfall.

The incident had also targeted Malahki for Panshinea's attention. It did not seem to bother the massively muscled Choya with the ebony mane. The excitement of what he'd almost accomplished and hoped to aspire to again one day brought out the gold flecks in his deep brown eyes, making them sparkle combatively. He would never be one to shave down his horns to follow society's fashions, nor would he have to. They had never been spindly or weak, a massive crowning rival only to Rindalan's rack. She could see them clearly now, spiraling about Malahki's head, as he leaned forward in the window and beckoned to her.

He slid aside a chair for her. "Moving up in the world," he observed ironically of her disguise.

Jorana flashed him a look. "My time is limited," she pointed out. "Why am I here?"

Malahki smiled broadly. The flecks in his eyes shone in the sunlight. "And a pleasant day to you also."

Jorana put her hands on the table. The veins at the back of them stood out with tension, aging them prematurely. As she looked down at them and exerted her will, her blood pressure dropped and the veins subsided. Then she took a deep breath. "I don't like being summoned. It jeopardizes all I've worked for."

Malahki poured her a glass of sparking blush wine. "Then understand I did it for your welfare, not mine."

She picked up the glass. She thought she could guess what was on his mind. "The three who died?" she suggested, without further subterfuge.

"Is that what really happened to them? I wondered. They were shipped off to camps so quickly." Malahki took a draft from his own glass. "They won't get much work done in that state."

"Malahki!"

"You're right. I should not make light. You should know, Jorana, dearest, that they were not mine, although I had some fleeting acquaintance with the one called Miska. Word on the street is hard to come by regarding the purposes of these three or their attack, but I do know this. They weren't assassins. Nor were they mine. And they all had a background of religious fanaticism."

Jorana sat back in her chair. "Religious—Malahki, that makes no sense at all."

He shrugged. "Any information I've given you is better than no information at all."

She took another sip of wine and let it linger upon her tongue, tart and sweet, light and full. "Then I thank you for that. My quandary is enriched."

"Since they didn't have Palaton's death as their goal, is this one puzzle which must be solved?"

She looked into his eyes. He did not seem to have aged

much, this Choya who'd fostered her. He must scarcely have been old enough to have been her father when he'd taken up those duties, though he'd not been the head of the home he'd put her into. He'd been more like an uncle. She had lived and eaten with another Choyan family, but Malahki's presence had always burned like a candle in her life. She answered, "You know me better than most. What do you think?"

"I think you'll search until you find the answers you need, or until a greater puzzle forces you to relinquish it." He uncapped the carafe and refilled both their glasses. A young Choya'i brought a basket of fry bread, hot and buttery. It steamed from the depths of its container.

He did indeed know her well. She sighed. "If only—" She bit off her words and reached for the bread tongs.

He looked up. "If only another knew you as well?"

Jorana did not answer. The warm bread stretched and tore in her hands. It took a kind of satisfying strength to break it open. She knew Malahki watched her and did not meet his gaze.

"What," he said softly, "have you done about Palaton since we last talked?"

"Nothing. If anyone shares his bed, it's me, but we're not lovers. Not in any deep sense, anyway. There is not enough time—and there is Rand."

The glass in his hand clattered down to the tabletop. Malahki caught it up just shy of disaster. He blinked. "He consorts with . . . with an alien?"

"No! No, of course not. No, rather I am reminded . . ." and this time she found the courage to meet his eyes, "I am reminded of the way you hovered over me."

"Really?" Malahki shifted, pondering that. "Really. And I wonder what a *tezar* would see in a humankind?"

"I'm not sure what Palaton's obligation is, but he feels it strongly. There is a bond between the two of them that I envy." Jorana paused as the young server came near again, bearing a tray with cold fruit salads, and dairy custards, still sprinkled with ice crystals on their creamy surfaces. She spread the plates before them and left without a word. Jorana said nothing further, but thought of the *bahdur* aura which occasionally touched Rand as well, an afterglow of his association with Palaton. She had noticed it fleetingly

and wondered, for all her information on the humankind
indicated their psi powers were far below the Choyan norm.
It had to be fed by Palaton, and that had to be draining
for him, yet she could guess why he did it: to shield the
manling from those who might pick his brain. To constantly
protect Rand as well as himself must be wearing on him.
Bahdur was not limitless. It burned out of its users, and
when it did, the wreckage it left behind was not pretty. But
she did not feel like voicing her worries to Malahki.

Malahki picked up his spoon and began to wield it
quickly as he changed the subject. "Jorana, you must get a
child from him. If he won't give you one, you must steal it."

"No." The last time they had spoken at length, he had
given her vials of a forbidden drug, pressed them into her
palm, and told her what to do with them. But she would
not force Palaton into fertility, into a progenesis he plainly
had not wanted. She could not. "What you suggest is out
of the question."

He licked a bit of juice from the corner of his mouth.
"Panshinea did not make Palaton the heir to protect him.
The emperor put his greatest rival to the fore in hopes of
eliminating him without dirtying his own hands. You guess
it, and I know it. The emperor is right in only one thought:
Palaton is an uncommon Choya. It would be a shame to
lose him and his genetic potential. If you cannot bring him
to you out of love, Jorana, then you must resort to duty."

"My duty, not his."

He lifted a shoulder and let it fall. "If that's the way you
see it. I see it as potential which can uplift all of Cho."

"You see it as an heir you can hide among your ranks,
teach and guide and suffuse with all your hopes and
dreams, and then topple the Houses with when the time
comes."

Malahki smiled. "We all have our dreams. I know you
have yours."

She could feel her skin heat, knew that a blush which
mirrored that of the wine she'd been drinking suffused her
translucent skin. "My dreams don't matter," she said, "if
he doesn't come to me willingly. That's part of what I love
about Palaton. He strives to find an untarnished truth, and
to act upon it. That's why Panshinea exiled him years ago,
and why the emperor had to bring him back. You can't

control a Choya searching after that kind of destiny. He's like Chaos itself."

"And do you think you can help him steer clear of disaster?"

"I hope to God-in-all I can. I'll die trying." She pushed away from the table. "I can't stay any longer."

"You've hardly touched your lunch."

"The palace is not short of food. Or intrigue." She leaned over and brushed a soft kiss across his brow. "You are a selfish brute," she whispered, "but I love you anyway."

Malahki grunted. Then he caught her hand. "I can't force you to do what I want you to. You're a grown Choya'i. But listen and remember. It will be best for us all if you decide to act upon it." He let her go before she could twist away.

Jorana left the bistro quickly. The parking arena had grown crowded since she left and it took a few moments to pick out her jet sled. She used those moments to calm her pounding heart. Too much wine, she thought, as she kicked the jet sled into operation and skimmed off down the street. Or too much love.

Palaton left Rand behind with no misgivings, but he undertook his journey with much trepidation. His grandfather's estates had ceased to be his home the moment his level of *bahdur* had been tested, and he had qualified as a candidate for flight school. But Palaton reflected that Volan's Householding had rarely been home to him even in the tender years before that. His mother's refusal to name his father had caused years of stormy communication between the two, and he had been tossed about on those seas of anger. Yet as he walked the grounds now and saw the wings being leveled, the walls of the houses being painstakingly rendered to individual stone pieces and brick and mortar dust, he felt an ache in his heart. The salvage work was being done carefully, for stone was not renewable. There was no way to salvage the time spent here.

There was more to a Householding than stone, however, and that also was no longer renewable. The new Houseds who had bought this land had homes of their own, and other needs for these fertile fields and orchards. Undoubtedly, the agriculture would still continue here, for Volan was the first to build on these fallow lands, which had been rested for some two hundred years before he'd earned them, and Relocation was probably another two hundred years away. It was good land to invest in.

Volan needn't have lost it, Palaton thought, as he crisscrossed between the various machinery and handlaborers working on the project. He had sent back more than enough of his earnings as a *tezar* to have paid off whatever gambling debts the Choya had had, and to keep the Householding afloat. What other needs for money his grandfather had had, Palaton couldn't guess, but it had flowed away from him prodigiously. It would have taken a family of *tezars* to provide him with the wealth he'd needed to keep this place.

The only wing which remained inviolate was the one where Tresa had raised Palaton and done her work in textile artistry. Even as he approached the outer walls, they were being sandblasted to reveal the face of the stone workings underneath, so that they might be disassembled. A stocky Choya, squat and dark-colored, a true son of the House of Earth, reminiscent of his friend Hat at Blue Ridge, wore a foreman's vest, despite the heat.

He saw Palaton out of the corner of his eye and swung around. His scowl immediately eased. "Heir Palaton? You have good timing. We've put these walls off to last, and the courtyard, but I can't wait forever."

"I am pleased you thought of me at all."

"My patron did. She owns two of Tresa's embroideries and when she found out the memorial stood here, she wanted to have it moved to her Householding. However, the stone workers have told me it will not survive such a major upheaval. She thought then that you might want to save whatever part of it you could."

Palaton wondered why his mother had commissioned such feeble workmanship for her memorial. He found himself blinking in the dust being raised. The Earthan took him by an elbow and pulled him to one side. "I can give you three workers."

"It's not necessary," Palaton told him. "I only came to pay my respects."

"Ah." The Earthan wiped away a rivulet of sweat from his forehead. "Your mother was a talented Choya'i."

"Yes, she was."

The foreman fell into step with him as he made his way through the wing, laid open to the sun and wind, stripped of all furnishings, dust curls skipping along the floors. She would not have been old, Palaton thought, if she'd lived, for she had had him very early in her youth. But she had not lived, for she'd taken her own life, without telling him or anyone else that she'd finally despaired enough to do so. Palaton often wondered if, in his absence as a *tezar*, his grandfather had driven her to it.

He paused in the doorway to the inner courtyard. The sun blazed down. Water in the fountain had long since ceased. It was a broken pitcher which had poured water in spite of its fatal flaws, an art form that, although traditional for fountains, also carried a profound symbolism. The plaque read "Do You Remember Me" and the dates of his mother's brief time upon Cho.

Palaton moved into the sunlight and knelt at the base of the fountain. He did not pray, he could not even really think, as he bowed upon the ground. He searched for her aura, her presence, which he had felt here in dreamtimes, in sendings, but found nothing. It was as though, with the razing of the Householding of Volan, her existence had been scrubbed away also. He would find more of her back in Charolon, in the palace's art gallery, than he would here.

The Earthan waited a respectful moment before saying, "I think I can get the plaque for you, at least." He brought out a mason's trowel and began to pry it loose.

Palaton almost put out a hand to stop him, for he was not ready, but he acted too late. The bronze plaque came off easily in the foreman's hands, and with its removal, the fountain began to crumble, to disintegrate.

The base which held the plaque toppled slowly, dustily, and Palaton got up, choking, his eyes and nose running. Then the broken pitcher fell open, like a blossoming flower.

For a brief, shining moment, a flame stood in its place. It collected the sun's light and reflected it fiercely, its red glow so hot it could have burned him. Palaton did not know if the foreman saw it also, although the other had stepped back with a gasp.

The base of the water pitcher had rested upon a starshaped lily pad, which remained. Now, it looked as though the star had birthed that fire. His throat went hard and dry as he looked at the message his mother had left for him. Did she tell him now, ultimately, in death what she could not bear or had not been allowed to tell him in life? Was he indeed a son of the House of Flame, and was that the genetic heritage he must seek? If so, this was all he had of the truth.

And then the fountain went all to dust, completely, every speck of it, ash-fine, except for the plaque in the foreman's shaking hands.

Chapter 7

The vibration of a heavy cruiser moving through space hummed through the metal plates under her feet as Alexa crept through the holding bay. Humidity made her shirt cling to her body. Sweat ran in rivulets under her arms. She put the back of her hand to her brow, in a useless attempt to wipe it dry. The Abdreliks had stepped up the ship's humidity. They'd been out in space a while and most Abdreliks did not bring their symbionts, their *turshes,* with them to keep their amphibious skins cleansed. The creams they used instead tended to irritate their hippopotamuslike hides and dry them out, so their answer was to flood their ships with heat and humidity. Alexa licked her lips, caught the taste of her body salt, and paused, listening.

Her brunette curls lay damply upon her head and neck, not as short as she liked, but thick and in ringlets, the humidity of the ship unable to defeat the natural body of her hair. She pushed her hair back from her ears, trying to catch a telltale hint of any noise beyond that of the ship's running.

She had her freedom, which she used cautiously, and was not willing to give it up for the sake of the one she now crept to visit. The Choya Nedar was of mild interest to her, but not enough for her to risk her privileges. They were both prisoners of a sort, but she had no delusions about who was of great value to GNask at the moment. The Choyan pilot commanded their attention and she was no more than excess baggage, to be handed over to her father when it proved advantageous to do so. If she were caught down here in the holding bay, she would be confined to her quarters, which were scarcely larger than a coffin, until such time as GNask found her of interest again.

The Choya, on the other hand, was a proud captive taken

during the Two Day War, presumed by his own people to have perished. No one mourned his loss, no one searched futilely for him. Not one of his people knew that Nedar still existed. . . . Alexa went to one knee, as something moved in the twilight of the bay. She held her breath and willed the beat of her heart to slow. To whisper. To pause altogether.

"Is that you, Alexa?" a voice drifted in the quiet, a dry, cynical, arrogant voice, with dual tonalities, a voice indisputably Choyan.

How had he sensed her? She did not know. Nedar had done it before. If he had been Abdrelik, Alexa would know that he'd smelled the heat of her blood and the pheromone of her body chemistry—always predators, the Abdreliks. But she knew of no such sharpness on the part of the Choyan. Oh, despite their lack of ears, they heard preternaturally well, but their eyesight was about average, and their sense of smell was not even as potent as a humankind's. So how had Nedar sensed her in the gloom, across the bay from the cell constructed for him. How had he known?

Alexa got back to her feet and moved deliberately across the metal-plating floor, making far less noise than the bulky Abdreliks did. The Choya sat on the floor of his cell, rather than on the bunk or chair they'd made for him. His shoulders were bowed, and he did not glance over when she approached.

"The surveillance cameras are off," Nedar said, as she dropped down near him and crossed her legs, settling in.

"I overheard their plans to do so. They are toying with you." Like him, she spoke Trade, but the Choyan were always remarkably formal in whatever language they spoke.

The Choya's head came up. His large, dark eyes glistened as he looked to her. She thought of Abdrelik eyes, hooded with heavy flesh, narrowed, keen, with a glint of a hunter's blood desire always deep within them. The Choya's eyes held a bit of a hunter's gleam in them as well. She remembered that Nedar had been primarily a combat pilot.

"They waste their time, and so do you. The secret of the *tezarian* drive will die with me."

"I think," she answered softly, closing her hands about the bars of his cage, "that death would be welcome after what they intend."

"No doubt." The pilot shifted his weight so that his body could follow the direction of his gaze. "I have, however, seen what the Ronins can do. They are most efficient. Yet they do not possess the *tezarian* drive, either."

He wore his flight suit still, though the Abdreliks had provided him with cleaner gear, hastily manufactured to fit his much leaner form. Abdreliks were nearly as tall as the Choyan, but their bulk and girth were far greater. Alexa could just imagine the redesigning done to make Nedar new clothing. She thought over what he'd said about the Ronins.

"Why?"

He did not blink. His dark eyes stayed with hers unflinchingly. "Because," he said, "we cannot give away our souls."

"You went up to protect Palaton. Why?"

"Not to protect him." The unflappable expression broke a little. "To keep him from getting all the glory. I am of the House of Sky. The throne of Cho will be ours. All the sooner, I hoped, for my actions."

"Was that what drove you to Arizar?"

He did not answer for long moments, and she knew he contemplated, as she often had, the ironic past they'd shared. Like Palaton, he'd come to Arizar. She was to have been his Companion, for cleansing and meditation. She'd been trained by the College of Arizar, for work she did not understand and for which no Choyan seemed prepared to offer explanation. She, Bevan, and Rand had not finished their training when Nedar had come, demanding, and the Choyan at the College had given her to him. She only knew that his violence had frightened her, and her lover Bevan had attacked Nedar, thought he'd killed him, and fled.

The campus had disintegrated into chaos, and the time, she'd thought, had come to bring in her allies, so she had called for the Abdreliks. But Arizar had had defenses which she'd known nothing about, and she'd been lucky to survive both the Abdrelikan attack and the Zarites' defense of their world. The College and its campuses had been destroyed. Any surviving inhabitants had fled, taking their secrets with them.

GNask and his war general rrRusk had come to the conclusion that the Choyan had perhaps been readying the

humankind to be pilots, for the campus and House holds
on Arizar had obviously been a dissident colony. Unable
to support their own meager population, they were recruiting. To spread across the galaxies, one had to first conquer
space. To conquer space, one had to have a pilot who could
navigate Chaos. Faster than light space did not fold neatly,
it collapsed into a miasma of Chaos, through which conven-
tional navigational systems could not see or plot. Only the
Choyan had broken its code. Only the Choyan could reli-
ably, time and time again, breach passage through it.

What would it mean to her people if they, too, could do
what the birdlike Ivrians, the Abdreliks, and the others
could not?

She stretched her fingers between the bars, as if she could
reach him. "Of what use to you would I have been on
Arizar?"

He blinked then, and looked past her, not quite meeting
her gaze. "As little use," he said finally, "as an oil filter,"
and lapsed into silence again.

Alexa watched him darkly. It was not an answer she had
hoped for. Her hands slid away from the bars. He still
frightened her, this Choya, for reasons she could not name.
Just as she had denied him his destiny, so now he denied
her hers.

But she would not be content. She would not let opportunity slip through her fingers. The Abdrelik sense which
coiled inside her began to rouse a little, like an emotion.
Alexa stood to leave the cage and its occupant alone.

Nedar looked up. "Will you be back," he asked, "with
the others?"

GNask sometimes brought her with him when the Choya
was to be interrogated.

"I don't know," Alexa said unevenly.

"Then I will see you another time." His dark eyes held
that steady gleam in them, a pilot gridding a target.

Alexa had no answer for that, and she left, making her
way unsteadily across the bay. When she reached the bulkhead and passed through the portal, she found her small
hands clenched into fists, her nails biting deep into her
palms. She couldn't abide the arrogance, the disdain of a
race who had little use for hers, save one which they kept
hidden, one for which they stole children. And the fact

that, though she'd been one of those children, she still had no understanding infuriated her.

The bulkhead closed behind her and she pulled her shirt out of her trousers, dropping her pants low on her hip bones, ripping at her flat stomach beneath her navel, pulling off the comset transmitter. The taping ripped from her skin. rrRusk rumbled in low amusement, "He knew, of course."

"How could he?"

"He knows you," the Abdrelik said. He watched her shuck her clothing with all the interest of a diner watching an oyster being shelled for consumption. She danced on one foot as she peeled the recalcitrant cuff off her ankle.

She stood, bare breasted, in her skivvies, her pale skin marred by the flaring patches where the wire had been taped. She sidestepped a spreading pool of drool where the war general had been standing, listening. The wire had been, even by Terran standards, somewhat primitive.

"I don't know what you proved."

The Abdrelik wore his fatigues, and the wattles of purplish hide that draped over his neckline deepened in color. "Perhaps," said rrRusk, "I did it not to get truth from him, but from you."

Alexa paused in her anger, her thoughts suddenly iced. She could not be confident that GNask remained strong enough to protect her, or even whether he would have the interest to do so if he discovered her minor alliance with rrRusk. She hid her discomfort by bending over to gather up the comset and her sweat-soaked clothes. By the time she stood, cold words were ready to spill over her lips. "If we're going to be allies, General, you have got to stop thinking of me as a meal."

rrRusk laughed at that, his tusks meshing open, shut, open, shut, as the humor came rumbling out of him. With a grace belying his size, he plucked the comset from her hand. She looked him in his little pig-eyes, turned sharply away, and left the area. She could not wait for a shower and fresh clothing.

Nedar ceased to listen for her when the bulkhead closed. Early in their confinement, he'd had some interest in the humankind, but it was clear she had little telepathic ability of her own, and he could not steal from her. *Bahdurless,* shorn of his own power, existing on what he could steal from others, he had little opportunity within the belly of the Abdrelikan ship to feed his needs, or even to plot an escape. As for the Abdreliks learning what they wanted from him, the idea was ludicrous. He had no more talent than a stone, and even if he told them the truth, he could not prove it and they would not listen to him. Heroics had little to do with his current situation though the Choyan race did not lack for role models. It was only that he, Nedar, had always walked a different path.

He closed his eyes and thought of beautiful Vihtirne and what the rulers of the House of Sky would do for him if he escaped unscathed. With such pleasant dreams he slipped into sleep and did not wake until the cage of his door opened with a resounding clang.

He caught only the mercurial figure of Alexa from the corner of his eye, then focused on the looming bulk of GNask, and next to him, the smaller, though scarcely feminine, body of the Abdrelikan physician who'd first attended him when he'd been brought on board. Kalak was no one's, not even another Abdrelik's, idea of a fetching mate. Her role on board the cruiser was strictly one of physician. She frowned now, her face folds etching deeply.

In his role as ambassador, GNask normally did not spend much time in space. Consequently, he kept his symbiont with him all the time and right now his *tursh* rode low on his torso, inching its slimy way across GNask's chest. Nedar felt his lips curl a little at the sight of the symbiont lifeform. There was no way in which an Abdrelik, inside or out, was not repellent to a Choyan.

Alexa stayed behind GNask, her dark eyes compelling him. Nedar looked away from her.

GNask asked, "Are you not feeling well, pilot? You did not wake for dinner last night or breakfast this morning."

Nedar looked down and saw the stacked trays upon the floor of his cage, their contents congealing. He had fallen so deeply into his dreams that he had never heard them being placed there. The unyielding metal floor beneath him had drilled its icy cold into his buttocks. He stood somewhat stiffly and felt his system respond sluggishly. He could smell himself as he moved, and the odor was not a pleasant one. Did he languish then, not eating, nor taking care of himself, the only lure of life the escape from it within dreams?

Or had they drugged him previously and he had not even been aware of it?

Nedar rubbed one lean hip. "I would invite you in," he said, "but there is hardly room. And," he looked at Kalak, with her tray of instruments and syringes, "I do not wish to come out."

The physician glared at him, even as she kicked a robo table into place and set her tray upon it. Her thick hands moved over the instruments as if checking their location.

GNask put out stubby fingers and stroked his *tursh* absently. "You are my guest, *tezar*, and as such, I have your every concern in mind."

"Do you? Take me home."

"That is hardly possible under the circumstances. It would be a considerable embarrassment explaining how we got you."

Nedar watched the thick hand caressing the large sluglike creature that fed upon GNask's skin. It put out a stalk eye and looked back at Nedar with an uncanny intelligence, and he could feel the hair at the nape of his neck stir. Like a bottom feeder, it continued its almost imperceptible track across the Abdrelik's torso.

"I could," continued GNask, "take you apart, but such severe methods of inquiry have had little effect in the past. The Ronins have traded information with us, and we with them, and neither of us appear to have devised a method of torture which will get us what we want. Drugs have not been compatible with the situation, either. So, Nedar, we stand at an impasse. You have information I wish. Will you not give it to me?"

Nedar let out a bitter laugh. Then he followed it by saying, "Not for my life could I." He watched as Alexa, who seemed to be in constant, restless motion behind GNask, paused solemnly.

GNask smiled. "As I thought. Well, then. I have an opportunity to try something which has only been done experimentally once or twice and never on a Choya. Truthfully, I doubt if any other Abdrelik has even considered such a radical procedure." His fingers curled about his *tursh* and began to peel it carefully away from his skin. "I owe you a warning. If you should survive this and, even if you should tell us what we wish to know, we can never let you go. You will be a part of us, you see, and I very much doubt your people would ever take you back."

The Abdrelik laid his symbiont upon the stainless steel tray which Kalak had cleared for it. "I don't know if you can be imprinted or not. Alexa here," and his voice dropped into an intimate tone, "was our first success. But my symbiont is at a stage of growth where imprinting is done among my people and it seemed fortuitous to me, as I have no heirs of my own yet, to go through with the procedure. What better reason to harvest this segment than to obtain the secrets of Chaos for my people?"

He ignored a tiny sound made by Alexa, but Nedar could not. He glanced at her again and saw the humankind was pale and trembling, her mouth open in horror behind a shaking hand, as if she could not bear to hear the Abdrelik speaking. Her reaction pierced Nedar. Fear began to grow in the pit of his stomach.

Kalak said briskly, "Where do you want the incision?"

"The upper back where, even with his double joints, he should not be able to tear it away," the ambassador answered, all business.

GNask brushed the back of his hand lovingly over the sluglike creature. He spoke softly. "You cannot know what a privilege this is," he said, then looked up to meet Nedar's eyes. "Truly. Abdreliks are not imprinted until we are certain they are going to survive the food chain. Each family guards their *turshes* with their lives. Through it, to you, will pass much of my familial knowledge. That's why," and the Abdrelik's lips stretched over his tusks, "I can't let you go later."

Alexa had sunk to her knees. She shook her head wordlessly, the expression on her face urging Nedar to speak rather than endure what the Abdrelik proposed.

The tursh moved across the silvery tray, a glistening trail in its wake. The coldness of the metal seemed to lend haste to its undulation.

Nedar's fascination with it was interrupted by the sound of Alexa's sudden retching. She bent to the flooring, her stomach heaving dryly.

"Now, my dear," GNask said. "One would think you did not enjoy being a part of me."

Nedar ripped his attention away from her. He had little choice.

Chapter 8

A shadow fell across Rand, its chill suddenness waking him from a half-drowse. He felt like a mouse pinned by the stare of a cat, and concentrated on shielding himself and keeping his *bahdur* damped down.

The Choya spoke, his voices stony. "They told me you sat vigil by our High Prelate. I did not give them credence."

Rand twisted his neck to see Qativar standing over him. The priest of the House of Star blocked his view of the monitors. Yet the appearance of the apartments he had come to know well remained unchanged as Choyan physicians moved silently just beyond his range of hearing, adjusting the atmosphere of the sick room, reading printouts, medicating Rindalan in ways Rand could only guess at. He could not forget the solemn atmosphere of the room, and Qativar's frowning expression amplified it.

"I thought I would," Rand answered slowly. "I miss him."

"After he helped Palaton mislead you? The capacity of the humankind heart is greater than we supposed." Qativar drew up a chair. "He would be pleased to know that."

Rand turned his face back so that he could watch the slow and steady rise and fall of the elder Choyan's chest. "If it pleases him, I hope it's because we're friends."

Qativar folded his hands deliberately upon one knee. "Friendship is valued among your people."

It was and was not a question. Rand did not honor it with an answer. There were wheels within wheels at work on Cho, and a stranger like himself could not begin to understand the intricacies, the underpinnings of the society. And because he was alien, much of that society had hidden itself from him, thinking he did not know its primary secret. Well, he had discovered it, and now, to save his life, he had to keep secrets of his own. He would not fence with Qativar. He decided to change the subject. "Will he make it?"

"I can't say. But I can't help but feel the God-in-all is not done with him, and although many things in life just happen, there is nothing about Rindy which is an accident. He was born to do great works, and I don't think he's finished yet."

"I don't think he thought about that when he went into the streets."

"Perhaps," remarked Qativar. "And perhaps he did what he did in the best interest of all concerned, and none of us will know what he wove until the work is finished, eh?"

They sat in companionable silence, the uneasiness Rand had felt at Qativar's presence being washed away by the lulling hum of the machinery which maintained and restored Rindalan's life. Its sound was almost subliminal, yet he could hear it, and he wondered what would happen if it stopped. The silence, the loss, would be jarring.

Qativar did not let his unease show, but his plans had been altered radically by finding the humankind at Rindy's side. Yet, as he sat and took note, other opportunities presented themselves to him. What would the outcry be if Rindy died suddenly, shortly after a visitation by the alien? How could Palaton protect the outsider then, in the face of the almost overwhelming evidence Qativar could arrange? If he could not turn the humankind against Palaton, then perhaps he could turn all of Cho against Rand. Cho would not continue to give sanctuary to a murderer.

The evidence would take time, careful manipulating, but the task was not beyond him. Qativar watched the ailing Choya, considering his options.

The Choyan embassy window for subspace communications finally opened. Traffic to and from Sorrow was always heavy, and although Choyan were high on the priority list, there was still only so much availability. His fingers ached for the keyboard of the *lindar* in his private study, Panshinea thought, flexing his hands carefully, feeling the pain and knots of them in his joints. Or perhaps it was merely the ache of age, not longing. He sat at the console of his

ambassadorial offices, and waited for his communications
link to become established. As he rubbed his hands together, he saw Gathon's lean and well-etched face come up
on the view screen. More yellow than ever streaked the old
Sky's sable hair. He was wearying, Panshinea noted, bowing
under the weight of his office and his duty to his people.

The Minister of Resource was even more valuable than
the resources of the planet he protected. He had long since
departed partisan politics. He was Cho, almost more than
Panshinea was, because Panshinea was and always would
be a Star, flamboyant in his warmth and enthusiasm and
bahdur, however erratic that had grown. Panshinea had
dared not leave home without knowing that the minister
was there, in place, doing the work that had to be done.

Gathon's face creased into a welcome expression, though
their link was not live, and what the minister had to say to
him had all been prerecorded. The emperor felt grateful,
however, for that small moment of warmth.

"Good morning, Emperor," Gathon said. "Rindalan's
condition is improving. Our physicians note that the brain
swelling is greatly reduced, decreasing the need for additional surgery, and our scans show that the bones are knitting as well as can be expected for one of his age. He
remains primarily comatose, though monitors recorded him
waking briefly during the night. He did not seem to be
cognizant of his surroundings, however, but the doctors are
still pleased. I would say his prognosis is good."

"In view of the Two Day War, the House of Earth has
seceded and relinquished all rights to succession to the
throne. I know we felt this would be inevitable, but a sealed
agreement has been delivered to Congress, so you can rest
easier on that score. Vihtirne of Sky, however, retreated
very reluctantly after Palaton met with her. Pan, we're
going to have to watch her. She can mean a great deal
of trouble.

"On the streets, the commons have generally gone back
to their homes and work and normalcy is returning. Construction and salvaging operations have begun, and the net
effect is a positive one upon the economy." Gathon paused
a moment, then commented dryly, "Perhaps we should
burn down a city every once in a while for the stimulation."

Panshinea found himself grimacing over the irony of the

statement. He made a note upon the transmission tape, flagging it for the content. He had no wish to spar with Vihtirne right now.

Gathon gave a fairly concise report of other matters. When it concluded, and the image faded, Panshinea pushed himself away from the console screen.

He did not fear losing the throne to Vihtirne of Sky, not yet anyway. He feared that he had already lost it to Palaton.

He had come to Sorrow to preserve the reputation of the *tezars*, to restore the influence Cho had upon the Compact to consolidate their position which the Abdreliks and Ronins had been steadily eroding. He had left his throne in the hands of an honest Choya.

That fact might prove to be his downfall.

Chirek was sitting at his console desk, pulling in the reports he needed to compile, when the call came in. He took it somewhat impatiently, irked at being interrupted, but the lowered voices on the line grabbed his full attention immediately.

"We've found her."

The Choya'i, located. He brought up a privacy screen and swiveled around in his chair to hide the expression on his face. "Where?"

"She's at Bayalak."

"Bayalak?" He smothered his response. "That's half a continent away. How did she get there?"

"I just found her. I didn't ask how she got here. Do you need me to make arrangements for you?"

"No. Yes. Wait. Let me think." For a split second, his personas as undersecretary and priest warred while he debated what his best course was. But he had to know what had happened to the Choya'i. Why had she fled? "No public housing. Is there a family, discreet, who can take me in?"

"In Bayalak, the streets are yours."

Chirek thought grimly that that was the last thing he needed. He did not wish to be honored, or singled out, or have his presence heralded among his people. "No. I want to come in quietly, leave quietly. Bringing the Choya'i, if I can."

There was a pause, and then his informant said, "I understand. I can arrange it."

"What's my best way in?"

"Without a charter, if you wish to be inconspicuous, the best way in is by airboat. The river is high, but the weather is good."

"All right." Chirek checked his chronograph. "Tomorrow afternoon. I'll be in whenever the airboat is scheduled to dock. And whatever you do, don't lose her."

The line clicked dead.

Chirek sat a moment, aware that usage of the shielding brought attention to his communications, but unwilling to lower it just yet. Should he contact Malahki and take a bodyguard with him? He shook off that consideration. It would be best if he went there alone, and dealt with the success or failure alone.

Chirek stretched out a finger and touched the switch which would lower the screens. Gathon, passing through the sector, scarcely gave him a glance.

Palaton had not seen his grandfather in three decades. As he walked the newly paved streets in the teeming community which now held what was left of his Householding, he watched the Choyan streaming past him. God-blind, most of them, workers with jobs that required no special sensitivity. Intelligence had nothing to do with it. A commons could be a meat processor, while the job would be so abhorrent to an Earthan, it would destroy him. And yet, Palaton thought as they passed him by, the empire so often excluded the commons in its decisions, as if they did not matter at all. It was no wonder, when he had offered them a voice, an ear, they had flocked to his cause. He had not really thought of what it was he had done. Perhaps the act had been one of those rare moments of destiny when it had not mattered who had made the call—the call would be made, by someone, and answered by these, and the destiny served. Rather like those pathways in Chaos when, regardless of what the random boil of stars and color and seas of time were like, a signpost could be made out. Random attractors, theory told them, that even Chaos was drawn to, making ripples or patterns that were a little less chaotic.

And he found it ironic that his grandfather lived here, in

this manufactured town, shoulder to shoulder with the very Choyan he had despised for most of his life. Did he lord it over them, Palaton wondered, making his neighbors miserable, as Volan had done with his daughter and grandson?

He found the pathway which would take him to the courtyard apartment address. Foot traffic eased. Motion sensors lit up as he passed them, screening him for weapons, identity. If he passed muster as the heir to the throne, they seemed not to know it. Those reading him either did not care or did not notice. If he had been wearing his *tezar's* uniform, now that would have been a different matter. The children would have escorted him all the way from the town's station and would only have left him at the doorway because he had shut them out. Almost all children dreamed of becoming pilots someday, before the realities of the world became ingrained in them and possibilities narrowed.

He paused just before the private entrance, gathering his thoughts. He wasn't sure why he'd come. It was definitely not because there had ever been any tender feelings between the two. Nor was it because his mother's death could reconcile them. She had died many years before. Her suicide had not brought them together then, nor had it been meant to. Tresa had done what she had done merely because she could not bear the burden of living anymore.

So what did he hope to find within? It was not in Palaton to harangue the old Choya over a past neither could change. Before he could make up or change his mind, the preview window in the door flickered, and he knew he had been seen by the occupant.

The doorway fanned open. A once tall Choya slumped within it, horn crown that creamy yellow color denoting the brittleness of age, large aquamarine eyes slightly clouded with the cataracts that came to all. A knobbed hand beckoned.

"Don't stand out there. I won't have family business done in the streets."

The voices, still imperious, still cruel. Palaton stepped forward as bid, and entered the much shrunken domain of his grandfather's house.

His grandfather sat without a word. Palaton took note that the chair was orthopedic, made to assist the occupant with rising, as well as adjusting to several different slants.

The apartment was government standard, a sitting room, a kitchen, a bathroom, and upstairs, no doubt, a single bedroom and storage closet. The lift in the staircase was reinforced for any who might be handicapped. The place stared back at him in the neutral colors of its starkly utilitarian appearance. His grandfather's private wing alone could have encompassed this place three times over.

He glanced about, seeing a few pieces of furniture he recognized from the old Household, and in the corner, one of his mother's earliest embroidery pieces. Art collectors prized that one as worth a fortune because it held the beginnings of several techniques she would later master and become extremely famous for. He felt a faint shock of surprise that it had not gone the way the rest of the Household of Volan had gone to pay his debts.

"Some things are beyond selling," his grandfather said.

He had been off-world long enough that he found the old Choya's presentiment of his thoughts eerie, although he shouldn't have. That sort of intuition ran strongly in his family lines. Palaton found an ordinary chair and seated himself, saying, "I didn't think you sentimental."

"I'm not." Volan looked to the corner. "That was before she turned on me. That was made by the daughter I loved."

"And I was made after."

The glance shot back to him. "Yes," Volan agreed shortly. He paused. "Did you know I get tithed less now that you're an heir than I did when you were a *tezar*?"

He would always be a *tezar*, until the day he died. But he did not correct his grandfather though Volan implied that he abandoned both of them by his actions. Volan had never actively opposed Panshinea, but Palaton knew of his private grumblings. "I would save what I could, if I were you," he answered instead. "You won't get much at all if I am dead."

Volan crossed his legs. The side table accompanying his chair held a cold drink. His frown deepened. "I smell thara on you. It's not grown here. I suppose you've been out to the old place, to look at my disgrace."

"Are you disgraced, Grandfather?"

The spine he remembered as being ramrod stiff had curved violently in the last few years. Volan could no longer put his shoulders back to sit up straight, but he could, and did, lift his chin defiantly. "Never. I built that Householding with the sweat of my brow and the blood of my hands when I was scarcely old enough to be an adult. My *bahdur* and my brawn carved a niche where there was none to be had among the other Households of Star." He took a long breath, to smooth over breathing which had suddenly become rough and agitated. "Not one of them broke a sweat watching me rise . . . or fall."

There had been few new Households created in the last hundred and fifty years of Choyan history. Volan had made history when he'd done so. No one would have put a hand out to aid him—that had been part of the test, the climb, the achievement. But that no one had helped at the last, Palaton could not believe. He did not argue with Volan, but he felt that the other had probably driven them away, as he'd done with his daughter and grandson.

Palaton shifted. "I came to see if you wanted the plaque from her memorial."

Something moved in Volan's expression. The corner of his mouth dropped slightly. Then he said, "They took it down?"

"Everything was leveled."

"They were supposed to leave the courtyard. It was in the contract." Volan seemed staggered. He paused. Then he said, "I thought I'd done that much." He took a deep breath. "You keep it. You have little enough of her."

"I want more," Palaton countered.

"What?"

"I want to know who my father is."

Volan looked away, his expression stark and harsh. "She would never tell me."

"You must have your suspicions."

"I spent a fortune trying to confirm my suspicions! I found nothing." Volan looked back, but his glance kept sliding away as if he could not meet Palaton's eyes squarely.

He had found enough to make sure that Palaton be sent away, sent to Blue Ridge where he would forever be separate from the Household of Volan, where he would either succeed or fail as a *tezar*. The strengths and weaknesses of all *tezars* were that they were more, and less, than their Households. Volan had been willing to share in the success, and turn away from the failure.

Palaton wet his lips, his words so dry he could hardly say them, "Tell me your suspicions, then."

The silence stretched between them. Volan put out a hand, passing his index finger over the controls to his chair, adjusting his angle. Finally, he said, "I meant to die without telling you anything. But I did not foresee that Panshinea would make you his heir. Because of that, and Cho, I owe you what little kernel of truth I know. Because Panshinea may well destroy you if he finds out and you do not. I will not have Panshinea destroy the last of the line of Volan!" He paused, voices breaking off, quavering, then began again. "We were not Householded, but we were always of the House of Star, merchants if not merchant kings, and our line was pure, traceable, through the last two millennia. I tell you what you already know, to remind you why your mother's obstinacy destroyed my love for her. There were always the rumors that I had fathered you, but she would never have allowed that, nor would I have attempted such an abomination. Yet I would rather have allowed those rumors than the actuality of what happened."

"She left in her nineteenth year, already a budding artist of some renown, to go study at the ruins of Maerlon. It was a half-year program, a scholarship, giving her the freedom to simply inhale technique, and be young and enjoy her creativity. I was proud she'd been chosen. The scholarship doesn't exist today." Volan's brows came together heavily. "I destroyed the foundation which funded it because, you see, she came back to me pregnant and refused to tell me the father's name."

"One of the other artists." Palaton leaned forward, intent on gathering every word, every expression his grandfather revealed.

"No. Nor one of the masters. The answer had seemed so obvious and yet not there. Tresa held steady through my rages, though I could see she was frightened herself. Even after you had been sent away to school, and then to Blue Ridge, even after you had made a name for yourself piloting, she did not tell me. It was not until after she . . . she died, that I began to understand. Not forgive, but understand. It was not that she would not tell me, it was that she could not." Volan cleared his throat. "She had been placed under a terrible compulsion, and trying to unravel it, trying to banish it, so that she could tell you of your genetic legacy, took her decades. And when it was done, finally, she was so destroyed by her efforts that she had become erratic, an invalid, her mind in shreds. And so she killed herself."

"But you had some inkling beforehand," Palaton interrupted. "You insisted I be tested, and she didn't want that."

"She had been a strong Choya'i. She wanted to be there to protect you." Volan took up his drink and drained it, the noise of his throat straining to swallow shattering the quiet of the apartment. His hand shook as he set the glass back down. "What I suspected could not have been, but it was based on all the evidence I had . . . your mother." He pressed a hand to his forehead, scratching an age spot high on his brow. "The compulsion which lay inside her, forbidding her to know or tell the truth, was the evidence itself. Only *bahdur* could do that, yet no Choya alive has talent which could be used in such a way." Volan's eyes fastened on him hotly. "We destroyed the House of Flame for having and using those abilities."

"Or the Houses thought they did." Palaton straightened, having finally heard enough.

"Genocide is a terrible thing. I don't think any of the Houses were proud of it. We don't mention it in our histories, but there are those of us who were told, and remember, and passed it down. If an entire House can be swept aside, a Householding had best be circumspect in its dealings. The fear set in us was passed down for generations among generations. And we weeded our lines carefully, lest we be thought to harbor a Flame somewhere in our heritage. Yet, as you say, I had no proof. Not even when the Prelates tested you, and your *bahdur* showed . . . talent . . . which it should not have."

He cleared his throat, but his gaze remained steady, an old Choya's gaze, the look of one who'd stared into many troubles and not backed down. "But it was the Prelate who suggested to me that there was hope yet for you, and who took money to see you safe. He was a powerful Choya, not only in the sense of influence, but his *bahdur* burned as brightly as any I have ever met. He convinced me that

God-in-all would not want you wasted. I listened to Rinda-lan, steeled my heart against your mother's wishes, and let you go."

"Rindalan? He knows?" Palaton moved in reaction, unable to reconcile his memories of his youth with the information. One could not forget having met Rindalan.

"He sent Choyan for you. Where you went, I did not know, at first. Tresa never forgave me. She never told me what happened to her. It took death to free her. It only took betrayal to free you." Volan gave his grandson a grim smile. "I did well, did I not, after all? You are a *tezar,* and one of the best. I may have ruined her life and mine, but not yours. You should never have been born, and yet now you live among the highest."

Chapter 9

The voyage to Bayalak sickened Chirek almost beyond his endurance. He wore the light, woven shirt and trousers of the area, but the humidity beaded on him like rain as the tropic air crowded close, and he found it difficult to breathe in the heat and mist. The airboat chugged steadily underfoot, the deck moving sluggishly, as the boat hovered its way over the turgid channels of the bayou. Moss from tree limbs hanging over the passage tore now and then, as the com towers on the boat snagged their ropy growths. He had flown half a continent away, but not from one season to another, and found himself mired in the thick of summer.

Those who had *bahdur* did not suffer quite so much from the heat, using their talent to maintain skin temperatures and suggest cooler climes. He would use his newly awakened skills if he knew how, and did not fear to attract their attention, but as he didn't know how, and he did fear to be noticed, he chose to stay uncomfortable and hidden. The passenger load was light, considering the season, and he had been left alone on the upper deck. He'd chosen to stand because sitting seemed to leave him a pool of rumpled sweat inside his clothes. Chirek used a panet leaf to fan himself, plucked from a bowl of them by the gangplank, for such usage. The thick, waxy green leaf did its feeble best, but it only seemed to stir a soup of muggy, hot, air. He reminded himself that the goal of the journey would be worth it.

Just before boarding, he'd intercepted a message that the Choya'i still remained in Bayalak. That was enough to drive him on. He clung to the airboat's railing and endured.

Beneath him, the brown-blue waters were stirred by the hover drive, and thick seaweed curled about. He saw a curious whiskered snout break the surface with a snort.

Two bright obsidian eyes met his. The creature's shadowy bulk stayed hidden in the water. The lily-eater disappeared back into the muddy depths with a flip of its wide and heavy fins. It would not surface again until the airboat was well out of its channel.

A Choya'i, in the uniform of the transport line, passed by with a tray of hot drinks. She paused by Chirek, waiting. He shook his head.

A smile quirked her lips. "It will help cool you down."

"In theory," Chirek croaked. "But I need something cold."

She looked back over one shoulder. "He's coming along. We're nearly there, sir." She passed by, cheerfully devoid of sympathy, for he could have waited several days and taken one of the luxury liners in, one of the faster boats with air-conditioned lounges, but instead he had chosen them. He'd either been cheap or a fool, and she wasn't concerned about either.

The Choya with the cold drinks came up to the deck eventually, his tray meager of choices, the glasses growing dewy as their chilled surfaces warmed before his very eyes. The youth's horn crown had been shaved down to near nothingness, and his mane with it, cropped to a lustrous brunet stripe down the back of his skull. He did, however, look arrogantly comfortable. "Drink, sir?"

Chirek dropped a credit on the tray and filled his hands with glasses. "Two," he said, and lifted them away before the Choya could protest or inform him of a limit.

But the other grinned. He swept away the money, saying, "You can keep the whole tray, if you want." He set it down on a deck chair, three drinks sloshing on it, and left with a piping whistle of some local tune Chirek didn't recognize.

One of the three remaining drinks seemed to be mere water. Chirek poured it over the top of his head. Then, as he quaffed a diluted fruit punch, he began to feel better.

The airboat picked up speed as it came out of the bayou reserves, and into the channels which the bigger transport used all the time. His drinks now long since finished, Chirek stood as the port town of Bayalak came into view. The hurricane walls were weathered by the generations, and panet trees hung heavy with scented blooms. Beyond them, the houses and buildings began, a fair distance away from the docks because their docks and fishing fleets were their lifeblood, and the shore was given to them. He could smell the brine, and the fish, and the panet blossoms, all intermingled.

On the piers across the way, trays of seafood, still wriggling with all the vigor of the newly caught, were being hauled off the fishing boats. Fishermen worked with cheerful shouts and waves at one another, their din carrying over to the airboat.

The commercial dock remained clear of all but a few personnel, waiting to rendezvous with the airboat. Chirek thought he saw Seli's broad face among the crowd, but as the airboat slowed and prepared to come about, he lost it. It did not matter. Seli would be there, if not on the pier itself, then waiting outside.

Chirek let the sparse crowd filter off the boat, then took up his overnight bag and came down the gangplank. Seli's wide face bobbed up again, and Chirek nodded that he had been seen. The customs examination was brief, the Housed Sky who gave it seemed disinterested in what he did.

Seli took the bag from him as Chirek was released onto the open streets. The air seemed a little less humid than it had upon the bayous, though not enough to give him relief. He dreaded the night.

"Where is she?"

"Let me take you to the lodgings, and then we'll talk."

Chirek paused in mid-stride, anger flushing through him. "I did not come to this hellhole to talk."

Seli, who looked as though Earthan and Star gene had been stirred about indiscriminately within him, though such a thing could never have happened, gave him back a morose expression. He shrugged. He wore a native shirt, light yellow with colorful blue flowers splashed upon it, and a wraparound skirt which came to his ankles and swung just above sandaled feet. Squat and chestnut-maned, his skin was as pink as if he'd been plucked out of a net and boiled along with the sea creatures for dinner. "I'm sorry." He ducked his head. "Dorea has gone strange, and I thought it best to prepare you."

Strange. Dared he hope it was a sign of the *Change?* He

put a hand out to the other's arm to steady himself, and his fingers tightened. "Don't worry. Just take me to her. After that, we'll plan."

The street was as far away from the docks as it could be. Filth had been ingrained into the stonework from years past, when Choyan could afford to be wasteful and slothful. The stench of it rose with the afternoon heat. Only commons lived here, and they passed him without notice, a quiet stream of them coming out to do their work as the day cooled slightly. A child ran past, shouting for his brother to wait. A wave of odor boiled up after him. Chirek put his sleeved forearm up to his nose as if it could filter the odor away. Seli paused briefly, looking back, saying, "This way."

Chirek followed the lemon and dark blue fabric around a corner, into a side alley. The line of buildings were little more than hovels, the wood blackened by years of preservative staining, leaning upon one another, windows like open sores draining misery and hopelessness onto the street. The roadway here was all but abandoned and sounds were muted behind shut doors. Chirek found himself thinking of the age of the place, and wondering why it had not come up for Relocation. Yet it was not dirty anymore; though dusty and old, it was not riddled with garbage heaps and middens. All of that had been scoured away a few generations ago. Perhaps this was only a collection of misery, and even being emptied for a hundred years or so by Relocation would not cleanse that away. It was soul, and lack of it, bonded into the wood and stone and mortar.

Chirek found his nose crinkling in spite of his resolve. And then the hairs behind his ears, where they were barbered short, began to stand on end. He could hear a keening within one of the hovels, a brokenhearted, wordless song, torn from a Choya'i's throat.

Seli stopped at the door. A single tear escaped down the Choya's face, a face which, although still young, had been toughened by life as a commons. He slid his hand into the palm lock and opened the door.

"She's inside."

The door slid open, revealing a low and mean ceiling, a lightless room with the exception of sun hammering through one window, ill-furnished and stifling in the Bayalakan heat. Wood creaked as the occupant of a solitary, four-legged chair rocked back and forth ceaselessly. She had not changed her brilliantly blue dress, after all, though now it was crumpled, torn, and filthy.

She turned her face toward the door as they entered. A red-soaked bandage gashed across her face, where her eyes should have been. Crimson rivulets streaked her face as though she had been crying blood.

Chirek sucked in his breath. "What happened? What's happened to her eyes?"

The Choya'i stopped keening. She cradled rust-tinged hands in her lap. "I tore them out," she said, her voices ragged with the sound of her agony. "But I can still see!"

The priest went haltingly to Dorea, uncertain whether she could meet his touch in her pain, but as he approached, she put her hands palm up to his in a kind of salute. Despite the dried blood caking her fingers, he grasped them.

The shock of their meeting thrilled through him. Dorea rocked back in the old chair, her mouth dropping.

Then she shivered. "What is it? For the sake of God, tell me what it is!"

Chirek leaned forward, quivering himself, until his lips were close to the base of her horn crown, and whispered, "It's *bahdur*. You've been Changed, my dear, and I wish to God I could have warned you beforehand."

Her fingers went chill and slipped out of his hands.

"Changed?" Her voices rasped in disbelief. "What do you mean?"

"I am Chirek, my daughter. Do you know who I am?"

Her hands now curled on her lap. One closed as if to grasp at a truth. "Our priest . . . our high priest . . . but . . ." and she shook her head slowly, as if taking care not to further wound herself. "You don't understand. It's the plague, it's in my blood. I can't be with anyone, you must go. It can't be the power. I'm Godblind, I—" She halted in mid-sentence, and her mouth remained open as if the words could no longer come out.

"Tell me what you see." Chirek coaxed the speech from her.

"It's different. I see . . . warmth, or the lack of it. Not like with my eyes. I . . . I couldn't stand to see what I saw before. Everyone was doubled up, and sometimes there were horrible things before or after them, and then I could see the life in the wood, the stones, the trees, the animals . . . I could see the fire in them and the pain when I touched them."

"Pain in the stone?" Seli repeated incredulously.

Her face turned toward him, centered unerringly on him. "Yes."

Chirek looked also. "And now you understand," he said, with a note of it in his voices, "why the Houseds pity us. They can see what we cannot, the life and the pain in every aspect of the world around us. Without *bahdur,* each of us is half-blind."

Seli backed up abruptly. A low table hit him in the back of the knees and he sat, and the furniture collapsed under him, sending him crashing to the floor. Dorea never flinched, as if she could see what was happening to him.

She put a hand up to the edge of her bandage. "It's not plague because I touched the humankind?"

"No."

"And you couldn't tell me this would happen?"

Chirek answered gently, "I wasn't sure it would happen. Or if it did, what exactly would happen. But I thought, I *hoped,* something would."

Seli sat on the floor, gasping like a fish out of water. His wraparound skirt had bunched up around his muscular thighs, and he looked thoroughly ridiculous. A tiny smile curved through the agony on Dorea's face as if she could see this, too.

"Do you realize," Seli finally got out, looking from the Choya'i to the priest, "what this means?"

"It means," Chirek announced, "that the alien Rand is the prophesied Being of Change. It means that our destiny has come."

"It means," Dorea corrected, "that he will be killed as soon as the truth is known." The room plunged into abrupt silence.

"What should we do?" asked Seli, rewrapping and adjusting his skirt.

Chirek chewed on his lip in concentration as he tugged a clean bandage into place over Dorea's eyes. "It means that we have to work very slowly, and very carefully, if we want to keep all of us alive." In the moments that had followed Dorea's declaration, he had felt the resonance of it through him, the absolute truth of what she had declared. The life of an alien would be of no more consequence than the life of a venomous bug if the Houseds wished to keep their exalted position on Cho. And though he had not wished to say anything in front of the Choya'i, he had no desire for Choyan unprepared for the *Change* to suffer as she had.

Oh, they had spent their lives getting ready, as had the generations before them. But none of them had really been prepared for the vast changes which could occur in them. The creation, or the unlocking, of the power within them took a toll, and the power itself, as it did in those trained, must obviously manifest itself in different ways. Dorea showed an ability to read truth and to forecast, giving her a double-sense of reality and perception, confusing her, driving her to eventually tear out her own eyes, the sense being so strange and horrible.

One would have to be very used to death to be able to *foresee* without reaction, for death waited, in one form or another, for all of them. As tragic as her reaction had been, it was not the *bahdur* which was flawed, but Dorea's perception of it. Chirek knew he would have to prepare his flock further or he would have mass hysteria and chaos on his hands.

"Malahki has to know," Seli said as he dusted himself off.

"No."

"No?"

"Not yet."

"But, Your Eminence—"

Chirek drew himself up to his full height. "Seli, you have to trust me on this."

Broad nostrils flared slightly. Then he gave a brusque nod.

"Good." He patted Dorea's hands. "Better?"

The Choya'i gave a weary nod.

"Good." He picked up his overnight bag. "Let's get her out of here, find those lodgings, and then I can make arrangements for Dorea." His people did not have the mas-

sive temple complexes of the Houseds, but there were
retreats, meditation centers, where she could be kept until
her wounds healed, and she could be fitted with sensors,
and she could be trained and tested carefully for the limitations of her new abilities.

Also, she could be kept silent.

Her chin lifted, as if she sensed his thoughts. Her lips
parted and she whispered, so softly that he knew Seli could
not possibly have heard her.

"Blood on your hands, three times over, Priest Chirek.
Be careful it does not spill into the streets, or all is lost."

He stared at her, stammering, "W—what?"

With voices as dead as stone, she repeated, "Blood on
your hands, three times over. Do not let it spill into the
streets, or all is lost."

A cold chill, as cold as the first black frost of the year,
iced down his spine despite the intolerable heat of Bayalak.

Chapter 10

There was no rest in the House of Flame. It raced through Palaton's mind, wild fire, orange and yellow, magenta with a glint of blue, but mostly crimson, blazing, racing across a marble of a planet hanging in a cobalt sky . . . flames consuming an entire world, visible from his perch in space.

Palaton woke with a jerk, found his face wet with night sweat as he put his hands to his eyes. His fingers trembled with the visions of his sleep. "God-in-all," he murmured, and his voices were choked with ash and smoke, as though he had actually stood amidst the destruction. He reached unsteadily toward the side table and dispensed a glass of water. As the glass filled, he swung his feet out of bed and sat up.

Had he dreamed or forecasted? Had he seen his fears or his future? Without *bahdur,* how could he know?

His head throbbed as he swallowed his drink convulsively, too quickly, the chill of it sending pains to his brow. The pain receded into throbbing as he sat in the dark of his room and looked around, grounding himself in time and space.

He had been dreaming of coming out of Chaos and finding Cho in the throes of destruction. He had been parting the swirling seas of confusion, the warship surrounding him thinned almost to nothingness, a reality fugue which happened often in FTL, and it had all been so clear, so *real.* . . .

He hadn't had dreams like that since his *bahdur* had been transferred to Rand. For a moment, he wondered whether it had come back to him, infusing his nerves, his very being, home, where it belonged. Palaton replaced the glass in the dispenser and listened to it disappear within the machinery. An emperor could command a glass of water out of nowhere in the middle of the night, but he could not command *bahdur*.

He lay back down, but sleep was no longer in the tempo of his breathing, the push of his blood through his body. There would be no more sleep for now. So, with a sigh, Palaton rose and dressed, informally, lightly, the heavy heat of the summer's night still shrouding the palace, and left his apartments.

He could no longer ignore the omens of his genetic origins. His father had been of the vanquished House of Flame, and his DNA ran as strongly in Palaton's body as did that of the House of Star. Considering that, he thought ruefully, and his mouth twisted in bitterness, it was well the *bahdur* had been rent from him. From the little he had uncovered about the Flames in Cho's past, they had been erratic and dangerous . . . talents not worth salvaging, though they had probably been the foundation stock for all of the Choyan who possessed paranormal ability.

As for the Earthans who'd hidden the few Flames able to survive the genocide, they'd only been interested in increasing the abilities of their House, manipulating genetic destinies in secret.

Palaton stumbled to a halt in the corridor, put a hand out to steady himself, and felt his breath come ragged in his chest. The Earthans—no wonder they had attempted to kill him on three separate occasions. They knew what he was! They had known of his parentage from the beginning. He had faced them knowing that, but not why. Not why! And now it stared him in the face. *They had known.* They had not issued a House assassination order against him because he had guessed their secrets. They had done it because he was an end product of all their planning and manipulation—and he was out of their control.

He had become the heir to the throne, supplanting their own Ariat, with no debt to them, no sworn kinship, no acknowledged genetic heritage for them to exploit.

Palaton straightened in the darkened corridor of the palace. Why, they must have begun seething from the moment he'd made *tezar*, which suddenly placed him out of their reach because he'd sworn to allegiances which even House lines were not supposed to meddle with. He had broken the back of their resistance during the Two Day War, but now he knew that they would not, could not, stop there.

The House of Earth would have retreated until they could decide on the best course of action to destroy the being they had most wanted to create, and whose existence they now feared most.

But why? What was it about the House of Flame that the Earthans, the Stars, and Skies had all feared?

The power was Rand's now. If any who knew his secret suspected that, his friend would become their target. Palaton had to do everything within his means to understand the abilities that might have been passed down to him, skills which had been hidden and left untapped, before Rand could hope to use them, and before he himself dared to take back the power. The ancient library hidden below the House temple at Sethu had been destroyed . . . but Palaton doubted, no, he knew, the information had to have been relocated.

His grandfather's actions of sequestering him within the ranks of *tezars* had undoubtedly saved his life. Palaton would have to try to find a way to protect Rand, as well. But he felt as he had the very first time he'd entered Chaos as a cadet, a fledgling master of the patterns—it had been as though a curtain had parted, and the light of life had been revealed to him as a truth which could never be altered or diminished.

His future seemed that clear to him.

Now, for the first time, Palaton was empowered to take his own action to regain himself.

Jorana woke as the doorway to her quarters whispered open. The footfalls coming toward her bedroom were not stealthy, and she edged to the side of her bed, hand ready to reach for her enforcer, uncertain of who could have been clever enough to breach her security without setting off alarms. She relaxed slightly when she remembered that one Choya had been keyed to pass unhampered.

Her eyes had not yet adjusted to the dark when she recognized the timbre of the intruder's voices.

"I could not sleep," said Palaton.

She felt herself smiling. "Nor I," she lied, the fuzziness of her voices giving away her gentle untruth.

He sat on the edge of the bed, and she moved back to the small hollow where she had awakened. Heat and energy rose from him, and she found herself responding, even though he had not yet touched her. But there was a curious emptiness to him, and she felt a chill where *bahdur* should have limned the power of his passion. It was not there, and she felt for him, knew he must be drained, tired, exhausted, in need of her for comfort and aid, as much as for sexual enjoyment. His relationship with Rand must indeed have affected him as she'd worried it might. Well, she could fill him temporarily and she would. He did not even ask. She put a hand out, felt it grabbed up eagerly, his lips on her palm.

"I think," she offered, "I know what might ease you."

"It's not ease I'm looking for."

Jorana laughed, and the laugh came bubbling out of her unexpectedly, from the delight she felt. He smothered her laughter with a mouth that was as hungry as it was tender, as passionate as it was promising, and she let herself go into his arms. She did not know what time he'd awakened her, but she prayed that most of the night was still before them, that it would never end.

In other rooms, in private quarters, Rand woke with a start, with a hand gone numb tucked under the crook of his neck, and with spasms in his lower back. His eyes fluttered briefly and then he knew where he was, sitting in a chair near Rindalan's medical créche-bed; he had fallen asleep there. The room was dimmed to twilight, and the Choyan monitors had gone, leaving the mechanical ones to do the job necessary during the night.

He shook his hand, feeling the pins and needles of circulation returning, pain and pleasure both, enough that it set his teeth on edge as he leaned forward in the chair to ease his back. Palaton had not spoken much at dinner, and Rand could tell there were some matters weighing heavily on him. Losing Rindalan as a counselor had been a blow. When Palaton was preoccupied as he had been since returning from seeing his grandfather, Rand suffered the loss of them both. He'd come here later, seeking at least physical nearness to Rindy. Qativar sat by the Prelate's side only when he needed to be noticed attending him. Rand had come more and more often, finding the sickroom empty except for the techs.

Rand got up and walked to the bedside. He scanned the monitors in view to make sure he wasn't interrupting the EMF fields, but it appeared his presence did not disturb them. They must be tuned to Rindy, and Rindy alone. He looked at the elderly Choya. His brow and cheekbones seemed even more gaunt. If the eyes were to open, would the pale blue color have faded even more? The sparse fringe of chestnut mane had grown thinner, salt-and-pepper among its red. Had the wise one colored his mane when well? Rand didn't know if the Choyan had employed that conceit or not. Age was nothing to be feared among them, that he knew, but he also knew they were very vain about their abilities and their self-perception.

A tangled strand of chestnut fringe hung down the old one's cheek, catching in the dry mouth, chapping now, despite the IV hydration. Rand reached down and gently moved it away from Rindalan's lips.

In the twilight, there was the tiniest spark of blue static as they touched, just the faintest visual acknowledgment. Rand snatched his hand away, not feeling the sting of a shock, wondering what he had seen.

Palaton had told him *bahdur* always called to *bahdur*. Rand checked the monitors, saw no spiking in the readout, and flexed his shoulders uneasily. Whatever power Rindalan had must lie deeply dormant right now. Palaton had also told him that no Choya had the power to heal, other than the natural healing flesh and medicine created. He found that difficult to believe, with all the other properties of the talents, but he knew that if it had been otherwise, healers would have been brought in.

Rand watched the High Prelate, felt himself breathe shallowly, so as not to disturb the Choya further. He should not even be here now, he told himself, bothering his friend's battle for life. The Choyan had done all they could, and that was considerable, Rand knew, looking down at the framework which cradled Rindy's body. Yet they had never tried to call to his *bahdur,* never tried to awaken his own natural ability to heal himself. Why not?

Power calls to power. Rand leaned over the bed. He wet his own drying lips. The atmosphere in the room was kept a littler drier than normal to discourage bacteria and viral growth, and his time in it had proven uncomfortable. He put his hands out, palms down. He thought of finding a flame in a dark room, and began to search.

His palms began to tingle with a nearly indistinguishable itch, but he kept his hands outstretched, sketching the outline of Rindy's form under the sterile sheet, not touching yet close enough to feel the other's heat. From the head he worked downward, feeling a "push" from the other, as though there was another Rindy, an outer shell, brimming with vitality, captured, bottled up, battling him back as if he might do harm.

His search took him to the foot of the bed where Rand paused, felt a drop of sweat roll down the side of his nose, and realized he had been moving by minute increments, the muscles at the back of his neck and arms tense with effort, and the perspiration running down his face. Far, far harder than finding a lit candle while blinded, yet the search tugged at him insistently. Rand blinked his eyes rapidly several times. Sweat glistened off the tips of his eyelashes as though he'd been drenched by a summer rain. What he'd begun, he could hardly be sure, but he could not stop, not yet.

As he began to move his hands away from the feet, back up Rindy's shrouded form, he could see faint lightning following him . . . a tracery of blue energy dancing upon the sheets, quickening to his fingers, his palms, his wrists. *Something inside Rindalan was answering him!*

Rand tossed his head back, felt the sprinkling of water upon his hair and down across his back, heard it splattering the floor—why, he was a damn rain cloud—and lightning and thunder danced from his hands.

The network of flashing blue energy tracked his pathway. Rand stared intently, thinking that it looked almost as if he had traced a neural schematic over Rindy's still body. What was happening? Were his efforts mapping the very flow of power through the other?

Rand found his movements growing slower and slower. The air turned as thick as mud, and then felt like wet cement, and he could not push his hands through it. They weighed tons, and his arms trembled as he tried to keep them outstretched, and the weight of both his hands and arms threatened to tear his shoulders out of his sockets. He breathed harshly, gusting like a hurricane wind, forcing his will upon that reluctant network.

Was he giving life or taking it? Could he possibly be helping Rindy, or was he killing him?

He had no way of knowing, no answers within his grasp. All he knew was that a pattern now gripped him, and he was as much imprisoned within the working as Rindalan was inside the medical créche-bed. Ha could barely see now, his forehead streamed water as if he were a fountain, and he could feel his throat going dry, his lungs burning as if they breathed hot powder, every bone in his body aching as he forced his way along the Choya's body. Yet still they came, fitfully now, sometimes spitting and sputtering, small blue sparks of energy darting this way and that and then tracing the fine network above the shroud, finding links to what had gone before, trailing open pathways to areas not yet awakened or liberated or healed, or whatever damn thing it was Rand was doing.

He came to a halt over the Choya's broad chest, hands shaking violently, the drops of sweat raining down now tinged with pink. Why, he was sweating *blood!* He had never heard of such a thing, but he could not stop until he reached the crown of Rindalan's head, he knew that. Rand bit his lip and prayed for the strength to go on. His hands steadied a little, it did not seemed to matter, the small lightnings of life and *bahdur* still answered to them, and then, suddenly, with a push and a shove, he was through the chest and up the throat, and most of the resistance had gone.

Rand took a last shuddering breath and brushed his hands gently over Rindy's tranquil face, and then, unable to hold their weight any longer, let them drop upon the Choya's horn crown, and found himself gasping as if he'd run a marathon distance and would never catch his breath again.

His clothing was drenched. He could smell himself, but it was not a rank smell. There was an odor like . . . flowers . . . yes, roses, reminding him of his mother and home, long ago. The faint tinge of the scent held in the air around him, and he wondered if it had existed before, or if he had created it out of memory.

The thin, witchery etching grew very strong, and then blinked out of sight.

Rand closed his eyes, afraid that he had killed his friend. He listened for the monitor alarms, concentrating with every fiber he had left which could function.

Rindalan reached up and grabbed him by the wrist.

Rand jumped back with a shout, but the old one's grasp about his hand was too tight, and he found himself staring into weary blue eyes.

"Drugs," husked Rindalan. "In the water. Don't let them give me water."

Alarms went off.

Jorana dressed with the quick, jittery motions of embarrassment, but Palaton had only laughed as the bulletin had come all the way to her apartments to find him. "If we have to be found out," he said to her, "at least it's with good news."

"He's awake?"

"That's what she said." Of all the staff physicians in the palace, this one, Ninever, was the one he liked best. Ninever had come to treat Rand once and, despite her initially xenophobic reaction, her practical good sense had come to the fore. On call when Rindy's alarms had gone off, she awaited him now. He would get clearer answers from her, he felt, than from anyone else.

He was dressed, though he did not take time to groom his hair. He leaned over and brushed a good-bye across Jorana's brow.

She looked up. "You go on," she said. "I'll catch up."

The doors closed almost on the last of her words. She flung a boot at them, then sighed and got up to retrieve it. At least they had had some time for themselves, and Rindalan was at last out of his coma.

Rand stood, wrapped in a lightweight blanket, looking as if he'd been a drowning victim. Palaton gave him a look of puzzlement, but then Ninever stepped forward, out of the subdued lighting from the instrument room. Her style was brisk, her silvered hair trailed down past her shoulders, and her heavily muscled frame took up the bulk of the spare room in the area.

She took a scanner from her pocket, checked the readings, and then said, "He's asleep again, but the readings confirm that it's only a light sleep. I can confidently say the coma is broken."

Palaton looked past her. He saw the grid screen display. There was a high spike pattern blown up in some detail. "His heart?"

Ninever swung about on one heel, a feat which every massively muscled part of her body amplified. She seemed to come to a halt with a slight sway. "No. That's the *bahdur* tracking. Old Rindy is almost off the scale. That's a good sign. We've had little reading off him since he was injured. We had thought . . . we worried . . . well, brain death was not an inappropriate diagnosis for some purposes." Her lips pinched together. "Rand here was with him."

"Rand?" The manling's turquoise eyes met Palaton's, tired and happy. He looked cocooned in spite of the evening heat. "What happened?"

Ninever answered, "He told us he woke up sopping wet, and Rindy was trying to sit up in the créche. From the spike, I'd say we had a spontaneous precipitation occurrence, rare, but not impossible for a Choya with the range of Rindalan."

Rand's mouth curved generously, behind the Choya'i's broad back, but he said nothing. Palaton thought of something uneasily, but did not voice it. He looked back to the physician. "How is he?"

"He has a very long way to go. We have to worry about moisture in the lungs, kidney function, liver function—it was severely lacerated by one of the blows he took—and, frankly, he may not make it yet. But now we have a conscious, cooperative patient, and some hope."

Palaton stepped over to the elder Choya's bed. He put a hand out and rested it gently on the bony shoulder. "He's lost more weight," he said.

"His systems are not functioning well. We thought some weight loss preferable to overburdening them, but we should be able to bring him more in balance."

"Good."

Doors slipped open and Jorana stepped into the rooms. He did not have to turn around to sense her, the faint musky perfume of their lovemaking she brought with her, or the way she entered the apartments. He tightened his fingers on Rindalan's shoulder. "Continue to let me know how he's doing."

"That," the doctor said brusquely, "is a matter of course." She added, with a sense of mischief, "As long as we know where to find you."

Jorana let out a muffled noise. Palaton turned toward her, bemused, and found her staring at a nondescript spot on the floor. Her uniform had been tugged into immaculate lines, her hair combed into perfect position, and her face glowed with a blush that did not come from any artifice. She absolutely glowed, especially for that time of night.

The manling, on the other hand, looked wrecked. Rand swayed within his blanket. Palaton left Rindy's bedside and put a hand out to steady him. "It's been a long night," the pilot observed. "I'd better get you into bed."

Rand leaned against him, and whispered, "Bring Jorana." Then he straightened.

The words concerned Palaton. He considered them for a moment, then said to Jorana as he passed her, "A word with you, Commander," as he moved to leave Rindalan's converted apartments.

Palaton caught Jorana by her elbow in the corridor, saying, "Screen us."

"Here?"

"Don't tell me you can't do it. We need to talk privately."

She wore her full uniform, and some of the devices on her belt could work small miracles. Her incredulous look took in the soaking Rand. Her hands moved to set up the white-noise interference. "All right. But—"

"I know the limitations," Palaton answered. He stepped within the screen's boundary, hauling Rand in with him, and for a moment, the three of them were sandwiched together with a great deal of intimacy.

Jorana's blush deepened. "What, by God, is the meaning of this?"

"I was there when Rindy woke," Rand said. He coughed a little, as if embarrassed himself. "He told me he was being drugged, something in the water."

"What?" Palaton echoed Jorana.

"That's all he said. But he was blocked, somehow, his *bahdur*—"

"Palaton," Jorana repeated urgently, "what does *he* know of *bahdur*?"

"I heard the doctor mention it," explained Rand hastily. "And whatever it is, it was blocked. He was struggling when I awoke. The monitors, all of them, were silent. I stood by him, and I didn't know what was happening." Rand paused, and Palaton sensed that he was choosing his words very carefully. "And then this began to happen, and there was a flash of blue fire—"

"Blue fire?" Jorana and Palaton said together, again.

"It enveloped him. And I got soaked, and when he woke, he grabbed my wrist. He didn't know me, but he knew he had to tell me that he'd been drugged. Was still being drugged."

Jorana looked up into Palaton's face. "A drug, a blocker, against *bahdur*? I've never heard of such a thing."

Palaton's face had gone grim. "An abomination, if it exists. Who do you trust on staff?"

"Ninever."

"I agree. She has exclusive care and treatment of him, then, until we find out what's going on. Are you finished, Rand?"

The other nodded.

Palaton stepped back, out of the boundaries of the screen. Jorana, with a shaky little breath, ran her palm over the square on her belt, and the invisible screen went down. Rand could feel a lessening of pressure as it did so. Rand shivered.

Jorana gave him an odd look. "You'd better get him into a decent bed. I'll brief Ninever."

"Tell her as little as you can get by with. She's sharp, so she won't ask questions she knows she's not likely to get the answers to."

The security officer's eyes did not leave Rand's face.

"Unlike myself," she said, and then nodded agreement.

Chapter 11

Palaton was waiting for Rand as he came out of the showers. He toweled his head vigorously, but the faint, sweet, musky odor of roses still hung about him, though it faded with every passing minute. His skin stung as he moved the towel down and dried the rest of himself. He padded barefoot into the room, moving quietly, in case the pilot had gone to sleep.

The Choya had leaned back in Rand's chair, put his feet up on an antique table of burled wood, and appeared to be asleep, except that his jawline had not gone slack and he did not snore softly. Though Palaton would deny it, he did snore at times. The tension lines in his face had smoothed. He appeared to be more at ease than Rand had seen him in a long time, or perhaps it was just general fatigue.

One of Jorana's officers had come in with them, done a sweep of the room, temporarily disabling any recording or listening devices that might be implanted, though Jorana had told them she could not guarantee the length of the blackout, and left. For security reasons, she could not leave the equipment disabled permanently. They would have hours, she said, but no more than that. Palaton had not invited her to stay and talk with them. Something hard had glinted at the back of her lovely eyes, and Rand had known she was disturbed.

In the excitement of Rindalan's awakening, Rand had not missed the fact that Palaton had evidently been summoned from her chambers. He swept his wet hair back from his forehead and skirted the couch.

As if reading his mind, Palaton said in subdued tones, "You're hard on my love life."

Rand knotted the towel about his waist, sat, and answered, "At least you have one."

The pilot sat up straight. Rand saw the cords on the powerful neck tighten as it once more took the full weight of the skull and horn crown. "Would you," Palaton asked mildly, "like me to import someone?"

Rand's face grew hot. "No."

"Good. Because I wouldn't and I can't." An expression washed briefly over his face. "This will all be over and done soon and you'll be free to go home."

Rand did not argue about the meaning of freedom if he were planet-bound, without hope of ever piloting himself. His future was tightly woven with the Choya's, and there was no immediate possibility of separation as far as he could see. In any case, he would not allow himself to be sent home without having his own destiny firmly in his grasp. But Palaton had other things on his mind tonight, so Rand did not pursue the matter.

The pilot wove his fingers together and set his hands on one knee. "Tell me all that happened tonight."

"I went up after dinner. You were preoccupied, and I needed something to do, so I went and sat with Rindy." Preoccupied was a difficult choice of words in Trade. The language, oddly formal, did not have the word he wanted. Brooding, he thought, would have been closer, over his visit to the Household of his childhood. Rand had given up on trying to communicate with the pilot and had finally left. Even comatose, Rindy had seemed better company. "I guess I fell asleep and the med techs just left me there. I woke with cricks and cramps everywhere. He was just lying there, so I got up. I felt like touching him, to see if he were really still alive, warm, I don't know." Rand felt his forehead begin to dew up again. He mopped it with the back of his forearm.

"He woke when you touched him?"

"No, but—it was dark in there, the lighting was low, and I saw this spark . . . static electricity. And I thought of what you told me, power calls to power."

Palaton frowned heavily. "You used the *bahdur* on him. How could you?"

Rand could not tell from the other's voice if it was accusatory, or if Palaton did not understand how the power could be awakened and directed by him. He paused, again searching the language of the star-born for the words he wanted. "I didn't try. It just . . . happened. I put both hands out, to see if I could bring the sparks up again, and I began to move them down across his form. The power flared up—how could I ignore it? Rindy was so still, so silent, yet this part of him seemed to awaken at will. And then, this resistance began as soon as I moved my hands through it and it got more and more difficult. But something was happening. I could see this field go up, a tracing of blue, as though his nerves were being outlined. It answered me, like lightning, I could smell it, I could touch it, I could raise it—" Rand paused. "It got harder and harder to do, but I couldn't have stopped if I wanted to . . ."

"Harder?"

"It was as though the air were turning slowly to stone. It got suffocating. I was afraid to stop before I'd finished what I'd begun."

"And the dampness?"

"Dampness? I felt as if I stood in the rain. Drops cascaded out of me . . . over Rindy, though he didn't really get wet . . . I had no control over anything that was happening. At first, it was just my face and I couldn't see well. I tried to blink my eyes free, and the cascade got worse and worse. I spouted like a damn cloud. And whatever it was I was pushing against got worse and worse. I thought my arms were going to drop out of my sockets. I had started at the chest, gone down to his feet, then back, and every inch of it had become torture. Then it stopped. It was over, whatever it was. My hands dropped to Rindy's head. I couldn't have lifted them if I tried. I didn't know if he was dead or alive—Palaton, I didn't know if *I* was dead or alive."

"I took about three breaths, and then he reached up and grabbed my hand. I couldn't tell if he knew me, but he said that the *bahdur* had been blocked, that there were drugs in the water. That took almost everything out of him, then the alarms went off and the med techs came rushing in, and you know the rest."

"He hasn't had water by mouth for days. I was told he had slipped too deep into his coma to be given liquid that way. We'll check the IV, but that's a sterile solution. It's unlikely it's been tampered with." Palaton unlaced his fingers, energized, thinking aloud. "Someone may have given him something early on. That may explain why he's made so little recovery. We have a lot of drugs which will do horrible things, but I've never heard of one which blocks *bahdur* in such a way. Alcohol will impair it, but alcohol affects many races."

Rand brought up a corner of the towel and dried his face. Palaton looked at him then, really looked at him, and leaned across to touch cool fingertips to his brow. He smelled his hand and then put a tentative tongue to taste. "This is what you precipitated?"

The aroma of roses had grown stronger. Rand shrugged. He put his hand to his forehead. "This isn't sweat."

Palaton got to his feet. He stretched, his Choyan lines a study in controlled elegance. "The phenomena is called spontaneous precipitation . . . it would be difficult for me to explain it to you fully, but suffice it to say, if any of us could do it on command, we'd have weather under our control. Though whether it would be wise to do it would be another issue altogether. Why it occurred, I couldn't guess, but it had to have something to do with the effort of freeing Rindy's *bahdur*."

Rand leaned forward. "Maybe your power isn't gone. Maybe it's just buried, blocked somehow. Could I do the same to you?"

Palaton looked at him. He had the most mellow eyes, and they glistened now in the nighttime lighting of the apartment. "No. I have no *bahdur*. Trust me in this. I've searched for it in every fiber of my being. As for freeing it in our old friend—I don't know how that worked either, except that you did it."

"A Cleansing?" Rand put forth the only thing he knew of Cho's religion, a ritual for keeping the powers the Choyan used pure and clear. The two of them had uncovered ancient evidence that what was ritual now, evidently had been reality in the distant past. With that loss of knowledge had gone a way to treat *tezars* for the neurological burnout caused by using their powers to the point of extinction.

Palaton shook his head. "No. My best guess is that, since

we're talking about a drug here, a neural blocker, you speeded up his metabolism to the point where he literally boiled it out of his system. The display you mention was indeed his talent awakening and responding to your call upon them. Your 'rain' may have been in reaction to that, keeping both your temperatures low in juxtaposition to what you were forcing his metabolism to do—" Palaton threw up his hands. "Guesswork. We don't interfere with cellular life by using the process of *bahdur*. Proscribed methods of gene therapy were codified by scientific method centuries ago. Most of us haven't the means to do it otherwise, but even if we did, it's expressly forbidden. Our powers are tightly interwoven within the very fabric of our being, to change that fabric, to modify it in even the slightest artificial way, is to invite havoc, to open up—"

"Chaos?" suggested Rand.

Palaton stopped. His mouth closed, then firmed, then opened again in realization. "A self-fulfilling prophecy, I suppose." He looked toward the windows, where the evening sky was now lighter than the room itself. "There isn't much left of the night. I suggest you enjoy it. I want to check on Rindy one more time, confirm with Jorana how we're going to protect him, and Gathon has to be informed as much as he can be about what's happened." Palaton added wryly, "I guess my day is just beginning."

Rand found himself yawning as the pilot went to the doors. He paused just before the secured threshold.

"Rand. Thank you."

Palaton caught him trying to rub the sand out of one eye. He stopped sheepishly. "It could have been you as easily as me."

"No. I would never have dared. For that, too, I hope I can one day thank you." The pilot let himself out.

Pondering what Palaton might have meant by that, Rand lay back on the couch, curled up, and was asleep almost before he had time to close his eyes.

Charolon and the warm summer's night were obscured by distance, scarcely more than a thermal blur on the horizon when Qativar stepped from his conveyance, agitation apparent in every movement. Forced to leave his apartments in the palace, he'd moved through the hidden passages as quickly as he could. He did not like being drawn away from Rindalan's side. His appearances there had grown scattered enough. Yet either he had made an impression as the dutiful young assistant, or he had not. Word had come, word that he must act on, or his plans for *ruhl* would fall to nothing.

He had made his journey throughout the night, swiftly and in stealth, to holdings no one knew he owned. In these tangled woods, few lived, not even lumber cutters, and his grounds showed neglect, the building a cinder block, hollow-looking thing, deceptive in its appearance. Security greater than that at the palace surrounded it. Shields had been let down to allow his hover car to pass within the gates.

His aide, a wiry, twisted Choya with lank yellow locks and dark gray eyes, met him at the door.

"How many dead?" asked Qativar wasting no time on preliminaries, pushing past Erlorn.

"All whom we harvested from the riots."

That stopped Qativar in his tracks, now inside the building, empty save for the echo of his hasty footfalls. "What? All thirty?"

"Two committed suicide after the first dose." Erlorn wrung his hands. "I told you I thought the dosage too high, too high—"

"Shut up!" snapped Qativar. He had gone to so much trouble. The riots, followed by the Two Day War, had given him so much opportunity, a Choya here, a Choya'i there, no one would be missed with certainty. He had gathered his test subjects from around the globe, and secreted them here. "Were you able to record *nothing*?"

"The first tests only. I'm sorry," the hapless Choya answered, bowing, his hands moving around and around themselves in distress, as well they might. His dirty yellow strands of mane fell over his brow, knotted up with the ungrown buds of horn which had been his since youth, a horn crown that had never grown, freakish, and yet perhaps representative of his perverse nature. "What do I do with the bodies?"

Qativar stood in the empty hall and thought about the shambles of his work and the fact that all this fool could think of were bodies. He put out a hand, caught Erlorn by the throat, and half-lifted him off the floor. "Let me see them."

Choking, Erlorn twisted out of his hold and sprinted across the room to the lift. Qativar followed, still seething, his rage like a thin red veil across his vision.

Rindy had not died. He had taken that dose, not once, not twice, but three times, and he'd survived, though none of the physicians held a hope the old priest would ever revive from his coma. Though few subjects would ever carry *bahdur* to match the sheer power Rindalan had, the difference in tolerance could not have been that great. He brushed through the lift doors, and the machinery jolted into action before his weight was fully upon the platform.

Inside the building's hidden laboratory, the scene was far different. Equipment sparkled, new, up to date, the rooms pristine and antiseptic. Erlorn did the work himself, alone, with the aid of the housekeeping robots. Qativar's eyes narrowed as he stepped out of the lift, trying to adjust to the sudden brightness, for the sun had come up, and the windows facing him captured its full glory. On the other side of the building, the forest would keep the rooms dim, gray, and cool.

Erlorn took to his heels as if reluctant to let Qativar get within arm's reach of him again, but the other did not need his guidance. The reek of death led Qativar on.

In the pathology lab, he could see two forms laid out, the suicides, he supposed, their cold wrappings not quite transparent with the chill they held. Qativar did not slow down. He followed his senses to the cells beyond, to where the subjects had been held.

Death must have been nearly instantaneous, from the look of the convulsed bodies awaiting him in the cells. They lay, sprawled or fallen, not far from the cups of water which had held their poison. Qativar examined them unfeelingly, his latest subjects, noting that Erlorn had harvested healthy, vigorous young Choyan. In that, at least, there had been no fault.

"Let me see the readouts," he ordered, pausing in front of one of the cells. "Before and after."

Erlorn hurried off. He came back, pushing the sheets at Qativar in haste but not in disarray. "See . . . see the *bahdur* readings. Each and every one a Housed Choya, though not prominent. No. We dared not harvest talent that was known. They would have been missed. Perhaps searched for. But look—look, see the spikings. I did well, did I not?"

"In this phase." Qativar could not begrudge him that. He retraced his steps to the pathology lab, pushed a door open with one knee, reading all the while, until he found a clear table and could sit and study. He knew what dosage would kill. He sought a safer dosage, one that would only cripple. Cripple, he thought, because a Housed Choya without his or her *bahdur* would indeed be crippled. Easily subverted and led.

The dosage had to be found, a universal measurement, by which he could make all Choyan equal and control the release of *bahdur* when he alone ordered it. No burn-out fever, no waste of application, and no House-born superiorities. The destiny was there for him, he could feel it almost within his grasp and yet, no matter what trials they had run, he could not determine the dosage.

The day was coming when all Choyan would be leveled, brought to their knees, by him and by the work they were doing now. They would beg to have their talents restored, and he alone would have the key. Their *tezars* and their emperors could not save them.

Erlorn cast a faint shadow across the report grids. Qativar looked up, annoyed, but no longer so infuriated.

"What?"

The Choya pointed a nail, curved and as yellow as his stringy hair. "See. The first to tolerance. Only these two reacted badly. I think they lost their *bahdur* almost instantly. But the others, although they showed some confusion and disorientation—look, see here, the readings. The blockers were not in place yet. The reinforcers you suggested," and Erlorn swallowed hard, his throat bobbing, "they have to be correct. The second dosage, though, perhaps if we cut it in half."

"Not good enough." Qativar put the heels of his hands to his suddenly tired eyes. "We'll have to start over with the second dose, a milliliter at a time."

"Subjects?"

"The difficult part." Qativar balled a fist and let it drop upon the table. "We wasted a valuable opportunity."

"Not purposefully. We'd worked very hard. It should have given us good results, the results we've been waiting for." Erlorn's eyes shone. His voices rang with fervor. He believed in his work. Qativar had promised him that the next step would be freeing and even creating *bahdur*.

"The problem," Qativar answered, "is in the taking of subjects. We simply can't take the risk that anyone might come looking." He paused. "There may be some opportunities in the near future. We will have to continue to be very careful, Erlorn. No more than one from any city. Damn. The riots were a perfect cover-up."

Erlorn stood on one foot and then the other, holding his breath as Qativar pondered. Then, as if he could wait no longer, he prodded. "The bodies?"

Qativar looked at him. "Cremation. Dump the ashes in the Brisan Sea. Stay calm, Erlorn, and all should yet be well."

"Cremation? But where would I find a facility willing to—" His narrow face collapsed even farther. "Surely, Qativar, burning in the forest would be noticed."

"Then I suggest a mass grave. But not here. There are fallow lands in the southern land masses, where you ought to be able to get in and out. Who knows?" Qativar rose with a short laugh. "Perhaps they would even contribute to the new fertility. But if you do that, the bodies must be shredded before they are moved. Messy, even cold-chilled. Necessary, however. The remains will be extremely hard to ID under those circumstances."

Qativar ran his hand over the readouts, as tenderly and lingeringly as if he caressed the body of a lover. "Take your time. Do it right. I do not want you harvesting new subjects until this is handled. Agreed?"

Erlorn met his eyes. The throat bobbed again with another hard swallow. "Agreed," the Choya finally said, although he did not look happy.

Qativar thumped him on the shoulder. "The ends will justify the means. Never forget that."

Chapter 12

For a second time, the emperor of Cho came to the ambassadorial offices of John Taylor Thomas. At one time in his career as ambassador, when he was young and inexperienced, he would have marveled at this happening. Now, he would have marveled if Panshinea had not come back. He had given up much to learn his diplomatic skills, yet he thought he wielded them well. Nor did the lateness of the hour surprise him, though he was a little stunned by the emperor's solo appearance, protected only by bodyshield. An ambassador's life on Sorrow was far more dearly bought than anywhere else should an attempt be made—but they were always made, and even Panshinea was not immune. That he should risk his life to come unseen, unnoticed, unrecorded, and unaccompanied told John more than anything the emperor might say.

John had stocked libations suitable to the Choyan physiology which was not actually that different from a human's. He believed that ibuprofen was toxic; it damaged their liver or what passed for liver beyond repair if taken regularly, but other than that, there were not all that many things which could not be shared between them. Choyan tended to be vegetarians, though they weren't purists. It was simply a matter of form and resource availability. John already had a pot of *bren* brewed, its strong odor and flavor similar to that of coffee, and he poured steaming cups as soon as Panshinea brought down his shielding and seated himself.

Panshinea took the porcelain cup, exquisitely cast just for the ambassadorial offices, and appraised the china. The ebony liquid within shadowed the translucent cup heavily. He looked up from its swirls. "Have you honey or other sweetener?" the emperor asked. "I confess I've developed a sweet tooth out here among non-Choyan."

John produced powdered honey as well as sugar and non-caloric sweetener. He watched as Panshinea deliberated and then chose the honey, after all. The packet dissolved quickly in the sable *bren,* disappearing from sight. John relaxed a little after that. The packaging was new and he had worried about the absorption, but the product had not embarrassed him. He did not intend for reminders of Earth's Class Zed status to intrude on this meeting.

Panshinea took a sip or two of his drink before setting it down to cool. As he brought his attention back to John, he said, "I've come to see if you've thought about my proposal."

"I've done a great deal of thinking," John answered. He sat back, balancing his drink upon his knee. "I'm not convinced that dropping the charges is in the best interest of the people I represent. But," he added, as Panshinea stirred restlessly, "neither is driving Choyan influence from the prestigious position you currently command. I have no desire to disrupt the present balance of power."

Tiny feathered lines about Panshinea's eyes and mouth faded a little, even as the emperor protested, "It would take more than your suit to shift our power blocks, Ambassador."

"Be that as it may, the charges are worrisome, or you would not be here."

Panshinea nodded in agreement. "My presence speaks for itself."

John paused to sip at his own drink. The protein- and caffeine-enriched brew surged through his senses. It took a moment for him to gather himself. He decided to put the drink aside as the Choyan physiology, he gathered, was much hardier than the human. He looked up into Panshinea's green eyes. The predominantly jade color, he saw was outlined by a thin ring of a much darker and vibrant green. Gold-red hair and green eyes reminded him of infamous temperament back home, and he wondered if it held true for Choyan as well. He would do well to treat Panshinea with the deference due him. "I know that you have gone to a great deal of trouble to present your position to me. Therefore, I would like to suggest a compromise."

"I'm listening."

Was the dual-toned voice as even as it sounded? John

wished he were an expert in reading the fine sound differences in the Choyan voices and any equipment he had which could have recorded and tracked those differences for him was not operational, by request of the being who sat with him. But there was no doubt he had the other's full attention.

"I suggest," he said, "a suspension of the investigation. Ten months. I can do so, claiming that my people have not had the time to organize the material and put in travel requests as needed. As you are well aware, Emperor, piloting contracts can be difficult to get when needed. The suspension will become, in effect, an extension, once we are ready to begin putting forth a case. It is not the total rescission which you've asked for, but this way I feel that I can protect my people and aid yours."

The panoramic view from the window had been closed off. John Taylor Thomas had wanted the Choya to look at him while they bargained. The emperor flicked a glance at the other end of the room, saw nothingness, and looked uneasily back. "It is a thing," Panshinea said at last, "which would help us greatly if it were done." He retrieved his drink and finished it.

John said nothing, letting the silence stretch. He would not speak first now and lose the advantage he had so painstakingly built.

The porcelain china cup danced a little as Panshinea settled it back on the table. His hand almost engulfed the cup, but he handled it with the deftest of touches. That double-elbow, John noted, made for a great deal of dexterity in upper body movement. "I would not ask your people," began Panshinea, "to accommodate us without offering some recompense in exchange."

"We ask nothing."

"That," the Choya responded, "we understand. But there must be something which we can do to help your investigations. We are, you see, convinced of our innocence, yet we are just as concerned as you that the truth be uncovered."

John Taylor Thomas found himself smiling widely. The solution to a conundrum had finally presented itself. "Find me the pilot who flies for GNask."

The Abdrelik cruiser continued its foray in space norm, heavy motors vibrating through the metal plating. Alexa wondered where they might be, knew it did not matter, and was thankful only that she did not have to spend her days drugged for FTL flight. Humankind took the reality plane shift of FTL flight with difficulty, and although the drugs made it possible to endure the procedure, she did not relish being drugged. Ever. She was a hunter, and hunters kept their wits about them, remaining sharp and alert at all times.

The makeshift cage did not stink as much as it had, and Nedar had been bathed and wrestled into clean clothes, but there was little life about him, Alexa thought, as she settled down by the bars to watch him. The Choya lay facedown on his crude cot. Actually, he looked as though he'd been broken in five or six crucial places and thrown down, so haphazard and limp was his form. But she could see the steady rise and fall of his rib cage and knew he breathed. He might be trying to will that away also, but she knew he still lived.

She could not remember when she had been imprinted. She'd been only a toddler in those days, and the memory had long since faded. She'd learned, her father told her, to walk and speak Abdrelikan and Trade at the same time. But when she tried to talk to him about those days, his face would go curiously flat and his eyes hollow, and she knew that, as casually as he spoke of it, the experience had marked him almost as deeply as it had her. He would change the subject or not speak of it at all.

But beyond that, they had never spoken of its consequences. Almost from the first, she knew that the cravings which possessed her, the waking dreams, thoughts, and ruling appetites, were not hers to share, that no one else in her life would accept them, not until she had grown and met the Abdrelik who'd infected her. There had been no one else in her life with whom she could relax and be herself because in many ways, she was not even human. Among the Droolers, GNask claimed her, but even GNask did not know her as well as he thought he did. Her life might well be forefeit if he did. The only one who had looked into her eyes and seen, buried there, a core of darkness, and not turned away had been Bevan. Vibrant, sensual, dark-souled himself, now dead Bevan.

If she had turned to Rand instead, hoping he would save her, she'd have destroyed them all.

Instead, only Bevan was gone. She survived. And Rand? GNask had told her that the Choyan sheltered him. A race, she thought, which despite all its hightoned preaching about integrity had made a virtue out of blackmail.

Though she knew it was more her Abdrelikan nature which railed at the thought of Choyan rather than anything in her own dealings with them. Within her own experiences, she felt ambivalent. Still . . . they held her world hostage, all worlds hostage, and the Compact let them get away with it. Cloaking their actions with high-toned philosophy made little difference to her.

Nedar stirred. Alexa's sharp chin shot back toward him, her gaze pinned on him, his frame in shambles, the natural elegance of movement gone. Forever? What had the *tursh* done to the Choya? GNask had forced her out of the holding bay when the *tezar* had reacted violently and gone berserk after the initial introduction. She had not been allowed to return in the days since. But if she could yet forge a bond with this arrogant being, she thought she could help them both. She would do whatever she had to in order to survive.

He was barely conscious, had not lifted his head to view his surroundings, yet he knew she was there. "You watch me," Nedar said weakly. "Like a . . . do you have carrion eaters on your world?"

"Vultures," answered Alexa. With irony, she added, "They're fliers, too."

Nedar gave a dry cough. She did not know if it smothered a laugh or not. She watched him roll to his feet and stand, wavering. The fabric of his suit hung on him. He had lost even more weight, and she wondered how he could bear to straighten. His horn crown looked as though he might topple under its burden. His gaze fastened on her.

"You know," he began slowly, "what this is like."

"I know."

"I have respect for you that I did not have before." Nedar sat down abruptly, the bunk just barely catching his weight and holding him. He put his hands to his head. His voices lowered. "This must never happen to one of my people again."

On hands and knees, she crept a little closer to him. "We have no control over that."

Nedar stared bleakly. "I have control."

Alexa rested her chin in the palm of her hand as she leaned against the bars. She watched as the Choya's body began to quiver uncontrollably, caught in a net of vast desires and hungers it could not accept. She watched as Nedar, groaning, began another battle, spirit over flesh, and knew that he would lose, as she had always lost, because the flesh would do whatever it had to, to *live*. Food, the hunt, the capture, the feeding, the sustenance, that was the primary drive. Whatever other drives his race had cultivated, the Abdrelik imprinting would sweep them away. Ambition, artistry, even sex had little to do with raw survival. The outcome was never really in question. Nedar would either live, or he would die.

Although, Alexa mused, being so primal also meant there was a new sensuality on many levels. As Nedar cried out and fell to the floor thrashing, she wondered if he would die fighting. He bashed his head against the flooring, his limbs flailing. His throat swelled with guttural cries of dismay. Her heart wrenched to see him, and yet she felt that dark core of her reacting as if a prey had been run to ground, fallen, and needed only to be gutted. She forced her own thoughts away.

"Give in," she advised quietly. "Conquer it by surrendering. Accept initially. Let it become a part of you. You'll find it has much to offer."

She dared not think of what it had taken from her.

John Taylor Thomas waited in triumph for the answer to his request. Panshinea reached blindly for his cup of *bren,* spilling the last of it and not noticing.

Then, "We cannot and will not do that," the emperor denied him. "Our pilots are not ours once they've been assigned. The contracts are reviewed for conflicts with the Compact and if there are none, and the basic compatibility of duty exists, *tezars* fulfill the terms." Panshinea seemed shocked that he would ask such a thing.

"Don't tell me you don't know who is flying for GNask." John could feel a vein in his hand pulse. "Don't start a diplomatic dance with me." Surely he could not be denied, so close to his goal. He wanted his daughter back. He wanted both the Abdreliks and the Choyan out of her head, out of her system.

Panshinea hesitated. "Certainly we would know. In actuality, there is no one pilot. The Abdreliks, for security reasons, requested and have been approved for a fairly steady rotation. This is routine with cruisers used for governing officials."

John slapped his hand down on the table which separated them. The finely made porcelain cups reacted, spinning wildly on their bases, and one clattered to its side. "Don't tell me what you want me to hear. I know you know who's assigned, and how to get a hold of him. I know you probably have a pretty precise fix on his position at the moment—unless he's crossing Chaos—regardless of the security which the Abdreliks have requested!"

Panshinea's eyes shut momentarily, then opened again. "I won't discuss internal matters with you." His timbre vibrated decisively.

"This is not Choyan security you're compromising. You will locate the pilot who is using the *tezarian* drive on the ambassadorial transport. And you will make arrangements to rendezvous with him. That is what you will do to recompense me, my people, for giving you ten months of breathing time."

The emperor of Cho regarded him. "You wish to board the ship."

John gathered his resolve. He nodded once. "He has my daughter."

"When we last spoke, you told me she had been taken to Arizar."

There had been no human survivors on Arizar after the attacks and the colonies' self-destruction. John had not bothered to tell him otherwise.

"Which she was, once recruited. And she was retrieved from the colony there by Abdrelikan forces."

Thoughts moved swiftly behind green eyes. The Abdreliks had living evidence of the Choyan purpose for being on Arizar. They had had it for months, to examine at will. John knew that Panshinea would reach the inevitable con-

clusion, which was that the Choyan could not afford to let
the Abdreliks keep that evidence. Panshinea made a small
protest. "But you are allies."

John smiled thinly. "If that's true, that guarantees me
that GNask probably will not fire on me once we locate
them. But, as a Class Zed member of the Compact, our
association with a charter member such as the Abdreliks,
or even yourselves, hardly constitutes an alliance."

"Won't this . . . strain . . . your relationship with the
Abdreliks?"

"Possibly. But I doubt it. The Abdreliks appreciate
power moves now and then, even from someone they consider fair prey. And if it jeopardizes our understanding, it
should only strengthen the new accord we've reached with
you, should it not?"

Panshinea reached out, picked up the overturned cup,
and set it upright. "This poses another problem. It would
indeed be worth our while to debrief your daughter on the
situation on Arizar. It is almost a certainty the Abdreliks
would never allow us access to her." He cleared his throat.
"Forgive my self-interest, but it would be valuable to my
own cause, as well as humanitarian to aid yours."

"Whatever motivates you," answered John briefly.

The Choya stood up. His movement was so quick, so
fluid, that the other scarcely anticipated it. Panshinea
looked down at him.

"You have no real idea of what it is that motivates me,"
Panshinea said sadly. "However, be that as it may, I came
asking a favor of your government, and I am prepared to
return one for your cooperation. I will see what I can do."

Chapter 13

Gathon came out of the hot room, the dry heat having baked away some of the various aches and pains in his knobby joints. He saw the message panel lit on the desk console and, belting his summer robe loosely, crossed the room. The relief from the moist summer day fled almost immediately and he wondered, not for the first time, if stress caused his aches as much as the weather and age did. Still and all, he feared the coming winter, feared it as much for its actual as its political climate. It was not beyond him to hope futilely that Charolon itself would come before Relocation and they would have to pack up and move elsewhere. Somewhere balmy and dry, where fiti trees grew, their leafy fronds barely stirring in a gentle breeze, leaning over white sand beaches. That would suit him.

He leaned over and activated the panel. A Choya'i in the com room looked up.

"It came in by ship, sir," she answered when he asked for his message. "From the emperor, Minister."

Gathon considered the urgency of that. Subspace calls could be delayed by as long as several days. If there had been a ship coming this way, Panshinea would have saved himself some time by having it hand-carried. Gathon would have to check schedules in order to reply the same way. No doubt he wanted an answer immediately.

The minister sat. "Have it relayed. Use the privacy shields," he told her. She nodded briskly and her fingers played across her board. His screen went dark until she could bring it up. He willed himself to be patient waiting for the transmission.

He did not sleep now the way he had as a youth, nor did he dream of flying in his sleep, like the *tezars* he had once hoped to join. Nevertheless, what sleep he got he generally relished, and it had been disrupted this morning by Palaton's early arrival. Gathon reflected that he would not, however, give back the recognition in Rindy's pale blue eyes. His old friend, awake, mending at last, and cognizant of Gathon by his side when he'd gone to see for himself if the news were true. Rindy had always had the most remarkable blue eyes, the minister decided, like clear rainwater puddles. That sleep, however, once lost, could never be regained, rather like one's youth. It had been foolish of him to try.

He'd awakened at mid-morning with a throbbing headache and an echo of it in all his joints. Without checking his desk, he'd gone to sweat it out in the hot room. Now he'd kept Panshinea waiting, for he had no doubt who'd called.

As if summoned by name, the screen illuminated. Panshinea was facing someone or something else in the room who remained hidden by the embassy screen. Abruptly, the emperor turned and sat down at the monitor. Impatient, Gathon thought, as always.

"Gathon, I need the name of the *tezar* who's currently piloting for GNask," the emperor said without preamble. "I know this is security, it's Jorana's realm, but I want to circumvent her. She'll fight this request, or want it as a matter of record at the very least, and I want this kept off."

Wisely, agreed Gathon. Not one of the Houses would approve of it.

Panshinea had paused, as if to allow the minister a reaction. He flexed his neck a little, showing signs of fatigue. "As soon as you have the name, I want him contacted. Use telepathy. There must be a Star with strong enough *bahdur* to do so discreetly. I want the current position and destination. There's someone trying to rendezvous with the Abdreliks. Lest you think my common sense has failed me altogether, this is not for an act of war."

Gathon had indeed so thought. Perhaps as a Sky himself, he should have had the failure of the current Star throne on the Wheel of Cho's many life cycles as his main concern, but he didn't. He did a job, well and good, and loyally, and to have Panshinea fail while he did it, meant that he failed. His quiet self-esteem went far beyond the boundaries of Houses.

"Do this for me," Panshinea said, "as quickly as possible. Haste is of the essence, and we will get some valuable time to prepare our case against the Abdrelik and Terran charge of tampering."

Ah. Gathon realized that the emperor had made a deal, of sorts. He sat considering his options as the screen went to neutral. The three flight schools maintained records of the contracts of their *tezars*. Blue Ridge would be the weakest of the three, as Hathord was a relatively new administrator there, easiest to pressure into releasing information Gathon hadn't any right to demand. The throne kept a record of contracts, but not of the individual *tezars* fulfilling such security sensitive rolls. He could back into it, he thought, by knowing who was employed and who was left to employ, but that might take days. A telepathic sending could not relay actual conversation, only convince a *tezar* it was absolutely necessary to make contact with home as soon as possible. But even that compulsion could not be relayed until they knew who to contact.

No. The shy, quiet Earthan who ran Blue Ridge would be his best target. Gathon ran a palm over the flatscreen, shutting it down. He would have to consider how to approach the problem. What Panshinea wanted was far, far easier said than done.

Qativar heard the news about Rindalan the moment he stepped out of his conveyance in the public garages. Broadcasting rigs from the various on-line communications services filled the area. Something had broken, something immense, but before he had a chance to wonder, he was approached.

"Prelate. Can you give us an idea how the news of His Eminence's awakening struck you?"

It nearly struck him dumb. He stared for a moment at the broadcasting equipment, then stretched a smile across his face, which had grown cold and drawn. "It is a wonderful step in what we all hope will be a speedy recovery."

"Palace sources tell us you have spent much of your time at his side."

His face warmed. That much, at least, he had planned well. "He is the elder of our church, and more than a father to me as well. It pained us all to see him struck down."

"You were with him, Prelate Qativar, weren't you, when he was attacked?"

Qativar kept his back to his vehicle, obscuring the control panel, where he had not yet finished changing the plans of his journey. He pulled the smile down, looked solemn and humble, responding, "Yes. When the rioting began, Rindalan was gravely affected by it. He asked me to go out with him and try to spread calm." He cleared his throat. "If you don't mind . . . I have hopes of catching him awake later this morning, and appointments to keep."

The communicator cut his line, tossed him a thank you, then raced for the public information access area of the palace grounds. Qativar watched him go, cast a glance about the garage, then returned to what he'd been doing. His fingers moved automatically while his mind sped ahead, weighing the implications. He secured the vehicle, double-checked the computer to make sure it carried the false program record, and sprinted to the palace grounds. Communicators swarmed the front steps, broadcasting medical bulletins and expertise. He had to push through them to get by, but no one else recognized him as Rindy's undersecretary and stopped him.

He took the lift toward the High Prelate's quarters, his heart thumping in his chest with anxiety. Security met him at the door. Two Choyan in body armor, with enforcers and serious expressions.

"Sorry, sir, no one goes in."

Qativar stopped in his tracks, jaw dropping. "I'm his aide. You've no right keeping me out."

"This area is secured. No unauthorized visitors."

His throat tightened. Could they know? How could they possibly know? His *bahdur* had shielded the monitors, Rindy had been all but dead. "Surely I'm to be authorized."

The Choya'i opposite him stepped back, and through the slide doors, and disappeared while the Choya holding him at bay stood firm and put the palm of one hand to his enforcer. Qativar held his half-smile frozen, willing benevolence, wondering what had occurred in his absence. The security officer's partner came back out promptly with a rueful smile.

"Prelate Qativar, His Eminence sends greetings, but the

physicians have confirmed that even you are not authorized at the moment. The situation will be better in a few days."

Qativar swallowed his bitter reaction. He inclined his head in what he hoped was a suitably humble manner, cursing himself for not having delivered a last, fatal, dosage to the old fool while he'd had the chance. "Please convey my joy to His Eminence at his recovery and that I hope to be with him soon. We have much work to catch up on." He spun around and walked away.

He calmed himself as he headed down the corridor, telling himself that if they had known, if there had been any evidence, they would have taken him instead of turning him away. Therefore, they suspected, but they did not know. And, not knowing, they had nothing on him. He had lost an opportunity, but he had not lost all.

Jorana returned to her quarters late in the afternoon. She pulled off her boots and sat, the solar fans complaining as she activated them, and felt the coolness begin to slowly steal over her body. The intensity of the season would soon be over, she reminded herself. Not that her days would be any shorter or easier, but at least somewhat cooler. Though, and she swiveled about in her chair and eyed the dresden blue sky from her view window, neither was she anxious for the gray-drizzle days of fall.

Jorana let the chair continue around in a lazy swivel and saw something across the room that hadn't been there that morning.

A messengered packet had been left for her on her desk. The seal showed it had been through security, though it was unopened, the privacy bonding on it still unbroken. If she had not been who she was, the packet would have been opened and scanned as well. Jorana sat, looking at the packet, too weary to get up. Finally, she summoned both the strength and the courage.

The packet contained no outward marks of who sent it, although it was in a common business envelope. Jorana hesitated, then decided to rely upon the security screening she helped to maintain, and slit the package open. It did not explode or emit poisonous gas once the seal broke, and she found she'd been standing tensely, her shoulders bunched, as if she had expected it to.

Instead, a travel voucher and a piece of paper slid into her hand. The voucher bore a round trip destination to Bayalak, and the note said only, "There is a new Prophet. Find her."

The note had been handwritten, an arrogant scrawl, really, and she knew it well enough that it needed no signature. Malahki.

His resources never ceased to amaze her. How he'd gotten this in to her . . . even if she attempted to trace it, she was certain the trail had been thoroughly muddied. And, obviously, it was too important to leave in the garden wall. The voucher could be traced, eventually, if found.

Jorana looked up and caught a glimpse of herself in a corner mirror, biting her lip pensively.

A prophet in Bayalak. Why did he want her to go? Charolon, and specifically the palace in Charolon, was her charge.

Yet forecasters had become rare indeed. Was this one genuine? And whether she was, or was not, what was her purpose? Did she foment trouble for either Panshinea or Palaton? What was the connection between her and Malahki? How had he learned of her? And how did he expect Jorana to find her knowing this little of her?

She tapped the travel voucher against the palm of her free hand. He undoubtedly expected her to seek him out for more information, to argue the request, to disclose information she might have gained on her own, all of which went against her grain. She was not Malahki's hidden asset within the palace. She would not act for him.

Jorana destroyed the note and placed the voucher back upon the desktop. Yet who among them would not want a hint into their future? She eyed the ticket, knowing that she had not destroyed it because she would go to Bayalak, and look for a gem among pebbles, hoping the brilliance of its shine would not blind her. She put a hand up to the back of her neck and rubbed it gently. The voucher was an expensive one, open to all availabilities.

Jorana checked her chronograph. No time like the present. Bayalak was not likely to be any cooler than it would be a few hours from now. She put in a summons for a jet sled to take her to the port, leaving her just enough time to effect a disguise and a little trail muddying of her own.

*　　*　　*

Dusk came with a heavy, cloying scent that struck her as soon as she left the port terminal. Trumpet flowers on vines opened in a nocturne pulse, flooding the area with their scent. The streets were dabbled with puddles from a short burst of hot, tropical rainfall. It had stopped just before they disembarked. Jarana paused for a moment, watching the crowds, thinking that Malahki would have anticipated this, too, and sent someone to meet her. No one, however, stepped out of the kaleidoscope of Choyan, no one sorted themselves from the myriad colors and scents that appeared quite different from more northern Charolon. Jorana found herself smiling as Choyan more striking than birds in full plumage moved past her, their summer cottons in swirls of prints and patterns that somber folk such as Palaton would never have considered wearing. It looked as though they dared the flowers and birds of the tropics to compete with them.

She shouldered her bag, preparing to go into the city, her enforcer secreted at the small of her back, reminding her of its presence, when she thought she saw a familiar head shape moving among the throngs.

Jorana swung about to catch him. As she did so, the Choya disappeared beyond the boarding portals, lost to her unless she wished to retrace her steps. She had not caught definitive sight of the other's crown or face, she could not swear it was Chirek, nor did she have any reason to believe he would be in Bayalak. One of Gathon's undersecretaries would have no purpose here, particularly a God-blind, which Chirek was, if she remembered correctly.

Loath to compromise her disguise by going after the Choya, she stayed where she was, telling herself she had not seen the other's face, but knowing that she had an intuition, a memory, for the way others moved, which bordered on *bahdur* itself as a recognition factor. Even if it had been Chirek, there was no crime in the other's presence. Jorana reshouldered her bag and pressed back into the departing flow of the port traffic.

Once outside, she could see a definite mixture of old city and new. The new lay back from the waterfront, cautiously placed to avoid damage from floods and hurricanes, not uncommon on this coast. It rose in multilayered skyscrapers, glittering windows, and solar panels.

The old city, on the other hand, lay low and lean, old and discolored, strong by dint of surviving over the centuries, battered by tide and wind. It did not glitter in the moonlight. It hunkered low like an animal stalking, waiting, slumbering perhaps, and perhaps not. Its streets looked narrow and unpromising. Jorana paused outside the travel port. She looked over the rentals. Conveyances appeared battered and haphazardly scattered. There was a newer jet sled leaning on its stall. She chose that, initiated the contract, signed it off, and took the machine, keeping an eye on the traffic as she did so. The Houseds tended to flow toward the new city, the God-blind toward the old.

She decided to try the wine parlors down in the old city first, mounted the jet sled, and kicked it into gear. It answered with a thrill of power and took her into the night. Dirty water sprayed as she drove down the narrow, hardpacked streets. Choyan watched her, eyes slit, expressions closed, as she passed, almost as if they knew she'd come to find their secrets.

"Valton blush," she ordered, stripping off her gloves and dropping into a clean chair, brushing away crumbs from the tabletop in front of her. The blush seldom went to her head, and this was the fourth parlor she'd been to, unable to pick up or solicit any gossip. If Bayalak had a Prophet, they were singularly unaware of it, at least in the old city. There might be prophets aplenty in the new city, but she doubted if any there would have the ring of authenticity. They would be milking whatever gain they could out of the flush Houseds living there. No. The Prophet she looked for would be among the poor, working not for gain, but for change and the future. Now Jorana knew she should not have been so stubborn. She should have gone to see Malahki first, to be briefed on the situation he wished her to investigate.

Her drink came, carried by a Choya'i, her stomach swollen in mid-pregnancy, her eyes sullen, for it was obvious that she had enough of the talent to recognize Jorana as being Housed. She had lank, yellow-white hair and eyes of deep sapphire, and her teeth had grown in crooked, spoiling her smile. She set the carafe of Valton blush and a glass in front of Jorana, looking her over carefully, slyly.

Jorana poured a glass and toasted the health of her unborn. "May your child's feet be swift, and his crown sturdy." The blush went down smoothly, a better vintage than she'd found at the other wine parlors, or perhaps it was simply watered down more skillfully. She did not have to manufacture the envy in her voices.

Something flickered in those jewel-dark eyes. The server watched as Jorana poured a second drink. "Anything else, honorable one?" the Choya'i said, her tone edging not on sarcasm, but on raw curiosity.

"Nothing you can bring me," Jorana said. She laid the bait out, wondering if the other would take it, along with the cold, hard coin paying for the drink.

The coin disappeared with sleight of hand that would do a trickster credit. The Choya'i said, "Do you want the credit back?"

"I'm fine, thank you."

The server should have left then, but she stayed, her hip nudging the table. She pitched her voices confidentially. "This is not a good part of Bayalak for you to be in alone."

Jorana looked up from her glass. "Thank you," she answered. "Your wine was recommended to me. When I'm finished, I'll go."

The Choya'i stood, baffled, then turned to leave. She bent back yet again. "Perhaps someone to talk to?"

"Again, no thank you. I'm not very good company tonight. I have a lot on my mind." Jorana faced the other as they spoke, but she also noticed the action in the half-empty room around her. No one particularly paid attention to them, though she knew they were not being ignored either.

"A Choya," the server guessed, and smiled, as if she'd divined that.

"Always. And what to do about him. I want children. He does not." Jorana shrugged.

"Not want children?" The server sounded a little shocked, as well she might. There were never enough children. The numbers dwindled yearly. Families celebrated each birth and prayed for the *bahdur* which blessed Cho to bless their progeny. She rested a hand on her own swelling belly. "I'm sorry."

Jorana moved diffidently again. "What can I do? I cannot

force him. Anyway, now I must decide." She looked about the wine parlor, simple, rustic, dingy. "This is as good a place as any."

The server sat down abruptly. She laid her tray on the table. "Better, perhaps." Her glance darted about. She leaned forward. "There are ways."

Jorana finished her glass and poured a third. She slid it toward the Choya'i, so that she might share it. "I won't use drugs. They might hurt the baby."

The Choya'i flipped her hand impatiently. "Not that. Listen to me. You're Housed. You know there is talent which can guide you, foretell your future."

"That talent runs thin as water in my family." Jorana shook her head in discouragement. "I barely passed the testing."

"Yet if I could find you such a one, would you use it? Would you value the casting?"

Jorana eyed her evenly. "I would."

The other stared intently, as if deciding the truth in her eyes and words. Then the Choya'i stood. She had not touched the offering of wine. "Good luck to you," she said in farewell, and disappeared to the back of the wine parlor, tray balanced on her hip.

Jorana sat musing the other's abrupt departure. Had she not passed the test? Had the other had enough talent to look past the surface truth of her words and see shadows lurking? She finished her final glass of Valton blush, not wanting to drink further, and sat for a moment, listening to the music in the background and the soft murmur of conversation, examining her minor triumph. At least here, she'd had a hint that there might be someone plying their trade at fortune-telling. Every city had them; she'd begun to wonder if the Bayalakans had any talents at all running in their veins.

Jorana stood, feeling the drink suffuse itself throughout her. She would leave the old city and return in the morning to begin again.

Outside, in a parking stall, her jet sled looked as though someone had been at it. Jorana cursed the security alarm for not sounding. She tucked her gloves into her belt and approached the bike. It had been shifted on its stand, and someone had tried to jimmy the fuel cell, but it looked as though no real damage had been done. Jorana clucked her tongue in relief. She had no wish to be stranded out here. The air felt as though it were gathering for another brief downpour.

As she leaned over the seat to release the stall's lock something moved behind her, too quickly for her to turn. It crashed across the back of her skull. She felt herself go, collapsing with a soft gasp across the jet sled, limbs limp, unable to keep herself from sliding into the blackness, cursing at herself for carelessness.

"Is she the one?"

A sharp set of voices, harsh against the throbbing in her skull, Jorana felt the grit of a dirty floor against her cheek. She ached, abominably and her arms had gone numb, unwilling to obey her. A toe prodded her ribs. "You asked for her, we brought her."

The sharp voices again. "Describe her face. Tell me what the jewelry looks like."

Jorana could not help but let a tiny moan escape, dismay at having been caught, like an amateur, certain they knew who she was and what value she might be. She'd been ID'd despite her care at disguise.

Someone put a rough hand into her mane and lifted her head, resting it on her pointed chin. Her neck cramped immediately, sending jarring waves of pain into her shoulders. The increased sensation woke her, though. She batted her eyes in awakening, could not see in the dim room, could not focus, and her chin hurt as the grit dug into it. There was a smell in the room, a stench she could not identify, an old aroma ground into the very fibers of the rough wood planking, a smell like . . . misery.

"Her jewelry! Describe it."

"Black onyx and gold chain," said the one whose fingers tore at her scalp. He described the inset pattern and then let her face drop back. For a moment, it felt blessedly better, then her head began to throb again.

A third said softly, "Leave us."

Feet shuffled on the floor, as though in reluctance.

Again, patiently, "Leave us."

"But—"

"I'll be fine. You can wait outside."

Jorana rolled onto her flank as Choyan paced around her and a door banged shut in their wake. She opened her eyes wide and saw dark stained planking overhead, blurred and swimming, and gorge rose in her throat. She squeezed her eyes shut quickly to stop the disorientation and her sickness.

There was a rustle of fabric. Someone inched their way across the room toward her, a warm body kneeling over her, a blessed feeling of relief as hands were placed on her, touching her brow gently, and Jorana dared to open her eyes again.

She stared at the ill-lit visage of a Choya'i, bloodstained bandage about her face hiding her eyes. She pulled Jorana into a sitting position.

The Choya'i smiled. "I've been looking for you," she said and moved back to a rocking chair where she sat.

A faint scent of *drath* hung on the air, and she wondered if the Choya'i had been taking it for pain. There was also a scent of what she could only describe as *bahdur* overburn, power out of control, a scent somewhat like wood smoke. Prickles of anticipation bit at her as she wondered what they had in store for her.

She put a hand to her chin and carefully brushed off the dirt, wincing as the scrape stung a little.

"You're surprised," the Choya'i said. "Why? You were also looking for me."

"I was—" Jorana halted. She narrowed her eyes "You're the Prophet."

"I am."

"And you know who I am."

The young Choya'i, who would have been pretty, had her face not suffered such a terrible ravaging, laughed slightly. "No. I don't know who you are, except that I knew what I must tell you, and what you looked like. I hoped you would come here. Then I felt you . . . so I sent for you."

Jorana got slowly to her feet. Malahki had set her up. What was transpiring back at Charolon while she wasted time here, she dared not guess, but anger flared in her suddenly at being used for another's purposes. "Don't waste my time."

The Choya'i snatched off her bandage, flaking dried

blood and scab from her cheekbones as she did so, exposing the terrible blood-black holes in her face. Jorana bit down on a gasp of pity. .

"Do I look," the other asked, "less than authentic to you?"

"I don't know what a Prophet should look like." Her own voices quavered at the mutilations as she added, "Who did this to you?"

The Choya'i put out her hands, and Jorana could see the rusty dried blood under her fingernails. "I did it to myself. I couldn't bear what I was seeing." The laugh now held a bitter edge. "I didn't know that it would not stop the visions."

Jorana felt guilt instantly, along with the pity. "It was seeing me that—"

"No. Others. Other things. Terrible things."

The acrid scent of ill-used *bahdur*. Jorana hazarded a guess. "You did not have the power before." Before what, she could not be certain, but the otherwise pretty, delicate young Choya'i sitting before her in agony had the look about her . . . almost childlike . . . sometimes *bahdur* came with the late onset of puberty. If it had rushed in, burning untrained, misunderstood, it was capable of destroying the life which birthed it. The condition was rare, but Jorana had seen it before. She wondered if she saw it now.

The Choya'i turned her face slightly, coming about a little to meet Jorana more squarely. "No. I was empty before. I could close my eyes and see peace. But not now. I wish to God-in-all I didn't have it! But I do. It burns like poison in my gut." The Choya'i looked unerringly at her as if she could see her clearly now. "I had you brought here so that I might tell you what I must."

Jorana felt chilled in the muggy tropical night. She rubbed her forearms. "Do you know who I am? And could I stop you?"

The other shook her head slowly. Her mouth curved slightly as she answered, "But you must know of what I speak, you must understand, because I don't, and yet someone must hear and understand and my . . . eyes . . . told me it was you."

The Prophet did not care what burden she placed on her.

Jorana forgot Malahki and his machinations, her suspicions of what brought her there, all else that had transpired, and braced herself. "Then I'm listening."

"Cho cannot have two emperors," the Prophet said. "There is Panshinea, and there is Palaton. This cannot be."

The chill turned to ice. Her teeth tried to chatter. She clamped her jaw shut in determination. "Palaton is only the heir. It's a formality for the succession—"

"Cho cannot bear two emperors," the Prophet repeated. "One of them must shortly die. You must make the decision which."

"How could I do such a thing?"

The Choya'i's voices rose in a bittersweet tone. "I know that you do because I have seen it."

"Then tell me what it is I do."

"No. You will do what you have to, but it must come out of you. I can't tell you. But when I felt you coming to Bayalak, I knew that I could bring you in, prepare you for what you have to do."

"Why must I choose?"

"If you do not—" Her hand went up to her ruined eyes, touched there as if probing the wound gently. "Ruin. Cho collapses on itself. The Abdreliks and Ronins sweep in like carrion hunters for the afterkill. The secret of the *tezarian* drive is lost. Our invaders, unable to recross Chaos, stay. Countless worlds, the same scenario. The death, the weeping. . . ."

"Don't do this to me," Jorana implored. Her tone cracked under the strain. "Tell me who."

"I can't! I don't know! There was too much to see, I don't understand—" The Choya'i sagged suddenly in the chair. Her chin fell to her chest. A thin line of new blood trickled from one socket, a bloody tear. Her tone crumbled into tears, which she gulped back into silence. With trembling hands, she tugged her bandage roughly back into place. The softness gone, she rasped, "Do you think I know? Or understand? Get out of here and leave me be. I've told you all I can! Now get out!"

Chapter 14

The late summer heat of Charolon felt cool compared to the sultry humidity of Bayalak. Jorana took a deep breath, smelled the city instead of the bayous and delta and panet. Bag in hand, she swiveled past the commonly used gates and prepared to leave through the freight bays, when a strong step caught up with her, and she felt a hand curl about her high elbow.

Her *bahdur* flared enough for her to know it was Malahki behind her, propelling her down a corridor. He must have been waiting for her ever since he'd discovered her absence. An empty office door slid open and he guided her in.

"You went without talking to me first," he accused, blocking her exit from the room.

Jorana scanned it quickly before answering. She saw no recording or visual systems in operation that she could readily identify, and then realized that Malahki knew this room was here, open, available, and uncensored, or they would not be standing here. She ignored the chairs and perched on the edge of the conference table.

"What more would you have told me about her?"

He sucked his breath in quickly. "You found her, then?"

"Didn't you expect me to?" His unexpected reaction cut into her belligerence.

He did take a chair, conquering more than sitting in it. He would not look at her. "I hoped you might. I didn't know what you'd find. I wanted to talk to you first, tell you why I had my suspicions." Then, from under stormy brows, he peered at her. "Is she authentic?"

"Oh, she exists, all right. How accurate her sight is remains to be seen. I didn't go equipped to test her."

"Tell me about her."

"She's young. She might have been beautiful. She has

the lines of a commons, but I think she merely came into her power very late. She's probably from a minor House-holding. Her talent's strong. It's burning right through her, and she's out of control. So, although I think she has ability, I don't know if she can use it or not. Or be of any use to you."

"That's not my concern."

Jorana could feel her forehead arch slightly. "Isn't it? Then why did you send me?" She thought of seeing Chirek at the port. "Is Chirek one of yours?"

Malahki flinched. Jorana realized she had ferreted out something and pounced on it. "He is, isn't he? So the question is, what has he to do with her?"

"That," Malahki said heavily, "I was hoping you could tell me."

Jorana lifted her chin. "If you need to know, then he's not one of yours." Thinking rapidly, she reached for intuition and declared, "Then you must be one of his." The luminary looked at her, glaring. She saw the pride, anger, and concern in him. It rocked her. "Oh, God. Malahki, there are few Choya who could top you, and I've found one of them. But I also know you wouldn't have faith in Chirek if he didn't merit it—so why trail him to Bayalak? Why seek out the Prophet? What's the connection?"

Shaking his head, Malahki got ponderously back to his feet. "I had forgotten how good you are in your career," he said. "Jorana, I can't tell you more. Your life is already dangerously close to forfeit as it is. And I won't have that, you mean too much to me." He started to leave.

She kicked out a boot, catching the empty chair, thrusting it, with an assist from her *bahdur,* across the room to block the threshold. Malahki stumbled to a halt. He looked back at her.

"Why didn't you know what he was doing there?" she repeated.

He took a deep breath. Then, "He didn't want me to know of the Choya'i. The ways of God are at least as devious as those of civil disobedience."

"Of God? Malahki, foster father, you have never bowed to the God-in-all in your life—" Struck, Jorana stopped. Stared.

"He's a priest of the prophecies of Change," Malahki told her, even as her thoughts plunged her into that same abyss.

"Renegade. That heresy was outlawed centuries ago."

"You're looking at a faithful follower."

Jorana narrowed her eyes. "You couldn't be."

He shrugged. "Perhaps not that faithful."

"Even if he was, why would he go to her? Why not send you, or someone else? Why risk exposure?"

Malahki put a hand up. "I don't have those answers. If you had come to me first, I could have given you some background, and you could have gone to Bayalak with your eyes open. We both might understand more now. But you've told me something valuable I didn't know before. I didn't know Chirek was involved with her."

"What difference does that make?"

"All the difference in the world. Look at your monitors covering the presentation, at the attack on Palaton. Look at your recordings very carefully. See if the Choya'i you saw at Bayalak is in the picture."

"Why?"

"Because, my precocious one, Chirek hired the Choyan who attacked Palaton. I don't know why. He never intended their deaths, I know that. But I'm told there was also a fourth, one who got at Rand, though she did not harm him. Look at the visuals. Tell me if she's the one you found at Bayalak."

"And if she is?"

The flecks of gold in Malahki's deep brown eyes seemed to glitter. "Then come and find me, and tell me if the Prophet told you anything. We may well stand at the brink of the Changing of the world." With that, he shoved the chair aside and left.

Jorana sat, stunned. The Changing of the world, when all Choyan were given prodigious *bahdur* powers, and nothing would be the same again, the apocalypse of Cho as they knew it. Many had predicted that such a coming would not be the beginning of a brave new society, but the cataclysmic end of everything. She blinked, and then marveled not that the Prophet had gouged her own eyes out, but that she had not taken her life as well.

*   *   *

The transmission from Blue Ridge flickered, interrupted by sunspot activity, but it was fitting, for Gathon had obviously caught Hat inconveniently.

Hathord gave Gathon a slightly harried look over the view screen. "That's information I can't give out," he argued plaintively in answer to the minister's request.

Gathon watched the flight school's master intently. There were many fine lines on the face which hadn't been there—what, ten years ago?—when he'd first taken over for the ailing Moameb. He had been the youngest flightmaster in Cho's history. The square, sensitive, strongly empathic Earthan had not been recommended because of his flying skills but because he had the temperament which seemed most desperately needed by the school. He was both father and mother to his cadets, nursing along each and every skill for piloting. It was to his credit that the attrition rate had been markedly less at Blue Ridge than at the Commons and the Salt Towers. Even Hat did not know how valuable he was. Still, it was not enough to protect him against the emperor's ire. Never enough. Gathon smothered a sigh and said only, "Hat, I cannot impress on you enough that this is not a request, it's an imperial demand. I can't tell you why we need it, but we do. I can assure you that no attack or other act of war will be planned with the information."

Hat ran stubby fingers through brunet hair that the sun had streaked with chestnut. His dark eyes shadowed deeper with indecision. He looked aside as if he might be consulting with someone else who sat in the comfortable, well broken in study at the school, but Gathon already knew the room was empty save for Hat and the view screen. The stubby fingers now pulled at the V neck of his faded flight tunic as if even that vee might feel too tight.

"I might not even have it on record," said Hat.

Gathon, ever the diplomat, knew a stall when he heard one, however unskillful it might be. He made a "tch" sound before saying, "Although the emperor does not involve himself in reviewing or assigning contracts, we know the three schools remain on-line with one another." He firmed his expression. "I don't wish to make an issue of this, Hathord, but I'm prepared to if I have to."

Hat, fortunately, had not been a diplomat long enough to know a bluff when he heard one. His expression crumpled. "All right," he surrendered. "But I'll have to get back to you."

"Do that," Gathon told him, and ended the transmission in relief. Short of invading the school and forcibly downloading the information, he had no way of enforcing an imperial decree. He didn't know what Hat expected of him. Fines, perhaps, or even reassignment. Gathon rolled back in his chair, flexed his brows a few times, and considered that, although he disliked browbeating, he had a certain flair for it. Panshinea would have his coordinates soon.

Hat moved away from the darkened screen with a sick feeling in the pit of his stomach. He could think of only one reason why Palaton, the acting emperor, would demand contracting and stationing information. They'd identified Nedar, knew that he was alive, and had begun to search for him. That Palaton would leave no stone unturned was apparent if he had stooped to using imperial decree even though he was technically just the heir.

Hat wiped his eyes. He could, of course, give Gathon what he wanted. Nedar's whereabouts would not be on the records. He did not regret sheltering his friend when the *tezar* had returned to him hurt and betrayed, hunted by Palaton and the renegades of Arizar, but now . . . now that Hat needed desperately to know where he was, needed his advice and guidance, where was he? He had obviously not died striking at Palaton or the body would have been found. He had not returned to the Choya'i who ran his House of Sky. He had vanished, as though he had never existed, and Hat felt heartsore with worry. He didn't know how much longer he could protect Nedar against Palaton and the throne.

Nedar trusted him and Hat would never willingly betray him, but he knew that if he did not comply with the latest demand, Palaton would come himself to investigate and that Nedar's presence at the school would be difficult to conceal. His rooms fairly brimmed with aura, an undeniable sign of recent occupation even though Nedar had kept himself hidden from the cadets, not hard to do in a school less than half-filled.

It would be better to give Gathon what he'd requested than to open the way to a line of inquiry which might prove

even more disastrous. Hat wiped his eyes again. *Tezars*
ought never to have to bow to this sort of pressure. Without
them, Cho would be a planet lost. He thought again of
Nedar's assertion that they should be loyal only to their
own, erasing all House lines, a power of their own, unto
their own. He had not supported Nedar before, but now
he knew that his own circumstances had changed, had been
molded by actions beyond his control.

With a resolved sigh, he crossed to his terminal and
began to call up assignments.

The gaunt form still reclined under sterile sheets, but
now the Choya snored lustily as Rand sneaked in and took
a seat, and found himself grinning ear to ear at the racket.
There was a snored and a gurgle as Rindy woke himself
and lay there a moment, uncertain, and smacking his lips.
Then his eyelids batted, and he lifted his head a little.

"Manling. Is that you?"

"I didn't mean to wake you."

"Nonsense. My own snoring woke me." Rindy's voices,
thin with weariness, argued with the same old orneriness.
He poked a finger into the side of the bed, energizing controls, and the head of the machine came up, bolstering him.
Pale blue eyes studied Rand with a clear, intent gaze. Then,
finally, the elder Choya spoke again. "Come here often,
do you?"

Rand could feel the color flushing his cheeks. Luckily
what passed for a haircut, Choyan style, hid his ears. "Yes,"
he admitted.

"One would wonder why."

"I was alone enough," Rand told him, "without losing
you as well."

Rindalan scratched the base of his crown. "Do all humankind pick friends so easily, with so lax a criteria?"

The embarrassment turned to irritation. "You told me
the truth, regardless of your feelings or mine. I count that
as a bond between us."

"Even if that truth misled you?"

"Even so."

"Ummm."

Rand knew suddenly, as if his borrowed powers had read
the other's mind, that Rindalan pondered the ability to

make good judgments about friendships and other matters without the intuitive sense Choyans had. Even the God-blind were not so handicapped. He realized how much the others had come to depend on that sixth sense, and how limited they thought him, unable to know. But they did not know either, not really, if *tezars* such as Nedar came to prominence among them. "We can be deceived," he said, suddenly mild. "Anyone can be."

Rindy blinked. Then his eyes crinkled at the corners with humor. "And is our friendship deceptive?"

"I don't think so. On Earth, we'd call it genuine."

The thin and knobby fingers of the priest plucked at his sheets. "I'm told," Rindy said, "that you awakened me."

How to tell him the truth of that? Palaton would never let him. While Rand pondered a lie, Rindy interrupted by saying, "I had a thorn in my dreams. It would not let me proceed along the Wheel, and the God-in-all did not speak clearly to me because of it. My attention kept straying from Him. I know now it must have been you, nagging me." The Prelate let out a tremulous sigh. "I cannot go until the question of you is answered and finished."

Rand refused to feel blame. "Good," he said briskly and stood up. "Because I'm not the only one here who still needs you."

"One would never know it," Rindy replied, "from the number of guests I have."

Rand had been about to leave. He stopped in his tracks. "They didn't tell you? Dr. Ninever? You don't remember?"

"Remember what?" snapped Rindy.

"You told me you'd been poisoned. The med techs couldn't find any trace of it, but the coma supports it—they thought you'd come out of it long ago. Your quarters have been restricted. Only a couple of us, Dr. Ninever, certain nurses, can get in and out."

"I told you?" The expression in the pale blue eyes wavered a little, and Rand could see the inevitable weariness growing. He did not want to stay much longer.

"They said it was a neural blocker. Something in your system." Rand did not say more, afraid to give himself away.

"A blocker?" Rindy raised himself in his bed, the fatigue

fled from eyes which now glinted fiercely at him. "I lay here powerless?"

Rand nodded.

"Who else knows?"

"Palaton. Jorana. Gathon. That's it. Even Qativar can't come in and see you."

The fury died a little. Rindy's lips pursed as he considered it. "That must make my secretary happy," he said, bemused.

"Furious, from what I was told. Jorana hasn't had time to clear him yet."

Folding his arms, Rindy settled back in his bed. "If my security is in Jorana's hands, I'll live forever. I trust her more than I trust myself."

"You should," Rand answered. "She wasn't the one who sent you out in the riots in the first place."

Rindy pointed a lecturing finger at him. "Those were my people. They needed my ministry."

"They nearly killed you."

The other looked tired again, and sad. "The commons are difficult to reach. It's our own fault. The Church drove them away long ago. It's still not fashionable for us to try and bring them back. But I couldn't let them destroy themselves."

"No," Rand agreed. "And that's one of the reasons I count you among my friends."

Rindy, whose gaze had dropped as he sat thinking, now looked up again and gave a sharp laugh. "Caught me, mauling, on my own horns. As neat a circle of philosophy and subtle intent as any I've had thrown at me. Point made, and taken. You may indeed count me among your friends." Rindy lowered his bed. "Now leave me to an old Choya's nap." He closed his wrinkled eyelids and before Rand had even reached the apartment's threshold, there was snoring from the hospital créche behind him.

Chapter 15

Eyes blearing with fatigue, Jorana sat before the micro-reader and went through the visuals. The security rooms were quiet, all other personnel gone to their barracks except for those physically on watch, the systems on automatic. The communicators and even the security systems were focusing on Palaton, naturally, for he was their heir, and the center of security concerns. Outside the grounds, the taping was sparse. She'd gone through a lot of tape before she'd found any camera that had Rand in more than peripheral focus during the parade and ceremonies.

Then she saw it. Jorana froze, tiredness fading, and leaned close to the screen, watching the vivacious figure in blue dancing close to Rand. It was plain to her, watching, that the Choya'i had the humankind as her goal, though her path wended its way through the throngs of commons and Houseds who were parading for Palaton's benefit. Yet that slender figure could not be mistaken.

Jorana ran her fingers through her hair and then, settling on one elbow, chin in hand, ran the tape back and watched the approach again. No. She was not mistaken. The Choya'i always kept Rand in her line of sight.

If she had only noticed this earlier, or any of her guard had—this was a textbook example of the kind of approach which should alert any of them, and they had all missed it. They should not have missed it. Of any of the procession, Rand's presence had aroused the most emotion. He was, after all, alien. Palaton's guardianship over him would not erase that. She *knew* that.

Jorana found herself biting her lip. The sweet, flat taste of iron on her tongue made her stop, even as she vowed that Rand would never again go so underprotected. She let the tape advance, and watched the Choya'i carefully. She brought up the frame, targeted the face, the horn crown pattern, trying to ID her more fully. It took a few long moments for the computer to pick up the scope and follow her instructions.

Then, suddenly, the face of the Prophet stared at her from the microreader screen. And the eyes, oh, they had once been startling eyes, hazel with flecks of green in their depths, laughing eyes, eyes which no longer existed.

Jorana ordered a few prints of the face, but she knew that Malahki, if he told her anything more, would not tell her all that he knew. She would have to go to Chirek, but that would take time. She would have to put him under closer observation, build a dossier, then see what answers she could get from him.

She wanted to, but could not discount, Malahki's own gloomy prophecy. Not without more information. She could not tell Malahki what she'd seen or surmised, but he would know, eventually, when she did not contact him. She could not predict what he would do to protect the Prophet, the Being of Change, or what he might force Chirek into doing. And, as far as what this Choya'i had told her, she would not bear that burden without doing all she could to avoid it nor would she tell Malahki.

No one, nothing, could force her to choose between her emperor's life and Palaton's.

She had very little time before Malahki would act on his own. Jorana snapped off the microreader, listened to the printer making her copies, and sat in the cubicle, her thoughts as heavy as the horn crown hugging her skull.

"We have your target in sight, Ambassador."

John, his ears ringing slightly from the combination of drugs used to combat the effects of FTL, came to a view portal. He saw the Abdrelik's vessel and smiled in satisfaction. He had him!

"Good work," he answered. "Get permission to board." Weak in the knees, he sat back down and waited for the heavy thumps and vibrations which would accompany the docking maneuver. GNask would let him board, if only for curiosity's sake. Leaving the ship might be another matter.

The look on GNask's face as he came to the docking bay and found John standing there, flanked by a company of fully armed Marines was perhaps worth it. The Abdrelik responded, charging into the area as soon as the adjoining air locks gave way, his purplish skin darkening in the equivalent of a flush. His tusks gnashed together once, twice, before the words came rumbling out.

"Ambassador. Might I have an explanation for this boarding?"

"Ambassador," responded John, "it's come to my attention that you carry passengers who would be better off in our hands. I commend you for their rescue from the dire conditions of Arizar, but for their continued health and proper medical care, I must urge you to let me take them." He was surrounded by well-trained soldiers, in deep space gear, helmets clipped to their utility belts, rifles cradled in their arms, weight lightly balanced on the balls of their feet, ready and waiting for action. Although John's words had been mild in tone, the Marines bore silent witness to his true intent. The only hedging he did was to avoid referring to Alexa by name and relationship, for that advantage he might still wish to hold, and he wondered if GNask caught the inference.

The alliance was being strained, but not broken.

Although, John reflected, if the Abdrelik did not hand his daughter over, it would be. The Marine closest to him moved slightly, mirroring his tension. The rifle rattled in his hands.

GNask's piglike glance darted to the weapon and back again. Then the alien spread his arms wide. "Naturally, Ambassador, now that their conditions have stabilized, it would perhaps be prudent to do as you suggest. They are survivors, after all, of a traumatic situation. We would not want to do anything to jeopardize their recovery."

John felt himself relaxing ever so slightly. He stepped forward. "You've done a great service," he said to GNask, "in retrieving them."

"We would not think of doing less," responded GNask, but his eyes narrowed, grew hard and flinty as John approached. The Abdrelik looked over his shoulder at the waiting adjuncts. "We have guests," he said, "who need medical care we cannot provide. Ready them for transfer."

Alexa lay in her cell, half-asleep, half-awake, thinking of nothing in particular. Drowsily, she'd heard the ships docking

and wondered what the Droolers were up to now. She'd left
Nedar in his cage, icily in control of himself again, the incision
where the *tursh* had been introduced in flagrant infection,
abscessing, and GNask chewing his tusks off that the imprint
had been thrown off somehow. She did not know if the
Choyan system had succeeded in beating off the invasion, or
if Nedar would survive the infection now raging through his
body, his gaunt form racked with sweats one moment and
chills the next, but she did know he was in no condition to
help her get out. And that meant she would have to monitor him carefully, nursing him along, hoping to reach that
point when she could convince the pilot to bolt with her.

Alexa opened her eyes lazily. It would do her no good
at all to take a shuttle and leave without a pilot. Any escape
depended entirely upon Nedar.

If the Choya had indeed defeated the imprinting, his system had little left to fight off ordinary infection. He'd lost
enough weight that he now looked like skin and bones, and
the luster had gone from his dark hair, leaving it brittle
and muddy. He would not eat the choice morsels of food
she'd been sneaking to him, nor would he deign to talk to
her often, suspicious of her association with the enemy.

Alexa wondered what she could do to turn the pilot, to
put him firmly in her debt, to anchor him to her cause.
Offering him freedom would not accomplish it—there was
no freedom from this cruiser without a pilot who could
take them across Chaos. Nedar knew his worth to her.

The portal to her quarters clanked open without ceremony. Startled, Alexa took her feet off the wall, swung
around, and sat up.

She did not recognize the Drooler who waved a thick
hand at her. "GNask wishes you," it said heavily. Its tusks,
predominant and pushing its rubbery lips out, made its
Trade difficult to understand.

She stood reluctantly, trying to decide why GNask might
have summoned her. She was stepping forward when the
Abdrelik added, "Get your things. Clear them out."

Her heart did a little skip jump as she realized she was
being transferred. With or without the ambassador? And
why? She pulled on her grav boots, stuffed a duffel with
the few items she had, and followed behind the adjunct.

She saw the Marines first, and then her father, and came

to a dead halt. GNask swiveled his ponderous yet graceful body about, saying, "Ah. Here she is."

She looked at their expressions, having come to learn those of the Abdrelik well, and instinctively reading those of her own father. GNask wore a mask of diplomatic neutrality and John Taylor Thomas' expression was no less manufactured. The show of arms was what surprised her most. She would not have expected it of him. What use would it be for him to take her? She was still the Abdreliks', would always be the Abdreliks'.

Yet she had to admire the attempt. She would go with her father because it suited her to do so.

GNask beckoned to her. She drew near, staying a carefully calculated distance away from either of the two, assessing the situation.

"We have only the sole survivor who is fit to travel," GNask announced, after a brief consultation with the adjunct. She knew the underling had had nothing significant to say, she could tell from the language they'd used. The Abdreliks had a strong dominant/dominated voice pattern.

Alexa wondered at that. She looked at her father, but he was not looking at her, his attention stayed upon GNask. Some political dance, she thought, whose meaning would become clearer if she provoked it a little. She decided to do so.

"What about the *tezar*?" she asked clearly. "I can't leave him behind."

The Marines' attention snapped to her, as did that of *tursh* riding on GNask's shoulder. Its antennae went up and the little stalk eyes emerged and homed in. Her father's intense gaze came to rest on her, then he focused all his attention on GNask.

"What *tezar* would that be, Ambassador GNask?"

"A case of burnout," GNask said smoothly, but the hide on the back of his neck was anything but smooth, its fat fold rippling with anger. "His craft was found adrift. We have been unable to notify Cho or its representatives, and truthfully, I don't think he will make it. Transferring him may cost him his life."

"But," John said smoothly, "I have a medical bay in my transport. We can offer him treatment which you, as serviceable as your cruiser is, cannot."

"His life . . ." GNask trailed off.

"I'm willing to take the risk," Alexa's father countered. "I don't think the Choyan will fault us on our attempt to help one of their own."

"The Choyan have an intricate body balance. We've been dealing with them for centuries, while you . . ." again, GNask let his voice trail away, this time his tone significant rather than at a loss for words.

"As a matter of record, are you denying him access to better medical facilities?"

"Father," interrupted Alexa brightly, "he's conscious enough to make his own decision. Unless, of course, the Abdreliks are attempting to keep him against his will."

GNask erupted in a rumble of dull thunder, vibrating even in the metal plating under her feet, but he got no words out.

John said soothingly, "I know that the ambassador could never be unjustly accused of such a thing. Still, GNask," and he looked at the Abdrelik thoughtfully, "if the Choya makes his own decision, you can scarcely be faulted if it leads to his death."

GNask found his voice. "Naturally," he said, "I protest the unnecessary risk to the pilot's welfare. But, as we do not keep our passengers prisoner, he is free to leave if he wishes."

Nedar watched Alexa through the bars. "And why should I trust you?"

"It's not a matter of trust. Stay here and you'll die. If the imprint's failed, you're a liability to them."

He lay on his side, the abscess on his shoulder hidden by the poultice, its foul scent making her nose wrinkle. She could see trickles of leakage tracing across his skin.

"You have nothing if you stay."

He considered her again. "I have nothing if I go."

Alexa lowered her voice again. "I am no more ready to become a prisoner of my father's than I am to stay here with GNask. But I'll do what I have to do to get off this cruiser."

"And I thought you were developing a friendship with me because you liked me," the Choya said dryly.

"Dammit! Are you coming or not? Any longer, and

they'll assume you weren't competent enough to make a decision and GNask will declare it in your medical best interests to stay. My father hasn't enough clout to take you forcibly."

With a sigh, the pilot sat up. "You drive a hard bargain." He got to his feet, staggered a step, and put a hand out to the bars to stay upright.

Alexa darted out of his reach. "I'll tell them. Keep moving. Drop, and I can't come back for you."

The Choya nodded. She sprinted for the bulkhead of the bay to let her father know the *tezar* had agreed to come with them.

She wondered how either of them intended to explain to the Choyan what they were doing with a *tezar* who had no listing on the current contract rolls.

GNask watched the bay doors close, and then listened to the noise of the air lock closing, preparing to flush. The adjunct nearest him cowered slightly, turning fearful eyes on him, but GNask only shook his head slightly.

He did not know what the girl had in mind, or hoped to gain by leaving, but he knew her as well as he knew himself, and there had to be advantage in it. She was of his lineage now, more than human, and he knew what he would do under the circumstances. He said aloud, "Ambassador Thomas will not be happy with what he has taken."

"What about the Choya?"

"That is another story." GNask put a finger up and gently chucked the forepart of his *tursh*. The creature responded with a sinuous shivering. "I do not think he will cause us trouble, but I cannot be sure." He shrugged. "My duty on Sorrow calls me. Have the course set accordingly. If I cannot work here, then I must ply Panshinea. The Choyan will give way eventually. Everything changes."

He paused. Then he added, "Contact our liaison with the Ronins. They've been searching diligently for the Choyan who fled Arizar. Remind them of our strong ties and mutual interests. I think it's time to stir up the waters and see what we can flush out. I've been lying in wait too long. I feel like hunting."

Chapter 16

Alexa sat on a stool, intently watching the Choyan pilot in the quarters they had set up for him, keeping him out of sight of the crew and away from the sick bay on ship, despite what her father had told the Abdreliks. Personally, she thought he had little choice. The *tezar* was in deplorable condition and might not survive the rigors of FTL, despite his heritage. It would be far easier to dispose of him if no one else knew he was aboard. She had spent a lot of time watching Nedar. In her human nature, she would have been bored, but in her dark side, in the Abdrelik nature, she was stalking, and she had all the time in the world, hunger her only spur.

Nedar roused a little from the stupor he'd collapsed into the moment he'd stepped on board. They were accelerating now to FTL. She would be medicated soon and confined to her own quarters. She wondered if the pilot could sense from the vibration of the ship what was happening.

His head turned slightly toward her. "Who's piloting?" he asked, voices raspy but still arrogant, as though he didn't deign to ask what they would do with him, though he as well as she knew that he had not stepped into any greater freedom than he'd left.

"Baros," answered Alexa shortly, after weighing the virtue of talking to him at all.

"A good Choya'i," he said grudgingly. "How long until we hit maximum acceleration?"

"Another hour or so. Hungry?" She lifted the wrap on a tray. Its aroma drifted out, a duplicate of Baros' dinner, so that she was fairly certain he would eat.

He sat up and reached for the tray as she slid it across his table. The Choyan meal was complete down to the odd utensil they used, a two-tined forklike instrument. He looked at her. "Order me some meat. Hot. Rare."

Alexa reared back a little in surprise, then left to do as he bid. She came back with a tray in its wrapper, heating as she walked down the corridor. The scent that leaked out set her own senses off like an alarm, and by the time she reached the Choya's quarters, she knew.

He had finished with the vegetable and cereal platter and shoved it to one side as she entered, almost as if he might be contemplating getting past her.

"I wouldn't try it," she informed him. "The security lock isn't coded for you. You'll be hit by the sonic barrier as you try to pass through."

"Am I well enough, do you think, to make a break for it?"

She set the tray down in front of him, stacking it on the empty one, and peeled back the wrap. The slices of meat, beef, she thought, lay in its bloody juices.

Nedar hesitated a moment, then jabbed at a slice and ate it whole, and Alexa sat back in triumph, assured that her suspicions were correct. She brought her knees up, wrapped her arms about them, and watched the Choya devour his carnivorous meal.

When he was done, she casually inquired, "How did GNask and Kalak miss the signs?"

He looked up at her quickly. A strange light blazed at the back of his eyes, one that was not a reflection of the cabin's indirect lighting. Then, more deliberately, he wrapped a slab of rare meat about his fork and ate it in several bites. After swallowing, he said, "What signs?"

"Of imprinting. Don't be a fool. I know what I see— hell, I know what you *feel*." She hunched forward over her knees. "They have no idea what a shock it is to become one of them, to hunt, to stalk, to hunger, to burn the way they do."

"Choyan eat meat," Nedar said noncommittally, stabbing a third hunk. This one he took the time to slice into neat pieces.

"Occasionally. But not like that." Alexa lifted her chin defiantly. "Don't tell me I don't know what I know. No wonder you're so thin. You must have decided to starve rather than reveal to them what had begun to happen. It burned in you so hot, you knew you couldn't control it once you started. Not as weak as you were. Not as stricken. So you elected to starve. To get weaker. In hopes—what? What did you hope for?''

Nedar ignored the last piece, lifted the tray up, and poured the juices into his mouth. When he set it down, Alexa could hardly tear her gaze away from the remaining filet of beef.

With a twisted smile, he shoved the tray over to her. "Go ahead," he said. "Take it."

She snatched it up and ate it much as he'd eaten the first slice, her bites shredding the slab of meat, juices released and running down her fingers, and when she'd swallowed the last bite, she licked her fingers clean. He did not speak until she'd finished.

"What I hoped for," Nedar said sadly, "was death."

"And now?"

He lounged back against the cabin bed. "Vengeance."

"Taking out GNask could start a massive war. And it will be difficult to achieve. There are other, perhaps more rewarding, options."

His eyes shuttered, then opened. "Not GNask," he said. "Against the *tezar* who brought me to this juncture. Against Palaton."

"Interesting." Alexa unwrapped her arms from about her legs and stood. "I wonder if you will feel the same way after."

"After what?"

"My father's research associates have concocted a serum which will eradicate the imprinting. Early tests are promising. I," and Alexa tilted her head, brunette curls bouncing about her shoulders, "will get the benefits of the treatment."

"How do they expect to do it?"

She shrugged. "I'm not a medic. They say the genetic memory was transferred virally. It establishes a foothold in the bloodstream and stays there, a permanent invader the body's immune systems can't overcome. So they shoot me up with this wonder drug and it cleans me out. Or so they say." She considered him. "Two or three treatments.

You're newly infected . . . perhaps less for you. If you go to them for treatment."

"And why wouldn't I?"

She made a diffident movement again. "Pride? Or perhaps you just like the edge it gives you. A lean and hungry edge."

His lip began to curl into a snarl, and then his face shifted, forcibly, as he contained himself. Alexa, of course, saw it all, and knew, and she laughed. "You don't have to make the decision now. We're docking at a station for a couple of days. Father is worried the Abdreliks may yet come after us. He figures that numbers will give us strength." She backed to the door and halted, leaning on the frame. "So you have time to think about it."

"What—" The word came out dry, harsh. He tried again. "What about you?"

"Oh, I've made my decision. A jolt or two, enough to take some of the edge off, and then I'm gone." She spoke quietly but with intensity. "No one, NO one, not even my father, is ever going to control me again. I have too much advantage knowing what the Abdreliks know. This universe is mine if I have the guts to go for it. And, thanks to the imprinting, I do." The doorway opened and swallowed her up, the forcefulness of her voice lingering behind her.

Nedar watched the doorway seal. She could not possibly make a break for independence without a pilot, just as before. She would take him along, if he agreed. He contemplated the unlikely partnership of the human nature with the Abdrelik nature. A shudder ran through him at the thought, and he shoved away the table, trays rattling. Yet he knew how she felt because it was how he felt. Like calls to like. Power calls to power.

She had not threatened to expose him. He pondered the possibility of their unlikely alliance. If he asked for treatment, he would betray the vulnerability of all Choyan to the Abdrelik imprinting. He knew, despite the apparently recently strained relations between GNask and the Terran ambassador, that the information would not be kept confidential. Either Thomas would use it for leverage, or he would give it to the Abdreliks for the same purpose. Part of the Choyan defense was its seemingly impenetrable invulnerability to attack and even torture by its enemies. The *tezarian* drive had not been deciphered. It would not be, unless the Choyan soul itself could be turned and blackened, as they'd attempted to do with his.

It was unfortunate they'd imprinted someone who already had little left to give, or lose, and refused to commit this one last treachery. He could continue to keep his secret, or he could seek treatment for it, hoping for a cure. But in this one matter, Nedar knew he had to weigh personal benefits against the damage to his people. It would take time to reach his decision.

He had fed, but he was not full. The lines of *bahdur* lay silent within his body, aching, longing. He knew the cruiser as well as if he'd crafted it himself, for it was Choyan made, and he knew how to gain access to the pilot through the fire exits. He could drain Baros of enough *bahdur* to fuel himself for a few weeks. With that, he could get back to Cho. Then, like a predator among grazers, he would have unlimited donors awaiting him. He would gather his strength and take Palaton whenever he desired.

He would be a fool to steal from Baros right before going into Chaos. Such an action could doom them all. The station promised more opportunities. There were always *tezars* at a station, changing duties over, resting, passing time while mechanical repairs were being made. The opportunity might be more difficult to initiate, but it would be there.

Nedar lay back and listened to the pilot give a one hour mark over the cruiser's intercom, for medicating and securing purposes, his thoughts an unpleasant buzz in his head.

Qativar did not flinch as, with no hand to propel it, a vase flew across his quarters' wall and smashed, exploding on contact. Scarcely breathing hard, he flexed his *bahdur* and mentally grabbed a painting, flinging it over the veranda to clatter down on the patio below. His hands convulsing in and out of fists, he snatched up a chair and let it fall to the tiles of the floor. Wood splintered. When his temper cooled, he stood in the wreckage of his apartment, pottery shards at his feet, furniture overturned, nothing untouched by the upheaval of his temper.

Three times he'd been to Rindalan's quarters and been refused entrance. His rightful position was denied as though it had never existed, as though he had not played those games all these years, and worked and scrubbed his very soul for Rindalan's benefit. Turned away like a commons. Ignored as though he were nothing more than an inconvenient mote.

More than that seethed inside him. Malahki had not answered a recent summons, and as a result Qativar had no idea what the High Priest of the cult was up to. Though Qativar hadn't been able to find out the cult leader's identity, he had narrowed down the possible candidates, and none of them had seen fit to keep him aware of developments.

The underground whispered of a new Prophet, a forecaster of immense if erratic ability somewhere in the God-in-all forsaken swamps half a world away.

And there was a persistent rumor that the *tezars* were closing ranks, preparing to make a break with the throne, and with their Houses, preparing to take up the power that their elite abilities had made them heir to. Who was behind that fomentation, and how could Palaton handle that?

Cho had begun to decay into Chaos. The end of an era seemed inevitable, and though he could work in such disarray, he would rather be in position before the end came about. He had to get to Rindalan again, and Jorana stood between the two of them, protecting the elderly Choya. She, however, would go wherever the heir or the emperor went, and so he must take care of Palaton first. It was time, no, it was past time, for him to do something with the information that a delirious Rindalan had passed to him thinking he was Palaton.

Word had come of the pilot's pilgrimage to his birthplace. Qativar folded up his legs and sat unceremoniously among the debris of his anger, thinking. If the pilot were indeed of the House of Flame, the Congress would turn against him. However, Qativar could not afford to make such charges frivolously, and he was all too aware he did not have the evidence he needed to prove it. But what about Palaton? How could he not suspect?

And if he did suspect, all Qativar had to do would be to lead him down the path a little, and Palaton would continue the journey to self-destruction very nicely. If he did not, then this one act might not be all that was necessary, but he could work on that later. Palaton already stood on shaky ground through his association with the alien. It would not be difficult to cause an abyss to open up under his feet.

He had the elements he needed to begin. Then he would turn his attention to Malahki and the rumors, as well as to picking up new subjects for his testing. Difficult times would be fertile ones for him. He did not fear a chaotic future.

It was time for him to use some of what he'd learned from Rindalan's fevered murmurings. He stood up, dusted himself off, and returned to the palace to set a trap.

Palaton returned to his quarters, longing for another shower to erase the day's heat and dust. As he put his hand on the lock, he felt distinctly uneasy, as if the security of the area had been violated. Without his power, he couldn't confirm it, and certainly the network Jorana had provided would have caught anyone attempting it. If he had had Rand with him, he would have had the manling probe the area, but after an exhausting day of training, Rand had gone to see how Rindy progressed. He could call up Jorana or one of the guards, but he knew that to do so would be to reveal his own lack of ability, a weakness he couldn't afford.

Nonetheless, he opened the door from the shadowed corridor hesitantly, not quite ready to face what might be waiting within. Nothing appeared disturbed from the morning. Housekeepers had been in, tidying up. He could smell the fresh, biting smell of newly laundered linens. Daybrights floated in a hand-blown goblet bowl on the center table, their petals beginning to fold with the approach of dusk. Nothing appeared wrong, but he knew that something was. He stepped inside, bracing himself.

The room had stayed relatively cool, and as he passed into it, he felt a trigger spot, something that even without *bahdur* made the hair at the nape of his neck stand on end.

Palaton whirled and caught the aura image projected from across his rooms, a Choya, tall and arrogant, ghostly, unrecognizable, his voices distorted by the psychic production.

"Son of the House of Flame," the image named him. "It's time to face the Chaos of your own destiny, to read the patterns, to chart your course."

Chapter 17

"Who are you?" Palaton's voices rang sharply in his own head. He heard fear and anger stretched by stress, and stood rooted, his heart pounding, unable to sense whether the projection was a live sending or a static transference. Either might have been triggered by his entrance. It did not matter, really, because whoever had done this knew the secret he had just ferreted out for himself. Whoever knew that held Palaton's life in his hands, and this projection was just as deadly as someone standing there with an enforcer in his hands aimed at the heir's heart.

He moved swiftly then, to a corner of the room, to see if the projection followed the line of sight, but it did not. The communication was not live. Transference, then, set up in advance and left for him. Set up very cleverly because he could not see the face of the Choya well enough, or hear the voices clearly enough, to know who'd left it. If he had Jorana with him to read, though she'd wonder why he could not read on his own, he might be able to tell if it was someone he knew, because although the aura had also been disrupted, there was always a flavor to a transference, which, once tasted, could be recognized again. Auras of actual presences were much easier to read, but he doubted if he'd have any luck with that, *bahdurless* as he was.

A part of him hoped it might be Rindy, that the elder had grown strong enough to attempt projection, but he knew that Rindalan was still not well enough. He hadn't yet had time to sit and talk with Rindy, to tell him what Volan had finally broken down and admitted to him. Even if Rindy had been strong enough, this projection held a tinge of menace. He thought of Nedar, but knew this had a level of subtlety Nedar had never favored.

The speaker had gone on and he'd missed the first words

". . . delay to establish yourself. Your fellows will not accept you. That which was condemned to ashes is better lost to all of us. The only way you can save yourself is to prove yourself, and then reveal yourself. What hidden talents might you have which will aid you greatly? The genetic possibilities are endless, Palaton. Without that wisdom, you will fail. I give you this: time. Time to learn and act. If you do not, I will grieve for you, because I and the others will pull you down and destroy you. Your destiny is inevitable. Succeed, or fail utterly."

Time? How much time? Far less than he needed or the projection would not be here. No, the projection was meant to nudge him, to tell him that time was running out. Its menace was indisputable. He did not think a friend had left this for him. Did the sender think to prod him into hasty action? Or hope that he would grow more discreet, losing whatever advantage he might gain from pursuing his heritage?

Palaton watched helplessly as it began to fade, leaving only a shimmering aura which eclipsed slowly and extinguished altogether.

Palaton felt for a chair and sat down. The speaker was right about one thing: if he had powers in his lineage that had weakened or did not exist in the other Houses, he had an advantage, whether he could use them himself or direct them through Rand. Indeed, Rand, untrained, unknowing, could be in trouble unless Palaton discovered the potential they shared. That aspect of the situation had not occurred to him before. How could he shield Rand from wielding powers he himself did not know he had? That decided him, more than the transference. The sender of the projection had motives which Palaton knew he couldn't fathom. But for himself, he knew that self-discovery was no longer a luxury. Maerlon beckoned.

He sat debating whether or not to take Rand with him, and how he could convince Jorana that he wished to go alone. She would fight him on that, especially after the incident at Sethu, where the Earthans had sacrificed their main temple in an attempt to get at him. Although he doubted that House would try again, as heir, he had sacrificed the ability to go where he wanted unheralded, unmolested. If he left Rand, he would urge Jorana to reassign

Traskar, the one-armed former *tezar* who'd guarded the humankind before. He knew and trusted that Choya; he was someone who'd been off-world and even liked the occasional contact with aliens.

He would rather take Rand along, for when they were together, the *bahdur* responded almost as if they shared it, rather than Rand being the sole carrier. It kept the intense emptiness and longing for its touch away. He could remain calm when Rand stayed near, not to mention the comfort he would feel at having a friend close by.

It struck him then. A friend. Not a child to be protected, but a brother-in-arms, a support as much as a burden. He wasn't sure when Rand's status had changed. Perhaps at Sethu. As Heir to the Throne of Cho, he had been told to obtain cleansing. The ambush set for him at the Earthan-held temple of Sethu would have destroyed him, if not for Rand. Perhaps the bonding had come later, during the riots. Perhaps Rand had always been that companion.

Palaton stood up, knowing Rand would not like being left at home. It seemed the wisest decision, however. Alone, Palaton might have a slight chance of exploring the ruins at Maerlon, and of talking to the residents of the small artists' colony which maintained it without being recognized or at least without being harassed. He could not take Rand to such a place. There would be no doubt in anyone's mind that they looked at an off-worlder, and who he might be. There was only one on all of Cho, had only been the one in the last century.

He thought he could convince Rand that he must stay. He knew, if he had to, he could order Jorana to let him go unescorted. That left only Rindalan, and the unsettled matter between them.

He checked his chronograph. Early evening, with the sun down and the heat dissipating this night. Rindy might still be awake, and if he was not, it would not hurt to awaken him for a while.

Rindy lay quietly as Palaton approached the créche bed. The med techs had looked curiously at Palaton, then turned back to their studies and monitors, disinterested in him after their initial recognition. He knew his conversation would not be recorded, that the unit had been wired mainly to keep tabs on Rindalan's condition. Still, he would have liked to have had more privacy, but it wasn't available to them.

"I'm not asleep," Rindy murmured irritably.

"That, I know," Palaton answered as he drew up a chair. "You'd be snoring if you were."

"Hah. I get enough from that young pup of yours, I don't need it from you." The bed gyrated into position, so Rindy's bright blue eyes were now on a level with his.

"Rand still comes here?"

"Often. They must not live long on his world. I think age fascinates him. He stares at me as if I have the answer to a great many things which baffle him."

"Don't you?" teased Palaton gently, as he watched Rindy pluck and tuck his sheets into place.

"Pull your chair a little closer. Maybe if I rap my knuckles across that thick skull of yours, I can teach you something." Rindy leaned slightly his way.

"Actually," answered Palaton, "that's why I came."

"Indeed?" Rindalan cleared his throat. "I might as well listen. I'm not going anywhere. At least not until tomorrow, when they tell me the underpinnings of this thing will be unwired from me, and I begin therapy."

"Walking?"

"Joyfully, yes. But I warn you now that I won't answer any more questions about who pulled me down. Even if I could identify them, I won't. Jorana's been after me and I wouldn't put it past her to sic you on me."

"There you have me again. I need your help against Jorana. I came to suggest an alliance," Palaton told him.

"Against Jorana? My boy, the battle of the sexes is one I never won when I was young, let alone now."

"It's not that." Palaton put his hand out and took up Rindy's, feeling the faint heat of a slight temperature, and the dry skin and knobby joints of his infirmity. "My Householding was leveled a few days ago. I had the chance to speak to my grandfather. He told me a great deal I never knew."

Rindy's blue gaze, normally very direct, looked aside. "Did he send you to me?" he asked, reluctance in his tone. It was clear to Palaton that if his grandfather had not told him, Rindy was loath to do so.

"No. He had the courage to tell me himself. I'm here because I need to go to Maerlon, to find out what I can about Tresa and whoever my father might be."

Rindy's hand tightened in his. "If he was a Flame, he won't reveal himself to you."

"If he knows who I am, possibly not. If I go with an entourage and a guard, there's no chance of it. I'm going alone, and I might need your backing to help me convince Jorana what I need to do."

"Have you told her?"

"I can't. For all that's there between us, she still works for the throne itself, and Panshinea still rules that throne. I don't want to put her in a position where she might feel compromised."

"You'd be surprised," Rindy interrupted, "what Jorana feels."

Palaton ignored that. He told Rindalan about the projection. The Prelate's gaze narrowed at that. "Who do you think it could be?"

"The House of Earth has strong suspicions. They've been behind several attempts at me, but I thought after the Two Day War, they'd given up overt action. There's a good chance they're trying to drive me into doing something rash, something which will reverse my support."

"I thought the attack at Sethu was aimed at the heir to the throne, rather than at you."

Palaton knew what the Prelate meant. He shook his head. "Both, from what I know. When we hid in the catacombs, I found the House library."

Rindy sucked a breath in deeply, then winced as it moved a sore rib. "I thought perhaps it might have been hidden there. Did the fire destroy it?"

"I doubt it. We had little pursuit getting out, once the fire began. I think they turned most of their attention to evacuating the area. But I saw the evidence. They'd taken in whatever Flames they could find, hoping to fill their own House with new, unsuspected talents. And when those talents turned on them, they began to eradicate them systematically. Although my lack of parentage isn't widely known, they must have suspected once Panshinea's eyes fell on me."

"There's another consideration," Rindy pointed out.

"What?"

"It might be your father himself, trying to suggest you find him."

Palaton let go of Rindy's hand. The suggestion startled him. He juggled his ramifications for a moment, then admitted, "I never thought of that."

"It's a possibility." Rindy looked thoughtful. "I tried to keep your secret well. You tested . . . how shall I put it . . . not extremely high, as a child, but richly. I knew that we not only had a potential, valuable *tezar* candidate, but something more, something undefinable, which could not be. Before I released your results to Volan, I sat for a few nights in my libraries, going over the literature, searching for the enigma that you'd become. I never did find what I truly wanted to know, just a suspicion." Rindy clucked his tongue. "Would that I could have seen the library hidden under Sethu."

"We're not likely to get an invitation now."

"No." Rindy chuckled. "Bless their hearts anyway, the Earthans. I can't blame them for their ambition. They've been getting short shrift from us for centuries. Like the God-blind, they're the salt of the land, but they're not bred to face the stars. Not like us, or the Skies. Even if they could ascend to the throne, it's not likely they'd keep it."

"What about the Flames? Could they keep it?"

Rindy paused, then shook his head. "Not as things stand now. We know too little and, because of our ignorance, could not trust. If there is someday to be a House resurrected, it will take a great deal of strength and example to build it. Is that what you had in mind, Palaton?"

"I don't know. I think perhaps survival is closer at hand."

"Good idea." Rindy shifted, and a line of pain passed across his expression. It faded slowly. "So you go to Maerlon. Alone?"

"That's the idea."

"Jorana, Rand, and Gathon will not be excited about that prospect. And, of course, you can't tell any of them your true reasons."

He intended to tell Rand, but he did not stop Rindy. "I'm open for suggestions."

"You'll have to pull rank with Jorana. Even if you tell her what you're going after, and don't think she doesn't know—I'm fairly certain there's a good security file on you—she won't let you go alone. Not after Sethu. You won't have any choice except to give her orders she doesn't dare countermand. But as for Rand, I can use his assistance here. He's about the right height to make a good crutch."

"I'll tell him," said Palaton dryly, knowing what Rand's reaction would probably be. As for Jorana, he could only hope she would forgive him. He got to his feet, as weariness began to replace the open animation on the other's face. "Good night, Rindy."

The elder looked at him intently. "I want to hear from you the moment you're back."

"You will."

Palaton stepped away from the bed as Rindalan cranked it back down into sleeping position. Rindy called out, a little breathlessly, "And don't worry. You're doing the right thing."

He left the Prelate's quarters, thinking that he was doing the only thing he could. But it helped that Rindy approved.

Freedom made Alexa feel giddy. It was a heady feeling being at a station again, one that even sitting here in the lab with Dr. Maren could not chase away. Her father was on the com deck, embroiled in Compact matters. She watched as the physician cleaned up the abscess on Nedar's neck, where the symbiont had been rejected. She put a hand back to her own neckline, fingers lightly tracing the fine-lined scar.

Nedar faced her, with that implacable Choyan mask, his dark hair freshly barbered and shampooed, brushed back from his high forehead. She thought that the Choyan must have been genetically designed to look both barbaric and vastly superior at the same time. He did not wince as the doctor neatly clipped out the edges of the wound and then quickly sutured it together.

Maren was not Alexa's idea of a handsome being either, but at least he was human. She watched his neat, efficient mannerisms as he worked, involved in his procedures. Professional, she supposed.

He put a plaster of synthetic flesh over the wound, saying, "This should hold it."

Nedar said gravely, "Thank you." He moved off the examination table as Maren bustled over to a robo table and selected an air inject. He looked up and eyed Alexa as if sizing her up.

She watched him holding the instrument with mixed emotions. To be done with the dark side of herself, never to dream, not to hear GNask's voice in her every thought, would be something to relish. But, on the other hand, she had been given superb survival skills, instincts that she had not inherited on her own. How many injections, she thought, could she endure before all that she was became totally erased.

One, surely.

As if sensing her apprehension, Dr. Maren said, "Three treatments, I think, with a booster in half a year's time. It's difficult to tell. The virus may regenerate itself somewhat, but if that becomes a problem, the formula will translate well to pills. You could take them regularly, if need be."

"Could I." She eyed the air inject, not liking its air quick needle qualities. Nedar had given no indication of his infection to the physician and she wondered if he would. Should she reveal what the Choya thought to keep hidden? The physician cut into her inner debate.

"I thought your father discussed the program with you," answered Maren, frowning, his wrinkle-free, slick face forcing an expression which slid quickly away.

Nedar stood behind the dispensing tables, his arms crossed over his flight suit, a new, clean uniform which had been taken from station laundry. His bones still showed in a terribly gaunt frame, but he looked like the *tezar* he was. "What kind of dosage would you give a Choya?"

"You?" Maren's face flipped a surprised look on and off, as though it were only a signboard, too polished to hold a permanent expression. "It depends on the infestation. Probably double her dose." The researcher paused. "Are you worried about the danger of imprinting?"

"They certainly attempted it," said Nedar in a reasonable tone. "I would be foolish to avoid treatment if one were available, don't you think?"

"Yes," responded Maren, licking his lips with a touch of excitement. "I've enough of the serum. There may be side effects. . . ."

"For which the Abdreliks, ultimately, will be responsible." Nedar rolled up the sleeve of his flight suit, preparing himself as Maren put aside the injector marked for her and loaded one for the pilot. Clever of him to avoid the issue of actual contamination, she thought, as she watched him take the dosage. She then bared her own arm and let Dr. Maren treat her. The drug spritzed into her system, and she felt nothing for a moment, then her blood turned hot, her skin flushed, and she experienced a momentary dizziness before she went limp in the doctor's arms.

Chapter 18

Nedar watched the girling drop with a faint sense of curiosity. He had thought the humankind stock a little hardier than that. For a certainty, the two of them had been through a lot and she had never proven so frail before. She had earned his grudging respect with her toughness and self-interest. He had almost begun to think of her in Choyan terms. She began to convulse in Maren's arms, semiconsciously fighting the drugs which washed through her system.

The Abdrelik contamination within him turned his thoughts aside, and he found himself watching her with an avid hunger. It grew into a craving with every unconscious flop and twitch of her body, like wounded prey. In dark, dense, smoldering bogs he wanted to stalk her, then capture, and rip and rend tender flesh until the blood, smoking hot, flowed out of her and into him. . . .

The pilot shuddered. A desire bordering on insanity to hunt and rip crashed through his senses. Like grasping onto a lifeline, he closed his eyes and thought of the Salt Towers and Blue Ridge, of the exercises they employed to calm and awaken their power, just before launching off a ridge to fly with eyes blinded by a deprivation helmet. He told himself to think of the wind, thin, blue, violent, under his wings, lifting him away from the muck and mire of the Abdrelik thoughts in his mind and soul.

His own blood felt as though it were going to boil. Sweat popped out on his forehead. His heart thumped in his chest as though he were running a tremendous race afoot in heavy gravity. His hearing dimmed. For a moment, he thought he would falter and drop as the humankind had.

Then it surged through him. Nedar threw his head back with a soft gasp. It took him like a shock, and he could feel tears spring to his eyes. It came as painful as circulation into frost-bitten flesh, as welcome as air to drowning lungs, as food to a starving being. His *bahdur*! His, not stolen from a hapless victim, but his, sprung from some hidden font he never knew existed, flooding him. He knew its soulfire well and reveled in it.

He was free again!

Nedar opened his eyes. The dazzling ceiling of the bay lab stretched overhead, but he didn't see it. He saw Chaos swirling, with all its infinite patterns, the Singing Choya'i, the Falling Tree, the Mountains of Sunrise, the Butterfly, and more. He could sense Baros resting in the pilots' lounge, and the minds of a good half-dozen more Choyan as they strolled through the malls of the station, their ships clustered at various docks scattered across the base. He could sense the girling's vicious fight with the viral intelligence riding her system and for a moment knew pity. Then a gigantic wave of triumph overwhelmed all else.

Bahdur!

Maren looked across the lab, his arms full of the flailing girl, saying to the *tezar* though Nedar could barely hear it, "Are you all right?"

"Yes," Nedar forced an answer. He crossed the lab and took the girl's convulsing body from the doctor, the strength of his Choyan body far greater even in his emaciated state, and laid her on the examination table. Her heels drummed the surface and then she went slack, her system exhausted. He touched her briefly with his talent, ascertained that she was already recovering, and took his hands from her.

Maren leaned over, fingers taking a quick pulse, afraid to trust the various monitors in his lab. He looked up. "You're certain you're all right?"

Nedar smiled. "Never better. I'll be in my quarters if I'm wanted."

"You can't leave me with her like this—"

"I'm not a vet," the pilot told him. "You've a com system. Summon the station med techs." The girl no longer concerned him. He could not stay. He needed privacy to assess what was happening to him. Had it been the new drug? If it had been, the implications were boundless. All *tezars* would be affected. He could not leave a discovery like this in the hands of a civilization barely considered eligible for the Halls of Compact. He had to think.

He turned his back on the scene and left, glorying in the walk down the familiar corridors where even the metal sang to him as it hadn't in too long a time. The nagging of his *bahdur* that all was not well, that a predator lurked just beyond the range of the docking station, that an Abdrelik presence thought escaped had drawn close once more clouded the edge of his perception. But it had been too long unused, barren, bereft, and Nedar was too confident in his joy to question the darkness.

rrRusk said, "It's confirmed. The Terran cruiser is docked at Sorrow Station A-11. We could pick it off if you so ordered, but I don't recommend it. We couldn't hide our tracks and it would be difficult to pass it off as an error. We're too close to the jump-off point for Sorrow and we'd draw unwanted attention."

GNask sat in his baths, feeling the sludge swirl comfortingly about him. "Recommendation?"

"That we wait until the cruiser disembarks, follow the set course, and pick him off before he enters Chaos."

"Probable destination?"

rrRusk clicked his tusks together with a little irritation. How could he guess where a humankind might go? But he had his theories and decided to put one forth. "Sorrow. Or his home base. But I think he'll go to Sorrow."

"For maximum protection?" GNask made a gargling sound at the back of his throat. "That's what I would do. He'll need it, that miserable parasite. Our only hope is if the Choya dies on him. Then perhaps we can catch him with an embarrassing body to explain and discredit him altogether."

rrRusk held his silence, watching his commander bathe in his private spa. His own hide itched abominably, the creams and chemicals far inferior to his own *tursh*, back home in the Abdrelikan colonies. His uniform chafed about his thighs and his stomach grumbled nervously. His own career was on the line here, and he knew it, but he could not act to save it. His life was in GNask's ungentle hands, and the only thing good about that was that the ambassador suffered from the same problems.

No one on Abdrela knew that GNask had done the unthinkable, splicing his symbiont into alien flesh. But once the fact got out, he would be anathema among his people unless tremendous advantage could be gotten out of it. rrRusk thought of the large-eyed, pale-faced girl who had haunted GNask's steps. She was almost more of an Abdrelik than his own misbegotten sister's hatchlings.

The unthinkable part of it was that the humankind had, unwittingly, been initiated into a major part of Abdrelik life. She knew their deepest secret, although she had seldom displayed any sign of it, and GNask should never have let her go. She could betray them. An Abdrelik who had not been initiated with his line's *tursh* was little more than a bog-mired killer. It was the symbiont which boosted them above the animal, which gave them the intelligence and capability to turn their cunning and stealth into a drive which would take them to the stars and beyond.

If ever the Ronins or Ivrians or even the Nortons guessed, the biological warfare which could be waged among the Abdrelikan colonies could conceivably wipe out the more delicate, extremely vulnerable *turshes*. rrRusk shuddered at the thought, his thick hide rippling down his flanks. Although once initiated, an Abdrelik could live without his symbiont, it was always much preferable to do so with it.

GNask's baggy eyes met his. "The girl has to be brought back," he stated. "Or destroyed. Post a watch on the station. Let me know when the cruiser leaves."

"Aye, sir," the general confirmed. He left for his watch stations, to relay the orders. It felt good to be doing something besides waiting. Even if they were headed for an FTL station, it would take the cruiser a while to build up enough acceleration. A completely armed Abdrelik warship ought to be able to overhaul them in no time.

Alexa felt herself come awake with a groan. Her skin felt like paper, burned brown as ash by the sun or some overflash, her nerves raw and eyes aching. Yet, when she got her lids peeled back and looked at herself, she was unchanged. Whether her eyes were opened or closed, there was a kaleidoscope of activity before them, primal, almost like looking into a microscope, colors and shapes coalescing without any rhyme or reason. They dizzied her. An atonal symphony accompanied the visual riot. Alexa groaned and let her head drop back to the examination table, longing for unconsciousness again.

"Miss Thomas?"

Alexa Taylor Thomas. That was her. Was the man an idiot, expecting her to respond to another name? She lay still, listening to the breath rattle in and out of her sore lungs. Like a death rattle, she thought. An IV pinioned one arm.

"You tried to kill me," she accused the physician, knowing without seeing that Dr. Maren stood at her side, checking monitors, adjusting the IV drip.

"The dosage. . . ." the researcher paused. "Too high and intense for the amount of concentration in your bloodstream. I'm sorry. There was no way I could have predicted the backlash."

"Try lab rats next time," suggested Alexa. She levered herself up on one elbow. "You damn near incinerated me." Through eyelids which fluttered beyond her control, she watched the man standing by her side.

"The infestation fights back. It's amazingly resilient. It's been reconfiguring. I can stay a step ahead of it, but it will take close to a half-dozen treatments before I can clean you out. And even then," he paused.

Alexa jostled him. "And?"

"It may metastasize. You may require medication for the rest of your life."

Having heard it before, she absorbed that with little worry. Alexa swiveled her head. The bones in her neck gave an irritating pop or two as she moved, but she didn't see the Choya anywhere.

"What about Nedar?"

"Gone to his quarters. The effect on him was much less than on you."

But Alexa saw a strangeness in the doctor's expression and wondered what he wasn't telling her. Had Nedar reacted the same way or differently? And why hadn't he been contained within the med facility—or had Maren been too busy with her to stop him from walking out? She wondered if he were still aboard ship.

Alexa sat up. Damn his hide, but the pilot wasn't going

anywhere without her. The IV line tangled and the monitor let out a soft beep. Clucking in dismay, Maren untangled the line and pressed on her shoulder, urging her to lie back down. She looked at him, the Abdrelik look, the look of black mud and dark stone, and saw him quail.

She swung her feet over the exam table. A sudden weakness spread through her and she conquered it by sheer dint of will. "Unhook me," she ordered. "I feel fine."

He reared over her, brows beetled. "Lie down."

Alexa lay back, not ready to show the doctor her true mettle yet. She felt her pulse thrum, then steady. Control came to her with an icy steadiness. The imprint had not been wiped out, but it had been greatly weakened. For the first time in years, she was alone in her mind, in charge of her destiny. She smiled. "When can I see my father?"

John sat at the view screen, hopeless, watching the outer pattern which Baros had brought up for him, pinpointing the vague, shadowy outline of the Abdrelik warship waiting on the verges of space.

The Choya stood over him at the console. "What do you suggest?"

He had not thought GNask would take his maneuver so harshly, but he should have known. He damned himself for being so headstrong, so sure he could outfox them. But would they risk an open attack here to take back their captives? "Nothing comes to mind," he admitted. News from Sorrow had not been pleasant, either. Their latest freight contract had been denied. Not enough pilots available, he'd been told, but he did not accept it. He turned his conform chair about to look up at Baros.

She wore strong obsidian jewelry under her translucent skin. Its tracings wove an intricate pattern on her face, and on her forearms, revealed because she kept her flight suit pushed up past her first elbow. Baros looked at the matrix.

"I don't think we could easily outrun him," she commented, "although he would be a fool to fire this close to a station. The Compact will know it wasn't accidental. He would risk fines, perhaps even loss of contracts. His home-world doesn't give GNask that big a leash, although he would like to think it does."

John had never met the Abdrelik head, one Frnark, by

name, although he'd been told the president was lean, even
by Abdrelik standards, mean, and quick. He had a mind
like a steel trap and he believed in letting his enemies, like
GNask, hang themselves. He wondered if GNask were
close to it, this time. He wasn't willing to put his life on
the line to accomplish it.

"What about the loss of contracts?"

Baros looked evenly at him. She was of the House of
Sky, her hair a dark brunette liberally streaked with even
darker raven, her eyes a smoky gray. She was not, even by
Choyan standards, beautiful, but she had an intensity about
her. She had come from the flight school at the Salt Towers,
she'd told him once, and had added that it was considered
the elite school of the *tezars*. This one, he thought, had the
stuff to rule Cho if anything ever happened to Panshinea
or Palaton. He wondered if the Skies had their eyes on the
Choyan throne.

"An economic threat," she said, "of some consequence."

"True enough . . . but it's getting common these days."

Baros hesitated. "The *tezarian* drive is intricate. Our pilots are spread thinly."

"And you're not providing enough of them," John interrupted. "What about cross training? Surely someone else
can use one of those little black boxes?"

She smiled thinly. "The question of the ages," she observed. "And the answer is still no. Not really. At any rate,
for GNask to be so punished, we would probably have to
be dead. Not a state I relish."

"But you have combat experience. Surely you've outrun
the Abdreliks before. Or the Ronins."

Her smoky eyes glinted with a silver sheen. "We Choyan
are generally escort pilots only, but . . . it can be done.
Even in a cruiser of this size. You would have to 'batten
down the hatches' the moment we push off, and I can almost guarantee you the backwash would affect the station.
We'd probably incur a minor fine."

"As long as I'm alive to pay it." John took the Abdrelik
shadow down off the view screen.

"Do I have my orders, then?"

"Not yet. But you'll be the first to know," the ambassador told her. The Choya'i bowed her head gravely and
exited the cabin.

John laid out the hard copies of his recent transmissions and tried to measure his response to them. Panshinea, he saw, was fighting hard to stay afloat in the halls of the Compact. The general overview of the scarcity of pilots was that the Choyan had begun a campaign which would not long be tolerated by those who could not contract the transport they so desperately needed.

Those little black boxes, thought John. The Choyan ruled the universe with them, but their subjects had begun to revolt. How tight could they squeeze before the breaking point was reached? Panshinea, in the thick of it, walked a double-edged blade of his own choosing. Where would any of them be without FTL? Locked in their own systems, with only a few out-planets to colonize, confined to their own stinking refuse, without any hope of new land, new air, new metals and horizons. John mused that it might do a few of the others good to suffer the fate of a Class Zed member. To know the hopelessness of being refused the right to traverse the stars.

He slapped a palm down on his console. He would offer support to Panshinea when he returned, but that support would have a price.

Chapter 19

"I need to make arrangements to go to Maerlon, and I need to go alone."

Jorana did not fight him as both he and Rindy had predicted, though she wore a disgruntled expression. Her eyes looked weary as the evening lengthened. They'd been talking about Rindalan before Palaton had told her what he wanted to do. When he'd finished detailing his plans, she said only, "Traskar is not available. I'll have to find someone else to escort Rand, although if he doesn't plan on leaving the palace, I don't think I need to worry too much. How long do you plan to be in Maerlon?"

Not having the former *tezar* to guard Rand might make it difficult, because of the xenophobia of many Choyan, but he would have to leave those details up to Jorana. He'd made his decision to go. Leaving Rand behind was better than taking him out in the open, if he went to confront the forces which had set his genetic destiny into motion. He could not, however, stay away from Charolon for any length of time. He chose his words carefully.

"I would like to say, as long as it takes me, but we both know that my primary obligation is here. I have to visit Blue Ridge and see if I can get a handle on the *tezar* situation, so I'll be back as soon as I can." Palaton felt relieved as, again, she did not argue with him. What existed between them could not grow, not when he had nothing more to offer her, but neither did he want enmity to take its place and flourish. He also felt grateful surprise that she didn't question the necessity of a trip to Maerlon.

She hid a yawn. "I'm not happy about it, but you're right. You'll probably achieve more going alone. They're academicians and artists. They'll be suspicious of authority.

You won't attract attention. If I check you out proper armor and weaponry, will you take it?"

"I don't promise to use it."

"Good enough. I hope you won't have to." She paused, jotted down a few notes, asking, "What do you expect to accomplish at Blue Ridge?"

Palaton sighed. Blue Ridge was another matter. He could not tell her about his hopes for Rand, although she knew of the research he'd begun about the school's program in general. He did not think she would argue with that agenda. "If I knew, I wouldn't have to go. But it's patently obvious we're not taking in enough candidates, and we're not graduating enough pilots. Although Hat has less attrition than any of the schools, it's still not enough. Maybe I can see what he's doing, what he's not doing, and go on from there. The pressure from the Compact is beginning to be extreme, from what Gathon tells me."

She tapped the end of her stylus on the notepad. "This didn't happen overnight."

"No . . . but if we're not holding Choosings, or some of the counties are holding back candidates as Malahki did at Danbe, then we've got part of the problem identified."

She looked up, amused. "We might need the commons?"

"We definitely need the talented among the commons," he countered her, knowing she needled him. "And since I'm now a voice for the God-blind, maybe they'll listen to me as well. They want a referendum. I need strength to give it to them."

"Trying to change all of Cho in your brief interregnum?"

"I made promises. I'm trying to keep them." He paused. "However brief my heirship is."

She gathered up her equipment. "I'll contact Rufeen and get her a skimship for Maerlon. Do you want me to call Blue Ridge?"

"No," said Palaton shortly, after considering it. "I think I'd better do that in person."

A spaceship in docking is never silent. The metal communicated constantly, through sometimes sharp, often muffled clangs and vibrations, the activity of other ships in docking and the life of the station itself. The constant noise was like a breeze, a wind promising freedom beyond the confines of the vessel, passageways worming into great, vaulted spaces. To a pilot, used to life aboard a ship, the noise was relegated to a nearly subliminal level, but at the same time, its significance could not be ignored. He slept on edge, his body reacting to the new energy burning within him, the way station of possibilities calling for him until he decided to answer. He woke in downtime and lay quietly, *bahdur*-scoping the craft until he was ready to leave. This time he did not ignore the dark patch pinging on his senses, but he could not verify his fears. He would do that later, as well, within the other base facilities.

Nedar escaped the ship with very little effort. He passed through the security locks and into the threadlike outer corridors of the station and took a deep breath of appreciation. Stations carried an odor all their own, dense with the machinery which maintained them, and the sweat of those who occupied them.

He had rested and thought out a course of action that depended on his being able to correspond privately with Hathord and Vihtirne, and the base was the only place to do that. He should be able to secure a private line at any one of several places along the mall. It would be cheaper to find the pilots' lounge and call from there, but he had no wish to be recognized just yet and there were Choyan here who might know him. Once into the main concourses, he was both hidden and exposed as a Choyan, but most aliens would not be able to name him even if he had flown for them before. The intricacies of Choyan physiognomy seemed to be beyond most aliens, as if all they saw were the height, the horn crown, and the strength and elegance of their general build. They would know him for what, not who, he was.

He had left the humankind behind because she did not fit into this part of the general plan as yet. That she would was almost inevitable, even if he planned her role more as hostage than conspirator. He had used his *bahdur* to touch her lightly before leaving the ship. She had not quite recovered from the treatment. His only doubt about her role centered on her recovery. He could not afford to drag along an invalid, but he would need her for a shield if John Taylor Thomas did not let him go.

He could see the stronger lights of the concourse ahead and feel the slightly stronger pull of gravity, and the noise of population pulled at him. Nedar hurried along. Time was of the essence.

Hat crossed his study, toweling off his mane vigorously, feeling the heady scent of the morning run in his nostrils and lungs. The benefit that came from his new exercise regimen would outlast the tiredness he felt. The early brisk-ness foretold the fall season which was not too far off, and a blessed relief to the summer doldrums which affected everyone, not just the cadets.

The view screen activated as he came within reach, star-tling him for a moment with its activity. Then he realized he had a message incoming.

As he sat down to take it, he noticed the comset panel reading telling him it was live, and that relayed transmission had a lag time of about eight minutes.

The image came into focus and he found himself staring at Nedar, gauntness edging his handsome visage into a knife-edge sharpness, eyes ablaze with his old intensity, and the Earthan's jaw dropped in amazement.

"Hat, I've billed this call to the school's account, but I don't want to take much time. Listen carefully. I want you to contact Vihtirne. I need a freighter from her mining co-op to dock here at Sorrow A-11 and pick me up. I know, you want to know how I got here and what's happened, but there's no time for that now. I've got to get two of us off A-11 and back to Cho with as little fuss as possible—and my companion is an alien. Tell Vihtirne that, and tell her I don't want any arguments. I need to use the House mines on Galern as a screen to bring the alien in. No one's to know where I am or what I'm bringing with me. I'll wait on-line to see that you received transmission."

Hat closed his mouth with a snap and found himself straining forward slightly as if he could make better contact with Nedar. "I understand, but I don't agree. Nedar, we can't bring an alien in! Anyway, I'll relay your request to Vihtirne and let her deal with you. Sorrow base A-11, use the Galern mining co-op as a screen, and I'll assume that you want to be picked up immediately." Hat took a quick breath. "And it's good to see you."

He sat back and waited the long, agonizing eight minutes for his transmission to reach Nedar and then bring confirmation back to him. The *tezar's* image changed to one of solemn amusement, and he added, "I'll know when the freighter's here. I'll make contact. Tell them not to reveal their true purpose. And there's an Abdrelik warship hanging out here, watching the station. Use caution."

The view screen went dark. Hat let out a whistle of a breath. What had Nedar gotten himself into?

It did not occur to him to ask himself why Nedar was asking for his aid. He paused at the comset long enough to determine Vihtirne of Sky's hailing number and place a call to her.

Her aristocratic features glared out at him, her mane of blue-black hair tumbling down on shoulders artfully bared in a morning gown. She frowned slightly, not recognizing him.

"*Tezar* Hathord," he introduced himself, "master of Blue Ridge."

"Good morning, Hathord," she said briskly. "How may I be of use to you?"

He wanted to confirm something first. "Are we on a privacy band?"

"You've contacted me through one. Is this Sky business?" she countered suspiciously.

Hat found himself smiling, knowing that he in no way resembled a Sky. "Actually, it is. I have some information I was requested to pass on to you, from *tezar* Nedar."

Her irritation fled, replaced by stark surprise. The expression did not do her face justice, showing the age which careful surgery had been trying to deny. She took a moment to gather herself. "Do I need to record this?"

"No, it's brief. He asks for you to send a freighter to pick him and a companion up from Sorrow Station A-11, as soon as you can do so. This is a covert request. He suggests using your mining interests at the Galern co-op to cover the flight. And he's bringing in an alien, and needs to keep that hidden as well."

Her brilliant eyes narrowed quickly. "He'd better have a bedamned good reason for that one." She hesitated. "Any word of where he's been?"

"No. Not for either of us."

Vihtirne considered him. Then she asked, "Would you do it, *tezar* Hathord?"

He'd already done more than he should, but he didn't hesitate. "Yes," he told her. "And as soon as possible."

A multitude of expressions flickered in the depths of her dark eyes. Hat knew that Nedar was counted among her lovers, for he'd told Hat as much, and that she had ambitions for him. Yet he could see her calculating the worth of the risk.

She evidently decided in Nedar's favor, for she nodded. "All right. I'll bring him at least as far as Galern. Then the three of us shall have to talk." She cut off the transmission abruptly.

He knew he should have her wariness, but he didn't. But then, she would never, ever, have ridden a thrust glider blind off a plateau, he thought in triumph, as he ended his own transmission. He was still a *tezar*, willing to take a risk.

Alexa dreamed of lovemaking. Her skin warm and satiny, her lover avid, sometimes Bevan, sometimes Rand with those honest turquoise eyes, and sometimes some faceless being whom she wasn't even sure was human. She awoke from her dream to the dimmed lights of her cabin, her lips parted, still half wet, and knew that she was not alone.

She rubbed the sand from her eyes and peered across the small room, to the heavily shaded corner where someone or something sat and waited for her notice. Alexa wrapped the sheet about her and sat up in the bed. The IV was gone, finally, leaving a purple bruise in its wake, and she had been brought here. Maren must be fairly certain she was well recovered. She thought that her father had made time for her at last.

Nedar emerged from the dark, hunching forward slightly from his position so that the dim illumination could highlight his distinctive face.

"You don't intend to have any more of the treatments," he stated.

She tucked her sheet about her more sturdily, feeling somewhat violated and vulnerable. She had no intention of revealing her plans to him. "I'm hardly in a condition to be making any choices."

"But you've already made yours." Nedar stood. He did

not approach, as if aware of her uneasiness, but stayed in the shadows, out of range of the security camera's focus.

"It seemed to have more of an effect on me than it did on you," she said.

"You were scarcely conscious enough to notice."

"You're still standing," Alexa returned forcefully.

"It could not be otherwise." Nedar paused. "You did not answer my question."

Alexa wiggled a bare foot which poked out from the sheeting. "Was it a question? You sounded as though you already knew what I was thinking."

"You came to me in my moments of need."

Laughter exploded from her. "This is a sickroom call? Nedar, I don't think so. What do you want from me?"

He shifted slightly, getting a little closer to her. She saw that he'd changed and was once again wearing a Choyan *tezar's* uniform. "We haven't much time. Tell me what the drug did to you."

Her moist lips had suddenly gone dry. She did not want to look into his eyes. "My blood boiled. I thought my heart was going to burst. And my mind—" she stopped, not wanting to share the intimacy.

"What about your mind?"

"What about yours?"

His glance shifted. "I was not affected in the same way you were."

"For which you should thank your lucky stars." Alexa folded her legs up under her.

The *tezar* gave a bittersweet smile. "No doubt. I want that drug, Alexa, its formula and the knowledge with which to manufacture it. He told you that it could be capsulated. Would he have that information here in the ship's lab, in his notes?"

"He should." Alexa watched carefully. Anything a Choya wanted that badly, she held an interest in. Anything which could make those arrogant bastards want to barter was valuable indeed.

"I'm leaving. I intend to take the information with me."

She rose up on her knees. "You're not going without me."

"I did not think." Nedar said gravely, "I had that choice. You'll be my shield."

"How are you getting off the station?"

Nedar paused, as though deciding what he would tell her and what he wouldn't. He answered, "A Choyan ore freighter will be docking shortly. They will smuggle us on board. There is an Abdrelik warship—"

"GNask," she murmured, barely interrupting him.

"—undoubtedly, hanging off the nearest quadrant. If your father intends to make a run for it, and I should think he would—he can't stay docked here indefinitely; the fees are too high—they'll catch him."

"They want us."

"As well as their vengeance for his invasion of their vessel, yes, I think so."

"But they won't go after a Choyan freighter."

"I hope not."

"What about my father?"

"What about him?"

Her chin went up. "I won't leave him to that."

"Your filial devotion surprises me." His chin also went up. She thought of locking horns with him.

"Don't be. My father used me when he needed to, and I'm no less his daughter. But I do love him." She paused. "I want the freighter to transmit before we hit FTL."

He gave a little nod of assent. "All right. That's reasonable. No one will be able to stop us then. GNask will not attack your father out of the remaining grievance. He's too smart for that."

"What if he thinks it's just a decoy?"

"Oh, he won't, I can guarantee that. Baros will be able to tell him otherwise." Nedar gave a brief smile.

"How long do I have to get to Maren?"

He told her the hour. Alexa digested it, saying, "That's standard downtime for us. The shift will be light. When do you think the freighter will be making its approach?"

"Sunrise, by your configuration. There'll be a few hours while it downloads, then they'll be able to take us on board."

"By then," Alexa told him, "I'll be ready." She slipped to the floor and stood, adjusting her wrap. "And by then I want to know just why it is you want the formula so badly."

"What makes you think I'd tell you?"

"Because I'm no more your hostage than you were ever

mine. That drug has some benefit you want, if only to protect your fellow pilots against further imprinting experiments. But there's something else to it, something that makes you sweat." Alexa smiled. "And I want to know about anything that makes you sweat."

Chapter 20

It must have been late in downtime when John awoke, startled, his knotting muscles bringing him out of that light stasis of dreaming. He lurched a little out of the reclining chair which held him and found both the room and the view screen dark as he grabbed for the lip of the desktop. He cursed himself for falling asleep at his work, one hand tingling back to life, his neck aching. The dominant lighting had dimmed considerably, so he knew it was downtime shift on the cruiser, but the small pinpoint light over his console, and highlighting the map board, stayed bright. He blinked at it owlishly, eyes trying to adjust.

He'd meant to look in on Alexa. After Maren's report, he found himself uncertain about the course of the treatment and seeing the taped backup didn't make him any more confident. Her violent reaction was not due to an overdosage, Maren assured him, but John couldn't see the difference. The violence, he'd been told, came from the cessation of the viral influence of the imprinting—an acute case of withdrawal. The Choya had showed no such reaction, but then Maren was fairly certain he had either not suffered imprinting, or the infection had just begun. As for Alexa's behavior, nothing in the tests he'd run had given any indication of such an adverse reaction. The physician researcher had cringed himself, reviewing the tape of her, and even more peculiar had been the Choya's abrupt exit after his own injection. Perhaps the pilot could no more bear her suffering than her father had been able to. Was it worth it, putting her through such an ordeal? Yet, if somehow he could get his daughter back, the loving and cheerful toddler he'd lost so many years ago, perhaps he could ask her to endure it.

John rubbed his eyes.

"Awake yet, Father?" queried a deceptively soft voice from across the room.

He swung about in his chair. Alexa lay curled on the small couch in the corner, her eyes cat-bright in the twilight, watching him.

"Alexa! How are you feeling?"

"You mean you don't know? You've a stack of reports at your elbow. I thought mine might have been in there somewhere."

"Compact business—it kept me late. I'm sorry. Maren told me you were resting comfortably, but I meant to come in and say good night to you."

"And tell me a story, I'm sure." She uncurled, standing up. "I don't need any excuses, Father. I know what you intended. If you hadn't wanted me, you wouldn't have taken me from GNask. We both know what you risked by doing that. I'd like to think you did it for yourself, rather than for your appointment." She came close and leaned over him, peering at the quadrant map. Although he'd taken Baros' report off the board, she reached out and put a fingertip to the darkened sector.

"There's an Abdrelik warship waiting here."

"How do you know?"

Alexa looked down on him, giving him a cold smile. "There is, isn't there?"

"Yes."

"GNask, of course, not willing to suffer the slight you gave him. He's thought it over and he wants us back, for reasons of his own which I might know or guess . . . and I don't think he's going to give up. If he can't take us, he may well attack."

John listened to the only child he had speak, in her light, icy voice, calculating, no less a predator than the being she talked about.

"You can give us up, or you can keep us, Father, but either way, GNask will see us dead ultimately. He can't afford to keep us alive now. We were taken once; he'll not let us be taken again. If you give us to him, he'll let you go in exchange for the pleasure of putting us to death himself. If you try to run, he'll have rrRusk blast us out of the quadrant, not as pleasurable, but final anyway." She stood back from the upright board. "Or. . . . ."

She'd thought of a third solution, he told himself, and although he did not want to hear it, for the chill of her voice put a tremor in his guts, he knew he had to listen. Just perhaps she'd thought of a way to save all their lives.

"What are you thinking of?" he asked, in spite of himself. *To lose her again!*

"I came to say good-bye."

He sat very still, watching her.

"No mourning? No objections?" She half-turned, peering back at him.

"Not yet. I'm listening."

"Good. Because somewhere around uptime, a Choyan ore freighter is docking here. When it leaves, Nedar and I will be on it." She paused, as if waiting for interruption, but none came. She took another stride away from him and turned. "We have a partnership, Nedar and I, uneasy at best. Choyan don't accept many as their equals. When we leave, we'll hail GNask to let him know we're gone and beyond his reach. He should turn away from you then. He might even attempt to pursue us. If not—"

"Baros is prepared," John said.

"I thought she might be." Alexa dropped back on the couch, drawing her legs up under her. In the dim light of the room, he was not reminded of anything so much as a leopardess at ease. "Nedar doesn't know I've come to you."

"He doesn't want me interfering."

"No. But I've a proposition for you, blood of my blood and flesh of my flesh." She smiled widely. "He wants that drug."

"What?"

"I don't know why yet, but I know he wants it badly. And, Father, anything the Choyan want that badly, I think we ought to be in a position to sell to them, don't you?

John was slow in replying. He wondered if Nedar's abrupt exit had been made to mask his own response to the pharmaceutical. "That depends on what it is."

"I don't know what it is yet, or what effect it has on him, only that Nedar is avid for it. He wants the supply on hand plus Maren's notes on the formula and whatever else I can get."

John felt the icy grip on his emotions begin to ease up

a little as his thoughts turned to this new development. The Choyan were fiercely independent, taking in little in trading, exporting the talents of their pilots as well as their technology. They had virtually every member of the Compact over a barrel with respect to the balance of trade. "What do you suggest we do?"

"Give him the supplies. Maren talked of being able to convert the formula into capsules. Go ahead with it. Be ready to make shipments when and where I tell you to."

"And you?"

"I'll be finding out just what it is Nedar craves, and how much they're willing to pay for it. They may be able to synthesize the formula in time, but I'm hoping most of the formula comes from what we grow at home. That's the one singular advantage we have. Even with their technology, it should take them years to synthesize the elements. If we can give him a ready supply quickly, we may just put the Choyan in a position where they'll have to bargain with us."

That position was something he'd barely managed to achieve diplomatically over the course of her lifetime. He watched her watching him over steepled fingers. "And what if we're talking about a drug we don't want distributed?" he asked evenly.

She shrugged. "It had little enough effect on me, other than attacking the Abdrelik imprinting."

"And from what I saw on the report, it had even less impact on him."

Alexa smiled again, this time the warmth reaching her eyes. "You took in a pilot who could barely stay on his feet. GNask gave him up so easily only because it was extremely probable Nedar might die on you, sparing him the embarrassment of disposing of the body and possibly giving him evidence with which to implicate you."

"The extremity of which condition the Choya might have exaggerated."

The smile grew. "I can guarantee you that he nearly died in the Abdreliks' tender hands. A few decent meals here, one treatment from Maren, and our near to death pilot was out on the concourse an hour or so ago, sampling the night life of the station, and placing a call home. You didn't even know he'd left the ship."

John digested the information. He ran a quick diagnostic on the cruiser's security systems. The boarding locks showed a malfunction several hours ago, although he could not place a humanoid form seeking egress. The aberration, however, was enough for him to believe Alexa's claim. Although he knew the strength of the Choyan race, he hadn't suspected Nedar could make so rapid a recovery. He thought of several pharmaceuticals which could be so effective not as cures but by their masking powers, and most of them he wouldn't want to traffic in. He looked back at his daughter. "I won't sell illegal drugs."

"We don't know if they're illegal or not. We've no idea of their potential, and we won't know what they did to him until he confides in me. And he won't do that until we're well away from here."

"Why is he taking you?"

"To ensure you won't follow."

She was hostage again, then. He guessed, however, that she would be gone anyway, that he'd driven her away. He absolved her. "You don't have to take any more treatments. It's too dangerous, until Maren gets more tests run."

She unsteepled her fingers. "You don't understand, do you, Father?"

"No, I don't."

"I like being this way. What the Abdreliks gave me is valuable as long as I can control it, and that's what you gave me. Your contribution is as valuable as theirs. But if I take any more, I won't be what I am, and I like what I am." Her eyes widened slightly, their catlike glow increasing. "Sharp, incisive, ruthless. I like having this edge, and I don't intend to lose it. So don't think about keeping me behind tomorrow. I won't let you. If you manage it, it won't be for long."

"And then what do you intend to do?"

Her head tilted a little. "Put the Choyan and Abdreliks at our feet, the same thing you've been trying to do, only I hope my methods are a lot quicker and I expect to benefit financially from them. Money transcends all barriers."

"You don't know what you're getting into."

"No. That's part of what makes it so rewarding. Do we have an understanding?"

He understood little except that she intended to leave him,

and that he had no hope he'd ever get her back again. The rest
of her he recognized only vaguely. He'd seen many rapacious
humans in his time, as well as the Abdreliks and Ronins with
their appetites, but she seemed to him to be some foreign
hybrid. He mourned his lost child. "Yes," he answered softly.

"Good. Wake Maren. I'll meet him at the lab. Tell him
as little as possible, but don't make it necessary for me to
give him explanations. I'll go with Nedar as planned, and
contact you as soon as I can." Alexa put her head back.
"Don't look so stricken. I'm as much your daughter as I
ever was."

"No." He shook his head. "But I can see I'm a fool to
hope that you might have been. What you are, Alexa, I
don't pretend to recognize, but you have my love. You've
always had my love."

"I know that. It's the one security that keeps me going.
I treasure it, whether you know it or not. I forgive you for
giving me to GNask so long ago."

"Do you?"

She went to the threshold, palming open the lock, without another look back. "Whatever it takes," she answered
faintly as she passed through.

The sunrise over Charolon flooded its east palace windows with rose-colored light. Rand, awakened too early for
his liking, watched Palaton ready his effects briskly. Though
he'd been told the *tezar's* plans, Palaton wasn't waiting for
Rand's approval or enthusiasm.

Rand stifled a yawn and made what little protest he
could. "You've probably already been through this with
Jorana, but I don't like the idea of your going out there
alone," Rand said unhappily.

"You're right," Palaton said with a half-smile. "I've already been through this with her. And I'm not going completely alone, Rufeen is piloting me." He had a small
duffel, which he hiked up on one shoulder. He wore one
of his older uniforms—faded, unimpressive, a little big on
him—for comfort.

Rufeen was one Choya'i Rand greatly respected, for her
blunt manners as well as her piloting skill, but she had her
limitations and he knew them well. "Rufeen will stay with
the ship. She has to. I don't."

"You'll mark me, Rand, and then I'll not only have to face whatever enemies I may have because of the questions I'm asking, but also anyone who has a grudge against the throne or against my recent decisions regarding the God-blind. You'll be a great liability."

"I'm also your greatest asset. I can bring the *bahdur* up now. I can give you the aura, sense the emotional balance of those around you—I can help."

Palaton paused in mid-stride and looked down at the humankind who was trying to keep up with him as they crossed the palace wing. "There's no doubt you could," he answered gently, "but if I can go in alone and remain unrecognized, I might never need that help. Your presence will precipitate things. Remember, I'll be going to a community which does not deal with aliens. I can take you to Blue Ridge—I *plan* to take you there—but not here. You simply cannot go everywhere I go."

The inner hurt was reflected in the turquoise eyes.

"What you do affects me," Rand said, "as what I do affects you."

"You'll know if I'm all right." Palaton referred to the bond between them.

"It's not enough! I can't be there to help."

Palaton put a hand on the other's shoulder. It surprised him to feel a certain bulk of muscle. "I know," he answered. "Nor I you. If Rindy were up and about, I wouldn't worry about you so much."

Rand read the note of finality in his voices. He said urgently, "If you need me, call. I swear, I'll find a way to get to you."

"That's all I can ask." He squeezed his hand tightly, then stepped forward, heading toward the side doors where a conveyance waited to take him to the private airstrip.

Unhappily, Rand watched him go. For a new day dawning with bright, clean light and a passionately blue sky, there were shadows which only his *bahdur* sense could feel, and they chilled him.

Above, on a landing, Qativar also watched. Once again, he had noted the disturbing closeness between the pilot and the off-worlder. It was not a sexual thing, although even thinking of that made his skin crawl, but it was something far, far stronger. Like a *durah,* he thought, though that kind of soul bonding was most common between lovers.

He needed to sever that bond, to leave each vulnerable and alone. Finishing Rindy off and putting the manling under suspicion of the deed would have accomplished his purpose neatly, but now there was no chance of that. He berated himself again for the loss of that opportunity. He would have to find some other way.

Qativar found his mouth twisting with dislike. He had been successful so far, but he had not counted on the alien staying behind. Since Rand figured so prominently in his scheme for Palaton's utter disgrace, this development did not bode well.

A step sounded on the marble flooring below, echoing loudly. Smoothing his face into neutrality, Qativar moved back quickly from the landing. He could speculate all day, but he would not know. He might never know. Whoever moved downstairs did so on a steady course, so Qativar turned away and went on about his business, still thinking.

Rand waited for the Choya to catch up with him, not sensing any menace in his approach. He'd come in through the employee entrance, and he still had his hand palm up, for the Ident read of his print, a case with papers and instruments in his other hand.

"Good morning," the Choya said, his voices faintly tinged with surprise as well as pleasure as he halted face-to-face with Rand. He blinked several times, his large, pale green eyes filled with innocence.

"Good morning," Rand answered. Something about the other nagged at him, but he could not place it. Surrounded by Choyan faces, he was just learning to pick out their individual characteristics.

"I'm early," the other commented. "Join me for a cup of *bren*?" His Trade had a slight accent to it, as though he wasn't that used to speaking it, although most of Cho was fairly bilingual.

Rand had developed a definite liking for the strong, coffeelike brew. It was early morning, and his stomach told him he'd probably appreciate *bren* and something a little more substantial. He'd missed the meal he normally shared with Palaton. Whoever this Choya was, and he had the slightly undefined, shaggy look Rand had come to associate with the Godless, he wore a security badge clipped to his shirt, meaning that Jorana's staff had at one time or another passed him. What could the harm be? "All right."

"Good." The Choya lowered his hand, trading off his case, beckoning. Rand led the way.

Chirek watched him go, thinking of his good fortune, his blood drumming through his horns, wondering where Palaton had gone so early in the day, guessing that he'd probably not planned to return immediately. After passing him on the side steps, Chirek had quickly thought of ways to get to Rand, to befriend as well as test him, and now here the alien was, practically laid in his lap.

For a tense moment, he thought the humankind had recognized him. He'd been banking that the other wouldn't, that the intense moments when they'd been thrown together in the Two Day War had not left Rand with memories he could readily call upon. If Chirek had thought for one moment that Rand could have picked him out, he would have quit work with Gathon immediately and gone elsewhere. There was too much at risk.

But knowing that many Choyan would seem only vaguely familiar to the humankind, in spite of their obvious outer differences, had been his best disguise. Within the palace, he dressed in his conservative business suiting, his manner scholarly and unremarkable. He was certain Rand would not recognize him for the Choya who'd pulled him out of a burning wreck, then taken him for safety to the old Abdrelik War Memorial in the sublevel just outside the palace and capital where they had then hidden from the first strikes of the Two Day War.

And he certainly bore no resemblance to the Choya who'd howled in distress as the Change had been worked in him, for Rand had had his own revelation. They had supported each other the distance of the Emperor's Walk to find Palaton and warn him of the impending Abdrelik strike, but Chirek knew Rand had not seen him, for his eyes and mind had been full of other sights and other faces.

So it was this morning that no obvious recognition had crawled across Rand's alien features, and Chirek had not been exposed. Given the opportunity which faced him today, however, the renegade priest was almost certain that things would not remain the same.

Over a cup of *bren,* Chirek hoped to change Rand's life as much as Rand had changed his.

Palaton moved quickly through the side entrance, his ordered conveyance waiting at the curbside, but a communicator saw him and bounded after, flamboyant red mane sticking out in all directions from his headgear, broadcaster to his throat.

Palaton quickly saw that the shoulder-mounted mobile unit was taping, although a live feed could be established the moment the communicator thought he had something, so he gave thanks for very small favors and slowed as the reporter called his name.

"Heir Palaton! Early day for you?"

He stopped reluctantly as the communicator loped near. The auto-focus went on and Palaton yearned for *bahdur* which might fog the broadcast, making any interview virtually impossible. But this was not a Godless, and chances were the Choya knew how to circumvent him anyway. He looked at the broad-nosed Choya, remembering his face from the crowd of communicators who stabled themselves near the palace and capital. Hurlek, he thought the name was.

"No," he answered. "I've appointments which need to be kept." He toned his voices to reflect routine, uninteresting tasks.

The communicator's live feed remained dark. "No security?"

"None needed." He checked his chronograph. "I've got a vehicle waiting."

The red-maned Choya flicked a look in that direction, noting the vehicle. Palaton knew he would have to alter the on-board computer, or Hurlek would be taking records off it.

"How about a couple of comments?"

Palaton stood patiently. The communicator smiled broadly as though he knew he had him. "What about the rumors that the imperial branch is leaning hard on the various flight schools, demanding confidential information and looking at massive restructuring? Word is that the *tezars* are becoming uneasy."

Palaton kept his face bland, although the Choya's words bit at him, distorting what he knew to be the truth. "Rumor overestimates the situation, as usual. The flight schools need our continued support and we need to open the schools up for students whose talent we may not be recognizing."

The camera reflected a taping light at him, his words going into technical storage. Unease began to fill him.

"What about pressuring for information the schools traditionally keep confidential, separate from imperial and legislative branches? As a *tezar* yourself, you're privy to the channels and you've been accused of misusing them."

Accused? Who would accuse him? And for what? Palaton drew back from the communicator. "I'm not aware of any pressure," Palaton responded. He took a step sideways, intent on moving out of range. Hurlek moved with him. "I can't comment on that."

"Then I gather you won't have any comment on the latest information that the three Choyan who accosted you during the memorial ceremony have all turned up dead in work camps? There are those who consider this a blatant betrayal of your earlier promises to the commons population."

"I'm aware there is an investigation into their deaths. These are three individuals who, despite the fact they were not carrying weapons, chose not to explain themselves or their threatening behavior. Detention in labor camps is routine while a case is being prepared. I see no conflict."

"What about betrayal, heir Palaton? Have you abandoned them?"

That, Palaton knew and feared. He said only, "My actions will bear me out." He ducked into the conveyance and slammed the door, locking Hurlek out. The vehicle pulled away and he caught a side mirror view of the communicator filming his rapid exit.

Chapter 21

Rand led the way to the kitchen area, where he usually ate, out of the way, quiet, not subjecting him to the stares he experienced in the massive dining room. But as he approached, the Choya caught him by the sleeve, saying lightly, "This way," and took him through a series of corridors to the office area of the palace, where Rand had never been before. The atmosphere here was one of work and purpose, the Choyan passing through looking at him curiously, but steadfast in their own pursuits. There was a high percentage of the God-blind here, he noticed, the underpinnings of the palace just as they were the stolid underpinnings of all Cho.

His guide took him into one of the offices and sat him down, pouring him a cup of *bren* from a nearby kitchenette, and sitting with him. Chirek put a hand up and brought down a privacy shield even though the partitioned area looked all but abandoned. Rand grew suddenly wary, and watched quietly, deciding on his next move.

The Choya smiled gently. "Please relax. You're my guest. You remind me of a rather large rodent we have in the grasslands—we called it *batrach*, large whiskers—it's a suspicious little beast, with good reason, for it's a favorite meal of the carnivores. It has large ears, too, but they droop when a *batrach* is at ease, giving the impression of even larger whiskers."

Rand pulled the hot *bren* toward him, saying, "I'm not worried so much if I'm a large whiskers but if you're a carnivore."

The Choya laughed. "With good reason, I'm afraid. Your stay here hasn't been an easy one." He brought his cup up, sipping gingerly at the steaming liquid.

Rand looked the desk over and saw materials, some in

Trade and some in Choyan which he could not read, relating to the Ministry of Resources. The privacy shield he now understood. Relocation and utilization of resources was a field in which a great deal was invested. Those matters, of necessity, had to remain confidential. He didn't understand why the Choya used the shielding now, except that it was clear he did not want to be seen or heard with Rand. But was it for Rand's protection or his own? He brought up his own cup, inky and pungent, and took a drink.

"You work with Gathon?"

"Most of us do, but I'm afraid you're talking to a relatively minor clerk." The Choya smiled again, and Rand felt himself haunted. He knew the other from somewhere, yet could not place him. With that nagging feeling came the worry that he ought to know if this were friend or foe and did not.

"I understand you've been spending time with Rindalan. How is he?"

The question distracted and disappointed Rand. Was palace gossip what this was all about? He lifted and dropped a shoulder. "He's making progress."

The Choya's light jade eyes fairly twinkled. "You're disappointed," he noted. "But, no, I didn't bring you here for gossip. Old Rindy is very dear to me. You were there, weren't you, when he came out of the coma?" And his companion sat forward, his casual manner dropped, waiting for Rand to answer.

Be careful, Rand thought to himself. Don't say too much, or too little. His mouth suddenly felt dry and he wet his lips so that he could answer.

Having surreptitiously made certain Palaton departed safely for Maerlon, Jorana paused at the bank of monitors, looking at the various entrances to the working branch of the palace. She didn't see the Choya she skimmed for. "Is Chirek in yet?"

The Choya nearest her ran fingertips across the flatscreen and said, "Yes, but he's already at his desk. His screen is up, so he's working."

"Working," she repeated. But at what? She had not been able to reach Malahki to confirm with him that the Choya'i she'd met at Bayalak as the Prophet and the one who'd

accosted Rand were one and the same . . . but she had
located the designer of the brilliant blue outfit the Choya'i
had worn and discovered the bill for the clothing had gone
to Chirek's account. So the Choya had known her both
before and after. It could be as innocent as courtship or as
deadly as conspiracy. She didn't want Chirek in her palace
until she knew. She hesitated, uncertain whether to interrupt him in his work, putting him on probation until she
knew what to do, or letting him stay. There was no connection as yet between Chirek and the three others who'd been
involved and then committed suicide. She decided to seek
out Gathon and have a talk with him.

Within the privacy screen, Rand decided what he wanted
to reveal to his new acquaintance. "Yes, I was with him,"
Rand answered.

"Alone?"

His *bahdur* began to warm inside him, a feeling much
like that of swallowing the hot *bren,* and for a moment he
thought he was confusing the two. But then he began to
welcome the intrusion of the power, and hoped he wouldn't
need it. "Listen," he said. "There's much I don't understand about Choyan society, and the palace, and what
ought to be private and what shouldn't. So how about I
thank you for the drink and leave."

He stood, the privacy shield shimmering as it quickly
adjusted to the increase in coverage area.

The Choya looked up at him and said, "That may be,
but there's a great deal you do know about *bahdur,* and
the fact that Cho is quickly reaching a crisis."

Rand sat back down, feeling as if his feet had been
knocked out from under him. How could this commons
presume to sit and discuss *bahdur* with him? And that echo
alone, of Palaton within him, sombered him abruptly. A
single Choya, with the knowledge of him that this one had,
could destroy all that Palaton had begun to work for. He
had no choice but to listen.

The Choya put a hand out, a long slender hand with
powerful fingers, and laced them gently about Rand's wrist.
There was a leap inside him, and he thought, *power answers
to power. This commons has the talent!*

"You don't remember me," the Choya said, "but I could never forget you."

"Who—" and Rand had to stop and clear his throat, "—are you?"

"It's who I was, rather than who I now am, that's more important. I was a God-blind Choya, and now, because of you, for reasons I can't scientifically prove or accept, but simply *know*, I'm Changed, filled with *bahdur*, because of you. I have to understand. Is that how you woke Rindy?"

Rand felt as though he sat at the brink of a chasm, an abyss which could swallow him and Palaton whole, and then dissolve the civilization for which Palaton had sacrificed his entire life. *Changed*, the other had said, as if he meant an entire metamorphosis. He fought for his voice. "What do you mean?"

"I mean that His Eminence wasn't expected to live. Even his *bahdur* readings were negligible. His whole life was slipping away from him, no matter how hard he tried to grasp it, no matter how much more work he was destined to do."

But Rindalan's state hadn't been common knowledge, except perhaps to those who'd come to see him—and to the one who'd tried to still him permanently. "You poisoned him," Rand accused hoarsely. He jerked his arm free from the other's hold.

"No." The jade eyes measured him. "Poison? Was that what kept him comatose? I didn't know. But I wouldn't have done that to Rindalan." He finished his drink, repeating, "Poison. No wonder he's kept sequestered now. What was it?"

"I can't have this conversation with you."

Chirek smiled mildly. "It's not in me to blackmail you, but I could. You protect Palaton as much as he protects you. Does he train you? Do all humankind have the potential and not recognize it?"

"No," answered Rand hoarsely. "Most of us have . . . nothing at all."

"I had wondered. There are no pilots from your world." He stared at Rand. "Just as Palaton needs you, so also did Rindalan. But why? Why you?"

"I don't know! He awoke when I was there, that's all, and told me he was being drugged."

"Do they know what was used on him?"

"No. Some kind of . . . blocker. Water soluble. Dammit." Rand slapped his hand down on the desktop. "Don't ask me any more. Just tell me what it is you want me to know."

"I'm afraid you'll find more questions in what I have to say than answers. I work for Gathon, but what I am is a priest."

"A priest? But you can't be, you're not Housed."

"Oh, yes," Chirek countered. "A Prelate much like Rindalan, although my religion has been outlawed on Cho for slightly over three hundred years. It's heretical, you see, to believe that there might come a day when all Choyan, no matter how basely born, might have *bahdur*. We wait for a Being of Change."

"I don't know what you're talking about it."

"Of course, you do. You must. You have it. I felt it in you when we touched. You hold that essence which has been denied to the Godless, which once was and should again be the legacy of everyone on Cho."

The Choya leaned ever closer. "My name is Chirek. We met in the Two Day War. Your craft was attacked returning from Sethu. You went down. The rioters were everywhere. I took you to safety, to the Emperor's Walk."

Rand felt his throat closing. He remembered the confusion and the smoke, and then the underground area known as the Emperor's Walk, where the remnants of an earlier Choyan civilization lay in silent memorial, where the Abdreliks had attacked before the Compact, and he felt again the gripping prescience which had overtaken him there. The memories held him still.

"You have to remember."

He looked up, feeling as though he was drowning, and said, "Chirek." A vision flooded back. "You lit the fountain."

"Yes! With *bahdur*, after you Changed me."

Rand well remembered the beautiful fountain, one of the artifacts from another age, when even the very young had had enough *bahdur* to touch and activate the sculpture. Palaton had never really told him about the gradual decline in Cho, but the evidence was everywhere. He could see all the maintenance systems that had once been activated by psychic power and now lay dormant, or functioned on manual backups. Gripped by a surge of *bahdur* which had torn loose from him, he could barely understand what had happened next, except that he knew the Abdreliks had been brought through Chaos to attack, and that he'd had to warn Palaton.

"I did nothing," he denied. Even if he had done it, it had not come from inside him, it had come from the power Palaton had entrusted to him. It was Palaton's power, Palaton's heritage.

"You did everything. You were Seeing what was to come, the next Abdrelik attack, and you grabbed me to tell me—and the blast of power that came through you changed everything that I was."

"It wasn't me."

"I would believe that," argued Chirek softly, "but then I sent Dorea to you. You changed her, too, by the barest of touches, and nothing will be the same for her, either. That's when I knew that I had to talk with you, had to make you understand what you had become: the Being of Change, the prophesied catalyst, the one for whom we've all been waiting."

"Oh, no." Rand shook his head. "You're not looking at a messiah. I don't know who this Dorea is, but I've got nothing to do with you or any of your religions."

Chirek did not argue with him this time. He merely palmed open a drawer, took a photo out, and slid it across the desktop.

Rand did not touch it. He looked down at the picture of a young Choya'i, with hazel eyes and wearing an electrifying blue dress, the skirt aswirl, like any young woman, showing off a beauty of which she was both stunningly aware and unaware. Rand deflated suddenly, recognizing her. It was she who kept him safe, momentarily, during the disruption.

He looked up, and his eyes met Chirek's. Silently, Chirek took another photo out and placed it atop the first.

Dorea again, only he would not have known her, for her eyes were bandaged, and she sat, still and frozen, in a dark hovel of a building, the stunning dress dirtied and in near rags tucked about her. Had he done this? His hand shook as he touched the edge of the picture, as though to push it away from him.

"What happened to her eyes?"

"She clawed them out, struck by visions she didn't understand and couldn't control."

"I didn't do this," he said, his voice barely audible.

"No," Chirek agreed. He looked down at the picture. "I did. I never thought that her experience might be as traumatic as mine, and I never warned her, I never prepared her for it, because I wanted to be certain the Change was real, not imagined. I'm a poor priest," he said mournfully, "destroying my people bringing them the very revelation we prayed for."

"I can't have done it," Rand repeated. He felt numb and twisted inside. "I'm not who you think I am. I can't be!" This was Palaton's power, he thought, not his. He could not possibly be what the other wanted him to be. "I'm not Choyan!"

"No. Outside of a few diplomats allowed here for conferences, you're the only alien we've had here for almost as long as my faith has been outlawed." Chirek gathered up the photos and secreted them away. "I can't explain it. I only know what happened to me, and to Dorea. And if you came to me, all puffed up and declaiming your ability, I wouldn't believe you then, either. But you didn't. This was forced on you as much as it was forced on us, but denying it won't take it away."

"I'm not even supposed to know what *bahdur* is," Rand said quietly.

"I don't doubt that. No one off-world knows. Can you imagine the shock to the Compact's scientific community when they learn we pilot by parapsychology? Those who are Housed know well the secret they keep. I'm convinced the xenophobia the rest of us share has been fostered by those who wish to keep us apart from alien communities. The secret is kept, one way or another." He paused significantly. "Rand, I'm telling you that your being here is interwoven with the destiny of my world, my people. You were supposed to come here. You're not an outsider. You bring the Change which can restore hope to all of us."

"It's not me," Rand protested again.

"Prove it. Come with me to Bayalak, to where Dorea sits and reads the future from her darkened eyes. Prove it one way or another, beyond a shadow of a doubt." Chirek sat back, waiting for his answer.

Jorana found Gathon stubbornly going through his transmissions from Panshinea, refusing to be disturbed by her. After cooling her heels for ·a reasonable time period, she decided she did not want to wait until he was free. She checked on Rindalan as she left the residential quarters.

"Well, well." The munificent horn crown with its sparse fringe of chestnut hair swung her way, and Rindy examined her with piercing blue eyes. Almost immediately, he added, "This isn't a social call." He seemed a little dejected.

"It is and it isn't." She looked around the apartment. Rindy sat on a power walker. The créche unit had been taken down, most of the monitors were gone, and only two med techs shared the room with him.

"Have you seen Rand?" the two asked each other simultaneously.

Rindy gave a wry look. "I thought I might get a visit today."

"And Palatan thought he might spend most of the day with you."

The elder dismounted from his walker. He stood, his spindly weight precariously balanced, and the nearest nurse took a protective stance, ready to dive in to his aid if needed. "There is a lot of mischief, even inside these walls."

Jorana gave him a look which brooked trouble for telling her her business. She turned away. "I'll send him up when I find him."

"Do that," commented Rindy, as she fled the apartment.

She returned to her monitoring stations. Barely across the threshold, she demanded, "Get me a tracer on the offworlder's current readings," as she took an enforcer from the weapons' cabinet and strapped it on.

The two monitoring nearest her ran the tracers together and both looked up blankly.

"No sign," the first Choya said. "Not since shortly after meeting up with Chirek this morning and going for *bren*."

Chirek. Jorana paused thoughtfully, then said, "Bring up the exchange, if you can."

The cameras from that angle barely showed the encounter, and it seemed benevolent even in enhanced framing. But the coincidence of the meeting bothered her, coupled with Rand's disappearance.

"All right, then. Where is Chirek now?"

"Still under privacy shield in his offices."

She said to the second Choya, "Check the lines. I want to know when that shield went up, and how long it's been up."

Upholstering the enforcer, she checked the current levels of charge, as the second security guard noted, "It's been up for the better part of an hour."

That made it a very long call under shielding. Jorana didn't like the sound of it. What if he had Rand . . . or Rand's body . . . hidden under that shield?

"Have the brace of guards on that floor meet me at the lift. I'll be right down," she ordered, going back out the door.

"I can't leave the palace with you," Rand answered. "There's no way to hide what I am."

"Actually, there is. A few bandages, a walker, no one would know. As for the trip to Bayalak . . . there's been word that a Prophet is there. She's already drawing pilgrims. You wouldn't be particularly noticeable there, either." Chirek paused. A faint hue lit up the shielding, notifying him that he was being monitored. The hue disappeared, then intensified.

"Come with me," he urged again, putting all the intensity of his newly developed *bahdur* into his voices. "Trust me and come see the possibilities."

Rand's lips tightened, then he made a decision which he knew he would have trouble explaining to Palaton. "All right. But only to prove you're wrong."

Chirek bounded to his feet, shutting down the privacy shield. "Good. But we have to hurry." He took the humankind by the elbow and steered him out of the office, taking back corridors at a fast clip.

When his monitors told him that Rand had not made an appearance, and that Jorana had left him, Qativar decided the time had come to assess his situation with Rindalan. If it proved to be untenable, he needed to get rid of the old

Choya before he grew any stronger, while his death might still be attributable to a sudden relapse.

The threshold at Rindalan's apartment was not closed to him this time, in fact, the doors were sprung wide open, and he could see the elder trundling about his quarters on a walker, steering it adroitly around the furniture. Qativar stepped inside hesitantly, knowing the security barrier could snap shut on him, but nothing happened.

The old fool looked hale enough. Qativar regretted not taking him out while he could, only God-in-all could know what trouble he'd make now. He wondered, though, with a perverse darkness, what Rindy would say if he knew his deathbed mumblings had sent Palaton into a dire trap. Qativar made no effort to conceal the smile his thoughts brought forth.

Rindy wheeled about a turn and came up short. "Qativar! Come to nag me about work?"

The younger Prelate gave a short bow. "There is enough of it piling up."

"The nurses here won't spring me for another day or two. Most of it can wait that long, can it not?" Those pale blue eyes examined him sharply.

"Of course it can. There is, however, the board to be selected for this fall's Choosings. We have a few more days yet, but I don't see how it can hurt you to think about it, do you?"

Rindy scratched knobby fingers through his wild fringe of hair. "I had almost forgotten. You're right. They do let me think, although not too long or strenuously, as long as I don't snore too loudly."

Qativar kept his smile frozen on his face. "Good. Now that I've seen you, my heart's at ease. Should I come back tomorrow and we'll begin sorting through things?"

Rindy shot a look at the nearest med tech. She shook her head. He sighed, then said, "Give it two days, Qativar. By then I should be strong enough to boot them out of here myself."

The nurse laughed, saying, "That's the general idea." She checked her chronograph, adding, "That's enough visiting. You need to park your walker, Eminence, and lie down."

Qativar began backing up. "Two days," he said. "It'll be good to be working with you again."

The nurse shut the door on his exit, and he did not hear if Rindalan had another exchange. He was free, then, of duty, until that time. Free to find another subject or two for Erlorn's tests, and oversee his plans. Then there was that water patent of Vihtirne of Sky's . . . the *ruhl* was not yet ready for distribution, but when it was, he needed free and easy access to the water filtration plants. Being in bed with Vihtirne would, so to speak, give him that. He was close enough, he decided, to approach her. She needed a few key votes within the system to free up the remaining court decisions. As High Priest on Cho, second only to Rindalan, he had the power to sway minds accordingly. If he waited much longer, Rindalan could begin usurping the power core he'd been carefully building. And what if Rindy suspected him? No, it was better to strike now, a bit prematurely, bait the hook and troll the fish along, than to miss the opportunity altogether.

He would take care of Vihtirne. Erlorn would see to Chirek, and find out what the other was up to. Although Qativar had no proof, he thought the quiet clerk was likely the head of the underground church, and Chirek had not been so quiet of late. He merited a much closer watch. Perhaps, if he could manage it without alerting Malahki, Chirek should even be terminated.

He took the nearest walkway to the garages.

The brace of guards met her at the corridors' intersection, just outside the kitchen. Their boot heels rang on the flooring as they hurried down to the office which Chirek shared with a half-dozen other clerks. Jorana entered first, hand curled about her enforcer, in case she needed it.

The desk sat empty, but she could read the auras as plainly as if the seats were still occupied, warm, the answer wafting in the air. Chirek and Rand had both been there, just moments ago.

But where they'd gone, she hadn't the slightest intuition.

Jorana kicked the wall. Was he in danger or not, and what was she going to do about it?

Chapter 22

"You have my daughter, and a supply of the drug. But I'm not giving you the formula." John Taylor Thomas stood alone, unarmed, in the freighter bay.

Alexa stepped back in surprise, her lips still warmed by his brushing good-bye kiss. "We had a deal."

"You had a deal," he responded, without looking at her, his face still and quiet, watching Nedar.

"We will be able to synthesize this," Nedar answered dryly.

"Until then, you have only what I can get to you by diplomatic pouch."

"You want a leash on me, Ambassador?"

"No. And neither do I want to deal in drugs without knowing their true effect. You Choyan are powerful and secretive, but you make the mistake of assuming the rest of us will bow down without asking questions. I won't, even though you have my daughter."

Alexa found herself holding her breath as the two faced each other. Then Nedar seemed to shift poses, ever so slightly, and a pleasant expression warmed his lean face.

"We will have to make arrangements for the future, then."

"And keep in touch to do it." Her father seemed to shrink a little in stature.

Nedar stepped back and took Alexa proprietarily by the elbow, as her father moved to the lip of the transport bay bulkhead, preparing to disembark. Klaxons sounded, warning of the freighter's imminent departure. Under cover of the sound and vibration, she heard Nedar murmur, "I took you on as an asset. Now you've become a liability. Your father knows more than I thought. You have talked to him, perhaps?"

"No," answered Alexa, but her voice quavered slightly, and she damned it. Choyan, with their dual voices, were masters at reading subtlety into inflection. She turned her face away as she felt him stare measuringly down at her. She watched as the air lock closed behind John Thomas Taylor, shutting her father away from sight.

"Compose yourself," Nedar told her. "We have a call to make as soon as Lathum has us in a shipping lane."

The view screen in the freighter was primitive by any standards, but it functioned well enough so Alexa had an excellent view of GNask's purpling hide, mottled with indigo and indignation, nor did she have any doubt that the Abdrelik saw her and Nedar equally well.

"As old and slow as this tub is," she said, "by the time you have a fix on us, we'll be out of reach. You might as well take your big guns off target, dear GNask. My visit with my father was brief and satisfying, but I'm onto bigger things." She could feel Nedar's presence behind her.

"It is good to see you both looking so well," GNask rumbled. The lowest registers of his voice blurred into static which the freighter's comset could not pick up well, but Alexa had heard him before, and she could imagine him now. He was like summer thunder, distant and frightening.

"And you, as well, Ambassador," returned Nedar smoothly. He paused, then added, "We would appreciate it if you kept our sojourn in your capable hands confidential. There are . . . surprises . . . which we would like to make."

The round, small eyes of the Abdrelik widened, then crinkled again. "As you wish, *tezar*, I'm always willing to accommodate a pilot of your stature." He beckoned off-screen. "And although I apologize for making a hasty departure, now that your welfare has been seen to, I have a pressing engagement elsewhere."

Nedar gave a slight bow. "We understand."

The view screen went dark.

GNask whirled in a fury, a movement that belied his bulk. "Blast them out of space!" he bellowed at rrRusk.

The other Abdrelik stood there, waiting, letting GNask's

blasting fury pass over him like a tsunami. When it was clear he would not move or obey, GNask railed at him until his breath failed him.

Then he sank down upon his haunches. He took a moment to compose himself, looked up at rrRusk. "If not the freighter, then get the other ship when it disembarks."

"You know we cannot do either. Not without a great deal of planning, and we haven't the time. I haven't come this far with you to sink."

GNask's anger still rattled in his chest, like the wheeze of a nasty ague. "Do you suggest something, rrRusk?"

"A crippling blow to the ambassador's ship. He'll know who sent it but will be unable to prove it. It'll be an accidental firing, if anyone should backtrack the logs . . . it will have to be, or we risk losing our pilot. And, Ambassador, I bring word that we have bigger fish to fry."

"What is it?"

"Our Ronin privateers believe they've located the survivors of Arizar. They have a freehold colony under observation."

"Choyan?"

"It would appear."

GNask rose to his feet. A colony of potential pilots, isolated, renegade from both Cho and the Compact. They would be at his mercy.

rrRusk was beaming about his tusks when GNask looked up. GNask smiled hugely in answer.

"At last! You bring me excellent news, rrRusk." He lumbered across the bay, headed for his private quarters. "Set the course accordingly. But don't forget that detour. I will have my revenge, however restrained."

rrRusk bowed to let the other pass. "I will make it so," he answered.

Nedar reached past Alexa to shut down the link, and they touched momentarily. Alexa felt the raw energy like a spark, and it began to smolder in her. She hadn't been touched in that way in a long, long time. Under no illusions that he'd brought her along as anything but a hostage, she knew she had to remain of value to him now that her father had devalued her worth. But more than that, she no longer wished to ignore the dark stirrings within her. She had been alone too long. Only Nedar could look at her other side and not flinch away, for he dealt with one as well.

She looked up quickly to see if Nedar noticed the quickening of her heartbeat under the touch of his hand, but his Choyan face stayed impassive. He disengaged. Alexa brought her primary emotion back in line and gave way, instead, to her curiosity. "Keep our visit quiet? What was that all about?"

"It's to our mutual benefit not to antagonize him further. If he thinks that we wish to keep this under wraps as much as he does, he may back off and give us the room we need to maneuver. When I return to Cho, I don't want to do it with an Abdrelik warship screaming on my tail." He led her out of the equipment niche on the freighter, stooping to pass through the bulkhead.

The vehicle reeked of raw ores and chemicals, its bays and conveyers opened and gutted like an animal carcass, its lighting system dim by necessity, and the crews' quarters they'd been stowed in held no amenities. Nedar held the door for Alexa to pass him, but she wedged her slim body in the threshold next to his, very aware of his form.

She put a hand on his wrist. "We have a few days before we reach Galern." It had not been her imagination. To touch him was to evoke a flame, and it must burn in him as well. It must!

He looked down on her, a glint at the back of his dark eyes, eyes which mirrored the sheen of his black mane cascading from his horn crown down the back of his skull and onto his shoulders. "Yes," he answered.

"I could suggest a way to pass the time," she offered.

When he did not immediately turn away from her, she knew he was listening.

It was a stretch to touch her fingertips to the forelock of hair which tumbled down onto his brow. "I have never," she added softly, "thought of sleeping with someone other than my own, but I find myself watching your eyes. Your body awakens me. And I wonder how your people make love with one another. Might we be compatible, do you think? Could I stir you as you do me?" She trailed her hand gently across his high cheekbones, down to his square jawline to the jut of his chin.

"We do not normally," Nedar began, his voices disturbed by an unaccustomed huskiness, and then he stopped.

"You find it difficult to say no."

"Yes." Nedar did not withdraw from the doorway and she leaned into him. As they pressed closer together, she could tell that, even through the flight suit, the similarities of their races were closer than their differences. She caressed him.

"I ask nothing but this moment," she said.

His hand came up, hesitatingly, his fingers digging into her hair, tangling in her curls, holding tightly, bringing her face up to meet his, her neck curving back as she did.

"I shouldn't do this." His voices were barely audible.

"You and I," she answered, "are different."

He grabbed her up, and she felt the intensity of an embrace which in itself was more intimate than any lovemaking she'd ever felt before, the double-elbowed curve of his arms fitting her tightly, bringing her so close that she gave a small gasp of pleasure. He kicked the servo door shut behind then.

Alexa gave a tiny shiver of anticipation. It would be strange, different, profitable . . . and perhaps even wonderful, she thought as he carried her across the tiny cabin. There were ways to conquer which GNask and her father couldn't even begin to fathom.

"You are so small," he whispered, his lips tickling at her temple.

She answered him with her hands and mouth and it was the last protest he made. After all, what was lovemaking but a different kind of hunt, and the kill could be so much more satisfying.

The tall, elegant Choyan who was both Vihtirne's lover and aide met Qativar at the door to the Sky's consulate in Charolon. Asten let him in, saying only, "She has little time. We are scheduled for an inspection of the Galern mines."

"I do not plan to cause her delay," Qativar answered smoothly. He appreciated Asten for what he was, but he did not intend to let the other dominate him. He shrugged off his summer jacket and stripped off his gloves, handing them to Asten and walking on ahead to the audience room.

Behind him, he could feel the aide hesitate, then turn around and drop the garments on an antique burlwood table in the entry.

Vihtirne waited for him. Always dressed in dark blue, she lounged on a couch, listening to a recording of Fathma, a *lindar* player currently in favor, the sounds subdued and low. She lowered the volume a bit more, swung her legs around on the divan, and sat up.

"Qativar! How good of you to come so promptly. I had little time into which to schedule you."

He took her hand, light, fine-boned, slightly chill. "It was good of you to see me on such short notice."

Vihtirne looked over Qativar's shoulder toward Asten, whose footsteps trod just behind him. "Wine, please, Asten dear, and then leave us."

There was a hesitation, a deliberate pause, and then Qativar heard Asten walk away.

Vihtirne fastened her gaze on him once more, luminous eyes, sable hair that shone, beauty maintained by careful attention to detail. He admired her for the work she put into it.

He took a detector from his belt and swept the room with it. Vihtirne's mouth settled into a tiny pout of amusement, but she sat back on the divan while he did so, content to watch. She had no recordings operational at the present moment. He replaced the detector. "So good of you to keep this confidential."

Her brow raised. "You asked. I complied."

Boot heels clicked sharply on the flooring as Asten entered, put down a tray on the divan table, and left without a word or a glance at either of them.

Vihtirne waited until the door closed again, shuttering them away. "A good youth," she commented. "But a bit sulky. He does not always differentiate between business and pleasure."

Qativar poured her a glass of golden silk wine, then one for himself. "Perhaps he is not far wrong." He saluted her with his glass.

"Oh? And I thought this was not a social call." Intrigued, Vihtirne took up her glass and sipped. "Perhaps I should cancel my flight to Galern."

She had no intention of doing so, of course, and they

both knew it. Off-world berthings were expensive, and rearranging a flight would cost her.

"It would be an expensive flirtation," he noted. "And I have more than that in mind."

"Do you."

"You've heard the news about Rindalan?"

"Who hasn't? Does he continue to recover well?"

"Too well," Qativar said frankly. He put his wineglass to his lips, reading her expression over it, and was glad to see surprise, then comprehension, then interest.

"You would," she said, "have taken his place had we lost him."

He topped off her glass before settling back on the settee at her feet. "We both have to deal with Choyan who have outlived their prime and their usefulness to Cho. Neither Panshinea nor Rindalan will give up gracefully, though the Wheel turns, and the House is clearly in descent. I want the power that is rightfully mine, and before Rindalan grows too much stronger, I can help you in the quest for what is rightfully your House's."

"I do not agree or disagree with you, but I am listening."

More than listening. She hung on every word, lips glistening, eyes avid. But did she do it to trap him, or did she sense what he might propose? Qativar could not read her thoughts, *bahdur* tightly shielded her, so he had no choice but to risk all.

"I can sway the court of appeals votes for you, so that you may gain the water patent. Although you cannot wield the totality of power having the patent will give you because of public outrage, you will have enough leverage to topple Panshinea, if it's used properly."

"And for doing this for me, you want . . . ?"

"An alliance. Access to your resources, if you join with me."

Vihtirne licked a drop of wine from her lips. "And what then?"

"I can bring the Houses to their knees," he said, and eagerness suffused his voices. "I have a drug which destroys *bahdur*."

Shock ran through her features, but she recovered quickly. "Permanently?"

"As long as the drug is administered. Remove it, and recovery is very slow, though eventual."

She set down her glass. "It seems I have little enough to offer you. Our alliance would be unequal." And unsafe, she left unsaid.

Qativar smiled. "Do not worry. I need your clever mind and your patent, Vihtirne." He paused. "The drug is water soluble."

She leaned forward, carafe in hand, to fill his glass. She smiled. "Perhaps," she said softly, "we can do business after all."

Maerlon once reigned in the northernmost mountains, an ice palace, where the air crystallized with every breath in the wintertime, and where the summers were hot and urgent, as only summers so brief can be. Palaton remembered it as battered down to ruins by winter winds as well as war; it lay half-slumbering, the tams in its peaks eyes of bottomless blue water staring up at the sky as if to ask what had happened to its years of strife and glory. Its mantle of blue-white snow on the background peaks never completely melted, nor were its frigid streams ever truly warm. Its rocky feet and hem of evergreen were seamed with time and scarred by conflict. Maerlon was as close to a monument to Choyan struggle as the planet still had. It reminded Palaton of Sorrow, of the alien people forever frozen in death.

And even if the Choyan never really came back to occupy the old fortress, neither did they ever truly abandon it. Its ruined walls outlined a hardy, if small artists' colony which braved the winds and howling ghosts of a brutal past. Winters, more than once, Palaton remembered, the colony had had to have supplies airlifted in, but the artists who stayed in permanent residence never left until they died.

Other visitors, far more transient, stayed in the spring and summer, learning. He looked at it, knowing he saw what his mother had seen, for time did not alter Maerlon in so quick a passage as years. Palaton watched over Rufeen's shoulder as she got landing permission for the small bluff overlooking the colony. Summer had already fled here. He could see that a recent snow from the last two or three days had already settled in on the permanent mantle, and the roofs of the houses dotting the ruins below were flecked with gray and white patches.

Rufeen flexed her heavy shoulders, saying, "Hope you brought your boots and jacket."

"You just keep the windows de-iced and the home fires burning," Palaton returned.

The pilot gave a low chuckle. She decelled and banked into a cold thermal coming directly off the mountain peaks, and brought the craft into a fairly decent approach to the plateau. There were recent landing scars across its runways.

"They're already taking the tourists out," she observed.

"What's the weather going to be like the next couple of days?"

"It should stay clear. Watch the slopes, though. It's warm enough that the weight of the last snow is unstable."

"I'll keep that in mind."

"Do that," Rufeen said gruffly. "I don't feel like digging anybody out." A conflicting thermal from below rose up and the craft waggled a moment as it hit pockets of disturbance. Palaton felt the deck pitch under his feet, and his stomach lurched with the sudden loss of altitude, but he rode it out as though he were still piloting himself. Although he couldn't feel it with his *bahdur,* he could still feel it through years of experience, and Rufeen was taking a swift, clean approach.

She brought them down with scarcely a bounce on landing and as they braked to a halt, he praised her.

"Good job."

"Why, thank you. For a minute there, I thought I was going to have your handprint permanently on the back of my neck."

Palaton looked down and realized he was gripping the headrest of her chair tightly. He let go with a sheepish expression.

Rufeen laughed. "Once a pilot, always a pilot," she said, unperturbed. She swung out of the chair. "I'm going to secure the craft. It's windy up here, but I'll be here when you need me."

Palaton stepped out, buffeted immediately by winds more chill than he'd figured on. He carried his jacket over his arm and immediately shrugged into it as his feet hit ground. She tossed his duffel out behind him and he picked it up.

Like Blue Ridge, there was a small cog rail which

brought cars up and down from the landing strip. He got into one, old and weathered and peeling, and rowed it into motion. As he descended from the landing strip, the wind calmed a little, but its bite was no less icy.

A Choya'i waited at the railway's base, hunched against the weather, her yellow-white hair gathered under a knit cap, and she looked up with disapproval on her heavily wrinkled face. It was like leather from the years spent in the thin atmosphere, wind, rain, and sun. He could not read a House in her face easily, so much had age obscured it.

The village elder bowed. "We are not used to visitors so late in the season, and with so little notice."

Her voices chided him. As the car bumped to a stop, he opened the side rail and got out, hoisting his duffel to his shoulder. "I apologize," he said. "I get so little time for retreat, and the temple of my Householding was closed for renovation. I thought to come here, instead. My sister wanted to paint here." He looked around and took a deep breath. The air, though thin, was inviting and brisk. "I can see why."

Some of the disapproval melted from the elder's face. She beckoned him to follow with a gloved hand. "We do most of our serious studies in the winter season, so you won't have a choice of homes to board in. We're just getting back to work after the students go. Do you mind?"

"I'll only be here for a few days, I hope," he answered honestly. "Any place I can lay my head down."

"Good. Then you'll be at Honry's. He works in textiles, you'll bother him least." The Choya'i hurried to stay in front of his long strides, her breath puffing foggy wisps upon the air. She did not bother to sugarcoat her words, he thought, as he followed after. He could not complain, anyway, for it would obviously do him little good, and if Honry was old enough, he might even be one of the artists his mother had studied under.

They reached a cobblestone pathway which widened into a street. Goldenweeds grew in the cracks, already lightened and dried to their autumn colors, reminding again that here time had a different passage. They crunched under his feet. Each hut, or huts merged together, had its own garden plot and immense woodpile, solars tilted to the sky bowl overhead, and water towers on stilts behind, giving every home a fiercely independent air.

Many of the artist occupants were on their porches, working in the light, and didn't even bother to look at them as they walked by. Palaton tightened his thumb on his duffel strap.

"Get snowed in often?"

"Often enough. We're prepared for it, though," the Choya'i answered, a little out of breath, as she chugged along the street. She paused by a large hut with a small gray fence. "This is Honry's."

Honry was neither ill-prepared nor modest, by the size of his hut. She leaned over the fencing and let out a whistle between her teeth. As she rocked back on her heels, she gave Palaton another frank look.

"I'm Baka," she said, giving him her hand.

"Teriot," he answered.

The look in her eyes did not change, so he did not know if she recognized him or simply did not care who he was. Another piercing whistle answered them, and Palaton looked around to see the hut's owner emerge, his clothes covered with lint and a thousand tiny fibers shed by the work he'd been doing.

Honry was tall and angular, his nose extremely thin and bent, his eyes small and beady by Choyan standards, his hair black and silver. He was easily old enough to have taught Tresa some of her accomplishments. Shedding as he walked gave him almost an aura. Honry strode down to them, his eyes curious. Here again, Palaton could not easily read a House in the Choya's face, although from the hair and eye color, he should have been a Sky.

"A late season boarder," Baka said. "This is Teriot. Can you take him in?"

Honry's nose pinched a little, but he shrugged. "Why not? How long are you staying? Who will you be studying with?"

"I'm just here for a few days. It's my sister who'll be working here, if she gets her name on the roles."

Honry looked him up and down, his nostrils getting whiter by the moment. When he spoke, it was as if through gritted teeth. "We won't audition for you."

"I don't expect it. Your reputation precedes you, although," and Palaton paused, sensing some artistic temperament, "she is also considering applying to the Falian society."

"The Falians! What do they know? The children go there for a vacation by the seaside, not for an education!" Honry's voices rose in belligerence.

Palaton gave a brisk nod. "That's what brought me. My father indulges her. She would be a foolish and vapid artist if she didn't learn to reach down and touch reality. This," and he took another deep breath of the brisk mountain air, "this makes you want to live."

Honry's disgruntled expression turned and he looked at Baka. "I guess I can take him for a night or two," he said.

"Good, because this is about all the choice he has." Baka sniffed. "Charge him enough, Honry. He's got a private craft waiting for him up on the strip."

Honry's bushy eyebrows arched as the elder Choya'i took off again, huffing and chugging her way down the street, her whole body in motion.

Honry unlatched the gate. Palaton could sense the muted *bahdur* in him, like a banked fire, as he entered the small yard.

His host broke into a no-nonsense stride toward the hut. "Your sister any good?" he asked, a little too offhandedly.

"Sometimes," Palaton said. "She likes to work in the style of Tresa of Volan." If Honry were testing him, that name, at least, was one he could throw at the artist.

Honry came to a dead halt. "Tresa?" he repeated. "Early period or late?"

"Early, she says. She has the youth for it, although I think she could mature into the later styles, as well. At any rate, her needlework could be good but she's too erratic."

"Tresa," said Honry with a great deal of feeling, "was never erratic, no matter how young she was when she came here."

It gave Palaton some comfort to know that, despite the years and seasons and students which this Choya must have known, Tresa still commanded his attention and memory. At the same time, although he'd lived his whole early life knowing she was a master, it felt odd to think of her now strictly as an artist rather than as his mother.

Honry stomped his boot soles clean from the scattered gravel and dirt of the yard as he went up the porch. Palaton imitated him. Great hanging hoops turned from the eaves, rough textile weavings upon them, tactile pieces, of wool and hair and fine, downy feathers, as well as coarse yarn. Hesitantly, Palaton touched one as he passed, and Honry said nothing but grinned widely as he went into the house.

There were hand looms and looms big enough to fill a small room, and embroidery hoops and frames, between which Honry expertly wove his skinny frame, leading the way into the rest of the hut. The size of the hut, Palaton thought, was explained by the need to house the extensive projects in progress. The other rooms were not so cluttered, although he had to duck going upstairs to where his room lay. It, at least, would be fairly warm, thanks to heavy tapestries at the windows, and the deep, quilted luxury of the bed.

Honry said, "Students' pieces," as he tossed Palaton's duffel into a corner.

"They show promise."

Another flashing grin. "All my students show promise. Alas, the potential does not always outlast the first bloom of praise. And artistry is not always financially remunerative."

At that hint, Palaton fished out a stack of credit notes, to pay for his board in advance. Honry took a portion of them gravely. "This," he said, "will buy some nice quality brandy to warm winter nights."

"That," Palaton told him, "I would be glad to pay for, as well. A brandy would go down smoothly this evening."

"Done, then. I won't quibble with a Choya who has the money to pay for his vices. I might even sell you a wall hanging or two to inspire your sister, eh?" He'd already turned away when Palaton said, "Give me the names of some other artists I might talk with."

"About your sister?"

"And about Tresa of Volan."

Honry faced him again, eyes gone very cold, money crunched tightly in his hand.

Palaton added lightly, "I'm very appreciative of her work."

Tension bled away from Honry's body very slowly, as if

he fought for control. The rims of his nostrils had gone pale again. Palaton pretended not to notice.

Honry said, "Try at the chapel. The luminary should be at his afternoon meditations." He left, his fist still working about the money Palaton had given him.

The chapel had been built of stone quarried from the mountains, rough, hand-hewn slabs brought down and stacked and mortared into position. The museum next to it, however, was relatively new, probably done in the last few centuries, its synthetic sides weatherproofed and well-insulated. Palaton went into it first, hoping to see a collection of the students who studied here, as well as the masters who'd stayed, and he was not disappointed. There was even an embroidered cloth by Tresa, a simple picture of one of the huts, singled out as though it might be the only one in town which existed, the cobblestoned road filled with goldenweed much as he'd seen it that day, leading to the door. The mountain backdrop and the setting sun seemed to backlight a fiery glow about the hut, and in the sky, a lone evening star shone down as well.

The paintings were magnificent, as were the mobiles and sculptures, but it was a display in a darkened wing which drew him finally, and then he stood in solemn mourning for that which had passed from Cho with hardly a whisper. The psychokinetic art gave him pause, sculptures and mobiles and other forms which should have been activated by *bahdur* and instead stayed static, for there was no longer anyone able to activate them.

Palaton took his leave when he heard the evening bells chime, a quaint sound, faint echo off the mountain ridges. No one came to the chapel, so he went inside hesitantly, unsure if he'd find anyone. It was not a cleansing temple, merely a meditation chapel, low-ceilinged and deafeningly quiet. He stood uncertainly just inside the threshold, believing he was alone, when a thin, spindly set of voices hailed him.

"You must be the newcomer, the one with money." Palaton narrowed his eyes, peering into the gloom. He finally saw the Choya, as wiry and old as his voices sounded, the pate of his skull as slick and bald as rocks that have been well-rubbed by a deep river. For a Choya this old to still have a position as luminary spoke for the depth and strength of his intellect.

"I flew in this afternoon," Palaton acknowledged. "I'm Teriot."

The luminary did not rise from his chair, violet eyes peering at him from a nest of wrinkles, and he replied, "I care not what name you use."

"Perhaps, then," Palaton returned, coming closer to the aged luminary, "what name I seek."

"That would be more appropriate."

"I've come about Tresa."

The luminary stared unmoving for a few, long minutes, then he drew himself up a little. "It's well," he said, "that someone finally did. And who might you be?"

"Her son."

That brought a sound from the liver-spotted lips, not quite a gasp, more vehement. "Her son is a *tezar*," the luminary added. "You're as barren of the power as a cracked egg of its yolk."

"I had the power once," answered Palaton painfully. He had known this moment was inevitable, that sooner or later someone would recognize him for the imposter he was. It seemed sharper from this aged luminary who presumed to judge him. "And I hope to again."

"Burnout doesn't heal."

"It wasn't burnout."

Another sharp glance from the elder one. "Who would steal from a *tezar*?" he queried.

"It was given, and one day I will find the way to ask for it back."

The old luminary harrumphed, saying, "If you don't have the courage to take what is yours, no one can help you." He stood up, wrapping his long coat about him.

"I didn't come about myself, I came about Tresa."

Another sharp look. "One is the other," the luminary snapped at him. "If you don't know that by now, I can't be helping you."

"One is *not* the other," shot back Palaton. "There are bloodlines and Houses and destinies I know nothing of.

"Then why did you come here?"

"I came to find my father."

The chapel stood silent for so long that Palaton began

to hear his heartbeat, and then that of the other Choya, and the sound of the breath laboring in his lungs.

"I cannot help you." The luminary stirred. He looked at the stone walls as if he could see the museum next door. "You must help yourself." He left, in a sweep of his long coat, his spindly, aged form skittering past Palaton as though he were some immense spider.

Chapter 23

"Chirek is one of my best and soundest clerks," Gathon said emphatically. "He can't have taken Rand."

Jorana repeated patiently what she'd already told him, and added, "There is some hope that the disappearance is innocent. We haven't had a ransom request."

"Ransom! Why would Chirek jeopardize his whole career? What could he want with Rand?" Gathon shook his head, iron-colored hair with its yellow streaking becoming disheveled. He clawed it back from his eyes. "Have you contacted Palaton?"

"I've not been able to get through," Jorana answered smoothly. She hadn't tried. She had some idea of the private mission he was on, and knew he would stop immediately and return if told about Rand. With any luck, she could find the manling and have him safely back before the night was over. "I think it's best this be kept confidential, for everyone's sake."

Gathon found his legs buckling and sat down hurriedly. He put a hand to his chest where his old thumper sounded like Rindy's did, sometimes, and he wondered if he should call for a physician. He swallowed down the discomfort. "You do what you have to, but keep me apprised. I don't want to have to explain another body. We've enough trouble with those three you had carted off to work camps. We may all be staring at riots again, and this time they'll burn the entire city down around our heads." He looked up. "You've searched Chirek's rooms?"

Jorana nodded. The residence had been in a more affluent section of the commons quarter, but nothing unusual had been found, and auras indicated no one had been there for days, not even Chirek. If she could have located the rooms of the Choya'i Dorea, she might have been able to establish where Chirek was spending his evenings, but she hadn't been able to track that down yet. Without evidence, she'd also said nothing to Gathon about the apparent link between the two. It was not, after all, his department. Security was hers. When she had her facts substantiated and cases built, then she would tell the minister everything she knew.

She started to leave, but Gathon raised a hand to halt her. Her surprise at seeing it shaking must have shown in her face, because he dropped it quickly and clenched his hands together tightly.

"Panshinea left a transmission for me this morning. His influence in the Compact is being sorely tried. GNask has filed a formal protest against the lack of pilots, requesting that the *tezarian* drive be made public domain and that Cho be required to train any and all qualified to pilot and navigate to do so. Panshinea thinks that the only way he can quiet the delegates is to return to Cho himself, on the pretense of massively overhauling the flight school system."

"But Palaton's already begun that," Jorana protested, and then stopped, interrupting herself.

"Cho can't have two emperors," Gathon said mildly.

She stared at him, thinking of what the Prophet had said to her. "What will he do with Palaton?"

"Set him aside, or perhaps send him to Sorrow, although I'd try to dissuade him of that. Palaton has not shown any great liking for the Halls of the Compact. I don't think he'd be happy there."

"He's a pilot," Jorana protested. "If anyone could go into the schools and ascertain what is happening, he could. Panshinea knows nothing of them."

Gathon blinked, as though he had not heard a word of what she'd said, and remarked, "I've suggested Rindalan as a replacement. Once his health is recovered, he should enjoy fencing with the likes of the Abdreliks and Ivrians. He brings a measure of wisdom and dignity no one else could."

"Rindy?"

Gathon nodded.

"Does he know?"

"I discussed it with him this morning. He is . . . intrigued . . . by the possibilities. Dr. Ninever said that travel is possible for him now, but that he should continue rehabilitation therapy for another week or so, and it's quite probable he will always have to rely on a walking cane."

"But he didn't say no."

"No, he didn't." Gathon found a smile. "He seems excited by the prospect."

She had known, of course, they all had, that they could lose Rindy. She hadn't anticipated his being sent to Sorrow. How could Panshinea think of such a thing, at Rindy's age?

One more support being torn away from Palaton. The more she thought about it, the more she realized Panshinea's ultimate goal. He would strip away all backing from Palaton, the *tezars*, Rindy, the commons if he could, so that when it came time to supplant him, the emperor would have no trouble stepping back in. No one would even protest if Panshinea had to kill him.

She might be the only thing now standing between Palaton and exile.

She looked up, to see Gathon's flinty eyes on her, and realized why the minister had said what he had said. He was giving her notice, so that she could be prepared. "Why," she asked, "did he even take Palaton as heir?"

Gathon looked away then. His mouth worked a little, as though his next words had a bitter taste. "I think he hoped that Palaton would eliminate a great many difficulties for him. I don't think he took into account the kind of Choya Palaton is, or that the Godless would give him the support they have. I don't really think Panshinea knows how to deal with integrity." The minister sighed. "Nor do I."

To that she answered only, "I have a job to do," and left, intent on finding Rand before she had to confront Palaton.

Rand watched Chirek sort through his belongings with an economy of motion, retaining only the sparest of possessions. Everything of value that the Choya was taking with them, he could carry on his back inconspicuously. Rand's head and face had been lightly bandaged, he wore thin cotton gloves over his hands, and his words came out slightly muffled as he noted, "You're not planning on coming back."

"No," said Chirek regretfully. "I don't believe it will be possible for me to. But then, I have waited for this my whole life. I can't mourn these changes, it would be hypocritical of me." He gave a bittersweet smile. "I'm afraid I have been a little too comfortable in my ways and in my ministry."

Rand examined the spartan, underground home. It did not look comfortable. Chirek stepped over to an alcove and removed clothes that looked as if they were vestments, and they were the last things folded away in his pack. He motioned for Rand to go up the stairs. At the top, he opened the recessed, carefully hidden door and left it that way.

Chirek did a half-turn. "It will all be gone in a matter of hours," he said, looking back on his life. "The needy will be stripping the place the moment we cross the street."

"Do you regret it?"

"Yes. And no. If you're not convinced, or if somehow I've been wrong, there is no coming back. Yet. . . ." The renegade priest took a deep breath. "Let's go."

Rand, unable to bear the guilt, took hold of the door and started to close it behind them anyway. Chirek stopped him.

"No," he said. "If it's not you, then it will be someone, and I must be preparing my people for the Change. I've gotten too complacent here, too worried about my immediate now. Leave it."

So Rand followed his order, and then the priest, across the street.

He worried at the port, for he was gathering curious stares, although he knew the bandages hid most of the obvious differences in his physique. Chirek guided him through the crowds, talking quietly, saying, "Don't worry. It's too early for anyone to be here looking for you. If Jorana even knows you're gone, she'll be waiting for someone to contact her, with demands. She won't be prepared for your leaving of your own volition."

Rand sidestepped an older Choya'i who called him youngster and gave him a sympathetic pat on the shoulder. He came barely chin high to her. Chirek took firmer hold of him to steer him through to the waiting skimcraft.

The Charolon summer's heat had begun to seep through the light wrapping of his bandages, and he could feel his face sweating uncomfortably. The eye slits obscured some of his vision. He'd been blindsided more than once trying to get through the boarding gates. He was conscious of the difference in class—the commons boarded through the more inconvenient gates, sat in the crowded portion of the fuselage, and he heard Choyan being spoken with its liquid syllables all about him, whereas to the front, with its better accommodations for those Housed, he heard Trade as often as he did Choyan.

He could understand a smattering of Choyan if he listened through *bahdur,* but he felt as though he were eavesdropping when he did so. As they settled into their seats, Chirek suggested he rest quietly, that Bayalak was less than a two-hour flight away.

Rand closed his eyes and leaned his head back, found the crown rest did not fit him at all, and wrestled with it for a few moments before shoving it aside in frustration and putting his head back on the harsh edge of the seat. The commons teeming around him reminded him of home. He felt a keen longing to see what he hadn't seen in years, and wondered about his father and the poverty he'd grown up in, not particularly overpowering but always present, the discrimination of disease and pollution ever near. One could not afford to be poor on Earth.

Being poor on Cho was quite another thing. One was poor if one was powerless, and being powerless, one did not receive the benefits of that power, and got slighted for it, and discriminated against. He could look out of the skimcraft's window and see the ashes of the city where the Godless had rioted and hurt only themselves, driving the wound deeper. He could sit among them and feel them worry, hoping, thinking that tomorrow might be better, fearing that it would not.

The very early morning hours when Palaton had awakened him to say good-bye took their toll and he fell asleep even before the skimcraft warmed up its engines for takeoff.

Bayalak was like stepping into a steam bath. Rand could feel the sweat pool in the folds of his neckline as he walked off the skimcraft, one foot still tingly from having fallen asleep in the cramped quarters. He smelled the strong, musky body odor of the Choyan shoving all around him, an ocean of taller bodies with free-flowing hair and large, flashing eyes, all intent on leveling him and walking over him if he didn't give way. Chirek crooked him about the elbow, saying, "Keep up."

A strong aroma, fruity and floral, hit the air as the port opened up and they surged through to the streets, where different conveyances sat at the curbs, waiting to be hired. "What is that?" Rand asked, trying to scout out the source, hampered by his bandaged face.

"Panet," Chirek answered. "It blooms heavily here in the bayous."

"It smells almost like magnolia," Rand told him. "A big white, delicate flower."

"This," Chirek answered, "is a creamy yellow, pale, its edges go brown as it fades. It opens in the morning and closes at night, but it can be very aromatic for as long as it blooms, and the night still holds the perfume. Small birds live in the hollow of the blossom once the pollen is gone, until the blossom dries entirely and falls, just before early winter." He seemed to be looking for something over the crowd, then pulled Rand aside. "Let's walk."

"How far do we have to go?"

"It doesn't matter. I want to see what's happening. I've never seen the port or streets so crowded. I told Seli to keep her hidden, but I think word has gotten out." He kept Rand with him, and they strode away from the facility.

Rand looked around. Many of the buildings were wood, soaked in what might have been creosote, darkened sable by that protectant, splintering and furring against the erosion of the wind and salt. Timber which hadn't been treated was bleached as gray as stone. A tang of the salt air and a rich effusion of the swamp hung just under the overwhelming scent of the panet flowers, yet none of it could hide the grind of the poverty he felt. Bayalak was a seaport, a town built on its freshwater and saltwater fishing industry, and no Choya needed *bahdur* to succeed here. He could see the coarser faces of the commons wherever he looked.

He could feel them weighing on him. These were the Choyan he'd tried to get Palaton to recognize and commit to aiding, but his friend hadn't seen them. He thought he listened, and he thought he spoke for them, but Rand knew that Palaton saw only what he wanted to see. There was God-blind and there was Cho-blind, he thought.

He knew there were those of the Houses here in the city, for he'd seen them board the skimcraft. Slightly out of breath, trying to keep up with Chirek's long stride, he pulled to a halt. Chirek immediately returned to him, face creased with concern.

"Are you all right?"

"Where are the Housed?" he asked.

Chirek looked as if he might point over a line of wharfs, then stopped. "You can't see the cityscape from here. But Bayalak is a city divided and to the northeast, on the edge of pink sand beaches, is another world altogether. The Houseds come here to play. There isn't much commerce here that they wish to indulge in."

"Is it like that everywhere?"

Chirek hesitated only briefly before answering, "Yes. They don't see it, of course. But we are relegated to doing those tasks which the sensibilities of those with *bahdur* don't feel they can handle. And we tend to overpopulate, hoping to breed into our young what we ourselves have none or little of. Yet what we do is crowd ourselves into smaller and smaller living areas, and opportunity, and hope."

Rand looked at his feet. He could see infinitesimal scales sparkling in the dirt. A drop of sweat ran off his cheek and dripped to the ground, where it immediately soaked in. Chirek flapped his hand at his face, fanning up the torpid air.

"It's not much farther."

A group of commons passed them on the walkway. Their shoulders brushed Rand, buffeting him. Chirek turned with them, listening intently.

He grabbed at Rand. "They're talking about her."

"Dorea?"

"Yes!" The priest hurried him, so they could stay close. He said in agitation, "She's been out in public several times, preaching the Changing of the world. The town guard has raided the neighborhoods looking for her. This is not good. I told Seli to keep her quiet!"

"If she has no control over the *bahdur*," Rand said slowly, knowing how it could burn out of control, "she might not be able to help it."

"I never had that kind of problem." Chirek stopped, letting the group of Choyan get ahead of them.

"What is it you can do that you couldn't before?"

"I can see the God-in-all. And I can tell the truth of things. If you stood in front of me and told me something, I would know if you were telling me the truth. And I can convince people to seek it out for themselves."

"Nothing earthshaking."

"Not to you, perhaps." Chirek smiled modestly. "What can you do?"

Rand thought about what Palaton had given him. He replied frankly, "I don't think we know all of it yet. I can cross Chaos. I can see when I'm blinded. I can feel the emotions of those around me. And you think I can Change others."

"I don't think, I know. Let me but find Dorea, and you'll know, too." The priest stood on the sidewalk, his eyes suddenly narrowed, and Rand caught the sense of him casting for the Choya'i, searching by way of his powers, like sifting through all the fine molecules of the neighborhoods. When he finished, Chirek put a hand out and said, "This way."

But the priest was no more successful than he had been before, and the afternoon grew hot and oppressive. Clouds gathered, spat out a quick, hot rain, and left. Rand's bandages got soaked and lay heavy against his skin. Chirek finally took pity on him.

He took Rand to a square, where several neighborhoods met, and sat him down at a bistro, ordering cold drinks for both of them. Rand watched the streets grow crowded, thin, and grow crowded again, as he sipped the fruit juice which somehow smelled a little like panet. The blossom's perfume must permeate everything here but the canneries. He could hear someone plucking at a hand *lindar*.

Chirek said wearily, "I can't find her."

Rand straightened in his chair, feeling somewhat revived.

"I can," he answered then, knowing what Palaton had told him to be true, that power called to power, something Chirek hadn't yet had time to truly learn. He stretched his legs out, relaxing in the chair, and sent his thoughts spinning away, looking for a Choya'i in a stunning blue dress, and where in the dark she might be waiting for him.

Like a spark arcing between two points, she responded. There was fear and desperation in it, and command, and power, and the strength of it alarmed him. Rand got to his feet, afraid of the force of the answer, and also feeling that anyone else nearby must have heard it, felt it, be driven to answer it also. "Come on!" He pulled Chirek up. "This way."

Clouds began to gather again. The sky grew leaden and menacing. He could hear the rumble of thunder and as he followed the call, he could see blinding flashes of lightning strike from the sky, from cloud to cloud, searching even as he searched.

Rain began to pelt them. It fell in steaming puddles. They splashed through it, hunching their shoulders against the strike of drops which felt more like a hail of bullets. He thought of the rain which had fallen from him when he tried to free Rindalan's *bahdur* and he wondered if this storm were natural or if Dorea had somehow precipitated it—if she even knew what she did.

Lightning crashed not two hundred yards from where they ran, striking into a wooden building with a flash of fire and splinters. The ground shook at the shock and Choyan ran screaming. The odor of ozone and fire filled the air. The sky seemed to have turned to a light green color, stormy gray and the lightning a vaporous green. Rand ducked his head against the sheets of hot rain drenching them and ran faster.

Chirek skidded on the wet pavement and started to go down. Rand reached over and half-hauled him back to his feet. The Choya's mane was slick and wild in the storm. "What have you done?" he cried over the torrent.

"Nothing. It's not me. It's her. She's trying to find us, but she can't control the power."

"Find us—or destroy us?"

Rand paused uncertainly. Then he shook his head. "I don't know!"

"It's your *bahdur* that Changed her!"

"But I have no control over what's happening."

"No one . . . no Choyan in our history has ever affected the weather like this."

A bolt lit the skies over the city, punctuating Chirek's

protest. Rand did not say the words which came immediately to mind. No Choyan allowed to live had ever played havoc with the weather before. Who knew what talents the Houses encouraged or weeded out? As thunder rattled the nearby buildings, he only said, "The closer to the storm center we get, the closer we'll be to her."

Chirek nodded his understanding, and they turned, searching through the curtain of rain, for the center of the miasma, found it, and headed across the streets. The storm reacted as if it sensed them coming. The clouds boiled in fury, sheet lightning crackled across the firmament, and day became night in the tempest.

Chirek let out a cry, and Rand felt the hairs prickle on the back of his neck, and he sensed a bolt arching after them, skimming the clouds and flying downward, and he turned abruptly toward the battered door of what appeared to be an abandoned warehouse, throwing it open, pulling Chirek into the shelter. The lightning struck the stone behind them. It shattered with a voice of pain, the air going white-hot with heat and energy, driving them both to their knees and blasting the door from the building. They scattered a small crowd of huddled Choyan, their faces turned toward a single one left standing.

The Choya'i cried, her high clear voices cutting across the echo of the lightning strike, her fear terrifying. "Help me!"

Chirek pulled Rand to his feet. The humankind reached out to his face and tore the bandages aside, heedless of those who might be watching, unable to bear their weight and dampness any longer. He shook his head and combed his hair back.

He'd just taken a step toward her when the thunder hit, a violent explosion in itself, and the building timbers shook to their very foundation. He thought the roof was going to slide from the eaves. Everyone went down, faces to the flooring, except for Rand and Chirek and the Choya'i known as the Prophet, her bandaged face upturned to the heavens.

With the storm battering around them, he knew the intensity of her terror. He denied that he could have done this to her, that he had the power, or ever could have had the power, but he could not deny the feeling in him that went out to her. Before Chirek could stop him, he went to her and swept her up in an embrace, trying to comfort her and quell the agony of her emotions.

As they touched, lightning struck them dead center, straight through the roof, blue as *bahdur,* immersing them, and Rand went blind.

Chapter 24

I ought to be dead, Rand thought. His hearing numb, a thousand tiny prickles and tingles fired his skin. His eyes watered, and the stink of scorched hair and wood and stone all around them filled his nostrils. He would be dead, if it had been lightning which hit, but he thought instead that it was a levin-bolt of pure *bahdur*, because he had felt it channeling through them.

He found himself standing, still, with his arms about Dorea, and she breathed heavily, spent, a runner with no more stamina. After a moment, he could see her, and what he saw shocked him to his core.

Alien. Wrongness in every joint. Thin, short hair, fleshy protuberances on the side of the head, the skin pale as a dead fish's belly, arms like sticks, small and parasitical being clinging to her, and then the turquoise eyes opened, and Rand realized with a jolt that he looked at himself.

Who are you?

Barbarian, destroyer, despoiler, plague-bringer. Stranger, uninvited invader, troublemaker, thief. A being of questionable intellect and hopefulness, tottering about like a Choyan child, yet with as much destructive power as an Abdrelik or a Ronin.

And more. Alone. Singularity. Always to be in solitude, never to be among true friends or to go home. Needy and begging, an aching emptiness pleading to be filled. Alone. Oneness. No mate or lover. Alone.

Rand caught his breath, sobbing in his throat as he looked at himself out of her blinded eyes, the bandage no obstacle to what she saw, the vision as harsh as a knife slicing him through the heart.

Alone, and so ugly and repulsive, not only externally,

but also in his soul, so that no one, no thing, would ever want to alleviate that solitude.

And he felt her take a deep, quavering breath in his embrace. *Who are you?*

She looked through his eyes and saw an alien, mane of golden brown tousled and brushed back from a proud horn crown that nestled her brow and swooped down both flanks of her skull, protecting the dual brainpan but also cupping cascades of luxuriant hair. An arrogant being, full of denial, punishing, judgmental, unnurturing of those asking only for a chance. A vessel of power, both spiratal and technical, unwilling to be poured, showering benefit upon the lesser.

An alien, strangely yet beautifully built. A highbrowed expressive face and what he remembered as large, lovely hazel eyes with flecks of green, now hidden by a rust-stained bandage that cut her face in two. A proud Choyan nose and a strong chin, and that lovely translucent almost salmon-colored skin, still unlined by wisdom and laughter. As tall as him, but not tall for a Choyan, the horn crown a little coarse as the sculpted edges went, the sign, perhaps, of a Godless. The dress, torn and drab now, hardly recognizable as blue, tucked about her shivering body.

A core of wild power, untarnable, unwise, needing only to be calmed, understood, helped, educated. Nothing to be feared but that which she created for herself.

Alien, but not alone. Strange, but not rejected. Out of control and to be pitied, but not beyond help. Among a boundless core of friendship, yet missing a half, a visionary without understanding, a face without eyes, a Choya'i without courage.

"I need courage," she murmured, repeating the thought, watching strangely her lips move in her face, still looking out of his eyes at herself.

"So do I," the alien thing said, and pulled her closer, tighter, as if it could give it to her. And their souls touched again, passing, like ships in full sail on a moonlight sea, touching, drifting back.

Rand let go, rocking back on his heels, shocked to the foundation of all his beliefs. The Prophet, released from his embrace, began to collapse and a handful of Choyan rushed to catch her.

Rand felt his own body go, and only Chirek dared to touch him. His weight was too much for the priest and the two of them went down in a gentle heap.

There was a black scorch mark on the floor where they had been standing.

"What happened?" pleaded Chirek near his ear as they sorted themselves out.

"I don't know. I don't understand. We should be dead."

The Prophet was carried to a reclining chair, and laid on it carefully. She put a hand up to quiet the thronging voices which began to rise in question and protest. "He brings the Change. He opens the gate inside each and every one of us, but you must know and understand . . . this is only half. We are part of what must become a whole, become reconciled, or we will destroy ourselves."

"Half," Rand whispered to himself. The Housed and the Godless. The Housed must teach them discipline and the Godless, once Changed, will give them back the vitality, the genetic variation which they so desperately needed. *Of course.*

Chirek dusted him off and said in a low tone, "Can you stand now? I don't think we can show them any weakness."

Rand stood up with the help of the priest. He walked to the couch, and Dorea reached for him. There was a calm and stillness outside, and no wind curled through the hole in the roof, although rain dripped steadily. The storm had gone.

"I could have destroyed us both," the Prophet said. "And still might, despite what you've shown me. Help me."

Rand could not quite meet her bandaged face, unable to accept what had been revealed to him of himself. Never could he trust Palaton or anyone else again, having seen what he was in their midst. He felt an ache, a wound, which would never heal. But he stepped toward her, knowing that he would help her.

She took his hand and pressed it into that of the Choya nearest her. "Change him," she asked.

Whether it was his power, or Palaton's, he did not ask. He knew how he would use it—if he could. But he still had no idea of what it was he had done to either Dorea or Chirek, and nothing flowed through him now.

The Choya's hand lay still in his, but the other faced him

wide-eyed and fearful, an older Choya, tinges of gray at the temple of his dark hair. He waited a moment before shouting, "I feel nothing!"

Even without *bahdur*, he knew what this Choya felt standing opposite him. He knew what clawed at the being's throat, what fear, what revulsion. Rand felt himself flinch and begin to turn away.

The Choya snatched his hand back, shouting again, "Nothing! Nothing!"

The hole where a door had been allowed Choyan crowding the street to flood in. They began to press closer and closer, the warehouse filling up, voices crying, "The Prophet! The Prophet!" And occasionally, "The alien. The off-worlder!"

His *bahdur* flickered awake in alarm. Chirek shouldered his way through and reached his side, saying, "Do something or we must find a way out quickly."

"I can't." The shock had finally gotten through to his system. His teeth began to chatter. He could feel the weakness and shaking in every joint. Despite the heat of the bodies, the air, the rain smoked as it dried from his clothing, and he felt cold, cold to his very marrow.

He was failing them. Her. Himself. Again.

"Come on," Chirek ordered, sensing something very wrong.

Rand stumbled a step away.

"The Change! She promised the Change!"

"Which one?" a hunched old Choya'i cried, bouncing into him. "Which one is the Bringer?"

Rand put his hands up to fend her off, the power in him surging to protect him, as she turned and hatred leapt in her weathered gray-green eyes and they touched, pushing into one another.

She fell back, crying, "What's happening to me?"

Chirek looked at him. "Power answers to power," he said. "To power!"

Rand looked at his hands. An eerie blue sheen danced along the surface of his skin. A Choya reached out and grabbed his hands, the clasp hard and desperate. Rand looked up in astonishment at the action. Their eyes met, but before the other could even blink, he fell to his knees and began to cry with joy, slipping away from Rand.

The *bahdur* rose in him like a tide. Rand began to move through the crowd, holding tight those who dared to touch him, feeling the surge and then the ebb as whatever it was in him, in that *bahdur,* rose to unlock what lay inside them. He began to work in a frenzy, knowing the power would not always be there, that it peaked and then left him, resting, and he had to touch whomever he could, Change everyone he could reach, heedlessly, praying that Chirek and the Prophet could somehow contain whatever damage he might do in his haste.

Before he fell in exhaustion, toppling slowly to his knees, the warehouse floor was littered with the bodies of those he'd transformed. The air filled with moans and tears, and Choyan clung to one another as though a disaster had swept through them. Chirek lowered him gently to the dirt near the doorway, and he could see that night had fallen. The warehouse was packed with the fallen, the Changed.

"I did what I could," Rand said, his throat hoarse, the skin on his hands raw and bruised.

"Tomorrow," declared Chirek, "we'll do more!"

The sun fled quickly in Maerlon, the towering peaks shuttering it from sight, and the temperature dropped rapidly as Palaton walked back from the chapel. The luminary had left him with nothing, no idea of what to do or think. He could blunder about, seeking for a House of Flame or its remnants, but that would bring him nothing but grief. If there were Flames here, they'd fight to defend their anonymity. He'd learn nothing by antagonizing them, no matter what the sending at his apartment had urged him. This legacy would be found in secrets and whispers, by circumspect searching, or not at all.

He would spend another day or two in the colony, hope he could find out something about the student who'd lived here and found a lover here, and then he would have to return to Charolon. He had Rand and Blue Ridge to attend to. He could ill-afford to spend this time elsewhere.

He hunched into his jacket, thinking that he should have brought all weather gear. If he had had his power, he could have kept himself warmer. His breath ceased to fog on the evening air as he grew steadily colder. There was a thin aura of warmth from Honry's hut as he drew near, and then Palaton stopped, looking down the street, his attention caught by a building.

It was by no means the only cottage on the street, yet it was on a curveaway, its back to the foot of a set of peaks, and if he looked at it in the sunrise perhaps he would see it as his mother had seen it. Solitary. Commanding. Standing out among the other homes.

There was a crunch of gravel behind him. Baka approached, her breath in great, gusty clouds. She panted from the exertion. "Recognize it?" she asked.

"From the museum. Yes."

"We call it the House of Flame," the Choya'i commented, watching the building, not him, or she would have seen him jump.

"What?"

"Oh, she had a gift with thread, that Choya'i did. She put a sunrise behind it that made the cottage look as though it rose from a fire, all golds and roses." Baka coughed and swung her arms about her ample rib cage. "Get up early and come see it then. You'll recognize the gift, then, too. She had a rare ability. Even the brief time spent with us was enough to show her the way, we like to think."

"And what about the morning sky? Is there a star up there?"

"Yes, although it'll be difficult to see tomorrow. A little late in the year. That's the morning star of spring—we used to call the artist that, young Tresa; our Morning Star."

A Star over a House of Flame. Drawn to it, brought down out of the sky, helplessly, by the gravity of what lay below it, a love which not even a Star could resist. Palaton felt hope leap in him. "Who lives there?"

"Why, no one. It's been abandoned for decades. We left it that way, in case he came back."

"Who?"

"Why the artist who lived there, that's who." Baka coughed again, her breath pluming out. "Come on. It's brisk tonight. We might even have snowfall by morning, if we get the clouds. Come on!" and she broke into a shuffling run, leading him to the warm safety of Honry's home and freshly brewed *bren*.

Baka left after her cup and Honry scarcely spoke to him during dinner. He left a glass of brandy on the tabletop and retired with a mumbled apology, but Palaton preferred to be left in quiet. He moved from the table to the settee, and reclined there, watching the illusionary heating panel, smokeless but not flameless, as the house lighting lowered.

Had his mother known what she did? Had she left a clue as to where her heart lay, even before she knew there would be disgrace and unhappiness at the conclusion of her love? Was she only reflecting the inner turmoil of her heart and her attraction, or had she fallen to him by then? He would never know for sure. He did know that, in the morning, he would enter that house and see what he could find of the Choya who'd lived there.

Jorana looked out unhappily at the curtain of darkness sweeping across the city. No word had come, and she hesitated still, knowing she had waited too long and that Rand either lay dead somewhere or spirited beyond her reach as head of security at the palace. She could bring in the network of county guards, and undoubtedly would be forced to once Palaton heard, but she didn't have the heart to tell him via a view screen what she'd allowed to happen. Nor did she want to interface with the various counties just yet. The throne in Charolon would be showing yet another weakness once she did.

"What should I do?" she asked of Rindy, who lay quietly on his chaise, having tired himself with a schedule of walks and exercises designed to build up his strength.

The elder chuckled. "I'll tell you what you should do, if you'll tell me what I should do."

She turned around, leaning one hip against the windowsill. "I thought you'd already decided to go."

He had his arm behind his head, pillowing it. "Panshinea," he said, and there were worlds behind his rendering of the emperor's name.

Panshinea. Erratic, brilliant, egomaniacal, resolute, clever, and sometimes absolutely blind as to the effects of what he hoped to accomplish. She'd seen him dupe Palaton and Nedar, exile Palaton, bring him back, toss away Nedar, set them against one another, knowing they were rivals for his own waning power. Nedar had known it. Palaton had not and when he'd finally taken up the mantle as heir, he'd done it only to give Cho some stability in Panshinea's wake.

Cho cannot have two emperors.

"If you don't go, Rindy, maybe he won't come back."

"Not good enough," Rindalan answered. "He would just appoint someone else. Gathon, probably, and frankly, I'd rather Gathon were here running things when Pan comes back. I would be little help at the administrative end of things."

Jorana hugged herself. "What will I do without you? What if he comes back and wants to begin stealing again? I can't go through that again, Rindy. I can't bring the young and watch him drain them of *bahdur* just so his doesn't fade. I can't do it."

A brow arched on the other's face. "I guess," he said slowly, "you've already made your decision, too."

She could feel heat warm her face. "He's not a bad emperor," she protested.

"He's just not a very good one anymore." Rindy sat up with a heavy sigh. "The spirit is willing, but my flesh is more than weak. I'm going to fall asleep on you, Choya'i, and poor counsel would I be then."

"What am I to tell Palaton about Rand?"

"Wait until morning. Maybe then you'll have all the answers you need. Old as I am, young as you are, even you ought to know that things are always clearer in the morning," He tottered to his bedroom and paused in the doorway. She saw, for the first time, how achingly age had begun to distort his body, silhouetted in the glare from his bedroom. He paused. "I haven't foresight, Jorana, but I have a great deal of experience upon which to base my intuition. Things will be all right."

Erlorn came to Qativar's bed, tiptoeing in fear and excitement, afraid to stretch out his hand to wake his master, but he did, and found his wrist gripped and forced backward by unforgiving fingers. His elbows cracked with pain.

Slowly, Qativar came fully awake. "What is it?" he said, impatience growling in his lower voice.

"Havoc in Bayalak, Master. The underground brings word. There is a Prophet, and a priest of the Change revealed—"

"Who is he?" asked Qativar sharply, getting out of bed.

Erlorn rubbed his released arm fretfully. "From the description and rumors, I think it's Chirek."

Qativar paused. He'd seen the fool go. It fit with his earlier suspicions and yet, he could not quite reconcile the information with his own feelings toward the clerk.

Chirek, the high priest of the prophecy? Chirek, heir to a couple of centuries of heresy? Surely someone stronger, or more charismatic, or more empowered.

Surely not *Chirek*.

But he could not let his doubt over Chirek obscure the bigger problem. If the Change were possible, if *bahdur* could be set free among the commons, then his plans for *ruhl* would be destroyed. He'd come too far to allow that.

And Rand in the middle of it, unless he'd secreted Rand away as a hostage. What had the manling to do with it?

"Are the communicators broadcasting?"

"No. Word came through the underground, but I haven't been able to confirm anything." Erlorn was still shaking. "A Prophet!"

Qativar backhanded the servant, sending him spinning across the room. "Details. Get me details. Remember," he snarled, "who owns your life."

Erlorn crawled to the door and lay there, supine, as Qativar stepped from the sleeping room into the rest of his quarters. He belted his shirt at his waist. "Find out where the manling is," he ordered. "Quickly."

Chapter 25

The Abdrelik part of her woke her, as it always did, silent but commanding, and she obeyed, not stretching or uncurling from the warmth of the thin bedding, but simply opening an eye alertly. Her breathing did not change. Any who saw her would think she still slept, her hair pushed carelessly into her eyes, obscuring them, her limbs folded under her. They were in Chaos, and the drugs she had taken to ease her perception of the reality lapses sang through her senses. Alexa stared into the downtime, and waited to see what had awakened her.

Nedar moved across the cabin, a tiny room by Choyan standards, but he made little sound. She saw him open the medical chest they had brought over, open it, and pull out an air inject. He checked the dosage, tapped it once or twice to clear it, and injected it quickly into his thigh.

Without stirring, she watched intently, trying to see his face, to see what the drug did that the Choya would risk so much to obtain it. He reeled back against the wall, unmoving, caught in a moment that was near orgasmic, and she could see the rapture on his face. Before it faded, she saw him open his hand, the air inject resting on his palm. A pale blue aura flared around his lean form. Alexa caught her breath at that, but he hadn't noticed, too involved in what was happening to him. He let out a slight, breathless laugh.

The air inject floated off his palm and returned to the medical chest under its own power. She blinked, wondering what he had done. Then, under the influence of that same unseen hand, the medical chest snapped shut. Nedar straightened.

Alexa shut her eyes quickly and resumed deep breathing.

She heard him cross the cabin and lean over her. A touch on her shoulder.

She allowed herself to stir then, and rolled over with a moan.

"I have to go forward," Nedar said. "We'll be docking soon."

"We're in decel?"

"Not quite yet."

"How do you know we're close?" she asked sleepily.

Nedar gave a dry smile. "Oh, I know," he said. "I know." He paused, and his hand did a sweep over her warm body, a light, massaging touch, oddly affectionate. "Go back to sleep."

Despite her suspicions, the touch awoke a renewed emotion in her, that she had finally found her match, her equal, a passion to encompass her own, and an understanding of the darkness which drove her. She didn't want to let Nedar go. She caught up his hand and pressed it to her lips. "Tell me," she said.

"Tell you what?"

"What the drug does for you. How it is you know where we are, without the *tezarian* drive."

Conflict crossed his face, and then he sat down on the edge of the bed. She immediately curled her body about the curve of his hip. He drew her into the bend of his elbows, remaining silent.

"They'll tear us apart," Alexa said. "You know that. We're caught between the Compact, the Abdreliks, and your people. If we have any advantage at all, we need to use it."

"We have every advantage," he answered quietly. "The world of Cho will bow to us, and the Compact will have no choice but to follow."

She did not try to contain her surprise. "Only the drive could do that."

He gave a dry laugh. "There is no drive. There is only us, the *tezars,* and because we're not machinery, and we can't be duplicated, we can hold the rest of the Compact at bay."

"No drive?" Alexa sat up, along the back of his flank, putting her chin on his shoulder. The soft silkiness of the fine hairs along his skin tickled her. "You don't use the black boxes?"

"No. That's a Choyan puzzle box, a subterfuge. It works admirably well, but it won't take you across Chaos." Nedar sucked in a proud breath. "Only I can do that."

"What does the drug do for you?"

"It renews me. It gives me the soulfire, the *bahdur*, we call it, to predict our navigation." He reached for her, drawing her into his lap and cradled her head against his chest. "There are no instruments which can defy Chaos. Only the soul, and its fire. We know where we are and where we're going because we *know*, instinctively. Our psyche tells us."

. She thought suddenly of poor Bevan, who was to have been Nedar's Companion on Arizar, who opened Chaos for himself and the Abdreliks, although it drove him insane to do so and cost him his life. "You gave it, the *bahdur*, to Bevan."

"Yes. The power is not without cost, tremendous cost. It renews itself slowly, and then there comes a day, when it won't renew at all. Burnout. Then the neuropathy begins, the wasting disease that destroys our neural pathways. Painful. Slow. Deadly. So when my power began to flicker, when I knew that I could no longer read the patterns of Chaos, I began to fear. All that I had was going to be ripped away from me. Too soon. There are Cleansings on Cho, but they do nothing for *tezars*. We could not find a cure."

His chest vibrated with the sorrow in his voices.

"What about the Companions? Was that what they offered you on Arizar?"

"What about them? I was told I could transfer my *bahdur* to a humankind, who would hold it for a period of time and then return it, cleansed, refreshed. Like," and he laughed again, "like an oil filter."

"No one told me."

"No one told any of you." Nedar paused. "No one thought you important enough to know, and all too often, the influx of *bahdur* destroyed your kind. So the College took steps to stifle your senses, so that you were little more than carriers, incubators. Understand that they were exiles, renegades. We don't colonize off-world. We don't tamper with other civilizations. When they came to me with their offer it was with the agreement that I would leave Cho behind and never look back. I agreed. None knew how it was that humankind did what they did, any more than we know how we produce *bahdur*. It's in us, genetically, but for all the study over hundreds of years, it's a mystery we haven't been able to decode. If it's born in you, it's there."

"And when it's gone, it's gone." Alexa stirred. "But now all you need is the drug."

"Yes! I had nothing, poured it all into Bevan for renewal when he stole it. I was like a bucket filled with holes so even when I could reach out and steal soulfire for myself, it slipped away. Now, I need nothing. No Companions, no religious mumblings which mean little and do less." He held her tightly and she could hear the slow drum of his heart through his immense chest. "I can offer all *tezars* what they most desire. I can build a House of my own, a House of pilots, the ultimate power on Cho."

The implications thrilled through her. "How will you tell them?"

"I don't have to. The treatment speaks for itself. One dose, and my fellows will know. I won't have any trouble finding converts."

Alexa shifted her head. "There might be side effects. There should be testing."

He lifted her a little so she could be on eye-level with him. "I know," he told her. "I *know*."

"Then where do we begin?"

"We begin with Vihtirne of Sky, and Hathord of Blue Ridge. I can turn the flight schools first. There's no end of candidates." He looked away from her, as if seeing into the future. "There's only one Choya who might think of stopping me, and I owe him one anyway."

She knew him well, the one who had first turned Rand away from her. "Palaton."

"Yes."

She could feel the fervor rising in him, a lust, whose faint heat and aroma came from every pore, and she felt herself answering to that. Power, power she could grasp and use to her own advantage. She leaned her taut body into his, felt the contact of her bare skin against his, her nipples growing hard, and said, "I have a score to settle there, as well."

He dropped his chin, and kissed the swell of her breast softly. "Another thing we have in common."

She closed her eyes, feeling the soft ecstasy he had begun. She thought of the *bahdur* and asked softly, "What else can you do?"

"This," he said, and opened his mind to hers, tangling their passion, letting her taste his dominion over Chaos as well as her body, and listened to her cries of pleasure. How odd to find his *durah* here, in this humankind, but perhaps that was just as well. If he could not bind her to his will and his needs, then he would have to kill her for what she knew. And he was loath to do that. Very, very loath.

When he slept, exhausted, his too lean Choyan body toppled across the bed, Alexa left him. She crept through the freighter bays until she found a maintenance closet, marked carefully by her so that she would note it. Inside, hidden, was the transmitter her father had given her.

Crouched in front of it, knowing that an awake and alert Nedar could possibly search her out and slay her for what she was doing, Alexa keyed open a line. Long minutes ticked past, then, blurred on the infinitesimally small screen, she saw her father's face.

"You're all right?"

"Yes." She brushed her curly, dark hair from her face. "I haven't much time. We need to open lines of distribution for the drug as soon as we can."

"I'm not—"

"Don't argue with me! Father, the Choyan will be lining up for this. We won't be Class Zed any longer. We'll have the pilot contracts we need, anything. I know the secret of the *tezarian* drive. It's not mechanical. It comes from them, from their minds. They navigate by parapsychology. They get through Chaos because they simply know what's going to be there."

His jaw dropped. She saw the age and weariness in his face. "That can't be. The Ivrians score much higher on all the scales, and their pilots are far inferior."

"Father, think. Any being with that much ability can mask it. They would have to. But their minds burn out. The ESP is not reliable. Our drug restores it!"

She saw the implications dawn up on him. "Alexa—"

"Do it. Do it for all of us."

She began to shut down the transmission, afraid to push her luck any longer. If the Choyan pilot for this vessel began to sense a signal, or if Nedar awoke—

"Alexa, what about you?"

He could not see her smile because she already had visuals off-line. She whispered, "I'm going to be an empress!" And ended her transmission.

Vihtirne pivoted slowly in front of the mirrored surface. She eyed her figure and hair critically. "Asten," she called to her aide. "What do you think?"

The Choya paused at his keyboard and looked over. He had been avoiding watching her dress for Nedar, because the jealousy ate at his very bones, but he also feared her and the power she held over him, so he looked and admired. "Your beauty endures," he said.

Vihtirne made an ironic sound, adding, "I'm holding my prime."

"Yes."

Her eyes flicked away from the mirror to him. Her dark eyes were outlined with wings of jewelry, emphasizing them, and keeping the fine lines of age away for now. "Thank you, Asten," she said dryly. She clicked the mirror lights off. "What's the ETA?"

"We should be leaving for the docks right about now. We have the freighter in tracking."

She gave a final fillip with her chin, saying, "He'd better be worth it," and signaled for Asten to get up and escort her to the hover sledge. Hathord's message had been less than cryptic, but she knew that Nedar did not make demands merely to flex his muscles. He had something, he needed something, and she wanted to be there when he set foot on Galern. She had offered to put him on the throne of Cho, and that was where she wanted him, as long as she could stand in the shadows beside him. The House of Sky was in the ascendant on the Wheel of Life, and she had every intention of taking that ride to the top. With the backing of Qativar, there was nothing that could stop them.

Asten kept the hover sledge to the less trafficked lanes, but it was a stuffy, bumpy ride and Vihtirne was glad when they reached the docking cradles and she could stretch her legs at the terminals and watch the freighters come in. Gal-ern's lesser gravity always revived her, although visits here had to be short unless one wore the pressure suits which provided each Choya with his own gravity, keeping the vas-cular and muscle systems fit. But for now, her skin felt tight, her spine stretched, her breasts rode high and firm and she felt the vibrancy of her youth.

Vihtirne held a keen appreciation for Galern and had thought, more than once, of opening a resort here. How-ever, the mining colony held little in the way of amenities and Choyan were reluctant to leave their home planet for any reason. True, the domes were necessary, and the sce-nery dreary, but, oh, that lovely lack of gravity.

Vihtirne smiled as her drone freighter came into view on the screens and she watched it settle clumsily onto a berth-ing cradle. Asten took her arm, escorting her to the locks.

An exchange of money had kept the inspectors away, and they had the terminal to themselves. If it was suspected she was bringing someone in illegally, she had the clout to make it possible, and to make others turn their heads away. She did not often use it, but she had this time.

She could hear the recyclers, the thump of metal plating, and the rumbling of the engines as they died down, and then the whine of the berthing cradle as everything moved into position. The floor beneath her shoes vibrated with the mechanics of actually docking the massive ship. Finally, there was silence, and then, with a click-click, the bulkhead air lock began to open.

Vihtirne stepped forward with a carefully manufactured air of elegance and welcome as the doors parted and Nedar stood, a humankind in the curve of his arm, an unmistak-able body language between them that shocked the Choya'i of Sky to her core. She would not have given credence to what she saw, but her *bahdur* read their shared aura, and she had no doubt.

She tore her eyes away from the humankind, who might possibly have been counted pretty among her people, and looked to Nedar, filled with repulsion and disgust.

"What," she said through tight lips, "have you done?"

Nedar gave her a cutting smile, stepping from the lock. "We've brought you the throne, my Choya'i."

*   *   *

He slept through sunrise. Perhaps it was the lulling effect of the high mountain air or because dreams chased Palaton so intensely all night, but when he woke, the sun was full in his face with its mid-morning light. He bathed and then dressed quickly. It had snowed during the night, but the sun worked to melt it, and there came a steady plip-plop of melting icicles from the eaves as he came down the stairs.

Honry sat in his front room, carding wool, his swiping motions quick and effective. He looked up. "Bren's on the hotpan. Too late for breakfast."

"That's all right," Palaton said, although his stomachpinched. "What's the weather like?"

"Warm. The road's treacherous, so watch your step." Honry frowned in thought. "Good day to see the ruins," he added. "Before another icing makes it impossible to get up there."

"Sounds intriguing. Is there a school or council where I can get a chance to meet the masters?"

"Not this late in the season. Most of us have gone back to our projects, what with the students gone." And with that, Honry went back to his work carding, all awareness of Palaton seemingly dismissed from his mind.

Palaton shrugged into his jacket and stepped outside, where a briskness in the air redefined his idea of warm. The upper slopes of the mountains looked refreshed, but the melting snow in the town had turned the streets and curbs into a kind of dirty slush. He walked carefully, picking his way around puddles and occasional skids of ice.

A corner grocer had fresher *bren* and hot, sweet bread rolls to go with it, and barbecued sticks, the meat peppery and sweet at the same time. Palaton sat in the corner at one of three small tables and watched the few shoppers come and go, picking up supplies for the day. The proprietor, a short, burly Earthan, watched him out of the corner of his eyes.

The streets were all but deserted when he ventured out again, and found the house which had haunted his dreams. Palaton stood on the walk, undecided about whether to go in, but he could see no signs other than one's own moral decency prohibiting entrance, so he finally strode through the arched gate and went up the path.

The cottage showed the results of neglect. The roofing

needed repair, and the walls were streaked with age. The windows had been permanently shuttered. The porch creaked in protest as he stepped onto it. But the door was not locked. Palaton palmed the latch and entered.

A dusty scent hung on the air, the smell of a place not opened in many years. Baskets of threads and flossing lay in the workroom, their brilliant colors dimmed by heavy curtains of dust. There were two long quilting tables in the outer workroom, and embroidery frames for large pieces standing in the next. Nothing had been left unfinished, however, and Palaton knew that whoever had been here, and left, knew that he was going.

He walked through slowly. Nothing cried out to him. Insects rattled away in surprise, disappearing into nooks and crannies gnawed gradually wider by their boldness over the years. The master had been a painter, as well, although the easels were empty, canvases stretched and left blank, stacked along the wall, waiting to be lifted up and begun. Paints, palettes, and knives were cleaned and filled a double-door cupboard. So also did the remnants of a rodent nest, its sides thatched with gnawings from brush heads.

He closed the door in quiet frustration. The loft upstairs was empty, devoid of any clue, stripped even of work except for a single basket, holding skeins of fine silver-tone thread. Palaton came downstairs, defeated, head down in thought. If there had ever been anything of his mother here, he had not found it, and even doubted if *bahdur* could sniff out an aura over forty years old.

"If you came to steal, your hands are empty," the spidery luminary commented from the doorstep.

Palaton glanced up quickly, reining in his surprise, not wanting to give the old Choya the satisfaction. "I thought," he said, "if she studied under the master, he might have been her lover."

"And you thought right, but if you're looking for him, he left long ago, and if you're looking for his work, we burned it. Although," and the elder followed Palaton out of the house and into the yard, "there might be some remnants of him in the cave where he did most of his painting. It lies in the cliffs above the ruins, just below the snow line. It should still be accessible."

"And you would send me there."

"I would," the elder teacher said sharply, "send you back to the throne of Charolon, but it's not my prerogative."

"You know me."

"I probably know you better than you know yourself, but then, I've been looking longer." The luminary gathered himself up, gave a wispy-sounding sigh with the effort.

"Why not just tell me what it is I need to know."

Eyes no longer clear focused on him as if trying to see him better. Then the other answered, "What one wants to do, and what one can do, are not necessarily the same." He leaned forward hastily, grabbing for Palaton as if pitching in a headlong fall. His thin voices gasped out. "Compulsion and possession are talents of the House of Flame. It rules Choyan minds and destroys will. It is like a webbing which catches the moth, and the more the moth fights, the more difficult it is to win free!"

Palaton kept the elder from struggling in his hold and when his breathing had calmed, he straightened him back on his feet. "What are you saying to me?"

"None of us," the luminary panted, his hands moving, clutching, as if grasping for words, "left behind can talk. You alone. . . ." He swallowed, gulping, and finished, "Find the cave." He fell back against the porch, sweating and trembling.

Palaton hesitated. The luminary waved him off, crying hoarsely, "Go on. Go on!"

"I cannot help you—"

"It doesn't matter. You must go. Most of us who stayed will kill to protect their secrets. They're undecided about you—you haven't the time!" The luminary leaned back on the step. "Please."

Palaton swung around. From the far end of the street, he could see Baka's thick form coming their way. The elder would not be alone for long. "Thank you," he said, and left immediately, his long legs carrying him beyond the village's perimeter in moments. He didn't look back to see if he was being followed.

By the time he reached the foundation walls of ancient Maerlon, the air had thinned to the point where he, too, gasped and reeled. He leaned his shoulder against the old stone, felt its glacial chill, and caught his breath. The fortress had been immense and thick, for how else to guard against fire throwers and levitators in warfare? Talent had been prodigious then, abundant in everyone, although not necessarily extremely powerful in itself. A Choya might be able to levitate two feet in the air, but not over thirty-foot walls. He might be able to start fires anywhere, but not hot enough to make stone crack and burn. He could teleport, but not well enough to guarantee he would appear inside the compound and not inside the wall itself, giving him a grisly and excruciating death. And so Maerlon had stood, in spite of *bahdur,* for centuries.

He steamed inside his jacket, ached to take it off, but the frigid air on his face told him that he would chill quickly and stiffen if he did. He pulled himself away from the stone and began walking the outer perimeter of the fortress, scanning upward. He found a pathway a springhoof might walk, scarcely wider than that, and needing the same agility, and took it. Soon, he was above Maerlon itself, looking down into the gutted interior, where treachery rather than might had brought the fortress down.

He shivered in spite of himself. *The talent of Flame is compulsion and possession.* To grip a Choya's mind tightly enough to turn him back on himself. The relization sickened Palaton. There were those with *bahdur* enough to suggest, to lead, to coerce, but actual possession was not possible and even if it were, it was abhorrent beyond reason. Was this what he'd inherited? No wonder his mother could never speak of it, even if she'd been left able.

His mother had never told who her lover had been, not because she did not wish to, but because he'd left her no choice. Like the web that tightened the more its captive struggled. Perhaps she'd even been stripped of the memories. He could think of fewer things more insidious than the invasion of another's soul.

Palaton came to a halt, as the cold fringe of the mountain's snow line pressed upon him, a physical presence. The ground emanated its frigid temperature, the mantle above had begun to spread across the path. He couldn't go much higher, not without climbing equipment, and this was not his terrain. He was a pilot, not a mountaineer. He pivoted to go back, and then he saw the cleft, a cobalt line among the gray and brown stone, and realized he'd found the cave.

A solar activated when he stepped inside, its panel

turned to the cleft opening, barely catching the early fall angle of the sun. Its panel had nearly expired, for the light it sent out was thin and richly yellow, shedding no great illumination. It was enough, however, for him to see empty easels and paint cases, a thick cot spread in one corner, with a canopy of silver thread, woven and knotted like a gossamer spider's webbing. Palaton went to the cot, for it was a lovers' bed, and across its head lay a shawl of crimson and violet. He picked it up. Even over the decades, its perfume-scented fibers exuded the aroma of thara tea.

Thara tea was a brisk, dry perfume, never greatly in fashion, seldom worn today, but his mother had worn it every day of the life he remembered with her. Palaton, his throat closing with sudden emotion, crushed the shawl to his chest.

Turning, still unable to swallow or breathe properly, he saw the easel in the best light, facing the doorway, a canvas in its cradle. Palaton went to it, and then stood, knowing he had an answer of sorts, for the artist had signed, not only his name, but also his destination.

If he had not also been there, if he had not succumbed to burn-out fever and been taken there for healing, if he had not found Rand there, if he had not met with the College of the Brethren, still he might know this was not Cho. Arizar was too primitive in its beauty, too new and achingly angled, its geological formations too sharp, too menacing, too clean.

The artist who'd painted this had known that only another who'd also seen these mountains, these forests, these plains could identify it and follow. Certainly not a foe.

Had he left it for his son?

Palaton put out a hand and touched the canvas. Not quite finished, it had still been signed. Aeliar. Not a name he knew, no indication of its lineage, but one he vowed never to forget. He would return to the ashes of Arizar and begin his search again.

The toe of his boot caught the easel as he turned and it tumbled over. The tubing split open, aged by temperature extremes and exposure, and a scroll inside fell free. Hand shaking, Palaton reached for it.

Nothing but a lineage chart. One side, he saw, had been painstakingly reconstructed, from the first devastation of the Householding when the Flames had suffered almost total genocide, to the present. The other he recognized as his own. More chillingly, each branch contained the strongest talents and from the projected union of the two lines he could read: telereading, discernment, teleportation, telemedicus, telempossession.

He had been bred to be a monster.

Outside, an explosion rang out, sharp, loud, cracking the very air. Palaton's head jerked up. He wondered if someone had been shooting at him. The earth began to rumble and shake beneath his feet, and the ceiling rained dust upon him as the whole mountain awoke with a deafening roar. The avalanche began, the first waves of it sweeping past the cave mouth, taking the solars with it, plunging him into a darkness which bellowed as it buried him.

Chapter 26

When Rand pried his eyelids free of the sandy glue which held them shut, he saw Chirek sitting across the tiny cubicle, his chin propped in his hand, staring out the window. The priest had already been out; he smelled of the tropic air, brine, and panet. As Rand sat up stiffly, finding aches in bones he didn't knew he had, never mind the muscles, he thought that perhaps Chirek had been crying.

There was a basin filled with fairly clean water, so he stripped his tunic off and began to wash. The sound of his dabbling in the water gave Chirek a chance to compose himself before swinging around.

Rand dried his hands. He hated to pull his tunic back on, then saw that Chirek had gotten a loose, native shirt for him. It swirled in blues and greens, pleasing colors, and he slipped it gratefully over his head.

"What happens today?"

"Today?" repeated Chirek numbly. "I'm not even certain what happened yesterday."

"It—it worked, didn't it?"

"Yes. I've been out today, calming and teaching what I can." Chirek stood up, agitated. "Rand, I never expected this—never. They're not prepared. They can't handle what we've kindled inside of them. It's wildfire, out of control, and the guards are looking for us amid the havoc."

"The Houses," Rand said. "We've got to go to the Houses for training. They're the only ones prepared to help us."

"Help us? They'll slaughter us in the streets," Chirek replied bitterly. "Do you think they want to share the power? If they did, they would have intermarried as much as they could, dispersing the genetic heritage. They would have combed through us eagerly to find those they could raise and nourish." He brushed a hand across his brow as if he could wipe away his fears. "It's my failure. I hoped that Dorea was an extreme."

"And she was," Rand argued. "I didn't feel that much power in anyone else I touched. Chirek, you can't give up. It's right, it feels right, it feels . . ." Rand spread out his hands, still tender from the night's work, and looked at them. "It's like shaping lightning. There's no good or bad to it—it's pure elemental. It just is."

And it was the only time he was not alone. The only time he felt connected, was when the power channeled through him, awakening the gift in another. He couldn't give that up easily. "We just need to make better choices."

"How?"

"I can't Change everyone overnight. We've got to find the steady ones, the responsible ones, who can be opened up and then become teachers later." He dropped his hands, stricken. He could not go back to Palaton, Palaton who would fear that his power was being drained beyond recovery, who would fight him tooth and nail on what he was doing, who could not possibly stand against the ground swell the Changing of his world would create.

The priest spoke quietly. "We'll have to go underground."

"Can we do it?"

Chirek looked at him steadily. "I can. You . . ."

"You'll have to find a way," Rand returned.

"It will mean constantly moving. Danger. Poverty."

"What about Malahki?"

The priest sighed and sat down abruptly on the edge of a cot in which he had apparently spent a very restless night. "I don't know. I don't know if we should Change him, I don't know if I can trust him. Malahki has always had his own agenda, and though I like him, I don't know him."

"Then that's a decision we can make later." Rand sat down and pulled on his boots. They still felt damp with perspiration.

Chirek watched him. "You're willing to do this."

"It makes no difference whether or not I'm willing. It has to be done. It was meant to be done." Rand stopped, as he heard a noise outside. There was a doorway into another room. "Who's in there?"

"Dorea and Seli, one of my underground. He was one of the first you touched last night."

Rand did not remember one out of a sea of Choyan faces. He didn't have time to search for it as a wave of alarm swept over him. "Someone's out there."

Chirek lurched to his feet. "What?"

Dorea appeared on the threshold, wearing clean clothes this time, a somber black dress, sweeping the floor, her bandage stark against her face. "Run," she urged, one hand reaching to steady herself. Seli came up behind her, put a hand around her waist.

"It's not the guard," the Bayalakan said, but he propelled Dorea forward anyway. "But she came awake with prophecy on her lips."

Chirek threw a bundle at Rand. "That way." He pointed to the rear of the room, where Rand saw daylight through thin boards. He put a shoulder down and ran at it, the priest beside him, and they literally burst out the back wall of the building.

There were shouts, and the beam of an enforcer cut past him. It sizzled harmlessly on the air. Rand felt its heat, knew it would not have been harmless if he'd been hit. Chirek grabbed and spun him around. A conveyance buzzed angrily past, just missing them as they spilled into the street.

Rand caught a glimpse of faces behind them. Qativar, to the fore, shouted in anger, words he could not hear, as Seli took them all across the traffic and the street and into the shadow of the next neighbor, where he strong-armed a hover sledge and threw Dorea onto it first, setting its direction as he did so. The three had to take running leaps as it rose and took off. Chirek made it handily. Rand hit the sled's railing mid-center and lay gasping, feeling the priest grab for his shoulders. He heaved aboard.

Seli missed the jump. He fell, rolling to the street. Rand crawled to the controls, reached for the resetting, to come about and pick him up, but Chirek cried out, "No!"

Rand looked back to see Seli blown apart on the street. The Choyan threw his arms in the air, with a look of pain and horror on his face, his shirt exploding into crimson tatters. Then he toppled, face first. Qativar held the enforcer, a look of satisfaction on his face. He looked up from the body and his eyes met Rand's across the distance.

There was a scream. A commons yelled, "The Bringer! Protect the Bringer!" A swarm of Choyan bodies flooded the roadway, heedless of the armed gunmen. Another yellow-red flash illuminated the daylight before the swarm engulfed the shooters. Rand saw no more as Chirek wrestled with the controls, swerving the hover sledge, and taking them out of reach.

John Taylor Thomas ordered the course set for Sorrow. Maren returned to the labs, to simplify and verify the findings of the last few days. Thomas returned to his offices, and sat, weighing his options. What Alexa suggested, what she demanded of him, he was not sure he could do. Despite his machinations, he thought of himself as a basically honest man. Yet he could say that neither Cho nor Abdrela had dealt openhandedly with him—or with any struggling Zed class civilization. He was searching his soul, trying to decide if he could do what he had to, when it happened. Neither man was prepared when the strike came out of the nether reaches of deep space.

The side of the ship blew. Air locks immediately ground shut and sealed, minimizing damage to the deck which had been hit. Thomas picked himself up off the floor, ears ringing, heart thudding. He hit the com switch, but Baros was already on it, reporting, her voices calming over the noise of damage control alarms.

"Ambassador. Take a deep breath, we're okay. That was just a parting shot from those bastards."

"Intentional?"

"With the precision they hit us with, I would have to say so, but we'll never prove it. I was just coming online to tell you we had an unidentified tail, possibly Ronin. The Abdreliks will only claim they were protecting us from assault and the shot misfired. The fact the scoundrels are always hand in glove will not matter. It's proof of intent we need, and we won't be getting that."

Thomas crawled backward, found his desk chair, righted it, and pulled himself into it. The com sounded fuzzy, and Baros' voices were fading rapidly. "What did they hit?"

"The com center. We have shipboard communications, but we're dead on the air otherwise."

Damn. Thomas ran a hand over his face, found it wet, and wondered in the dimly lit cabin if it were sweat or blood. "Anything else?"

"There's a fire in one of the smaller labs. It's under containment." Baros paused. "Damage control tells me the technician you were working with, Maren, died of smoke inhalation."

Damnation again. Thomas clenched his fist. He had the information saved and stored. A store of the drug in capsulated form lay in the bottom of his diplomatic pouch.

As he listened to the general quarters alarm subside, and smelled smoke faintly through the air recycler system, he made up his mind. Neither Choyan nor Abdrelik was going to hold him hostage again.

He would begin with Panshinea, desperate to hold his throne, faced with fading power. John Taylor Thomas wondered just what the drug would do for Panshinea. He opened his comline.

"Baros."

"Yes, Ambassador."

"Just get me back to Sorrow as quickly as you can."

"We're en route, sir. A few patch jobs, and we'll hit FTL as soon as we can."

"Good."

He sat back. The future was in his hands. Finally.

"I'm not lying," Rand repeated, then leaned over to pick up his cold drink. "Why would I lie?"

"It couldn't have been Qativar you saw. He's Housed, he's the highest of any of us, he has his position with Rindalan. What would he have to gain?" Chirek paced, upset, his face streaked with dirt and sweat, and his furious pacing did nothing to calm him down.

"I know Qativar. It was him."

Chirek threw his hands up, unconsciously mimicking Seli's death fall. "It couldn't have been him. Listen, you've not been among us to know our faces that well. Subtlety of crown, jewelry, eye shade—"

"Why couldn't it have been him? And if he was Housed,

why was he a member of the Church of the Prophecy? What would he gain by being a heretic?"

"Because he barely passed testing. He was sent down once, but then his family begged for retesting and he finally passed. His *bahdur* is so weak as to be almost nonexistent. He went into the church because he could function there, but his Householding disowned him. He knows what it means to become a commons, to be threatened with that, to be redeemed from it. He knows what we all lose, what we all gain."

"I know what I saw." Rand set his jaw stubbornly.

Both had ignored the Prophet. She tugged fretfully on her bandage. "Chirek," she said mildly, and when she somehow knew she had their attention, she added, "I saw him."

"Describe him."

She gave a description that fit the Choya perfectly, right down to his icy blue eyes and the fancy clothes he preferred to wear instead of his robes of office. "And," she announced, "he intended to kill us." When she finished, Chirek looked staggered.

He collapsed next to Rand. Rand passed him a cold drink. The bayou slid by, green, steaming, panet heavy on the waterside, the airboat they'd exchanged the hover sledge for chugging through steadily. Instead of drinking, he pressed the cold glass to his forehead.

"Seli," he said. "I left Seli behind."

"I don't think," Rand told him, "any of us could have helped him."

Tears slid down the priest's face. He did not respond, instead began to drink.

Dorea tilted her head a little as if listening. "We're on the run now," she murmured. "Bayalak is in flames."

"What?" Chirek twisted about in the deck chair, looking back. Storm clouds grew in the distance, obscuring the towers of the Housed part of the cityscape, as the swamp obscured the wharves and old town. They began to blot out the blue sky, roiling, mottled and ominous.

Rand took a deep breath. "Those aren't rain clouds," he said. "That's smoke."

"Why? Why?" Chirek appeared to be at a breaking point.

"To protect the Bringer," Dorea remarked. "And the Prophet. They're fighting in the streets because of what Qativar did."

"With any luck, he won't get out alive." Rand stood up and went to the railing. "And we won't get far without help."

Dorea looked overhead, her bandaged face searching the sky. She put out a hand, seeking, grasping, and caught hold of Chirek. "We're found."

The sound of a skimcraft whistling near pierced the chug of the airboat, and Rand saw the dark splinter of a shadow arrowing down at them. He leaped the railing, landing on the deck where the bridge was, scattering other passengers. He could hear the scream of the diving plane as he lunged to the control panel, slapped his hands down and sent the airboat hurtling into the swamp, across the channels. Birds fled with a colorful burst, taking wing, throating cries of distress, and the airboat bogged slightly as the vegetation threatened to overwhelm them.

The skimcraft whizzed past, put a wing down, and prepared to come about. Rand looked through the bridge and saw an impenetrable forest, trees and moss arching to form a cavelike entrance into the depths of the swamp. Anything wanting to take them on would have to follow them into the heart of the morass. He set the course and took them in headlong.

"Personally," Vihtirne said, her face tightening in disagreeable lines, her mouth drawn down, "I think we should offer this opportunity to the Salt Towers." She crossed her legs, the drape of her skirt following the action, but only her aide looked appreciatively her way.

Nedar's and Alexa's attention centered on Hat, sitting miserably in the middle of them, his shoulders hunched against confrontation.

When the flightmaster looked up, he said, "You're asking me to betray Cho."

"No. Absolutely not. I'm telling you, old friend, that the throne has betrayed you. Me. All *tezars*. And only we can save our world. Only we."

Hat did not look comforted, even in the sanctuary of his study, and indeed, Vihtirne and her brace of House guards, Asten, Alexa, and Nedar crowded the study. But he set his shoulders resolutely. He had made a remarkable recovery since they had invaded the base and his offices. "We've discussed this before, Nedar, and you make a good case. But where are we without the support of the Houses and our Householdings when our careers are done? They gave us support at the beginning, and it's to them we go at the ending. What you ask will plunge Cho into total chaos."

"No more." Nedar crossed to him and crouched on the floor to look him in the face. There was nothing humble about his posture. "We gave our Houses everything we had, let them drain us until every last spark of soulfire went out. They owed us the end of our lives then, and more. We're a long way from collecting on that debt! But I'm here to tell you that we don't need them anymore. They will always need us, but we're free of that yoke."

"What do you mean?"

Alexa spoke up. "My people have developed a drug which chemically cleanses *bahdur* and restores it. There will never be such a thing as burnout again."

Hat's head swiveled as he looked up in shock. "What are you saying? Can this be true?"

"Believe me," Vihtirne said. "My *tezar* Lathum flew to Sorrow A-11 to pick them up. He brought them back to Galem, where I met them, and we came straight on to Blue Ridge without so much as a layover. You know the rigors of that crossing."

Hat wet dry lips. He looked at Alexa. He looked back to Nedar. Nedar nodded. "It's true. You met Lathum at the field yourself. Did he look fresh to you? Relaxed, happy?"

"He couldn't have made that crossing."

"Ask him." Nedar reached out and keyed open the comline at Hat's side. "Where's he staying?"

"In the Red Flight wing."

"*Tezar* Lathum. Respond to the flightmaster's line."

It was a long moment before the Choya's deliberate voice came over the com. "This is Lathum."

Hat did not want to take his eyes from Nedar's face, but he did so to speak into the com. "Lathum, you flew the ore freighter to A-11?"

"I did and back and then here." Lathum gave a pleased laugh. "So they've told you, have they? It's true, Hat, every word and more. Believe!"

Nedar took his fingers off the keys, cutting the line off. He raised a brow at Hathord. The Earthan flightmaster looked as stubborn as the element his House had been named for, stone and dirt, solid, eternal.

"What more can I tell you?"

Hat blinked several times. He looked at Alexa. "Why bring her?"

"Because I desired to. Because her House developed the drug and until we can synthesize it, they will be our main suppliers."

"It's not permanent, then."

Vihtime uncrossed her legs and stood. "We're wasting time. We need to get organized as soon as possible." Her dark eyes flashed. "Bayalak went up in flames this afternoon, Master Hathord. The commons are on another rampage, and I'm told Panshinea has already left Sorrow. He'll wrest the throne from Palaton by any means he can, and we'll be left with the dregs at the bottom of a cup of *bren* if we hesitate any longer." She looked to Nedar. "If he doesn't want the opportunity, let's get on with it."

"Wait!" Hat mopped his forehead on the cuff of his sleeve. "I—I just—Nedar," and he threw the Sky a pleading look.

Nedar put a hand on his shoulder and clasped it firmly. "If I tell you it's all right, it will be."

Hat put his face into his hands. "All right," he agreed, his voices muffled. "God help us all."

Nedar straightened. "We'll start with the veterans. Get me everybody who's on downtime, and bring them in one at a time. As soon as we've got a good fix on whether they'll side with us or not, we'll give them a treatment. That should swing them over. I've got a hundred doses calibrated. After that, we'll have to hope our supplier meets his deadlines." Alexa nodded encouragingly. Nedar swung back to the Earthan. "Hat, I want you to ground the cadets temporarily. I don't want any green fliers up there. As soon as I know Blue Ridge is solid, then we'll contact the Salt Towers. But, under any circumstances, Ridge is the main hub of operations. Understood?"

Vihtirne said nothing, but her lips grew thin and pale as she watched Nedar take charge.

*　　　*　　　*

As soon as Gathon told Jorana that Panshinea had left Sorrow, she knew she could not wait any longer. The news from Bayalak was jumbled, confusing, but by the time her sources could be verified, she could have Palaton back in Charolon. She contacted Rufeen aboard the palace craft.

Rufeen appeared unhappy. Jorana immediately thought of the way she'd looked when there'd been an attack at Sethu. She wasn't wrong.

"I lost him again, boss."

"He hasn't checked in."

"No. I wish he'd pick someone else to pilot him if he's going to take off and get killed. There's been a massive avalanche on the cliff face above the ruins. All I can gather from my eavesdropping equipment—" Rufeen referred to the surveillance gear aboard the craft, "—is that they're fairly sure he's in the middle of it."

If the weight of the snow didn't suffocate him first, a Choya could survive. With *bahdur,* the temperature could be maintained for a while, and the breathing rate dropped down to a near cryogenic stasis. He could make it, if they got to him in time.

"I'm on my way," Jorana said. "See if you can hustle their artists' butts up that hill and get him out!"

She found Rindy in his rooms, leaning on a walker cane, contemplating the packing of crates to take with him to Sorrow. The atmosphere in his quarters was even graver than it had been when he'd lain there comatose. He lifted an arm and she snuggled in under it, for a moment feeling more like a child than a grown Choya'i.

She felt his reluctance as well as her own. Jorana stood back, saying, "I don't want you to go."

"There is some inevitability in every life." Rindalan looked over the activity. "This is best, for now. What have you found out about Palaton and Rand?"

"No word on Rand yet. Palaton has been delayed at Maerlon. I'm going to see if I can extricate him."

"Good."

"I won't be back before you leave." There was a hardening lump in her throat which made it difficult to get words past. "Don't you die on me out there, old friend."

Rindy looked at her, eyes suspiciously bright. "Die! I'm only a hundred and sixty years old. I have at least twenty,

thirty good years left in me! And, if my genetic line holds
true, perhaps as long as another fifty. Long enough to see
your children find their *durahs*."

"Promise?"

With great dignity, Rindy took her hand and kissed it,
saying, "With all due care, I promise."

She rushed him then, and gave him a tremendous hug.
"I'll hold you to that," she choked out before leaving
quickly, not allowing another word to be said.

She went to her room just long enough to change into
sturdier clothing and boots and to switch weapons. The vial
of *ruhl*, forbidden and unwanted, sat in a hidden drawer
where she kept a rather lethal power blade. She slid the
blade into the shank of her boot and stood, looking down
at the aphrodisiac. It could muddle the senses of anyone
with *bahdur*, as well as add to intoxication, besides performing its primary function of breaking down the self-
imposed fertility barriers of any Choyan. She didn't know
what kind of help she might need getting Palaton back, but
she'd take whatever she could get her hands on. She swept
up the *ruhl* and placed it in a pocket.

Chapter 27

As soon as the rumbling stopped, Palaton became acutely aware of the rapid drop in temperature. A chill immediately began to gather. He found himself crawling on his hands and knees, unaware of exactly when he'd been knocked off his feet. Inky darkness surrounded him. Grit tore into the palms of his hands and he reared up. The cave entrance had disappeared completely, and the only way he could distinguish where it had been was by an eerie dark blue glow that seemed lighter than the black of the stone walls.

He'd been buried alive. Panic rushed in, and for a moment he couldn't breathe. He fought for control. Maybe the opening had just been obscured by a thin layer of snow and ice. Maybe he could push his way out. The solars glowed warmly as he passed them. He put out fingers experimentally, grabbing an edge of the paneling, cursed it for being too warm, and then was immediately sorry. It would grow cold all too soon. There was the bedding of the cot, old and mildewed and rotting as it was. It seemed best to stay on hands and knees, and eventually he ran into the bedding.

He debated crawling into it, then decided to drag the pallet back over to the center of the cave where the solars lay. It took precious minutes to get the one to the other. By then, he'd stabbed himself once on a shard of the broken easel, and knocked into the artist's chair, but he was beyond small injuries. He had to think about suffocation and freezing. The air in the cave would be limited also, though he thought hypothermia would be his greatest problem.

But only if he decided to sit and wait for someone to come and dig him out. From his memory of a sharp crack or explosion just before the avalanche, he did not think anyone was coming soon. The warming and then icing and then warming again had made the snow water heavy, unstable. Someone had set off the avalanche deliberately and any plans to rescue him were probably being stalled, if they were being made at all.

He put a hand to his jacket pocket and pulled out his remote or, rather, pieces of his remote. Signaling Rufeen had just moved beyond the realm of possibility.

He had one advantage, and that was that he could stand in a stable threshold and attempt to dig himself out. But it meant bringing the cold environment in. He didn't know if that would decrease his chances once he was too exhausted to dig any more, or not. Snow could be insulating . . . provided body warmth could be maintained at a certain level. He had only the natural resources of a Godless.

First, light. He stayed on hands and knees and carefully began to explore the small cave, gridding it in his mind. The bedding tangled him up once; he kicked free in a fluff and rip. Then, his hands and legs growing cold, he sat for a while, huddling by the solars until the numbness stopped. It was on the third grid that he found a lamp. It responded even more weakly than the solars had when turned on, batteries at a very low ebb. Considering the age of the lamp, he was lucky it lit at all, unless someone else had come up here now and then to observe from the painter's viewpoint. He smashed the artist's chair.

In an orange glow reflective of a late fall harvest moon, he staggered back to the cave front with the chair's back in his hands, like a large spoon, and began to ladle the snow out.

He worked until the jacketed part of him was dripping with sweat and the exposed part of him, clad only in slacks, grew numb. Then he forced himself to retreat to the rotten blankets and wrap himself, trying to gauge the time. His chronograph had disappeared during his first crawl around the cave, and the light was too weak to help him find it again. His hands filled with splinters and blisters until even holding the wooden chair back filled him with agony. He took strips of the bedding and wrapped his hands, praying that infection wouldn't set into the open blister sores.

He stopped once to laugh at himself. He was better

equipped to be adrift in space than he was for surviving in this faraway part of his own world. Hysteria edged his efforts, and he knew it. He pulled back once with a thin cry as the orange glow faltered and then caught back on. He did not want to be left alone in the dark.

The pile of snow growing by the cave wall brought its chill with it, as he knew it would. It looked clean enough, so he ate from it from time to time, but the cold made his throat close in agonizing spasms, and his stomach feel icy, so, as thirsty as he was, he stopped. Inside the jacket, sweat ran down in rivers, soaking his shirt, and he knew he was dehydrating rapidly.

Time bled away. He dug, he stopped, he shivered, he warmed, he thirsted, he dug and dug. His shoulder and elbow joints ached with a pain beyond imagining which would, like magic, ease the moment he stopped, and burn like fire the moment he began digging again.

Palaton lurched away from the icy wall and fell into the bedding, dragging it over the solars, to gather the very last of their warmth for they'd cooled to the point where there was no danger of fire. He felt like a fevered man and resisted the temptation to tear off his jacket, to cool his torso, while at the same time attempting to bring soothing warmth to his hands and legs and feet.

He couldn't think of any reason why he shouldn't sleep, so he did.

The airboat barreled into the swamp. Vines tangled across the windscreen, obscuring the view, and Rand drew upon the soulfire to give him insight on bringing the boat through. It needed little draft, designed the way it was, but the thick, knobby-kneed tree roots which protruded from the water, as well as the overhanging branches and dripping mosses, made it almost impossible to proceed faster than a crawl. The airboat had to keep up a certain surface speed or it would lose its hover and stall altogether. The ship's captain shoved him aside impatiently, taking back the controls, cursing him to the two Choyan hells of fire and ice. Rand leaned back, concentrating on the skimcraft.

The thick cover defeated it. He could not sense its immediate whereabouts, but knew that they would not be safe for long. He left the bridge and made his way back to

Chirek and Dorea, who'd taken shelter underneath the top deck overhang. Vines slapped down at them.

"We're hunted," Chirek said.

"We should be safe, for a while." Rand ventured to the rail and looked over. The airboat had smaller craft, life-boats, lashed to its side. They were lean, shallow-drafted boats which would hold six passengers comfortably. Rand was not a sailor, but that which was Palaton inside him itched to hold the wheel of such a boat. Piloting was piloting.

The airboat made a noise, like a throttling groan, and Rand knew they were going to bog down. He'd been wrong about their safety. He waved Chirek over, saying, "We're going down. When we do, help me cast this off."

"Do you know where you're going?"

"No, but I do know that if we stay, we're targets. Qativar wants us dead. He won't care how long it takes to find us and kill us. He'll go through these swamps with whatever it takes—and with *bahdur,* it won't take long. They'll find us if we don't keep moving."

The airboat settled suddenly, listing as it landed, tangled in tree roots as well as swamp water. It made it difficult for Rand to get at the lifeboats and their ties. Chirek worked frantically beside him. "We could stay," he said. "We're not sinking, just beached."

"We'll draw Qativar to us no matter where we are. I like our chances a lot better out on open water. You told me that the Housed resort is on the other side, by the sea. There has to be a way to get there." Rand tore a nail off, sucked on the bloody finger with a muffled curse, then renewed his efforts. Suddenly, the boat came free. He looked up at Chirek.

"Put Dorea over."

He scarcely needed to speak, for the Prophet had appeared at the railing behind them, and was already climbing over unsteadily, her hands searching for holds. Chirek's hands circled her waist and he lifted her down to Rand who'd already taken up a stance in the lifeboat. Her smile was a pale slash under her bandaged eyes.

"Adventure," she said. "It'll make a good memory."

He helped her seat herself, then put a hand up to brace

Chirek, who climbed down a little less awkwardly than had the blinded Choya'i.

Rand put his hands on the controls, letting Palaton's senses spin out of him, telling him what to do. He started the engine up, heard it purr into life for him, and steered the craft away from the airboat just as it gave another moan and began to slip dangerously in their direction. Rand gunned his engine, sending up a high-spraying wake, and the airboat crashed into the water where they had just been, with another loud groan and the thin screams of the remaining passengers.

The Prophet turned her face to the prow, saying, "I can guide you."

Chirek's expression underwent a series of changes from dubious to unhappy, but Rand said, "Tell me," as he slipped the boat into high gear, steaming water churning under them, and the swamp closed its jaws about them even tighter. He needed Palaton, but the bond which had been between them was empty when he reached for it. Stripped away, destroyed. Had it happened when he met the Prophet? Or had it always been just one-way, when Palaton needed him? Rand stared bleakly into the swamp.

Rufeen met Jorana at the airstrip's edge, and helped her dismiss her pilot as late afternoon threatened to give way to the edge of night. Jorana pulled a cap down about her hair and tucked in loose strands.

"What's the word?"

"They won't go up. Two have tried, I'll give 'em that, they made an honest effort after a couple of hours of dancing around, but they brought down another mountain of snow. The peak is obliterated all the way to the foundation wall of the ruins now."

"How helpful of them," Jorana said scathingly. She looked across the peaks, where night's edge gave them purpling shadows. "What's the weather going to be like tonight?"

"Temperature's dropping again, which is good. No weather to speak of, so that's a help. It's windier here than down in the valley." Rufeen paused, then she turned to Jorana and said, in her frank way, "He's either dead or unconscious. There's been nothing by remote, and not a single flare of *bahdur*."

Jorana felt the wind stinging her eyes. She turned out of it and pulled her gloves on quickly, jamming each finger into its sleeve. Finally she turned back and said sharply, "Get me to where they think the trail starts."

She did not speak again, not even when a delegation of the elders who ran the colony came rushing out to meet them at the village's edge. She did accept a steaming cup of *bren* from one of them, drank half of it, and poured the rest on the ground. They stood in shock as though she'd insulted them, but all the time, her eyes were on the mountain, as if she could by sheer will pick up the beacon of Palaton's soul.

Rufeen said, "There's enough light to get about halfway up to where they think he might be."

"And where is that?"

"There's a cave up there one of the artists used to use to paint in."

"A cave? Well, that's something, anyway, if that's where he's trapped." Jorana pulled her scarf tighter about her throat. It looked as if the mountain had been blown, like an ancient, snow-topped volcano had suddenly given way, the aftermath sweeping down upon the ruins like some cataclysmic tidal wave. If he'd been caught in the snow itself, the weight would have crushed him. Jorana turned to the elders. "Who's coming with me?"

The eager welcomes quickly turned to shuffles and downcast eyes. Rufeen watched them. "No backbone here."

A Choya'i with beady eyes almost hidden in a cascade of wrinkles said sharply, "We didn't ask him to go up there. If he'd told any one of us where he was going, we'd have warned him away. New snow, melting snow, that's the most treacherous. He was a fool to go."

"And how do you know where he is?"

Her face flushed deeply. "He was seen climbing the springhoof trail."

"And no one stopped him then. I see." A hover sledge would never survive the wind and the rapidly changing thermals as the valley and peaks cooled further. She'd have to go up on foot. Jorana took a climbing rope from someone's arms, tied a loose harness about her shoulders and waist and said to Rufeen, "Anchor me."

"Do you know what you're doing?"

Rappeling buildings was not mountaineering. No, she didn't know what she was doing, but it was better than doing nothing, which the questioning villager had been all too good at. Jorana turned a scowl on the questioner, and that Choya moved aside, clearing his throat. Someone shoved snowshoes across the gravelly road and she picked them up. Time enough to use them when she reached Maerlon.

She hadn't expected an escort to the ruins, and they didn't get one. Only one Choya made the walk with them, a spindly, frail elder who looked as if the wind might blow him away. He went with them until the ice made the way hazardous and then paused, touching her lightly.

"Bring him back," was all he said. Then he hunched his shoulders into his coat and skittered away, disappearing far more quickly than she'd have given him credit for.

"Well, boss, it's just you and me," Rufeen commented.

Jorana threw her head back, looking up the mountain's side. "Any suggestions?"

"I wouldn't slip and fall if I were you."

With a humorless laugh, Jorana bent down to put on the webbed snowshoes. When she straightened, she surveyed the peak again. She didn't know what she expected of an avalanche, but what she faced was a slide which had poured off the mountain ridges, and it bore no contouring as to the actual slope under it. It could be drifted quite high. Jorana let out a gusty sigh. It could be quite hopeless.

But someone—who, the Choya'i with the vast wrinkles?—had said he'd been following a springhoof's trail. Springhooves she knew. She'd chased and bounded after them her entire childhood along the Danbe River. They liked steep slopes, but they never went straight up. They always crisscrossed back and forth, on rock, if they could. Jorana said a soft prayer for guidance and set off, playing the line behind her, walking across the snow, angling across the way a springhoof buck would.

Palaton woke, confused, shaking with cold, yet he'd been dreaming of bog water, steaming, and mosses, and trailing vines that tangled every movement, the intense need to escape . . . and he had no idea where the dream had come from. His power had called to him as only his own soulfire could, and he, repulsed by what he'd been bred to become, had rejected it. Severed it. Shoved it away. He would not be his father's son, no matter what the plans of the fallen House of Flame.

Behind the dream of *bahdur,* there had lain another appeal, but he had not seen anything but the shadow of it, and that too, he had pushed away, denied. Fever dreams, he thought, when he woke. Nothing more than fever dreams attempting to strike at his very soul.

His teeth chattered until he clenched them shut successfully. He'd kicked his rags off, and took a moment to rewrap himself, just long enough to grow warm. He would have to dig now, and dig until he either dropped or freed himself. He'd lost too much body warmth and water. He could not afford to sleep again.

The orange glow of the lantern had grown even weaker. He found the chair back and began to shovel again. Within minutes, his muscles burned in protest, and his joints ached, and his chest hurt, and his mouth was dry enough to be filled with sand. Palaton set his jaw and bent to the work. He would not die here, although perhaps it would be easier and better. But his *bahdur* lay in Rand who was unaware of its horrific potential. It was his burden, and Palaton knew that he had to take the ultimate responsibility for it. He would not let the mountain take that away from him.

He'd been spooning until everything had gone numb except for a fiery band across his chest as even his heart had begun to protest, when the quality of the snow began to change. Drier, crisper, infinitely colder—Palaton did not understand it until he realized he was reaching the surface, which had begun to ice up with the dropping temperature of the coming night. The knowledge that he was close to breaking through, as well as being iced in if he tried to stay, spurred him.

He ate two or three mouthfuls of snow in an attempt to quench his thirst. Then he renewed his attack. He thrust himself into the snowpack giving all he had with every shovelful and then, suddenly, the snow gave way. He slid head and shoulders into the open.

A last, fiery glimpse of the sun over the crests of the mountains struck him in the face, dazzling, even as it threw long, blue shadows across the snowfields. For a second, he knew why his father had liked to paint here, and what it was he must have seen. It was an epiphany, a connection with a parent he had never known, he had never thought he could know. Palaton stood, stunned, surrounded by the snow, until his violent shivering woke him up. He looked back into the cave. The lantern went out with a last, amber shimmer.

"You're right," Palaton said, and his voices surprised him, dry, husky rasps. "There's no place to go but forward." He took a deep breath and pushed himself all the way through, out onto the slope.

The force of his movement took him over the edge, plowing across ice-edged drifts, out of control. He came to a stop, breath sobbing in his lungs, against a tree which had held against the push of snow. Down below were the foundation walls of the ruins, and he knew he would have gone over, to his death, if the evergreen had not held so stubbornly. He found his feet. The drifts had thinned here, to waist high, only about four feet or so, and he could push through them, as long as he kept moving. Angling sideways against the mountain, he shoved forward.

Jorana shaded her eyes, casting more with soulfire than with the limited visibility. Blue shadows had gone to purple. The rope harness chafed her lightly even through her winter jacket's padding. Rufeen had let go long ago, the few hundred feet of the rope more than played out, and it trailed limply behind her, no good to anyone unless she, too, were caught in an avalanche, and then it might flag her unless buried also. She was too tired to recoil the rope over her shoulder. She edged sideways, the snowshoes gaining good purchase on the rapidly icing crust, and saw nothing, felt nothing. Even unconscious, the *bahdur* should have smoldered, banked, a reserve which would answer hers. Only death or burnout could have silenced it.

The Prophet had been wrong if Palaton were dead out here. There were not two emperors on Cho, and would not be. No choice had come to Jorana, and she reflected bitterly that she would give anything if the forecaster had foreseen correctly. Anything for there to have been a choice to be made.

Resolutely, she started up again, determined not to stop until exhausted or the black curtain of nightfall turned her back. The glimmer of dusk hung overhead, and she could still see her way.

She heard the sound before she saw the form, the harsh, rasping breathing. Jorana looked up, up, and saw a darkened form coming downslope, across the angle, not fifty feet above her.

"Palaton!" she cried and it was as if the mountain shook to hear her, for the snow, began to shift and the form went down, sliding. Jorana leaped back, found a boulder face, and clung to it. The slide flowed past in a churning of ice and crystals and when it stopped, she looked up, and saw that he survived, through he lay facedown, unmoving. It had even brought him closer into her reach.

Jorana snapped on the remote and cried into it, "Rufeen, I've got him. Get a hover sledge warmed up. I can get him back that far." She ended transmission before Rufeen could do any more than let out a startled gust of sound.

She scrambled upslope, going to her knees beside him. His lips had gone blue and his jaw chattered helplessly, as she turned him over and cradled him onto her lap. Hypothermia threatened him as abruptly as any assassin.

She pulled her hands out of her gloves and jammed his into them, uncaring of where fingers went, anything so long as they warmed. She placed her palms over his face, feeling the icy chill of his skin. He was found, but nearly too late, and she didn't know if she could save him. She reached for his soulfire, to warm it with hers, to keep him going, and found him empty.

Jorana snatched her hands back in shock. Her thoughts went blank. Then she tried to reach him again, and knew that she was right. He was as empty as a well gone dry.

Palaton groaned. His eyelids fluttered and then opened. That drew her over him again.

"Work with me," she urged. "I can't do this alone. We need to lift down to the hover sledge."

His head moved imperceptibly. "No . . . power," he husked.

"I can't do it alone!" Her voices rose in panic, and Jorana heard herself and buried her hands in the collar of his inadequate jacket. "Palaton, wake up. Come back to me," she called as his eyes rolled back again.

Visibly, he made a tremendous effort to refocus his consciousness. Jorana put her arms around him, channeled her *bahdur* as narrowly as she ever had, concentrated on a lift, bringing their bodies off the snow. They barely cleared the surface, and she could feel the drain, it was like drowning with a two-ton boulder on her chest, trying to pull her down, trying to keep her from swimming to the surface.

She could feel his body's shivers within her embrace as they grew weaker and weaker. "Don't do this to me," she begged. She broke concentration long enough to search again for his inner spark, to hold onto it before it threatened to extinguish altogether.

But she hadn't been mistaken. He was empty of *bahdur,* gutted of it, as devoid as a commons. There was nothing for her to hold onto if he started to slip away. Hot tears began to flood down her face. She was going to lose him, if not here, now, then when Panshinea returned and found his heir helpless. The night air turned the drops chill before they could fall.

"Damn you," she said to him. "You leave me nothing."

Rufeen had the hover sledge ready and she slipped the unconscious Palaton onto it, fatigue apparent in every limb. Her horn crown ached with the effort she'd pulled out of herself and she collapsed beside him. She lay close as the pilot threw heated blankets over both of them.

"To the village?"

"To the hells with them," Jorana said bitterly. "Take us back aboard ship." Then she laid her pounding head down, and felt the small ferry shudder into the air.

By the time they drew near the plateau, Palaton had stopped shivering. He rallied enough to say, "Jorana?" and draw her closer to him. She lay still, wondering if he would live or die and which would be better for him.

Without *bahdur,* he could never withstand Panshinea's return. He would have no future, either as an heir or as a *tezar,* and she asked herself when it could have happened, how she could not have read the signs. Surely protecting the humankind could not have burned him into nothingness?

Rufeen brought the hover sledge to a stop. Jorana got out and let the pilot load Palaton into the plane. She followed, her hands pushed deep into her pockets against the cold, her shoulders bowed in thought.

Palaton was awake when she entered. Rufeen grinned and said, "I have piloting to do," and disappeared up front into the cockpit.

Jorana closed off the corridor between the areas, drew up the door and secured it as the plane vibrated into warm-up. She returned to him, tucking in reheated blankets and he caught one of her hands and held it tightly.

She could not keep the sorrow from her voices as she asked, "Why didn't you tell me? Why couldn't you tell me you'd lost it? Or was it Rand? Did he strip it from you?"

Palaton let go of her hand. "Not Rand. He . . . helps." His lips had regained their color as his body returned to normal, but every once in a while, his body threw off a convulsive shiver. He struggled through one now before he said, "No one knows. Not even Rindy."

"Panshinea?"

"Him, least of all."

She looked at his eyes, eyes of brown and gold, more gold than any other. He had not told her, but she knew that Rand knew. He'd known about Rindalan's *bahdur* when he'd come out of the coma. She'd not asked questions then. She wished now that she had, that she had not let trust blind her. "How could I not have seen it? Any of us?"

"You saw what you expected to see, I hope." He managed to sit up and reached for her.

She went stiff, then forced herself to relax as he embraced her. He smoothed back her hair. "I couldn't tell you. You know that. You work for the throne. I couldn't command your loyalty."

"You're going to go back, as if this had never happened?"

His lips curved slightly. "I'll try."

"You can't do it. Panshinea is coming back."

He held her away a little so he could read her face. "What?"

"Rioting broke out again in Bayalak. It's like a flashfire.

We could erupt all over again. Pan gave notice he was returning as soon as he settles affairs on Sorrow. You can't face him without *bahdur*."

Palaton pulled his blanket closer about his shoulders. "Why didn't Rand come with you?"

"He's missing. He left the palace yesterday morning and I haven't been able to find a trace of him. We think Chirek took him—"

"Who?"

"He's a clerk in Gathon's ministry. But why he would take Rand . . . I don't know."

"Malahki," said Palaton explosively.

"No. At least, I don't think so. I keep fairly good tabs on Malahki's movements. No. Someone else may be planning to use him as a hostage, but it wasn't Malahki."

"Have you heard anything?"

"No. The only rumors flying are the ones out of Bayalak. There's a Choya'i, a powerful forecaster, but she came out of nowhere. No one had heard of her before, then all of a sudden, she was there."

"We have to find Rand."

"I'm trying."

Palaton shivered again, losing half his blankets. Jorana felt a stab through her heart for him. She rewrapped him, knowing that he would never survive what Panshinea would do to him. She would lose him yet.

Quietly, she came to a decision. She stood. "Let me fix you something warm to drink." She walked past him to the galley, slipping her hand into her pocket, where the *ruhl* lay waiting.

If she could not have him, if she could not keep him, then at least she would have his child.

Briskly, efficiently, she took down a bottle of wine and honey and spices, and began to warm two goblets, mulling them, until the aroma filled the cabin. She returned to him, pressed the mulled wine into his hand and leaned forward. "When you're finished with this, let me massage those knots out, and get you into some warmer clothes. Then we'll decide what to do about Rand and Panshinea."

He took the wine and drank deeply.

Chapter 28

The heat of the Bayalakan swamps permeated everything, even dreams. It stole the restfulness from them, leaving them limp and tired upon waking. Chirek would dream and rouse, then lapse back again, trying to find some kind of personal peace.

Blood on your hands, three times over. Do not let it spill into the streets, or all is lost. Chirek came awake with a start yet again. The craft rocked under his movement. The light scarf he'd folded over his face to protect it from the sun and bugs wafted into the air and went overboard, where it lay like a fallen leaf on the water before swirling away.

Blood on his hands. Chirek lifted them and looked at them as if he could see it. First, Dorea's. Then Seli's. He carried that onus, he had to, but he could not bear the thought that he might be responsible for yet another tragedy. Who else might be in harm's way? His thoughts led his gaze to Rand, and he shuddered. The humankind had slowed the vessel and now stood at the wheel, weaving the boat in and out of the root caves and massive tunnel branches like threading a needle.

Panet so thickened the air that Chirek could hardly breathe. He rolled on his side and sat up, head throbbing. Dorea still sat in tranquil repose in the bow, every now and then suggesting a turn to Rand with an acuity that indicated she *saw,* despite her blindness. She was bringing them back to Bayalak, even Chirek could sense that, as turned about as he was. The increasing smell of smoke was beginning to cut through the panet. Beyond Bayalak lay the open sea. Was she taking them to escape or back into the jaws of their enemy?

And whose blood must he fear for?

The boat slewed around in the water to a sudden halt. Rand said something pungent. Chirek did not understand the alien words, but could guess the meaning as the other leaned over the bow and poled away from a root. Chirek looked over as well and saw the mottled brown face of a lily-eater watching them from the shadowed water. It flipped its body over sleekly and slid away as the boat came free and the motor churned noisily again.

"If we get caught in here at night," Rand said, "we're done for. I won't be able to see well enough to get through, with Dorea or not."

The Prophet broke her repose, turning her face slightly toward Rand. "I don't think we need to worry about that," she remarked, and pointed off across the torpid waters of the swamp.

From out of the myriad pathways, around islands of root and bark, a raftlike craft glided toward them, ably propelled by its Choya rider, pole in hands. Rand slowed the boat to idle and let the Choya approach.

He was obviously a God-blind, his horn crown coarse and heavy, curled at the edges, even covered with a fungus that looked like gray-green moss along the tips. His clothes bagged, thin and stained by swamp water. But he smiled as he poled the raft to them, and leaned forward, holding his hand out to Rand, the alien, without fear.

"Bringer," he breathed, with reverence.

Rand reached out in answer without hesitation, clasping hands with the boatman. Chirek could see the tiniest of blue auras sparking when they met. He flinched at the sight, knowing what Rand had done. His reaction surprised him. Wasn't this what he had wanted? Wasn't this what he had dedicated his life to, paving the way for the Bringer of the Change to all of them?

The Choya let go with a stifled cry, joy transforming his rough features and he shook his head, braided mane flapping about his shoulders. He let go a second shout, and tree branches waved in answer as birds took flight from them, and water splashed as lily-eaters dove in surprise. His chest heaved as he fought for composure. "Follow me," he begged. "Please." He maneuvered the raft about.

Rand looked over his shoulder at Chirek. "Well?"

He could not have answered no. He lifted a shoulder. "What else can you do?"

Their boat purred smoothly after the boatman, at scarcely faster than idling speed, Rand leaning carefully upon the throttle. The waterways began to open up, the claustrophobic tunnels giving way to patches of blue sky. The tree groves began to straighten, their canopies no longer obscuring the expanse. As great a relief as that was, Chirek knew it must bother Rand because the manling started looking overhead from time to time, as if tracking the enemy, whoever and wherever they might be.

In his heart, Chirek could not believe it to be Qativar, but his mind coolly argued otherwise. He might never know the whys and wherefores. The only reasoning he could accept was that the Housed Prelate had retreated to old precepts, the inferiority of the commons, the God-blind, the street Choyan, despised and facing betrayal as their innate lot in life. He knew that could not be the whole of it, but perhaps it was the kernel which had given birth to the rest. He had never entirely trusted Qativar, but he did not feel vindicated. He wished now that he had confided everything in Malahki, even his suspicions about Rand's ability. If he had, they might not now be in the situation they were. Malahki's resources were vast.

"Chirek," Rand called gently.

The priest, alerted from his thoughts, looked out. Along the waterways, he could see objects skimming the water toward them. Floats, rafts, boats, anything that could navigate. The swamp filled with Choyan. He rose carefully to his feet, bracing himself on the rim of the boat to scan their faces, but he saw nothing troubling on any of them. They slid across the still, warm waters of the bayou, and let Rand pass, then fell in behind. Occasionally one of them would lean precariously over his or her craft and put a hand out in appeal. Rand answered with his touch, and they would cry out and fall back with the shock of that contact, but never did they protest. Some of the larger craft were crowded, carrying whole families. They would cradle the transformed member within their midst, faces streaming with tears.

"Tell me," said Dorea to Chirek. "Tell me everything."

The Prophet laughed as Chirek described the scene to her, the sound gentle and uplifting, reminding him of the Choya'i before her Change. She leaned forward to Rand, saying, "They heard your call."

"But I didn't—" Rand stopped his protest. His face paled.

"Didn't you?"

He looked at Chirek. "I called for Palaton," he answered. His hand moved on the throttle, bringing the boat down to an even slower pace as the bayou channels grew crowded.

"You called for help," corrected Dorea. "And they came."

Chirek sat down, the boat rocking as the wakes of other vessels stirred the waters. He thoughtfully folded his arms across his chest.

A smaller version of their own boat drew close. A Choya leaned out. "Father Chirek?"

"Yes?"

The Choya grinned widely, a young, brash male, scarcely out of the clothes of a child. "Malahki sent us."

"Malahki!" His own prayers answered! "Where?"

"In Bayalak. Or what's left of it. The old port is burning like tinder. He's secured the airstrip, the port, and most of the new town. He says he can protect you. And he wants me to tell you that he's underestimated you again." The Choya's grin flashed hugely, taking some of the sting from his words.

Rand had overheard. "How far?" he called out.

"About an hour. You'll smell the fires."

The smoke had never really left them, but Chirek did not correct the youngling. He said gratefully, "Tell him we're coming."

The boat circled about, instead of joining the flotilla, and shot forward through the growing procession, pinpointing its openings and taking them with a daring that threatened to engulf more than one raft, before disappearing beyond a bend of overgrowth.

"Malahki," repeated Chirek disbelievingly.

"Did you doubt?" the Prophet asked softly.

"Yes," the priest answered. "Yes, I did."

*   *   *

Dreams of tropical waters, with leaning trees and trailing mosses, invaded his fitful slumber, brushing away earlier dreams of ice and snow and darkness. Palaton woke, warm at last, soothed and invigorated, the effects of exhaustion gone but for aching muscles. Despite Jorana's tender care, he would hurt for days. As for the rest of her ministration, he would remember their lovemaking as long as he lived, ardor fired as much by care as passion. He had not thought he would live to make love with her again. She had risen to his lust, matched, and surpassed it. He had not know it could be so exquisite without the enhancement of *bahdur*.

He moved carefully off the couch when he sat up, because she slept in the chair opposite, her head back, hair still tousled from his caresses. He folded the blankets and stowed them. His flight suit fit poorly, too wide and too short on him, one of Rufeen's issue, but he had no complaints.

Jorana had not asked him what he'd found in Maerlon, and for that, too, he was grateful. He was not sure himself what to think, now that the first shock was wearing off. The proclivities of the House of Flame were either not as dominant in him as Aeliar had hoped, or his training had subdued them. The disciplines of a *tezar* had molded his life perhaps even beyond his knowing. But the potential was there, would always be there. Would it be enough to be forewarned, to have caution? He had no way of knowing without taking his powers back from Rand, and he had no idea how to accomplish that.

What had the luminary of Maerlon said to him? If he didn't have the courage to take what was his, no one could help him? Was it only the conviction he lacked, or had the elder merely been spouting platitudes of encouragement?

Jorana must have heard him rustling about the cabin. She lifted her head, smiling shyly. "Feel better?"

"Infinitely."

"Good. I need to get back to business. I want an ETA from Rufeen." Belying her words, Jorana stood and stretched languidly for a moment, then dodged past Palaton as if knowing the response she ignited in him. She opened the doorway to the pilot's cabin.

Rufeen swung around, backlit by the glow from the control panel. "You two awake? Good, because I've got news. I've found Rand."

"Where?"

"In Bayalak."

Palaton's thoughts swung back to his waking dreams of sultry swamps. "Safe?"

"Malahki has him. He sent you a transmission about half an hour ago."

Fury flared up. He slammed his fist into the side of the fuselage. The sting in his knuckles did not even slow him down. "That explains the rioting! Damn Malahki's hide. He doesn't care who he expends. He flexes his muscle to show us the streets are his any time he cares to take them. I should have brought him down when I had the chance. We had an agreement!"

"You don't know what happened down there."

"Don't I? I want Rand pulled out of there, now. Change course, Rufeen, and use a military offensive if necessary. Don't let Malahki tell you you can't land."

"Yes, sir!" Rufeen saluted. She swung back around to her instruments.

Jorana looked upset. She reached out. "What are you trying to do?"

Save Rand, save himself. And others. "Lives," he said, "are at stake. When Panshinea comes in, he won't sit down and negotiate with the commons. He'll arrest and execute. You know that as well as I do, and he'll do it as much because they backed me earlier, as for civil disobedience now. He'll have to, if he wants to regain the support of the Houses. There will be no revolution for the God-blind."

"Even Pan couldn't be that ruthless." Jorana sounded as if she did not believe her own words.

The skimcraft tilted, dipping a wing as it changed course. Palaton could still feel the anger surging through him. "I'm going up front," he said.

She did not respond.

The airstrip had been lit in the growing dusk. Palaton could not see signs of devastation at the port, though outlying areas still smoldered orange-red at night's edge. Even before Jorana kicked the hatch open, they could smell the burning. The air lay thick and heavy with heat, panet fragrance lacing the oppressive stench of smoke. Palaton paused in the bulkhead.

Malahki, his massive frame towering over the Bayalakan Choyan who accompanied him, looked as though he'd been in a fight. A bandage was wrapped about his right forearm, and he was wearing chest armor that had taken more than one hit. Palaton also took note that one of the Bayalakans who accompanied him wore county guard insignia.

He stepped out of the plane. They met halfway on the tarmac.

"Where's Rand?"

"Actually," responded Malahki, his sketched greeting ignored, "I don't have him yet. He's being brought in."

"Brought in? From where?"

"The swamps. Come with me to the south docks. He should be here any moment." Malahki's steady gaze left Palaton momentarily, looking past him to Jorana, but the Choya'i brushed by him without returning it. He pursed his lips. "Rough day?"

"For both of us, from the looks of it." Palaton let his longer legs set a pace that the other had to work to keep up with as they strode to the conveyances idling in wait for them. "How much of this city lies in your hands?"

Malahki laughed heavily. "Not my hands, Palaton, not mine. I think you'll be surprised to see who the conqueror is." He returned his forearm to the sling lying empty upon his flank, and swung one-handed aboard the conveyance, a large flat car, open to the tropic air. Jorana entered without a word.

Palaton settled himself inside. "Are you telling me you didn't start this?"

"Not I, but it's a good thing I was here to finish it. Although," and Malahki's jaw bulged a little as he added grimly, "it isn't quiet yet. It may never be quiet again."

"Don't give me riddles," Palaton returned, refusing to look at him longer, instead staring out the conveyance at signs of damage as they edged away from the terminal. Rather than wholesale looting as Charolon and most of the other major cities had suffered months ago during the first commons' rioting, it looked as if there had been street fighting here. Barriers were strewn across streets, and there were signs of enforcer fire and shelling. "What happened here?"

"This quarter of Bayalak was attacked, and it fought back." Malahki shifted around a bit as if uncomfortable, then finally settled into the seat cushions. "I won't tell you more until we pick up Rand and Chirek."

Jorana swung to face him. Her expression stayed bland, but her eyes had sharpened. "Chirek?"

"Yes."

"He still has the manling? I thought you communicated that you had him."

"Actually, I think it's more a question of Rand having us." Malahki leaned back with a thin smile, refusing to say anything more.

Jorana's expression smoldered a bit before she subsided sullenly.

Palaton watched the shoreline, lit as the airstrip had been. There were lanterns of every imaginable shape lining the quays and shore. As their conveyance whined to a stop and settled to the ground, Palaton got out to survey the growing crowd.

As a *tezar*, he'd grown used to attention and adulation, but this unnerved him. He could not understand what they were waiting for with such quiet expectation, looking not to him or even Malahki, but to the water. They were there, filling every available space along the docks, except for a channel Malahki's men made for them by literally forming a wall of flesh as they saw him descend from the vehicle. Malahki motioned for them to join him. They walked down the uneasy corridor, jostled from time to time as the press of flesh grew too great. Malahki hissed in pain once as his arm was hit, but his men held the avenue well enough as they went to the end of the quay.

"Look carefully," Malahki warned. "The world we know is changing today." His voices vibrated with pride.

He pointed off the quay, to where the swamp waters mingled with the seashore. Out of the trees and moss-roped channels, a convoy bobbed into sight. Anything that could, floated. There were lights on the water as a procession boated toward them.

The flotilla was hung with lanterns of its own, golden harvest moons reflecting on the night-black water. They dipped and wove as poles propelled the rafts forward, as oars skimmed, as engines churned, depending on the type of craft.

Jorana stirred. "There they are. At the fore."

Palaton craned his neck anxiously to see. He spotted Rand at the wheel, guiding his vessel into the harbor area, features indistinct across the water, but clearly the humankind. "Who's that with him?"

Jorana answered before Malahki. "Chirek. And the Choya'i known as the Prophet."

He saw the swathe of white about her head. "She's been injured."

"No," replied Malahki. "She did that to herself."

He did not know what to think, or expect. He watched Malahki as if sorting out the truth, then looked back toward Rand. Already he could feel the *bahdur* reaching out to him, the bond that connected them strengthening. Just as he knew that was Rand approaching, Rand must sense him among the crowd.

The Choyan began to call out, words he could not distinguish, even as Rand cut the boat's power. He tossed a line to a rafter to be towed into the dock, water slurping at the sides of the vessel.

"What's that they're shouting?" Jorana asked faintly.

"I'falan," Malahki told her. "The Bringer."

Hunger for his *bahdur* almost obscured what was happening around Palaton. He heard Malahki but faintly. The crowd animated suddenly, and their fervor worried him. He wanted Rand safe and out of there, before whatever revolution it was Malahki wanted stirred up could flare again. The dock, built for freighters, towered over the boat as Rand bumped it close. The manling stared up at Palaton, then reached out to grasp the crude, wooden ladder nailed at the quay's end.

"Palaton!" Sweat and moss streaked his pale face, but he grinned in welcome, and his turquoise eyes, those remarkable eyes in the face of an alien, lit up. Palaton could feel an answering swell inside of him.

Malahki stooped awkwardly to offer a hand, but a youth dodged in first. He put his hand out, shaking.

"I'falan," the youth cried.

Rand smiled and, instead of climbing the ladder, took the other's fingers. There was a moment Palaton could feel as if he himself pressed the flesh, a flash, a singe of *bahdur* so sharp it made him gasp. The young Choya cried in exultation and fell back. Others caught his body and bore him away as Palaton stared in astonishment. They buffeted him as they passed, and he stood stunned, trying to identify what it was he had felt.

Jorana shouldered up beside Malahki as the press became almost unbearable. The dock creaked with the weight of those standing on it. "What's happening?"

Palaton felt his chest and stomach grow tight. He could not have imagined the brief blue aura which had encircled the clasped hands. He could taste the soulfire on the air, as acrid as the prevading smoke and ashes. It tasted of hope, and fear.

Rand ignored the hands now grasping at him and climbed to the pier. He stood, turned about to hand up Chirek and the wounded Choya'i, her eyes bound. Jorana reached for the Prophet, shielding her from the jostling which had intensified. Malahki pushed his way through and put his hand out.

An odd look passed over Rand's begrimed face. Then he gave a lopsided smile, and began to reach back.

Palaton could sense, could see, the beginning of an arc. He did not understand what was happening here, and it shook him to his core. "No!" Lunging forward, he knocked Rand's hand aside, battling the unknown.

The crowd gasped with shock. Palaton found himself facing hostility on every face.

Malahki drew himself up gravely to stare him in the eyes. "Surely you, Palaton, of all Choyan, cannot deny me this."

Hunger for his *bahdur* sweeping him, ruling him as though he were starving, his thoughts churning, Palaton knew that he did not understand what was happening. Malahki had spoken of their world changing, and he knew now that Rand was at the crux of it. He faced him. "What's going on?"

The third Choya, the one Jorana had known as Chirek, had been standing quietly behind the others, his back to the water. He came forward now, carrying a presence that Palaton knew well, a presence Rindalan had often carried. As their gazes met, he knew that Chirek recognized him, as he recognized something in Chirek. The Choya gave him a comforting smile. "Let me explain, if I can. A time has

come that I never thought to see in my lifetime. Heir Palaton, I'm a priest of the Prophecy of Change. The Bringer
has come to us, and that Bringer is Rand."

Before the import could sink in, Jorana hissed, "Heresy,"
and the Prophet flinched in her arms. She twisted about,
turning her blinded face to Jorana, speaking. "You asked
for my words before. Did you not care what it was that
transformed me, that burned through me, that shaped me
as a vessel for those words?"

Jorana's jaw tightened. Uncompromisingly, she answered, "*Bahdur,* pure and simple."

"For you, perhaps," countered Chirek. "But not for the
majority of us, until now. He brings the Change, and with
it *bahdur* to any Choya with the courage to ask for it."

Suddenly understanding, Palaton grabbed for Rand. With
the manling in his hold, he began to strong-arm his way
through the crowd. Chirek's voices rose after them, pro-
claiming, "The day when all Choyan shall have *bahdur* is
come, and no one shall be denied who is here!"

Rand spoke. "Palaton—"

"Keep moving." He could feel Rand's reluctance in
every fiber of his hold on the other. Just under the flesh,
he thought he could also feel his *bahdur* answering to him,
in turmoil, igniting, and he feared it.

The manling whispered hoarsely, "Don't do this. These
are your people."

Palaton would not listen. The corridor Malahki's men
had held open by sheer brute strength began to collapse
around them. At his heels, Jorana said, "Go, go!"

The cries of "I'falan!" changed into protests and hoarse
shouts and threats. Hope mutated into anger. He could feel
the wall rise against him, his own people hating him, what
he was taking from them. He knew now why the streets
had been barricaded for war, and who fought. The Housed
against the commons, those with power against those who'd
always coveted it. His world was shattering before his very
eyes, and Rand had been drawn into the conflict.

Using his *bahdur,* his cursed talent from the cursed
House of Flame.

He shoved Rand free of the crowd. With a jump, they
gained the hovercar. Jorana sprang to the driver's seat. She
pounded on the control paned, shutting the doors just

ahead of Malahki and Chirek. Under Jorana's handling, the conveyance put on a burst of speed, and spurted into movement. Palaton saw Malahki turn away, but knew they were not safe yet.

Rand said urgently, "You don't understand—"

"No," he erupted. "*You* don't. You're tearing my world apart. We're on the precipice of civil war, an abyss that will swallow us."

"Things have to change—"

"Things can't change, not this way, not now, or did you learn nothing from the Two Day War? Strength is the only key to our survival."

Rand settled onto a seat. He looked out. "They'll just follow."

Even as he spoke, Palaton could see another conveyance surge away from the crowds and docks. It swerved down a side street.

"Jorana—"

"I saw it," she said tightly. She urged the hovercar to its maximum speed. She focused on keeping the conveyance clear of the obstacles on the streets, weaving back and forth among the barriers and damage.

Rand wiped his face down, trying to clean it on his tattered sleeve.

Palaton found himself trying to deal with emotions he wasn't entirely sure of. Words spilled from him. "What were you thinking of?"

Rand looked at Palaton. "What were you? Why should I deny them their legacy? They were dying in the gutters for it. Their religion's been underground for nearly three hundred years because you guys didn't want to hear about it anymore. I didn't ask for this. I didn't ask to be the Bringer, but I am." He held out his hands in front of him, battered and scarred as though he'd been bare-knuckle fighting. "You're going to have to accept it."

No, he wasn't. Whatever Rand was, whatever he did, it had been with Palaton's power. Didn't the manling understand that there was no limitless reservoir, that when the *bahdur* burned out, it was gone forever? Or did he simply not care, caught up in zealot fervor? Palaton shook his head. "No. This goes no further. I'm taking you back to Charolon. Home, if I can get you off-planet."

"It won't matter." Rand looked out the side of the vehicle, and Palaton followed his line of sight. He could see the Choyan, not a crowd but a following, react as they passed. He could hear their voices faintly under the whine of the conveyance's engines.

Jorana took out her remote. Her tone was brusque and clear. "Rufeen, fire up and keep her ready. We're leaving in a big hurry."

"Again?" responded the pilot's hale voices. "We live in exciting times!"

Jorana put them down at the edge of the tarmac, but Choyan spilled in there as well. As Palaton got Rand out of the vehicle, he saw the other hovercar at the airstrip edge. Chirek and Malahki blocked the boarding ramp to the skimcraft. He had no time to wonder how they'd beaten them to the port.

He put a hand out to Jorana. "Give me your enforcer."

"No. I'm the better shot, and I'll use it without hesitation." She smiled thinly. "You think too much." She withdrew the weapon from her holster.

The Bayalakans pulled back as she stepped out, drawing a bead. The hard looked on her face opened up an avenue that they took to the boarding ramp where Chirek stepped forward, brave beyond his trembling and pallor.

"Don't do this," he begged of Palaton. "You can't take him away."

"If there's any denial here, it's yours," Palaton fired back. "Are you blind? Look what you're doing to Cho. He is an alien among us. He doesn't know what this means, but you do. I can't let it go on. Move aside." Palaton steeled his hand firmly about Rand's arm, felt the muscles and nerves quiver slightly inside his hold.

Chirek hesitated. Malahki, behind him, did not. Saying only, "I'falan," he moved forward. He went to one knee in supplication.

Rand twisted away sharply. Palaton lost hold of him, surprised at the manling's sudden strength. Malahki reached for him. Their hands touched before he could be stopped, and Rand lifted Malahki to his feet.

Palaton lunged at them, knocking Malahki aside. He put his shoulder into Rand's stomach, bodily hoisting him over his shoulder, and broke into a run up the boarding ramp as

Rufeen opened the hatch. Palaton tossed Rand inside and Rufeen bent over him as he landed sprawling at her feet,

With a roar, the crowd launched itself on Palaton, engulfing him. Chirek stood frozen by horror, speechless, but Jorana charged through shouting, "Move it! Or I'll shoot!" She pointed the barrel at Malahki's forehead.

He froze as if nailed to the tarmac. Their eyes leveled, held one another.

Chirek found words. He tried to shield Palaton with his own battered body, crying, "Not this way!" His voices gathered timbre and cut through the growing fury of the mob. He staggered back from a kick and threw a forearm up to catch a body blow. He clawed Palaton free and covered him as they backed to the ramp.

Malahki began to raise a hand, but Jorana warned, "I do mean it."

He dropped his hand.

Palaton, shaken, backed up the ramp. Jorana chanced a look over her shoulder, saw his movement, and began to edge back as well.

"You can't get all of us," a Choya shouted at her.

She did not blink. "I don't need to," she said steadily, watching Malahki. "All I have to do is hit one."

He twitched again, this time with a hand signal for quiet. The barrel of the gun never wavered, even when Jorana hit the ramp's edge and found it lifting under her feet.

She turned and sprinted up the closing ramp.

Rufeen had dragged Rand inside, but he was up, jaw set and face flushed with anger, as Palaton pulled Jorana through the hatch. She dropped the enforcer and locked the bulkhead behind her. Rand looked at the weapon, then stepped back.

The plane vibrated as it taxied forward. He stepped to the view portal, looking down at the tarmac and the surging crowd of Choyan trying to give chase.

"I'll be back," he vowed softly and put his spread hands to the clear window. A faint, blue fire outlined them.

The assembly shouted in response to the display, answering as clearly as if he'd spoken to them.

"The Change will come whether you want it or not." He shouldered past Palaton and went to sit alone at the back of the plane.

Chapter 29

The noise of Bayalak was echoed in Charolon. Jorana's guard got them to the palace, but once they were within, the walls were surrounded. Palaton shut the windows of his apartments against the shouting, but he could not force it out entirely. Charolon had not gone up in flames a second time, but the heat, the fury, remained.

"How can you deny your own power?" Rand asked quietly from behind him.

Palaton swung about. "I never could have done that with my power! You've twisted it, subverted it—"

"Liberated it?" suggested Rand.

"No. And nothing good will come out of this day's work."

Rand went to the far end of the window, looking out on his own panorama. Beyond the palace walls, Choyan moved restlessly, their shadows darker than the night itself, but they could still be seen. "You don't know that."

"Don't I? I don't know what you think you were doing out there, but you weren't changing anyone. Malahki used you, elaborately, heedless of the cost of life, put you up in front of those Choyan who desperately need a miracle of some kind, any kind, to change their lot in life—"

"There was nothing fake about what I did! And Malahki didn't arrive until long after. You weren't there, you didn't see."

"I saw enough. And you're more naive than I thought if you don't realize any one of us can pull strings from a distance. He has his resources. He needs to mobilize his people, and he chose to do it through you." Palaton turned his back on Rand. He knew his soulfire, he knew now what it was capable of, and he knew in his heart that what he'd seen Rand do, what he'd heard about the Changes, meant what he feared most had come to pass. No one had been Changed, no one had been converted. They had been *possessed,* held in the grip of Rand's power, believing what he wanted so desperately to believe, the worst kind of mental rape done with the best of intentions. He had imprinted them with the *bahdur* so strongly that they truly believed they'd been transformed. It was the curse of the House of Flame, that and the ability to kill through the same cellular disruption as healing. He could not tell Rand that his genetic legacy made a monster of him, but neither could he let Rand keep believing that he was fulfilling a prophecy. That would be the worst heresy of all. But Rand would have none of it.

"You saw *nothing* and you understood even less. I thought I knew you, I thought we had this bond between us, I thought—" Rand's voice broke strangely, and he crashed to a halt.

"Then tell me."

"You would listen?"

"The bond is gone. In Maerlon, when I needed it, I never thought of using it. Perhaps I'm the one who destroyed it, by rejecting it. I don't know. But I won't willingly turn from you."

"Then you have to understand I didn't start the rioting in Bayalak, and neither did Malahki. It was Qativar."

"Qativar?"

"Yes. He's one of the supporters of Chirek's underground. Chirek doesn't know why he turned on them, but he came after us with the intent of killing us. The crowd—you have to understand, Palaton, that they waited for me, even when I slept, searched for us and when Qativar attacked, they went after him. We got out with our lives, all except for Seli." Rand swallowed as though it were difficult for him. "It happened so fast, it made no sense, but my *bahdur* was pinging and then the Prophet came into the room, telling us to run—we made it out two jumps ahead of the attack. And it was Qativar, no doubt of it. We got out of the neighborhoods and smuggled ourselves onto the airboat, but he came after us by skimcraft and fired on us. I took us into the swamps to lose him. I don't know what happened in the streets after we left. I suppose the guard came in and the commons fought whoever they had to."

Palaton tilted his head in skepticism. He knew little of Chirek and even less of the Choya who'd died. "Why would Qativar risk anything by attacking you, or revealing himself?"

"Why would Qativar lead Rindy into the riots? Who sent you to Maerlon?"

"I don't know who sent me to Maerlon, and we don't know what happened between Qativar and Rindalan in the riots. Qativar could have left him in the streets to die, but he didn't. He brought him back."

"Somebody poisoned Rindy."

"And again we don't know who. Or why. And even if I had enough evidence to suspect Qativar, it doesn't make him guilty of attacking you. Is it possible he was acting on Jorana's behalf, that he knew you'd been taken from the palace and was attempting to rescue you?"

Rand looked at him. Then he shook his head. "I know what I know;" he repeated stubbornly.

"Nedar worries me far more than some cleric."

"Clerics nearly killed us at Sethu."

Mixed emotions warred in Palaton. He no longer knew how to deal with this alien friend he'd brought to his world. If Rindy were there, perhaps the bridges could be rebuilt. He was alone in this. He relented enough to say, "It's my fault. Training takes years, and I abandoned you before we'd even begun. I knew you were spilling. I knew I should have done more then just warn you."

"It wouldn't have made any difference. It's something which has to be done, and I have a chance to make a difference."

"And if it was real, if you did Change anyone, how many millions do you think you can touch in the next twenty-four hours?"

Rand looked at him uncomprehendingly. "Millions? In a day?"

"That's how long you'll have to live when Panshinea returns. Maybe less. He doesn't suffer fools." Palaton shifted. "I won't be able to protect either one of us, let alone *them*," and he jerked his head toward the window, and the faint cries of the mob.

His next statement was interrupted by the alarm of an

incoming transmission. Rand moved out of focus of the view screen in case it was live, as Palaton sat down to answer it. he put his hand over the flatscreen, activating it.

The angry face of his emperor filled it. Panshinea, proud, arrogant, handsome, the colors of his Star heritage high in his face, his green eyes hard and his red-gold hair fairly sparkling, looked down at Palaton.

"I gave you a trust," the emperor said. "And you return me a shambles."

"What you left me had already began to crumble," he answered. "You hoped I might be able to contain what you couldn't." And he waited for the response.

Pan's eyes narrowed. "When I hit dirtside, you'll be re-scinded as my heir. I've already notified Congress. If the commons are in full-blown riot again, you had better find yourself a deep hole to hide in, because I will make you fully responsible. And the other had better be dead."

Without his naming Rand, Palaton knew exactly who he meant.

"I won't fight you for the throne, but I will fight you for the streets. I won't let you put out the fires with their own blood."

"I'll do whatever I have to," snarled Panshinea, and the transmission cut off.

Palaton sat, his hands growing cold, feeling defeated before he had even begun to fight. There was no one to bring to his side, not even the commons, unless he gave Rand back to them, and he couldn't do that, he couldn't bring his world to the brink of civil war. He keyed Jorana's comline.

The apartment rang empty, but a message came on, coded for him because it began transmitting as his ID came through. Jorana's recorded face looked shadowed with worry, and she did not quite meet the screen squarely. "I'm going," she said. "I know you won't understand, but it's what I have to do," and she signed off without another word or explanation. The screen showed him an emptied room, drawers still open, shelves stripped. She had already left.

Rand stirred. "She can't have gone far."

"It doesn't matter. She won't be found if she doesn't want to be." He sat there, mourning his loss. He had no

one to turn to, no sanctuary for himself and Rand. There
were few who would take them both in. Only one home
had he ever had, and that one—

Palaton reached out and keyed another comline. The
screen lit, and he faced a very sleepy Choya.

"I need a safe house," he said before the other could
protest the call. "I've lost the throne."

There was the briefest of pauses, and then Hat answered,
"Then you've got to come here. Blue Ridge will take you
in."

"Expect us," Palaton told him, then ended the call. He
turned to Rand. "Get ready to leave."

Hat turned as Nedar came off the couch at the far end
of the room, out of screen's range, leaving Alexa still curled
in sleep. The Earthan rubbed his eyes, commenting, "And
you were wondering how to lure him in."

"Straight to us," exulted Nedar. "He'll never know what
hit him. And when Panshinea returns, he'll be facing a
House like he's never faced before. We had the conviction.
Now we'll have the power."

Hat asked, "Who's going up?"

"I will," answered Nedar. "And I'll let the other wing
pilots know. Surprised or not, it won't be easy to take Palaton down." He paused, and put a hand on Hat's shoulder.
"Are you all right about this?"

The chunky Choya faced him squarely. "I might not
have been," he answered frankly, "but after what happened in Bayalak ... . the rumors, the lies. . . ." His voice
trailed off.

Nedar tightened his clasp in comfort. "I know," he said.
"I know what it must feel like." He added, "He won't
betray any of us again."

Hat stirred. "I'll start a brew going. We'll need it if we're
going to make plans."

Alexa did not leave the warm couch until Hat left the
room. Then she crossed the study. She wrapped her arms
about Nedar's waist. "Now what?" she asked, her voice
low and throaty with sleep.

"I call Vihtirne and let her know what's happening. She
won't be pleased at the hour, but I can't help that. I need
to be in the air just after dawn. Then all we need worry

about is how long it takes her to establish a supply route with your father for the capsules."

She looked troubled. "What if he didn't make it?"

"From the transmissions we picked up, the ship took only minor hits. Trust me. If the Abdreliks had wanted to bring him down, they would have."

"But—"

"No. Listen to me." The corner of Nedar's mouth pulled slightly. "It only means that until he makes dirtfall on Sorrow, we have to keep control of the drugs."

"We have them hidden. Don't you trust Vihtirne?"

"She will sacrifice whatever she has to, to get the throne of Cho. This way, she'll be motivated to establish negotiations with your father. Otherwise, she might take the risk of hoping to duplicate the drug on her own."

"If she has the throne, we have the House."

He kissed her brow. "Yes. Do you doubt me?"

"But Palaton stands in our way."

"Not for long."

"You're taking me up with you."

He paused, slipped around in her embrace, to watch her face. "I hadn't planned on it."

"I have the same taste for vengeance you do. I want Palaton, and then I want GNask."

He smoothed her short, vibrant hair from her eyes.

"Indeed you do," he agreed. "And who would I be to deny you?" He bent over to kiss the curve of her throat.

Gathon smuggled them out, through tunnels even Palaton did not know existed. He took them to a deserted street, where a jet sled waited. Palaton paused, looking at the aged minister, and then said, "You won't get in trouble for this?"

"How is Pan to know? Anyway, I've suffered through more of his tantrums than you have years." Gathon grimaced. "He can't run Charolon or Cho without me, and he knows it. This way I can tell Rindy I helped, or risk having him threaten to haunt me the rest of my life. Rindy frightens me more than Panshinea. Now go on, before the mob senses you're out here."

Rand looked at them. "They're already on the move," he commented in a subdued voice.

Gathon gave Palaton a light shove, moving them to the jet sled. Rand mounted the forward seat, Palaton at his back. The pilot kicked the vehicle into high speed, taking them rocketing away from the curb.

Rand gazed into the night, but what he saw into was himself and Palaton. Just as the Prophet had shown him, he was alone on Cho, condemned to his alienness through no fault of his own. Palaton had but one reason to save his life, and that was to protect his own *bahdur* against the future when he would be able to retrieve it.

And he would never have the courage to do with his soulfire what Rand had been doing.

The jet sled swerved. Palaton brought it around, down a deserted lane, and Rand recognized an airstrip outside of Charolon. A skimcraft lay waiting outside the hangars.

He stirred. "Rufeen?" he shouted into the wind, as it snatched his voice from him.

Palaton's voices buzzed near his ear. "No. I don't need power to pilot a skimcraft, and I don't want to involve her."

The jet sled came about again, settling on the edge of the airstrip. Rand dismounted.

"Let me go," he said, as Palaton opened the hatch and brought down the inside boarding ramp.

"What?"

"Malahki and Chirek will hide me."

The pilot's face closed, his eyes showing anger. "This is not an option."

"Perhaps it is for me."

"You're going with me if I tell you you are."

Rand shook his head slowly. "I'm the one carrying the power, Palaton, Don't make me use it on you."

"Would you Change me?" Palaton's voices got higher, sarcastic.

"I'll knock you on your ass if that's what it takes. But I don't think the commons are the ones who're God-blind. You are. You and all the Houseds who have some kind of ingrained idea that you're all superior. You treat subclass worlds in the Compact like you treat your own people There are layers, privileges, where there should only be opportunity. I belong out there, giving them back what's been taken from them."

"Panshinea will fry you up and have you for breakfast," Palaton shouted, and reached for Rand.

Rand put up an arm, and they hit, crossed like swords, staring into one another's souls, blue fire raging between them. It was Palaton's *bahdur,* he could taste it, sweet as honey and pungent as lightning. It crackled over them, enveloping them in a cage of discharging energy. Palaton ached for it. He reached out and hooked into it, taking it back.

Rand could feel it draining from him, and he gasped. Palaton felt it surging into him, and he accepted it, he needed it. More than that, he had to strip it from Rand, as one would a deadly weapon from a child who could destroy everything if he used it. No longer caring whether it was elixir or toxin, he drank it down. He took his power back, regardless of the genetic destiny pledged with it. He wanted it all, the bad with the good, because it was a part of him, and he could deny it no longer.

The *bahdur* flooded into him. He staggered back a step, charged with it, his head roaring with the power. His back arched with the shock. Rand let out a tiny sound and crumpled at his feet.

Palaton knelt beside him, felt the heart beating like a wild thing inside the manling's chest, picked him up and heaved him over his shoulder. He mounted the boarding ramp, a *tezar* again.

Rufeen felt the vibration as a skimcraft took off from the limits of Charolon. She paused in her work on her ship's mechanics, and let her power spin out to tell her who it might be. She caught the thin edge of Palaton's signature. She dropped her stylus, knowing that he must be leaving ahead of Panshinea's return.

Pilots were supposed to be neutral, to have loyalty only to their House and the Householding in which they'd been born, putting aside those loyalties for space and the patterns they wove and unwove to traverse it. But there were times, Rufeen told herself, when a Choya came along who commanded a greater loyalty, and this was surely one of them. She had no intention of letting Palaton go alone, his flank exposed.

She kicked aside her notepad, went up front, and set the engines to warming. In moments, she, too, was headed skyward, following the vapor trail of the other plane. The flight board rattled agitated warnings in her ear about unauthorized takeoffs until she finally shut off her comline and flew in silence. The world turned below them as they flew, keeping them at the edge of night for what seemed forever.

Chapter 30

Rand woke with his guts churning and his head on fire. Never had he felt so disconnected from his soul, or been in so much bodily pain. It was as if the two parts of him, spiritual and physical had been fissioned apart. He sat up, holding his skull.

Attacked by Palaton! The betrayal cleaved through him. He had nothing, and no one. A bereft feeling assailed him, doubling him over, sobs tearing his throat. He as lost.

The surface cradling him vibrated smoothly and it took a moment to place, to remember, his whereabouts on a skimcraft. He choked back the emotions tearing him inside out. He wiped his face and found, to his surprise, that it was dry, as though his eyes could no longer bear to shed tears.

He pulled aside a shutter and saw the sky and clouds, alight with all the fires of sunrise and dawn.

Out of habit, he reached for the *bahdur* inside of him, and felt a dizzying sense of vertigo. His mind slid one way and his body the other. There was nothing. He was raped, stripped, gutted. Rand immediately quit trying and subsided, holding his head and attempting to ignore the throbbing. But he knew then what Palaton had done to him. All they had been through had come to nothing. What would happen to him now? Choyan who had soulfire and lost it often went insane. They, who'd been disciplined from birth to use and renew their abilities, who wore a rigid facade of conduct . . . if they could be so affected by its loss, what lay ahead for him?

Had Palaton even cared?

All that the Prophet had seen for him had come to pass. The disaster, not the triumph.

Weakly, Rand put out a foot and tried to stand. He toppled to one knee.

The door to the cockpit was open.

"Rand? Are you all right?"

He would not answer. What did Palaton care now? He was useless to the pilot. He had nothing left in his guardianship, and the friendship between them had been stripped away. Ignoring the query, he clawed his way back onto his feet. He would not give the Choya the satisfaction of seeing him utterly defeated. As he stood, the shutter he'd opened flapped wide again, revealing the dawn.

Rand stared at it.

He saw the fighter wing coming at them out of the rising sun.

"Palaton!" he screamed in warning.

Palaton looked down at Blue Ridge, saw the plateau devoid of thrust gliders, no cadets warming up for training, saw the airstrip empty of skimmers, and then he heard the alarm tearing from Rand's throat. He turned his head even as his screens came on, warning of targeting on his flank. He put his weaponry system on automatic, as the grids came up.

He checked the winds and thermals, as well as topology, preparing to come in low under sensors, in evasive action. His newly won *bahdur* flared, filling him, steadying him.

"Blue Ridge, this is Palaton. Come in."

Nothing answered him on-line, but he thought he could hear the scream of fighters coming in. He brought the plane about, head on, remembering the plane which had engaged him once before, stolen from Blue Ridge. The comp system chattered at him, giving him a steady update of positions on the four planes.

Nedar, he thought. It had to be. The hatred which had lain smoldering between them could never be excised. Always his nemesis. And he'd involved Hat in it this time, up to his neck. What had he said, how could he have persuaded *tezar* to turn against *tezar*?

Using his voices in command, he yelled for Rand. "Get in here in and strap down."

Rand stumbled into the cockpit and half-sat, half-fell into the empty chair. "What is it?" He would not look at him.

"Ambush. And at four to one, it's one hell of a trap."

The targeting headset settled over his right eye with a whine of servos, and locked him in.

His first system came on-line and Palaton fired a burst. The warning shot went wide and he had little hope of bringing the plane down. He drew return fire, but he was already turning away, out of range.

Colors filled his screen. Red wing. He knew which one held Nedar, the point leader. Even if he hadn't been filled with *bahdur* again, he could tell by the style of flying.

"You clever bastard," Palaton murmured. He leaned on the stick abruptly, yawing, and in his wake, he could feel the bump of an explosive burst.

Rand hit the instrument board and Palaton snapped, "Belt yourself in if you're staying up front!"

The sight came loose. He pulled it back down, refastening it over one eye. The weapons system gave him another warning that he'd been targeted.

Palaton went up this time, pulling back on the stick and watching the plane go nose up, sluggishly, but quick enough to get him out of harm's way.

"What about heat missiles?"

"Don't use them. Don't have to, with *bahdur*."

Rand shakily buckled the safety web about himself. He looked at the screens. "We've got another player," he commented.

Someone came in on his flank from below. Palaton reached out with his senses, blue fire tinging his peripheral sight. He caught an image of Rufeen, hunkered down determinedly over her controls, thoughts scattered, but it was the Red wing she had in her sights. He drew the *bahdur* back in gratefully. She let out a burst that took out the cadet flagging in the rear of Nedar's formation. He went down with a scream of *bahdur* which seared them all.

Hat paused, nailed in his tracks, looking skyward when his student died. He had his hands full, guiding the younger cadets to the great hall, the eating hall, built as the center of the school hundreds of years ago, fortified against war and strife which had long since left the Choyan Houses. He heard Koar's scream as she died, then counted split seconds and heard the plane itself hit, and a rain of debris. He could smell the destruction.

The cadet nearest his outstretched hand began to cry. The sniffling brought Hathord back, and he put his fingers on the youngling's thick-maned crown. "Don't cry. You're safe here." He waved the others past as the youngling clung to him a moment, gulping back sobs. He patted the child.

"This," he said quietly, "is what it takes to form a new House, a House of *tezars,* a House where no one will ever again use us badly. You must be strong!"

And he gave the youth an encouraging squeeze before pushing him on into the safety of the building. He wondered where Vihtirne was, why she was late. Nedar had said she would come, backing them up. But where was she? After Blue wing, he had no more seasoned cadets to send up.

He looked toward the sky as the last of his younger charges ran past him into the hall. *Oh, Palaton, and Nedar. You are breaking my heart.*

He followed after his youths, afraid to his core that he had made a wrong decision, that his loyalty had been misplaced.

Palaton watched the impact. He circled, wagged a wing, and went on open channel. "Evening the odds, Nedar."

A dry chuckle came back. "I knew you would know it was me. Welcome back, Palaton."

He took the plane farther around even as he answered, "This is destructive. It hurts all of us."

"I don't care who else it hurts at the moment as long as it brings you down."

The plane bucked as it flew through a thin cloud of fire. "Nothing hit," reported Rand. His face looked sickened, and Palaton wondered briefly if he had heard the cadet's dying scream. Perhaps he was atuned enough that the cry had wrung him through as it had Palaton.

Rufeen said, "I'm on your tail, boss."

He could see her loosen a burst of chatter-fire at the cadets, who were falling behind Nedar, unable to keep up with his maneuvering.

"Thank you," answered Palaton. "I could use a little backup." The target grids gave him a shot. He studied it, reluctant to take down the inexperienced. He modified the grid. The comp system argued with him, reseting the coordinates. Palaton cursed.

Rand flinched in his chair. He swung about to face Palaton, who paid him no attention. The *tezar* keyed in manual override and took the shot he wanted. He fired, and another cadet went down, his craft letting off a thin, gray line of smoke as it spiraled downward. The craft wobbled desperately, then the cadet righted it.

"What are you doing?" asked Rand thinly.

"Grounding him." Palaton resumed automatic targeting. He broadcast, "Two to two, Nedar. I'm beginning to like the odds."

No answer. Palaton swung around in his chair, eyed the instruments. "Where is he!"

"He's off the screen," cried Rand.

Rufeen let out a muffled curse, and then she cried, "I'm hit. Damn all, here comes the Blue wing. Who's letting those babies up?"

"Forget them. Can you stay up?"

"No, boss, she's coming apart. I'm losing hydraulics."

"Can you take her down?"

"Don't have much choice! I can walk away from any landing, boss, but you—" and the comline fizzled into static, losing her reply.

A cold chill ran down the back of Palaton's neck.

Rand said, "He's right behind us."

Palaton already knew. He looked at his grids. The skimcraft wasn't as responsive as the fighters Nedar had brought up, but then, neither was it as old, nor had it been worked on by amateur mechanics like the green cadets at Blue Ridge.

Rand said softly, "She's down. Looks okay."

He received the news gratefully, but his comp system told him four more fighters were pulling within range. He yanked off his sight and looked at the instrument panel, getting a better read on how the four operated as a unit. They were sluggish and uneven in formation. What did Nedar think he was doing bringing such young fliers up with him? Or did he even care? "There's still time to end this, Nedar," he said smoothly as he thought out the possibilities.

Nedar growled in response. "I'm not finished until you're dead. And then, maybe, I can finally pick up my life and lead it."

"On the throne of Cho? It's a rough ride." He brought the plane on a hard rudder, Nedar staying with him, though the targeting system told him he was still in the clear, that Nedar hadn't managed to lock on yet.

"We have our own House now, Palaton. We *tezars*, the way it should be."

His words shot an icy bolt through Palaton. He said, "What about the concept of duty and service?" Below him flashed the fields, hangars, and buildings of Blue Ridge, the only real home he'd ever had.

"What about sacrifice?" Nedar flung back. Palaton watched in horror as the fighter craft turned, looping about, coming up behind Nedar's own Blue wing. The sky streaked red-orange, and then the craft went down, screaming, plumes of black and gray smoke and crimson flame. The world flamed.

His own *bahdur* screamed with theirs—the dying young. His eyes ached with the need to tear, and could not, as the fighter craft sheered downward. Their needle noses exploded into Blue Ridge, one after another, the airstrip disappearing, the second taking out a row of hangars as it disintegrated, a third following in its path, and the fourth bursting into the outbuildings, leveling most of the main structures of the school.

Rand cried, "Oh, my God." He held his hands to his head as though he might fragment.

"You'll get the credit for that, Palaton," said Nedar. "Now it's just the two of us."

Without waiting for an answer, he brought the skim-craft's nose up again, screaming straight up, climbing in protest, and over on its back.

Then he stalled it out, putting it beyond centrifugal force and into the hands of gravity, and let it plummet.

"Shit!"

Alexa jumped, as the cold calm in Nedar's voices shattered. "What is it?"

"I've lost him, he's off the screen. What in the two hells

is he doing?" Nedar scanned his grids furiously, bringing the fighter about. "Get me a reading, anything! I've got to—"

Alexa searched the grids desperately. She saw nothing. Nedar pulled his plane upward. Gravity clawed at her, made her ears ring, her eyes blur. Then, with a cry of triumph, "Got him!"

Nedar secured his targeting sight, a split second before an explosion rocked the craft. The air shattered. Wind screamed past them. Anything loose was flung against the fuselage with a chilling fury.

Alexa felt it coming apart. A rush, a spin out of control, her ears bursting with the change of pressure, Nedar shoving her out of the cockpit with one hand and all of his *bahdur,* pushing her back into the depths of the fuselage— and the wind came screaming their death.

Palaton brought the plane down on the flat land outside of Blue Ridge. The school lay in flames, bombed out, cadets running and screaming in terror. He climbed out of the plane hurriedly and hit the dirt. Rand followed him silently, and they looked at the destruction.

"For *bahdur,*" Rand said bitterly.

"No," Palaton answered. "For power. There is a difference." He cast about, uncertain where to go next. Emerging from the smoke and debris, he saw a figure. He gave a shout and went running. Rufeen was there, half-carrying Hat on one shoulder, and Palaton gently took the Earthan, lowering him to the grasses.

"He didn't mean to," Hat said, his eyes filled with tears. "Oh, God, Palaton, tell me he didn't mean to."

Palaton smoothed his friend's hair back from his forehead and crown. He'd taken quite a blow, but the horn crown had done what it was supposed to, and protected him from most of it. "I never understood Nedar," he answered softly. "You came the closest, and he used that."

"He told me you lied about Arizar. He told me that you tried to kill him, steal his *bahdur.* He told me he would build a House of *tezars.*" Tear squeezed down Hat's bruised face. "He killed my children!"

Palaton rocked him. "I never lied to you, Hat," he said

gently, "but even if I had, I would never have put Blue Ridge in jeopardy." He looked around as cadets ran in panic, flames licking at the dorms, smoke thick.

"And I don't lie to you now when I say we'll rebuild it. Bigger and better than ever."

Hat closed his eyes as if he could not bear to stare into Palaton's face. Palaton put a hand over his friend's face, willing him some meager comfort.

Rand made a noise in his throat. "Is he . . . ?"

Palaton looked up, drawn back to the world around him. "No. No, he'll be fine, providing his head's thick enough, and most Earthans have thick skulls." He lay Hat down carefully in the grass. "I have to see about Nedar," he said, as if anything could have survived the crash.

He picked his way through melted stone and slag, and wood beams burning like winter's deep logs. Everywhere the guts of the flight school lay scattered, the entrails of centuries of cadets. Rand followed him. He found Nedar's plane at the edge of the airstrip. The cockpit had been cracked like a shell, and a Choya's body spilled out, sable hair coated with blood, limbs twisted at impossible angles.

Yet he still breathed as Palaton knelt by him. He sucked in a gargling gulp as the other turned his face to the new day. There was no longer a roof overhead, and through the black plumes of choking smoke, a brilliantly blue sky shone down.

Nedar seemed to fix on that for a moment. Then he turned his gaze on Palaton's face, and said, "Finish it."

Palaton hesitated. The Sky pilot added bitterly, "They can't repair what's left of me. I won't live crippled, not the way I'd have to. As one *tezar* to another, don't let me live like this." He sucked in another fierce breath. "I won't beg."

"I've never asked you to. All I ask is that you give Hat a Sending. Tell him the truth so that he can rebuild."

Nedar's black eyes flickered as pain rushed through them. Then he said, bitterly, "You ask for something I can't give."

"Hat believed you. Hat loved you. You want me to take your murder on my hands; you must do this." Palaton's face remained unmoved, as stern as a father's. Rand watched the two.

"You were always better than me," Nedar spat out. Blood foamed with his words. He twisted his eyes shut, then opened them. "All right."

Rand felt the singing of power in the air, dimly heard Hathord cry out, knew that something, somehow had been sent or done to him.

Palaton straightened. Nedar's neck lay over his hands. Palaton knew the weak spot. He gave it a quick, convulsive twist, just below the burden of the horn crown, heard the crack of vertebrae, and Nedar went limp in his hold. He lowered the pilot.

A woman screamed. "Nooo! You son of a bitch! You killed him!"

Palaton looked up to the twisted fuselage and saw a humankind standing there, drenched with blood, but on her feet, with all the hatred of the ages flickering across her face. She held an enforcer in her shaking hand. "You killed him!" she cried again and raised the weapon.

Rand dipped his hand among the debris. He stood up with a spear-sharp length of metal in his fingers. "Alexa! Don't."

She looked at him. A half-crazed smile creased her bloodied face. "What would you know?" she charged. "What do you know about anything?"

Rand took a step closer. "You're not alone here." He ached for her, could feel the outpouring of her anguish. Could nothing be salvaged out of this, out of everything he'd given his life for, to become a pilot, a Companion to Choyan, out of the life he'd spent with her and Bevan. Would he be utterly alone among the stars, or could he help her, take her in, be loved by her again? "Alexa, listen to me! I'm here."

"You never wanted me," Alexa answered with curdling self-hatred. "You just took away the only thing I ever had." She choked back another word, bared her teeth, and aimed at Palaton.

As her finger tightened, Rand let fly with the metal shard. It speared through the air. It hit her hard, throwing her backward into the fuselage. Her body disappeared into the rippling heat of the wreckage. Then the flames hit the fuel cells. White hot and searing, the explosion knocked both Palaton and Rand off their feet and into the ashes and bruised grass. Flames washed over them. When Rand could stand, there was not enough left of the plane for anyone to have survived in.

Rufeèn came to get them, and the Choyan leaned on one another, helping each other out of the flame and smoke and into the sunlight, to begin to heal. Rand followed, alone, blindly, through the rain of his tears.

They pitched camp in the mess hall, the only building still intact, built with fire walls out of necessity, because of the kitchen, and remaining whole because it was away from the main sites of the crashes. Nedar's death and the destruction of Blue Ridge shocked the cadets with the reality of what warring against one another meant. No one accosted Palaton as he carried Hat in and tried to make him comfortable.

Rand spoke no word to him, and there was a look in his turquoise eyes which told Palaton that he had witnessed sins for which the pilot had not been forgiven. Perhaps could never be forgiven.

Palaton did not know what to tell him. Now they had no place to go, no place to be safe. He would have to find that for them later.

The mess kitchen filled with the smell of soup and fry bread, and a Green wing cadet gave him first serving. He took it to Hat and leaned over his friend, coaxing him to eat.

Hat took his hand. His grip was weak, but the flesh was warm and firm. "They found a treatment to restore *bahdur* . . . it seemed to put the world in our hands, when everything was going wrong . . . how can you forgive me?"

"You did what you thought you had to." Palaton broke off a corner of fry bread and dipped it in the soup.

"But we were friends . . ."

"All of us were, once." Palaton found a smile. "We have to concentrate on tomorrow." He held the bowl closer and put it in Hat's fingers so he could sip from it. "Blue Ridge needs a foundation. You'll be flightmaster again."

The doors to the mess hall banged open. Palaton looked up. In silhouette, he saw the figures in body armor, weapons up. A cadet screamed in fear. The guards came thundering in, shooting. Cadets fell like straw in the wind. Rand went down an arm's length from him. Palaton was trying to reach him and still protect Hat's body, when the dart pierced him.

He fell, thinking how odd the weapon, when the paralysis surged through him, and his heart did all it could to keep pumping. It sounded like a drum inside his head, and the *bahdur* slipped away from him when he tried to touch it. He looked down to his thigh and saw the dart piercing it.

A drug of some kind. He did not know if it was supposed to have been fatal. Then he saw Vihtirne of Sky walk in.

The blue dress she wore carried a sheen of steel, like the barrel of an enforcer. It made her look as if she were made of the smoke of the destruction outside. She strode between the bodies and disarray, her lip curled in disdain, until she reached Palaton. He could not move a muscle, but he felt every nerve in his body when she kicked him in the flank.

"You'd be dead, but I have more use for you alive."

Hat, lying sheltered by Palaton, groaned in his agony. Vihtirne spit on him.

"Fools who thought to offer me crumbs, when I already had a House at my feet. Do you know what you laid to waste here? Do you know what you destroyed when you killed Nedar and the woman?" She looked back over her shoulder at the Choya following her into the bombed out building. "You left me but one choice, to find a partner who owes a real sense of his worth to me."

Qativar moved out of her shadow. Palaton tried to blink, felt the pain as his eyes dried, tried to keep the traitor in focus. "I have the drug to make you powerless," the Choya said, and he smiled in humorless triumph, his eyes like glass.

"And I have the pill to bring it back," Vihtirne told him. "So we are meant for each other, wouldn't you think? But first Qativar has a pleasant little duty."

The Choya reached down and picked up Rand, who hung limp as a sack over his arm. It was not a loving embrace. "For crimes against Cho, for instigating civil war, for messianic interference in our religion—only a trial in the Halls of the Compact, on Sorrow, will do him justice. Don't you agree, Palaton? A trial before his peers, if the Abdreliks and Ronin don't get to him first. How much chance do you think he has without you?"

Palaton summoned up all his will, all his power, all his anger and thrust it outward. His body answered, cramping painfully, and brought him upward. Qativar laughed harshly and kicked him down again, leaving Palaton to lie, panting, helpless as a newborn.

"John Taylor Thomas will want to deal with us when we bring him the humankind who murdered his daughter. You came close to ruining a lot of plans. Close, but not close enough." Qativar laughed again.

Rand stirred in his arms, gave him a look. There was no hope in his turquoise eyes as Qativar bore him away.

Vihtirne kicked him again, in the skull this time, and that, mercifully, took him away.

He awoke in the night. The school had been stripped of all other bodies. He knew not who had lived or died, or what had happened to Rand. Beneath him, Hat lay as if dead. Next to them lay Rufeen, on her back, face ashen. He sensed a spark in her, but knew it weakened. They'd left his friends to die beside him. He crawled out of the smoldering wreckage where they'd left him. He clawed himself to his feet, coughing.

They had given him this burden; too, the destruction of Blue Ridge, the destruction of the *tezars*.

Well, he wouldn't take it. If they wanted to wage war on him, he was finally ready to fight back. He had his *bahdur*, legacy be damned or not, and he would use whatever means he had in his grasp. He threw his hands in the air and let it stream from him in defiance, the power of the House of Flame, blue fire, blue flames, *bahdur*, pure and untainted.

Behind him, Hat cried out weakly. He could hear the Choya crawling out of the debris, crying, and he shouted back, "Get on your feet, Hat! By God-in-all, get on your feet!"

His friend grasped him around the knees and, using him as support, got up. He stood, swaying next to him. Rufeen gasped. Hat reached down and pulled her up, and the two stood in unsteady embrace, Palaton left the aurora dancing in the air before them, washing over them, burning them with its chill force, cauterizing them, filling them with a spark that could not easily be extinguished. Rufeen put her head back, gulped it down as if it were air. He could not explain what it was that touched them next, but he could feel the strength growing in them, could feel the *bahdur* pouring around them, weaving them into something more than they had been.

He was the House of Flame.

The past had been shorn from Palaton, never to be touched again. He stood at the point of no return. Only the future stretched ahead of him.

Soulfire

Chapter 1

Palaton received two summons the day after Blue Ridge flight school burned down. Both were imperative, and he was disinclined to answer either.

The first came from his emperor, so timely on the heels of disaster that it seemed Panshinea had been prescient considering the time lag of subspace bulletin boards. But Pan had not foreseen the destruction of the pilot's training grounds. He sent an ETA from Sorrow and the Halls of the Compact, demanding the return of his throne, ordering Palaton to relinquish the heirship formally, setting a time and place for their meeting. If Palaton had once thought he could dissuade his emperor from this action, that thought had gone up in smoke with Blue Ridge. As soon as Panshinea learned of that, as well, the heirship would definitely be taken from him.

Most likely over his dead body. The emperor would not want any disputes later. The Choyan line of ascension must remain unmuddied.

Even more distasteful was the summons from the Prophet.

The biotox crew came in the next day, late, almost as though they did not wish to acknowledge what had happened. By the time they arrived, the ashes had cooled, a temporary morgue had already been set up in the only building which still stood, and Hathord, as master of the flight school, was scanning the bodies and matching the dental records with his on-line files. His square, stolid body stood at the screen impassively while the scans did most of the job.

Palaton worked outside, with the main task force of the biotox crew, for the reek of spilled fuel and flame-fighting foam lay spewed over acres. He had done what he could to put the wreckage of the planes to one side, though he received no thanks from the crew for his efforts.

They were his people, Choyan, but the majority of them were the Godless, the God-blind, those Choyan not gifted with the extrasensory perception and talents which made them sensitive to the life which lay with their surroundings. They could not hear the ground soil moan under the scorch of fire and chemicals. They could not feel the tremble of the organic world about them, the silent screams of the ecosystem so damaged and disrupted. They had no senses to detect the vibrancy of God which ran through all things in creation, and it was just as well, for if they had, they would not have been suited for their work.

But that did not mean that the stench of fire and spilled fuel and death did not bother them. He could read it in the lines of their faces as they jumped from their cruisers and readied their shoulder tanks, preparing to lay down detox foam. He could see it in their wiry bodies as they bent their double-elbowed arms to the task of spraying, then plowing, then seeding the damaged earth. The bio-techs gave him scarcely a glance as they went out on survey to determine the environmental impact.

Thanks did not lie in their Choyan eyes. Instead, if anyone met his face, it was only for a brief, flinching moment and then they looked away. He set his jaw and worked harder at his task despite the injuries he'd taken in the disaster, despite having lost his Companion to the enemy, despite knowing that the emperor was about to return home and rip the throne away from him, despite everything.

He deserved the condemnation. He'd brought civil war to Cho. Pilot had turned on pilot, destroying Blue Ridge, one of the finest of the flight schools. He had brought aliens here. He had failed to discharge his duties as heir. He had given status to those who were God-blind, and then he'd barged ahead as though he, too, were blind to the patterns of life which the God-in-all had woven through every fabric of Choyan being.

He had been the most blind Choya ever born.

And Palaton was still uncertain if the veil had been lifted from his eyes. In the last few months, much had been revealed, but even more had been clouded. *A wise man knows that he knows very little,* the *tezar* thought as he leaned upon his hand-plow and let the biotox crew part around him like a tidal wave and pass him upon the fields. They sprayed down their enzyme cleaner with an efficiency that was almost lulling in its rhythmic motions.

There was a movement behind him. A tall, chestnut-haired Choya watched him, sprayer held across his chest in a dormant position.

"*Tezar* Palaton."

Tezar. Said grudgingly, as if Palaton had not sacrificed all that he had been to gain the title of pilot. But after this, after all this, how could he blame the other for the bile in his tone?

"Yes." He straightened. The hand-plow vibrated down to idle in his hands, purring quietly.

"I have a message for you." The Choya's face was already soot-streaked, muddying the fine jewelry accents tattooing his cheekbones. "The Prophet says you must come to her."

His lips peeled back from his teeth before he caught himself, smoothed his mouth, and considered the matter. "No," he answered quietly, after a long moment of thought.

The faintly green eyes of the other lit up, as though already knowing what the answer would be.

"She says to tell you that you *will* come to her. Only that you must ensure it is not too late."

"I have no business with the Prophet." He thumbed the plow back up to speed, and its mechanical voice grew loud.

The Choya dared to lay a hand on him, callused fingers gripping him tightly on the lower wrist. A tiny spark of blue arced between them, like a zap of static electricity, *bahdur.* Power calling to power. Palaton looked down at the crewman's hand and then up to his face.

"I was *Changed,*" the Choya confirmed. "By Rand. You must return him to us. He is the Bringer of Change. He is the catalyst which gives us all the power, which brings sight to the God-blind, faith to the Godless."

Palaton felt as though he'd been gut-kicked. He shook the Choya's hand off roughly. "The humankind has been taken from me! Tell your Prophet that. Tell her that if word travels throughout Cho who and what the Bringer is, his life will be worth no more than a piece of yesterday's garbage. Tell her that! Without her silence, I have no hope of finding and restoring him."

Disbelieving, the crewman rocked back. "No. . . ."

"Do you think Blue Ridge was destroyed over nothing? Do you think I brought civil war to my home because I was bored? Or because of petty jealousy against another pilot? They came after us because they wanted to devastate us, and from the ashes they took Rand to ensure my silence, my complicity. But they don't know exactly what they have in him. They don't know what he's capable of, and if your mistress and her crusade endanger his life further, not only will I meet with her, but she will regret every moment of that meeting!"

His voices roared over that of the hand-plow and other Choyan nearby looked up from their task.

The messenger stood with thinning lips, then gave a brusque nod and turned away. Palaton, unblinking, watched him work through his sector, before turning off the hand-plow altogether.

He decided that his presence was superfluous and turned his equipment over to one of the crew so he could go check on Hat, who was still trying to get control of his emotions. The Choya'i who wore the bars of crew supervisor met him beside the equipment pallets.

"You in charge inside?"

"One of them."

"Good." Her nostrils flared slightly as she handed him a notepad. "Sign for supplies. I need a tally of how many you're sending out, so I can arrange for transport."

"You're not hauling them?"

No.

It was strange, but he did not remark on it. He didn't have to; he saw the flicker of awareness deep in her eyes. He looked over the supply roster. They were being given field packs, not the usual crisis supplies. He did not like the implications, but he made his sweeping signature across the lightscreen anyway. "I'll get back to you on departees."

She turned away, leaving him facing the burned-out hulk of the school.

Duty leaned heavily on him. He still had not decided his course of action, but it seemed best to take one step at a time. The first step began here.

The dining hall smelled, not of death, but of disinfectant. Palaton came to a halt, felt his nose wrinkling with its pungency. Even if that had not been offensive to him, his *bahdur* reacted strongly. The aura of death and destruction permeated this building. It pooled in the sooty shadows, scraped along the splintering floor, hung from the massive overhead beams. The psychic vibrations of the disaster which had descended upon them resounded so strongly that even those Choyan who had no ability, the God-blind, could feel them.

Palaton swung his head about as Rufeen's booming voice resounded from the galley area. As soon as he tuned in to her, he began mentally reciting almost word for word her lecture—they had rounded up the cadets who were waiting for transport out and reassignment and she was teaching, returning the flight school to as much normalcy as was possible. A whispery scribbling on the scribe boards followed her bombastic speech as the cadets raced to keep up with her. A smile tugged briefly at the corner of Palaton's mouth. Even though these were no longer Blue Ridge students, even though some would flee reassignment and join with the House of Tezars, she was giving it her all and would see that they did, too.

At the far end of the dining hall, plastisheet rippled in the tent structure erected there, catching Palaton's eye as Hat moved in and around the tables within, scanning and identifying the dead.

If he noticed the stench of burned flesh, he did not reflect it. It was as though he were carved from the Earthan matter which represented the sign of his House. Palaton alone knew what an effort it was for him to identify the bodies of the dead cadets. These were his children, in a way, taken in and taught and groomed to be star pilots, *tezars*, masters of the Patterns of Chaos. Each and every death diminished Hat in a way he could probably not have expressed with mere words, but he felt it keenly and Palaton knew it because he felt every death twice as sharply.

Palaton strode across the immense and now far too empty room, a room which had always evoked in him memories of hot fry bread on cold winter days, and mugs of steaming *bren*, dark and fierce as poet's ink, just the way he liked it. The tables and chairs had been previously

shoved aside for barricading. What was left when the front
doors had been blasted open by Qativar's entrance still lay
tossed over. His boots crunched on dirt and ash. By the
time he reached the medical tent, the smell of disinfectant
had grown disagreeably strong. He paused again, head up,
his horn crown aching.

Hat made a note on his scribe board and ordered out a
chip. When it was produced, he took the end neatly on his
scalpel-implant and punched the chip under the dermaline,
just below the horn crown of the corpse. Their skulls being
what they were, hard and thick to protect the dual brainpan, and the scalloped edge of the horns which arose from
that, were nearly indestructible. The scans of the horn
growth, coupled with dental records, made identification
incredibly accurate. And the chip containing the medical
information, ID, student records and the official report of
the disaster, once implanted into the beginning of the horny
outgrowth, would stay firmly with the body for whatever
official need until interment or cremation when the chip
would be removed and stored. Hat worked with a brisk
detachment as he made sure the implant was secure, then
closed up the coffin bag before he looked across the table
at Palaton.

His dark brunet mop, shaggy about his own low scalloped
horns and showing a touch of gray at the temples, hung into
his eyes. He shook his head impatiently. "How's it going?"

"I came by to ask that of you." Palaton found himself
somewhat amazed by Hathord's resilience. He had expected his friend to collapse in dismay, though perhaps this
frenzy of activity was itself a denial of all that had happened. "The enzyme foam is down. I don't think the contamination was too bad. You'd have gotten more if a raw
recruit had panicked while taking off from the plateau and
dumped a planeload of fuel. The crew chief told me they'd
be out of here before sunset." He hesitated.

Hat had been reaching for another gurney. He stopped
and looked up sharply. "What is it?"

"I'm not sure. It's their attitude, I think. They were not
happy to be here."

"Our cleanup contract is current. We're in their sector.
I don't think Blue Ridge, given the circumstances, has been
too demanding of their time."

"It's not that, Hat." Palaton looked out of the dark plastisheet tent rigging, away from the gurneys with their still, silent bags. "They responded a day late to the alarm, as it was. Maybe it's me, maybe it's what I perceive—they didn't want to run into our enemies, then or now. They're not taking us out, although they'll arrange flights for the cadets."

Hat blinked. "Not taking us out?"

"No." Palaton watched his statement sink in. As neatly as the biotox crew could have said it without saying it, the three of them were on their own. "They left us a pallet of journeypack rations and water filters."

"We're on our own," responded Hat slowly.

"Yes."

There was another pause, then Hathord drew a long, shivery breath. He held it a second, then sighed it back. "Well," he said "We thought this would happen once the emperor got back."

"We wouldn't be standing here talking if he were," Palaton answered dryly. Their emperor was not one to mince words or actions. The treatment by the biotox crew went beyond that.

"Then I've got time to finish this." Hat hooked a thumb, pulling a gurney into scanning position. "Rufeen's got the wings under control until the biotox crew takes them out. I guess you've got to find us sanctuary."

"Leave me the easy job, will you?"

Hat flashed him a quick grin. "Always." His expression became somber. "This is the last of the idents. The humankind's body was not in the wreckage."

Palaton felt a twinge, as though Hathord had been speaking of Rand, but he had not. He had been speaking of the other, the female who had been a Companion to the traitorous pilot Nedar. She should have been among the dead.

"No? Do we need to sift the ashes?"

"No. It didn't burn hot enough to cremate remains. She should have been there."

Alexa gone. Palaton pondered the meaning of that. Had Qativar taken the corpse for some reason, as well as taking Rand from him? Of what good would a dead humankind avail a living one? If Rand were still alive.

He had to be. Palaton would have felt his death, and he

had to go on believing that Rand survived. That Qativar
and Vihtirne had a use for their hostage or he wouldn't
have been taken.

"Palaton."

"I'm thinking." He looked back to Hathord. "The ambassador was notified of his daughter's death. All we can
do is send additional notification that we cannot turn over
the remains. We're going underground anyway. I can't do
anything more for him."

"But why do you think—"

"I don't know! I can't possibly know what Qativar intends to do. He has his House of Tezars now. Allied with
Vihtirne, I can only guess that they intend to use the water
patent for leverage if they need it. They have Rand to keep
me from their throats—" Palaton bared his teeth slightly
as he thought aloud, as if tearing their throats out sounded
appealing.

Silent tears began to course down Hat's face. He staggered back a step, bolstered unintentionally by a wall of
gurneys, their bagged remains already processed. "I'm
sorry, Palaton. So very, very sorry." His voices dropped to
a husky whisper. "I let Nedar and Alexa use me. I didn't
know! I couldn't see what they were doing. . . ."

Palaton reached out to take his friend by the sleeve and
draw him close, embracing him in a warm hug. Hat, square
and bulky in the way of all who descended from the House
of Earth line, stood quietly for a moment in his arms and
then hugged back. Palaton, whose genetic qualities came
from the Houses of Star and Flame, stood taller and much
thinner. He braced himself to support his friend. He could
feel Hat's shoulders shake as the Earthan began to cry in
earnest for all that he had lost.

His job as flightmaster for Blue Ridge.

Blue Ridge itself, with its hundreds-of-years-old buildings
and traditions, refitted for the age of star-faring.

His students, some dead, most alive but taken from him.

Nedar, flamboyant *tezar*, who'd schooled with both of
them, Hat's friend and Palaton's enemy. It was Nedar who
had led several wings of cadets into the sky to slug it out
with Palaton and Rufeen, an ambush whose jaws should
have closed irretrievably about them but had failed. Palaton
would not miss Nedar. Though the Sky had been an excel-

lent pilot, he had never been admirable, but he knew Hat would miss him. The bond between the two of them had been strong, though it was something Palaton could not understand any more than any fellow Choya could understand the bond between himself and the humankind Rand.

All of this, and more, Palaton's actions had taken from Hat and from Rufeen and from himself. He patted Hat's thick shoulder. "It is I who should apologize to you," he said, and held his friend close while he cried.

Hat had lightly suggested that he had the easy job of finding sanctuary for them, but both of them knew what lay ahead of them immediately. Theirs was a psychic race, secrets were difficult to maintain.

With the emperor returning, there was no room on the throne for the heir. And Panshinea would not brook his living to provide a focal point for dissidence. His life was now forfeit.

With a House of Tezars formed, breaking all precedents, and Palaton alone to stand against it, his life was now forfeit.

Among the Housed, his life was forfeit for the effort he had spent elevating the second-class citizens of the Godless.

Among the Godless, whose psychic abilities were genetically less or blocked or totally nonexistent and who had spent generations waiting to be delivered, for taking Rand away from them, Rand who seemed to be the catalyst and the messiah predicted to them, his life was now forfeit.

They had no place to go, and no one would suffer them to live.

Not an auspicious beginning for a rebirth.

Chapter 2

A hand gripped Palaton's shoulder from behind. As he felt its warmth and aura, he realized that Rufeen's lectures had ceased.

The pilot said, as he turned, "What's left of Red wing is ready to be pulled out."

"They've eaten?"

"Rations have been distributed. No one's eaten yet nothing looks too appetizing. The biotox crew is packing up. How many are they taking with them?"

"None." Palaton caught the flash in her eyes. His roughhewn friend had come to the same conclusions he had, only she did not voice them. "They're calling in transports."

Hat paused in his examination of the remains on the gurney. "I'm almost done here. There's nothing either of you can do at this point."

A muscle worked in Palaton's jaw before he answered, "Except get the cadets out of here. Come on. I think I have some heads to bust."

"Oh, goody," Rufeen said at his side. "It's about time."

Palaton went outside for a long moment. Clouds had begun to gather on the horizon and a lowering sun tinted them a fiery orange which would, like burning embers, turn to crimson and then darken to ash with the night. The biotox crews had nearly finished packing up their cruisers. He scanned the silvery planes.

With an expert eye born of his years of piloting, he knew for a certainty that they could take out two dozen of his cadets. They had brought in pallets of equipment which, now used, would be broken down into scrap, and the pallets of supplies now sat at the airfield's edge, meaning the cruiser bellies were even emptier. He said to Rufeen, a bare second before she spoke to him, and her voices were an echo of his, "Two dozen."

Rufeen grinned then, adding, "Easy."

He nodded.

"That would cut our responsibilities in half."

"Umm." Palaton was already back in full stride and Rufeen had to double-quick to, keep up with him.

He caught the crew supervisor by surprise outside the freight doors of the first cruiser.

"We're done here."

"Not quite," Palaton said. "You're taking some of the students with you."

"We told you we were only prepared to call in transport. It's been ordered for you. You shouldn't have to wait more than five or six hours."

"Any wait is too long. You know what transpired here. Lives were lost. *Tezarian* lives."

The Choya'i looked him steadily in the face. She'd cleaned the soot away, though she was still a bit sweaty and begrimed along the forehead and temple. "Any loss of life is regrettable," she responded.

"And we are still in peril from further attack. I want these students out as soon as possible."

"That is your problem." She handed her notepad to an adjutant who came quietly up behind and shadowed her, eyes on Palaton and Rufeen, one hand resting comfortably close to a hip holster.

"It's going to be your problem. Rufeen, call out Red wing. We should be able to get all but one or two senior cadets aboard."

"Yessir." Rufeen turned, put her fingers to her lips, and let out a skull-splitting whistle that lanced through the dusk.

Red wing came on the run, packs on their backs, eyes wide and expectant.

Palaton said to the biotox supervisor, as the cadets ran toward them, "You explain to them why you intend to keep them in jeopardy. You explain to them that you haven't the guts to do what they pledged to do the moment they left behind their Households and entered a flight school. You explain why they left behind homes and family and property in order to expend their lives and their *bahdur* for fellow Choyan who don't give a damn that some of them died yesterday and many of them will die in some tomorrow, offplanet, alone, piloting. You explain to them why you don't care that they are *tezars,* the only beings who can navigate Chaos, and bring home honor, trade, and glory to Cho. You explain to them why the very soulfire which gives them life, which burns in their veins as brightly as blood, why it isn't good enough for you that they have pledged to drain every drop of it *in your service*?"

He kept his voices low, pitched so that none but the three of them might hear, and he used his vocal cords well, underscoring one timbre with the other. Rindalan, of the stentorian priestly voices, would have approved. He missed Rindy, could have used the elder Choya here and now, but it appeared his voices had hit home. The biotox crew chief trembled slightly beside him as the Red wing fell into place, eyes intent on Rufeen and Palaton.

Rufeen had done her job well. The horror of yesterday's air strike, *tezar* against *tezar,* had faded from their fresh, young faces. She had reminded them of their calling, their destiny, and they were once again ready and eager to fulfill it. If not at Blue Ridge, then perhaps at the Commons if there were room enough.

Palaton could not predict the status at either Salt Towers or the Commons. If they had realigned their traditional neutral positions which had been intended to prevent the Houses and branch Householdings from using the *tezars* as leverage during various wars and political strategies, Palaton might simply be sending the youths off to the enemy camp. He strongly suspected the Salt Towers, long an elitist flight school, would probably play right into the hands of Vihtirne of Sky.

If he thought Vihtirne was holding Rand hostage at Salt Towers, he'd commandeer a cruiser on the spot. It was ridiculous to think that Qativar and Vihtirne would hold his Brethren at such an obvious site, however. But the commandeering might just have merit. . . .

Sotto voce, he nudged the biotox crew chief. "I know how much room you have. You can split this wing into two and take them, or perhaps you would rather I took one of the cruisers and let you make do with the other?"

"My ship!" started the chief. She composed herself. "You have aircraft."

"Not for passenger transport. Take it either way, Chief, but my cadets are getting out of here. You can assimilate them among your crew, or I can take the cruiser we need."

He felt another tremble run through the body of the Choya'i, but the chief swallowed tightly before snapping out, pointing, "You dozen go this way, you dozen that. Quarters will be cramped. If you need to sleep, do it sitting up. When we get back to dispatch, I'll arrange for further flights."

Palaton murmured a thank you, but the supervisor had thrown herself into action, and he was not entirely sure he'd even been heard.

Rufeen watched the cadets load. She slapped Palaton lightly. "I'll stay," she added, "until takeoff. Just to see them off."

"Whatever it takes," he responded before heading back to the mess hall.

Inside, Hat was sealing the last of the temporary coffin bags and shutting down the morgue. They would be sent out on more appropriate craft. The Earthan looked up, fatigue and sorrow deeply etched into his square face. "Everything all right?"

"It took a little persuasion."

Hat pulled up a stool and perched on it. His barrel chest heaved a sigh. "What do you think will happen?"

"If we had comlines open, we'd have a better idea, but since we don't—" Palaton paused. "I imagine Salt Towers is probably the new base of operations for the House of Tezars."

Hat rubbed his brow wearily, just below the bulge of his horn crown. "That would make sense," he agreed. "Not that I want to see Vihtirne firmly entrenched anywhere. When it was just Nedar, one of us, I could see it. I should have known that wherever Nedar stood, Vihtirne hid in his shadow. I should have known that."

"He could scarcely help it. He was the foremost of his line, and she the head of the House. He was never her puppet, but I doubt that any move he made was unknown to her."

"Alexa was."

Palaton drew up another stool. "The humankind?"

Hat nodded. "I heard her arguing with Nedar after they

came here. Vihtirne wanted him to be rid of the alien. He would not have it. There was a bond between them—it makes me cold to think it, but I think she was his *durah*."

"They were lovers?" said Palaton in shock.

Another weary nod. "I think so. I don't mean to speak ill of the dead—but I can't overlook that possibility."

Memory played out an awful scene in Palaton's mind. Yesterday's crash, Nedar's broken body thrown from the wreckage, and his pleading for a fellow *tezar* to end his agony. It no longer mattered that only moments before they'd engaged in armed combat, that Nedar had led a wing of raw recruits into the air to bring Palaton down. In that time, there had only been the two of them, Palaton shadowed by Rand, his humankind link, and Nedar broken upon the burning ground.

He'd ended his classmate/nemesis' life as Nedar had begged, only to have the disheveled human girl burst out of the aircraft wreckage, screaming in hatred and distress. Rand had saved his life and Alexa had died when the fuselage exploded. Palaton had not understood her actions fully then. If what Hat mused about now were true, though unthinkable, it explained much.

"I didn't know," Hat concluded, "that such things could happen." He looked up then, and met Palaton's gaze. "You and Rand—"

"No," answered Palaton firmly. "Though what it is that binds us, I cannot quite explain."

"Oh," Hat mumbled and lapsed into silence.

Palaton could explain, but he chose not to. That Rand had taken his *bahdur* and borne it, and cleansed it was beyond Choyan understanding. How could their soulfire be transferred in its entirety? How could an alien race with practically no extrasensory abilities whatsoever be involved in such a procedure? Did it mean that the inevitable burnout of the power and the awful neuropathy which accompanied it could be postponed indefinitely? Did it mean that *tezars* no longer had a future of disease and emptiness facing them? Palaton wasn't sure. He only knew that retrieving his *bahdur* from Rand had left the humankind crippled and bereft, nearly as mindlessly numb as suddenly losing the soulfire would do to a Choya. Palaton would not choose to benefit at the risk of another, nor would he let anyone else do so.

However, it made the mission to recover Rand, who was hurt and vulnerable, that much more desperate.

Rufeen interrupted their companionable silence, bearing a tray of mugs. The steaming odor of *bren* filled the air. "We've still got work to do."

Hat shook himself as though stepping out of a cold shower. His dark eyes were bloodshot as he snagged a mug and rolled a glance at her.

"Supper," she suggested. "Then we need to bed the other wings down."

Palaton lurched to his feet. "I'll see the pallets get unloaded. Maybe something hot can be made out of those ration packets." It felt welcome to target his thoughts on the immediacy of the action needed. He would worry about Rand later. This had to be done now.

The ordered-in ships touched down around midnight. Their beams lit the one airstrip and pad which had not been destroyed by the combat. Palaton stood in the night which had rapidly grown chill, and he greeted the pilots who stepped down.

"There's a storm front moving in," the graying Choya, a son of the House of Star, like Palaton himself, said. He removed his helmet. "I'm Jago." His hair of bronze and red flowed back from his forehead, streaks of age lightening it. There was a slight weariness in his aquamarine eyes. "I can take two dozen. Maybe a few less, if they're carrying full packs."

"They're carrying everything they can salvage," Palaton told him.

The first pilot indicated the second, a slender Choya'i, of the House of Sky, ebony-haired and light-eyed, so much like Nedar that she might have been the late *tezar's* sister . . . or she could have been his child, Palaton thought, reminding himself of the years which had passed.

"I can take nearly three dozen," she said.

"Coffin bags?"

"I have room in the cargo hold. Two dozen, then, if you have bags and equipment to go. *Tezar* Palaton," she began and hesitated.

"Yes?"

Her lips pursed, then she finished, "We would advise you strongly not to travel with us."

"We have no intention of doing so."

Tension fled abruptly from the carriages of the two. Palaton had swung around to signal Rufeen to start the remaining cadets boarding, when Jago asked, "Should we call in more cruisers?"

"No. I'm afraid that's all we need taken out."

Their faces went bleak. Blue Ridge, the first and greatest of the flight schools, had had its ranks decimated. Dwindling due to the ever growing scarcity of enough talented recruits, now their ranks were being thinned even more by civil war. The elder Choya nodded brusquely and replaced his helmet.

"I'm ready when you are."

Palaton returned to the mess hall where Hat and Rufeen were rousing the sleeping students. He made himself useful checking packs and accepting salutes from the cadets as they formed a line by the makeshift doorway, their faces crusted with sleep and dreams.

A clatter came from the galley. Pans went rolling and a young, panicked Choya cried, "*Tezar* Rufeen! Help!"

He entered the galley from one end, Rufeen from the other. The brawny Choya'i knelt down as one of the Blue wing lay on the floor, frothing from the mouth, body writhing in convulsions. His classmate knelt at his flanks, trying vainly to capture his flailing hands.

"What is it?"

"He just—he just collapsed."

Rufeen frowned heavily at Palaton, then muttered, "No one just collapses." She tried to cradle the cadet's head on her knee, keeping him from bashing the floor repeatedly in his agony. "Head injury?"

"N-oo."

Palaton thought he recognized both cadets as pilots whom Nedar had foolishly taken into the air with him, the only two survivors of the opposition who'd ambushed him. If they had been flying combat, then this one on the floor could not have been an epileptic. He would never have passed the physicals and training to this point.

Foam spattered the Choya's light blue flight suit as he

writhed in their arms. His agony cut to the quick to even watch. Hat leaned in past Palaton.

Palaton pushed him back. "Get the others loaded."

"What is it?"

"Convulsions. We'll take care of it."

"My student—"

"Hat. We'll take care of it." Palaton stood to block his view.

Hat's dark-shadowed eyes deepened a second, then he gave way. He left the galley without another word.

Rufeen met Palaton's gaze as he knelt back down. Wordless agreement passed between them: Hat did not need to handle the death of yet another of his charges.

Rufeen had her fingers lightly pressed on the major pulse point of the Choya's neck. She said softly, "I'm losing him."

Palaton swung on the sobbing wingmate and grabbed him up by the neckline of his flight suit. "Tell me what's happening!"

Chapter 3

Even with his wingmate's life at stake, Palaton could feel deceit throbbing through the cadet's aura. He shook the youth. "His life for your lies!" he warned. "Tell me what you know."

"It—it won't help him."

"Are you so sure of that? Are you ready for the weight of his death? It's a heavy burden." As if accenting Palaton's words, the dying pilot's heels drummed on the galley flooring. "What brought this about?"

The cadet twisted slightly, trying to see his friend's body, then looked back to Palaton. "He took the . . . he took the drugs Nedar brought back." He clawed a hand at the front of his flight suit, trying to loosen Palaton's grip a little.

"Drugs? What drugs?"

"Nedar said—Nedar said they would be the foundation of the House of Tezars. No more burnout. No more layovers waiting for the *bahdur* to freshen. No more borderline talent hoping to fulfill lesser piloting jobs."

Palaton relinquished his grasp on the youth's neck enough to set him back on his feet and let him take a gulping breath. Rufeen rebutted what he could not.

"There is no such thing."

"Nedar brought them from off-world. He took them. One or two of the elder *tezars* tried them as well. They work! And when Kano heard we were shipping out, he wanted to make sure his *bahdur* tested high, that it burned as brightly as it could. I told him not to . . . that Nedar said the drug was only to be taken if the soulfire was dormant. But he didn't listen. He was desperate! He's been on the edge all year. Hat warned him he could wash out. He wanted to be a *tezar*!" The cadet's eyes filled with tears that began to slide down his pale face.

Rufeen said quietly, "Palaton. Look."

The cadet in her hands had ceased to convulse. Now he lay sprawled and still, his heaving chest the only proof he still lived . . . that and a network of bahdur-laced fire that seemed to play over him, It sparkled from head to toe, lacy cobalt blue lines that danced and hissed as energy burned freely.

It brutally mimicked the Patterns of Chaos that all tezars must one day learn to master if they wished to be space pilots. It tangled and untangled in the swirls of random matter motion, yet Palaton could look into the net and see the signposts by which he navigated FTL flight: The soulfire twisted and formed, then re-formed the Butterfly, the Singing Choya'i, even the treacherous Arachnae. With each coil that broke and re-formed, the dying student let out a gasping moan.

The *bahdur* network grew darker and darker, as the cadet's face grew paler and paler, the soulfire leeching the very life from his body. It glowed midnight dark and then, with a hiss, it was gone, leaving a shell of a body behind.

Palaton let the other youth go, and with a wail, he fell to his knees beside his friend's hulk.

Rufeen's jaw had dropped. She worked a moment to form words. She looked up at Palaton.

"What in hell has Nedar done to us?"

"I don't know," he answered, and an icy finger of foreboding brushed the back of his neck.

Off-world. Nedar partnered with a humankind woman, a woman who had been known to have been allied with the Abdreliks. Off-world and intergalactic. He rocked back on his heels. Had the Abdreliks hoped to instigate civil war here, seeking to conquer from within what they had spent hundreds of years trying to conquer from without?

He could only hope that, with Alexa and Nedar dead, the House of Tezars had no destiny, no miraculous if deadly panacea, that the link to this drug had been severed. He could hope that, but he knew he could not count on it.

"What are we going to do?"

He gave Rufeen a hand up. "Hat's equipment isn't sophisticated enough to do an autopsy here. Besides, I wouldn't put him through that. But we need to know what really killed him, and why."

She nodded, a stunned expression still on her wide face. "I'll get a coffin bag." She started to push past him, then stopped.

"What if—"

"If what?"

"It works. It kills some of us, but it works on others. What if it works on a lot of us?"

"That's our soul, Rufeen. No one can chemically create what doesn't exist in us."

"But what if it can restore . . . ?"

Palaton looked back to the sobbing youth and his dead friend. "Then they'll own us," he answered briefly. "Choyan will do anything for soulfire."

Rufeen gave a shudder. She stopped. "I know that look. What can you possibly hope to do?"

"For one thing, I'll have to change my travel plans."

"You can't stay here."

"No. But I won't be going on with you and Hat, either. I've got to meet with Pan. This issue gives me no choice. The emperor has to know what's been sown here, what's at stake."

"He intends to kill you, Palaton."

"I know that. But first, he'll damn well have to listen to me."

Rufeen looked at him silently, and he could read her thoughts as clearly as if she had sent them to him. The emperor was the emperor. Panshinea did not have to do anything he did not wish to do. Anything she might have decided to say was interrupted by Hathord, who paused at the door to the galley, and finally said in a broken voice, "By God-in-all, I hope this is the last of my dead."

He took his student by the shoulders. "Go and get me another bag."

The Choya looked at him with a stunned and pale face. Hat gave him a rough shake. "Go. Then get your kit. The last transport is waiting for you."

Finally, after the weeping cadet had recovered enough to bring sheet and coffin bag for his friend, and they had tucked the body in, she said, "You have three days, four at the most, before he arrives. You should be in place before then—"

"In place?"

Her face averted now, as her hands busily prepared the body, she continued, "In place. Arrange that whatever confrontation Pan wishes is in public. Use the broadcasters to keep him honest. If he attempts to bring you down, let it be in full view of everyone. Unless he has branded you as traitor and is prepared to offer incontrovertible truth, he won't dare lay a hand on you. Find whatever allies you can—"

"With Jorana out of the palace, I can't count on anybody."

Her gaze leveled on him then. "You can count on a good many more than you think. The only problem you might have is that Vihtirne and Qativar will strike, making it look as though Panshinea has done it." She finished with the seal on the coffin bag and stood. He drew up with her. "You'll have to be in place with the Choyan you can trust."

A glimmer of what she was saying touched him. He shook his head. "No. You and Hat are not going with me."

"You can count on us."

"No. No, I won't risk the two of you. If Qativar is using drugs to build the House of Tezars, there won't be anybody left to train true *bahdur*. He's going to leave Cho in shambles. The two of you need to be able to rebuild, pick up the pieces. If I have only one legacy to leave behind me, it's going to be that. Do you understand me? You and Hat have to take the jet sleds and get as far away from here and the capital as possible. Don't look back."

From behind him, Hathord said, "Don't do this, Palaton. Don't go."

"I have to. I have to relinquish the heirship, and I have to let Pan know what's happening. There can't be two emperors of Cho. Our world can't survive that—it's already fracturing under the strain. Pan can have his throne, but he'll keep it only if he's strong enough to face Qativar and Vihtirne. I'll do anything I can to give him that strength, but I'll have to do it alone."

Rufeen commented quietly, "That's why they took Rand. You know that. As soon as they suspect you're moving against them in any way, he will become expendable."

He didn't know that, but he also had no doubt that was why Qativar had taken his Brethren, his humankind . . . his friend. "I know. Which is why I have to go alone. I

have to send you two on as decoys and attract as little
attention as I can. As much as I need your help, as much
as I want it—I can't afford to have it.''

His friends fell silent. The three of them bent to grab
the corners of the coffin bag and transported it to the storage room where the other dead lay. They stood for a moment, aware that they were the only beings left alive in
the ruins of the flight school. Palaton could hear the faint
afterburn of the last transport as it circled once, took its
bearing, and disappeared into the midnight sky. He realized
belatedly that it had been doing a flyover in mourning for
Blue Ridge.

He encircled his hand about Hat's wrist. "I pledged to
you once before, and I do it again: Blue Ridge will be
rebuilt.''

Hat looked at him, eyes shining with emotion. He nodded wordlessly in understanding.

The Choya'i who, in her former life, had been a Commons and had had beautiful blue eyes, eyes the color of
the sky after a refreshing rain, sat quietly in a straight-
backed chair, head tilted to one side as if listening, a cerulean band of cloth covering scarred eye sockets. She raised
a hand, a crackle of *bahdur* accompanying the gesture. The
Choya who had been approaching her paused as she halted
him in his tracks.

Her name had been Dorea. She was young, barely out
of her teens, and she should have been flirting with other
Choyan, dancing and laughing, her life stretching ahead of
her. Instead she sat as still as if life had already used her,
filled her with wisdom and care and strife and memory, her
skirts demurely about her ankles, her back pressed to the
chair as if seeking solace against some unseen burdens
weighing upon her shoulders.

Or so it seemed to Malahki—lately wrenched from his
destiny as one time mayor-luminary of Danbe, head of the
underground which sought to free the common people from
their second-citizen status-as he felt his own *bahdur* answer
to hers. Power to power. It was no wonder the Housed felt
superior to the God-blind. They were superior, in many
ways. No wonder they feared the religion and revolution
which had driven Malahki's people into hiding. *Bahdur* un-

leashed was a fearsome thing. When the humankind known as Rand had touched Dorea, Changing her, opening up and unsealing her bands of power, she had become the Prophet. Dorea no longer, young and carefree no more, unable to understand or bear her new foresight, she had gouged her eyes from her face.

Yet she still *saw,* and was *seeing* even now, as she waited for Malahki to join her.

He did not stir until she dropped her hand to her lap and straightened, turning her blind face toward him, nostrils flaring slightly.

"He will not come," she said.

"Palaton? Why do you say that?"

"Rand is no longer with him." Her voices were flat. Like most born of common blood, she had not had the auditory sensibility or *bahdur* to teach her to use the dual pitches of her double larynxes to full ability. Her voices twinned one another. Malahki was keenly aware that another Choya'i, one born into her power, would have used one voice to convey one emotion, the other to underscore it, or seduce or even scold, at the same time.

Of foremost importance, however, was the whereabouts of Rand. "He has him secured somewhere. Gone to ground, where we cannot sniff him out."

The Prophet considered that before shaking her head slightly. "No. I cannot sense Rand. He is lost to me, and Palaton refuses to respond to my plea. He will not come to me, will not listen to what I have to say."

Malahki hesitated, thinking to offer to be a messenger, but he knew better; the Prophet did not yet have a message for Palaton. She would, and knew she would, but more than that . . . his presence must be needed to stimulate the full import of her foresight. He could not think that Palaton would knowingly ignore her, despite all that had happened between them. He might have been wounded in the attack on Blue Ridge. He must surely be caught up in the events which would precede Panshinea's return to Cho.

"Prophet. Let me carry another summons."

One hand went up. Her fingertips gently touched the cloth which bound her empty eyes. Patted the cloth as if reassuring herself. Then Dorea dropped her chin slightly, and her forehead wrinkled.

"All right," she said finally. "But do not go to Blue Ridge. He won't be there. Look for him at Charolon. Look for him in the eye of disaster."

Malahki did not like the sound of that. He'd turned and left the tiny room when her voices caught him at the door.

"And Malahki."

He turned.

"See if you can bring him to me alive."

His blood chilled. "Yes, Prophet," he promised, and left.

Chapter 4

The day on Sorrow was pleasant enough for GNask to lower the frequency of his bodyshielding as he strolled along the quartz river path to his ambassadorial wing. His bodyguards lumbered along behind, grumbling quietly to one another, unable to understand his predilection for this walkway, his fascination with the sentient life frozen forever inside the rivers and lakeways of the planet. He did not take the time today to meditate, as he would have liked to have done, to philosophize about these people and what they had done to attract such a powerful enemy. He did not pause to watch and stalk as a predator would, imagining the skillful prey one of them would be, bipedal, upright, lithely mobile as they must once have been.

Nor did he indulge himself in cataloging the various facial expressions preserved for eternity on their slender, oval faces. There was a certain serenity as well as fear to be found, giving any observer pause.

It was those expressions, those bodies, which had wrought a truce between the Abdreliks, the Ronins, the Choyan, and the other quibbling races of the Compact. Here a civilization had died and been entombed by a technology which none of them could yet match. Somewhere, out there, was an enemy more vastly powerful than any of them.

It had been a sobering thought centuries ago. It still was today.

Who had these people been, and who had been so almighty as to bring them down? The crystals of Sorrow did not tell them. They could only hint and warn.

Truth to tell, GNask had to admire a predator who could accomplish such a massive kill, with no need to take any sustenance or reward for the effort. The planet of Sorrow was nearly pristine with the exception of its network of frozen waterways. They were not an amphibian people, yet they had stepped into this liquid and died nearly instantly. Nearly, GNask thought, because his minute observations over the years had revealed a few bodies, here and there, showing abject pain and terror. Not quite instantaneous enough for some, it appeared.

GNask always took the lesson of Sorrow personally. He had an enemy to meet, one that would demand the very best he could offer, and he had a fine line of compromise to walk in the meantime while he grew strong enough to meet the challenge. He did not allow himself the luxury or complacency of thinking that Sorrow's history was in the distant past. It would forever be as fresh to him as the moment in which their lives had been snuffed out.

His bodyguards uttered a grunt of relief as he turned away from the walkway and jogged up the steps to the ambassadorial wing. He lowered his bodyshield as he entered and one of his aides darted out to meet him.

GNask came to a halt, his massive bulk settling into a sudden stealthiness, all his instincts directed momentarily on the preylike movements of the aide.

The youngling, not far from the egg or initiation with his *tursh* blushed, turning his dark hide even darker. His sluglike symbiont turned color as well and hugged close to the nape of his neck, eye stalks pulled in and quivering. The *tursh* had more sense than the aide did, though the youngling finally seemed to catch wind of his predicament and stammered. "I b-beg your pardon, Ambassador."

In their wild days, this one would not have lived to leave the nest. GNask made a noise at the back of his throat, noncommittal as to whether pardon had been granted or not.

"That damage report you wanted just came in. Class Zed cruiser, currently being leased and operated by Ambassador John Taylor Thomas is anchored at bay station 17 for repairs. A report detailing a minor skirmish with a Ronin privateer is on file."

GNask could feel the warmth bubbling inside of him. As he'd thought, Thomas had not had the guts to report a direct attack by them. It had been a warning shot only. If GNask had commanded rrRusk to take them out, there would be no one to make reports. The point had been made, and understood, that Thomas was not to play lightly with the alliance they had made. The Terran ambassador had stolen two agents from him. GNask had vented his anger. Now they were even again, though their little alliance was somewhat in doubt. Thomas would have to convince him that there was still an advantage in their association. Meanwhile, his aide waited.

"Good. Is that all?"

"No, Your Eminence. You have a call waiting, of high priority."

GNask nodded and rolled past his aide, leaving him trembling in his wake, making even more preylike movements to attract the attention of the bodyguards following.

GNask saw the scramble link when he sat before the screen and knew that no one higher among the Abdreliks could be waiting for him to pick up. He licked his lips, jowls rattling, as he settled down and powered the screen.

The Abdrelik president sat hunched and glowering. GNask recognized the deep meditation of a classic stalk as a flicker of light came into the other's eyes as Frnark launched into words. "With the human girl gone, we have lost our link into Cho."

GNask grimaced, his lips skinning back from his tusks, and he made an effort to keep from revealing more ivory than he should. It would be an egregious breach of etiquette to do so. And, furthermore, it could cost him the ambassadorship which he had won so dearly four decades ago and had no desire to give up until he was ready to place himself even higher. Damn John Taylor Thomas for tampering with his agents, even if the girl had been the manling's own daughter. "That is so. But not all is lost. What I have gained in information was worth the time, the risk. . . ."

Frnark glared at him, small piggish eyes in a face of purplish hide, a lean face like and yet unlike GNask's. He had fought for his position and would fight to keep it. Neither had any doubt that they looked into the face of their most probable next opponent. However, neither was ready for the inevitable battle. Not yet.

GNask felt a string of spittle cascade from the corner of his lips. He mopped it away delicately on the back of one

large, well-muscled wrist. He was easily twice the bulk of
Frnark, and aware that he gave away in agility what he'd
built in strength. He did not blink voluntarily, but rather
let his eyelids drop ever so slightly, in a subservient manner, breaking his stare so that the president would not
think himself challenged. Not yet, not at this time or
place.

He lowered his rumbling voice a notch. "I am not so
new from the egg that I cannot see this unfortunate death
as a set back; but neither am I so hidebound that I cannot
accept the loss and move on. The consequences of the girl's
death to the Choyan far outweigh any inconvenience to me.
Panshinea has been moved to leave the safety of the Halls
of the Compact. Leadership on both Sorrow and Cho are
now in jeopardy."

"Do not lecture me."

"I did not seek to do so. Only to encourage you."

"I do not need encouragement! I need results! Any upheaval on Cho that disrupts the availability of pilots is disastrous to us. The Ivrians are the only ones who can make
do for any time at all without piloting—do you want to
leave us open for an Ivrian invasion?" The Abdrelik across
from GNask paused for a moment, then began to laugh at
the notion. The reedy, avian aliens could scarcely conceive
of an attack on Abdrelikan holdings and the thought of
one was so ridiculous that both GNask and the president
lapsed into deep, rumbling laughter.

The speaker waved away his humor finally, saying, "Be
that as it may, they're the only ones who can even come
close to fulfilling Choyan contracts, They may not come at
us militarily, but they'll sure as hell be in our pockets."

"I can arrange a deterrent."

"I'm sure you can." Frnark dipped a hand down into a
gurgling pot by the side of his chair, plunged a talon into
the turgid waters, and pulled out a struggling *scriff* which
he stuffed into his cheek and began to chew with great
enjoyment. He swallowed, aware of the avid attention his
actions drew. When his throat was clear, he said, "Do not
think, GNask, that we are unaware of your actions of the
past few days. We fully expect the humankind ambassador
to file a protest with the Compact in a matter of hours."

GNask had thought that that action might have gone unnoticed. He should have known better. No matter how he had weeded out his crew and command, there were always spies. Always. "He can prove nothing. There were Ronin privateers in the sector. His ship was a casualty of friendly fire."

"Mayhap. How badly damaged was he?"

"Enough to remove him from the sector. Not so badly he would have suffered casualties of any degree. If he is alive, squawking, perhaps not badly enough."

"Perhaps you would care to explain to me your course of action. I would like to share in the rationality of such an attack."

GNask got to his feet. His bulk, in motion, was a majestic achievement of which he was well aware. He would, when the time came, quash his foe as easily as the president had eaten the *scriff*. "I think not. You have granted me certain autonomy of movement and action. I would like to hold onto that independence a little longer, but I assure you that you will be pleased with the final results."

He was gazed at darkly. The president's lips thinned, his ivory glistened whitely. "Tell me some some particle of your ultimate objective."

It was a request which he, for the moment, dare not refuse. GNask leaned close to the viewing screen. "Nothing less," he said, "than the *tezarian* drive itself."

"A goal which has been in our sights for centuries."

"A difference," GNask returned. "I know what it is. I quest now to learn how to control it."

The president sat back with a hiss.

GNask waved a palm over the controls, closing off the view screen and ending transmission. He stood by the chair, watching the blank screen for a long moment, pondering his boldness. The president did not renew the signal.

He had either succeeded in his statement, or he had just cut off the last of his ties. Either way, it would not matter, if he succeeded in this final mission. He had almost had the secret of the drive when he had Nedar in his hands. The implantation and imprinting of his symbiont in the pilot had been as successful as it had been in the human girl. He knew it, though Thomas had taken the two out of his grasp before he could complete the experiment on the Choya. His *tursh* was strong and resilient. It could withstand another segmentation for implantation.

All he needed was another pilot.

He headed out of the communication deck, bellowing for rrRusk as he lumbered along.

Chapter 5

It seemed the cruiser had barely stopped vibrating from the bay station launch when his commander called him to the con deck. Thomas stood wearily, feeling the buzz in the soles of his boots, the sway of the ship disorienting him ever so slightly, the weight of his years and his loss upon his shoulders. A dull thrum continued to sound through the vessel from repairs being made internally while in flight. Major hull repairs had been completed before disembarking from the Compact bay station. They'd already had trouble. Frankly, John Taylor Thomas had not expected to draw any more.

"We're being approached," the commander told him.

Surely not the Ronin and Abdreliks again. Thomas felt himself twitch defensively, away from the screen projection of their deep space position. They were beginning acceleration for the FTL run even as they continued making repairs, but were still hours, perhaps even days, from being able to make the jump. The laser dot of light which indicated their position shone strongly. Pulsating ever closer on the 3-D screen came another pin of illumination.

"Any ID?"

"Not at this point in time, although our pilot doesn't seem particularly worried. But whoever they are, they deceled, looking for us, or someone. I'd say it was us as they've set an intersect course."

Out of Chaos, looking for them. They'd have the speed advantage, decelerating as they were. His vessel's own engines were laboring to pick up the acceleration they needed to gain FTL. Thomas stood, musing, thinking so deeply that he must have missed something, for his commander put his hand on his shoulder, saying, "Ambassador?"

" 'Yes?" Thomas looked up. He'd been thinking of

Alexa, dead, lost to him finally, lost to him in more ways
than he could ever imagine, even more forsaken than when
the Abdreliks had taken her. He was wondering who could
possibly threaten him with anything more devastating
than that.

"What do you want us to do?"

"ID and hail them as soon as you can. I'll be in my
quarters. Wake me if necessary."

His commander nodded. "Very good, sir."

Thomas shrugged wearily and left the con deck. Sleep
beckoned, but he would not get much. He could not, thinking of Alexa's legacy. He found it ironic that on this voyage
of endless night there would be little, if any, rest for him.
I regret that I have but one life to give for my country. . . .
Would that it had been his own instead of his daughter's.
Would that he had had anything to give which could have
spared her the course she had taken. Would that anything
but power would have pleased her.

He must have slept the deep, unconscious sleep he had
hoped for, because the clang and jolt of a hard-docking
woke him. The hammock bed swung uneasily as the ship
moved and echoed with the metallic hammering. Boarded.
They were being boarded. Forcibly? Surely not, or his commander would have woken him. But then, his pilot was a
tezar and there were bounds there which crossed the contracts of commanding a vessel.

Had his commander betrayed him?

Thomas had gotten to his feet, hammock still swaying
violently behind him as he went to the sink and scrubbed
his face. The cold sting of the water woke him a little. He
stared at himself through red-rimmed eyes. Had he cried
in his sleep, dreamless ease giving vent to emotions he had
not been able to allow himself otherwise? He washed his
face again, more carefully, then dragged a comb through
thinning hair. The downtime light in the cabin made him
grayer than he remembered. Distinguished. More like the
experienced ambassador he portrayed. Less like the grieving father.

He had finished straightening his jacket when the commander called for him.

"Ambassador. We have guests from Cho who respectfully request audience with you."

His heart squeezed a painful beat. From Cho. No wonder his pilot had allowed boarding. The Choyan were not in the habit of initiating warfare. They did not need to. Their mastery over Chaos was enough in itself. So what Choyan came to treat with him? Not Panshinea, or his commander would have announced the emperor. "Where?"

"Bay deck D, sir."

Just beyond the docking deck. Why not come into the vessel, into the belly of the beast? Why hover near the exit? Thomas put his shoulders back and chin up, and went to meet his guests, wondering.

"I don't like this, Qativar." Vihtirne paced just beyond the bulkhead, looking back frequently as if she wished to leave, with or without him. Her sable tresses swung with the agitated movement of her graceful form and her long, midnight blue dress swept the deck with every step, She was beautiful, elegantly so, and used to being obeyed. It was etched as much into her movements as her race and her sex.

Qativar straightened the line of his trouser. "This act would seal the bond between us."

"We have no bond with humankind! You would deal away the only bargaining chip we have—"

"No. Need I remind you that we could not keep him if we wished, that Palaton would go to the ends of Cho to find him eventually, no matter what blackmail we hoped would stop him. We must use him while we have him—if we wish for the House of Tezars to succeed. We do wish that, don't we, dear Viihtirne?"

She'd pivoted neatly and now leveled a sapphire gaze into his eyes. Cold as any gemstone. Vibrant but icy. Multifaceted but unliving. She had had a House at her beck and call, and had forsaken it to build a new House with him. She had known what she was doing, he thought. Known that with him she'd have but one person to deal with as she plied her strategy to change the fate of Cho and Choyan instead of the tradition-bound infrastructure of along established genetic bloodline. He would have to remember to be terribly careful in the days ahead.

"Yes," she said icily. "We do wish that. But you leave us scant protection."

"Boost will be our protection. They'll do anything for it, for a steady supply. *Anything.*"

Her lips thinned. She swung away from him, a tiny movement underlying the major one . . . had it been a shudder? A grimace of distaste?

No matter. Qativar heard footfalls nearing. The ambassador must be coming to meet them. He checked the lines of his suit, especially tailored for moments like this. He was Choyan, that bespoke his lineage in itself. And now he was the establishing head of a new House, a feat which had not been accomplished successfully in hundreds of years. His robes of priesthood in the House of Star had been thrown aside. He was newborn, he was the foundation of the House of Tezars. It did not matter that he had never been a *tezar,* that he had not the soulfire to pilot. Without him, none of them would pilot. That would suffice.

He stood. As the two figures drew near down the dimly lit corridor beyond the docking area's bulkhead, he could easily distinguish between the tall, loping form of the commanding pilot and the awkward straight-armed stick figure of the humankind. The manling walked with all the gawky attitude of a child hoping to become an adult. The only graceful feature about him, when they drew near, would be the eyes. Like Choyan eyes, large and luminous and expressive. Among all the races, none had eyes quite like Choyan did—with the possible exception of the humankind. The Ronins were full of slit-eyed guile, the Ivrians double-lidded like the birds they so resembled, and the Quinonans had eyes of tar that dominated their skull-like heads though little intelligence or compassion lit the depths of the hive-consciousness aliens.

The ambassador stumbled crossing the bulkhead, then caught himself, and Qativar clenched his jaw to squelch any possible derision at the action. He could read an aura of fatigue from the manling, fatigue and sorrow. Vihtirne caught his eye as she joined him and he knew she'd read the same emotional psyche. He'd planned correctly, he thought triumphantly.

As the pilot and the ambassador came to a halt in front of them, Qativar thought he recognized the *tezar,* a Sky from his sable hair and silvery eyes, an older commander, one Dilarabe, if he recalled correctly. Not wanting to be in error, he let Vihtirne greet them first.

"Ambassador Thomas, *Tezar* Dilarabe," she said warmly in Trade. "Thank you for allowing us to dock."

Pleasure spiked in Qativar's chest. He'd been right again. It augured well for the meeting they were about to conduct. As Vihtirne presented him, the humankind ambassador turned to face him, weary expression sparked by a momentary curiosity. Fleeting, yet it had been there. He bowed fluidly in greeting,

"Forgive us for intruding, Ambassador. I know that you are in mourning, and we join you in your inconsolable loss."

Thomas' eyelids fluttered slightly. "Thank you, Mistress Vihtirne, Your Eminence Qativar. However, I hardly think you have flown this distance to sit with me in my grief. Forgive my brusqueness, but I have little patience left. What do you want here?"

This was a being, Qativar thought, who was plumbing the depths of his soul and found he had little left to lose. He would take careful handling in the future, if he ever reached these depths again. The manling might decide that he had nothing to lose.

Qativar inclined his head, and tried to project understanding. "I trust you are somewhat familiar with the history of my home world?"

"I have a working knowledge of it."

"Then you must know, and sympathize with from your own history, the strife and difficulty concerning the raising of a House. Our people came to terms with aggression long ago. We do not colonize; therefore, it behooves us to keep the peace so that our planet, as well as our people, do not suffer. Yet incidences do happen from time to time. It is most regrettable to us, Vihtirne and myself, that your daughter Alexa was caught in the midst of our actions. Although we are not personally responsible, we bear the onus of her death." He paused, allowing the weight of his words and the pitch of his voices to sink in.

One of the manling's hands twitched a little, as if urging him to say what he had to say, and finish.

"To that end," and he moved, gesturing to a crewman

who stood silent guard at the far bulkhead, "we have done the only thing we could, and brought you her remains."

The air lock door opened like a giant metal maw, and issued forth an honor guard of Choyan bearing a coffin between them. They paced slowly and with great dignity, their boot soles scarcely drumming on the metal plate of the deck. The coffin moved between them as if borne by nothing but air. It was draped with a silken ebony cloth, simple but effective. Though both he and Vihtirne had moved to face the guard, Qativar slipped a glance to the side to see the look on the ambassador's face. It was all he hoped for. He had brought a father's child home.

Thomas took a furtive step toward the casket with a smothered cry, but Dilarabe caught him, saying, "Sir. The coffin is sealed. You cannot see her." He held the manling still for a moment, looking over Thomas' shoulder at Qativar and Vihtirne, his face stony, then he released his employer. "You cannot see her," he repeated.

Thomas took another halting step, then seemed to recover his composure as the pacing guard reached him, did a step in place and came to a stop. With their voices echoing one another, the Choyan counted off and lowered the casket to the deck. It settled without a sound, yet with its lowering, an atmosphere of gravity fell too; an oppression so dense that for a moment Qativar believed a sending or curse had come with it, though humankind had no such abilities.

John Taylor Thomas stretched out a hand and laid it gently atop the ebony drape. A moment of silence, then, "Open it."

"We cannot, sir." The honor guards looked imploringly at Qativar. He stepped forward.

"The coffin is sealed both for quarantine and aesthetic purposes, Ambassador. What is inside does not resemble the daughter you bore and raised. We have," and Qativar beckoned forward one of the crewmen at the air lock bulkhead. He offered a small package which Qativar took. "We have samples for DNA testing which should allay any questions you have about the identity of the remains."

Thomas had gone pale, so pale he seemed translucent. "I want it opened," he repeated.

"You would not want to see her," Vihtirne said. Her

overvoice was silken, compassionate, but her underlying pitch was one of stern command which Qativar heard well. He wondered if the humankind could hear it so well, or if he would just find it compelling.

Thomas stared at them now, his eyes like burning coals in his face, dark and searing. "Who are you," he said, "to question what I want." .

It was a moment which went beyond diplomacy or even the alienness of their races. He was a father. He had a murdered child in the casket in front of him. He had a need to know the truth of her death.

Qativar swallowed. "Very well," he said. He reached inside his jacket for the key.

Vihtirne moved, her dress of darkest blue swirling about her, as she placed her hand across the ambassador's. She was barely taller than the manling, and they looked into one another's face. "You can do this if you wish," she said, "but I would advise you not to. You have memories of her now which will be changed forever by what you see within. Trust me. We have nothing to gain by bringing you another's remains. I ask you not to do this for your sake, and your sake alone."

"I want to see her."

"As any father would. But it is not her you will see."

"I cannot believe. . . ."

"You do not want to believe, and we understand that. But we have made the identification and have brought samples so that your staff can confirm it. Besides," Vihtirne added firmly, "we were there. We saw her heroic death, trying to defend Nedar, who was the foremost *tezar* in my House of Sky. There is no doubt." She took her hand away from Thomas. "Qativar."

He held out the key which would open the hermetically sealed box.

Thomas looked at it for a long moment, then took a quavering breath. "No," he refused it. But he did take the package of testing samples.

"Believe me," Vihtirne breathed. "This is for the best."

Dilarabe called out for crew to take the coffin and stow it away. Thomas watched it go with extreme longing etched into his face. Qativar recognized the expression with satisfaction. He had high hopes for what would follow. He waited until the bulkhead doors had closed again before speaking.

"Our commiserations, Ambassador. We extend our sincerest apologies for the actions of our colleagues and hope that what we offer next will help begin healing the breach between our governments."

Thomas seemed to be standing on his feet with a power that had gone beyond his own meager strength. Color had begun coming back to his face, however, though new lines etched into his cheeks did not appear to be smoothing. "What action?"

Qativar said, "As you know, Nedar and Alexa had begun an alliance, an alliance with us which would allow the birthing of a new House, the House of Tezars. No longer would pilots be slave to or subject to the whims of the Houses and Householdings of their birth."

Dilarabe seemed to draw himself close behind Ambassador Thomas, though he remained silent. The humankind closed his eyes a momemt, swayed, and then pulled himself tall again. "For the return of my daughter's body, I owe you thanks. But I don't owe you anything else, Qativar. I know what Alexa wanted from you and what you probably sought from her, but I do know that if I return to the Halls of the Compact and announce to the worlds in general that the *tezarian* drive, the mechanical discovery of the millennia is nothing more than paranormal drivel, space flight will be ruined. So you have my silence. For the moment. I cannot give you anything more."

Dilarabe jerked in surprise and looked down on the man he shadowed.

Vihtirne began, "You rave—"

Qativar interrupted her. "The truth is not quite what you perceive it to be."

"Oh? It isn't You don't navigate Chaos by esper perception? You don't get from jump-off to decel by merely having a hunch that you're where you want to be? Explain to me, if you can, just where I've gone wrong."

Qativar opened his mouth to respond, but it was Dilarabe who answered, "We do not guess, we *know*."

Thomas took a step back, as if suddenly aware that his humankind crewmen had all left the docking bay and he was surrounded by Choyan. He looked at his commander.

"We *know* because we are masters at reading the Patterns of Chaos. There are random patterns, fractals, attractors which are loci for us. We can read them, though they are never the same, readable even though normal space has collapsed, contracted into an unnavigable miasma. We can read them because it's in our bloodlines to do so. We can guide a ship through FTL because the *bahdur* burns in us. There is no doubt in what we do, and when the power leaves us, when the soulfire is gone, it's as though the very heart is cut from us. But until it leaves me or is torn from me, when I tell you that I know where we go, no matter how we're to get there, I *know*."

Thomas moved back yet again, his voice defensive. "I know what I know," he repeated, though his tone, already thin sounding to Choyan listeners, was barely audible.

"You may know," Dilarabe answered sadly. "But you do not understand."

"It doesn't matter what I understand." The flush which had come back into his cheeks now began to blaze. "It matters that I have the means to produce a drug which can revitalize your *soul*."

Dilarabe's jaw dropped. "What?"

Qativar said smoothly into the sudden silence, "You grieve, Ambassador, but I have misjudged your head for the business at hand."

"We have no business."

"You are a Class Zed planet. You have difficulty obtaining piloting contracts. You've been permitted to remain a part of the Compact temporarily, by the grace of your Abdrelikan status, but that probationary status is soon to come before review. We can help one another greatly."

Qativar was not sure what he read in the depth of the other's eyes, but he stood his ground confidently. He had leverage yet to reveal.

Thomas started to respond, then laughed without humor and shook his head. Then he managed, "You don't get it. If word about the *tezarian* drive gets out, your piloting contracts won't be worth the material they're recorded on."

Qativar shrugged. "You don't seem to get it, either, Ambassador. Without us, there is no intersystem trade. Colonies will wither and blow away like so much chaff in the galactic wind. You can't get off-planet without us."

"It would perhaps be better than being lost in space."

"Not with boost," Vihtirne put in hurriedly. "Ambassador, we can help each other greatly. Hundreds of years of the *tezarian* drive can't be overlooked, not even by one so new to FTL as you are. You may not fully comprehend what we do, but it is undeniable we are successful until fatigue or permanent burnout affects our abilities, and even those vagaries are offset by boost."

"You've even named it."

"Our pilots have. You must understand that it does not give soulfire to those who do not have it, or to the untrained who cannot use it. You are only augmenting a skill, not grafting one."

"I want nothing to do with it. It's a drug, untested, and its effects are unknown."

Qativar said softly, "We know what it can do."

They looked steadily at one another and then Qativar added, "We need the drug. We need a provider. And I think you will want to give it to us, for reasons even other than the advantages we have just pointed out."

"Why?"

"Because," said Qativar even more softly, leaning forward so that only Vihtirne and the ambassador could hear him. "I have come to gift you with the humankind who murdered your daughter. Want him? He is yours, if we can come to an understanding."

Chapter 6

Thomas leaned over the cryo chamber. He had not answered Qativar's question, but neither had he turned the Choyan crew away when they brought in the medical equipment. The honor guard had wheeled it in with considerably less ceremony than they had his daughter's coffin. It was bigger, built for the needs of a Choya, and it dominated the small bay. Its slate gray sides radiated an unemotional frost. Its observation window drew him now, closer, a fatal attraction. He felt as though he were standing on the edge of a tall bridge, unable to fight the gravity which would pull him over and down, down into an uncertain but surely deadly fate.

The chamber sank a chill through Thomas' clothing as he brushed its surface. Its drone was nearly out of his register of hearing, but hung there, an irritating noise that made him clench his teeth as he leaned against the side and bent closer to look into the observation port. He should not look, knew he should not, but he could not help himself. Like a moth nearing a flame, he bent close enough to position himself over the window.

Cold flesh. Even the recent bruising had dulled to purplish charcoal streaks along an alabaster complexion. He had been in a fight or a battle, and had been put down still disheveled, streaks of soot and grit across the backs of his hands, across one brow like a chevron or badge. The dark hair lay unruly, the eyes were closed, the flight suit was torn open along the neckline revealing only a few fine hairs lying curled on the upper torso. He was—he had been—a good-looking young man, Thomas thought. It was no wonder Alexa had taken him for a lover, once. What had Randall thought of her then? Had he been grateful for the gift of passion, of life? Had he loved her back? Had he known

and understood her in the ways a father never could . . .
duplicitous Alexa, Alexa with a dark side she kept well-
hidden from all but the most intimate. What had he thought
when he'd murdered her? Did he, in a sleep beyond dreaming, have the slightest idea of who watched him now, who
hated him beyond even the boundaries of time and space?

"Do we have an understanding? Do you want him?"

The ambassador found himself standing with his hands
clenched on either side of the observation port window,
clenched until the skin across his knuckles went livid. With
a slow deliberation, he took his hands away, breathed deep,
and stepped away. But it was too late to back away from
the brink. He had fallen and knew he would never hit
bottom.

"Yes," he answered. "And yes."

*   *   *

The Halls of the Compact bustled with life, teemed with
sentient races which were, for the most part, at the top of
their respective food chains. Rindalan thought that that
made them more or less secure about their position in the
galactic scheme of things as he watched them file into the
subassembly room where a good many things would be
decided concerning their fate, and he could not tell them
the truth.

The horns upon his head seemed to bear the brunt of
the burden he felt, sending a dull throb through him. Perhaps he had not convalesced enough before taking up this
position. Perhaps he was not diplomat enough to be here
at all, he thought, once more scanning the hall's interior.
Sharp eyes met his glance and turned aside, some defiantly,
most resentfully, a few curiously. He had claimed what few
favors Panshinea had left in his wake to call this vote, and
now that he had it, he was not at all sure he could sway it
in his favor.

He watched the Abdrelik contigent enter, the heavy amphibious bulk of GNask and rrRusk swaying with each ponderous step, but he was no more fooled by their size than
any other member of the Compact. The Abdreliks were
quick, rapacious predators, swift as lightning, and as vicious
as any primal race still struggling to escape the gravitational

ooze of their world. No, the Abdreliks could not be escaped
easily, except in the long run, where stamina and strategy
could be brought into play. Thus the Choyan had survived
their first encounters with the Abdreliks, and stayed ahead
of them, though the long chase had begun to wear on them.

Rindalan reminded himself that he was not in the Halls
for Cho alone, but for all races, for any who chose to face
the Chaos created by FTL flight. Without *tezars* to pilot
the nether regions, no race could spread its wings wide
enough to span the galaxies, all the galaxies, known and
unknown. Without the *tezarian* drive, there was no destiny
for any race beyond the mundane, and without *bahdur,*
there was no safety. But after the centuries of Cho's monopoly, even the lowliest of Compact members had come
to chafe under the secrecy the *tezars* maintained.

What would these fools do if they even guessed that the
Choyan piloted, not by superior navigational devices and
drives, but by the psychic skin of their teeth, Rindalan
thought with a grim satisfaction. And he was here to save
them once more from the disaster such a revelation would
bring. His head continued to throb, and he wondered again,
if it was worth it, all the subterfuge, the manipulation.

The Ivrian ambassador fluttered in, all atwitter. With a
swirl of color and down, he settled at his voting pod.

"Order," stated the Ronin chairperson. His empty quills
rattled at the back of his neck as he looked upon the assembly. This committee had once been Panshinea's to chair—
he had lost it to the Ronin. Rindalan turned jaundiced eyes
on the former assassin who now occupied a podium of
power as if born to it. Faln narrowed his gaze back, his
pointed nails ripping at the notes in front of him, then
looked away as Rindalan met his stare squarely.

The elder wondered what the worlds were coming to. He
stifled a sigh and folded his hands across his lap. Below
him, the Ivrian caught his attention and stared, boldly, for
a split second.

That was a vote he had, Rindalan thought. He gave a
tiny nod in acknowledgment. Immediately in front of him,
the voting pod activated.

"I wish to state my objections," the Ronin said, his voice
vibrating with the strain of reproducing Trade, his tones
rusty as though he had not spoken the language for a long

while. He always sounded like that, the result of a throat wound he'd taken, the wound which had ended his career as an assassin. "This vote has been taken once, and settled, and I do not feel an appeal is necessary in this committee."

Rindalan braced himself for a reply, but GNask took issue instead, interrupting, "Not all of us feel this way, Faln, or the appeal would not have been allowed. Step down and let the process evolve."

The Choyan did not look across at the Abdrelik, lest he show his surprise at the unexpected support.

GNask sat back in the booth, rumbling quietly in his pleasure. rrRusk said, "The old relic is pointedly not looking at us."

"He would not. The prey knows better than to let the predator see the whites of his eyes." GNask put up a hand, caressed the symbiont life which was curled behind his ear. The slug warmed to his touch, stirred, and shifted its footing upon the amphibian's purplish hide. "Nonetheless, he wonders what we are up to."

rrRusk, whose career in the diplomatic pits of Sorrow was nonexistent, said, "What are we up to?"

"We are observing the Choyan ambassador in crisis." GNask took his hand from the *tursh*, which pulsed in a kind of contented purr, and tucked his hands under his heavy jowls. "Do not you, my general, be like these short-sighted fools and ignore the real purpose of this vote. Cho teeters in an uneasy balance, and if she falls, her mystery will crack and perhaps even the *tezarian* drive will be revealed to us."

"I will listen closely, then." The Abdrelik war general grunted and shifted his weight upon the massive bench which held them. Unlike the ambassador's, his symbiont had been left at home. He depended on the various moisturizing and exfoliant creamicides to keep his skin comfortable in space. They did not, nor did the distance from his *tursh* improve his temper any. He looked forward to a mud bath and a cool bottle of beer, one of the few contributions of Terra that he had any use for.

GNask panned the gallery. Though Faln protested the appeal and considered the matter done, the subcommittee had drawn nearly its full roster. There might be some major shifts among the diplomatic blocs this session . . . or there might not. Rindalan, revered though he was on his home planet, hardly held the charismatic abilities of the emperor himself or even of Panshinea's ill-fated predecessor. In the months of his appointment, he had not yet proved to be the torch which illuminated them nor the glue which bound them together.

All of which did not mean that Rindalan did not have the support he needed to sway this vote. He must have, or he would not have called the appeal. Still, GNask thought to himself as he surveyed the hall, there might be some good to be had by adding his own sway. It would be a reversal of his earlier position, but he thought he could explain it if it gained the advantage he needed. If not, well, his career and rrRusk's were already on the line. The only thing that could save him now was the *tezarian* drive.

Cho was undergoing a massive upheaval in its internal politics and alignments. The dearth of eligible pilots had suddenly changed and become, almost overnight, a flood. But the sudden availability of pilots for Compact contracts made GNask as suspicious as it did hopeful. He knew the rigid Choyan standards, and realized that many of those coming into the job were not as qualified as they had been in the past. They had what they wished—more pilots to use the *tezarian* drive—but they did not have what they needed: safety crossing the chaotic zone of warped space. He hoped to be able to press the point over the next session, lobbying for the secret of the drive itself to be made available to all, arguing that piloting was a difficult skill which even the Choyan could not always guarantee, and that it was a burden which should be shared for the good of all.

He perceived the situation like a cracked seal on an air lock, enough pressure and the whole thing would blow skyhigh. The Choyan had begun to fracture along what was once a seamless society. He, among others, could apply the pressure.

GNask rolled back onto a haunch and watched the sharp-faced Ronin ambassador. Faln betrayed little emotion except the bright-eyed attention which typified all of his ilk. He still watched with a hunter's eyes. GNask did not flinch when the Ronin examined him and moved on. Faln had once tried to assassinate GNask within these very halls, and if it had not been for the quick reactions of a Choyan patrolman, GNask would not be alive today. It was the second time in his life a Choyan had saved him. He did not hold it to their account. The patrolman had done it because it was his job within the Compact. Palaton had done it because a Norton assassin had come after the two of them, and it was necessary to save both to save the one. GNask had no illusions. The personal amplifications mattered little to him. He allied with Choyan rarely, and Faln had his uses.

"Order," called the Ronin for the second, and last time. He signaled for the assembly doors to be shut and locked, and the room became muffled and oppressive as the members were sealed in. As the silence shrouded them, Faln pointed his chin at Rindalan.

"I trust the ambassador from Cho has gathered the support he needs to call this assembly."

"I have, your honor," the Choyan said, as he got to his feet. "Or we would not be here."

Faln scarcely acknowledged the formality, eyeing the electronic roleboard in the podium. "Sign in accordingly," he ordered the delegates.

GNask watched Rindalan closely, from a three-quarter angle, searching what he could see of the aged ambassador's face for signs of worry or hesitation, and saw none. He could read nothing in the Choya's body language either, beyond Rindalan's advancing years. The naturally wiry musculature had given way to gauntness, the fringe of hair steadily losing its red-gold luster, the horn crown, bold and impressive even by Choyan standards, seeming somehow diminished. By the egg, Rindalan was old enough to be GNask's grandfather, for the ancient enemy was incredibly long-lived, outside of a pilot's span, and that made Rindalan old indeed. Old but not infirm, never infirm, and GNask could not count on any weakness there.

The Abdrelik leaned forward and punched his own signature on the board. He wiped the corner of his mouth with the fleshy back of one hand, catching a tiny string of spittle from his tusk as he did so. Sitting back, he stared overhead at the screen, waiting for results. Nothing would be projected until all votes were in, so as not to influence those still undecided on the question.

Out of the corner of his eye, GNask saw the first undeniable reaction as Rindalan jerked in surprise as the totals flashed into visibility. The vote was close, extremely close, near enough so that GNask might have been the deciding vote which meant that Rindalan had lost support he'd been led to count upon. The Choya looked as though he fought with himself to not turn and survey the assembly, to see who had defected.

As the ID came up on the voters, however, the Choya's body jerked again, then swung about stiffly as if unlocked, and Rindalan leveled his gaze at GNask. The Abdrelik peeled his lips back in a half-smile. The other knew how he had voted, and that his unexpected support had given the Choya the appeal he asked for, though the question of why the Abdrelik should support Rindalan surely gave the Choya reason to pause.

Faln called for attention and stated, "The vote goes in favor of Rindalan's request, and we are now prepared to hear the appeal."

"I am prepared to give it at this time." Rindalan swayed a bit, then settled back in his chair. The neck which had been slightly bowed, now straightened with determination.

"State your position."

"Ambassadors and delegates of the committee, I would like, first, to thank you for this opportunity," Rindalan began, his voices dry but commanding. The richness of the Choya's throat, with two vocal cords resounding and two voices, subtly underlying one another, filled the small assembly room.

"It was approved by this committee, several days ago, to negotiate with a second pilot contracting group from my world, a group which exists outside the framework of the three schools which have trained *tezars* since the beginning of flight. This was a decision which, I know, was not undertaken lightly, but which I must respectfully request you to rescind. Although the sudden influx of available pilots for contracting must seem a boon to many of you, I must stress that these are not necessarily qualified pilots, and that crossing the void does not leave room for error."

From a dark swirled corner of the assembly, a being stirred, a lithe, sinuous beast which unslitted green eyes, and leaned forward from the shadow. Its Trade was accented with a sibilant hiss. "Does the ambassador suggest that any Choyan pilot is inferior to the challenge of the *tezarian* drive?''

Rindalan looked toward the Norton delegate which, with feline grace, had resettled into the inky backdrop of its area.

"I suggest," the Choya returned, "that you do not know who you're dealing with, and that the current state of internal politics on my world makes normal negotiations considerably riskier."

"Are we to understand that the Vihtirne group is unreliable?" asked the Ronin ambassador sharply.

"I do not have enough facts to prove so, Your Honor, but it is not facts I seek. Those facts, each and every one of them, would mean an unmitigated disaster. I wish to prevent such statistics before they can occur."

The Norton gave a lash of its whiplike tail, but subsided into silence and said nothing further. However, Fain was not finished.

"If we made laws or negotiated by innuendo," the Ronin said, "we would never be done with the process. This appeal was granted on what should have been more concrete offerings. The Compact is aware of a power struggle on Cho, and that the Vihtirne group is but one of several contending against the emperor for control. The Compact intends to stay neutral with regard to your internal politics, but we have been offered what seems to be a good faith opportunity to hire pilots. Unless you provide me with incontrovertible proof that hiring those pilots would be reckless endangerment and downright stupid, I would hesitate to even call this appeal for a vote." Fain cleared his raspy throat after he ground to a halt.

"The proof," Rindalan said, "is that we cannot cross space without the *tezarian* drive and qualified pilots to use it. Those of you who have, over the centuries, tried to discern our navigating process know the truth of what I'm saying. Few can use the drive. Even amongst ourselves, there are those who are borderline in ability, which is not good enough when lives and valuable cargo are on the line. Chaos is an unforgiving phenomenon. It does not give up its dead, or our mistakes, easily."

"You contend that the Vihtirne group offers up ill-qualified pilots."

"I do."

Fain brought up a reading on the podium screen. He looked at it for a moment, then said, "Is Birgnan of Sky an unreliable pilot?"

Rindalan hesitated only a second, but even that hesitation made GNask grow alert. "Your Honor, he graduated from the Salt Towers, but suffered a severe bout of what we call burnout fever and, yes, I would call him unreliable."

"Dangerous?"

Rindalan's spine went stubbornly rigid. The Choya paused before nodding his head once. "Yes."

"What about Lilen of Star?"

"From Blue Ridge. She quit the school voluntarily and returned to run her Householding. She never finished her training."

"And Paes?"

"A stellar pilot. Too old, however, for the job."

"One might say that of you, Rindalan." And Faln glowered down at him.

Rindalan looked back with pale blue eyes. "One might. The difference between the two of us is that this assembly is not going to disappear forever from space norm simply because I requested the hearing."

"Yet, based on the reports I'm bringing up, there have been no complaints from their current contractors."

Rindalan said patiently, "As I've stated, Your Honor, when there is a complaint, it will be because there has been a disaster, perhaps an irreversible one. Shall we sit and wait for it to happen, or should I take action and prevent it?"

GNask listened to the Choya fence with comments from others in the assembly hall, but his attention had become internal now. Rindalan was not telling the truth, entirely, and GNask knew evasiveness when he heard it. But there was a kernel of truth in his statements which had brought the Abdrelik fully awake.

It was not the *tezarian* drive. Perhaps it never had been. The issue here was clearly not the availability of the drive, but of those interpreting and using it. All those centuries, all those lost decades of research, knowingly misguided. *It was the pilots themselves.* And Rindalan had been handcuffed by his own people's secrecy. He could not say what it was that had gone wrong, only that it had and even his own people were no longer to be trusted. It was not in what he had said, in whatever it·was he was going to say, the truth lay in what he could not say, not matter how this council went.

And GNask had had a pilot in his hands and let him slip through. The Abdrelik clenched his fists. John Taylor Thomas had wrenched both his human daughter and the Choya pilot Nedar right out of his grip. As his pulse surged, his *tursh* made a slight murmur of awareness, and its antennae came out, stalk eyes peering about in alarm. GNask reined in his anger and put a soothing finger out to stroke the symbiont's chin. He told himself that if he had done it once, he could do it again, and what better timing than amid the confusion of Cho's own civil war? A great many crimes could be committed in such a climate.

He closed his eyes and prayed to the bogs which birthed him that he had not grown soft in his years as an ambassador, that he would be able to seize this truth and make of it such a victory that his people would never be able to forget it.

When he opened his eyes, to the sound of vigorous piping and arguing by the Ivrian delegate, the vote of the appeal had been postponed. The doors to the assembly hall opened, and the delegates began to leave. Rindalan sat in his booth, unmoving. GNask waved rrRusk off and waited until the Choya finally got to his feet. He stood as the other passed.

Rindalan halted. "Don't think I did not notice your vote," the Choya said, his voices deep, if somewhat thin.

"I knew that you would have," GNask returned.

"And do not think you will gain an advantage by it."

GNask let his lips curl back against his tusks. "I do not," he said. "None that you will give me, anyway."

Rindalan's expression changed, as if he would answer that back. Instead he clamped his lips shut and leaned into motion, moving past the Abdrelik. GNask felt the satisfaction that comes with successfully tracking and cornering a prey. The kill might be postponed, he might toy with the other a bit, but the end was inevitable. Any good hunter knew that.

Chapter 7

"Two things." Panshinea entered his palace, with the bent elderly minister scurrying to keep pace with him, and he paused long enough to let Gathon catch up. "Rindalan was to call a vote. I want to know from him immediately what the outcome was. Secondly, I want to know if you or anyone in security has heard from Palaton." He had just arrived, and the smell of burn off from the landing pads was still on him.

The palace at Charolon was vast, built and rebuilt over the centuries from its early years as a fortress, to a high tech center, and now retrofitted into its past glory, though it would not be inaccurate to say that it was probably a hundred times bigger than its predecessors. Yet, Gathon reflected, Pan filled it. He always had, and even in death, probably would still.

The ruling head of the House of Star cast an aura of charisma and vigor that went beyond finite limits. When he was gone from Charolon, the palace was bereft. When he was home, it seemed bursting with Panshinea's presence. Although, Gathon reflected with a small bit of irony, it did not necessarily indicate Pan's fitness for the throne he occupied.

He took a deep breath, for keeping up with the emperor had winded him somewhat. He was well aware of what he looked like next to the other: spindly, hair thinning from black to yellow-white strands of age, his shoulders bent from the burdens of his job and his scallop-edged crown beginning to grow brittle. Another looking on him might think of retiring him, but Gathon found comfort knowing that Pan did not. Gathon had long ago crossed the threshold of his House. He was not a Sky, he was a Choya in the service of Cho and the emperor of Cho, and if the job were a harness, he wished only to be allowed to die in it. He did not wish it because there would be no retirement for him, no returning to the fold of his Householding because they had forsaken him as he had forsaken them. No, he desired it because it was fitting for him to die as he had lived, in dedication to his office.

He became aware, as Pan's forest green and jade eyes sparked a little, that the emperor had tired of waiting for him.

He cleared his throat. "I have an open line to Rindy, but have not had any word yet on the vote, although he did transmit that a vote had been called."

"Success in that, then, if limited. Hopefully, more news will bring greater success."

Gathon nodded, looking down his notepad, scarcely paying attention to Panshinea's words. "No word from Palaton yet, and I have to replace the head of security. I've taken the liberty of hard-copying some rèsumès and putting them on your desk for your earliest review."

"What's wrong with Jorana?"

"Nothing that I'm aware of. She left her resignation when you announced your return." Gathon lifted his chin, watching Pan.

The emperor's jaw moved. He looked through the massive marble lobby of the entrance hall. His bronze hair curled back thickly from his forehead, a typical Star, gold cast with auburn highlights, face delicately pale, eyes of green or blue, square jaw, tall and wiry of strength. There was aging apparent in his neckline, to be sure, for he was no longer young, but neither was he old. And, even if he were, Panshinea would never have admitted it. Losing Jorana, though, had been a blow. Gathon could see it in his aspect. Though the emperor had not yet taken a wife because his throne took his time and devotion, at one time, he and Jorana had been lovers. He had never admitted it to be more than a dalliance, but Gathon knew that Panshinea's mixed feelings toward Palaton had as much to do with Jorana as they did with the undeniable fact that Palaton represented the future beyond Pan's time as emperor, a future which Pan was trying as hard as he could to delay.

"Is she . . . all right?"

"I could not say, sire. I have not heard from her, or of her, since she left."

"Did she give an explanation for her resignation?"

"Only that it was a personal reason; and that she could not serve with divided loyalty."

Pan's jaw ticked. He stared, into the palace lobby as if seeking an answer written on air, before looking down at Gathon. "I'll look over the files. I take it you recommend promoting from within rather than searching outside the ranks?"

"Jorana left you an excellent security force. There are half a dozen candidates who ought to do well in her position."

"All right, then." Panshinea paused, then gathered himself. "The rest of the business we should conduct in my music room."

The music room, along with a small and intimate library, were the only rooms in the palace guaranteed to be secure against all manner of eavesdropping, both high tech and psychic, although Gathon sometimes wondered to himself how such a thing could be guaranteed. It mattered to him because if the security of those two rooms could be breached, then his own life would be worth very little in the emperor's eyes. Still, for all the conversations they had had in those two rooms over the decades, no word had ever been repeated. Perhaps Panshinea's faith was not misplaced, after all.

Pan sat at the self-standing *lindar*. He splayed his right hand over the keyboard, barely touching it, and producing a plaintive strain. He stared at the keys a moment as if contemplating another stroking, then put his shoulders back and lifted his head to gaze across the room at Gathon.

"No word from Palaton."

"Not yet."

"It would not be well advised if he were to hold his peace."

"I agree with you," Gathon remarked, though both knew well it did not matter if Gathon agreed or not.

"But he does not respond."

"I have had no word of him since he left Blue Ridge five days ago."

Panshinea flinched. His verdant gaze moved past Gathon to stare out the music room window, at a garden few if any even knew existed within the palace walls. Because of its secrecy, even the landscapers did not tend it. Only Pan, in sporadic moods of floral creativity, or Gathon if the drought withered it too badly. It was feral and somewhat seedy, and altogether beautiful because it had not been so carefully sculpted. It simply *was*, and that in itself was quite an accomplishment. "Blue Ridge in ruins," he murmured.

"Yes, sire."

"How could that have happened?"

"Not by Palaton's design."

"No. No, I think he would sooner have cut off his right hand than destroyed a flight school. Although neither Qati-var nor Vihtirne have proved any more agreeable to an interview than Palaton, I will lay the blame in their laps. They will feel no guilt, of course, using the martyrdom of Blue Ridge to help build the foundation for their new House." Panshinea's thick neck muscles rippled as he looked back to the keyboard. This time, he deliberately stroked the *lindar*, evoking a sinister chord. "What about the drug?"

"It's called boost on the streets."

"Does it work?"

"Only if one has *bahdur*. The commons have no real use for it."

The *lindar* quieted. Panshinea met his eyes. "Do you think it will help me?"

This was a conversation Gathon suddenly knew he wished to have no part of. He shifted weight. "I . . . don't know."

"I understand it banishes the fatigue which blocks *bahdur*. That would seem to be something quite desirable."

"It's an off-world drug. Supplies, now, are limited. I have not been able to obtain any for analysis, but even if I could, we don't know that we could duplicate it. Pan, it is like wondering if sleight of hand and illusion can substitute for *bahdur*. It may seem adequate on the first flash, but its substance is entirely different and transient."

"But you don't know that."

"No. I don't."

Panshinea became very quiet, and Gathon knew he was pondering what the drug might mean to him if it were genuine. His gift of *bahdur* had been prodigal, but his days as emperor had steadily drained it, and now his body felt the creeping agony of neuropathy, the death of the nerve field which created and fed soulfire. As surely as a *tezar,* he was burning dry, and as surely as any pilot who'd lost it, he felt the edge of the madness and the emptiness which accompanied the condition. But while there were Householdings which would take back their sons and daughters who'd mastered Chaos and been fortunate enough to return, there was no niche for failed emperors. Cho never had more than one emperor at a time. Death was Panshinea's only future, if the soulfire guttered out completely. His enemies, and perhaps even his successors, would tear him to shreds.

They would do so even sooner if they knew that he perpetuated what little *bahdur* he had left by stealing it from others. Gathon did not approve of Panshinea's actions, but he was an accomplice in them nonetheless, and had been for twenty years, because until this juncture in time, Pan had been the emperor for Cho. Now, he was beginning to have his doubts. Now, he did not know how far he was willing to continue to go to keep the throne occupied. He stood, with a face as blankly solemn as possible, knowing that if Pan could read his thoughts, he would be dead before he crossed the threshold of the music room.

But theirs had been a long association. Gathon had never had any indication that Panshinea, though rumored to, had ever possessed that particular Choyan ability. Few did. Perhaps it had been eradicated when the House of Flame had been destroyed centuries ago, a talent erased along with others, good and bad, out of fear and jealousy. "I have to do something, Gathon," Panshinea said softly, his voices shot through with desperation and longing.

"I know, sire," Gathon responded with compassion. "I know you do." His communicator let out a low buzz and he clapped a hand to his belt. Stepping to the desk near him, he picked up the comline and found that the transmission from Sorrow they'd been waiting for was now coming in.

Pan let out a sigh. "I'll wait," he said, and beckoned for

Gathon to go retrieve a printout from decoding. He looked back to the garden and the walls which harbored it. "I'm not going anywhere."

Malahki found Father Chirek in the second bolt-hole he searched, a squalid, odoriferous excuse for a home in the undersection of the commons' quarter in Charolon. He had not thought to find Dorea's priest anywhere in the capital, but his objective had been to find a place from which he could operate business of his own, and the priest had been there, sleeping on a low-slung cot which had seen better decades.

The boat trip from the harbor city where Dorea quartered had left him stiff and tired. City security in Charoion had been alert and he'd taken back streets, wending his way into the inner quarters. He'd thought for a brief moment that he was too old for this, that he was nearing the age of being a grandfather, that he ought to be sitting in a solarium watching his grandchildren romp, but he had no family left. Jorana had been his fosterling and he'd thought perhaps to share her family, but once she had gained the talent necessary to become Housed, he'd been forced to carve a new destiny for her. His work with her had its successes and failures, but it had changed the relationship between them forever.

As a security agent, she had been his contact as well as his enemy. He could not fault Jorana. She had managed to walk a fine line, serving both her emperor and her foster father well. But how did she now serve herself? Malahki had no delusions that he had followed Dorea's instructions as much to find Jorana as to find Palaton.

And all he had done so far was to find another strife-worn revolutionary. Malahki smiled gently and leaned forward to awaken his old friend.

A spark of *bahdur* jumped from Malahki's hand to the other's brown-clothed shoulder as he touched him into waking. Power calling to power. The phenomenon never ceased to amaze Malahki, though it could be something as simple as static electricity being released. He had never been aware of it in all the years of his life among the greetings of the Housed. Did they even notice it? He wondered if his newly awakened soulfire were perhaps stronger or greater than the average.

Father Chirek opened heavy eyelids and groaned when he saw Malahki leaning over him. He sat up, slumped against the rough adobe walls of the room, and rubbed his eyes clearer. "Took you long enough," he remarked.

"She sent you here as well?"

"Indeed. Said that we were a pair, useless at anything without the other." The renegade priest smiled wryly. He was at the crossroads between youth and age, his face just beginning to acquire character and wisdom, his eyes still clear and unlined, a face of earnestness and honesty, Malahki thought. Father Chirek had lived for years working for the future which blind Dorea saw so well, and he had been far from ineffective with or without Malahki. The room which held him now was quite different from the home which he had occupied formerly—before the Change had been wrought in him, and the prophecy for which he had trained his whole life had begun unfolding about him. That home had been abandoned, for he had left a life as a mere data clerk in the employ of the government and gone in search of a Prophet—and found her.

Malahki pulled up a stool and rested his weight upon it. "She chides you inappropriately."

"She chides all of us, the child suddenly become parent. As for the appropriateness—she has the Sight, I do not. Like a tapestry weaving, tomorrow is far more subtle and varied than I could guess." Chirek took a deep breath and then let it out. "I doubt that Palaton will contact us, but if he is here, thinking to respond to the emperor publicly, then he will need to have some sort of network in place. He won't come to us, not after taking Rand from us, and may well avoid all commons because of that. No allies there. Yet, despite all that happened at Blue Ridge, I think I may have found it."

"Who would he go to?"

"Who else would a pilot go to but other *tezars*?"

Chirek's statement took Malahki aback. "Surely not, after what Vihtirne has done. There is no refuge there."

"Not pilots who can work. There is too much chaos there, at the moment. I mean pilots who cannot. Retired *tezars*."

"Ah." Malahki scratched his brow. "Few and far between. Reclusive. Embittered. Nor particularly sane, any that I ever met."

"All it takes is one or two. There was the *tezar* who worked as bodyguard for young Rand. . . ."

Malahki searched his memory frantically for a name that fit the image: *tezar* in his prime, cut away from service by an injury which even their medical technology could not reverse, fitted with an arm prosthesis he sometimes used and sometimes shunned. The name came to him in a flash.

"Traskar!"

Chirek nodded. "If we can find him."

Traskar had not suffered burnout, he had suffered amputation. He had *bahdur*, he had tolerated, even developed a friendship with Palaton's alien companion—yes, Palaton might well feel Traskar an ally to be sought out.

For the first time in days, Malahki felt as though Dorea had not assigned him an impossible task. He rubbed his hands as though anticipating the pulling together of the hidden reins of Chirek's network. "Oh, we'll find him. Let us hope that Palaton finds him as well."

Chapter 8

"Vihtirne of Sky awaits, Your Majesty," Gathon said.

The emperor of Cho looked up from his console, responding to his friend's tone. "Do I detect a note of disapproval in your voices, Minister?"

The aging Choya raised an eyebrow, adding another knifelike crease to the many in his face. The yellow-white streaks in his dark mane had increased, Panshinea realized, multifold during his absence. "You do, Panshinea," Gathon returned. "By asking her here, you lend her authority she does not need."

"You think this private council legitimizes the House of Tezars?"

"I think this meeting will confirm several of her suspicions, as well as lend weight to her usurpation. However," and Gathon bowed stiffly, "what's done is done."

"What would you suggest I do now?"

"I would suggest," the minister answered quietly, "that you not keep her waiting." He stood in the doorway, shoulders hunched slightly.

Panshinea took a deep breath. He did not like crossing the instincts of his minister, and bearing Gathon's disapproval now was like adding a heavier weight to the burden which already threatened to overwhelm him. Anger began to shove his regret aside. Where was Gathon when these momentous decisions had to be made? No, that was when he, Panshinea, stood alone. He always had. He always would. The emperor motioned with a hand. "All right. Show her in."

After a moment of silence, she filled the threshold. He would, Panshinea reflected, have to have been a dead Choya not to feel her presence charging the room. As a faint drift of perfume reached his nose, he turned and beheld her.

Viihtirne of Sky was still a Choya'i of great beauty, he thought. If the genetic imperative to stay within one's House were not so great, he, a Star, might even have considered her a potential mate and empress. He had flirted with that consideration many times during his long reign and association with her. She was, like him, no longer firmly in her prime, but it scarcely mattered to a Choya'i. If they wished, they could be fertile until far past their middle years. Fertility among the Choyan was not a gender issue. The female, as well as the male, had complete control over her ability to conceive and bear children.

Perhaps, Panshinea reflected, he should simply have asked Viihtirne to become his mistress. No untoward mingling of their Houses' genetic heritage would have been called for, though the arrangement would have been just as unconventional. The couplings of ambitions, as well as sexual drives, would have been spectacular. But he doubted that she then, as she certainly would not now, would have accepted such a proposal.

She wore a sheath of deep, shimmering blue that accentuated her eyes and the still jet-dark mane of hair that cascaded from her horn crown. Her shoulders remained as smooth as her neckline, her peach-toned skin firm and unblemished. As she stepped forward, there was something more to her regal and sophisticated carriage, an air of expectation, and Pan knew with a sinking heart that Gathon had been right, more than right. Viihtirne thought this meeting of greater import than he'd intended.

Another mistake, for a throne already mired in mistakes. He threw back his shoulders, then stood to take her hand, remembering all too well why he'd never asked her to be his mistress. She would never have been happy in the throne's shadow. She intended to have it for herself.

And she would have it yet, over his dead body, if she could contrive it.

"Emperor. It has been too long." She offered him a hand, which he took briefly.

"I agree. You look as lovely as ever."

Her deep-set eyes considered him. "I wish I could say the same for you," she returned finally. "But I do not think the burdens of the throne are good for a Choya of your temperament. The confinements of the position have worn on you."

He led her across the chambers and let her choose where she would sit, on a divan or the *lindar* bench or a high-backed chair upholstered to look as though it were the feathered tail fan of a *ferentar*. She chose the chair. The multihued splendor of the tail fan set off the dark sheen of her hair spectacularly, giving him pause and her an advantage which he was not willing to grant. As he caught his breath, he deliberately chose the *lindar* bench, sitting before the keyboard instrument as if the meeting were incredibly casual. The briefest of frowns creased her face and then was smoothed away.

"The position," he admitted, "has duties and obligations more wearing than most Choyan could imagine. Even without interference, it would be difficult to do one's best. Yet, if you or anyone else were to ask me if I wished to give it up, I would have to be frank and tell you that I am not yet ready. There is much I think I can still accomplish."

Vihtirne arranged a fold of her skirt about her ankle. "Perhaps I can be of assistance."

"No. I don't think so," Pan told her easily. He put an elbow on the *lindar*. A faint note tinkled from the keyboard.

"Then, please, Your Majesty, tell me why you've summoned me. I assure you I cannot possibly guess." The natural arrogance of the House of Sky rose in her face, intensifying her blush.

"To warn you, not once but twice."

The hard glitter in her eyes did not soften a speck. "Warn me? Pray tell, Emperor, am I in trouble?"

"I will not recognize the House of *Tezars*," he told her. "Nor will the Congress."

She put out a hand, smooth, relatively unlined or freckled with age, and stroked her knee through the fabric of her skirt. She looked back up at him, unruffled. "Perhaps once," she said, "you could have known that, with whatever assurances and guarantees came to the emperor who sat the throne of Cho. Now, however, our world is upside down. You cannot threaten me with any great surety, just as I," and she smiled coldly, "cannot threaten you."

Panshinea let his face move in an unanswering smile of equal chill. "Do not make light of this, Vihtirne. I'm busy. I didn't summon you here to trivialize matters. I have word from my ambassador on Sorrow that the Compact there has agreed not to accept piloting charters with your House, pending investigation."

He expected her to show the blow he'd dealt her, perhaps even to surge to her feet, voices ringing as she declared, "You have done what?"

But Vihtirne of Sky did not even twitch an eyebrow. The moment of silence stretched between them. Finally, she stirred. "The Great Wheel, with only three Houses to turn upon it, is unbalanced. You can't be so much a fool as to ignore the *tezars*."

"I find it in the best interest of Cho to do so."

Vihtirne now moved her head, stretching her graceful neck, to look at him slightly askance. She turned her hand, palm up, on her knee as if she cupped something. "The courts have returned the water recycling patent to my House. More specifically, to me. Do not make me use something so vital as clean water as a tool to have the House of *Tezars* recognized."

Her declaration struck him to his core. She had him, if she chose to use her power. The recycling patent had been made public centuries ago, for the common good, but he knew she had been pursuing its return. Damn Gathon, who had not told him the decision had finally come through. And damn the courts, who normally could have kept this ball bouncing for a decade or so, if they'd wished. The House of Star was in its descendant. He knew it, they all knew it. The only question now was how long, how far, the fall.

Vihtirne returned his stare evenly. He felt something turn in him. She did not have him, or she would not be sitting here so meekly. He did not know what it was, but there was something holding her back. She had hoped, not demanded, that he would recognize the founding of the new House. There was something she had *not* said which was equally as important as what she had. There was danger here, but not necessarily defeat. Panshinea sucked in his stomach as well as his resolve.

"You cannot be of two Houses," Panshinea told her. "Either one or the other. If you leave Sky for the *tezars*, think very carefully on what it is you leave behind." He stood. "And that brings me to my second warning. You presume, because of our chaotic situation, that the Wheel must be balanced, but you've assumed there is room for your ambitions. There is not. The fourth House has returned to its rightful place on the Wheel, a House risen from out of the ashes of its downfall. What you Skies, we, and the Earthans feared most has come about, regardless of our past. The House of Flame has returned to Cho."

He heard, with satisfaction, the tiniest of gasps from Vihtrne. When he looked back at her, he saw she had paled.

"How is this possible?"

"A genetic selection which could not be denied, however destructive it may be." He shrugged. "Who knows? If any were left or hidden, there was bound to come a time when they would gain enough strength to be felt again. And if they were the tree from which we all branched, we would be fools to ignore them, my dear. We learned some difficult lessons in our past about genetic manipulation. It appears we are still students to the God and nature which carved us."

Vihtirne did stand then. She mouthed derision. "Don't spout platitudes at me, Panshinea. There could be no Flames today if someone had not hidden them during the scourging. What was destroyed once before can be destroyed again. They will not take my spot upon the Great Wheel! The *tezars* have made Cho—they will have a House, if I have to build it stone by stone. If there are Flames, they can't be in force, not yet, or they would have shown their hand. What do you know of them?"

"I know," said Panshinea heavily, "that they won't be put down again. We have, both of us, tried to deal with Palaton before."

"Palaton! A Flame!" Vihtirne spun about, her dress shimmering around her slender form. "That explains much," she commented softly. Her eyes met his squarely. "And you, fool, made him an heir to the throne."

"A warning," repeated Panshinea, as though what she said had not stung him, though it had. "Make of it what you will. Before you threaten the throne, and the fabric of life on Cho by rescinding your patent, I think you had better consider the enemy a little more closely."

Vihtirne's eyes narrowed, and her voices dropped into a faint purr. "Do you suggest an alliance, Emperor?"

Panshinea dared to turn his back on her, spreading his slender hands over the *lindar* keyboard, keeping his fingers suspended over the instrument. "I suggest only," he said, "that you have more options to consider than you believed." He then dropped his hands lightly down and began to play, drowning out whatever her response might have been with music, an imperial dismissal. He did not sit, but let the keyboard take his leaning weight.

Gathon came, in response to the *lindar,* and escorted Vihtirne out. She looked back once, eyes flashing, over her shoulder. Panshinea, swept up in the beauty of the song he was playing, tossed his head back and caught a glimpse of her look before she swept out the door. It sent a chill down his back, and he frowned in concentration to keep his playing from faltering.

It was as though he'd looked Death in the face and won only the barest of reprieves.

Still, he must have set her to thinking, and hesitating about weakening his position further. For the moment, she would be pondering what to do about Palaton and the possible rise of a House of Flame. The corner of his mouth quirked. Not that Palaton would do such a thing by design. Wherever the heir to the throne was, he must surely be focusing on more elemental matters—like staying alive.

If the imperial guards could not ferret out the pilot, perhaps Vihtirne's more numerous and less scrupulous contacts could do the job. Then Panshinea could throw him a lifeline, if Palaton acquiesced to his will and terms. And if Palaton destroyed Vihtirne instead, so much the better.

Gathon returned.

Sharply, Panshinea broke off playing. "Why didn't you tell me the decision had come in on the recycling patent?"

"Has it?" Gathon knotted his face tightly. "I was unaware. I knew it was pending. . . ."

"I don't think she was bluffing, entirely," Panshinea remarked. He sat down heavily on the bench. "She wants that House."

"Did you think she would renounce it for you?"

" 'No," he answered to the minister's dry tone. "Not really. Do you think, old friend, there's room on the Great Wheel for five Houses?"

"I imagine," Gathon told him, "that the God-in-all would have room for any number of Houses, if we had the strength to found them. It is we who are limited, not the Wheel of Life."

The minister's words hit him like a refreshing spring breeze, and he gave out a soft laugh in response. "Are you sure you wouldn't want to consult with Prelate Rindalan before you answer so quickly?"

"No," said the other solemnly. "We've traded philosophies before. I believe we would be of the same mind on this matter." Gathon did hesitate, however, before leaving. "Anything else you wish at the moment?"

Panshinea knew that the other was going to check his court reports, as well as attend to other duties. He sighed heavily as the moment of lightness inevitably fled. "Find her, Gathon, find her and bring her back."

"Who, Your Majesty?"

"Jorana."

"I'm afraid that's not prudent at the moment, but I will issue the orders, if that's what you wish."

Pan's eyebrow flew up. "You know where Jorana is?"

"No, sire. I can issue the order, but I'm afraid it won't do much good. Rindalan might be able to unearth her. He has resources we cannot count, as well as abilities. He seems to be doing quite well on Sorrow. Perhaps a prelate is not so different from a diplomat after all, eh?"

"No. No, I guess not. And from what sideline might the best emperors come?"

Gathon answered with scarcely a pause. "I always thought that those who wanted it most fiercely ought to be given the throne. You were a natural. Vihtirne, too, would have been, if she had been a Star instead of a Sky. The Houses should stay in order."

"And after the Stars, who do you look for?"

He scratched his chin quickly. "The Flames. The Earthans cannot compete within the Compact. If your House must give way, then it should go to the Flames. The Skies have had their turn.

"And what about blood?"

"I have never approved of a succession. Emperors ought to fight for what they want, like the rest of us. May the strongest one win."

"Only the strongest? What about the best?"

"It scarcely matters, Your Highness. We have a representative system in place. Checks and balances. No. The strength, the desire, that's what should win out. It's the only rock which will withstand the weight of the office." Finished, the minister began to walk out the door. He paused on the threshold. "Don't you agree, sir?"

"I'll let you know," Panshinea said dryly, "when I'm finished."

Gathon sketched a bow and left the study.

Chapter 9

Berthing at Sorrow with a crate big enough to handle both the coffin and the cryonic casket under the seal of a diplomatic pouch was difficult only in the actual physical transference. Deep space cruisers were not allowed dirtside on the Compact planet. Ambassador Thomas had to wait for a shuttle with a large enough cargo hold to give him transport down. He'd asked legal to meet him and Maeva was at the dock, a dash of a frown line marking her young face.

"You do know you're pushing ambassadorial rights bringing that in. The boundaries of our probation are being stretched very thin."

Thomas watched as robot arms unloaded the massive crate, their cables groaning in response to its weight and unwieldiness. "It's my daughter's remains," he answered slowly. "I do not feel like putting my life on display, at the moment."

His legal counsel shifted uneasily, then said, "Then that's the biggest damn coffin I've ever seen for . . ." She paused.

Thomas tore his gaze away from the crate and looked down at her. Young, he thought, as Alexa had been. And, in her way, equally ambitious. Her boss had sent her in his place to greet the ambassador. Thomas did not normally appreciate youth and inexperience, but felt it could work to his advantage in this instance. "Yes? For what?"

She blushed faintly. "For someone supposedly burned to death in the wreckage of a crash."

He could feel himself blink. Anger, such as he'd had, and tears, had been replaced by a core of iciness. Her statement hit home and found an emotional vacuum. The corners of his lips pulled. "Yes," he agreed. "It is. The biggest damn coffin I've ever seen. But I don't want the seal on that pouch broken."

"It won't be. That's why I'm along," Maeva said confidently. She took an extra half step to keep up with Thomas as he took the walkway out of the docks. Compact customs inspections looked up, scanned their notepads, matched the bar codes on the crate, and frowned almost in unison, but no one stopped the barge which carried the diplomatic pouch through the docks. A forklift took it from the hover barge as it emerged from the warehouse without incident.

Maeva let out her breath in a tiny puff. Thomas looked down, amused that she had been so confident and yet so tense. "Primed for a fight?"

"If necessary." She had her notebook open. As the forklift transferred the pouch to the embassy's own hover barge, she flipped the notebook closed and sealed it, and slung it from its strap over her shoulder. "I have a car, Ambassador."

"Good. Is the freight barge programmed as I requested?"

That intense little dash-line of worry reappeared. "Yes, sir, but it's highly irregular—"

"I'll take care of it. This is my business. I don't want Quinonan or Abdrelikan spies looking over my shoulder."

"Yes, sir."

The car door opened for them. Thomas offered her a hand in and then, ducking slightly, seated himself. The car was from their own embassy, nonetheless he ran a quick scan for bugs before he settled back into the upholstery, the attorney watching him closely.

"Ambassador."

"Maeva."

"How much interference are you expecting?"

"None, if the freight barge follows its delivery programming." The delivery programming took the crate to their warehouse where, ostensibly, it would be left. However, Maeva knew that cloaking had been ordered, and that the crate would be transferred later, in stealth, to the embassy. Uncomfortably, she wondered just what else was being brought in.

She shifted uneasily. "I must protest, Ambassador, if anything you're doing jeopardizes our diplomatic mission here on Sorrow."

"You must?" He looked down at her.

Maeva felt her lips going dry. His seniority was unquestionable, as had been his integrity and his service. That had been his reputation, but now, as he looked at her, she could see the years in him, and the death which his daughter had brought to him, and the emptiness in his eyes. She tried to swallow, and did not find it easy. "Yes. I must. If only to protect your own rights, as well. This procedure is highly irregular and—"

"Necessary."

"Necessary?"

"Yes. I brought not only a body back with me, but a life. The life of the man accused of my daughter's murder. But he's more than a murderer, he is the only one of us to have lived successfully among the Choyan. He is the only surviving eyewitness to the firestorming of Arizar, to the attempted invasion of Cho by Abdrelika, and to the current political turmoil surrounding the throne of the *tezarian* empire. Now tell me, Maeva—how far do you think this young man will get if we do not give him full embassy protection?"

Thoughts flashed by. "Not far," she answered briskly.

"Then are you reassured that there is a method to my madness?"

"Yes."

"Good." He sat back in the car again, eyes glittering. "This information is given in confidence, and I expect it to remain confidential. Even from your supervisors. When the crate has been delivered successfully, you and I have an interview to conduct."

Maeva nodded. She sat back as well, still and quiet, and wondered what she'd gotten herself into.

Palaton had thought to leave Charolon for sanctuary at Blue Ridge and the irony of returning to find haven, even if only temporarily, did not escape him. After sending Rufeen and Hat reluctantly away, he had worked his way crosscountry by jet sled to the capital. He decided to hide among the crowds of workmen from the God-blind classes, construction crews who had been brought in to rebuild the quarters devastated by the rioting of months past. The regeneration of Charolon was in full swing, and he found it fairly easy to pass on the streets and in the lunchrooms among the workers even though the city teemed with security.

It was not only the commons who were blind, he thought, as he made his way through the crews. Security looked through him and his rugged coveralls and the ragged shag he'd cut his hair into, his shuffled steps and chin down walk, looked through him as though he did not exist. Perhaps it was his discipline as a *tezar*, but the inevitable calling of talent to talent was one which he could keep under tight control, and he thought perhaps it was one of the ways in which they'd hoped he'd betray himself. If that was what they wanted from him, Palaton determined, they would not get it. He was a master and when he came to Emperor Panshinea, he would do it in his own time and his own way. So their sharp-eyed sight looked straight through him, never identifying their prey. In the meantime, he walked the streets of the commons, ate with them, slept at the work camp sites, and searched the city.

At night, he slept fitfully, his dreams invaded by the countenance of the Prophet, her eye holes bound from sight by a rusty cloth, yet looking for him. The summonses she sent him remained the same when they reached him in his slumber and he kicked them off as fitfully as he did his meager flophouse covers. He awoke cold and shivering, his jaw clenched in determination not to answer her, not to reveal himself despite the inhospitable condition of his surroundings, as though her displeasure had visited it upon him in punishment.

He had little enough coin. Hat had pressed it upon him when they parted, dear stumpy Hat whose crust had dissolved when the last of his cadets had gone. It had been as though Hat had kept going only as long as there had been the least facade of his school. When the last pupil left, so had his competent exterior. Rufeen had clucked and taken him under her brawny wing, so to speak, and that was when Palaton knew he could never have brought them. Hat could not have managed, at least not at the moment, and Rufeen had to manage for Hathord, so he could not ask her to abandon their friend.

But Hat had torn up plaster at what had once been the

doorway of his study and unearthed a stiff, leather bag of coin and split it two ways, tucking the major portion into Palaton's hands.

"You'll need it," he said.

Palaton had been unable to dispute that. He would need it, to live, at least until he faced Panshinea. After that it depended on how well he'd planned. He'd curled his fingers over the money. "Thank you."

Hat had nodded brusquely, as though his neck were stiff and disjointed, and turned roughly away. Rufeen's lips came together in tight sympathy, as her eyes met Palaton's for a last time, and she turned away also.

Now, awake in the early morning hours, aware of the workers beginning to stir in their rough cots around him, Palaton fished out a coin for *bren* and held it between his knuckles as he completed dressing. He took everything with him in a meager kit. He'd stayed there three nights in a row, one night too many for caution, but he'd been tired and lazy last night. He would not come back to this sleephouse this evening.

He rubbed sleep from his eyes as he passed the house's doorway. The sky was streaked charcoal and blue as dawn fingered its way into being through clouds. He could smell *bren* brewing from a sidewalk shop down the street, strong and substantial, just how he liked it. He made his way there and plunked his coin down on the counter.

The commons server did not look at him twice as he dipped out a huge mug and passed it over. He did not look at Palaton at all until their hands accidentally touched as Palaton reached for his drink.

A tiny spark shot through them. The server's chin jolted up and his eyes flew wide. He looked at his fingers and then at Palaton. He blinked.

"You," he said quietly, containing the word with difficulty, as though he'd wished to shout it.

Nearly as startled, Palaton had jerked his *bren* back across the counter, hugging it to his chest to keep it from spilling, shocked that a God-blind would have provoked such a reaction from his *bahdur*.

He swallowed. "You mistake me."

"Never. But that does not matter. I must talk with

you. . . ." The server's gaze left Palaton's face as the door opened, and a crowd of eager workmen came in, calling loudly for their mugs to be filled.

Palaton stepped back, thinking of disappearing in the crowd, knowing that the server would never find him if he did. But something held him back, tugging at his curiosity and also his duty. He found a corner and sat, unfolded a plastisheet to look over the synopsis from the local broadcasters, and waited for a lull in the activity.

More than an hour passed before the servers finished with the demand, and dawn streamed fully in the windows as the crew stamped out of the *bren* house. The last dregs in Palaton's mug had gone cold and muddy, and the broadcasters' words had been tossed to another table when the server straightened his apron and came from behind the counter to sit with him. He left a Choya'i to fill the last few orders of stragglers and brought a fresh pot with him, filling Palaton's mug anew and then his own.

He tapped a packet of sweetener into the *bren* and even then drew back his lips after swallowing, as though its bitterness was not appreciated. Palaton reflected that perhaps only a pilot could fully appreciate *bren* for the subtlety and depth beyond its bitterness. He could see the other prepare to speak.

"Do not use names."

The commons answered, "I do not intend to. However, I know who you are."

"You might be mistaken."

"If you're a laborer, you've missed the opening of your shift."

"My skills allow for flexibility."

"You're lucky at that, then. I have a friend with skills similar to yours, but he's no longer in demand. With only one good hand—" The server shrugged.

"One hand." Palaton could only think of one *tezar* with whom he had a relationship, and that had been one-armed Traskar. He'd brought Traskar back into the palace to guard Rand temporarily. Did this commons claim to know both Palaton and Traskar?

"One arm," the server corrected congenially. "But even shortchanged as that, he does not have to work among the commons."

The hair prickled at the back of Palaton's neck. This one need drop no more hints. He knew Palaton for a pilot, even if he did not know him for the heir to the throne of Cho, although Palaton thought perhaps this one knew him for all that he could lay claim to.

"What," he returned, "can I do for you?"

"Meet with my friend. His skills might be to your advantage."

"Somewhere public. I am a bit shy, at the moment."

"The fountain at Cliburn Street," the server returned promptly.

"That will do. Noonish?"

The server looked out the bank of windows where the cloud-streaked sky looked as though it were trying unsuccessfully to warm. "I think," he answered carefully, "that could be arranged. But I would urge you to act with caution, shy or not, for public places can draw attention neither of you will wish.

"I'll keep that in mind." Palaton stood, set his empty mug down, and dropped a small denomination coin into it. "Thank you for the *bren*."

The God-blind server picked up the cup. "It is my job," he answered simply. "I was Housed once, but showed no talent for it. I have a great-uncle who was Housed as well, and left it to serve the throne of Cho. We agreed not to mention names, but I am proud of my uncle Gathon. He says that each of us should serve the destiny of Cho as best we can. He would be pleased to know we had this conversation."

Before Palaton could quite comprehend all that the Choya had said, the server had left the table and disappeared into his kitchens, where the rattling of pans indicated he had begun brewing *bren* again, for the next wave of morning workers.

Palaton left, musing. So canny old Gathon had thought to put him together with Traskar. A good thought. Probably one the minister had never hoped would come to fruition, but which he had scattered throughout his many networks, hoping that if anyone came in touch with Palaton, it would be passed along.

And it had.

Gathon, Palaton thought, would have been a far better

emperor than Panshinea. He shrugged into his jacket, letting his mane slump shaggy and matted over his forehead, and shuffled against a brisk wind as he walked crowded sidewalks.

The server watched him go through his window banks, then walked to the rear of his shop and opened a comline. When Chirek answered, the server said only, "It is done." Without waiting for answer, the Choya hung up and then looked at his fingertips where the talent had zapped him gently, as if chiding him, reminding him. He stopped by his sink and laved his hands thoroughly before going back out front where late breakfasters would soon begin to clamor for *bren* and fry bread.

Chapter 10

Even looking for him, Palaton did not find it easy to spot Traskar. He was wearing his prosthesis, which filled out his jacket naturally, and he walked through the lunchtime crowd with an easy swing of his arms that belied his artificial limb. It was the walk itself which gave him away as he approached the fountain, the walk of someone who had strolled cruiser corridors, who had dealt with artificial gravity and zero gravity, who carried his body with a different sense of symmetry than a Choya who had never left the dirt of his birthing. It was a swagger not unlike a sailor's swagger, as distinctive as the plowman's trudge of a farmer, or the balanced carriage of a dancer.

Palaton's senses knew it almost before he recognized it, knew it and alerted him. Then he recognized the horn crown and brow. It was Traskar and the former *tezar* was just as carefully looking for him as he crossed to a seat below the famed fountain of Cliburn and sat down to wait.

Palaton did not suspect treachery, but he allowed himself a quick sweep of the area. Because it was a little after noon, and because he had had only *bren* that morning, he bought himself a twist of vegetable stew and, cup in hand, joined Traskar at the fountain's base.

Traskar flinched as he sat down, then, eyes trailing over him, flicking away and coming idly back, the pilot gaped in astonishment.

Palaton smiled around a forkful of lunch. "Time doesn't change you much."

"Necessity warps the hell out of you." Traskar stuck his natural hand out. "Good to see you again. I heard you've lost the manling. Need some help trailing him?"

"Had him stolen, and no. No, whoever's got him is keeping him for leverage, I fear." The falling water of the fountain kept their voices from carrying, but Palaton watched as they spoke, nonetheless. "He's gone and now is not the time for me to deal with it."

"Then what can I do?" Traskar sat back against the limestone, eyeing him somewhat warily. There were shadows under his eyes, faint bruises of sleeplessness, but for all the wear and tear caused as a result of his career, he looked fit.

"I want you to protect me against the emperor."

"What?" Traskar could not contain a sputter. Then he composed himself and shook his head, crossing his arms over his chest. It was a most un-Choyan gesture, but Rand had done it often and it startled Palaton to see the other had picked it up.

"I'm going to meet him, but on my terms."

"Ah." Warmth glowed in the depths of the other's eyes, kindled by interest. "You won't survive the meeting, not without help. My help, I presume."

"Yes, and don't you dare ask what a one-armed Choya can do."

Traskar showed his teeth in a smile. "If I asked, I would not have been much of a pilot, even when I was able."

"Can you stand by, then?"

"What did you have in mind?"

"I want a levitation, then a simple hook and snatch."

Traskar's well-tanned face blanched. With an effort, he asked, "Where?"

"The Emperor's Walk. I won't face Panshinea anyplace less public than that."

"There's nothing simple about that." Traskar scrubbed his hand over his face, as if he could wipe out the fear that way. "There will be crowds, security. We'll be drawing fire."

Palaton had not stopped eating; two days of very short rations had sharpened his hunger, but he paused now, utensil in hand. "I can take care of security."

"How?"

He called for his *bahdur,* felt it answer him like the warmth of the meal which slowly began to fill his stomach with comforting heat. He shaped an illusion and then moved quickly to Traskar's other side.

The former pilot never noticed, watching the shape which Palaton had left behind him.

"Traskar," murmured Palaton gently, as he placed a hand on his friend's shoulder.

Traskar exploded with a curse that Palaton had not heard since his days working on contract deep space freighting. Traskar ended his curse with a fit of coughing, doubling over, sending the curious glances of other Choyan past him. When he'd finished, he sat up sharply.

"What in the—"

"A talent," Palaton told him. "Not well known in my House."

"Nor any other." Illusionists could rarely solidify their projections, or make them look much different from holograms, projections out of time and space that inevitably gave themselves away. This image *was* Palaton, in every detail and way, paused as though listening intently to their conversation Traskar looked from the illusion to him and back again. "How did you get behind me?"

"It's an echo of the original illusion. It's as though I'm simply there and nowhere else."

"How long can you hold it?"

"Not long." Palaton smiled grimly. "Let's hope long enough."

"Well," returned Traskar. "It ought to draw their fire." He stood up. "I know a place where we can plan a little better."

"No." Palaton tossed the remains of his lunch away and dusted his hands. "I've endangered you too much already. Listen to the broadcasters. They'll let you know when Pan and I intend to meet. Then, if you can do what we've discussed, you can. If not," Palaton tilted his head and shrugged, "we *tezars* have more lives than most Choyan."

"Aye," agreed Traskar sourly. "But ill spent." He stood in the misty shade of the fountain and watched Palaton walk away.

"Will it work?" asked Malahki intently.

"I don't know." Traskar had been pacing uneasily, difficult enough in the low-roofed hovel of their shelter, but he seemed to fill the place to bursting and now stood hump-shouldered as he paused. Malahki, who knew he was bigger than the pilot, had never felt that confined. He moved in the chair he straddled, and it creaked as though to confirm his presence in it.

"I can't tell you if it will work," Traskar repeated.

Chirek had been sitting quietly in the corner, his chin dropped to his chest, so quiet and small that his presence was nearly ignored. "We'll have a network spread all through the crowd at the Walk. I'll see to it." His voices dropped like a pebble into a still pond and rippled outward toward the two of them.

Malahki growled back, "I still don't like it."

"Nor do I, but he asked me for what help I can give and, by the God-in-all, I can still do this. *This*, I can do." Traskar fisted a hand and pounded it into the palm of his other hand. Synthetic flesh smacked into skin. "And it is daring enough that Panshinea would never anticipate it."

"At least," Father Chirek said as he stood, "it gives him a chance." His wrinkled robes smoothed about his form as he straightened. "That's all she asked of us."

Malahki closed his eyes for a second in thought. "When?"

"He would not tell me, but he said the broadcasters would carry it. I won't have much time for preparation, but I think that's what he intended. Less chance for anyone else to decipher what we're doing."

Chirek consulted his chronogram. "Then all we can do is wait. Prepare and wait."

Traskar went to the doorway. "After I've pulled him out, if I pull him out, then what do we do with him?"

Malahki let out a rumbling sigh. "That part is easy enough. *She* wants him."

Traskar's bulk shadowed the doorway to the small cottage like a thunderhead. "As long as she knows that once I've taken him from Panshinea, there will be no place on Cho safe enough for him—or anyone who knows him. One doesn't have to be a prophet to know that." He left the doorway, and bright sunlight slowly filtered in to replace him.

Malahki blinked once or twice, then scratched his jawline. "The truth," he said, "is hard to dispute."

Father Chirek crossed the room briskly to close the door. "As the Prophet would tell us, the truth is changing from moment to moment, decision to decision. The Emperor's Walk is both terribly open and terribly closed. You and I have some planning to do if we want agents in place there, in case Traskar cannot carry out his role."

Malahki watched the tabletop as Chirek called out a line diagram of that part of the capital. Infiltration would be difficult among the government buildings which dominated the north side of the Walk, but it could be done. He would have more confidence in the entire operation if he but knew where Jorana was.

He was almost certain she had fled to avoid this moment, hoping never to see the time when Panshinea would return to destroy Palaton. He'd had no word from her nor had the Prophet yielded to his pleas to look for her. But if anyone could sway Palaton from his suicidal course, it would be Jorana, his Jori.

Chirek looked up, caught his eyes. "Malahki, are you listening?"

"Listening," Malahki confirmed heavily. "And thinking."

"There is little margin for error."

If not Jorana herself, he still had the benefit of the years she'd spent at the palace. Malahki took the map pen from his friend's hand and began to sketch along the diagram. "There are secret ways, here and here and here. . . ."

*   *   *

The chill of the cryo chamber seemed to permeate the entire lower level of the embassy. Maeva ran her card through the door locks, containing a shiver as she passed across the last threshold, and the smell of the level hit her fully. The ambassador was waiting for her. He looked better than he had before, rested, shaved, barbered, and wearing clean clothes, but he had lost a few more pounds, she saw, and his eyes were still and dead.

She resisted the impulse to hug herself for warmth, glad she'd worn red because it reflected its heat and passion inwardly back into her, and she needed that in this sterile environment. "Do you think this is such a good idea, sir? Keeping him down would be far easier."

Thomas turned about to face a viewing window into the medical lab. "I want," he said flatly, "to see the man responsible for my daughter's death. I want to *talk* to him. I want to—" Thomas swayed slightly.

She rushed to bolster him up, pushing him back gently against a wall and taking his arm.

He took a deep breath.

"Are you all right?"

"I will be." He shook her off.

Maeva stepped back, uneasily aware that she had crossed some kind of line which the ambassador had drawn. She turned away from him as he peered once more into the lab room as the automatic créche prepared its occupant for waking. From the healthy color of the face, she could see that the procedure was nearly finished.

An attendant came into the room, an androgynous construct of a being, leaned over Randall's sleeping form and checked the vitals and shunts, preparing to disengage the creche completely. She restrained a shiver at the sight of the medico. Neither human nor inhuman, it was one of half a dozen such beings who worked in the secured depths of the embassy.

Dead men tell no tales.

And what the construct did could hardly be called living. Maeva knew that every embassy here on Sorrow had its share of secret servants, beings who would ask no questions, tell no truths, hear no lies, speak no betrayals, formed out of whatever clay their particular race had chosen to shape them from. She did not like it and before she'd taken this assignment on Sorrow, she would have been hard-pressed to admit that any race could ever do such a thing.

In the absence of thoroughly reliable and independent robotics, such beings had become both necessary and indispensable. Still, it did not mean she had ever become used to their presence.

The medico turned about as if attracted by her thoughts of it. However, its blank, almost completely unformed face looked for the ambassador and, finding him framed in the portal, the creature gave a beckoning wave.

"He's awake," said Thomas. "Let's go down to the interviewing room." He strode off briskly down the corridor, his momentary lapse of strength forgotten.

Maeva pushed away reluctantly, catching in her peripheral vision the sight of Randall being sat up and groggily sliding down from the créche to his feet, supported by the unyielding form of the medico. He might be awake, but she could tell he was not yet aware, and she felt a pang for him as she hurried away from the window to catch up with her employer.

The interviewing room was little more than a turn in the corridor, a bay, which opened up to the cell beyond. Its front had been structured with a beam latticework, hardly more subtle than old-fashioned metal bars. Thomas indicated a chair for her but stayed on his own feet, pacing in a tightly constricted circle, waiting for the prisoner to be brought out.

The erratic sound of their progress preceded them. When they finally came into view, she could see the medico stoically steering the weaving steps of his charge down the hallway and into the bay. The medico stepped back unobtrusively, face as unlined as that of the wall behind it. Rand came to a sudden halt and pivoted toward them, dark hair ruffled from his long sleep, face alert from some sense other than vision, for she had the sudden, piercing intuition that he saw them by other means than his newly awakened eyes.

"Who's there?" His voice was deep and clear, and she wondered if sleep had deepened it beyond his normal range. She moved as if to answer him, but the ambassador twitched a hand at her. She realized that there was a lightscreen between them, filtering them from view.

Rand extended a hand. "Holding me won't do you any good. He'll do what he has to do, you know that."

Maeva kept silent as indicated. The ambassador moved a step closer. The sound carried, for Rand reacted. He repeated sharply, "Who's there? Who's watching me? What do you want from me?" He stared at them without seeing them, his eyes so intensely aquamarine it was like watching the shore of a Caribbean sea. Maeva looked away.

Thomas paced across the barrier and back as though his silence bottled up more than words, more than mere emotion.

At first Rand followed the movement, head tilted, waiting, but then a momentary disorientation seemed to overcome him. Maeva had seen a few come out of cryo; the drift was normal. In fact, his lucidity had surprised her.

Without putting his hand down, he said, "Come to me if

you want to. I can't do it anymore. Is it the Change you
want? I don't have it, I'm empty. Is that what you want to
know? *I don't have it in me anymore.* I can't do it. Not for
you, not for *her.*"

Thomas made a sound under his breath like an angry,
spitting cat, a noise which Rand could not hear because
of his rambling. Maeva heard it, though, and got to her
feet quickly.

"Amb—"

He sliced her words off with a savage, hacking gesture.
She came to a complete halt, afraid.

Rand stopped talking and stood, swaying. He blinked
once or twice. "I'll prove it to you," he said, and he lurched
forward. "Take my hand. I'd give you anything, but I can't.
I'm empty. Take my hand and see."

He hit the barrier, hands outstretched. He dug his arms
into it up to the elbow as if not feeling the surge, though
his back arched and his hair stood on end from the contact.
The energy sizzled once, twice, striking back. Flesh
scorched. She could smell it burn. See it open up in black
and crimson gashes, raw nerves exposed. She heard him
scream in a pitch so high it went silent from a throat achingly contorted with his agony.

Thomas shouted at the medico. "Get him out of there!"

The construct hesitated, dumbfounded by the crackle and
sizzle of the attacking levinfire. A smell of ozone and blackened skin and molten copper filled the bay.

Thomas stepped forward as though he might shake the
other loose himself. Then Randall bounced back from the
field, shaking, fingers curled in pain, and when he screamed
a second time, it was in full voice.

He fell back into the cell, but the barrier wasn't done
with him yet. It followed him, a crackling maw of gold
and silver sparks. He rocked back on his heels when the
phenomenon erupted.

Energy crawled over him, electric blue, spitting lightning,
covering him from head to toe, wild static energy. It answered the attack of the first and swallowed it down, consuming it, then turned on Rand himself. Like a flame it
devoured him until he stood cloaked in blue sparks. Maeva
stared. She'd never seen anything like it. Her throat ached
rawly in sympathy with his agony.

Rand thrust his hands above his head, reaching, and the energy followed his gesture, twirling overhead, arcing as though he controlled it with his will. It swirled about his hands, and then she saw the livid angry welts bubble and begin to heal.

"Get out!"

"Ambassador—"

"We can't help him from here."

Thomas grabbed her shoulder and pushed her out of the interviewing room, stumbling after her. She turned her head, watching the bluefire consume Rand, imprisoning him, cocooning him, as his cries grew weaker and weaker.

She lost sight of him just as he collapsed and the construct medico gained enough confidence to come forward and collect him.

Her last view was of him lying on the floor, as the bluefire subsided and faded away, his scarred and throbbing hands and forearms akimbo, flesh healing more rapidly than was humanly possible.

In two or three days, the scars would be gone. She knew that instinctively.

If he lived two or three more days.

What had just happened to him? What had she seen?

Thomas escorted her through the tunnel of the secured level. She had to quick-step to stay with him, his hand roughly on her elbow.

"What was that?"

"I don't know."

"Ambassador, you can't just leave him here."

"I can and I will. The medico will see to him. You see that you're ready to depose him in two or three days—or whenever he's coherent."

"But—"

"We don't have any choice! Until we know what he's done, what's been done to him—we can't let him loose. You know that."

Not on Sorrow, at any rate. The Abdreliks or the Ronins would snatch him up and, from what she'd heard, they were not averse to vivisecting other races if they felt it was to their advantage. Maeva grew breathless keeping up with the ambassador, but it did not matter if she could not speak.

She didn't have words to express the emotions running through her.

What had she just seen happen? How much of Randall remained that was human? How could he have survived it otherwise?

Chapter 11

Rand did not wake for three days, and when he did, he was profoundly disoriented. Maeva stood at the observation win dow, something cold growing inside her, as the medico tried to cope with the flailing body and mind of its charge. While Rand wheeled about, fighting aimlessly and weakly, there seemed to be no evidence of any mind behind his actions. She watched until she could stand to watch no longer, made a note of the waking and feeding timetable posted by the medico, and resolved to return the next day.

And the next and the next until she found a subject whole enough to interrogate, to *understand*.

In the meantime, her trade law files were backing up, and she had to reapply for security to this sector of the embassy, as Thomas had only granted her a temporary pass. She realized as she made plans for the application that she could be becoming involved in something that might absorb her completely. It was as though she stood at the edge of an abyss and willingly contemplated the downward slope.

She had to know. She had to understand, and she had to resolve. If she had to jump to accomplish those goals, she would.

*　　*　　*

Rain showers swept through the Charolon sky just after dusk, accompanied by occasional rumbles of thunder, muted, and quieting as though easily spent. Malahki and Father Chirek worked until the priest sat back with a sigh and said, "We've done all we can."

Unsaid was the worry that it would not be enough. Malahki watched his friend pad off to the sleeping nook where their crude pallets lay waiting. Sleep, however, did not seem to welcome him that night, not even after Chirek's gentle snoring filled the room.

Malahki sat with his hands resting on the table and played for a moment with the *bahdur* sparks that resulted if he pushed his palms close enough together. So he had talent. Foolish Choya, how often he had thought that having it would be all that mattered. He had all but moved the sky and Cho to get to Rand, to experience the Change for himself. Now, having it, he had no idea what to do with it. What his genealogical heritage for the soulfire was. Was he Earth, Sky, or Star? Or had he perhaps mutated from the lost House of Flame, destroyed so many centuries ago? Oh, yes, he had the talent, but no head for it, and he was like a child with an enforcer, dangerous and lethal but not particularly effective. He could beam death anywhere he wished, without knowing what he should wish. Jorana had warned him of such consequences.

And, realizing that, he was not so fanatical as Chirek and the Prophet Dorea to find Rand and return him to his role as the Bringer of Change. Change wasn't enough, it wasn't all, and if the streets were filled with Choyan brimming with untrained power, he could foresee anarchy. For once, he thought ironically, he shared a reaction with Palaton. The *tezar* had been horrified at what Rand could do, had been doing. The *tezar* had already looked down those roadways and seen the pitfalls awaiting them.

So, as necessary as it was to find Rand, it was even more necessary to prepare his own people. To find those among the Householdings who would be willing to train those newly empowered. Dorea would be disappointed in him, that his agenda was not hers or Chirek's. Malahki wondered if she suspected it or had *seen* it, and so sent the priest along to ensure her commands. Keeping Palaton safe was the key to finding Rand.

It was not necessarily, in Malahki's mind, the key to restoring Cho.

He needed to find Jorana as well. Brought out of the common stock, tested and rising to the status of the Housed, she more than any would know what he and all those who had been Changed faced. She would understand how his mission had evolved.

Thinking of Jorana drowsily, wondering where she was

and how, he caught a sense of her. A wispy feeling of green growth and flowers and Cleansing prayers . . . she sat among a garden of rocks and blossoms and looked up sharply as if she sensed him watching her.

He caught himself spiraling downward into sleep, leaning on his elbows on the table, jerked back into awareness.

A dream, he told himself, a dream with his eyes half-closed and his own throat beginning to sag into stentorian breathing. The day was finally ending for him, too, and Malahki shrugged off the fancy that he had viewed the Choya'i. In his wanderings, he had nearly leaned over the computer board and wiped out the maps and placements they'd been working on.

He took a moment to store their efforts of the day and then cleared the screen. He pulled up the newsline and sat, waiting for it to come on-line, bouncing among the various networks he used for cover until it came to him, untraceable, broadcasters looking solemn.

"A public meeting tomorrow at noon in Charolon, where Emperor Panshinea is expected to strip the heirship to the throne from his once favored protege, *Tezar* Palaton. We will bring it to you live from Emperor's Walk. Once again, the rumors surrounding the forced abdication of *Tezar* Palaton from the heirship to the throne of Cho are evidently well-founded as Panshinea has demanded a meeting and Palaton has agreed. This meeting will take place tomorrow at noon, from the capitol grounds and war memorials on the Emperor's Walk. Stay tuned for coverage on your local weather."

Tomorrow. Malahki shook his head, felt the weight of his crown, and got up. He entered the sleeping nook quietly and stood over Chirek for a moment, debating, then leaned down and put his hand on the priest's shoulder.

Chirek came awake instantly. "What is it?"

"Tomorrow," Malahki told him. "At noon."

"We'll be ready." Chirek cleared his throat. "Coming to bed?"

He sounded like Malahki's deceased wife, and the burly Choya hid his amusement. "In a moment. I have one last thing to attend to." Malahki left the cubicle and closed the sound curtain behind him, muffling Chirek's quick return to snoring.

He put on his jacket, found it growing tight across the shoulders and around the arm joints, and grimaced uneasily. Not muscle, he thought wryly. Not at this point in his life. He shrugged into the garment to stretch it a little, then stepped into the damp night.

He did not believe in visions or dreams, but now he had power, and perhaps it had been the power in him calling to the *bahdur* in her. He could not discount it; he needed her assistance too much, and if she were where he'd seen her, then it was indeed a hiding place he would never have thought of looking for her. He would have to hurry.

Jorana sat among the slab boulders, listening to the silence, breathing the soft aroma of the flowers which had been strewn upon the temple grounds, and contemplating the cleansing of her soul. Although it had been years since Rindalan had presided here, his resonance could still be felt. If she were not newly with child, she would be tempted to go to Sorrow and spend her waiting days at Rindy's side, so keenly did she feel the need for the other's tempered wisdom

Instead, she would abide here, seeking cleansing, doing the daily rituals, hiding, given sanctuary which not even the emperor's security forces could pierce, contemplating her own life and the one she had stolen from Palaton. She did not think there was enough forgiveness in all the temples on Cho to filter the black marks from her psyche. Jorana reconciled herself to the fact that she must seek mercy instead.

An uneasiness stole over her. Protectively, she curved the palm of her hand over her stomach where the life she anticipated did not even show. She peered up through the carved stone arches and saw nothing, heard nothing, but sensed . . . something.

As she continued to look up, it seemed to home in on her, focusing more intently, and hackles rose on the back of her neck. She shielded herself quickly, but knew she had not reacted soon enough.

Someone knew who she was, and possibly where.

Jorana rose from the stone couch where she had been curled, and hurried down the temple corridors, out of the maze of meditation chambers, and toward the living quarters. She would have to leave and in a hurry, but not so much in a hurry as to arouse suspicion. The priests were circumspect, always, but they could be political, too.

She secured a comline and arranged to send herself a message summoning her, making sure its origin could not be traced back. She was resting in her room when the Prelate came, bowing, apologizing for the lateness of the hour, with news that she had been called away from her retreat. He had been awakened for his task and stood, sable hair rumpled, creases on his face imprinted from the embrace of his bedsheets, his robes knife-creased, fresh robes he'd laid out to wear in the morning.

Jorana got to her feet reluctantly, with the air of one both worried and loath, and reached for the small piece of luggage she had brought with her when she'd first come to the temple, opening its catch to pack it."

The Prelate caught her slim wrist. "There is no time," he said. "I'm sorry. Someone has come for you and waits in the outer garden."

Jorana froze. "Someone's here?"

"The matter must be most urgent. He asks that you attend him as soon as possible."

She glanced sharply about the room, deciding if she should flee now or take her chances and leave from the outer garden. She was still deep in the sanctum, trapped in the rock it had been carved from. In the garden, at least, she was only lengths away from freedom, even if closer to her pursuers. Her skin chilled as she made a decision.

"I'll send for my things."

He nodded. "We will keep them here for you. Do you . . . wish me to accompany you?"

"No. I . . . do you know what it is?"

He shook his head. "No, my dear, I have no details. Whatever you fear, God-in-all will give you strength." He blessed her as he followed her from the room and locked it behind them.

There were things in that room she did not want to leave behind, but nothing of personal consequence. Those items she had cached when she'd fled the palace. There was nothing which had been in her possession long enough to absorb a telltale aura or give her away. She would be inconvenienced, nothing more, though she did not know when or how she would be able to stop and replace the necessities.

She took a deep breath as she hurried down the corridors leading to the surface and the outer gardens and the ancient temple gates. The smell of night and dampness came to her. It must have rained since dusk when she'd first gone to meditate after a light supper. The footsteps behind her, the Prelate returning to his own chambers, faded. She could flee now, but she was in the throat of the temple grounds and all she could do would be to return the way she'd come, a dead end, or go on, past the teeth and hope she could get by whoever waited for her.

Expecting palace guards, she stepped into the grassy glen of the garden and saw but a single burly figure waiting, back to her, bent to examine a fruiting shrub near the wall. She thought she knew the body language of the hulking Choya. Her heart did a tiny flutter, and Jorana came to a halt, her breath catching momentarily in her throat.

He heard the sound, however, and turned. "Jori."

His face reassured her even more. "Quiet. No one here knows me by that name."

Malahki smiled widely. "I should have known." He spread his arms.

She walked into them, thinking of her childhood, as well as of her adulthood. One, he had fostered, the other manipulated for his own needs, but she could not help loving him or responding to him. He was the only father she had ever known. "Malahki," she whispered into his jaw.

He said softly, "Palaton meets Panshinea at noon tomorrow. Had you heard?"

She shivered. "No."

"We need you, Father Chirek and I. *He* needs you."

He kept his arms loosely about her, though she no longer surrendered to the reunion.

"I can't."

"We have no time, Jori, and you know the importance of this."

"I can't."

He bent back slightly. "Why?"

"I'm with child."

His eyes widened. Then, "His?"

"Yes."

"Does he know?"

"No." Her shame rose to her cheeks, flooding them with heat, despite the chill she felt elsewhere. Malahki would know then, that she had used the drug he'd given her and stolen Palaton's fertility from him, conceiving a child in a union not meant to bear fruit.

Malahki cleared his throat huskily. "Well," he said. "Your timing."

He had wanted this child as badly as she did, but even he knew now was not the time.

"If not now, when," she began, and he hushed her with a rough finger to her lips.

"I understand. But you must understand that I am reluctant to undertake any kind of rescue without your deft hand. Panshinea can't let Palaton leave their meeting alive."

Jorana stepped out of his hold, looking back toward the temple complex. She had to leave, not giving herself a choice, but did not know where she could go. Dorea had told her, foreseen for her, and she had not wanted to hear it then or now. *Cho cannot have two emperors. You must choose.* The Prophet had not meant for all of Cho to make the decision, but for her and her alone.

She didn't want this!

He reached for her hand, and there was a familiar tingle as their flesh met.

She looked down and then up, into his eyes. "Was it you who found me?"

"Earlier, in the caves. Yes. I don't know how—"

His newly awakened talent was untrained, unhoned. If he had found her, others would. For the moment, perhaps there would be safety among the numbers and chaos of Chirek's and Malahki's network. That might bypass any *bahdur*-augmented search as well as the usual methods security forces had at their disposal. She stopped his words. "It doesn't matter. I'll come, but I can't stay. You understand that, don't you?"

"No, but I'll accept it." Malahki stood back and opened the temple gate. "Don't you need to get your things?"

"There is nothing here," she said, passing him. Not even sanctuary, any longer.

Chapter 12

Shortly after the midnight hour, Traskar went in search of a miracle. He would have pledged his aid to Palaton regardless of whether or not Malahki had come to him, but it helped to know that future years would be soothed by Malahki and his network. Although he had medical coverage in perpetuity, he was not a Choya who wished to be a debit upon the system. He wanted nothing more than to work again, to pilot, to use the soulfire he had been born and trained to. Malahki had promised him work and usefulness. Palaton had always given him respect. Those three things, he had found in his years since forced retirement, he needed more than air. He made the arrangements he and Palaton had agreed upon the moment the meeting had been announced. Now, he decided upon additional measures.

He drew on a rough cloak against the weather, a cloak good not only against the inclemency, but also proof against the quarters which he would travel. It would hide the swing of his walk and give him passport to the areas he sought and, because of its looseness and flexibility, might even save his life if someone thought to knife him. He had other tricks which were more dependable and skills he'd learned while piloting for various trade ports, but even a humble cloak might have its purpose.

As he, himself, might.

Palaton had not asked much of him, only something that any second-year cadet in flight school would be able to do, but Traskar wanted to be certain he would not fail.

As he brushed through coarser elements in alleyways and substreet dives, where Choyan waited the tables and counters instead of servos, their faces heavily tattooed and jewelry-bedecked to hide the ravages of the lives they lived, he made inquiries and followed a trail of whispered clues.

He had heard only rumor previously, but rumor was confirmed, and it led him to a shop in a section of the commons which had suffered most during the riots, a shop which was little more than a lean-to set up against a burned-out frame.

The shop, like the night, would be gone with the dawn. Possibly to set up at a new location with the next evening, or perhaps never to return again. Traskar shrugged deeper into his cloak with a grunt. Satisfaction would not be guaranteed with purchase. He examined his motives and needs before he stepped into the shop. The Choya who sat crossed-legged on a crude mat was gambling at sticks with another who looked enough like him to be his son. They were both beady eyed, with their manes roached and their horn crowns shaved so close to their skulls as to be nonexistent. *Family business*, thought Traskar to himself. There was not likely enough trust to bring in anyone else.

"Who are you?"

"It does not matter, any more than it matters who you are." He snugged his cloak at his throat. "I am looking for something, and I am told you have it."

The younger commons drew back on his haunches and sat warily, watching. The elder crossed his arms about his chest, at which action Traskar calmly requested, "Keep your hands where I can see them."

An unpleasant look crossed the seller's face, but he eased his position in response, flashing his palms. "What do you want?"

Traskar told him.

The seller rocked back a little. "Who told you I had it?"

"Does it matter?"

"It might. Describe him."

"*She* wears amber and onyx, highlighting her cheekbones in strata. Possibly a common, more probably a Housed who didn't have enough talent to stay there, even through marriage, black hair, bleached at the ends."

Recognition flickered in the other's muddy gaze. "All right. Perhaps I have what you want. How do I know you have enough buying power?"

Traskar felt his body react with an annoying flinch. The muscle movement was picked up by his prosthetic, which reacted as well, much more openly. The commons stared as he raised his arm and made a fist.

Traskar relaxed and the arm settled back. "I haven't time to waste," he said. "Name your price."

The seller named a price that was twice his monthly pension.

Traskar surprised them both by agreeing. He dipped his good hand into the pouch at his waist, punched in a credit amount on the disk and tossed it at the seller's feet. He had been uneasy carrying the disk around as a blank, anyone could have punched in any amount. He had his retirement online with that account, he could have been wiped out.

As it was, his capital took a hit.

The seller kicked the disk over to his son who picked it up and eyed it carefully. He pulled a crate off a hidden processor and ran it through, looked up and said, "It's real, and funds are verified."

The commons pulled a packet out of his waistband. "Two doses. All I've got. They're yours." He tossed it over.

Traskar neatly caught the packet in midair. Two tabs. He could feel them through the envelope. The elder watched him keenly, saying, "Too bad you're in such a hurry. Word says in a moon's time, they'll be as common as *bren*. They call it boost. The House of *Tezars* says it works miracles."

Traskar secured it in a shirt pocket. "Let's hope," he answered.

The storm had cleansed the air. Day bloomed brilliantly clear. Palaton rose from the private room he'd secured and stared into the reflective screen, then set about grooming himself as much back to normal as possible. He shook his dress uniform out of his duffel bag. Light, durable, made to be compressed into as little space as possible, it unfolded immaculately. He straightened the neckline, thinking of Blue Ridge's colors. *May they be worn again with pride long after me.* He did not think that anything he did this day would sully them. At least, he hoped not. He owed Hat that much, at least. Not to mention his promise to resurrect the school.

He bathed, in what little water he'd been allowed to decant for his usage. He fastened a utility belt around his right wrist, not much in the way of weaponry, but the rope it carried might come in handy. He dressed, reviewed him-

self, then pulled his bulky workman's coveralls over the
uniform. It would do no one any good to plan if a patrol
spotted him and picked him up on the way to the meet.
Then, it was only a matter of finding some breakfast and
waiting until it was time to cross town. There was no safe
way to reach Traskar. He had either done what he'd agreed
to do, or he had not been able to. Either way, Palaton was
committed to his own course of action.

He bought breakfast and fetched it back to the loft room,
where he sat and brought his journal up to date while he
ate. Then, he posted the journal to a safe address that he
knew of, and fished for the last crumbs of the sweet buns
he'd been dunking into the *bren*. Thinking that he should
have purchased one more bun, he sat back and watched
the day blossom. There were Choyan he wished he could have
by his side: Rufeen, Hat, Jorana. He thought of Jorana for
some time, her luxuriant bronze hair, her fine-boned face
with its strong jawline, her eyes. She had hoped for his
understanding when she'd left. He did not understand, but
Palaton took that as a fault of his own rather than hers.
He *should* have understood. God-in-all, one day he would
see her again, and she could explain.

Gathon, whose hand kept the throne steady despite all
the turmoil within the one who sat on it, he would see
when he met Panshinea. There were only two he had no
hope of seeing again, to whom he had not said good-byes.
Rindalan was beyond communication, the tall, spindly,
proud priest who was now a reluctant diplomat. And then
there was Rand, not Choyan at all, but without whom he
was not really complete. Their bonding had gone beyond
the sharing of his *bahdur* in a way he had not known until
the manling had been taken from him.

He had brought Rand to Cho because he'd had no
choice, Rand had been receptacle for his power, cleansing
it, holding it until they could figure out a way to transfer
it back. The humankind had been a survivor who had
needed his guardianship, the pilot was an heir to the throne
who desperately needed to hide his lack of *bahdur*. Their
bonding of necessity had become one of respect and friendship—and more. Was it the *bahdur* which had tied them
together? He didn't know. It was as though Rand had become the Brethren he had never had. Taking his power

back, literally ripping it from the manling, had nearly destroyed them both. And then Qativar had stolen Rand before Palaton had had any chance to pick up the pieces of their lives, to make amends for what he'd done.

He was not ready to die. He had not made his peace with his friends and settled with his enemies. He would have to cheat Panshinea this day.

He was content when the time came.

He stood and stretched, then took his chronogram off its alarm, already knowing the time in his head, knowing he was ready to meet Panshinea. He'd taken a room near the quarter of the city which was ruled by the palace and governmental structures. A brisk walk would take him there.

Traskar settled into the single engine skimmer. He'd bulked out since he'd quit flying, the seat felt a little hampering, but on the panel in front of him everything responded as he stretched out his hands. He'd swallowed down one of the bitter pills just before climbing into the plane. It sat in the pit of his stomach like a glowing ember.

He set his view screen on the local news channel and saw a pan of the crowds growing below Emperor's Walk, waiting to see the emperor and his heir. Broadcasters stalked the area, on foot and in communications towers. Cams were everywhere, gobbling up the sights. Traskar turned the engine on to warm it, secured his harness, and watched, listening, waiting for the time.

It was just a little game of lancing, played by second-year cadets, a skill of flying, with a backup of *bahdur*. The skill he had. The power . . . it was difficult to explain what losing a limb did to the talent. He had used very little of it since waking in rehab, permanently altered, never to be the same again, unable to be restored to whole. The one time he had—

Traskar shuddered, and the burning in his stomach splashed up the back of his throat. He swallowed it down tightly. It had been like bleeding to death, having an open artery, out of which the *bahdur* flowed, taking everything, even life itself, with it, the soulfire determined to fill a phantom limb and draining into nothingness. A black void which had sucked eagerly at him. . . .

He was not so newly healed now. It had been decades.

He'd managed to keep a thready use of soulfire going, off and on, to keep himself both sane and useful. What he had to do today would demand very little from him, just an edge to his senses and skills. He'd taken the boost just to ensure that nothing would go wrong.

He sat, keeping an eye on the fuel and energy cells, waiting for the emperor and Palaton to make their appearances.

Panshinea appeared, in full regalia, his gold-red hair flashing in the sun, bent Gathon a half-step behind. The emperor wore muted green robes, green and gold, which would accent his own coloring, and upon his shoulders lay a collar of gemstones which were worth the price of the entire capital. Gathon, moving stiffly after, wore a somber ebony robe and under that, shirt and trousers of charcoal and umber.

But it was Palaton who drew the eye of the cams, the *tezar* in his dress uniform, a glorified flight suit, nothing spectacular, simple and utilitarian in its lines, edged by gold thread, the fabric a rippling palette of blues. He wore no jewels, his horn crown and forehead bare of all but his mane of hair which a light breeze teased while the sun lent glints to its malt-brown depths. The cams brought his face into sharp focus. No ornaments, no tattoos, just a leanly handsome face dominated by clear, amber eyes. The stare from the eyes was steady. Traskar knew there was no way Palaton could see him through the cam, that Palaton was not looking at anybody or anything beyond the emperor, but he felt as though the pilot looked right into his depths, and he answered that look.

"I won't fail you," Traskar vowed, and put his hand to the throttle of the skimmer.

The instrument panel flashed a light, indicating the engine had warmed properly. He taxied out to the end of the strip and sat, waiting.

"We are not well met," Panshinea said, as Palaton drew close. He signaled the pilot to halt on the Emperor's Walk and although close to two hundred thousand watched and listened, they did so in utter silence.

"To my sorrow," Palaton answered, and truth rang in his voices, because he truly felt it. He caught a glimpse of Gathon, where he stood behind Panshinea. The minister looked pained. Age had sunken his cheeks, and the yellow-white streaks in his dark hair had nearly overwhelmed his brow.

The emperor, however, looked stunning. If the flight from Sorrow had tired him, it did not show in his face, his flamboyant mane of red-gold fire, or in his jade eyes. This was his stage, the only one he'd desired to hold or had trained for, the role which had consumed his entire life.

Palaton felt a tiny stretch of humor at the corner of his mouth. Though the emperor was playing to the crowd, he had not forgotten to take precautions. Panshinea's collar reflected brilliantly in the overhead sun. Palaton knew it, though he had only seen it once before. Its usage was more than ornamentation. When activated, it soundscreened the area around it. When the emperor let him come forward and kneel to be disinherited, the screen would be activated and whatever final words they exchanged would be private.

Panshinea lifted his chin arrogantly, as if tired of meeting Palaton's gaze, and lifted his hand. "On this day, let it be known that the heirship to the throne of Cho, held by myself for the House of Star and all Choyan, is rescinded from Palaton of Star. The heirship is surrendered, voluntarily resigned, to me by *Tezar* Palaton who admits no wrongdoing, but must now face inquiry. Do you resign your office and obligation and duties, Palaton?"

Pan glanced at him quickly. "I do," replied Palaton evenly.

"Then come forward and kneel, and relinquish your burden."

A murmur began through the crowd of watchers as he stepped forward, an underlying current of faint noise which was truncated when he stepped into the broadcasting influence of the soundscreen. He dropped to one knee.

"What have you done to me?" asked the emperor.

"Nothing. A house built on quicksand is doomed to sink, sooner or later."

"You call my work, my life, quicksand!"

Palaton looked up, though he knew he should not, but he had to know when Pan would strike at him, and he had to look him in the eyes to know that. "Not your work alone," he said. "But we cannot live as a people divided. The commons are as much a part of us as ourselves. If we do not unite, our powers will continue to fade, and we will find ourselves in a system of master and slave—and the masters too weak to survive inevitable insurrection."

"You think to lecture me?"

The tiny smile widened. "I think that, if you were ever to listen to me, now would be the time."

"I entrusted you with Cho's peace."

"You put me on the throne as a shock absorber or, if it came to that, a scapegoat. Let us be realistic about what you expected of me."

Pan tilted his head slightly and pursed his lips. He looked back to Gathon. "The child matures."

Gathon inclined his head. "That, too, is inevitable. With maturity comes wisdom. Even an emperor cannot afford to turn away wisdom."

Panshinea looked back at Palaton. "My minister counsels me to listen to you. But your words are like bitter poison to my hearing." A storm began to gather in his eyes, darkening them.

"I don't have much time," Palaton responded. "The House of *Tezars* is using a drug. There's already street slang for it: it's called boost. It affects *bahdur* in those who have talent. Supposedly, it rejuvenates the power."

Panshinea's green eyes glittered. "And that is crucial news to a *tezar*?"

"The hope of unlimited power is a false one. The drug can be fatal. It comes from off-world. There may be additional side effects which we cannot possibly anticipate. You have to know this. It wasn't manufactured for the purpose for which it is being used—the consequences could be catastrophic."

"Fatalities?"

"A cadet at Blue Ridge. He died in my arms in convulsions. Nedar brought the drug in; Vihtirne and Qativar have it now. Consider its off-world origins. Consider what can happen if we grow dependent on it, or if the Abdreliks learn about and take control of the supply."

"Only the one death."

"Is one death so insignificant?" He stared at Panshinea, knowing what the other had planned for him.

The emperor was the first to look away. "Perhaps not," he said quietly. "Consider yourself heard."

"Good." Palaton got to his feet and backed out of range of the jeweled collar. He raised his voices as Pan flinched in surprise.

"As of this day, I am no longer a son of Panshinea. I relinquish all claims to the throne of Cho. And, on this day, I declare myself no longer a son of the House of Star. I am a *tezar,* and my heritage comes from the lost House of Flame." Those last words dropped like a blazing comet into still water, exploding into the silence.

The expression on Panshinea's face in reaction to his declaration was thunderous.

The watching crowd reacted with a roar of startlement, a noise which threatened to wipe out all other noises, even Pan's shout of displeasure. Palaton put his hands up, let his *bahdur* free, let it shine. He stepped before the crowd to give his farewell—and Panshinea's first blow hit him. It knocked him off his feet.

"Remand yourself into my custody!"

Hoarsely, determined, he got out, "No."

He staggered to right himself, gasping for breath, feeling the immense power of the emperor. Measure for measure, if *bahdur* could be so weighed, Panshinea was, had been, incredibly powerful. Though his last decade or so of rule had drained him, had made his use of his talents erratic and desperate, Palaton hoped fervently he had not underestimated his opponent.

He turned around, facing Panshinea, and saw the emperor standing with his palms upraised, his red-gold hair streaming about his horn crown. All pretense of civilization had been stripped away, the imperial robes shrugged off in a heap at his feet. Gathon had been shoved away and struggled to right himself, his robes of office disheveled and imprisoning him in their twists.

Before he could shield himself, Panshinea struck again, with *bahdur,* a strike few could see. It hit Palaton like a juggernaut, driving him to his knees.

"You leave me no choice," Panshinea declared.

The very air in his lungs knifed through tissue. He saw red for a second, then his sight cleared. He looked up. Pan reared over him in triumph, and Palaton realized that the emperor would, indeed, kill him. He had thought it possible all along, but had not believed it, not in the core of him, that Panshinea would murder him in front of all these witnesses.

"I've done nothing wrong. I've brought you no treachery!" His voices, reedy and brittle, protested.

But he realized now that he had played into Panshinea's hands. He had declared himself son of an outlaw House, declared that he was a survivor of genetic manipulation, for how else could a fallen House be resurrected? His freedom would be taken from him, if not his life.

Pan was free to unleash his imperial powers, the *bahdur* of legend which only emperors could use.

Bahdur the sole use and purpose of which was to kill.

He had not seen it used in his lifetime, nor, he supposed, had it been used in the last several hundred years. As he fought for breath now, as he wheezed and flailed and resisted with his own soulfire, his head pounded in time with his heart.

Pan would kill him.

Palaton staggered to his feet. The crowds, limited on the capital side of the walkways, and thronging the other side, surged, held back like a floodtide by security troops. Through blurring vision, he sought help and saw no escape. He looked up, his hearing muted by his agony. *Where was Traskar?*

Panshinea gathered himself for another blow. Palaton could feel it in the atmosphere, like the dulling change of pressure just before a lightening strike. He braced himself with his own power. When it struck, he gave way, staggered back helplessly, and yet his shield held, and *bahdur* sprayed out, like wildfire, scorching the crowd about them.

He heard screams of panic and pain. The crowd turned away from them, away from the spectacle, and ran in fear, but there was no place to go. Bodies began to clamber and shove. He saw a Choya'i go down, her muffled screams cut short.

Pan blasted him again. He absorbed what he could, but he could not contain it, and wildfire sparked everywhere. Horrified watchers turned and stampeded from being destroyed themselves by the emperor's powers gone mad.

Their panic deafened Palaton. He looked up wildly and saw a glimmering of what he hoped to spy.

He took a deep, hurting breath and began to recreate

himself. His heart fluttered wildly and his vision blurred again, head ringing. If he didn't get out now, if Traskar's ploy did not succeed, he would be too weak to resist Panshinea much longer.

He let out a throaty yell of defiance and, hands upheld, rose into the air. Stately levitation, not quick, but steady, above the Walk, above the tumultuous crowd, above the murderous emperor. Cries of surprise followed him.

Palaton took another stabbing breath and concentrated, his *bahdur* answering him with pain of its own, the soulfire telling him that he was nearly drained, finished, empty, burned out.

He continued to rise above the crowd. Twenty feet, thirty— Panshinea commanded the security forces to begin firing, but his bodyshielding took the brunt of that. Only *bahdur* could bring him down.

The droning roar of a single engine grew closer and Palaton could see it now, dipping low over the roof of the palace. Painfully, he threw a loop upward from the utility belt strapped around his wrist. It defied gravity just as his form did. The needle nose of the skimmer pointed for him, and it was clear it would thread that loop and draw him away, safely out of Panshinea's reach.

Panshinea let out another roar of pure rage and frustration. He unleashed a wave of *bahdur* that engulfed Palaton's form, the loop, and fogged the skimmer as it hit.

Palaton could feel Traskar's determination. The pilot answered with *bahdur* of his own, trying to break Palaton loose. There was a second when Palaton hung in the sky, caught in a tug-of-war between the two, his body like a bright shining star brought down from the heavens.

Panshinea's strength was unquestionable, but the pilot had fresh power, untapped, unused, uncalled for, and threw it into the fray.

Then, abruptly, Traskar began to bleed to death, his *bahdur* draining. It flooded out of him, a rushing torrent of power being lost. He was failing Palaton, himself, everything, the boost no good. His hand wobbled on the stick. He had the pickup, but he could not carry Palaton free.

He would die with Palaton, and when the skimmer went down, it would take out half a city block with it. A city block crammed with surging, stampeding, trapped Choyan.

As his life geysered from him, and his vision darkened, he *sent* his regrets to Palaton.

Caught between Traskar's dying power and Panshinea, Palaton felt his own heart slow to a thready beat. He looked up at the plane, knew he could not let Traskar fail, and sent what last *bahdur* he could summon.

He fell. His illusion soared at the rope's end, and Traskar broke free, his drain of power abruptly cauterized. The pilot could feel the emperor's hold on hiin snap. He grabbed the stick and brought up the plane's nose abruptly, taking it out of hover and accelerating as fast as he could. He had Palaton on the loop and bore him out of harm's way.

Or so he thought.

Palaton, body and illusion separated with a cold slice that seemed to tear life from death, plunged to the ground.

He hit the Emperor's Walk and lay, unable to move, hearing the crowd running below, stumbling and screaming as the plane flew off. His plan had failed, done the opposite of what they'd schemed . . . he was to have sent his illusion plunging to death at Panshinea's feet and himself flying to freedom. Now he lay in a crumpled heap, hurt, powerless, nearly senseless, invisible for a few moments as the illusion carried his semblance to freedom.

At least Panshinea could not hurt him any more.

He rolled onto his flank and saw Panshinea topple, wheezing for breath as though his heart had given out. Gathon bent over him in concern.

"Guards! Guards!" the minister called, to no purpose, as the crowds had carried them away.

"Panshinea," Gathon cried beseechingly. "Ah, God, what have you done, Pan?"

The emperor let out a broken noise that echoed what Palaton felt. Palaton tried to crawl toward the emperor, thinking that they had killed each other. But his senses reeled and then closed in on him. His last thought was of Rand. Palaton felt he was dying as but half a being, and if he had only kept Rand with him, he would have had the strength to save both himself and his emperor.

All went black.

Chapter 13

Jorana thought her heart would snap in two when the emperor collapsed and Palaton fell. She dropped linked arms with the riot guards around her and ran over to the walkway, staring at its surface. Then she looked up and saw what appeared to be Palaton, still holding to the loop which the skimmer had captured, being borne off safely, and she blinked.

The skimmer's flight stuttered and bucked in midair, and then it turned on one wing. It made a slow, downward turn and crashed into the free ground just beyond the Congress building. A resounding explosion followed and flames rocketed into the air.

Palaton, gone.

She shoved the visor off her riot helmet, jostled and pushed as Choyan around her reacted in sheer frenzy. She stood and swayed, eyes closed, thinking that he'd almost made it. He'd almost survived what Panshinea had planned for him—

"Oh, God, Pan, what have you done!"

Gathon's agonized voice brought her eyes open again, and she turned from the flaming crash as sirens began to sound and fire units dispatch automatically. The minister had gotten to Panshinea and the scene filled her with a dull shock. Everything was different now. Palaton, gone. Panshinea, perhaps dying himself. The throng around her coming and going in disorganized terror. But even as she stared, she thought she saw something nebulous on the walkway, some . . . cloud, or shadow . . . which was not right, which had not been cast there but which had plunged out of the skies.

She reached up and vaulted onto the walkway, her patrol uniform sensors reacting to the guards' devices which had been put up on the Emperor's Walk, allowing her access. As loath as she had been to put on this uniform, it let her move unnoticed into the thick of things. Pan had gone down, moaning and making a broken sound as though dying. No one on the walkway could read her face through her helmet. She snapped a hand out. Choyan faces stared at her, frozen. A handful of guards lay unconscious, their forms charred and maimed by the backlash of Panshinea's killing stroke.

"Get emergency teams landed here now!" No one moved. "I said NOW."

They unreeled from their stupor and ran for dispatch. She shot a look. Gathon cradled the emperor on his lap, crying in despair. He would recognize her if she went to him. She pulled her visor back into place.

"Who knows CPR?"

From below, one of the patrol raised a hand. She bent down off the walkway and gave him an arm up. "Go help the minister. Let's see if we can get Panshinea back into sinus rhythm."

The guard nodded and ran to the emperor's side. Jorana sidled along the walkway backward a foot or two until she reached the area which was wrong somehow. A distortion shimmered off it and she knelt down.

She could not see it, but she could feel it as she reached. A warm body, cooling rapidly. She pushed her hand deeper into the illusion and found a pulse, barely markable. More than a pulse, she touched an aura, a sense of being that she recognized almost as intimately as she knew herself.

Palaton. It had to be. She felt it with every fiber of her being, and as she thought of him, his image began to flicker into sight.

She took her hand away quickly. Let him be cloaked but a moment longer, so she could get him out of here.

Jorana stood, her throat closing with fear and love for him, her eyes and heart and mind searching. The crowd had thinned by nearly half, but there were bodies everywhere. Some were clearly dead, lifeless, trampled by others when fleeing Panshinea's power surge. Others flailed and cried out for help. The curious and the hardened had begun to push toward the Walkway again.

She knew Malahki and his network would reach her

soon, if she signaled. But she was also aware that she would be giving Palaton into a custody which he would not thank her for. Malahki had an agenda. He was not here to rescue Palaton for the altruism of it, and even though he worked for the Prophet now, there were shadowy underpinnings to everything he did. Malahki was her father, who knew him better?

She swallowed down her indecision. Palaton would die if she did nothing, and he would soon lose that last spark of *bahdur* which empowered the cloaking which hid him. When that happened, security would execute him the moment he was revealed.

Emergency techs landed on the walkway. They surrounded Gathon and Panshinea with all the fervor of their lifesaving activity. Jorana took a freight hover and dislodged their gear from it, setting it close at hand and making pretense of getting the hover out of the way while they worked.

She rolled a guard's body over and heaved it onto the freight hover. Then she pulled at the nebulous shadow which she knew to be Palaton. Without clear vision, it took her more precious moments than she had, but finally, she got it loaded. She kept a hand on his chest a second, felt the shallow and racked breathing.

She looked up, saw a guard watching her curiously. She jerked a thumb. "Get these bodies out of here, call in techs for the injured down below."

The Choya closed his jaw, then nodded. She kicked the hover into low and took it off the walkway. She paused to pull on another dead body, in case anyone questioned her actions later.

A burly form brushed past her as she paused for breath, bent over and head swimming with uncertainty, and she straightened. Recognition flooded her, and gratitude thickened her voices as she said, "Hey there!"

The Choya did not know her, but she reached out and caught his arm, and his partner swung in behind defensively. The Choya'i was bigger than her *tezar* friend and flexed her shoulders warningly.

Jorana put up her visor and gave a brittle smile.

"Take the hover and get as far out of Charolon as you can."

The two stared at her.

"*Do* it," she said. "I know who you're looking for. Take the hover and get the hell out of here. It's the only way you can help him."

Rufeen moved while Hathord could only stare, entrapped by the horror they had just witnessed. The Choya'i sat down in the driver's seat. Jorana boosted the other onto a free area.

She kept her voices low and tense. "Don't look back. Do you understand?"

Rufeen nodded and kicked the freight hover into high gear. Jorana jumped back as it bucked out from under her. She watched them wend their way out of sight.

Hat hugged himself around the knees, inundated by more death than he had ever hoped to see in his life, keening to himself that, although they'd come to help Palaton, they had not succeeded. He stared at the charred guard, the second sprawled across him, his nostrils full of burned death and his stomach sickened.

He shoved a leg out to kick them over the side of the freight hover. The guard rolled off the edge and made a terrible noise when he hit the street below. The hover rocked a little under the change of weight.

"What are you doing?"

"Getting rid of the dead weight." Hat made a funny little giggle deep in his throat at that, and with a second nervous laugh thrust his foot toward the remaining body.

He hit something solid that he could not see. It groaned, and Hat realized that he was looking at a cloudy outline and the more he concentrated on it, the more it coalesced.

He grabbed at Rufeen's elbow. The freight hover skidded sideways across the air lane.

"We've got him!"

"Got who?"

"Palaton!"

Rufeen craned her head back, as the illusion shredded completely.

Hat crawled forward on his hands and knees, rolled the second dead body off the hover and then pulled Palaton's crumpled form onto his back. He slid a hand inside the flight suit.

"Heart rate's bad. Really bad. He's shocky . . . Rufeen, we've got him, but we could lose him."

"Will he make it?"

"The last few days . . ." Hathord rubbed his free hand over his chunky face, wiping his eyes dry. "I've seen more death than life. I don't know, I can't tell. He's comatose. I won't know anything until he wakes, if he wakes." He met Rufeen's frown. "We can't keep him, Rufi."

"Where else is he going to go? Why else did we circle back and come here?"

"He needs medical attention."

"We can't risk it!"

Hat felt his eyes shift back and forth, unable to meet Rufeen's intensity. "He's from a House that was destroyed. Pan tried to—"

"Have you a spine? Or are you still full of the lies Nedar tried to feed you?"

He knew he ought to flare up, ought to feel insulted, but he didn't. He did have doubts, some of them planted by Nedar, some grown by himself. He thought he should know what to do, would know when he agreed to come back with Rufeen. But he didn't.

Rufeen let out an exasperated sigh. "Hat, quit back-pedaling on me."

Hat bit his lip. "I'll try. At least they won't be looking for him. And we can't tell him about Jorana. She would have stayed with him if it had been safe. All we can give him is shelter and warmth. There isn't anything else we can do for him."

Rufeen set her jaw. "Not if I have any damn thing to say about it." She jammed the freight hover into overdrive.

Qativar turned away from his view screen in satisfaction. "One down, one to go." He relished the safety of the opulent suite they had chosen to watch the abdication. The broadcasters were still showing the EMT efforts to tend to those trampled in the panic.

Vihtirne had left the divan and gone to the window of the suite. She stood pensively, hugging herself, her face in shadows that showed her age. She turned painfully to face Qativar, keenly aware that the same sun which gave harsh-

ness to her features outlined his with vigor, youth, and a
petulant handsomeness. He did not wear the robes of his
office as a priest for the House of Star, he'd thrown them
over long ago for the tight fitting trousers and silken shirts
and jackets of the fashion-conscious. But for all his beauty,
there was no light in his eyes. No soul. As for herself, the
spectacle they had just witnessed left her riddled with
doubts. Experience against youth, she thought wryly.

"Are you sure of that?"

"You saw the crash."

"I know that Palaton has more lives than anyone has a
right to." She rubbed her temple gently as if suppressing a
headache. "If he is gone, we can concentrate on the throne.
With Panshinea down, we have opportunity we did not
have before. . . ."

Qativar waved a hand. "Please enlighten me as to your
logic. The emperor lies near death, recuperating from the
expenditure of his imperial *bahdur*. We don't dare move
openly now. Before, we might have had a chance, but he
gave his all trying to destroy a traitor, a genetic aberration—his approval rating will go through the sky now. He's
a hero, albeit a comatose one. Too bad. He's extremely
vulnerable."

"Fool," she said icily.

He tilted his head, but there was no whimsy in his posture. "What do you mean?"

"Panshinea expended everything he had. If he survives . . .
he will need us, Qativar."

His eyebrow quirked.

Vihtirne smiled thinly. "We have boost, and the emperor
needs *bahdur*. He'll be ours for as long as we need him."

"Ah." Qativar sat back and put the heels of his boots
up on the small table fronting the divan. "I shall have to
think on it. Gathon is canny, he won't let us in easily. But
once we are—" He smiled widely. "I suggest we not leave
this to chance."

Her feet wearied. She drew up a small upholstered chair
and perched upon it, spine straight, slender neck held just
so to balance her head and horn crown. She knew how she
must look, yet it fatigued her, this constant fight to maintain
her looks, her poise. She smothered a sigh. Her companion

must be coaxed. She wished for handsome, passionate young Asten instead of this self-absorbed cohort, but he was elsewhere, tending to her business. "Tell me."

"I have a supply of *ruhl* on hand. Let's assert your right to the water patent and visit the local pumping plant."

While boost had come from off-world, *ruhl* was strictly Choyan, an aphrodisiac which disrupted *bahdur* and loosened inhibitions. Normally it was used for lovemaking, to unbind the fertility of either partner, since among Choyan both male and female controlled their fertility. It was dangerously easy to overdose to the point of death, but Qativar had been working with it to alter its effects. "Distribute the *ruhl* now?" It would be potent, she thought, and when soluble in the water, no Choya who drank would be free of its numbing effects. *Bahdur* would be masked almost beyond the endurance of its possessor. They had talked of this before, but she had just thought it talk. Other than surreptitiously distributing it among the *tezars* to keep them demanding the boost, she had not really put much stock in Qativar's grandiose plans.

"What better time? No one knows what the side effects of imperial *bahdur* are—but you and I both know he had to siphon that much energy off someone. Maybe the entire population of Charolon. We will be here during the emergency, of course. Available. With the medication which enables our *tezars* to recover so quickly and completely that their flight time is doubled—no, tripled. Of course, the ordinary Choya is scarcely a *tezar*. But," and he looked down his nose at her, "I can guarantee we will have them lining up in the streets for boost."

"And the emperor will scarcely ignore what is happening."

"Nor is Panshinea likely to accept a populace more powerful than he."

"That is a hook," she agreed, "upon which we might persuade him to hang himself."

* * *

The call came late in the night when dawn first begins to tug weakly on its edges . . . and on an old Choya's bladder, Rindalan thought wryly as he staggered up to answer the embassy alarm. The view screen lit up as he approached it, and Gathon faced him as soon as the scrambler decoded the incoming signal. Gathon, light-years and seasons away. His old friend did not look well, and Rindy's heart sank. There was no good news behind this urgent sending.

Gathon spoke. "Eminence Rindalan, Rindy, this is to inform you that Emperor Panshinea today met with the heir to the throne, Palaton, and took back the heirship, which Palaton voluntarily abdicated."

As the words trickled in slowly, synchronized with Gathon's face, yet unreal because Gathon did not speak slowly and deliberately—that was the decoder's fault—and because the nuances of the blended voices could not be transmitted well, Rindy's mind raced ahead. How could Palaton have so cut himself off from Panshinea, unless Pan left him no choice? And what then . . . civil unrest over which to follow, the head of a House in its descent on the Great Wheel, or the *tezar* who had proved himself time and again?

"Palaton then declared his true genetic heritage—the House of Flame—and Panshinea declared him outlaw and an abomination and attempted to use imperial *bahdur* to destroy him."

Gathon's words struck deeply into Rindy, shaking away the last of whatever drowsiness had been nestling in him. There would be no going back to sleep this night, or perhaps even the next. Imperial *bahdur*! Rindy had only heard of such things in the old texts, describing the wrath of the God-in-all or some of the old emperors, whose powers had been legendary. There were depths to Pan that Rindy had never guessed. And the use of terminology describing their esper powers was forbidden over subspace transmission, scrambled or not, for there was no knowing how clever the Ronins and Abdreliks had gotten in their spying. Gathon was desperate indeed if he discussed their soulfire . . . but perhaps there was hope somewhere in this message. The keyword was *attempted*. Rindy narrowed his eyes, the better to listen to what followed.

"The use of that ability has felled Panshinea temporarily. I am assuming his duties for the next span of days. He lives, but is weakened. Details to follow. Palaton escaped the wrath of the emperor, but his skimmer crashed and he and his accomplice are presumed dead. I am sorry, old friend."

There came a lengthening silence. It took a moment for Rindy to realize it was not the fault of the decoding program, that Gathon had stopped speaking.

He grabbed the edge of the desk before him, leaning forward intently into the view screen's focus. "I will assume that word of Pan's disability will be kept confidential before the Compact because of our opportunistic friends. However . . ." and he stopped, searching his heart as well as his mind for words. Palaton, dead. He rejected it. He had not saved the boy from his brutish grandfather and from his own blemished heritage, to have him inducted into flight school, and succeed from there, only to see him die before his time. No. "Palaton *cannot* be dead. Gathon, I know that I have not your cold logic, but I would know if he were dead. I would know it! I can only give you assurances that all is not lost. Do not despair."

He sat and waited for Gathon's reply, long, long minutes during which his feet grew cold upon the tile flooring, and a cramp came and went fitfully between his shoulder blades (heart, he thought, and knew he would have to take his medicine before he did anything else), and his bladder pressed with urgency upon him.

Finally, Gathon's image moved upon the screen. "I hope and pray you are correct, Rindy. Try to keep a vote on the pilot contracts from being called until Pan is recovered. I will let you know the minute I hear any further developments."

The screen went dark. Rindy sat back on his chair and flexed his shoulders.

He, too, hoped and prayed he was correct.

Chapter 14

He had offended the Prophet. She stared at him with her blindfolded face, in a long room with many doors, and he could hear trouble outside those doors, danger coming like thunder rumbling in a stormy summer sky. Palaton knew he could not face her or the looming menace, and he turned to run down the length of the hall. As if in a dream, his limbs obeyed, but the gravity was strange.

She pointed commandingly at a door. He knew he could not listen to her, for he had a destiny of his own, and she did not respect that. He ran the other way, while anger creased her face. The menace came closer, thunder booming louder. One of the walls exploded, splinters and debris flying everywhere. He dodged, grazed, but the Prophet stood implacable.

"Stop!" she cried and pointed again.

He could not bow to her wishes. His destiny was not written yet, he still had things he needed to do, obligations he had to fulfill, and he could not go the way she wanted to send him. Sometimes leaping, sometimes running, he fled.

Palaton threw open a door and great, yammering *things* surged after him. He slammed the door in their faces, and stood a moment, heart thudding, taking stock of which way to go.

The Prophet stood aloof in a whirlwind of storm. She raised her hand and pointed a third time.

He would not yield. Palaton took a deep breath, dashed across the hallway which grew longer and more dangerous with every footfall. The floor beneath him was dirt, and it heaved as though quake-ridden, breaking away from him as he raced over its surface. There was no safe passage anywhere.

The *things* chasing him down drew nearer with every

stride. They nipped at his heels, threw dirt clods and more dangerous weapons at his shoulders. They harried him as he took evasive action, their hot sulfurous breath roaring at him, their howls and yips of the hunt making his head ring. The hall stretched before him in a gentle curve, walls wavering and re-forming as he neared them until he had come full circle, winded, spent, wounded. He did not know when he had been gashed and stabbed, but he ached as he struggled to breathe, and he could feel hot blood trickling down his side, his shirt hanging in tatters.

Finally he threw open the door she had shown him. He had no other way to go. It opened into an immense, columned room with an empty throne, and the Prophet stood before it.

"Come to me," she said, beckoning.

Palaton ground his teeth. He could not turn back, the howling pack would be upon him in a moment. He could not go forward, because he knew what she wanted from him, and he did not have it to give. Rand was not his, and even if Rand were to be found, the manling was a free entity, not a commodity to be traded.

He halted and stood, torn, tormented, unable to go forward or back.

The pack of things' howling grew to a frenzy. He heard them as they gathered for a leap and came at him, barreling down on his shoulders with the weight of the world. He went down to his knees under the assault, eyes still upon the Prophet.

At last she turned away, whispering, "If you survive . . . come to me."

The pack bore him all the way to the ground. As he rolled, he put his hands up, wrestling and flailing with *them,* their hot, slavering breath all over him, fangs flashing, tusks slicing the air, closer, closer, closer. . . .

He woke with a shuddering gasp.

A hot compress sloughed away from his brow as he opened his eyes. Hat leaned over, looking closely into his face, his own visage blurred and wobbly.

"He's back," the Earthan announced over his shoulder to someone. "I told you."

"You weren't so confident yesterday. Or the day before."

Rufeen's melodious voices, deep for a Choya'i, filtered into Palaton's hearing, though he could not see her.

He lay back upon a hard pillow, his head throbbing. He knew the feeling which permeated his very bones. His *bahdur* had been expended almost to the point of permanent extinguishing. He put a hand to his horn crown, hoping to still the throbbing or at least make it bearable. Traskar had nearly killed both of them. What had happened?

"How—" the word stuck in his throat. He tried to clear it, choked and coughed harshly. Hat helped him to sit up, pounded his back until he coughed again and spat it out, then wiped his mouth and fed him an herbal tea. The tea went down comfortingly.

"How long?" Palaton said, when he felt he could talk.

"Ten days, and counting."

Ten days. He looked about the low-beamed room. Its modesty was readily apparent. "Where?"

"Semola. I was raised here." Rufeen leaned into his frame of view. She had an apron around her thick waist, looking incongruous over dungarees. "I doubt if anyone's looking for us here."

"Traskar. The plane." The *tezar* had been in distress. "Did he get clear?"

Hat was busy cleaning away compresses and a wooden bowl of scented water. He paused, then said apologetically, "He didn't make it. The plane crashed just past the Congressional dome."

"He should have done it," Rufeen added. "Just a simple lance and snatch. Any second-year recruit could have done it."

Palaton swung his legs out of the cot and sat up. The touch of his feet on the floor grounded him, but sent his equilibrium swinging for a second. He was weaker than he thought, as he gratefully took the hand Hat quickly put out. His own wrapped around larger, his fingers and palm slim, but Hat's were thick and callused and warm.

"Something went wrong," Palaton said. "He tried to shield me from Pan. The *bahdur*—it was like a dam burst. It all came rushing out of him at once. It was fatal. He knew it, I knew—I tried to cut it off. He couldn't control it. I thought I'd succeeded when I broke away. I could feel it seal off. It must have been too late. Why didn't he tell

me he couldn't handle it? What was he thinking of?" Palaton closed his eyes, his head filled with the image of the
very life flooding out of Traskar, out of the stump which
had once been a part of him.

"He didn't want to fail you. You gave him purpose, I
would guess. Not many ex-*tezars* have that."

Hat squeezed his hand gently. "You can't live our lives
for us," he said.

Palaton looked at him. His friend's stocky face blurred a
second, then focused sharply, as his senses weakened and
then sharpened. "No. And I wouldn't want to. God knows,
I have enough trouble with this one."

Rufeen thumped down on the end of the cot and thrust
a steaming mug at him. "Traskar may have brought the
skimmer down on purpose. No one knows you're alive."

That struck him as probable. Traskar would have thought
the sacrifice fitting, after his initial failure. Palaton looked
down into his *bren*. He would never have asked another to
die for him, but it was too late to alter the event. "And
where did you two come from?"

They exchanged looks as if there was something they
weren't quite willing to tell him. "You didn't think we were
going to let you face Pan alone. We followed you to
Charolon."

"I thought we had agreed something to the effect that
we would be stronger split apart."

Rufeen wrinkled her nose. "You agreed. We listened. I
don't remember saying anything definite."

"It's a good thing you didn't. Tell me what happened."
Palaton put his mug up to his lips, hiding his smile.

"Pan used imperial *bahdur*. He went out of control. The
backlash killed a handful of the guards, sprayed across by-
standers. There was a stampede to get out of harm's way,
and more were trampled. It was pretty awful, but it looked
as though Traskar pulled you out of there."

"He tried until I had to break loose to save him. I remember falling. Not much after that. How did you find
me?"

Hat said quickly, "I stumbled over you. There wasn't
anything there but a kind of . . . distortion. I reached down
and your aura was plain. We commandeered a hover

brought in to transport bodies and got out of there as quickly as possible."

"Poor Hat," Palaton murmured. "More bodies."

Hat shuddered and let go of Palaton's hand. "I'll never get used to it."

Palaton got to his feet, as the strength of the *bren* coursed through him. "You've nothing to be ashamed of. There are depths to you that I never suspected."

Rufeen echoed his words with a slap to Hat's shoulder, a blow that rocked the narrow pallet they sat on.

Palaton decided to stay on his feet. It seemed easier than negotiating the two or three steps back to the cot and sitting down. "What about Panshinea?"

"Collapsed, like you. The official word is that he's awake, resting, but has everything in hand. Unofficial buzz says he's still out, but Gathon is running everything." Rufeen added, reflectively, "What are you going to do about it?"

"I tried to tell him about boost. He would not hear of it. So we're going to have to take stock and see what happens."

The two Choyan exchanged uneasy looks again."

"What is it?" Palaton asked sharply.

"Boost. It's everywhere. Overnight."

"Side effects?"

"No one knows, yet. But from my own view—" Rufeen paused.

"What?"

"Anyone who's had the power, and felt it diminish, would do anything to get that old feeling back. It has to be highly addictive, Palaton, emotionally if not physiologically. It has to be."

As *tezars*, they had all seen the ravages of drug addiction in other societies. "Not here," Palaton said. "Not here."

Rufeen lifted her eyes to him. "Sooner or later," she answered back, "someone had to find our weak spot. Do you think we're beyond the same grievances everyone else has to struggle with?"

"I think, with our powers, that we have to be." He fought to stay upright, on his feet, and steady. "It's off-world. That gives Pan a chance to cut it off before we find a way to synthesize it. I have to find a way to convince him to do what he has to do."

"It will be difficult. I don't understand about imperial *bahdur*, I've never seen it used before—"

"None of us have," Hat put in.

Rufeen gave him a look before continuing. "It appears Panshinea was able to siphon off *bahdur* from unsuspecting donors all over Charolon. There was massive power loss all over the city."

"Havoc in the streets," Palaton said slowly. He knew what a Choya was like without his power, with the sudden loss of it. Mindless terror. They would turn to boost. Eagerly and desperately. "Any deaths?"

"None that are being reported. It doesn't seem to be an issue. They could be hiding side effects."

"It's a cycle," Palaton said. "One that needs to be broken. We have to find a way to do it. What about Rand? Any word at all?"

Rufeen looked at her knees. "If Qativar thinks you're dead," she responded, "he may think he has no use for the manling."

"No!"

"Without needing to control you, Rand's too big a liability for the two of them to hold onto him."

"Then my first order of business is to let them know I'm still around. And to let Pan know. We need to go after the pipeline bringing in the drug."

A silence fell, broken only by the loud gurgling of Hat's stomach. Rufeen snickered.

"First order of business would seem to be to eat that stew I've been simmering."

Hat got up with a grateful look, offered his shoulder to Palaton to lean on. "Food first. Planning later."

Palaton found himself agreeing. He put an arm around his friend's shoulder, leaning heavily as they traversed the small room to the kitchen. "Have I thanked you for coming after me?"

"No," they answered together. "But we're sure you'll get around to it," Rufeen added.

Chapter 15

They came and woke Rand, quietly, shadow-people with rough hands and voices, and told him to clean himself and dress, that he had an appointment later. Rand woke slowly during this process as he always did, as if he rose from the dead, so stiff and cold and weak did he find himself. His senses seemed to thaw slowest of all. His handlers would be gone before he could identify them, but he thought they were human. Sometimes.

Like himself.

It couldn't be, of course, because he knew he was still on Cho. Off-worlders were not allowed on Cho. He was being held, perhaps to bring pressure on Palaton, and without the *bahdur* the pilot had shared with him, he could no longer protect himself from the prodigious telepathic powers of the Choyan race.

He found the shower and used it, his mouth brackish-tasting and dry, even when he stood under the showerhead, mouth open, water running from his lips. He could never have used water like this on Earth, but he could here, and he let it pound him awake. He creamed his face for stubble, washed his hair, then stepped out. New clothing had been laid out for him, and a breakfast tray.

He looked at the food, scrambled eggs, bread, and fruit, and what smelled like coffee, real coffee. He did not remember ever having a breakfast like this on Cho. Someone evidently wanted him on their good side. Someone wanted him badly enough to import coffee.

The rich smells drifting toward him turned his stomach. He could have eaten but he was not ready to, yet. *Drugs*, Rand thought. He'd been kept out on drugs, as well. He toweled off briskly and dressed and then sat at the small table which had been put into his holding cell.

He could only remember having been up once before. He still had welt burns across one thigh and the palms of his hands from testing the barriers of the restraint center. The sonics had been only partially effective, but the laser bars still left pain lashing through him. He looked at his hands. They'd healed partially, and he knew that the incident had to have been a few days ago, or longer. Yet this was only the second morning he remembered awaking.

Was Palaton looking for him? He knew the other would never leave him vulnerable in enemy hands. Despite the upheaval of Panshinea's return, and the destruction of Blue Ridge, Hat's and Palaton's beloved flight school, Palaton must be searching for him. Having so crudely stripped Rand of the *bahdur* they had both shared, he must now feel tremendous guilt for letting the enemy take Rand. Theirs was a bond which went deeper than shared power, or common enemies. They had developed a deep friendship which went beyond all barriers. Palaton would leave no stone unturned.

If any good were to come out of this, it might be to drive the *tezar* into alliance with Malahki and the network of Chirek's underground religion although they had argued bitterly over it. Did the Prophet see him in her visions and help the search for him? What happened on Cho without, or because of, him?

Palaton would not involve himself in the metamorphosis of Change, but Rand could not turn his back on the plight of the millions of Choyan who could not access their hereditary powers. Now he had nothing, though he owed them everything. He owed them that right to live as equals. Emotion washed through him, leaving him feeling bereft in its wake. He was not what he had been, and he didn't know if he could deal with being less . . . and yet he would have been nothing at all, if it could have saved the Choyan the grief he'd seen.

Rand pushed his plate aside, barely touched, but drank the bitter coffee down, hoping to clear his head. He looked across the neutrally colored cell, beiges and taupes, the woven fibers of his bedding and furniture in pale blues, and watched where the wall intersected with what appeared to be an open corridor, though its bend went beyond his field of vision.

He sat and watched, saw an occasional flicker of the laser bars, a silver tracking, like the trail a snail left on walkways after passing, nothing more than a hint of the deadly force which kept him imprisoned. He sat and waited for the Choyan who held him to come, tall as they all were, even the squatty Earthans, tall and arrogant, handsome, with a sculptured crown of horn upon their brows to protect their dual brain-panned skull, aliens who held the only method to traverse space when warped, waited for those beings to come and tell him why he was being held.

His ears told him when they were coming. First, the slight change of pressurization in the chamber, and then the foot-steps. Two, one long-striding and measured, the other hur-rying to keep up. Male and female, probably. Rand watched the corridor intently to see who his captors were.

When they came into view, he sat dumbstruck, then got to his feet so hastily the small table overturned and the food tray clattered away sharply, bringing the young wom-an's eyes to his face in alarm.

Human. They were human. They were more than human, for the man who walked to the fore wore the black and gray, and white bars upon the shoulders of his jacket, and Rand had seen his face on view screens for most of his life: Ambassador John Taylor Thomas. It was that mature vis-age which held his attention, the slowly receding dark hair-line, the eyes lined at the corners, the jaw tight. The chiseled resemblance to his daughter was uncanny.

Rand felt bowled over. Who had him, who could get permission to bring down outsiders to Cho? No one outside of the palace ever entertained aliens, and even those occa-sions were rare. Had he been bartered to Panshinea? If not . . . who else kept him prisoner?

Thomas stopped just outside the laser and sonic barriers, distaste flickering over his face quickly at the food scattered across the cell floor. He said to the young woman, "Get that cleaned up as soon as possible after we're done."

She nodded and jotted down the instruction on her note-pad. She was also, Rand saw, fitted with a minicam and recorder. Her fair blonde beauty seemed more alien to him than human.

Ambassador Thomas looked at him. "Randall."

"Ambassador Thomas." Rand paused, his voice rusty in

his throat, thinking oddly that if the ambassador had been
Choyan, with his coloration, he would have known he was
a Sky, and how to deal with him, knowing his inherited
temperament from his genetic House, but he wasn't, he was
human, and suddenly Rand felt adrift among his own kind.
What was he to say? He had seen the man's daughter die.
He reached desperately for that bridge. "I'm sorry about
Alexa. Words aren't enough, but I—I'm so very sorry."

The ambassador blinked tightly. Rand wondered for a
moment if he had even known, but as the man composed
himself, he realized that Thomas knew. Perhaps not every
detail of her death on Cho, but he knew. "She chose her
own course."

"Does that make a difference? I would have changed it
if I could have. I think you would have, too."

Thomas cleared his throat. "You have other concerns."

"Is that why you were brought to see me? Who holds
me here?"

The ambassador answered shortly, "Your perception of
'here' is probably a bit skewed. You've been brought to
Sorrow, and you're presently a guest in the holding cells of
my embassy."

Sorrow? What was he doing in the Halls of the Compact?
"I don't understand."

"Which is precisely why it's important you remain in protective custody."

The young woman had been watching Rand intently and
her concentration distracted him. She was pretty enough,
perhaps a little older than he was, her hair that golden-
hued color which was neither blonde nor brunette, but
both, depending on how much sun she'd been in, touched
with honey tones. She wore a navy suit, a red scarf curled
at her neckline, giving her a brief fountain of color. Her
eyes, outlined in dark blue pencil, were a light sky blue,
reminding him of Rindy's eyes. Like the elder statesman,
she had the appearance of a seeker of truth. She listened
to every word, every nuance with intensity. Rand found
himself staring, and turned back to the ambassador.

"Who else knows I'm here?"

Rindalan had been appointed to Sorrow. He, at least,
should have been made aware. If Rindy knew, then Palaton

would know. And if Palaton knew, then his release was imminent.

The ambassador took a slight step away from his assistant, giving Rand a view of his profile. Thomas cocked his head a little as though considering his answer. "No one," he said shortly.

Rand felt as though the floor under his feet had given way. He put a hand behind him, found the chair, and brought it up so he could sit down. "No one," he repeated.

"That's right. We thought it best, considering the charges against you, and the charges to which you could be witness, when the time comes."

He was witness to the fire-strike of the Abdreliks upon the renegade Choyan colony on Arizar. It was for that Palaton had taken him in, and protected him, and befriended him. It was because of that they had exchanged *bahdur* and the Abdreliks had later hunted him down and tried to strike against Cho itself. But Rand knew that the Abdreliks would not, could not, touch him here on Sorrow, cell or no cell. "Why am I being detained?"

"For your own safety," the young woman said, her voice melodious and low.

Rand did not look at her. He stared at Ambassador Thomas. "Why am I being detained?" he repeated.

The older man frowned. "For crimes against Cho," he said, "at their request, pending investigation." Thomas pulled himself up briskly. "I think, Maeva," he said to his assistant, "that we'll postpone deposition for a little while longer. Give him a chance to clear the cobwebs out, and think about his options."

"I want to speak with someone, let him know I'm here."

"I'm afraid that's not possible," Thomas answered. "Not for the present."

It began to dawn upon Rand that, his own people or not, he was not among friends. "Will it ever be possible?"

The young woman gave him a startled look, but the ambassador showed no emotion as he answered, "That depends upon the findings of our investigation."

"I have rights—"

The ambassador had begun to turn away, to leave. He now swung back and leaned dangerously close to the im-

prisoning barriers. "No," he said tightly. "That's where
you're very much mistaken. You have no rights. For the
murder of my daughter, for the inciting of riot upon Cho,
for the attempted overthrow of a government sanctioned
by the Compact, for meddling in the treaties of senior races
of the Compact," and the ambassador took a deep breath,
adding, "and for other crimes I haven't the time to deline-
eate, you have no rights. You gave up your citizenship
when you became a member of an outlaw colony. The only
right you have now is the basic right to continue living until
tried by your peers—and I wouldn't press that too hard if
I were you."

Rand sat, bathed in the venom with which the man
spoke, his heartbeat growing slow and steady as Thomas
ground to a halt.

The ambassador shook and forcibly calmed himself.
Rand stayed silent.

Thomas finished. "Have you nothing to say to that?"

Rand knew Maeva watched him closely with those
Choyan-like eyes, those eyes which sought for truth. "I
gave my life for my world," he said slowly. "I gave up my
childhood, my family, because I wanted to be a pilot, and
I thought I could bring that back to my people—the way
through, safe and clear, the *tezarian* drive. I thought that,
if I studied hard and learned swiftly and worked beyond
endurance, I could bring it back and lay it in your hands
and it would be worth it—worth all of it—to know what
I'd made possible."

"You're alive. Alexa is dead. And we have no drive."

"Does that make my sacrifice any less valid? The ashes
of the dead are strewn all over Arizar. Does that make my
life less valuable? Do you have me locked up here because
I breathe and she doesn't? Do you intend for me to die,
so that you feel avenged?"

"You sicken me." Thomas whirled about and left. His
assistant hesitated a moment, flung Rand a look which he
could not read, then hurried after her employer.

He stayed very quiet in his chair, the wreckage of his
meal strewn about him, as though it were the wreckage of
his life, and listened to the footsteps fade. Of all the ambitious and contentious races of the Compact which he
feared, he knew that it was his own he feared the most. If

only he could get word to Rindalan. If only he still possessed the *bahdur* to attempt a cry which only those with six senses could hear. If only.

She found herself not believing in the charges of sedition as she ordered up a janitorial drone, and then began disconnecting the recording equipment. The medico had been dismissed as soon as Rand had gained more than random consciousness. Thomas had ordered the medico out, wanting nothing living around the prisoner. The tapes and files would remain, like the prisoner, in his highly secured underground vault. As she laid them in the steel drawer and slid it into place, locking it, she was never so much reminded of a morgue as now. The ambassador inserted his key in the second lock.

"I think perhaps," she said slowly, "we'll get farther with the deposition if you don't attend."

John Taylor Thomas drew himself up. "I'm too emotionally involved?"

"Something like that. Also, your visits to this secured area could draw attention you don't want."

"He's dangerous, Maeva. He has no scruples."

She gave a tiny smile. "As an attorney, I'm not supposed to, either." She stowed away her key. "But it remains that you have other work to do, and your time is already divided in too many directions. Let me get the deposition, and then we'll build the case together." She met Thomas' examination steadily, trying not to think of the tall, somewhat inelegant young man down below, with eyes of clear, earnest turquoise. She could not abandon her own sense of judicial fair play and the writ of habeas corpus. She repeated evenly, "Let me handle this."

John Taylor Thomas looked at Maeva. "I don't care what we have to do. He's never to leave the holding center. Never."

Chapter 16

Maeva reentered the holding cell to see that the prisoner had cleaned up himself, everything in a neat pile waiting for the medico. He was in the process of cupping up a last bit of scrambled egg, back to her, when he heard her step.

She lowered her terminal board which she had been carrying clasped across her chest as if it could shield her from the other, and said, "I can order some more for you."

"I'm not hungry," he answered shortly. He righted the chair. "I thought Thomas was done with me."

"He is. I'm not." She drew up a stool from outside the barriers and sat down.

"I don't think I have anything further to say."

She turned off her audio equipment. "Then perhaps you'd like some company. Or information. I can give you a little, if you wish."

Those light turquoise eyes looked at her. His voice was deeper than she thought it would be—mature, crisp, and clean. "Should I sit down?"

"Only if you want to be more comfortable." Maeva felt the corner of her mouth twitch a little in dry amusement. Between them, the invisible barriers let out a warning pulse of light. Its faint reflection deepened the blue in the other's eyes, overriding the faint greenish tone.

He sat down with a fluid grace most humankind could not imitate. She wondered if he'd gotten it from the years he'd spent among the Choyan who, with their double-elbowed arms and other physiological differences, were among the most graceful of the alien races she'd seen in the Compact. He could be a dancer or an athlete; he was that much in control of his body and unconscious of it at the same time.

Rand sat. He rubbed his hands together and she could

see the burn wounds scarring across his palms. He followed her line of sight. "I found out about the barriers the hard way."

"Do you need medical attention?"

"No. They seem to be healing quickly. Or . . ." He paused. "I'm sleeping longer than I think."

They'd had him in reduction most of his conscious time, waiting for him to return to rational behavior. That was one of the things she could tell him. She dropped her chin slightly. "If you're asking, yes, you've been in suspension most of the time you've been here."

Rand rubbed his hands across his knees, as if drying them. "Passive exercise?"

"I beg your pardon?"

"I haven't lost much muscle tone. Have you had me rigged up?"

"Oh. Well, that's not really my expertise. You got whatever was needed to keep you healthy."

The turquoise stare regarded her. "Freedom," he said, "would help."

"I can't—" Maeva began, then stopped, slightly unnerved. "I have no control over that," she told him. "At least, not yet."

"At least give me my call."

"We're talking IG law here, not your basic Bill of Rights."

"Which is your way of telling me I have no rights." He sucked in a breath. "What is your area of expertise?"

"I'm a trial lawyer."

"Prosecution or defense?"

Maeva could feel herself rise to the edge in the other's voice. She curbed it and said, "Whoever needs me most."

Rand gave a dry laugh. "Right now I think I'd have better luck throwing myself on Abdrelikan mercy."

Her jaw clenched and her throat tightened. They stared at one another for a very long moment, before she cleared her throat to ask, "How can you say that? You know nothing about me."

He answered steadily, "You're with the ones who conspire to keep me here. I think I know all I need to." But he blinked, just before he looked away.

Maeva watched him, thinking of all that he was supposed

to have done: brought down a firestorm attack on Arizar, a world which should have stayed off limits to all of them, according to the technology level of the Zarites; participated in an illegal invasion and colonization of the same world; then gone on to Cho where he had incited civil unrest and been part of an attempt to usurp the throne. Not to mention the attempted destruction of the order of pilots which all of the Compact worlds depended upon—and that he'd been present when Alexa Thomas met her death, details of which were sparse and unavailable at the moment. Did he really think he was innocent of all those actions?

Maeva felt her hand tighten on her terminal. She had become who she was because of her need to know, to understand, so that she could act upon the truth. Part of her job lay here, shuttered behind that face which had turned away from her.

Technically, she was part of the team which would present him with a defense when he went before the Compact. Realistically, she knew that the ambassador wanted to hang this young man out to dry.

"Like it or not, I may be the only chance you have," she told him.

Rand looked back. For that instant, she saw the echo of the Choyan in him, of the grace and gravity with which they carried themselves, particularly the burden of the horn crown they wore upon their heads. Did he know how he mirrored his association with them? He remained silent.

"It's your choice," Maeva persisted. She got to her feet. "It may be the only one you'll be offered."

"Things change," Rand answered.

She was not quite sure what he meant by that, so she decided to take it as an opening. "I'll be back," she told him. As she left, a little servo janitor unit came wheeling in to clean up the debris. She punched in a new order for breakfast, without knowing exactly why she did.

Rand listened to the fading footsteps. He stood up and moved away when the janitor came in, watching carefully how it pierced the barrier. There was no cessation in the fields. The robotic unit merely appeared immune. He did not take his eyes away from the unit as it cleaned up the mess, stored it within its canister body, wheeled about, and left. If he thought to leave with it, taking his chances, he changed his mind as he saw the shimmer of the laser field off the janitor's metallic shell. If there was a weakness, he could not perceive it.

And even if he could escape, where could he go? This was Sorrow. In all its teeming population, he could think of only one who might be his ally—and there was no way to let Rindalan know he was being held here. There was no one else he could trust, and thousands who were his outright enemies. He might be imprisoned, but he was also being protected.

Ironic, he thought, as he moved back to his bunk. On Cho, alone, he would have given anything to be among his own people. Now he would give anything to be allowed to return to Cho.

*   *   *

Gathon answered the door of the suite with some irritation. Though Pan had told him that he would receive the contingent from the House of Tezars, he thought privately that the emperor was too weak to be dealing with enemies. But he also understood Panshinea's reasoning. Vihtirne and Qativar would spread the truth of his refusal if he had, well seasoned with rumors. The emperor had decided that he must meet with them to quell thoughts that he was on his way to his demise. *Show no weakness, no flank, no fear.*

Pan sat propped on his divan, the lighting set slightly lower to flatter his features. His convalescence had been long and difficult, the *bahdur* stubbornly refusing to rejuvenate rapidly, and he was lucky to be conscious. He had managed, by sheer dint of his will, which was considerable, to look as if merely resting after a mild illness and not as if the war he had waged against Palaton had nearly killed him as well.

Gathon stood back to allow Vihtirne and Qativar to enter. Vihtirne had shed her affection for blue and wore fuchsia, its rose hues flattering the artificial blush upon her face. The neckline was higher than usual, imparting a regal quality to her carriage. Her raven-wing hair had been knotted up and pinned with quartz jewelry and lay twinkling among her scalloped crown.

Qativar followed her, dressed in caramels, somber, but not at all reminiscent of the priestly robes he used to wear. Gathon had not thought much of Qativar as a priest. It was no shock to see he had shed his offices as a snake did its skin. Privately, the minister still held the opinion that Qativar had tried to kill the elderly Rindalan during the commons riots which had racked the city weeks ago. He was not pleased to be letting these two close to Panshinea now.

He announced them. Pan raised his face from the book he had been reading—Shakespeare again, Gathon had fetched it up from the music room library—and said nothing.

Vihtirne swept across the suite and came to a deep curtsy across from the divan. "My dear Panshinea. Let us be the first House to bring our wishes for your speedy recovery to you in person. Thank you for allowing us the inconvenience of seeing you this afternoon."

Bluntly. "What do you want?"

Qativar had caught up with Vihtirne, sketched a bow, and now stood at her side. He gave the appearance of one looking over the imperial suite as though he might one day desire to be an occupant. "We wish you well, nothing more."

Gathon closed the door and took up sentry duty, though if anything were to happen, he would have to call the guard. He could not protect Pan's personage alone, not any more.

Pan smiled thinly. "Everything is something more. If I recognize you as the first House to visit me personally, then the least of what I do is recognize the House of Tezars."

Qativar inclined his head. "A side effect, a ripple, of our visit, perhaps, but not our intention."

"Then what is your intention?"

"Your recuperation," Vihtirne answered lightly. She sat down on the long couch opposite, without invitation. The smallish fire in the fireplace reflected itself in the glowing hues of her dress.

"I do not look well enough to you?"

She smoothed a sleeve. "The whole city suffers, dear Pan, from the drain of imperial *bahdur*. You, of all Choyan, could scarcely do better."

The atmosphere of the room crackled and the fine, red-gold hair on Panshinea's head seemed to rise in a gentle aura, blue sparks contrailing through the air after each strand. Vihtirne swallowed tightly and moved back on the sofa, as if hoping to pull herself out of striking range. Qativar stood, looking thoughtful.

The power went out abruptly. Gathon moved two or three steps closer, knowing what that expenditure had just cost his charge.

"I take your well-wishes," Pan said dryly, "and thank you for them."

Qativar appeared unmoved. "No one of us is a *tezar*," he remarked. "Yet we understand that each of us burns as a torch, and when the fuel is consumed, it is gone, never to return. Do you not wonder, Panshinea, what it is we offer our pilots that their own Houses could not?" He leaned forward intently. "Limitless power," he said, and his voices hissed with the seduction of it. "Never to falter again. Never to face the void of emptiness inside when the power is gone. Neuropathy defeated. We have a House because we can cure what no one else has been able to."

"You have a cure for burnout?" Pan's green eyes fixed on Qativar, a predator's stare which Qativar either did not care about or did not notice.

"As close to a cure as is ever likely to be found. We have a drug that will boost the recovery time ten—no, a hundred—times faster. It won't restore *bahdur* to those who have totally gutted themselves, and it won't help the God-blind, but it *will* rejuvenate you. Or any *tezar* who choses to take it."

Vihtirne leaned forward. "Isn't it about time?"

Pan's glance flicked to her, then back to her companion. "And what to you propose to do with this . . . miracle?"

"Extend a supply to you, to aid you in your convalescence. Make it available to those in the city who are currently struggling through difficulties of their own."

"And you would do this out of the goodness of your own hearts?"

"No." Vihtirne and Qativar exchanged glances. "No," she repeated firmly. "We do it to prove to you that we *are* a House, a House which will stand."

"I was not aware," Pan murmured, "that anyone had been working on such a drug." He still watched Qativar's face closely. "Although I had heard word of Rindalan's long, difficult, comatose recovery after the rioting. There was some talk of his being *bahdur*-impaired. You were, as I recall, banned from his quarters, were you not, Qativar?"

Qativar's face warmed. But he gave a nod. "Your intelligence is, as always, impeccable."

"That must have been difficult for you to accept and work around, as you were his closest aide." Pan slid aside the ivory-colored throw and stood. He wore gold and blue, and the gold seemed to hold the heat of the fireplace within it.

"The facts of Rindy's injuries and recovery are no secret, Your Highness. My difficulties with the office are unimportant. Rindalan is now your ambassador to Sorrow. And I," Qativar smiled, "I am one of the founding heads of a new House."

"Be that as it may." Pan put a hand down lightly on the back of his divan as he walked around behind it. Gathon knew instinctively that he was leaning on it without giving that appearance, propping himself up before his enemies. "My understanding is that you have already been overly generous with your drug."

"We have supplied those Choyan who seemed in dire need. How could we do less? There is an illness. We have the means to cure it." Qativar produced a small, ornately jeweled box from his jacket pocket. He laid it on the divan. "As you may see for yourself."

"Take it and get out. See that your charity on the streets is completed as well."

"Our people need this."

"You have no license to distribute it. I want it off the streets."

"You are defeating yourself. We've invested much in seeing Charolon recover—"

"I'm sure you'll be recouped by the black market."

Qativar bowed to Vihtirne and offered her his arm. She swept up her skirts and stood.

"Very well. We will withdraw boost from open availability. But you will not cut us off. I will remind you again of the water patent I hold, and this time, the upper hand is mine. This is a House which will stand. Make a move against us, and you will live to regret it." Vihtirne inclined her head slightly, adding, "May you be fully recovered next time we meet, Panshinea."

"I will be. Have no doubt."

She let Qativar escort her from the imperial suite.

Gathon slammed the door on their heels after ordering the guard to see them from the palace. He crossed the room briskly, reaching for the jeweled box. "I'll dispose of this."

"Leave it," Pan ordered.

"Surely you don't intend to—"

"No. I don't intend to do as they suggest." Pan reached out and caught up the box. "But neither will I be in the dark about what it is they are doing."

"But you don't intend to take it."

Pan's eyes held a smoldering in their depth. "No," he repeated. "Now leave me, Gathon. I think I'd better lie down again." He tottered slightly as he turned his back and wove across the suite toward the bedroom.

Gathon watched him go, thinking that he was probably the only Choya in the world upon whom Pan would turn his back.

Pan needed *bahdur*. Now, more than ever. Something twisted knifelike in his guts as he pondered what the emperor would do to retrieve it.

rrRusk brought the hard copy of the intelligence report in with him when he went to disturb GNask. The ambassador's muscular bulk soaked in the inner suite's spa, the temperature reflecting the heat and humidity of their home world. For a moment, rrRusk basked in it, before GNask's eyelids went up and the ambassador regarded him.

"The Ronins owe me a pilot."

rrRusk swallowed hard. Their uneasy alliance with the quilled assassins had brought them little satisfaction. The Ronins had reported traces of the Choyan colony fled from Arizar, but they had been in error. The rogue colony had gone to ground somewhere, untraceable. GNask had hoped to pick up specimens for observation and experimentation much as they had done with Alexa and Nedar. rrRusk did not condone it, himself. He had given his *tursh* up to be able to stay in deep space for long periods of time. The sluglike symbiont was a valuable commodity, possessing all of the wisdom and shrewdness of his line, as GNask's *tursh* did for his own. But unlike GNask, rrRusk was unwilling to segment his symbiont for implantation in an alien, no matter how intriguing the outcome might be.

While it was true that Alexa had been a successful outcome, the effect on the Choyan had been dubious. rrRusk could not see jeopardizing his symbiont further in experimentation. But then, the war general surmised, GNask had different ambitions than he did. It was not for him, ultimately, to question GNask's actions.

"There may be more reliable ways of suborning a pilot than the Ronins," he suggested.

"Yes?" GNask's eyes narrowed.

"You supported a vote to accept no contracts from the House of Tezars, but that was in your official capacity. Unofficially. . . ."

Water sloughed about the ambassador. "Mmmm. You suggest that it would be wise to establish clandestine diplomatic ties with the new House, to conduct an investigation of my own into the availability and reliability of the piloting? There could be an accident. One of the new pilots could be . . . lost. They would have no standing to protest. That is perhaps a viable option, rrRusk. Yes. Very viable. Thank you, General." Deep in thought, GNask sank to the bottom of his tank, buried up to his eyes in turgid liquid. After a moment, he noticed that the other had not moved.

"What is it?"

"I thought you might be interested. Ambassador Thomas was observed making a visit to his consulate's holding cells."

"And we, of course, could not get a recording."

"No. They are too well shielded. But our observations do not show that they, at the present time, have any prisoners."

GNask, who had been mopping at his tusk, stopped. "Visiting an empty cell? Not likely. Our old ally is much too busy." He half-reared his form from the water. "I wonder what he is hiding from us."

"I knew you would be interested," said rrRusk confidently.

The ambassador's *tursh* had been resting on GNask's flank, just below the waterline. It stirred now, as though awakened, and its two tiny pseudo-stalk eyes poked out curiously. "We will make every effort to discover what Thomas has down there, will we not?"

"I already have intelligence working on it."

"Good." GNask reached for a rough towel and began to dry himself vigorously. "You look dry, rrRusk. Why don't you come in for a soak?"

"Why—why, thank you, Your Honor." A blush of pleasure warmed rrRusk further. GNask took the report from him as he began to shed his suspender straps and short pants.

GNask moved to a sedan chair and sat back. He tapped a finger talon against his teeth as he read. "Yes, indeed," he said thoughtfully. "I very much want to know what he's hiding down there."

Chapter 17

On a half-moonlit night, Palaton paused on the brink of entering a bar which was darker inside than out, its atmosphere oozing out onto the street, murky and muddled. His gaze swept the neighborhood. Streets, littered and dirty. Buildings, some half-built, some half-burnt, others shadowed with disrepute, a slum. The sight tugged eerily at him, not unfamiliar in his travelings but nothing he ever thought to see on his home world. Not on Cho, never on the life-giver itself. The recognition left a bitter taste in his throat, which he swallowed down.

They had come back to Charolon to announce his rebirth. The danger was inherent, but he intended to send Pan an unmistakable message. It had been a scant four weeks since their meeting. It had taken him that long to regain his strength and to acquire the jet sleds, and to decide where to hit.

Palaton shrugged into the collar of his jacket, uneasy out of pilot's clothes, his horn crown throbbing with intuition. He prepared himself to step inward when the shadows boiled. A figure stirred at his feet, a youngster, thin and hunched over as though in pain.

He jolted to a stop and looked the beggar over soundlessly, his voices trapped in his throat by outrage and compassion. The streets and doorways of the capital had never held beggars before.

A hand wavered in his direction, fingers as thin as sticks waggling. "Can you help?" asked the Choya'i. "I'm hungry."

Angry and helpless, he looked down at the young one, saw horns thinned by malnutrition, rags about the slender figure. That one of his own should be found begging—*Emperor, that you could see this as well as I*—Palaton began to press money into her hand, enough money to carry her for several weeks. He froze as they touched, and the distance between them could have spanned Chaos itself. He could fathom galaxies, he could cut between the curtain which separated time and space, but he could not see this poor one's destiny.

"No drugs," the pilot said finally, curtly as if he could dictate the other's future. Then he pushed his hand into hers.

Their fingers met, curled tightly for a moment, then the youngster wrestled the money away. She stowed it within the layering of her rags and got up, whispering, "*She* says to come to her. She says that she is not truly blind."

Palaton stiffened. "Who?"

The Choya'i looked into his face, her eyes the only thing about her not starved and wasted. They were deep, luminous pools of knowledge one so young should never have had. "She says you'll know how to find her. As for me— the guard's about. They'll have your horns." With that, the beggar bolted into the night.

He looked after her, rags flapping in the night air, her flickering of talent setting off the streetlights sporadically, highlighting her as she fled among them. She was not used to *bahdur,* he thought, for she was doing the opposite of what she wished: illuminating rather than shadowing her flight.

And yet the irony was that for most of the last century, few Choya could have lit any of those bulbs simply by thought, despite their design. This was one Rand must have Changed. How far they had come, and fallen, and yet reached again.

He waited a heartbeat while his eyes readjusted to the darkness. The threshold, sluggishly sensing his presence, opened and let him in. He entered and moved to the right with the grace of one trained for gravity-less flight.

There were no guards inside the bar, but that did not make the warning any less potent. His own senses traced icy fingers of alarm across his nerves. The crude *bahdur*-laced illusion which disguised him would not fool any who really knew him. The bar was rife with power.

As accustomed as he was to *bahdur,* he could not grow used to scenes such as this where the atmosphere fairly crackled with psi power ill-gotten and ill-used, a symptom of the epidemic raging across Cho. The hairs at the back of his neck rose in response. This, even for Choyan, was not normal. He stood amidst power undisciplined, unwarranted, untrained.

He was a *tezar. Bahdur* was his legacy. Bound into his genes, it made him master and reader of the nether world between navigable real space and time, and unnavigable Chaos. He was what he was because of his abundance of talent, yet he was perhaps more aware than any of his race of what it meant to have not been gifted . . . or to have had the talent burned out, seared from his very being.

Unlimited *bahdur,* once a dream, was now a nightmare mesh which bound them together. Palaton could smell the faint odor of the drug in the air, an off-worldly perfume which clung to every user, sweated off through every pore. The bar reeked of it.

They could not live with the power the drug gave them, and they could not live without boost once addicted. Yet the surge of *bahdur* left many rocketing out of control, living on a fiery edge of uncontrollable psi abilities. Drugs to boost them, drugs to bring them down again, the only control users had. In a few short weeks, his world had become nearly unrecognizable to him. Addicts, beggars, traitors. This was a Chaos he could not master. His world had changed so quickly that none of them could cope with it. It was still changing, like a river in floodtide.

He did not know for sure what he could hope to do— stemming the tide seemed impossible—he only knew he had to be there. Had to do something. He was a *tezar,* once elite, once proud, from a time before any fool who could swallow boost could pilot a starship.

Palaton moved again, unwilling to attract attention by standing too long in any one place. He found a table and ordered a drink from the servo. His contact either had not seen him or had not entered the bar yet. Palaton forced himself to lean back into his chair, lounging, disinterested in the muddied whispers in other parts of the room. As he relaxed, his hand brushed the end of his jacket, confirming that the enforcer, charged and ready, was still in its holster.

The drink came. Palaton took the chilled bottle, twisted the cap off, and poured it into a none too clean glass. Wary of ambush, he wouldn't have drunk it at all if the container had come already opened.

He felt a brush against his thoughts as he took a sip. He'd taken care to shield himself before entering the bar; now all the intruder would feel was a slight eddy of weariness and satisfaction, emotions rather than defined thought. The rebuff would be barely noticeable rather than if Palaton had suddenly flung up his barriers. The difference in reaction could mean his life.

"Tezar?"

Palaton looked over his shoulder as the speaker sidled up from behind, coming around and finally stopping, the table between them. "I'm Lescal." The Choya stood, hunched over to speak to him, his frame emaciated, his mane wild and uncombed, his cheeks gaunt hollows in his face. His horn crown looked as though it had begun to thin and curl. Most of all, Palaton hated the look in the eyes, the whites too gray-blue, too visible under the irises, intelligence fled, replaced by desperation: the look of a Choya addicted to boost.

Palaton smoothed over the revulsion he felt. Dealing with pilots addicted to boost was becoming a facet of life he'd never thought to face. But pilots who'd been through the proud flight schools of Blue Ridge, the Salt Tower, or the Commons were professional, highly trained, and, if such a thing could be said, they used boost in moderation. They sought after nothing that was not already theirs.

This Choya was nothing more than a street user, who, after having tasted boost could not endure living without it, no matter what the drug did to his system. He wore the patch of the House of Tezars, meaning he piloted because he'd suddenly been thrust into the powers which enabled him to do so—but though he could now perceive the Patterns of Chaos, Palaton knew this Choya could never master them. One day soon, under boost or not, he would lose himself and a flight.

Lescal would be dangerous, Palaton told himself, and forced a thin-lipped smile in response. "I am," he confirmed the other's inquiry. "Have a seat. A drink."

The Choya wiped his dry lips on the back of his hand, looked about, then sat quickly. "All right."

Palaton ordered another bottle. He sat, watching his

guest, wondering where Rufeen was, if there should be trouble. He hadn't seen her in the bar, but he knew she'd entered before he had. His companion would be there, somewhere, backing him up from the depths. He could search for her with his *bahdur,* but didn't dare. The room was already too charged with power.

"What do you want?" The Choya perched at his chair's edge, one foot tapping the floor in a frantic, rhythmless beat.

"Information. And boost."

"The boost I've got." The other gave him full attention. "It's only been cut twice."

"Twice? You told me once yesterday."

Lescal licked his lips nervously. "I had to go to a different supplier. Twice is still good. Very good."

As indeed it was, Palaton reflected. The average supply was usually diluted three to four times. "I'm not happy, but I'll take it."

Lescal's eyes narrowed. His lip curled and even the intrusion of the servo with his drink did not stop his reaction. "You're all alike. You want it, but you act like you're too good for it." His gaze lasered up and down Palaton. "You're probably Housed, but can't burn enough *bahdur* to get anywhere, right? So use a little boost and make everyone take notice. We're not that much different."

Palaton felt his muscles tense, but he forced himself to stay in his chair, relaxing his body nonchalantly. "Maybe not," he agreed. "Price the same?"

"Yes."

"Done, then. Give me your deposit code and I'll have the money transferred."

Lescal showed his teeth. "Credit in hand, or no deal."

"All right. Show me the boost."

Lescal slipped a hand inside the jacket, showed him the corner of a tightly sealed packet. Palaton could see the fuchsia powder. He took out his money disks and slid them across the tabletop to the Choya. With barely a movement of hands, the exchange was made.

Palaton secured the packet inside his jacket.

"We're done," Lescal said.

Palaton struck, moving from his chair so quickly he had the other pinned to his seat before the streetrunner even knew he was moving. "Not quite," he said quietly, through his teeth. "I also need some information."

Lescal's eyes rolled. No one else in the bar paid any attention. If he were to let out a death scream, no one would even turn or raise an eyebrow. "What?"

"Your supplier."

"Trevon the Black. But you won't find him. He doesn't need boost. He can stay clear of you or anyone else." The Choya's jaws chattered in fear as he ran out of words.

"Then Trevon doesn't need to worry that you told about him, does he?"

"No-o," answered Lescal, unconvinced. "What else?"

"A stranger, an alien."

"Off-worlder?" Lescal blinked. "Hiding?"

"Possibly." Palaton watched the other think, knowing that there had only been one off-worlder at large on Cho in the last generation, and Palaton had lost him. He'd brought Rand to Cho to keep him safe from the stewpot politics of the Compact, and lost him to a traitor among his own people. If this boost-laced Choya could think, he'd put Palaton and Rand together. If not . . . Would the query unmask him?

Lescal licked his lips. Most common Choyan were xenophobic. The reaction now showed in Lescal's eyes. He shook it off briskly. "I haven't seen anyone like that."

"But if you do. You know who's looking for him."

"Tezar."

"Palaton. Remember the name."

"But you're—dead."

"You're sure? Look at me closely. Look and remember. Panshinea will pay for that memory. Sell it wisely."

His captive pulled away.

Palaton let go and Lescal bolted, chair overturning in his haste. He fled the bar, never looking back.

Business done, Palaton finished his drink, dissatisfied. How could one humankind be wrenched from his guardianship and hidden away so thoroughly? And for what ransom? That was a failure he could not stare in the face, not yet.

Peripherally, he saw a shadow detach itself and drift his way. She took a chair and their eyes met.

Rufeen was frowning. "You take too many chances, boss."

"He was a burned-out boost addict." Palaton could feel his nostrils flare slightly with the disgust he felt. He could still smell the stink of it on him, the ooze from the other's pores, the chemical wrongness.

Rufeen faced him. She opened her mouth to say something more, then snapped it shut, and opened it again to warn, "If Jorana were here, she'd have your hide. The little street rat couldn't wait to get out of here. That ought to tell you something."

"But she isn't," Palaton said sharply. Rand had been taken from him, but the sting of Jorana's fleeing was just as sharp. She'd abandoned him, left him to face the wrath of the returning emperor alone. He'd failed as guardian to Rand. As heir to Panshinea's throne. But how had he failed Jorana?

What Rufeen said returned to niggle at him. Lescal couldn't have escaped quickly enough. He wondered if he'd stepped into a trap and stirred, agreeing with the Choya'i.

"No, he couldn't." If he knew imperial guards, his informant wouldn't get far. Aloud, he observed of Lescal, "He won't get far enough to spend his money."

Rufeen snorted. "If he's colluding, Panshinea will have his liver for breakfast."

Palaton did a quick psychic sweep of the table, altering the aura of his presence and hers as carefully as he could without attracting attention. As he finished, Lescal's attitude and the beggar's warning came together. Palaton stood. "I'm done here."

They got no farther. A hand of imperial guards broke in the door, awash in light from their helmets and belt lanterns, eyes coldly sweeping the bar. Rufeen melted away into the shadows with a muttered curse, heading toward the back. Palaton continued with a soft step toward the front as though the guards had not alarmed him, knowing that they would be night-blinded as he had been upon entering.

Another Choya did not take the invasion so calmly. He came to his feet with a shout, and the guards swung around in a united front, enforcers in their hands. Palaton hit the deck at the first discharge, heard tables and chairs avalanche about him. Footsteps ran past. He saw regulation issue boots as they went by. He rolled over onto his flank and peered cautiously over a tabletop. The guards had their target surrounded and were, none too gently, searching their prisoner. The downed Choya got a beam in the face and a boot shoved in his ribs.

Palaton shot a glance toward the rear, saw Rufeen waiting near the archway, thumb hooked nonchalantly in her belt. She had the exit secure, for the moment.

He got to one knee, catching her eye, and signaled her to go on out and free their transport. As she moved out cautiously, the guards watched her go but did nothing to detain her.

Palaton doubted he would be that lucky. *Bahdur* tingled under his skin like a fiery network of energy and he drew on it, crafting the illusion of himself standing, readying to fight, staring them down. When he'd finished, he threw the aura at them, knowing it would hold long enough to get him through the back doorway. After that, he was in trouble.

As the illusion went up, he scrambled across the barroom floor on hands and knees, pitching upward at the back door. The guards were engaged in firing at the illusion, crying out in disbelief as their target failed to go down.

He caught his hip on the corner of the serving bar. It swung him around, a physical blow that brought a gasp of pain to his lips. As he moved, he saw a Choya'i react, a beautiful face to the rear of the bar, a familiar face swinging past. . . .

He went to one knee in pain, sucked his lip to stay quiet, and craned his neck to look, to see if it *was* her, drinking alone, Jorana, her bronze mane tied back from her crown and her exquisite face. . . . The blinding white arc of light thrown out by the guards had sent the room into shocking light and dark patterns, and he could not see her well, but he knew the way she moved. He could feel that burned into his mind, moving to him, with him . . . was it her? The Choya'i turned sharply away, and he lost her entirely to the shadow.

Then the guards started across the floor, their boot stamps drumming and he knew he was out of time.

Palaton drew a soft breath, focused, and threw one last illusion at the barroom's front counter. It would last far longer than the other, orange flames, gushing upward, engulfing the counter, guaranteed to send the remaining clientele bursting for the exits, a cold fire which would dwindle down to a single blue flame, burning icily from the ashes of its casting. He wrote his name within the flame. He felt the *bahdur* leaving him, an icy hole into which nothingness plunged, a weak, giddy feeling of expenditure that made him reel. Palaton caught himself, pivoted, put a shoulder to the back door, rolling through and onto his feet in one fluid move even as screams and shouts exploded behind him.

Quickly, he moved around the building to find Rufeen at the jet sleds, firing them up. He panted too hard for the simple exertion, but with his *bahdur* nothing was as simple as it had been, once. He put his chin down to catch his breath and saw the forms at Rufeen's boots. Two guards littered the backstreet. Her nose wrinkled.

"They'll sleep a while," she said. Her knuckles were split and bloodied. She swung a leg over her sled, and added, "But I suggest we get out of here anyway."

He put his transport into full throttle, and she followed in his wake. Palaton signaled to Rufeen when they'd moved uphill, decently out of range, past a burned-out shell of a building, and they brought the jet sleds down to idle hover. He brought scopes out of the tool bag, keyed in the night filter, and put them to his eyes to watch. Night shadows hid them as imperial guards stormed outside the bar. He did not like having to leave his psychic fingerprint behind, but he'd been left no choice. He would rather have come and gone without Panshinea's finest knowing he'd even been there. But he saw no sign of Jorana. He trained the scopes on all the exits, watching those who carefully and not so carefully fled the scene. He tarried too long, watching, but he could not tear himself away.

Rufeen brought up the idle on her jet sled. "Boss, we've got to get out of here."

"I know." He watched the building, saw a few more occupants slither out and disappear. "I don't like to leave unfinished business behind."

"You're going to leave your behind behind if we don't get out of here." Rufeen glared at him, her face large and square and homely, but honest, and boost had never dimmed the truth in her eyes. "Let's go."

Nodding, Palaton reluctantly turned his sled about and

followed her lead out of the ruins. A Choya more wanted than any boost dealer, a prize the emperor would stop at nothing to acquire, the former heir to the throne stole away in the night.

The emperor sat bowed at his *lindar,* his hands curved over the keyboard as though prepared to play . . . or perhaps to throttle. He turned his head slightly, bringing his green gaze to rest on the nervous captain of the imperial guard. The captain was new to his post, promoted when the former head, Jorana, had abruptly disappeared. That did not make Namen any more secure in his position. He set his jaw as Panshinea stared at him.

"He's alive."

"We got a handful of gutter rats leaving the bar. They've all reported the same thing." Namen felt his knees grow weak.

"What about the dealer? Have you found him?"

"He's in custody, awaiting questioning."

"I will," stated the emperor, "be there when you take your deposition."

"Yes, Your Highness." Namen could feel the burn in front, and back, as his own guards stared at him from behind.

Panshinea took his hands from the keyboard. He massaged one lightly. He was not old for a Choyan, but his hands had begun to show his age. The veins stood out in ropy lines, his knuckles had begun to knot. His luxuriant mane of reddish gold, however, remained undiminished. "What good can you tell me, Namen?"

"Little. The bar was so rife with boost users we could not pick up an accurate aura reading. If this was Palaton, why here? No descriptions, and this facility has made a policy of not making visuals. There was only the fire illusion. . . ."

Panshinea finally looked away, and Namen suffocated the sigh of relief in his throat. The emperor gazed down the length of the room to the garden beyond the arched doorway. "Do what you can," he said, finally, his voices fading.

Namen dared not take it as a sign of weakness. He knew that Panshinea's fury toward his heir was unabated. He saluted and turned away.

"Namen."

The captain stopped in his tracks. He spun about as if twirled by an inexorable force.

Panshinea looked upon him again. "You will find him, won't you? Because I have no choice but to believe he's alive." Alive and flaunting the House of Flame in my face. Alive and unpredictable. Alive and out there somewhere.

"If he's on Cho, Your Highness, I will find him."

Panshinea launched himself to his feet. "He's a *tezar*, burn your hide, Captain! He has the universes to hide himself in."

"He's Choyan," Namen replied evenly. "And I have reason to believe he would not abandon his home."

"Do you, Captain?"

Namen felt his chin go up. "I have my convictions, Highness."

"I used to, once." The fire left Panshinea's eyes. He sagged into his chair. "Get out of here."

Namen left swiftly.

Panshinea listened to the rapid fade of the footsteps of his guard. Jorana, gone. Had she fled before Palaton's fall from grace to save her own hide, or had her pilot lover sent her away? None of Panshinea's intelligence within the palace could give him the answer. She had come to him young and beautiful, and matured into an experienced, intelligent Choya'i. The beauty had only strengthened. But once he had brought Palaton to the palace, she had never looked at him again in the same way. Panshinea knew then that Palaton had taken her from him.

As for the throne, Panshinea had given it to him, knowing the burden would destroy him. Instead, Cho itself had split asunder and the rival factions were tearing at its flesh like ravenous carrion eaters. Panshinea had destroyed the very thing he had hoped most to save.

The emperor swallowed his emotions, bitter bile in his throat, swearing to himself.

Palaton would pay for that with his life, and any and all who dealt with him, no matter who they were, would fall also.

No matter who.

Chapter 18

It was like keeping the carrion hounds at bay, Panshinea thought, and wearily put a cold glass to his temple, to ease the pounding.

Palaton alive, and harrying the black market for boost. The broadcasters had caught word of him and now he was some heroic phantom, fighting to reestablish himself and the lost House. They were making an icon of him. He was waging the war against boost that Panshinea ought to be waging, and could not.

The news of the water patent reversion had been the subject of the last three Congressional sessions, and though Vihtirne had apparently done nothing, the possibility of the privatization of the public utility held all the representatives in tension. But overshadowing all was the threat she had left with him. *Cut off boost, and I'll cut off the water.* Pan felt powerless.

The guard had sent out a detail, reasonably sure that they had finally netted Palaton, but their unconscious bodies had been found in the common quarter of the city, and nothing they said upon recovery made much sense. The doctor examiner had told Pan privately that he doubted full memory could ever be restored. The emperor was not certain that the Choya they had encountered had been Palaton. He did not think the *tezar* had it in him to treat even an enemy that way.

Rindalan's latest reports from Sorrow were not much more encouraging. The demand for open contracting with pilots was building and if it came to a full Compact vote, there would be no way to keep any of the space-going races from treating separately with the House of Tezars.

Even the comfort of his garden library did not bring him the ease he'd hoped for. He had given up his post on Sorrow to return, but his presence had done no good. He no longer held the control from the throne he once had, and his own people knew it, the Abdreliks guessed it, the Ronins lusted for it. The Great Wheel of God was rotating slowly about, his House was on the descendant, and when the Wheel rose again, another House would be uplifted. An emperor in descendant could ruin all that Cho had striven for these last few hundred years.

Panshinea looked at his reflection in the gleaming wood panels of his desk. Blessed by prelates after the God-blind had carved it, this desk had stood in the palace for, what, most of the three or four hundred years he thought of? The core that underlay all their *bahdur* was the acknowledgment of things organic, of the once living, of all which reflected the spark of God. He could not sit here and not know that this living thing had been sacrificed to make an object for his use. It would not live again, except in the essence of the God-in-all which lost nothing that had ever been created—except for those lost crossing Chaos. They were irretrievable.

Still . . . Panshinea put his dewy-sided goblet down and drew across the heavily polished wood with a fingertip. Why him? Why was it he who had been doomed to be emperor at a time when the Wheel turned to its downside? Had he not worked as hard as anyone, no, harder, to keep the carrion hounds at bay, both upon Cho and in the Compact? Had he not sacrificed his youth and his prime? What more could he have done?

Anger flared in him. He curled a fist and slammed it into the pattern he'd traced upon the desktop. Who were any of them to judge him the dregs of his House! It would not be over until it was over, and not until then could any presume to judge him. And when the dust had settled over his coffin, his descendants would look at one another and say, "The House of Star never had a more brilliant emperor."

He would not quit. They would have to defeat him. And, by so doing, they would bring their own doom upon Cho.

Panshinea glared at his reflection in the desktop. The burls lent new lines to his face, new heaviness to his eyes. He lifted his chin and downed his drink, then put his head back and bellowed for Gathon.

*　　*　　*

The prime minister must have been napping, for when he came in, there were lines on his face which the bed linens had imprinted there, and his yellowing mane of hair lay uncombed upon his forehead. His jacket looked as though it had been pulled hastily upon his wiry frame.

"What is it?" Gathon asked softly, as though he had not been interrupted.

"I need you to make a little journey for me." Panshinea studied his minister. He saw the tiny signs of distaste he had been looking for.

"It is late."

"So much the better." Pan cleared his throat. "I would have Jorana do this for me, but . . ."

"Your Highness, is it necessary?"

Pan drew himself up. "Look into my eyes, Gathon. You tell me what burns there, and you tell me if this is necessary."

The prime minister stole the briefest of glances, and turned away, as if he did not like what he saw. Speaking almost in an entirely different direction, Gathon said reluctantly, "I do not like doing this."

"We haven't any choice. Would you rather I started using boost? What a field day the broadcasters would have with that, would they not? They would love to bring me down and let Congress and the commons dance on my bones. The emperor must absorb *bahdur* from the defenseless to maintain his throne and his powers. The fall of the House of Star, at last." Panshinea thrust himself to his feet. "Well, they can't have the throne yet. I'm not done with it. And I'll do whatever I have to do to keep it within my grasp."

"You risk much," Gathon answered him.

"I know." Panshinea's voices leveled. He paced across the room, away from the elderly Sky. "Your loyalty is remarkable."

Gathon's dry voices followed after him. "I try."

Panshinea turned quickly. "I only need one tonight, Gathon. But I do need him. I can't face tomorrow without him."

Gathon swallowed tightly, then said, "I don't . . . I'm not sure if I can find a suitable candidate. Finding unsullied talent is getting more and more difficult."

Panshinea looked out the garden room windows at the velvet blackness of his atrium. "I know," he answered finally.

"Perhaps the alternative is preferable."

"Never!" The strength of Gathon's response surprised them both, and Panshinea faced him. Color had risen high in the prime minister's face. "The drug is off-world, we know that much. If you came to depend on it, and that dependency were known—"

"The throne of Cho would be a puppet on a string for anyone to manipulate," Panshinea finished. "So, disagreeable as tonight is, we're agreed it's necessary."

Gathon dropped his chin down in silence.

Pan took a deep breath. He crossed his hands behind his back. "Take the back ways," he said. "I'll be here waiting."

The faint sound of shuffling steps told him when Gathon left.

He had decanted a bottle of the wine known as Imperial Gold. It was rare now, Imperial Gold, the vineyards in an area forced to become fallow, the vines stored for that future when the land could again be used; the wine prized beyond value for its like would probably never be fermented again. That was the tragedy, and the success, of Relocation. The lands, all of them, and fishing lanes, and cities as well, were forced to cease and desist so that the land and water itself could take a breather, lie wild, rest, without occupation or disturbance. The vines which had produced Imperial Gold might be replanted successfully in the future. Or they might not. Grape vines, as Panshinea recalled, could be difficult and stubborn.

He had glasses waiting. The inside basin of one had been discreetly rubbed with *ruhl*, the aphrodisiac which quite disabled *bahdur*. It did not take much of the illicit drug to confuse and fog the mind. The glasses were placed so that he knew which was which, for the obvious reasons. He had retired to his chair and was reading a translated volume of Shakespeare, marveling at the richness of thought and emotion, telling himself that the humankind race proved the theory that all races, whether space-going or not, had the ability to reach spiritual maturity when he heard the voices and steps outside his study.

Gathon came in, face grayed with the cold, hunched under his jacket and hood, with a bracing young Choya on each arm. Pan set aside his book and stood. They were wilders, off the street, their hair roached, shining with the luster of newly fallen raindrops, the brown of newly turned earth, rich and virgin. They did not have facial jewelry as was the custom of the Housed, but they wore open-throated vests rather than jackets or cloaks to display their pectoral jewelry. They shook off the rain, scattering it like diamonds across the carpets of his solarium, and turned their green-gold eyes on him and waited.

He could feel the charge of their sexual energy, and felt the corner of his mouth twist a little in response. Gathon bowed his head without introduction and left, closing the doors firmly behind them.

They both had *bahdur,* borderline, and from the swagger of their walk, they used it, whether consciously or unconsciously, to enhance their appeal. The knowledge of their virility rippled beneath their musculature, and flashed in their eyes. Pan looked at the whites, could see little of the blood-shot appearance of those addicted to boost, and decided that Gathon had brought him appropriate subjects, after all. It only gave him a momentary pause to wonder how and where Gathon had known to look for Choya like these.

"I'm Farren," said the bigger of the two, and hiked a thumb back at his shadow. "And this is Syman."

Panshinea took down a third glass as he stepped to the liquor cabinet, dashed a drop of *ruhl* in it as his back was turned, and then filled all three of the stemware with Imperial Gold. He said, dryly, "No need to give you my name, is there?"

"No, sir," echoed the two commons.

Panshinea turned about, and handed around the glasses. "This should take the chill off." He drank deeply and watched as, nervously, they took the delicate glasses in their work-callused hands, and sipped at the wine. They were probably used to coarser brews, but an immediate appreciation of the wine bloomed over their faces.

Nice, he thought, to have both the brashness and the innocence of the young. He leaned his hips against the corner of the bar. "Now, then. What did you have in mind?"

Syman kept his nose buried in his glass, but Farren answered, "Nothing, sir. But we met your Choya on the down-side, and we got to arguing, and then he told us he could get us this opportunity to meet with you ourselves. Said you like to keep in touch with the commons."

"I have been known to, from time to time." Pan swirled his wine and finished it. He held the bottle out and topped off Syman's glass.

The youth gave him a look, from gold-green eyes, and Pan gave him a level look back, from eyes which he knew were cold jade green. The other shrank back into Farren's shadow a bit, as if suddenly realizing that, despite their fitness and brawn, Panshinea stood over them by a good shoulder and crown.

Farren flexed inside his ebony leather vest. "So we're here."

"Indeed you are." Panshinea refilled Farren's glass as well. The wine flowed inside him like a river of sun. He let that wealth pour outside of himself as well, fueled with the last, flickering vestiges of his own *bahdur.* He could feel it cascading about the two youths, drawing them closer, intimate, warming, calming. He looked into their eyes and smiled. He had seduced far more important and intelligent Choyan than they with that smile; indeed, the impact of that gesture had been felt oceans of starlight away. He knew its power.

It did not startle him when Farren flushed, then put his hand to the throat of his vest, opening it, as if suddenly too warm. Syman cleared his throat huskily, responding to the charge in the air. Then Farren went to his knees, and Syman made an odd little noise and toppled, crashing head-first among the shards of his glass. Farren looked up at Panshinea, terror striking across his face.

"Wha—" He did not finish before falling backward across the torso of his companion. His eyelids fluttered closed.

Panshinea stood over them a moment, waiting until their frightened breathing subsided into puffs barely sufficient to keep them alive. "There are many ways to serve your emperor," he told them, before kneeling next to their unconscious bodies and draining them of the soulfire which fueled them.

* * *

Rand jerked awake in his cell, gasping and choking, eyes staring starkly into the darkness of downtime, heart beating so wildly in his chest he thought it might burst. He put his hand to it, as if he could somehow quiet it that way, like he had once petted a dog, and felt his chest heaving under his palm.

He hadn't dreamed of vampires since leaving his father and Earth, but now he had. The terror had invaded a peaceful dream of Rindy discussing philosophy with him, a tract of peace and help and friendship, when something dark had pierced their togetherness. That darkness had grabbed him, ripping him away, had thrown him down, and with a cold, wet kiss, had begun to devour his soul. It had sucked him inside out, until his blood had grown cold and tired in his body, and his heart barely flickered. Down, down, it had reached inside of him and peeled him away from—what?

His *bahdur.*

But he had none. His only gift had been lent him by Palaton to be cleansed and taken back when Palaton's need was greatest. He had nothing.

Rand leaned back against the wall of the sleeping cubicle.

His hair was slick and wet down his neck. He put a hand back to try and wipe it dry, without luck. His heart quit drumming, but his pulse still hummed loudly in his ears.

Nightmares. Or memories?

Subconscious memories. Did he think of Palaton as some subliminal rapist?

But the presence which had attacked his dreams had not felt like Palaton. Or even dead Nedar.

Vampires. Bogeymen. Rand forced a laugh as he pulled his knees up and hugged them, staring across the cell and wondering when uptime would lighten the corridors. He wondered if Maeva would come that day, even as he told himself the chances were that she could not.

In his fear, the rest of his dream, the part of the dream telling him of friendship and aid and peace and comfort fled completely.

Chapter 19

"He saw me. I know he did." The Choya'i paced the room of the tiny warren, her stride swift and sure despite the growing bulk of her body. Her distress was written all over, from the pallor of her expression to the sweep of her steps.

"And how could he recognize you? If indeed if was him. He was under attack at the time. He might have been busy trying to survive." The immense, sable-haired Choya who watched her sat at a table which he dwarfed, his work-worn hands in front of him, playing at a child's game of beads and sticks. He played at divination, and bright flashes of *bahdur* power struck sparks now and then. A game it was, but a game meant to measure the talent of the young and untested. He played it as though it were new to him, as indeed it was, for he had been born a Godless, a commons, until the Change came over him. Malahki watched the game patterns fall before him, as if he could not believe the fortune which had struck him. "And if it was him, then you are twice the fool for not turning him over to us when you should have. He gains nothing by taunting Panshinea now. The Prophet has things to tell him, but he refuses to go to Bayalak to see her. He is playing with fire, Jorana, and you won't be able to save him from himself a second time."

Jorana paused, put a hand to her stomach reflectively, noting the rounding of pregnancy, and said, "I couldn't have given him to you, you know that. He would never have forgiven me."

"I understand. That doesn't mean she would, which is why I'm holed up here with you." Malahki gave a wry smile. "We're both in trouble."

She combed her fingers nervously through her hair, loosening the forelock from its ribboned braid, colored like river clay, far from the natural luster of her gold-fire mane.

Malahki intoned, "It would be stupidity beyond measure to come back to the capital, well within Pan's grasp. Our *tezar* is many things, but I did not count stupidity among his faults."

"The guards were looking for someone."

"A boost dealer, no doubt. Panshinea hesitates to take a stand about the traffic, but whether he intends to shut it down or control it himself, I haven't been able to figure out. And I won't find the answer here!" Malahki shoved himself back in the chair, taking his eyes off the game and looking squarely at Jorana. "Perhaps Palaton would behave differently if he knew he was to be a father."

Jorana took a deep breath. "Malahki," she said softly. "I stole a child from him. If he knew then, or if he knows now, do you think he would forgive me that? Do you?"

"The only thing he knows is that you abandoned the palace before Panshinea returned. As far as he knows, you left so as not to be a pawn between the two of them." Malahki tapped a finger upon the tabletop. "What do you fear?"

"His hatred. His disgust and pity. You did this to me, Malahki, with your insistence that I take a child from him. . . ."

Malahki continued to level his gaze at her, until finally it was she who turned away. He said, "We each have our own destiny. Would you deny it?"

"I wish that you'd left me orphaned and destitute. I wish that you'd never raised me or sponsored me to be Housed. That you'd never educated me. Bullied me. Driven me to be that which I can't be anymore!"

"Or loved you?"

His voices were like a gentle hand under her chin, lifting her face back up so that she could look him in the eyes again.

"Yes!" Jorana gasped out.

"You are not worthy of love?"

"No." She looked askance again. "Not from anyone." A single, dewy tear escaped her right eye and began to slide down her cheek.

Malahki tilted his chair back on its legs. He put his hands behind his head. "You remind me of my Dara, rest her soul, when she carried my own children. This is not you talking, it's hormones running amok, preparing a nest for your young. You're an educated Choya'i—you should know this. It brings tears to the surface, like the quickening of a heartbeat. It stirs up storms. Yes," and he gave a rueful grin. "I remember Dara storming."

"I might know it, but I've never experienced it." Jorana collapsed onto a chair opposite Malahki. "I can't even be myself!"

"Of course you can. But you're tired, and worried, and you've been drinking. What do you think your system can do under an overload like that?" The immense, burly Choya reached across the tabletop now, his wrist brushing over the game pattern of beads and sticks. "I should get you a midwife. Let her tell you what you won't believe from me."

Jorana took another deep, shuddery breath, and realized she had been on the brink of sobbing. "I've months yet."

"Yes. But the life within you is brimming over. It may be unborn, but it has the same potent *bahdur* you do, that its father has. It's spilling out, affecting you, along with everything else. If only Dara were alive to talk with you . . . you're isolated here. I think we should move you. Cross continent, if we can. You need to be out, among other Choya'i, and working. You've a fine mind, Jorana. You were the captain of the guard! Why do you think you were out, unwisely, tonight?"

She made a tiny sound which might have been ironic, or a hiccup. "I was restless."

"You see?"

"I see." Her voices sounded a little blurred, weary. She pulled a handkerchief from her pocket and blew her nose. "How long does this insanity last?"

Malahki shrugged "Motherhood goes on as long as the mother does, from the way my Dara behaved."

"Oh, God-in-all!" Jorana leaned forward and let her head drop to the table. "How could I do this to myself?"

Malahki cupped his hand over her hair. The color, which had been so beautiful once, was now as common as the river clay it mimicked. She had changed it to hide herself.

But the texture of the hair had remained, and despite its drab appearance, it filled his hand with soft, luxurious waves. "We could not let that spark which made Palaton what he was go out. The genetic heritage—"

"I know!" Muffled, yet emphatic. Softer. "I know, I know."

"Yet do you?"

Jorana rested her chin on the table's edge, still hunching her body over, and put a finger out, where she stirred the pieces of beads and sticks. As if repelled by a magnet, the game pieces fled ahead of her touch, though she left a pathway behind of ordered patterns. *Bahdur,* if it was used, did not glow at all, so powerful was she, that she made her passage silently. Genetic heritage was so crucial to the Choyan way of life, yet its crossing and bastardization was blasphemy, so that she hesitated but a second before saying, "And I suspect that you've known it all along, too." And she canted her glance upward slightly, watching Malahki for his reaction.

The Choya sat back, shock on his broad, yet handsome face. After a long pause, he answered, "I was never certain."

"And what heritage is it, do you think, that I'm bringing into this world?"

He mumbled slightly. "I'm not sure. Whatever it is, it will be powerful."

"Powerful enough that it might be handy to have a mother who was formerly head of the imperial guards to protect it." Jorana sat up then. "Oh, Malahki. We don't know what will come of this mix. My DNA traces back to some long ago bastardization of a Star Householding, but this child . . . what can a Flame do? Why was the House set upon by the other Houses and destroyed? What happened—what will it do to me and my baby?"

"I don't know." He looked down at the table, and read fully the patterns which Jorana had stirred into existence. It showed the Great Wheel, its turning and destruction and reformation. He hoped that it was not prophetic. "But whatever the talents, they managed to elude complete genocide. They managed to survive, Jorana, and so must you." He swept aside the beads and sticks. "We need to do some planning. I can't stay here with you for long. Father Chirek is starting another campaign. The Prophet will forget her ire at both of us, and I'll once again be of use to her."

"Others need you," she echoed faintly. Then she drew her chair closer to the burly Choya. "All right. Let's make some decisions. I overheard something else, and I'm not sure what it means."

"Tell me."

"Palaton was asking for word of an alien. I think he was looking for Rand."

Malahki rocked back in his chair. "Rand has left him?" He rubbed a thick finger between his eyes. "They would have to burn Blue Ridge down to get Rand away from him. That could explain much. Although why Dorea didn't tell me this—surely she *saw* it—"

"She's a Prophet, not a God," interrupted Jorana.

Malahki halted, then shrugged. "Then we have to wonder if Palaton does what he does because he's been directed, or because that's the course of action he's chosen."

"If he were being directed, his supposed death in the crash would have allowed him to go underground and stay there. He didn't choose to stay dead. It also means Pan doesn't have Rand, or the meeting on Emperor's Walk would have gone far differently." Her eyes widened. "It has to be Qativar and Vihtirne. They initiated the fight at Blue Ridge, then came in to pick up the pieces."

"Possibly. The House of Tezars remains relatively secure, at the moment. Of course, that might only be because Palaton has limited resources." He dipped a fingernail into the divination game in front of him, and a spark flew up. "He might have his hands tied, but I do not. Rand is as important to me as he is to Palaton."

"We do not play at games, Malahki," Jorana said softly.

He looked up at her. "I know, foster daughter. Believe me, I know." He frowned heavily, concentrating on his palms. "If Palaton is of the House of Flame, then I choose to become a Flame, newly empowered as I am. He won't have me, I know, because of our past enmity and my ties to the Prophet, but that doesn't matter. I will follow him, and all those linked to me will do as I do. Wherever Palaton takes a stand against boost or the emperor, a dozen others will do likewise. He will be mirrored wherever he goes, whatever he does. For his, and our sake, I pray that the good of Cho goes with him." As Malahki moved his hands apart, the illusion of a blue flame burned on the table in front of him, as like to the signature Palaton had left burning for Jorana to see as if she had copied it herself.

Malahki stood up and shook himself, sable mane ruffling. "I have work to do."

Chapter 20

"You take chances," Rufeen said, her face pulled into a morose expression, her hand curled about a mug of steaming hot *bren*. "Chances that you shouldn't."

"A *tezar* not take chances?" Palaton injected humor into his reply, though weariness had settled into his bones as he sat down opposite her. The tiny room seemed bursting with them, though they were only three. The silent third went about filling two more mugs and sliding one of them in front of Palaton.

Rufeen rolled her eyes, looking at the Earthan for support. "You know what I mean. *He* knows what I mean, but he won't allow it to sink in."

Hathord sweetened his drink and then sat down heavily, both elbows and nearly his chin, too, on the tabletop. "*I* know what you mean but I'm not so sure *he* does."

Palaton put his fingers into his topknot, combing it away from his forehead. Even as he did so, he wondered if the forehead had gotten higher . . . the topknot thinner. He could tell without looking that the lines across his brow had gotten deeper. God-in-all knew that his horn crown felt like a ton of rock settled upon his head and shoulders. He flexed his neck slightly at the thought. This last recovery had taken him longer and had been difficult, though when the power came back, it always seemed stronger than ever.

Rufeen said, with satisfaction, "We're not talking about navigation, and you know it. We're talking about here and now. Your hide is too valuable to waste. And if you haven't noticed lately, we have imitators."

"I've noticed." Palaton thought of Jorana. Was she shadowing his deeds, giving a resonance to his campaign against Panshinea's seeming indifference, or was someone else hiding in the echo of his defiance? "We all need to be a bit more circumspect. No more kidnapping of broadcasters, though I will admit that was a stroke of genius."

"Thank you," Rufeen acknowledged modestly. "You needed to get that ugly mug of yours on the air. You will be pleased to know we put him back just where we found him, too." She took a cautious sip of her drink, pronounced it good, which by pilot's standards meant that a spoon could stand upright in it, and added, "You have a duty to remember what you are to Cho."

"I remember only too well," Palaton told her. "But you can't go in alone, and Hat's not good at it."

"No," Hat agreed, unabashedly. "Not at that." He blinked. "Not that I wouldn't cheerfully kill anyone pushing boost."

"There is that, but you don't need to be chasing down the black market while you're doing it."

"It seemed opportune." Palaton cleared his throat. "From what I saw in that quarter, boost has already eroded deeply into Charolon. I can't hesitate any longer. You didn't see what I saw."

Rufeen put her mug down thoughtfully. "I think the problem goes deeper. I've been talking among the few I can who will keep my confidence, boost or no, and there's a phenomenon we haven't heard much about. The broadcasters have been keeping silent under duress. Panshinea has a blackout on the media."

Palaton's gaze riveted on her. "What?" He wondered how much more damage could be done to his people.

Rufeen shook her head. "Pan's use of imperial *bahdur* has evidently created a drain through all of Charolon. Maybe even planetwide, though his effect is less farther out from the Emperor's Walk. The House of Tezars came in, offering the drug freely, which explains why the capital fell into it so easily."

"And Panshinea let them?"

"My intelligence says that Pan made them pull out after a week or so, but by then the damage was done. The need was created."

Hat said, "That doesn't explain *us*."

Palaton looked at Rufeen, then remarked gently to the Earthan, "You haven't flown the schedules we have, Hat. You don't know what it's like to have a few hours, or days, of downtime and then be needed elsewhere, and to always have to be master, in control."

"Maybe I don't, but—"

Rufeen put her hand on his wrist. "You don't. It's that simple. No one of us wants to be the one who burns out and loses a shipment in Chaos. But it happens."

"Boost is no guarantee it won't," said Hat stubbornly.

"It's as close as we can get."

Rufeen lifted a shoulder and let it drop. "There's something else. Pilots aren't allowed to fly regular schedules. They're using a second medication with the boost. I don't have a name for it . . . but my friends told me that, in order to pilot, they're forced to use it in conjunction. And," she paused, her eyes thoughtful, "it doesn't increase *bahdur*. It wipes it out. They say it's necessary to use both, to avoid the rather undesirable side effects of boost alone."

Palaton's mug slipped from his grip, crashing to the table. Hat reached out to steady it as Palaton's expression grew very grim. "Vihtirne's got the House of Tezars wired like a damn circuit switch. What's the coercion?"

"The coercion is that those who've resisted boost are fed the other stuff first." Rufeen looked at him levelly. "You know what we're like without *bahdur*. They're creating the same need in us that Charolon had after Panshinea's drainage."

Cold fingers traced down his spine. Oh, he knew very well indeed what it was like to have the power stripped away or burned out. Stronger Choyan than he had been broken over the very prospect. Under different circumstances, even Palaton could not swear that he would not eventually reach for boost himself.

Hat commented, "*Ruhl* can do that."

Despite her tough pilot's demeanor, Rufeen blushed. "It's an aphrodisiac, and outlawed at that. We're not talking inhibition in bed."

"Stronger doses."

Palaton shook his head. "Stronger doses are invariably fatal."

"Somebody's concocted something." Hat pulled his keyboard and terminal over. "And more likely than not, that somebody is Trevon the Black. He seems to have the pipeline into Charolon and it's probable he's supplying Qativar and Vihtirne as well." He brought up files they'd been gathering and named the most common cross-reference.

"Not a Housed name that I recognize," Palaton told him.

"Or I," chimed in Rufeen. The blush was fading slowly from her craggy features.

Hat did not take his eyes from the flat screen monitor. Tonelessly, he said as if it were something they'd discussed and turned down many times already, "We're going to have to network. Malahki or someone else."

"No," answered Palaton firmly.

"Malahki has the resources."

"He doesn't know where we are, and I want to keep it that way. If he gets his, hooks into me, he'll set me up to directly oppose Panshinea. I won't do it." Palaton had always known Malahki had his own agenda and now that there was bad blood between them, Palaton would be another expendable pawn in his plans. The famed rebel leader of the common forces would never forgive him for taking Rand away. As far as Malahki knew, Palaton had the humankind secreted somewhere, out of Choyan sight and politics.

Palaton swallowed down a throat that suddenly felt lined with thistle. But no matter how driven, how desperate he was he would not turn to Malahki, to be used in a plot to further plunge Cho into turmoil.

"That's your final word?" asked Hat.

"I've learned better than to say never. For now, while he has the advantage, that's my final word."

"What about Chirek?" Rufeen ventured.

"Too close to Malahki. And Chirek's religion is even more explosive than Malahki's politics. No," and Palaton paused to rub his eyes thoughtfully. "No, I'm afraid we're in this alone."

"We can't stay alone long," Hat responded. "I'm running out of resources, and we're running out of places to hide."

"On-world, yes. But off . . ." Rufeen let her voices trail off as she felt the other two look at her. She shrugged.

"That way we'd lose everything," Palaton told her.

"Our cause isn't much good if we're found by Panshinea." The pilot narrowed her eyes and looked into her mug. "Retreat can be a good tactical maneuver."

"I won't do it. You two can leave, but I'm staying."

"What if," Hat said softly, "what you're looking for can't be found here?"

Palaton pushed his chair away from the table. "When I've looked everywhere, when I've exhausted everything, then I'll go. Not before." He stood. "Why don't you two get some sleep? I'll take first watch." His *bahdur* flared into use, its aura about him like a faint, bluish flame, so powerful it was to those near him who were sensitive to the power. Hat had to turn his face away, as Rufeen squinted against the brilliance. Its presence flickered behind him even as he left the room.

Rufeen kicked back in her chair as the door closed. She looked at Hat. "He won't leave," she said.

"I know." He shut down his computer and locked it away. "But I thought we'd all decided we're in for the duration, however long it is."

"Oh, I'm in," Rufeen told the flightmaster. "But all I can do is navigate space. These political waters are much too murky for me, and I would like to see some allies. I don't know how much the three of us can achieve, even if we have shadows."

Hat answered, "Don't think he doesn't know that. But he won't give up easily, and he won't retreat until that or death is the only option."

"Sometimes death doesn't give you that much notice." Rufeen moodily poured herself another cup of *bren* and frowned into its depths.

Chapter 21

Maeva keyed in her entrance code and stood, weight shifted to the ball of one foot, the only sign of the nervousness she felt, waiting for the security door to open. She told herself there was no reason Ambassador Thomas would have her locked out, but there was no particular reason she should still have a valid access code, either. If he were with her, there'd be no problem. But if he were with her, there would *be* a problem, because she couldn't be doing what she intended to do now.

She told herself, while the electronic interface on the door blinked at her, that she was doing what she had to do for her client. Seeing Rand again was necessary. He had refused to be deposed, but she could bring him in as a hostile witness. Her dealings should be over and done with. But she was convinced that whatever he had to say would be so much more valuable if it were open, unforced, genuine. Both Rand and her client would benefit from that course, if she could only persuade him to cooperate.

Are you for the prosecution or the defense, counselor?

Maeva felt her eyes begin to water slightly as the retinal scan slid past. Good question, she answered herself. No answer. Not yet. That's why I want in. In! And she slapped her palm upon the grid as it lit up in soft inquiry.

Who, besides himself, could Rand be trying to protect by being uncooperative? If his actions, as he'd claimed, had been unintentional and undirected, then who would he harm? Could he be trying to protect the very Choyan he had been working against?

He was like a very complicated knot which could only be worked on a hitch at a time, she thought, and bit her lip slightly as the door gave her an affirmative entry and let her in.

Next time, she would have to erase the log entry. She could afford no more attention. *Next time!* she chided herself, as she pushed past the threshold and entered the myriad corridors of the underground facility. Just in, and already she was planning to come back again.

Strand by strand, both she and Rand were coming undone.

Maeva paused just inside the gates. She could turn back now, it was not too late; whatever might happen would not happen if she turned around right now and asked for egress.

She felt her spine stiffen even before her mind rejected that option. She had never turned back from a challenge in her life, and it was challenge she'd read in those turquoise eyes. Challenge and honesty and desperation. He did not believe that there would be any justice here on Sorrow. She feared that, if Ambassador Thomas got his way, Rand could be right.

Could she live with that?

No. Not without knowing as much of the truth as she could obtain. She would never know all of it. Truth was not black or white, it was gray and subjective and it faded with time, despite what she occasionally told jurors. But now, from one of the major participants, she could grasp a vivid enough accounting to make a judgment. And perhaps she could help him as well.

Counselor for the defense. Maeva felt her lips thin in an ironic smile. She'd made her choice without even knowing it. Having made that choice, she knew she would have to inform the ambassador as soon as she could. He might even deny her access altogether. What was she doing here? Trying to jettison a career which had brought her across *space,* for God's sake, a career whose student loans she was still paying off—and, if she stood frozen in hesitation in the corridor much longer, security-authorized access or not, she would bring the system alert on-line.

She put one foot in the front of the other, picking out the corridor which would take her to the elevators, to the lowest and most secure levels of the facility, walking as though she knew the cameras were taping her. She felt as though she had jumped a chasm. Her heart sped up a little.

She could feel her pulse throbbing slightly at the base of her throat.

What was the worst which could possibly happen? Thomas firing her? She could go to the Compact and demand satisfaction on her contract or apply for a grant to work directly for the Halls. Something would be negotiated. One-way tickets home were expensive to come by, given the scarcity of pilots for the runs.

Plus there was pressure she could bring to bear. The ambassador would not do much overtly, she knew, rather than risk the revelation that he had Rand secreted away. That either made her very safe, or very much at risk. There were steps to avoid that, as well, and as soon as she left the interview, she would begin to take them.

For the defense.

Vihtirne slowed her pacing along the marbled flooring to throw yet another epitaph at her companion, then pivoted and began another circuit. Qativar leaned indolently against a column in the spacious room, watching the blues of her dress washing up and down her body, rather like watching rain blend into a stormy ocean.

He did not muster an answer until she halted again. Then he said quietly, "If I had not given over the alien to his consulate, we could bait Palaton and draw him out. Panshinea has his price. We can meet it."

Vihtirne of Sky slowly faced him. Qativar pushed away from the column, standing straight. He was at least as well dressed as she, in black and silver, forging the somber style of his true office of priest. "You might as well have dropped the manling in a black hole. There's been no word of him from Sorrow. The humankind has disappeared. I've not been able to find out what plans Thomas has for him."

Qativar waved a hand. "It doesn't matter. We can't afford to press Thomas. We can't afford an interruption in our supply yet, we don't have it synthesized successfully. But," and he met her icy glance, a smile growing, "we have Charolon in the palm of our hand. Panshinea is sure to follow. Palaton will operate as though we do still have our hostage."

Vihtirne smoothed a hand across her neckline. "Don't play at bluffing him. He's too powerful for that."

"Ummmm." Qativar rolled his voices deep in his throat. "I may not have to. There might be other bait to draw Palaton out. I shall have to do some research, my dear Choya'i." He leaned close to her. "Will you miss me?"

Her glance flickered but a second, downcast in false modesty which, somehow, suited her anyway. "You will take care, won't you, Qativar?"

"Oh, I'll be very careful. We have a House to build, you and I." Qativar trailed a fingertip across the very hollow she had just touched, brushing the caress across territory which he knew she could have him killed for trespassing.

A light kindled in her eyes, one which he had hoped for. Qativar's smile grew wider. "It's unfortunate plans won't allow me to stay." He straightened. "I'll contact you in a few days." He moved past her briskly, and was out of the room before she could protest.

But she wouldn't. She had the pride of her House, as well as her sex, and her ambition. Qativar wouldn't have worked with her as a partner if she did not. He needed a Choya'i with a heart and mind as chill as his own, who would not crumble under the pressure Panshinea was sure to bring as he saw his empire torn apart. If she were the type who would run faint-heartedly after him, he would not stop, and would never return.

He had not put most of his adult years into subterfuge to be turned aside by an elegant face. If truth be told, she was a little too mature for him, but her strengths were too great not to let her play the role she'd fought for. The financial and intelligence resources of her Householding alone made her invaluable to many of his plans.

Plans could be changed if she became inconvenient or weakened. However, he could not discount that she was correct. He'd erred in giving the humankind over to John Taylor Thomas so quickly. He'd thought to force an open trial, revealing the peccadilloes of the Abdreliks, the Ronins, and those Choyan who were supporting a coverup of the incidents on Arizar as well as on Cho. He'd thought it would have been even more to Thomas' advantage than to his own; he had been mistaken. He had not gotten where he was by making mistakes. Not killing Rindalan during the commons riots in the capital was one. Handing the alien over was obviously another. He would not succeed in supplanting Panshinea if he continued to err.

He had a stake in Thomas and the ambassador's actions. Heretofore, he had not interfered with the other. But now, perhaps, a nudge in the right direction might force the ambassador into motion. He passed Asten in the corridors. His blueblack hair combed back, revealing the strongly masculine cut of his horn crown, Asten's eyes barely met Qativar's. The tall, handsome Choya scarcely acknowledged his presence as he strode to Vihtirne's chambers.

The corner of Qativar's mouth pulled tight. Hardly gone long enough for his aura to have left her rooms and she had summoned her lover to join her. It is well, he thought, that we have no illusions about our real importance to one another.

"You don't need to be here," Rand said flatly as she pulled up a chair outside the barrier. "Whatever you have to do, you don't need me to do it."

Maeva tucked her ankles in, staring at the young man Thomas intended to bury from sight forever. Was Thomas so bent on vengeance that he dared not trust justice in a trial? Did he think he could circumvent habeas corpus here on Sorrow? Looking at Rand, she could not see the menace to the Compact and national security that the ambassador had described. She did not see the manipulator and fabricator who had cold-bloodedly murdered Thomas' daughter.

She did not know who she saw.

Maeva leaned forward. "Tell me how Alexa died."

Rand flinched slightly. His hair waved forward as he did, threatening to drop into his eyes, hiding them from her scrutiny, but almost in the same movement, he brushed his forehead impatiently. Emotion, she thought. Real, not manufactured. *Give me more.*

"Are you recording?"

"I'm not. I cannot guarantee security isn't. In fact, it probably is." She slipped a small handheld white noise generator from her pocket, put it on her knee, and switched it on. "This should help."

"What is that?" A fleeting expression of both pain and surprise crossed his face so quickly she wasn't sure she'd seen it.

"It's making white noise."

"Ah." He rubbed his jawline, just in front of his right ear once, then shifted in his chair. "Why should I talk to you?"

"Because I'm here, now, and I'm listening."

"The Choyan have no ears," Rand told her. "But they heard everything I said, and more."

"More?"

"What I meant. Barring cultural differences. They're older . . . different."

"Alien."

"Not as alien as many of the races." Rand leaned forward on his elbows. "I still have no reason to answer you."

"How about your life? Gaining your freedom isn't important?"

His lips thinned slightly. "You work with Thomas. He isn't about to let me go. I know it, you should, too, if he hasn't already told you. If he weren't who he was, he would probably already have killed me with his bare hands."

"And what if I told you that, regardless of his plans for you, I think the law should come first."

Something in the depths of his eyes adjusted. Rand smiled slightly as he said, "Sounds like you have a conflict of interest, counselor."

Maeva could feel the heat rising in her cheeks. She turned away slightly, not wanting him to see her face. Her glance fell on his hands . . . hands which had healed remarkably over the last several weeks, even when he had been in reduction. The barest tracing of the burn scarring remained.

"What are you looking at?"

"Your hands. How did you do that?"

The young man followed her line of vision and held his hands and wrists up. "Oh. I'm . . . not sure."

Even with medical care, he couldn't possibly have healed like that. Maeva looked at his pale skin. He wouldn't even have a permanent marking. She remembered seeing the process begin and thinking of the outcome, but even then, she hadn't really thought it possible. She made a note. She looked up. "Did they teach you to do that?"

"No." He folded his hands across his arms and leaned on them again. "I wouldn't even know how to do something like this and neither would they."

"The Ivrians—"

"Are not Choyan," he interrupted.

Maeva sat back in a flash of her own irritation. Why should the mention of healing augmentation by thought control close him off like that? She opened her mouth to argue with him, then closed it without saying a word. Perhaps what offended him was that he'd been imprisoned and injured in the first place, as well as abandoned.

"I can't do this, if you don't want me to," she said, softly, finally.

"Do what?"

"Help you."

"And why would you want to help me?"

"Because I don't understand what's happening, and I'm a terribly curious person."

"Maeva," he said gently. "You won't get far in the Compact being overly curious."

The advice sounded as though it came from a terribly old, terribly weary personage. Maeva straightened her spine, felt her muscles move in a kind of knotted tension, and eyed the barriers which separated them. She took the sound generator and pitched it neatly through the bars. It thunked onto the table in front of him as she got up.

"What is this for?"

"That," she answered over her shoulder, preparing to leave, "is in case you want to talk to anyone else. Ever. You might need it, if you can find someone else interested in your story. It's got a twenty year warranty."

"Not that it'll do me much good if it breaks," he said.

"No. So I'd take good care of it if I were you. It's innocuous enough they'll probably let you keep it."

He got to his feet, still holding the generator. "I'll keep it for the next time then."

Maeva was in the hallway. She paused. "There won't be a next time, Rand. You've misjudged me. I am interested, and I would like to help you, but neither of us have the time to win each other's trust. Either you do, or you don't, and you've chosen not to. So I won't be back. I can't take the risk if it's not going to do any good, because every second here is stolen, every word precious, and you don't want to participate."

He took a step around his small table, terribly close to

the barriers of his cell. The warning colors came on, notifying him of the placements and danger, but he ignored them. He was already all too familiar with the deterrents, she thought.

"If you want to help me, get word to Ambassador Rindalan."

"I won't do that without your talking to me first." She swung about. She could feel that tiny tic in her throat which started up when she was intensely involved. It throbbed with every heartbeat. She waited while he stared at her, as if committing every line of her body to memory. She'd been given licentious looks before, but there was nothing sexual in this. It was as though he could see *through* her, or into her.

He backed away from the barrier and sat down, placing the generator in front of him. "All right," he conceded. "How Alexa Thomas died." Then he waited for her to return to her chair.

Maeva was so stunned she could not move for a second, then, flustered, she moved too quickly and the chair clattered loudly as she took it. Rand seemed not to notice, though, as if gathering himself. He licked his lips and cleared his throat.

"I killed her," he said, "but it wasn't murder. There was . . . it's very complicated." He rubbed his hands together. "There was a *tezar* . . ."

"Did this have anything to do with the destruction of the Choyan flight school known as Blue Ridge and the founding of the House of Tezars?"

"House?" Rand looked at her, almost numbly, as if watching two realities at once. "Is that what they did? Try to raise a House of pilots?"

"Tried and accomplished, as far as we can tell. The Compact had been doing most of its contracting with them, although that's been temporarily halted."

Rand nodded as if he understood. "We were trying to save Blue Ridge. There was a dogfight—"

"Dogfight? You mean, with airplanes? Like the videos?"

"Something like that." Rand looked at her clearly then, a light in his eyes. "You can't imagine how they fly. They're absolute masters at what they do."

"And two of the best met?"

"Yes. Nedar attacked. Our plane was crippled, but Pala-ton managed to pull it out of a spin and retaliate. They took a direct hit. We didn't know he had Alexa on board . . . we didn't know that Alexa was even involved. I thought I was the only human on Cho. . . ." he stopped again, dry-voiced, and she caught a sense of the terrible isolation he must have felt.

"I'm still listening," she coaxed softly.

"Yes." He swallowed. "We went down, too, but their craft was all but annihilated when it hit. I was thrown clear. Palaton bailed out of the cockpit and ran to see if he could bring anybody out alive. Nedar was critically injured. I don't even know how he could have lived, but he did. His remains spilled out of the wreckage. He asked Palaton to finish him off. He did not want to live a cripple. Palaton did what he wished. But she was in the plane, too. She survived. She saw what Palaton had done. She came out of this hole in the twisted metal, her hair burning with sparks and smoking, and she didn't even know it, didn't even care, all she wanted to do was kill Palaton. He didn't . . . he couldn't defend himself against her. I had a . . ." Rand looked at his right hand as if he could see it still. "I had a piece of metal in my hand. Sharp, like a knife. I screamed at her to stop, and threw it. She took it in the shoulder. It stopped her. She staggered back with the pain, back into the fuselage—there was an explosion almost immediately, and there was nothing left of either of them but ash."

"Self-defense," said Maeva. "And the wound did not kill her, the explosion did."

"Yes. But I don't think it would matter to Ambassador Thomas."

"No." Maeva stood up again. "But it matters to me." She found her eyes very moist and resisted the impulse to dab at them. "I'll contact Ambassador Rindalan as soon as I can. I don't know what good it will do."

"Neither do I." Rand's voice remained quiet, halting, as if the effort to speak had taken a great deal out of him. He held the sound generator and stroked its plastic body. Then looked up. "You'll be back?"

"Yes."

Rand closed his eyes. "Good," he said.

Chapter 22

He slept more than he was used to. Rand knew that he was being kept in reduction, a lighter form of cryonics, because it was the only thing which could account for the gaps in time. It was part of the imprisonment to be without the anchor of time and place. He accepted it, for the moment. He accepted as much as he could, knowing that there would be a time when he would be unable to accept. Unable to bear what they had done to him. The solitude, the timelessness, these were things he could deal with. He did not know if he would see the edge of his sanity growing thin. He did not know if he would be aware when it crumbled away altogether.

When he dreamed, he dreamed mostly of Cho. It was a verdant world, kept that way by hard work and a delicate balancing act. The Choyan built mainly of metal, stone, and rock, those things which either endured or could be recycled over and over again. The cities were peppered with technology which was meant to be triggered by psionic powers, and which few now could activate. Beyond that, power used tended to be as clean as possible, and regenerative.

Most civilizations would have chosen to colonize other planets, lifting the strain from their native world while expanding elsewhere. The Choyan were adamantly against that. He did not understand it when Palaton first brought him, but he'd grown into it, just as he had come to understand the various esper systems which functioned only sporadically. Expansion of a race beyond its native boundaries invariably brought in genetic mutation, adaptation to new surroundings. No world could ever be found which would exactly duplicate the home world, so this change was taken for granted.

But not by the Choyan, into whose very genetic fiber was woven their power, their legacy, the ability which gave them the stars. They had no tolerance for any variation in their abilities. Perhaps that was why they had destroyed one of their own Houses. They feared that by leaving their home world they would lose all that they had been, so afraid that they dared not embrace all that they could become.

A few had splintered off, unknown to the rest, perhaps remnants of the lost House, perhaps visionaries, perhaps renegades. Rand doubted they numbered more than thirty or forty, given the air strike on Arizar which destroyed their experimental work. Somewhere in time, a Choya had discovered that, when paired with a human, his powers of *bahdur* could be cleansed. Instead of burning out, they could be renewed. It wasn't a permanent solution, like an oil filter for machinery, it would have to be used periodically, but the results—ah, the results.

The results had been enlightening. Rand dreamed of being filled with Palaton's power once more, so strange and yet so wonderful. The Zarite college had not been entirely successful. They had stolen humankind to perfect the transferal method, but even then, had not wanted the subjects to know or understand what was happening. Humans filled with *bahdur* often could not hold or contain it. They were chemically blinded in order to physically restrain their abilities, to make them dependent upon their Choyan companion, the same companion who had given them their powers and who would take them back.

More often than not, it was ultimately fatal for the human subject. He and dear, dead, strange Bevan and Alexa—of them all, only he had escaped unscathed, if this imprisonment could be called untouched. If the sinkhole which seemed to have swallowed his heart and was now working on his guts and his sanity could be called unscathed.

He had been lucky in that the treatments to chemically blind and mute him had not been completed, and the *bahdur* which flowed through him had defeated them. He had been lucky that Palaton was who he was, and had chosen to have Rand alert and aware, a true partner, a *durah,* as the Choya would have explained it. A soulmate.

But in the long run, even Palaton had been blinded by his fear, afraid of the possibility of living permanently with his power burning inside Rand, afraid of the use to which Rand had evolved it. They had parted, quarreling. He wondered if he would ever see Palaton again, could ever convince his *durah* that the soulfire they had shared should be used to transform any who desired it, even if it changed Palaton's world forever.

As he mused within his dreamtime, he saw Dorea, the reluctant Prophet, her blindfolded face turning toward him as if she sought the warmth of his memory. She sat upon the crude rocking chair as she had in Bayalak, her dress new and unstained by the fires and riots she had passed through, her hands working on a kind of knitting in her lap.

He felt as though he stood on the threshold, watching her. The weathered wood of an old seaside shanty framed him. It was daytime, a clear morning, the air still humid from the tropical weather earlier. He could hear the cries of the kites as they hung in the air over the harbor. It still smelled of fire, riot-burned as Charolon had been. *Did the burning follow him wherever he went?*

But there was peace in here, within and without, on the streets. Bayalak had settled down again and perhaps it had been due to her influence.

She must have been pretty once, before the Change. He was no judge of Choyan beauty, they were all an elegant, graceful race to him, even the square and stocky Earthan branches, but he thought she had been before the eyes had been torn weeping blood from her face, and the power she embraced had worn her thin. Her cheekbone structure dominated her visible expression. She turned her face, thick hair stirring as if blown by a sea breeze off Bayalak Harbor. Dorea reached up slowly, hand moving as if by some cause other than her own willpower. The fingers plucked at the blindfold, digging into the edge of the cloth.

And then ripping it down. "I see you," she said. The shadowed depths of her scars looked blankly at him.

He recoiled in shock and surprise and it was as if a vacuum had inhaled him. Wind rushed past his ears. He fell backward, fell and fell and fell.

What if she had seen him? *What if she had?*

Had she summoned him, or had he called for her? And

if she had seen him, could she tell others? Was he truly alone and abandoned, or could he—somehow—make contact?

Recoiling ever faster, he found himself in chill darkness, hurtling through time and space at such a rate that the stars and suns became narrow pinpricks and then, suddenly, he found himself beyond the speed of light itself, and Chaos yawned around him.

The sensation of speed disappeared. So did the feeling of being torn backward. He floated about, ungainly and awkward, swimming through the swirl of color and darkness.

Palaton had told him there were patterns in the Chaos, patterns which his psionic powers could discern and use as landmarks. But those patterns were never the same, and migrated as constantly as space evolved, and every *tezar* viewed Chaos from his own reference point.

There *were* no Patterns of Chaos. That was the whole concept of the random activity of objects pushed beyond the speed of light. The Choyan only perceived that there were, foreseeing events and arrivals before they occurred, and arranging them to happen as seen. Rand swirled from one whirlpool to another, tossed back and forth, swallowed down and spit up, a miasma without center, beginning, or end. As he grasped for some sense of what was happening to him, he righted himself and found an edge of awareness that he was not alone.

Rand managed a turn and saw a cruiser, its slim lines blurred by the arc of reality where real-time met Chaos. The vessel lost its integrity; it was as though he stared inward through transparent walls, and saw the proud Choya standing at its helm.

He knew, albeit briefly, what it was to helm a starship. Knowing what he knew about *bahdur,* he also realized he would likely never pilot again. The power to navigate Chaos could not be grafted onto ship or man. It was not a computer-driven black box that plotted and shifted rudders, accelerated or decelerated engines.

It was flesh and blood. Heir to all the errors and promises thereof.

The Choya he watched had been born in the House of Sky. His dark hair was roped back off his shoulders, and the epaulets of his flight suit delineated his campaigns, contracts, and awards. His silvery-light eyes scoured the Chaos before him, never seeing Rand, never sensing him, though they stared nearly face-to-face. He wore only minimal onyx facial jewelry under his cheekbones and he might have been of an age with Palaton, young, but old enough to be experienced, to be in his prime. Worry furrowed his brow unnaturally, shadows of fatigue clouded his expression.

And there was fear in his eyes.

He can't see me, thought Rand, *and he can't see the Patterns of Chaos. He is lost, lost and without hope.* Rand was just outside the skin of the ship now, balancing beyond the transparent skin of the con, and he reached out, his hand going through the skin, stretching the membrane, as if he were pushing outward from an egg without breaking the molecular surface. Fingers wiggling, he stretched closer, closer, closer.

"This is my third run on boost," the *tezar* said. Rand jumped, startled, realized that he was not being spoken to, that the pilot was recording. "I'm experiencing a complete and total breakdown and failure of pattern recognition. I cannot *see* where I am going. I'm jettisoning the cargo, in hopes that an eddy might carry it back to the mainstream and it will someday be salvaged. If anyone finds this recorder, I am Jilaro of the Householding of Abran, of the House of Sky, of the House of Tezars."

He paused, licking dry lips. His hands roamed the control board and the vessel shuddered. Rand could feel it as the cargo hold broke loose, jettisoned away as Jilaro had said he would do.

He watched as the square compartment, gutted from the center of the cruiser, floated clear. It dropped quickly into the nebulous swirls of Chaos. He looked back to the Choya who broke open a packet of crushed powder and tipped it into a cylinder of water. It turned the water a brilliant color before Jilaro gulped it down.

The Choya shuddered as if he had swallowed a bitter potion. He spoke to the recorder again. "Forgive me, my House, for my failure. The boost is potent, my desire for it unslackable. But it no longer fills the emptiness within me."

Rand tried once again to touch the pilot, but although

the membrane stretched so thinly as to be nonexistent, he could not break through.

The cruiser shuddered.

Jilaro looked ahead and pain etched his face. "The Web. It expands for me, like a flower blooming in Chaos. I am lost." He set his jaw grimly and piloted to his fate.

Rand bumped off the hull of the cruiser, pushed aside by forces he could feel but not see or control, as the ship swept past him. He'd heard of the Web. All *tezars* dreaded it. It was either a hole in Chaos that swallowed matter, like a black hole, or death itself. It had come for Jilaro.

The ship veered away from him, speeding farther and farther away, distorting—and then it was gone.

He fell.

The fall accelerated, faster, faster, until he was snapping back into himself, heart pounding, as if he'd been pushed off a cliff and knew that death awaited him as he hit—

and he sank into himself, found everything cold, colder than ice, still and frozen. But he, himself, was not frozen, his heart still thundering hotly, his pulse ringing like a hammer on an anvil, his breath smoking from his mouth.

Without substance, he was yet trapped, spirit bound into the flesh by a connection he had never understood, but as his spirit heart slowed, he could yet hear, see, touch. Shapes, all around him. Not the boundaries of himself, which contained his journeying soul after its return, but other shapes. Jagged. Rounded. Familiar. Strange.

He knew he should be alone. He sensed that his soul had taken him, all of him, someplace where he should not be. Someplace deadly.

Someplace still. Lifeless.

Among the dead.

He lay among the crystalline bodies of Sorrow. He could sense them all around him, harder than his cold flesh, far more dead than alive. His cell was not near them, but his current state had brought him among them. Rand took a slight, shuddering gasp. He fought for calmness. He was trapped in the quartz, his own molecules slipped in among the others and soon he would cease to exist, and although he did not actually breathe, it was the most conscious part of the process of his life, next to his tripping heart, that he did breathe. He had to.

He felt himself sliding away, gliding among the dead. He recoiled from the touch, yet it was not unpleasant. They bumped back as if they pushed him, no, guided him, among them, out of the quartz into the more familiar stone and sand of Sorrow, and then into the air, and then into the cell which held him.

At the realization that he had joined his body proper, his heart began to slowly descend into the rhythms of reduced metabolic function, not cold sleep, but the next thing to it. Alone, losing all sense of himself, he thought vaguely that, frightening as it had been, the dead of Sorrow offered more comfort than his cell.

In the subterranean holding cells, the computer noted a variance in the reading of the limbic activity of the subject in reduction. It made a note and medicated to counter the unusual activity, and produced a printout to confirm its action. After long moments, the subject's readings fell back into normal columns again. The creche computer noted that also, humming slightly as it performed its watchful calculations.

Chapter 23

"I want to try dosing the Eastern continent," Qativar said. His voices reflected his mood, indolent, casual, truculent. "That damned Palaton keeps showing up everywhere and going back underground. With any luck, we'll catch him long enough to put him out of commission. That should dampen his blue flame!"

"His actions are aimed at Pan. They shouldn't worry you much."

"They don't. But he is like a splinter in my hand." Qativar looked at his hand, at the long, elegant fingers, and flexed it, then made a fist as if crushing the object of their conversation. "*Ruhl* would knock the wind out of his sails, don't you think?"

"I think he's done half our job, harrying the emperor." Pages rustled as Vihtirne worked.

"And I could finish the other half if we dosed the outlying areas. The Eastern continent, Bayalak, the outer portions of the South."

Vihtirne paused in her study of the pilots' roster. "I think we've done enough."

"Don't forget we've created the impression of a ripple effect from Panshinea. That cloaks everything we've done, but suspicion will be roused if the pattern breaks. We'll lose that if we don't pursue it." He had been leaning on the doorjamb, watching her, but she refused to meet his glare.

"We're causing panic in the streets. We haven't enough boost for the market we've created . . . there is a point at which we're doing ourselves more damage than we are good. And what about your production of *ruhl*? We may need it for a concentrated attack later."

Qativar waved off her objection. "Don't worry about me. I have what it takes to do what we want." Not all at the correct concentration, but she needn't know that. He had been laying his plans for years before the sudden advent of boost and his alliance with her. "We need to make a point."

She laid aside the printout, and lifted her eyes to his. "I think we've done that. The demand for boost is growing by leaps and bounds. Ambassador Thomas is protesting the production shipments he's making to us. Sooner or later, the traffic at Galern is going to raise eyebrows among the Ronins and Abdreliks. We don't have a Compact-sanctioned trade agreement with Earth. My mining operation won't be able to withstand much scrutiny. And . . . there is always the possibility that Thomas could change his mind."

"We'll have it synthesized by then."

"There are one or two elements giving my biochemists a considerable amount of trouble," she pointed out. "Until that time when we can stabilize supply, I think we should be more conservative. The demand within our own House is greater than we had planned for, and while we're on this discussion, there is something which has been troubling me . . ." Vihtirne paused as Qativar responded with an immense grin.

"I amuse you?"

"No. No," and he shook his head at her icy expression as he crossed the room. "Our House. The thought delights me. Does it not you?"

"Not if there are problems within our walls. They're too newly erected to take much strain."

He perched on an antique chair, not noticing the strength of her disapproval as it creaked under his weight. "You see trouble in everything. That's why we complement one another. I am the risk taker, you are the worrier. What bothers you?"

Vihtirne pushed her chair a little away from her desk. She crossed her legs with a rustle of the long, silken panels of her dress. "Too much boost. Our pilots are using a greater quantity and more frequently than we estimated."

His lip curled. "Pilots are spoiled. They expect to always operate at optimum ability."

"They're addicted, Qativar. The drug addicts quickly and thoroughly."

"All the better. We need to keep them bound to us—"

"I'm serious."

"So am I." He flashed another smile. "Vihtirne, they can't be so dependent. It's only been weeks."

"I have pilots here refusing to fly without an increase in their rations. Pilots who can't fly without boost. And we lost a *tezar* last week at a bay station, overdosed. The autopsy came back clean, so I suppose I can thank the incompetence of the Compact doctors for not detecting it, but I read the report from the others who were on layover. She'd been taking boost heavily without detoxing first by taking the *ruhl*. It's not the first death, it won't be the last. What if something happens on contract? We've got an alien substance here which bonds itself to our neural systems and we're pushing it as though it were honey candy."

"It built us a House. It's given us the finances to withstand almost anything Panshinea can hope to throw at us—"

"Unless he decides to outlaw the drug."

"He won't."

"Won't? Or can't?"

Qativar shoved himself away from his chair. "He won't touch us! Even the Abdreliks are picking up contracts the Compact isn't monitoring. As for the Compact, there is enough pressure now to bring a general vote, and you and I both know the ban against our pilots will be lifted. They can't afford not to."

Vihtirne repeated flatly, "If Panshinea is forced to take a stand against boost—"

"He won't. He'll fall first."

"I have *tezars* missing."

He shrugged. "It happens. Even with boost. The hazards of Chaos are eternal. The Commons still hesitates to join the House and we're working with some pilots who are substandard. Bring the Commons in, gather up the remnants from Blue Ridge. You do your work, mistress from the House of Sky. Let me do mine." He stalked to the doorway of the room and paused at the threshold with controlled fury.

Vihtirne's gaze fell away from his face. She resumed her interest in the paperwork before her. "Just so you understand," she said, "that I have concerns."

"Understand then, that I will take care of them," he answered tightly, before leaving.

* * *

Maeva decided to apply for body armor, and found, to her surprise, that the Compact permits to obtain it were relatively simple. They did not even require her office's signature or proof of need. Her word was enough. Armor was, after all, she reflected, strictly defensive. What they did require, and this surprised her more, was that she make an appointment to be outfitted in person rather than send her holographic measures over and take delivery later. She scowled as the message came up on her terminal screen and said to herself, "So that's the catch. They don't say 'no,' they'll just intimidate the hell out of you when you show up." She keyed in her positive response, plugged in her signatory thread, and signed off as soon as an appointment time was assigned.

Maeva checked her watch. She had time to kill, with no place to go. She could try, for the fourth time in three days, to get an appointment with Ambassador Rindalan. Earth's status as a Class Zed planet did not give her any rank at all, and the Choyan at the embassy had been very uncooperative. At the moment, she did not understand what Rand found so enchanting about the race. They were stuffy, overly formal, and without compassion.

And she was not about to give up without a fight. Maeva signed out of the office complex and left the building.

The weather in the office complex was brisk. The air, a little thinner than she'd grown up in, giving it the feel of high mountains, was clean from a recent pounding rain. The demisphere of peaks which crowned the complex grounds wore an icing of white, which would not stay, as winter was not yet here in full. Grass edging the walkways crunched under her steps, the stalks growing brittle with the approach of frost.

No matter what the season, there would always be the frozen crystalline lakes and streams of the main continent. Suicide or genocide, it scarcely mattered—an alien race inhabited the waterways of ruined cities, encased, inert, a warning against the ultimate enemy, whoever it might be.

Maeva did not often have the courage to look in the canals or the lake which ran under half the Compact grounds. She could not bear the distorted, ethereal, haunting looks of a vaguely humanoid people caught in the deadly crystal embrace.

Like her own people, caught in Pompeian smoke and ash, these people had not died in private. But unlike the excavations of volcanic disaster, there was no knowing what had happened here. How had the crystal been created? Who had done it to them, and what had they done to deserve it? There were no overt scars of war on the planet's face, yet genocide on such a scale could hardly be the result of anything less.

Sorrow had been found that way, and taken by both the Choyan and the Abdreliks, space-faring and quarreling civilizations that the planet could be taken as nothing less than a warning against the ultimate fate. The ending which faced them all. The power of an unknown enemy which could strike at any of them unless they found a way to cooperate among themselves, and so the Compact had been formed.

The quartz had been analyzed. It could be broken down, if they wished, but that would destroy its occupants, and there was an unspoken agreement among all the races who joined the Compact and walked its Halls that the dead would lie unsullied. Scientific knowledge would be put aside for respect and monument. Without knowing for sure, it would be assumed that these who had died should not have done so in vain, that those who lived after would work never to see its like happen again.

She did not view the canals now, catching only a blurred glimpse of them in her peripheral vision, the ghostlike figures of the aliens caught in their depths unrecognizable, not even visible, perhaps, except in her imagination. Maeva found the afternoon teeming with other Compact members striding to the more major consulates, as well as the massive complex of Halls and wings which made up the main buildings. Many wore body armor, their outlines shimmering as they moved, but vastly more did not. Was she a coward?

No, she did not think so. What she was about to involve herself in could bring risk from the Abdrelik contingent, the Ronins, the Choyan, and perhaps even her own government.

She told herself she was giving herself the freedom to act as her conscience dictated.

At the Choyan embassy, she barely got in the door. The screen lit up, and a personage said, "Pilot requests are made through contract."

"I' m not here for a *tezar*." Like the French, the Choyan were fussy about their language and she made certain to pronounce the word as authentically as possible.

The on-screen personage frowned slightly. "What do you wish?" The Choya's Trade was faintly accented, and she could not tell if the disapproval was inherent with the accent—or typically arrogant Choyan.

"I need to make an appointment with Ambassador Rindalan."

"I am sorry, but what you would like to do is not possible at this moment." Bored, the secretarial image began to turn away from her.

Maeva slapped a hand on the screen, setting off a buzz of static. "I did not say *like to,* I said, *need to.*" She could not get much stronger in the public lobby without attracting attention she did not want. "It is vital," she insisted, leaning forward, looking into the image now frowning heavily at her. "I have already been refused several times."

"And you will not take 'no' for an answer," the Choyan observed dryly.

"I cannot," she corrected him.

There was a very long pause. She did not know if the screen had been freeze-framed, with the image in place while the real-life secretary withdrew and made inquiries, but after a long moment, the screen thawed, and the Choya said, "I will take your request under advisement."

Maeva let out her breath. Not permission, but no longer a flat-out denial. "You know where to reach me," she answered and keyed in her comline. "Thank you."

Outside, it was later than she had expected and she wondered if a privacy shield had been thrown up about her while she stood motionless in the lobby. If so, she had not even realized it. Long, long moments had gone by with no recollection other than a vague awareness. If she didn't hurry, she would miss her armor fitting, and she knew that would not bode well if she had to reapply.

Indigo shadows stretched out as she cut across the

grounds, eschewing the normal security gates and slidewalks. Foot traffic had thinned considerably as dusk began to settle its cloak over the Halls of the Compact, and globe lights had begun to warm. Maeva trotted briskly to keep warm, as a keening autumn wind began to rise.

Someone just a little behind her also began to hurry. She could hear their footfalls as the L-shaped wing of permits lay ahead, its black obsidian walls in sharp contrast to the surrounding greenery. It cast the deepest, longest shadow yet across her path.

Maeva was within earshot of the building when she was caught by the arm and spun around. A Ronin crouched in her path. Its grin was accented by its rodent-sharp teeth. Its quills lay flat along its sloping head and shoulders, but it rattled them warningly as she prepared to defend herself.

"You will come with me," the Ronin said. "Your appearance is requested."

For a wild moment, she thought perhaps the Choyan ambassador had sent the Ronin after her, to bring her back, but then she realized how stupid that was. There was no love lost between these aliens.

"And if I refuse to accompany you?"

The Ronin gave a shiver of delight. Its quills made another tintinnabulation of noise. "I can tell you that I have never been devenomed," it said. "Any one of my barbs will paralyze, perhaps even kill you, most excruciatingly. More than one will certainly bring death."

Ronins weren't allowed off-planet until they'd been devenomed. Their quills were never supposed to be lethal. Was she to believe that here, on Sorrow, an assassin dared to walk freely?

On the other hand, could she afford not to believe?

Maeva sighed and took an obedient step forward. It was already too late for body armor.

Chapter 24

The Ronin glided forward to put a hand on her sleeve, when the rich, rolling voice of a Choya spoke out of the shadows, startling both of them.

"Your appointment," the Choya said apologetically, and bowed into the faint light of a nearby globe. "I beg your pardon, but the ambassador will see you now." The deep shadows of the architectural garden had all but hidden him until he'd revealed himself. Unlike the Ronin, his eyes were large, expressive, inquisitive, and quite benign.

The Ronin snatched his hand back, his quill headdress chiming slightly as he did so, his coal black eyes squinted up the height of the Choya, who waited, as if to see what both their reactions might be.

The Choyan voice, she'd been told several times, came from the richness of a double larynx and two voices, one underlying the other. She could not separate them, just as she was tone-deaf and could not produce a decent rendition of a song if she had to, but now she could almost hear the irony layering the politeness.

Maeva turned her flank to the Ronin, though it made nearly every hair on her body stand on end to do so, exposing her blind side to the alien. However, the pivot took her from between the Choya and the Ronin, as well as presenting her face to the embassy secretary. "My apologies," she got out smoothly, despite the sudden dryness of her throat. "I didn't mean to keep His Eminence waiting."

"There is no problem," the secretary said. "He had a cancellation and thought this would be an opportune time, if a bit earlier than we had scheduled."

"We must hurry, then," she told him. She left the Ronin behind, saying, "I'm so sorry to be leaving you this abruptly."

The Ronin made a deep sound at the back of his throat for answer as Maeva swept past the Choya, down the walk, back toward the ambassadorial wings. She did not breathe easier until she had the Choya's graceful and athletic frame between them.

Within the bright glow of the building, she opened her mouth to speak, but the Choya said dryly in warning, "Say nothing. Tell it to the ambassador. I am unimportant in this matter."

"Unimportant? You have no idea what you just saved me from."

The Choya gave a slight bow as he opened the lobby door for her. "Actually, neither do you. It would be wise to remember, in the future, when walking alone or doing business in the outlying sectors, to request an escort. That could save you many anxious moments."

Maeva came to a halt. She tried not to grind her teeth at the other's mocking tone. "Do I have an appointment?"

"Not yet, but you will. The ambassador requested that I follow you, as he was a bit curious about your insistence on seeing him. He will make time for you, I think, once I've reported to him."

"Good." Maeva looked around, saw a basalt bench planter and sat down. "I'll wait."

The secretary bowed and left. No less physically imposing than the pilots she was used to, he was dressed considerably more humbly. He wore somber robes of gray and white, but his hair was that glorious yellow-gold with red highlights, an echo of Emperor Panshinea's color, which she had been told was a prime genetic characteristic of the House he belonged to. If she understood right, the secretary's dress was that of their religious order, for Rindalan was not only the ambassador, he was the High Prelate. She wondered if the Choyan equivalent of the Pope had as dry a sense of humor as his younger priest did.

She found out moments later as his voices boomed across the lobby, stopping traffic dead, as other embassy staff and visitors quickly bowed to the ambassador. Rindalan swept through them, a tall, gaunt alien who dismissed them all with a wave of his hands.

He had the most grand horn crown she'd ever seen on a Choya, but the mane of hair tumbling through it and cascading down his back was considerably thinned and graying, and had more red to it than blond. He reached for her hand with a sweep of his double-elbowed arm, saying, "Madam Attorney Polonia. I am so pleased you could accommodate me."

The jewel-blue eyes fairly twinkled at her as he pressed, then released, her fingers. Of all the alien races she had met, none had eyes like she did, even the Choyan, though they were the closest. Their eyes were larger, more liquid, with very little whites. Typical of the Choyan, she thought, to be abundantly gifted in every way. She let herself smile. "I take it that perseverance is also a virtue on Cho."

"My dear. Everything about you would be a virtue on Cho. Come up where we can be a bit more private." The ambassador bent a little to offer his arm. "Prelate Timero here told me that meeting you would be an experience."

"I know that meeting him was one for me."

Rindalan let out a laugh, totally unpretentious and free. "I shall have to tell him. He does not appreciate the small errands he runs for me, you know." The intense eyes looked down on her as they entered a lift. "You must call me Rindalan. None of this Eminence nonsense."

"It isn't nonsense, and you know it. You earned every bit of it."

"Ah. I see. No sympathy for me, Timero has already been at you." Randalan let out a sigh.

Despite the levity of his words, she could feel the tension in the arm she still held. She looked up at him, and immediately understood that she had to keep up the pretense. She made herself laugh then. "Your secretary is extremely efficient, Mister Ambassador. I would let him chide you, if I were you. It will probably save time in the long run."

"Ah, efficiency. If Timero has indeed discovered that elusive virtue, he could bottle it and make a fortune here on Sorrow." Rindalan patted the back of her hand as if comforting her.

She could tell that he had measurably altered his stride to accommodate hers, and made an effort to keep up. The lift took them high into the building and then disgorged them on a floor which appeared almost deserted. Young and somber Timero, however, awaited them in front of a doorway.

Rindalan steered her into it, saying, "You know, my

dear, I had not meant to put you off so long, but business always comes before pleasure."

The heavily paneled door closed almost on his words.

Maeva found herself ankle-deep in a plush cream-and-blue-patterned carpet. A wall fireplace crackled cheerfully in illusion, putting out homeyness instead of heat. A sedan chair was littered with hard copy, and a coffee table held the remnants of a modest fruit plate. She was in the ambassador's private quarters rather than in one of the embassy conference rooms. She blinked.

"Timero tells me he saved you from what could have been an unpleasant situation." As the door sealed, Rindalan's tone changed from jovial to serious.

Maeva shivered. "I don't think I was a target," she said, thinking about it in retrospect. "But I don't think I wanted to go with him, either. I can't thank you enough for seeing me."

The ambassador waved his hands to the chair opposite the sedan. "We can talk here, in complete confidence, unlike most of the rooms in the building. I have had the apartment secured."

"Good." Maeva let her bones melt. She waited until Rindalan perched opposite her. She could see the imprint of his bony knees through his robes as he sat.

"Now then. What is it you want from me?"

She was not used to blunt talk, especially not from the formal, almost flowery Choyan. It startled the words from her until Rindalan said, almost impatiently, "The appointment I canceled to see you was actually a late dinner. But I do have appointments waiting. . . ."

"I'm sorry." She looked around. She wished desperately for her white noise generator, in spite of the elder's assurances. She licked dry lips. "This could mean my contract," she began.

"Serious." Rindalan sat back on the divan. "You must have grave problems to risk a confidence with someone you've no idea whether you can trust. Who are you, madame attorney?"

"I'm on Ambassador Thomas' legal staff."

"Not with the business contracts wing or lobby?"

"No. Although the staff does lend us out, once in a while. My main work is with treaty and protocol."

"I see," said Rindalan, and she thought almost that he might. "And we do not need to step on any toes here, do we?" He smiled, and like the laugh, it was so fresh, so genuine that it could not help but evoke a smile in return from her. "How can I help?"

"I bring word from someone who—" Maeva plowed to a halt. There seemed to be no proper way to say this, although Rand had warned her that what she would say might be shocking to the aged ambassador. "Your Eminence, there's no easy way to say this, and I can't give you all the information you might want because of my position, but Rand asked me to get word to you. He's being held in security detention at my embassy."

Her words hit the Choya like a physical blow. She could see the translucent complexion go dead pale, and then gray, and the air leave his gaunt frame like a stuffing, as he sagged on the couch.

Then, Rindalan managed, "Alive?"

"Well, yes." There wasn't much point in holding a corpse, but she decided perhaps the Choya knew more about galactic diplomacy than she did.

Rindalan had been resting an elbow on the arm of the divan, and now he put his hand under the curve of his jaw as though the weight of his head had suddenly become too momentous for him to hold without help. "Will Thomas bring him to trial?"

"No. He intends that Rand never see the light of day again, although he will use whatever information he can get from him to consolidate his position between you and the Abdreliks."

Rindalan took a deep breath, muttering, "Would that Pan was here. He likes these games. Even Gathon. But no, they would send me, an honest Choya, here." He looked back at her intently. "Did he ask you to carry other messages?"

"No. He's putting his whole faith and trust in you."

"Is he?" Rindalan sounded faintly pleased, and the color had begun to seep back into his face again. "I shall have to see it hasn't been misplaced. He is too young to be thoroughly disillusioned by circumstances." The Choya rubbed his jaw thoughtfully, massaging the knifelike wrinkles along its jutting length. He looked then, to Maeva. "And what about you? What is your stake in all of this?"

She had thought about it, but had no resolution. She answered faintly, "I don't know. I may lose my contract."

"Have no worry about that. I'll see our embassy picks it up if necessary. That is, if you would not mind working for us."

She looked into the large Choyan eyes, so clear, so pure of color. "No. If it comes to that."

He gave a dry laugh. "We're the last resort, eh?"

She felt her face warming and shook her head quickly. "It's just that—I have other projects—my people—"

He reached over and patted her hand. "After being around Rand, I think I can truthfully say, I understand. Emotion often outweighs logic among you, eh?"

"Well . . ." Maeva took a deep breath. "It did this time, anyway." She stood. "I don't know what you can do for him, or even if I can get back in to see him, to let him know that I've reached you—"

"That won't be necessary," Rindalan answered. "He'll know if I have any success at all. What you need to do now is determine what course Thomas intends to follow, and how you'll react to it. Leave the dear boy to me."

She searched his face, saw none of the machinations, the facades, she'd become used to since graduating from school and beginning her practice. Becoming an adult, she thought, had been more of an education than getting her degree. But here was a being who either had transcended that, or had stayed within simple childhood confines of honesty and loyalty. Either way, could she trust him? She decided, emphatically, that she had no choice. "Thank you," she said, and knew the bargain was struck as Rindalan settled back on his divan, nodding vigorously.

"I'll have Timero escort you. You were on your way to a previous engagement." Rindalan crossed his hands as the apartment doors opened almost simultaneously with his words, and the secretarial Prelate entered. She had seen nothing rung or signaled, but Timero took her by the elbow after saying good evening to the ambassador, and steered her out of the apartments.

"You were," the Choya said to her as they entered the downward lift, "en route to the armor shop, I believe."

"Yes, but—"

He continued smoothly, saying, "I took the liberty of informing them you would be delayed. They're awaiting you, at your convenience."

Maeva felt herself blink. "I didn't know," she said slowly, "that the Choyan were so devastatingly efficient."

Prelate Timero did not answer, but he could not hide the wide grin of amusement which bloomed across his face. She reflected that there was a great deal none of them knew about the Choyan, not the least of which was how they navigated across Chaos.

*   *   *

Jorana stole into the rain, while Malahki slept, exhausted from implementing the planned move of his headquarters. As new as he was to the awakening of his power, he did not have their rooms warded, nor did he sense in his dreams that she rose from a light nap, packed the few things she owned, and left as silently as the misting drizzle which had begun to gray the late afternoon.

He would be furious when he awoke, and as unable to stop the flight he had put into motion as a piece of drift-wood to move against a floodtide. He himself had ordered the evacuation, and now he would be borne away with it. It would be days before Malahki could pull out, return, and search for her.

Even if he did find her, she hoped that she would be able to accomplish what she wished before then.

Jorana shouldered her pack and cloak against the weather and narrowed her eyes at the broken horizon of Charolon. Lights had begun to come on, fitfully, as the mild storm darkened the capital. The Change had not come to the city. Choyan with unawakened power still slept. And as much as she had wanted to be by Malahki's side when the Change was brought to all her people, she knew that the catalyst, the Bringer of Change, had been torn from them and would not be coming back. Malahki knew it, too, having seen it himself. Father Chirek, the underground priest who ministered to a flock of millions, knew it as well.

She did not know whether or not to believe Malahki's assertion that Rand had been that Bringer. She knew only that when Palaton had taken guardianship of the humankind and brought him to Cho, circumstances had begun to evolve at an astronomical rate, and none of them could predict the future. It had all become too momentous.

So, while she was skeptical that Rand's touch could open closed pathways of *bahdur* inside the commons, she knew that he had done something to all of them. She also knew that Palaton had taken Rand from Malahki and Father Chirek, and even Dorea, the blind Prophet, could not see where his pathway led. If Malahki could use her to force Palaton to return Rand, he would do so, for even as he protected her, he would use her.

Jorana stood at the corner, under the eaves, listening to rain patter upon the broken concrete. This part of the city decayed. It had been left to the poor, the broken in spirit, those who had had the *bahdur* burned out of them and now reeked of *boost* in their attempts to restore it, and those who had never had power, and reeked of honest sweat, in hard-laboring jobs the more skilled threw them like scraps to a carrion eater. Here the drain of imperial *bahdur* had not been too devastating, for there were few here who could have been affected. Life itself had been the enemy here, eroding, destroying. She would be scared, but she could not afford to be, not for the life she carried inside of her.

Three million Choyan populated Charolon. She could not hope, even with her abilities, to single out a particular one so quickly. But she did hope, and it was not with her ability alone. Pregnancy affected her talent, making it ebb and flow as the tides did, but the child within her glowed as brightly as a small sun. She could feel it pulsing through her with every tiny beat of its still forming heart. It fed her as much as she nurtured it. She dropped a hand over the swell of her stomach. *I have to find your father,* she thought, and as though it answered her, she could feel a rising glow of warmth.

Supported by its acknowledgment, she pushed away from the corner and into the growing rain. Thoughts trickled through her head, unformed, bare, wispy things which tugged her this way and that, against the direction of the growing tide of Choyan who were heading home from work sites or bars. They shouldered past one another, horn crowns open to the elements, hair growing wet and running into strings down their heads and backs. If they lifted their heads long enough to look into her eyes as they passed, they would pause, and then smile gruffly, unknowingly, as warmed by their touch with her as she was by the child she carried. And they would pause to let her pass unmolested.

Jorana strode into the traffic of the late afternoon unaware of their responses, every sense tuned to that within her and to what she sought. With a precognition she had never had before, she knew that soon she would meet Rufeen on a corner, somewhere in this city. And where there was Rufeen, there could very well be Palaton.

But when? Where?

The drizzle stopped, gray clouds hung low and leaden, threatening, as she crisscrossed the city streets. She left the quarter and passed into another, even worse, burned out by the street riots of last year, the sickening smell of its ashes and fire scars rising as rain puddled among the ruins. It would take a monsoon to wash the smell clear of the carnage left behind. When she left there, however, she entered a crowded section of the capital, where the commons had built and lived and worked, crowded, busy, vibrant, a massive portion of the new city which had grown up around the ancient fortress which Charolon had been in almost prehistoric times.

Here, briefly, the rain had cleaned the streets. Window canopies had been lowered over storefronts, and Choyan shared the shelter as the rain began again, and she was not only stepped aside for, but often found a helping hand to bring her up over the curbs of the streets as she crossed them. As she passed from neighborhood to neighborhood, she met Choyan who were the backbone of Malahki's movement. Not downtrodden, but industrious, not powerful but seeking empowerment. The ordinary, the good-hearted and open-spirited. Yet as she moved among them, she could sense the depression, the furtiveness, the burden of recent upheaval bowing them down. It was as if Panshinea stood on their backs—had, all these years, but now this burden was too much and threatened to break them.

As captain of the guard, she'd had little to do with these citizens. They were neither prey nor predators, except by accident if one of them should stray. They were the foundation of the capital, and she barely knew any of them at all.

Someone caught her as her boot heel skidded on a wet patch, and righted her. She got out a, "Thank you," then froze, looking diagonally across a square of small shops. The Choya'i who'd helped her let go and continued past, leaving her looking at a corner, heavily shadowed by the clouds and rain and time of day, and it was from there she knew she would see Rufeen.

Chapter 25

She rented a small room across from the square, its windows facing down on the corner. The landlady asked her little, even when Jorana told her that she was a composer, though oddly lacking in instruments, recording equipment, or even luggage of any consequence. The Choya'i merely told her in a flat voice, as she coded the palm lock on the apartment that there were several artists' lofts and co-op studios for musicians a block or two away. Jorana had chosen her occupation because she had already done a spiral recon of the area and the fact that the landlady treated her in such an unremarkable way meant that she'd done her research well.

Jorana recoded the lock as soon as the Choya'i left, then went in and lay down on the stiff bed. The room was chill, but she did not feel like getting up and adjusting the warmer. Somewhen, somehow, she would be on that corner she could see from that bed, that window, and when she was, seeing in real-time that which she'd foreseen, she knew that Rufeen would lead her to Palaton.

What she did not know, what she could not summon up from within her, was what would happen then. Would she follow, and if she did . . . ?

The child stirred within her. It was not a kick against confinement, nor the first barely felt quickening of life she had felt a month or so ago, but it was like . . . a stroke, the stroke a swimmer gives when beginning to leisurely cross over an expanse of water. The child was not yet big enough to be cramped and hampered by the limitations of the Choya'i who bore it though formed enough to swim the environment of her womb.

Jorana regretted that she had never listened to the tales of other mothers and mothers-to-be. The folklore of motherhood had never interested her before. There had never been time for that, and even if there had been time, She wouldn't have taken it. She rested both hands gently on the curve of her stomach. Her talent for foresight had never been very measurable. If it had been, she would have trained as a *tezar*, regardless of any other career she'd had in mind, for Malahki would never have let the opportunity to have a pilot under his influence slip past. Beyond that, she had never let any limitations in her *bahdur* slow her down as she'd found her niche and risen in it. But she did have her regrets now which had nothing to do with her usage of her power, but her misuse, or her neglect, of her own sexual identity. To be a Choya'i inherently meant to have a capacity to bear life, to nurture it, and she had never had that realization until now.

When it was almost too late.

This child might well be the only child she could have. She was not past her prime by any means, but neither was she as young as she had once been. Time had fled while she had thought she was in command of it, and all the options it had opened to her. Foolish me, she thought, to think I could reorder even Time.

Was it as foolish to think she could change Prophecy?

Jorana rolled onto her side, propped her head up on her hand, and looked out the window. The rain had stopped momentarily, and the air smelled of its dampness, of the air it had swept clean, and the wind it had captured within its storm clouds. The challenge of foresight was not in the doing of it, though that was difficult enough. It was in the interpretation and, also, in the strength of it. Easy enough to *see* what one might do in the next five minutes or half an hour. Difficult to *see* beyond that, as the skeins of other Choyan became entwined and entangled, wrapped and unwrapped, impossible to separate all the choices which might be made and unmade. Unless one's path through life were so blazingly clear that it was impossible to turn from it, to make other decisions, to have others impact upon it, forecasting was nearly impossible.

She had heard of only one Prophet in her lifetime, and that was a newly risen one. Despite the rarity, she had not doubted Dorea once she met her. From still raw eye sockets from which the Choya'i had torn her own orbs out, because she could neither comprehend nor contain the *bahdur* sight within her, to the anguished words of confusion and self-contempt at their last meeting, the Prophet had been real. More genuine than any Choya Jorana had ever met in her life, with the possible exceptions of Rindalan and Palaton. The Choya'i did not know what she said until she said it, and professed no great understanding or portent of it—but foreseen she had.

Cho must not have two emperors—and you must choose.

With that, Dorea had placed upon Jorana a burden unthought of, and unthinkable. How could she make such a choice, and to what dire crossroads must she come that she would face that decision?

Despite the Prophet's assurance that ruin would come to Cho if she did not, that Abdrelik and Ronin hounds would harry the planet, that nothing of the world in which they had grown up would remain, Jorana had turned aside from the burden. It was inconceivable that such a choice should be in her hands. Who was she that it would come to that? How could she, if it came to Panshinea and Palaton, turn her face from one to the other and say, this one lives, that one dies—for the good of Cho. She had fled, rather than face that which was prophesied for her.

Yet, in her heart, she knew she had already made the decision, and that also was what had driven her from the palace. Palaton was no emperor. He was a *tezar,* his soulfire burned most fiercely there, and he had never wished the throne, though Panshinea had thrust it upon him.

If only Dorea had given her other options, but she had not. *One must live, and one must die.* To save Cho, Jorana knew that she had to condemn Palaton to death.

But she would not stand flat-footed in the palace and have that fate pushed upon them both. If she could run, if she could somehow change the turning of the Wheel of the Houses, if she could prove the Prophet wrong. . . .

And if not, then at least Palaton's child lived within her.

So what was she doing here and now, waiting for Rufeen? Would it lead her to that which she'd tried so desperately to avoid? She did not think so, but she did not know. All she knew was that love for Palaton burned inside her as fiercely as *bahdur,* and she wished to see him one last time. She would tell him what she had done, and then, whatever fate he walked into, he would do so with full knowledge.

Perhaps it would save him. Perhaps it would drive him deeper into the web of his destiny.

She could only hope.

Jorana sat up. The child within her made another tiny stroking movement, as if reminding her that she was hungry, and hadn't eaten yet that afternoon. There was a tiny bakery just beyond the corner. Afternoon *bren* and fresh fry bread with honey sounded delicious after all her dark thoughts of fate and prophecy.

One moment at a time. She would settle for that.

Jorana picked up her wet cloak, shook it out, listening to the drops patter to the wooden floor, and wrapped herself up. The inner layer of the cloak was dry and warm, and she shrugged into it as she left her room and hurried downstairs

The fry bread buns were sandwiched around a filling of soft cream, into which honey and fruit juice had been whipped. She bought a bag of them, more than she intended to, unwilling to stay and be limited to only one or two. The store owner filled a jug with freshly brewed drink, capped it, and handed it to her with an understanding look which Jorana ducked away from, not wanting to be seen well enough to be recognized later. The rain had stopped, leaving the sidewalk tables and chairs dotted with drops, too bespeckled to be sat at, so she headed across the square to return to her room.

Instinct halted her at the arched hallway to the building. After standing still a moment, she could hear the timbre of other voices, voices which shivered through the old building, and, although she could not hear words distinctly, she knew from the pitch that questions were being posed, and the landlady was answering them unsteadily.

Cautiously, Jorana came inside and looked up the landings. Guard, it had to be the guard, although how they had found her so quickly, or even at all, she had no idea.

She put the sack of buns inside her cloak to muffle their scent from drifting out onto the air, as good a giveaway as any noise she might make, and stood indecisively. Go or stay? Bluff or run?

What little she had taken into the world with her lay in that room upstairs. God-in-all knew it wasn't much, but it was all she had. Jorana sucked in her breath and held it, thinking and listening.

Then the sound of boots on the landing drew her attention, and she realized that the guard was not outside her room, but on the fifth and top floor above . . . nor were they searching any particular apartment, but going door-to-door. The landlady trailed unhappily in their wake.

Jorana shrank back into a corner of the archway. They were not looking for her, then; they were making a general search.

She stepped back out onto the street. There would be no reason to go door-to-door unless they were fairly certain that their prey was somewhere in the vicinity.

Rufeen. Palaton.

Rumors. Thorough work would turn up the quarry if rumors were accurate enough. She knew the drill. Sometimes she thought she'd invented it.

She slipped a hand into her bag, now warm against her chest, and withdrew a bun. Retreating back across the street, to the fated corner, where she could safely watch the guard searching her building, she stood under the eaves and nibbled on a food which, though her stomach still craved it, her mind no longer savored.

The sweet, cheesy filling spilled onto her tongue as she watched the windows, saw shadows moving, saw the search go from floor to floor, saw an intruder pause even at her own window to look out briefly and move on. She leaned against the storefront with a nonchalance her pounding heart did not echo, as a light sprinkle began again, and then she saw Rufeen.

Jorana dropped the sweet to the ground, took a step forward, preparing to call out, to warn, but the rangy pilot did not see her, intent on her own sweep of the square. However, framed in Jorana's own room window, one of the guards watched.

Jorana moved back into the shadows, knowing Rufeen was out of earshot unless she yelled loudly, and that would alert the guardsman for certain. She swallowed hard, a little surprised at the taste of the fry bread and honey in her throat. Rufeen looked at her, directly at her, unseeing, the glance slid away, and then the pilot was going, down the alleyway, past the large artists' co-ops, and toward a dingy underground station.

She checked the line destinations. Outlying towns she was unfamiliar with, industrial sectors where many of the apartments were as much belowground as above. Jorana herself had canvased the area earlier and dismissed it as too borderline for her to feel comfortable as a Choya'i alone, though she had not felt unsafe there.

Jorana turned a shoulder and sat down at a bakery table, even though it was still dewed with rain, as the guardsmen came clattering out of the building and gathered in the square.

She could feel the flare of *bahdur* as they began to conduct an aura search, and she knew from his body posture and then sudden spin-around, to talk to the commanding officer, that the hound had picked up on Rufeen. In formation, they fell into a dogtrot toward the transport station. If she hurried, she would not be far behind them, as they were not far behind Rufeen.

There was nothing Jorana could do now but follow. She dropped the sack of buns on the table, put a hand inside her cloak to the small of her back, and undid the safety on her enforcer.

As soon as the square cleared, she bolted across the street and up the landing to her apartment. Inside the one bag lay something she'd thought never to use again. She put on the armored vest, found it difficult to secure over the curve of her stomach and left the side lacings loose. It was better than no protection at all. She found a heat knife and slid it into the shank of her boot. That was all the armory she could afford at the moment.

Jorana hurried back downstairs and, using her own tracking sense, picked up the hot trail of the guard, who had made no effort to disperse their aura. The dark and sooty-smelling tunnel transport swallowed her. She occupied a single car, no grand linkage of commuters at this hour, though later it would be another matter. She sat down as the car rocked into motion. Flashing lights told her of her progress. Where would she need to stop: Semola? Trivan? D'albalen?

She watched the begrimed and nearly burned-out screen

showing her car's progress through the system, and the tiny, winking lights of cars preceding her. One of them was Rufeen's. Another held a handful of the guard elite, intent on killing when they reached their destination.

"I've got him," Hat said triumphantly, shouldering his way through the narrow door, cloth bags of supplies swinging from his elbows.

Palaton looked up from the graphs he and Rufeen had overlaid on the wall and frowned, refocusing both his vision and his thoughts. "Who?"

"Trevon the Black."

The smell of Rufeen's cheap beer permeated their living quarters as she picked up her mug and took a deep drink. She put the back of her hand to her mouth, to dab away the mustache of foam. "We were just trying to pinpoint the most logical base of operations." The grids of the projection reflected oddly across her fair skin. She frowned and told Palaton how to manipulate the program when a glitch disrupted the grid.

"When'd you pick that up?"

"I made a scavenging trip into Charolon today."

"Oh?" Hat grinned slightly. "Brought back some beer, too."

"Naturally." Rufeen added, "there's a concentration of Sky Householdings here. It's something to consider."

Hat dropped the groceries down into the storage bin, obviously bursting with his news, and Palaton kept his attention away from the projection, waiting for the revelation.

Hat straightened, his face aglow with triumph. "But you're wrong if you're looking for a Sky."

"Trevon the Black," Palaton observed, "would most likely be from that House."

Hat shook himself all over. A winter drizzle had dampened his jacket and his bare head, his hair hanging limply. "But we've known that for weeks, and without much success. The info you got the other night was no more specific."

"No," Rufeen answered for Palaton. "But the contaminant they used to cut the boost is."

"Well, this is even better." Hat drew up a chair without shedding his jacket. "When I was a child, we had an uncle

in my Householding, a dour Choya, as dark of temperament as any Earthan could be. I got to thinking—what if
Trevon the Black referred not to his coloring, but his manner. We're not looking for a Sky here, we're looking for
an Earthan. So I started asking around—and I found him!"

"Where?" asked Palaton.

"East on the continent, near the fallow lands of S'laneen,
a minor industrial and agricultural area called Bitron."

Palaton shifted uneasily. He looked to Rufeen. "That's
too easy. Better backtrack him a bit. See what you can
pick up."

"Will do, boss." The pilot got up and shouldered Hathord out of her way as she went out the door into the wind
and rain, heedless of the weather, intent on picking up
auras.

Hat pivoted in bewilderment. "What—you think my information is no good?"

Palaton lifted a finger to silence him, saying only, "We'll
discuss it when she gets back."

Hat clamped his mouth shut and resumed throwing groceries into the bins, his good humor gone, his frustration
venting itself on their goods. When Rufeen shoved her way
back in a few minutes later, he had his bags folded across
the counter.

"Not a thing." Rufeen looked to Palaton. "And I've
been thinking . . . if we haven't been set up, that fits the
profile of the cutting agent. Since this is consumed, dried
milk is not an uncommon extender. We're talking dairylands
here, pasturing, is common around the fallow lands in the
east. It could be processed on the edge of the S'laneen well
enough. Cheap enough, too." She sat down and retrieved
her mug, eyeing Hathord.

Hat took a deep breath, as if trying to settle himself
down. He said defensively, "The Earthan I've found manages a large penning and storage area there. More than
one or two Earths I've talked to describe him as Trevon
the Black."

"A stockyards manager?"

"More or less."

Palaton scratched his chin. If any of the Choyan could
be called the salt of the planet, it was the Earthans, a
House well suited to agricultural careers. Their empathy

with the land, its ecosystems, and its animals was the main-stay of the House. He and Rufeen had just come to the conclusion that the cutting agent used in the boost, pow-dered lactose, had been rather low-tech, harmless, and ele-mental—almost echoing the description of the House of Earth itself.

Although, he reminded himself, they had spearheaded three assassination attempts on him in the past, not nearly so harmless as they might appear. And it had been the Earthans who had gleaned Flames from the ashes of the destruction of the lost House, intending to "beef up" their own genetic pool. They had done it so slyly that the other two remaining Houses had not even guessed at their duplicity.

He decided that Hat's prospect deserved some attention after all. "He might have something." Rufeen's thick lips pursed in thought as he said to her, "Can we get there?" Jet sleds wouldn't manage the amount of territory they needed to cover.

"Everything big is monitored. You know that."

"I also know we can't jet sled across an entire continent. What about going off-world, to the mines, and then coming back in? Would that be easier?"

The heavyset pilot rubbed at her eyes. "Don't know," she mumbled for an answer. She shied a glance at the Earthan before clamming up.

The pleasure bled completely out of Hat's face. He stood up abruptly, and went to the storage bins and began to shuffle through them again, as if to make sure the groceries were stored correctly. The damp back of his jacket, pre-sented to them, seemed stiff and hurt.

"I'm not afraid to talk in front of Hat," Palaton told Rufeen.

She gave a shrug. It rippled through her abundant shoul-der muscles. Then, in voices light for her frame and looks, she said, "I didn't mean anything by it, Hat."

He separated the packaged goods from the perishables. Without turning around, he answered, "Of course you did. You don't trust me. Because of Nedar. . . ."

"I trust you." Palaton's voices cut across the silence of the cramped housing.

"Maybe you shouldn't. Nedar made a fool of me. I was

ready to turn the school over to him, the cadets, the train-
ers, everything. I listened to him."

"There was enough truth in what he said that you would
have listened. As for giving the school over, who among us
hasn't thought that we deserved our own House, that we
are what vitalizes Cho. We *tezars* have two major traits:
we're pilots, and we're arrogant. Our abilities give us that.
Our hardships earn us the right to keep it. I think," and
Palaton leaned forward to retrieve his ever-present cup of
bren, "you heard what you wanted to. You thought with
your heart instead of your mind, and which one of us hasn't
done that?"

Rufeen heeded the conversation closely, her glance going
from Palaton's face to Hat's and back.

"I'm a flightmaster," Hat protested. "I had students to
protect." He swung about, and his emotional agony was
clearly imprinted across his normally stoic face. Lines of
character had been etched deeply into him and Palaton
realized suddenly that the years they had spent as cadets
together were far behind them. As good a pilot as Hat had
been, he was one of the few who had not minded leaving
space before his time. Becoming master at the school had
been his dream, and he had excelled at it—and the war of
vengeance between Palaton and Nedar had destroyed that.

He could not bear Hathord's agony. "Which you thought
you were doing. And if you had not listened, Nedar would
have taken you out. Nothing was gong to stand between
him and what he wanted. You were able to temper his
plans and judgment. You are probably the only proud asset
in Nedar's life. I'm the one who feels guilt here. Because
of me, Blue Ridge was destroyed. I'm the one who needs
to ask forgiveness, and trust. And so I do now, old friend.
Will you forgive me for losing sight of what it is to be a
tezar? For letting myself get embroiled in the machinations
of the emperor and others, and jeopardizing the lives of
tezars to come?"

Hat's face contorted, his mouth opened to interrupt or
accept the apology, but closed again without uttering a
word.

Palaton added gently, "As the God-in-all is my witness,
I'll rebuild Blue Ridge for you. Panshinea told me more
lies than Nedar could have ever hoped to utter if he'd lived

a hundred more years. And my listening was just as dis-
criminating as yours. Sometimes I think all I've been doing
is some fancy dancing to Pan's *lindar* playing."

Rufeen muttered, "We should all dance so well."

Palaton gave her a quick glance, then turned his face
back to Hat's, searching it earnestly. "We need this settled.
Am I forgiven?"

Hat made a movement that shrugged throughout his entire body, averting his face. "If you forgive me."

"Done, then." Palaton swung his chair around. "Where
on this damn map are these stockyards and our elusive
Trevon the Black?"

Rufeen had gotten to her feet and was headed to the
storage bins, trading places with Hat at the graphics projection, when she froze. Her hand went to her thick waist,
where her enforcer was always holstered. Her hiss cut
through the air as Palaton and Hat began to wrangle over
the map.

"Ssssht." She tilted her head. "It can't be. I backtracked.
Either of you hear anything?"

Hat lifted a shoulder. "I don't think so."

Palaton began to clear the table. "Both of you have been
out. Either one of you could have attracted attention." The
map faded off the wall as he downloaded the projector and
locked the keyboard. He threw a bag to Hat. "Pack everything you can."

"But—"

"No time! Rufi?"

"I'm not quite sure." Her face unfocused slightly, as she
sent her *bahdur* in quest of the unknown.

Neither Choya waited for a definitive answer, gathering
up what they could get their hands on quickly. Before she
straightened and frowned, saying, "A hand or more, coming down the alleyway," Hat and Palaton were ready to go.
Hat had never even had a chance to take his jacket off and
Palaton tossed Rufeen hers.

They almost made it clear, but the door blew open, and
the uniforms of imperial guards filled the shattered threshold to bursting.

Chapter 26

"Put your weapons down by order of the emperor," the Choya in front shouted, to which Rufeen responded by going to her stomach, and dropping him with a single, clean shot. She rolled out of range immediately.

Palaton shoved Hat aside and dove in the other direction as beams split the air. The burly Earthan went down behind an overturned table with a grunt and sat up, blinking, clutching a bag of groceries to his chest.

Rufeen spat back, her voices gravelly but level, "Next one moves gets his head sliced from his shoulders."

Seeing that they had not been able to wound or immobilize any of the quarry, and that they now stood in a cross fire, the guard paused to assess the situation. Their commander writhed in front of them, grasping his thigh and attempting to stop the flow of blood from a none too neat and bulging wound. The sound of ripping fabric filled the air as he tore his tunic and tried to fasten it about the wound.

Rufeen slid across the flooring and behind the table barrier where Hat sat, muttering something about the lack of manners and ancestry of the imperial guard, as well as proper search and seizure notification, when the second in command snapped out, "You have no rights."

"You have a Choya bleeding to death," Palaton observed dryly. "I will give you the right to withdraw expediently and take care of your wounded."

Rufeen took Hat's enforcer from its holster, primed it, and put it into Hat's palm. "I think," she said calmly, "you might need this."

Hat swallowed hard and took it, still clutching his bag of supplies as if it were a shield. His hand shook a little. They both watched the guardsman, as if divining his thoughts by the look in his eyes.

The guard stayed between them and freedom, but Palaton knew that they had been sent to capture, not kill. Panshinea wanted him brought in alive, tortured exquisitely, and then executed. Nothing less would suit the emperor. He was not certain that the order would cover Rufeen's and Hat's lives, but the opportunity to gain information from them would probably protect them as well. So the only fear here was how much damage they would do before being taken in, or getting out.

He did not want any more on his head than he already had. He took his voices and *pushed,* feeling the *bahdur* leap to ready use, saying, "Take your Choya and get him clear. Then deal with us."

To his surprise, the guardsmen responded. The nearest one bent and grabbed his superior's arm and began to drag him back out onto the street. Surely, they would have been shielded against *bahdur,* surely they would have their defenses up—but he had either punched through, or they had not. Another guardsman wavered as if he would help the first drag out their comrade, but the second in command barked, "Stand your ground!" and he stayed, a look of torn loyalties across his face.

One less body blocking the doorway. One less between them and the street. Still, there would be no getting out without further bloodshed. He could try his influence again, but from the tightly set jaw of the second in command, and the way his bronze mane fairly bristled above his horn crown, it would not work.

Hat broke the stalemate. At Rufeen's sudden nudging, his burly form staggered upward and he broke into a shambling run toward the rear of the rooms. Palaton let out a coarse yell, feeling it rip at his throat, even as the guard fired.

The enforcer beam seared its way across the room. Rufeen shoved the table in its path, shearing it astray, as Hat went down and rolled to safety behind a bedstead, and suddenly there were three less guards in the doorway.

Palaton got up, moving quickly, and grabbed the second by his neck, pulling him in and holding him to his chest. Looking out on the street, he saw three guardsmen down, one of them still holding that messy thigh wound, and a fourth on his knees, arms about his head. Someone had come to their aid, and taken advantage of being at the backs of the imperial guard.

In a swirl of midnight cloak, the Choya turned, and Palaton caught a full face glimpse of his, no, *her,* features.

"Jorana," he breathed, even as he shoved the Choya he held out the door. He called back, "Rufeen, get Hat and whatever the two of you can carry."

The doubt that he had seen her before was replaced by the wonder of seeing her now, so that he could not think, but only feel. She looked, against the gray foggy drizzle of the day, like the edge of night, or perhaps the glory of the storm itself, come to rest and create havoc in this alleyway.

"Don't just stand there," she said, and her voices were clipped and dry. "You've got to get out of here."

"How did you—"

"Find you? I saw Rufeen." Jorana flashed a look at the rangy pilot. "What you don't know, Choya'i, about backtracking, nearly got all of you killed. You left an aura trail a burned-out hound could follow all the way from Charolon."

Rufeen had the grace to flush in embarrassment, before she leaned down and stripped the guards of their weapons. Jorana turned slightly to watch her movements, and Palaton saw the slight roundedness of her outline. More than that, a spike of *bahdur* touched him, not hers, but from within.

With child. The realization stuck in his throat, along with the thought that it could not have been his. Whose, then, and why? She looked up, as if in response to a gasp, and their eyes met.

Jorana closed her eyes softly a moment as if to gather herself, then looked back at him.

"Jorana—"

"There's no time. I came to see you, to explain, but now there's no time!" Anger flashed like lightning through her words. "You've got to get out of here, and I've got work to do."

Their names, other details, would be leached from the minds of the fallen. It would take time and effort. Her role would be betrayed. He could not leave her behind. Not now, with so much unknown and at stake.

"Come with us."

Jorana shook her head. "Not now. Later. Where—"

He did not know how well she worked. He did not want to leave a trail. "After Trevon the Black," he said, finally, knowing that if anyone could trace the dealer, she could.

Jorana gave a curt nod. She pulled the second guard from Palaton's hold and clubbed him behind the cusp of the neck and crown. The Choya went to his knees with a soft grunt, then collapsed onto the bodies of his fellows. Jorana went to one knee, putting her hand across his forehead, already beginning to narrow her thoughts into what must be done.

Palaton had to touch her, to stroke the softness of her skin, to lightly trace the gold chain and onyx pattern upon her cheeks. His question surged wordlessly through him. Jorana caught his hand and held onto it for dear life, squeezing his fingers tightly enough to drive away the blood and bring pain.

"It's your child," she said softly, breathlessly. "Dear God-in-all, I don't know what it does to you to tell this, but I can't let you go without knowing."

"My child . . ." It could not be. Never with her or anyone else, had he prepared to conceive a child. The enormity of her words left him speechless.

"Believe me," Jorana begged. "Now go. I can't keep you safe much longer."

"You—"

"I'll be all right. I'll follow. Somehow." She released his hand. Blood sprang back to life with a stinging pain, an echo of the stabbing she had just wrought in his heart.

A child. Cursed with the blood of the Flames, as he was. Damned to unknown possibilities.

A child. To live beyond his own death, to carry on, to have a legacy. . . .

Did she know what she had done to him?

It had begun raining again, softly, upon Jorana's upraised face. She dashed the drops away and said roughly, "Get out of here."

He turned abruptly, shoved Hat into motion, and grabbed Rufeen by the elbow. They ran down the alley to the garage where the pilots had stowed their jet sleds. He did not look back, though he could feel Jorana's eyes on him still, smell the faint perfume of her hair, see the rain upon her face, and the well of her body beneath the cloak.

He could not leave her!

Palaton turned at the garage, preparing to go back down the alley and get her, but she was gone, the bodies of the downed guard left in her wake, and there was nothing to show she had ever been there.

Rufeen joggled his elbow. "Come on, Boss. She gave us a chance, let's not waste it."

"I can't—did you see her?"

"I saw her," answered Rufeen gruffly. "But she didn't want you to drag her along, and you have to let her go. Now let's get out of here before backup arrives."

"I can't. Even with talent, she can't possible wipe their minds enough to keep herself in the clear. At least one is bound to recognize her, later."

"She can do it if she has *ruhl*," Rufeen bit off impatiently.

Palaton gave a slight shudder, an involuntary response to the use of the drug which muddled those with *bahdur* almost beyond the point of sanity, depending on its dosage. Despite the fact that death was not uncommon, its popularity as an aphrodisiac among the God-blind was legendary. And if she had it to use. . . . His thoughts roiled in his mind, paralyzing him. "You two go on. I have to go back. I have to talk to her."

"I'm not going anywhere without you," Rufeen argued.

Hat added faintly, "I think I was hit." He stood, hunched over, face growing rapidly more pale.

The pain echoed in his voices. Palaton looked down, and saw the blood tracing on the hand Hat held clutched to his flank. The splotch was thin and pink, a flesh wound in the squat Choya's side, no doubt, but nothing to be trifled with. He took Hat gently by the arm. "Can you drive?"

Hat gave a convulsive nod.

"All right." Palaton mounted his jet sled. "Where to?"

Rufeen bared her teeth. "After Trevon."

"I can make it," Hat said tightly, before being asked.

Rufeen kicked open the unloading door to the garage, saying, "This isn't my idea of fun. I never thought I'd draw down on one of my own. A Drooler's my idea of a target."

She grabbed Hat's sled by the handlebars and slung it

past her, opening up the doorway, for Palaton to leave. They exchanged glances, and then Rufeen ducked away, unable to meet his eyes.

"It'll be all right," she muttered, and kicked her vehicle into tandem with Hat's, guiding him through the alleyway.

Rain came down in sheeting curtains. Palaton, caught without a jacket or coat, shrugged his shoulders against the downpour. The weather was all the better for washing away their presence and hiding their escape.

But it did not keep him from thinking that the sky wept for him.

*   *   *

The night was late when she returned to the legal wing of the embassy, having missed dinner and late tea. She would have to order something up to her rooms, which were little more than a hole in the wall, nothing more than could be expected to be provided by contract. She had a kitchenette, a bed, a bathroom, and an office/study. No window, of course, though she did have an imaging wall to keep her from feeling claustrophobic.

Maeva clutched her package tightly under her elbow despite its bulk, trying to free herself of the idea that anyone who looked her way would know what it was she carried. It was not as though the armor was unwrapped or marked conspicuously, but she could not shake the feeling as she made her way through the security lobby and into the general lobby, that anyone who looked could identify the package.

The traffic was light, due to the hour, and she squinted her eyes against the white-flood of illumination, after her walk in the gently lit night. She knew no one she saw as she hurried into the scanner. Maeva felt her chin go up defensively—how many scanners had she been through in her life, starting from her earliest school days until now—how many security portals, many of which were no promise of protection at all, but simply there to keep the masses quiet? She stepped out, feeling it was ironic that having crossed oceans of star systems, she was not that far from home, after all.

As she passed through the portal, a dark mass of a being

rose to greet her, a being of vast bulk and yet infinite grace, and she plunged to a startled halt as it met her.

"Good evening, madame attorney," the Abdrelik said. "As you would say in your language, if Muhammad will not go to the mountain, then the mountain must come to Muhammad." GNask smiled greatly, and drops of saliva cascaded from one ivory tusk.

Chapter 27

"What do you think you're doing?" Maeva retreated nervously as the Abdrelik drew close to her, a Ronin in his shadow. *The* Ronin, unless she was very much mistaken. Maeva swiveled on one heel, looking about wildly for assistance. The lobby had become deserted, and she quelled her initial reaction, realizing that this was a senior member of the Compact who could not possibly act so publicly, nor should she, not wanting to cause an incident to embarrass herself. She chewed on her lip, before turning back slowly to face GNask.

"I have a pass," the ambassador said mildly. "And if I were you, madame attorney, I would compose myself and listen to what is being said. Attracting undue attention at this time and place may not be in your best interests. Authorities such as myself, with passes, are not looked upon unfavorably in the Compact. I have a right to be here, and so I am." He lowered his rumbling voice even more. "And it might even be said later that I was never here at all."

Maeva hugged her package close. Though she could feel herself, shaking (with fear? or anger?), she managed her next words with the calm the Abdrelik suggested. "I'm honored by your presence, Ambassador GNask, but one of my status can hardly be of any assistance to you."

GNask smiled warmly. He returned to the massive couch which had been his chair and beckoned for her to sit down next to him. Maeva perched on the cushion's edge, balancing the packaged armor on her knee. "How may I help you?"

"You are one of the legal counsel on staff here, are you not?"

She nodded hesitantly, wondering where he was leading,

and what he wanted, and thought that if assassination were on their minds, she would now be dead and her body hidden in one of the phone cubicles off the lobby's main entrance. With a privacy shield down, it would take days to find her. An Ivrian pilot had been killed like that in his own consulate. Maeva felt her mouth getting dry.

The Ronin stayed in her peripheral vision. It occurred to Maeva that he might be doing that on purpose—or he might be unaware she had as much side vision as she did. Without giving away that she could see him, Maeva kept her attention directed toward the huge alien close to her. "My status on the staff could hardly be less junior. I doubt if I can be of any value to you." She paused, and added, "And I couldn't divulge anything to you without permission of the head of the staff, even if there were something I did know."

GNask put up a hand to stroke the sluglike creature at his throat. Maeva had not seen it there before, so perfectly did the fleshy purplish color match. She had thought it the wattle of his neck, and now saw the creature pulsate wetly. Its stalk eyes came out and flicked a look at her. She knew that the thing's main purpose seemed to be as a pet, and as a skin-fungus-and-bacteria feeder, although there were rumors the symbiont also leached blood from time to time to complete its diet. Revulsion rose at the back of her throat and Maeva felt her glance flicker away. She forced herself to look back.

One of the ambassador's thick fingers stroked the creature as he spoke. "You underestimate yourself. My allies and I have observed you in the company of your ambassador, John Taylor Thomas, a great deal lately. Therefore, you must be capable of some standards of hard work as well as loyalty. My old friend can be very demanding. And it is not likely he would prefer the company of a junior employee unless her abilities were superior."

Or unless the threat of having your contract sold out from under you made you very pliable. Maeva closed her lips tightly on her thoughts. Feigning disinterest, she eyed her watch and said, "Ambassador GNask, with all due respect, the hour is growing late, and I have some work to prepare for tomorrow."

GNask smiled again, the grimace exposing his gums as well as his teeth. "And a cumbersome burden to put away as well, I see."

"Yes," she replied evenly. The Ronin moved slightly on her flank, as if closing in on her. He halted as she turned her head involuntarily in response. He *was* trying to circle her. Her grip on her package tightened, despite her effort to look relaxed. What did these two have in common?

"I will try to be brief," GNask said expansively. He spread his thick hands. "What I need from you is information which will not compromise you at all. My associate here tells me you had a meeting with Ambassador Rindalan of Cho."

She could hardly claim confidentiality there. Besides, Timero had not kept the meeting a secret out there on the pathways. Maeva nodded smoothly. "Yes, the ambassador was gracious enough to set aside some time for me."

"And you will tell me why."

She eyed the Abdrelik closely before saying, in her best clipped tones, "I think not."

"Do you claim that to do so would betray your secrecy and loyalty oath to your embassy?"

She had not fenced with an Abdrelik before, and had not given them much credit for subtlety, and GNask was pointing toward something, something oblique that she instantly felt would be very dangerous for her to be cornered into. "What would you have me claim?" she countered quickly.

That took GNask back a moment, as his lips came down over his tusks, and his jowls sagged again. The beady eyes blinked once or twice.

"May I remind you," he said, "of my position."

"But you see," Maeva pressed, "that's what I can't understand. Why an ambassador of your position would be the slightest bit interested in a counsel of my position."

"Perhaps I am curious as to why such a junior member of the staff was recently assigned the embassy's highest security rating and clearance. Perhaps I am curious as to what you intend to do with it. Or are already engaged in."

Maeva let out a short laugh. "And you would expect me to tell you?"

"Yes."

She stared into the Abdrelik's broad, purplish face for a long moment. The alien did not flinch from her examination, although the symbiont had begun to ripple its way up the throat and onto GNask's jawline. It became clear to her that GNask honestly did think she would confide in him.

The Ronin moved. This time Maeva shifted her weight and looked directly at the creature. "Ask once nicely, and then torture?" she said lightly, although her throat had begun to tighten, and she knew her next words would be difficult to force out.

"Something like that." GNask smoothed his jowls with the back of his hand, patting away the ever-present moisture. "I am well acquainted with your ambassador. We have had, from time to time, some informal dealings. I do not think you too terribly naive about the internal workings of the Compact."

"Not terribly," Maeva echoed.

"I do not expect you to confide in me tonight, here, and now. But I have come to make you an offer. I know Thomas. His moods, his expectations—his shortfalls. There may well come a time when you need a safety net, madame attorney, when you find that your home world does not provide what you need to stay alive. May I make my own humble offering of assistance when that time comes?"

"Assistance? Provided I tell you everything I know."

GNask lowered his head slightly.

"And if I don't accept your generous offer?"

The ambassador said nothing, but he raised his head and stared at the Ronin who skinned his lips back from his teeth and rattled his quills. GNask then added, "Perhaps you will allow me to convince you. We will talk again." With speed belied by his bulk, the ambassador beckoned to the Ronin, got to his feet, and made his way to the security portal.

The archway lit up and let him exit without any deterrence whatsoever. The recording sensor stayed dim, and Maeva realized that what GNask had told her was true. There would be no record of his presence tonight, except those who saw him, and those few would probably not bear witness.

The package of body armor slid from her knee, and she let it drop to the floor as she realized she had just been

offered both the carrot and the stick. How had the Abdrelik known about her security clearance? And if he knew
that, did he in truth have the slightest suspicion of what
she might be doing for Thomas?

To hell with the ambassador. Did the alien know about
Rand?

She had begun to shake again as delayed adrenaline
began to flood her body. She leaned over to pick up the
package. It took three tries to coordinate her reach with her
grasp, and another two tries to stand up holding the armor.

About one thing GNask had been correct. If Thomas
ever found out what she had done, what she yet planned
to do, he would cut her loose from the embassy. She would
have no place to go for safety. She would be at the mercy
of the reassignment courts of the Compact, and GNask no
doubt had a great deal of influence there, as well.

Although the Choyan had been gracious, she doubted
she would find refuge there. She would be outcast, just as
Rand had been, and along the tide of adrenaline came a
new emotion, one deeper than the compassion she had felt
earlier. She knew now the despair and disillusionment he
had tried to convey to her. She was alone among her
own people.

Maeva walked to the lifts for her apartment tower. The
halls were strangely quiet, abandoned, and her footfalls
echoed loudly. She thought she could hear her heartbeat
pounding.

The body armor didn't have a chance in hell of saving
her.

The midnight hours brought little rest to Rindalan. He
lay on his divan, rather than his bed, head elevated on the
crown pillow, taking the weight off his aching neck and
shoulders, and thought behind the blackness of his eyelids.
He would rather have slept whatever hours he could, for
he had reached that elderly portion of his life where even
sleep could be a rare commodity. He could sleep in chambers where the arguments droned on and on, but he could
not find rest in his own bed, during his own time.

Rindy sighed gustily and opened his eyes. He did not
mind his age. With it had come a certain amount of wisdom, he hoped, and a great many memories of which he

was excessively fond. But memory would not serve him now. Rand was with his own people, and though Rindy could not comprehend the logic of his treatment, the elder prelate was entirely uncertain of how to deal with it. He could no more delicately dislodge Rand from that imprisonment than he could wake the frozen race of Sorrow. Not without creating a great deal of turmoil, anyway.

Rindy shifted his weight on the divan. One hip was a little tender with arthritis. He moved off it slightly to assuage the pain and pressure. If Panshinea were not so avid a xenophobe, the emperor would be able to deal with the problem. Pan, though his *bahdur* burned erratically, affecting his entire temperament, was nonetheless shrewd and capable with these problems. Rindy couldn't hold a candle to him. But he could not ask Panshinea. The emperor would manipulate Rand to his doom.

As for Palaton, Rindy had no idea where he had gone into hiding, although there was that spark within the elder which told him the pilot still lived. If the *tezar* continued to wish to live, he would remain just as elusive. No, he could not reach Palaton though that was Rand's best hope of rescue.

No, no matter how he worried at the knot of problems and troubles, he kept coming back to the same conclusion. Rindy had no allies for this undertaking, and the burden was his and his alone. He sighed again, not liking the odds.

There was the humankind, of course, who'd come to him. Pretty little thing, if knowing Rand had taught him anything about that race. He thought them all rather awkward, though their eyes gave him pause, wide-eyed innocents like his own people's children. If eyes were indeed the windows to the soul, humankind was a deep well of psyches, and the Abdreliks an absolute drought. Maeva had risked much in coming to him.

Well, then, perhaps he did not stand alone in this enterprise. Maeva could be counted upon for something, surely, if not for more information. Unless he could read little of them, she had an interest in Rand. He had touched her. Though whether deeply enough so she was as willing as Rindy to risk all, the elder Choya could not tell.

Two, then, against the clever Halls and entrapments of the Compact. Rindy shook his head slightly. He still did not like the odds. He closed his eyes again. The problem with solving conundrums at night was that the possibilities, like the sky, tended to be dark. He decided to drift determinedly into sleep, and work on solutions in the morning.

Knowing that Rand was not possessed of psychic ability, he sidestepped the embassy shielding, and sent him a thought anyway, of hope, of help coming, of comfort. Perhaps the boy had been around Palaton long enough to have absorbed something of the *tezar's* soulfire. If not, no harm done.

As he sank deeper into the rhythms of his mind, his thoughts went coiling out, visualized as a rope of smoke, curling through nothingness until it might find its recipient. It sank, through the warmth of his being, down, down, until it was seized and a shocking chill shot back into Rindalan.

He sat up on the divan, clutching at the upholstered back of it, feeling as if he had been doused in icy water. Dropped into a wintery pond, the surface had given under him, dunking him under its treacherous lid. He could not quite catch his breath, and his limbs reacted to the mental cold by thrashing about in violent shudders, throwing off the blanket he had tucked about his legs. Rindy gasped and his aged heart did a stutter step which frightened him almost more than the cold.

But worse, he found Rand in the center of it, frozen among lifelessness, like an anchor. The other's consciousness caught onto his, a drowning man reaching for a lifeline, pulling him under as well, immersing him in the chill aftermath. *Fool!* thought Rindy. *He's in cold sleep or reduction.* But this was more, less than cold sleep, but worse.

He lay among Sorrow's dead. Rindy could feel them as well, a realization which startled as well as frightened him. With all his psychic acumen he had never sensed their crystalline being before. The God-in-all had gifted him with the ability to sense the vibrancy of life in everything, even stone, but here on Sorrow those vibrations had never been felt. Shielded, perhaps? He caught an echo of intense sadness, and longing, and reluctance to let him go, to let him take Rand up with him.

As if rescuing a foundering diver, Rindy wrapped his thoughts about the lad and brought him up, kicking hard to reach a surface which existed only in his mind, his lungs laboring, his heart thudding. Rand lay in his embrace as if one of the dead, and stirred only when Rindalan finally broke clear.

They touched thoughts briefly, a faint brush against one another, and then Rand left him. Rindy felt him float away sluggishly, knew that wherever he was, he was indeed in near-cryonic suspension.

He opened his eyes to the familiarity of the diplomatic suite. The needlepoint upholstery of the divan which he had clutched until his knuckles turned white. The dim lighting of the room, the burlwood table, the Ivrian watercolor on the far wall, a light and feathery subject amid the tailored striped wallpaper. His chest heaved with the effort he had just expended.

He did not understand what had just happened. He only knew that if he had not been searching for Rand, the boy might have died imprisoned there among the mysterious people of Sorrow.

He could not wait to free him. There were things here which Rindy did not understand, and which might prove fatal if left ignored.

Chapter 28

"Did you dump the bodies?" The question came from the depths of the massive chair pulled up to face the fireplace. Its reflected heat did much to chase the chill from the wintry atrium room, but Gathon did not feel warm.

He hugged his spindly ribs with hands nearly blue beyond the cuffs of his robe. "I did," he answered, and he did not bother to filter from his voices the self-anger and repulsion filling him. The youths were alive but, with their soulfire drained, they were little more than warm hulks. The chore repulsed him, and there was the niggling feeling that this time, he'd been sighted. This time, his efforts had been watched. This time, the emperor had been found out. He shivered, trying to dispel his unfortunate thoughts.

Panshinea swung the chair around. Despite being at ease within the upholstery, he did not look rested. He appeared coiled, ready to spring, overflowing with energy as he had not been in weeks. Color blazed in his face and it was as if the fire itself danced in his glorious golden hair. It was the stolen *bahdur,* Gathon knew, and though he had the knowledge of where the emperor's well-being had come from, he felt no better for the knowing.

"That extra dose," Gathon added, "might very well kill them." He detested *ruhl*, with all its possible misuses.

"Perhaps they would think it better if I had." Panshinea curled his fingers about his wineglass, cradling it to his chest. "I tell myself it would be no great loss, that if I had only found those Flame bastards and treated them the same way, I would not be facing what I'm facing now." He let out a sigh, which was more a hiss. "But I agree with you, Gathon. I do that which no Choya should do to another, and I cannot help myself. There's no other way for me to continue." He drained the glass of Imperial Gold.

"You could step down," Gathon responded mildly.

Panshinea, who had begun to look down into the depths of his drink with a melancholy expression, snapped his glance back at the prime minister. "That is never a consideration."

Gathon could feel drops of sweat beading on his forehead, yet his arms and hands and feet remained icy, and shivers rippled up and down his aged body. He said, recklessly, "Perhaps it should be."

"And have you anyone in mind to replace me?"

The internal heat which had flared began to cool rapidly. "No."

"You're certain?"

"Do you doubt me as well as yourself?" His recklessness gave one final spurt.

Panshinea looked as though he had something to reply, but he closed his mouth on it, and his lips thinned as if he reconsidered. His gaze did drop to the glass he held close. "How could I expect to treat you better, dear Gathon, than I treat myself?" he murmured, barely audibly. He drained the wine. "Any word on our quarry?"

"None." Gathon took his hands from under his arms and chafed them together lightly, as pins and needles began to warm them. "If you do not mind, Pan, it has been a long night for me. I need to retire."

Pan said abruptly, "You do not like pimping for me."

"No. No more than did Jorana. But you are Cho, and Cho ails if you ail, and so I would wish for you to be well."

"I'm a parasite."

Gathon thought of the bodies he had disposed of in the outer slums of Charolon, the fourth such group in the weeks since Pan's attack on Palaton. "Yes," he agreed.

"But a necessary one."

Gathon did not answer.

"Perhaps not so necessary."

"Your Highness. The hour is late, and my duties are many in the morning. May I go?"

Wordlessly, the emperor of Cho nodded, but Gathon did not wait for dismissal. He simply turned and left.

Panshinea watched the door close, then put his finger into the wineglass and stirred the tip of it around the bowl's bottom where a faint residue had been left. He licked the

fingertip clean of the gritty powder, with misgivings. Vihtirne and Qativar had been right. This, *this,* was the wellspring from which renewed power could flow. With this, he
no longer needed to do what he'd done that night, and
every week since he'd failed to destroy Palaton. With this,
he could rule as surely God had intended him to. With this,
nothing was impossible.

He would never have tried it, without catching the taste
of it in the youths he was draining. Their *bahdur,* weak and
fragile as it was, had left him more hungry than sated, aching with the need to be filled. But their power had had an
edge to it, a promise, and he had gone to the drug in search
of that promise. And, Pan told himself, he had found it.
This evening he fairly burned with potential, having found
his prey inadequate, and trying the drug in Gathon's disap-
proving absence. What the old Choya did not know would
not hurt him.

Gathon had sensed nothing, or if he had sensed how full
of *bahdur* Panshinea had become, he would attribute it to
the callow youths he'd just disposed of. It was just as well.
He already felt condemnation from the elderly Choya. If
Gathon discovered he'd used boost it would only have
added to his disapproval, and Pan had no intention of letting the minister persuade him to leave the course he'd just
begun. This was power, and this was his!

He had only to make sure of an uninterrupted supply.

Pan refilled his wineglass and sipped at it slowly and
pensively.

Walking the streets, Jorana cautiously continued the perimeter search, fulfilling her need to know if her newly
chosen quarters were safe. She had taken the guard and
their hound by transport to Trivan and dumped them there,
but she wanted to backtrack their aura as much as possible,
confusing the trail when the hound awoke, so she had returned. She had found a new bolt-hole in outer Charolon,
far from the musicians' quarters, and although it was seedy,
at least no one had asked any questions when she had
checked in.

The rain threatened to turn to sleet, so she kept her head
somewhat bowed as the cold of it iced her face. She had

not returned to the little apartment across from the bakery, could not, and mourned what few items she had left there. She could go back to Malahki, but knew the wrath she would face. No. She had taken this road, and did not wish to retrace her steps upon it.

She skirted a dark alleyway, then heard the faint moans issuing from it, and paused. This time of night, few traversed the city but burned-out boost addicts and beggars with nowhere to go and no prospects but another's misfortune. No one of any good intent might be hovering in the alleyways. Hard times, in Charolon.

She heard the moan again. Intuition prickled at the base of her neck, but she turned anyway, and stood in the alley's mouth until her vision narrowed to the velvet depths. She saw two tumbled heaps, and stepped closer.

The auras had been dispersed, but it did not matter. Two forms lay sprawled in the back of the street, dumped like offal, left to live or die as they would. She could smell the drugs on them, and the even rarer, more distinctive smell of Imperial Gold, and Jorana knew what had happened here. She used to bring the emperor his victims herself.

She bent over them and felt for the pulses throbbing sluggishly in their necks. She stood for a long time, measuring the strength of the life ebbing through them.

They would make it, she decided, and straightened, drawing her cloak about her. They were young and vigorous, and even a night in a slush-filled alley would not harm them permanently.

But as to whether or not they would survive what Panshinea had done to them, that she could not predict. Those commons who had some *bahdur* but not enough to pass testing to be brought into Houses did not always even know what it was they had. They often thought it luck. Those who did, who used it and depended on it, erratic though it might be, were the ones most affected by the method the emperor had used to drain them. He did what he did not only to temporarily recharge himself but also to destroy the neurais within the victims. They would know the yawning hole within themselves which would never be filled again. They were not dissimilar to *tezars* of much greater power, who suffered neurological damage and burned out over the years from the usage of their soulfire. Those *tezars* who died in the line of duty were far luckier than those who had to face the depths of their scarred souls, and could not.

She could not know if these unlucky youths faced a mirroring reaction to what had happened to them tonight, and even if she were to know, there was nothing she could do to assist them. Even boost would not help. It could not spur what no longer existed. She wondered who was disposing of the bodies for Panshinea now.

Jorana tucked the cloaks in tightly about them and left them in the alley.

This quarter of Charolon was not safe for her if the emperor hunted here. She pulled her hood about her face, and walked off into the stinging wind.

A solid darkness arose from the corner before her, blocking the street.

"The emperor leaves his spore in the oddest places, don't you agree, Jorana?"

She looked up into the winter-cold eyes of Qativar. He added, "You know, of course, that many of us have been looking for you. I think it would be best if you came with me."

*   *   *

The jet sleds carried them into the storm front, bucking against the aboveground thermals, and sleet-filled wind. Palaton kept an anxious eye on Hat, curled painfully over the handlebar grips, feet braced on the floorboards, but the Earthan kept his sled steady, so there was little Palaton could do but watch.

Rufeen tried to cut a path for them, attempting to draft Hat's vehicle in her wake. Her thick form was barely visible in the night despite the yellow beams from the sleds. Her mane flew loose from her coat collar, but it did not banner in the wind, for it soon frosted in icicle patterns. Palaton would have worried for them all, but his sense told him that the storm front only covered a few hundred miles and they would soon be out of it, even if it traveled with them a ways. They could not turn out of its path, and it covered their leaving far better than they could have hoped. Only someone as desperate as they were would fly in the face of the wind, sleet, and rain.

The front fell apart just as dawn began to creep through the sky, and Palaton saw Rufeen shear aside, taking the sled so close to the ground as to nearly plow it, searching for a lee. She turned about, he saw her face, frosted and pale, and knew she needed a fire and rest, even as she beckoned.

Hat did not respond, but he followed, and when Palaton brought up the rear, braking the sled to a halt where the other two had come to a stop, he saw Rufeen dismount stiffly. Hat stayed crouched on his sled, frozen to his grip on the handlebars. Palaton reached the Earthan before the pilot did.

He ran his hands over Hat's and gently pried the fingers loose. "Come on," he coaxed. "Rufi's getting a fire going. Let's take a look at that bleeding."

Hat turned a tortured face to him. "I brought them."

"No. I won't even blame Rufi for that. They were searching for us." Popping open the vehicle's tool compartment, he found the aid kit and slung it over one shoulder. He took Hat's arm gently and put his other shoulder in under, taking the other's weight carefully and lifting him from the vehicle's saddle.

"If it hadn't been for Jorana—" Rufeen was there, suddenly, helping him from the other side. They walked Hathord to the fire she'd already laid and had banked. Its sputtering warmth was taking hold amongst the rocks.

Hat tried to take a deep breath, coughed in discomfort, and let his weight sag upon their shoulders. Rufeen said nothing, but shot Palaton a worried look over the top of their comrade's head. He felt himself frowning. Hat felt terribly cold in their embrace.

Rufeen went to one knee so that Palaton could lay Hat down on the ground. Their companion fell back, his face so gray that he would have been camouflaged among the stone. She put his feet close to the bed of rocks which had begun to warm under the wood-fed fire, as Palaton stripped off his jacket, rolled it inside out, and put it under Hat's head and shoulders. He let the aid kit drop to the ground beside them.

Then his fingers went to the bloodstained coat front to peel it back.

Hat put his hand over Palaton's. "Don't," he pleaded.

"We have to take a look at it."

"I don't want to know."

Palaton kept his hand still. As a cadet, Hat had never been very bold. He had not taken risks. He had never liked surprises, and Palaton knew what frightened him now.

Rufeen rubbed her hands briskly and hunched over the fire, feeding more substantial deadwood into it. She'd found a copse among the broken rock field, and though the wind still howled steadily, the gray of the dawn had given way to a faintly blue light, and the chill of the storm could not be felt here. They'd come enough miles to be outside even the capital's agri district . . . perhaps even to the fallow parklands. The trees rattled thinly, much of their foliage lost to the fall, their branches as dark as *bren* against the sky. In the lee of an immense marble-streaked boulder, its mates broken about it into stones and pebbles, there was a kind of beauty to the place.

Hat had followed his line of sight. He said weakly, "This would not be a bad place to die."

Rufeen snorted and then said, "Now that's what I need to hear."

Hat's face had been gaining some color. Now he flushed darkly, though the anger paled almost as quickly as it came. His fingers curled tightly about Palaton's hand. Before Palaton could say something to comfort Hat, Rufeen added, "We really need to be digging graves now, Boss. See if you can get a plug in him, okay? I'm gong to look for lightfoot, see if I can make some stew." She got up and sauntered away, her thick hips swinging.

"Lightfoot," Hat whined. "I'll be spitting out fur for a week."

Palaton looked back at him, and realized what Rufeen had been doing. He felt the corner of his mouth draw back in mild irritation even as he put Hat's hand aside and skinned back the bloodstained cloth.

Jorana's initial assessment back in the alleyway had been correct. The wound, though it seeped gently, had all but seared itself shut, and had done little damage, having cut into that portion of Hat's waistline settling over his hips, which the commons called love handles. He needn't worry about the fat roll on this flank for a while. It would be sore, and it still wept, but it looked clean, for all the slice it had taken out of him, and it wasn't even close to being life threatening.

Palaton told him as much in clipped, unsympathetic tones. Hat's face settled into a sulky, yet relieved expression as Palaton left his side. He found moss among the stones which had tumbled close to the edge of a tiny freshet at the edge of the copse, scraped it loose, brought it back, and bound it to the wound. Hat let out a quavering hiss as the cool lichen began to draw the heat from the puckered tissue. Palaton rocked back on his heels and waited for his friend to finish.

Hat touched the compress with tentative fingers and tried to look at the work Palaton had done. He let out a short laugh. "I was never very brave, was I?"

"The one reason you didn't make an excellent pilot. You've always been a little hesitant about the unknown." Palaton wrapped a bandage about the Earthan's waistline to anchor the compress and clipped it off.

"But I was a *good* pilot, wasn't I?"

He finished the bandaging with an antibiotic radiation spray, capped the flare to return it to the kit, and answered, "Of course you were. And you're one of the best flightmasters we've ever had."

"Without a school," Hat said mournfully as Palaton wedged him upright. He tested the position a little gingerly, then gave a relieved grin. "I can't go anywhere, or you'll build me a memorial instead of a school. And you did promise me a new school."

"That I did." Palaton repackaged the aid kit. There were no oral antibiotics to give Hat, but if he needed that kind of medical care, they'd have to find it for him. Another day or two on the jet sled to find Rufeen's bolt-hole, and he thought Hat would be all right.

"Rufeen knows," Hat continued.

"What?"

"That I haven't got the nerve."

"It's not that you haven't got nerve," Palaton said, sitting down beside the wounded Earthan, and stretching his legs out. "It's a different kind of nerve. Rufeen wouldn't have the courage to run a school, coordinating the fragile egos of incoming cadets with half-burned-out pilots and cocky wing leaders. Balancing budgets. Going among the God-blind and testing for *bahdur*—it hasn't happened recently, but there've been terrible riots over the tests. You have courage all right, Hathord. It's just a different kind."

Hat settled his back to the smooth side of the immense, fractured boulder. He blinked as he patted the bandage once as if to ensure it stayed in place, and answered, "I hadn't thought of it that way."

"Maybe it's time you should," Rufeen said gruffly, as she came around the granite- and marble-streaked structure. She threw two half-skinned lightfoot rodents onto the dirt by the fire. "We don't have time to keep mending falling egos."

"Well," Hat returned slowly, "if we have time to hunt for enough supplies to fill your dinner plate, we should have some time to set aside for me."

Rufeen shot him a look, then lapsed into a chagrined expression as Palaton began to laugh. Then she pointed at him.

"Laugh all you want, but these morsels aren't fully skinned yet. You want to eat, I need some help."

Palaton shifted away from Hat, took up a lightfoot and began to apply his heat knife to it. Tufts of fur swirled around the fire, *pfffting* as the heat destroyed them. Rufeen squatted beside him and finished the second. She pushed her chin at Hat.

"He's going to live, eh?"

"Looks like it."

Hat wrinkled his nose. "If your cooking doesn't kill me first." He wiggled around until he got his back to a boulder and sat up straighter. "Where do we go from here?"

Rufeen spitted her carcass. "I think I have the answer to that, too. There's a Relocation depot not far from here. It's got transports being fueled. Place looks fairly empty. I'd say it's probably under minimum maintenance."

"It would have to be." Relocation was a traumatic process of uprooting whole communities from their geographic location and transplanting them. In this way, the country itself was being recycled, bit by bit, territory by territory. There had been talk for years that Charolon was overdue for Relocation, but because of its position as capital, it was thought Panshinea had been fighting Relocation off successfully. This depot must have been built for the eventuality, which had never come. Palaton added, "We'll have to take a look at it in the morning. I think you may have found a way to get us to Trevon the Black."

Chapter 29

He summoned Vihtirne from her nocturnal chambers. It
was so late at night as to be early the next morning, he
thought, as he waited for her to come down. Her humor
would not be good, but Qativar cared little about that.
When she did appear on the stairs, she was wrapped in a
purple robe of deep color, its silken folds whispering as she
came down the stairs, its high collar hiding her neck but
not her face. He realized with shock, when he saw her, that
she must use a firming net, applied electrically, before she
saw anyone for the day. She was awake, but not made up,
and the sagging of her cheeks and jawline surprised him.
As she neared the bottom step, seeing Qativar and what
he had hidden in his shadow, her eyes widened. The faint
smell of sex, of sex and lovemaking, came with her, perfum-
ing her skin and robe. Qativar did not particularly care for
the odor, but that dislike said a lot more about himself
than it did about Vihtirne, he thought.

"What have you brought her here for?" demanded Vihtirne, the unexpected awakening not having dulled her wits
at all. Or her tongue.

To keep you busy and out of my way, Qativar thought,
as he bowed slightly toward Jorana, who stood, cold and
sulking, in the foyer. "We needed leverage."

"She's more trouble than she's worth."

"Thank you. I try." Jorana smiled thinly. Her own
beauty, though pale and wan, was fresh and dewy compared
to the artifices of Vihtirne. Qativar wondered if that accounted for the incredible amount of tension which had
built in the air.

"You won't do anything to harm her," he said.

Vihtirne had paused on the next to last step. Now she

descended one more step, and stopped, drawing herself up, pulling her robe about her. She stood above both of them. "I would not presume. It's a raw night out. Wherever did you find her?"

"Doing the emperor's dirty work."

Jorana chafed her wrists lightly inside her shackles. Vihtirne glanced down at the bonds with distrust.

"It will be difficult to hold her here for long."

Qativar lifted a shoulder, let it drop. "I doubt that we will need long."

"You will consult with me, will you not, as to our plans?"

He looked up at Vihtirne. "Naturally. When both the hour and the weather are more hospitable. In the meantime . . ." he waved at Jorana.

"Put her in downstairs storage. It's dry and warm enough. Throw her a blanket and some cushions from the salon. Keep her shackled. I'll be down later to check on her." Vihtirne twisted about on the step to return upstairs, then paused. She tilted her head toward Jorana. "You are pregnant."

Her accomplice started, but Jorana did nothing. Her jaw moved as though she clenched her teeth, and there was defiance in the set of her face. Vihtirne gave a knowing smile.

"Poor timing, Jorana. It gives us an advantage we'll not hesitate to use. That abomination would be well off ripped from your womb. Do not tempt us."

Qativar laughed. It was without humor and as icy as the night they'd come in out of, and he did not stop until after he'd locked the door behind Jorana.

* * *

John Taylor Thomas awoke from uneasy dreams of Alexa, her dark eyes shining with a brittle light that seemed to pierce him. He could not remember what she had been saying to him, and for that he gave rueful thanks, for her words to him had never been kind since that fateful day when he had turned her over to GNask's ungentle hands for imprinting. From the chubby, toddling, child he had given over, he never saw his daughter again in Alexa, never saw anything of him or her mother in her eyes or words. She had always been a shadow of the Abdreliks, a predator, hiding behind a mask, and terribly aware that she was different.

Perhaps it was better that she was dead now.

Perhaps.

The readout of incoming messages told him that the embassy had had a lot of traffic during the evening. Most had been dispatched elsewhere, one or two items were slated for his eyes only, and there was an appointment for incoming. The alarm had not yet gone off for it. He checked the time, saw that he had risen early, and neutralized the alarm, acknowledging the appointment. He had just enough time for a shower and shave. His hands shook as he scraped his face clean, tiny drops of blood welling up where he nicked himself.

The president awaited him as he sat down at the view screen. "Good morning, John. I trust I have not inconvenienced your schedule this morning."

Thomas did not reply, he was not meant to, but this was a real-time transmission and as he held his remarks until the president indicated he could speak, he wondered what had occasioned the call.

Gerald Mitchell had come into his office long after Thomas had, but he wore the robes of his authority with an easy familiarity. "We have been informed that one of our cargo shipments has been lost by the contract pilot. The incident occurred under FTL conditions and it is not probable that we will be able to recover our goods. As is customary, we have sent the Choyan our deepest regrets for the loss of their *tezar,* and we have filed insurance claims for the shipment." The president paused. He was sitting in the high-backed chair of his office, the windows behind nearly obscured by the protective weaving of the glass. The chair was permeated with keflex. It would stop most bullets, even hollow-nosed atrocities, although it was more probable the bodyshielding of the president would make such precautions unnecessary. But the chair was an antique symbol of the office.

"He was not under attack, John, and from preliminary investigations, he suffered from burnout. Normally I don't get involved in these incidents, but because of the nature of the cargo and its destination, I was notified. I've been

sitting in with the Economic Council most of the night."
The president leaned forward, bringing his face into close-up focus in the view screen, the salt-and-pepper coloring of his bushy eyebrows suddenly clear, the gold flecks in his brown eyes, and the shine of his thinning pate.

"What in the hell are you doing sending pharmaceuticals to the Choyan?"

Thomas felt his eyes close in sudden fear. He forced them back open, smoothing his face into neutral lines. He was a diplomat, after all. Bland neutrality had been schooled, ingrained, into him. He spoke. "Mr. President. Please convey my assurances to the Economic Council that this transaction is all very aboveboard. We have begun a preliminary trade agreement with Cho as benefits our status upgrade from a Class Zed. I have worked diligently for decades to improve our status and to open trade channels with those who will most benefit us. The pharmaceuticals lost in shipment are for a restorative remedy which the Choyan themselves requested. It is but a foot in the door for us, but one which should prove invaluable."

He sat back in his own chair, waiting for the long, long moments between transmission, his thoughts racing wildly. Boost lost in transit. The demand had risen sharply in the past few weeks, he could not keep up with it, had shifted a whole Terran-leased bay station over to the production of the remedy and hidden the paper trail for it as well as he could. Ironic that a pilot in burnout should drop a whole cargo of the drug which would have cured him.

He split-screened the view screen and scanned backup traffic while waiting for the president to respond. Nothing else seemed to be of any import to him except that Maeva Polonia had made another visit to the holding cell. Thomas felt a twitch in his composed expression as he viewed the authorization record. He would have to set up an interview with her to check on the status of the deposition. His attention distracted, he missed the first words of the president's response.

". . . without proper testing on alien physiology or field samples, are you crazy? Thomas, we come from a planet which has struggled with self-destructive chemical dependencies for most of our race's history. Without conducting a survey, how can you know what it is we're exporting to the

Choyan and how it will ultimately affect them? I have to protest your actions—"

Thomas put his hands on the console in front of him and broke into the president's transmission. "I beg your pardon, sir, but we are now trading with the Choyan. We now have a currency to barter with, a leverage to get their attention. The *Choyan,* sir, without whom we cannot ship or transport anywhere."

His words had overridden the president's but now Mitchell's voice came back powerfully. "Without any knowledge of their biochemistry or long-term effects, you cannot convince me or anyone else, let alone the FDA, of the harmlessness of any drug you might be selling them. I can well understand your urgent desire to effect trade with any one of the major groups of the Compact, but as you're aware, under the Compact's own rulings, the trade of foodstuffs and pharmaceuticals are among the last to get officially sanctioned because of the ramifications. There will be no replacement cargo sent out. I have stopped any authorization on future shipments. John, I don't think even I can protect your ass on this one."

Thomas forced himself to remain within the lens' focus for the view screen, inwardly seething, outwardly calm, finding it impossible to argue with an ages' long interval between transmission and reception. He found himself blinking rapidly as if he could time the minutes flowing past. President Mitchell seemed to move in strobelike flashes, out of sync with what he was saying. When Mitchell's voice had halted, he sat quietly for another long moment.

"You don't need to protect my ass, Mr. President. It's been my job to convince the Compact that we are a developing, responsible, sentient race which deserves membership here and not just a stop on the galactic food chain. I have sat in my office, doing my job years before you even thought of running for your office. My ass, as you so elegantly put it, was on the line some thirty years ago. As far as replacing the shipment, I don't think you want to tell the Choyan that we don't want to deal with them any longer. We have finally established a foothold of value with them, and I won't let you stop that. If I have to, I'll go to the Compact to get authority. All I have to do is tell them that this drug is needed by the Choyan, that it's a restorative that will keep their pilots flying, and the Compact will crack you open like an egg. But I think," and Thomas leaned forward, lowering his voice a little, "you won't want that, because we'll lose whatever advantage we have now. The Choyan predicament will become public, and they're a very private people, Mitchell. Very private. What I have begun between us is a bond which will prove absolutely invaluable to us in the coming years, and I won't let you ruin that."

In the next lapse, Thomas could see Mitchell listening closely, and, at the same time, noticed his attention diverted off-screen. There, Thomas realized, must sit the head of the EC, or someone of like stature.

Mitchell finally replied, "Am I to understand that the Choyan have asked you for utmost confidentiality in this matter?"

"Yes."

An incredibly long wait for his one word answer. Then, Mitchell put his shoulders to the back of his antique, bullet-proof chair. "In making that request, the Choyan have assumed full responsibility for the consequences of this commerce. Under those conditions, providing we will be allowed to conduct field surveys and tests in the future to protect our own interests, we will allow you to continue to conduct business." Mitchell scratched an eyebrow. "Don't make us pimps, Thomas."

"I won't, sir." Thomas waited, out of courtesy, but he knew the president's last words had been both a warning and a signoff.

Mitchell's request had been pointed toward the future. From where Thomas sat, it was already too late.

*　　*　　*

Panshinea woke just after dawn, his head aching, his dreams fading so quickly that he was not even sure if he had had any. His limbs responded woodenly as he got out of bed and he stood unsteadily, gathering strength to keep his balance. His tongue felt dry and heavy and he cleared his throat several times. Too much wine, he thought, though he had a head for wine and the fruits of the vine did not affect Choyan as it did many of the races of the galaxies. Still, there was no denying he throbbed and suffered, the sensation a most unpleasant one.

Too much Imperial Gold, he thought, and before the thought was spent, he knew he was wrong.

He stumbled out of the bedroom, to the communications console in the corner of the suite's living room. He kicked aside the small, wooden-framed ottoman irritably as he banged a shin on its corner. It skidded away from its companion chair and table and he skirted it a second time, weaving toward the console.

Gathon had the day's agenda already posted. Panshinea looked at it in despair. As full as he had been, he was that empty now, and as he eyed the meetings and negotiations awaiting him, fear pulsed through him. How could he face them, face them down, without those instincts and intuitions which would give him the key to his opponents, to the compromises they would accept and the ones they would not—which gave him the foresight to know the future to which Cho should be guided. How could he function? He had nothing on which to draw. It had seeped out of him in the darkest hours of the night, and he had not even felt it go.

He could cancel the majority of his appointments, postponing them for another day or two. But there were meetings here which had already been postponed past prudence, and he knew he must meet those obligations. One or two of those, he might be able to bluff out—after all, this was his career. There were things ingrained in him down to the very bone which even the loss of *bahdur* ought not to be able to negate.

Even as Pan leaned over the console, looking at the display of the agenda, he felt as though he were disconnected, unable to stand because he was nothing more than a shell of himself, and that shell had begun to collapse, to implode, from outside gravity and pressure.

He took a step back from the console and half-fell, half-sat, on the edge of his divan. His head suffered another lingering throb as he shouted for Gathon. The com came on at the sounds of his voices, and after a moment, he heard the blurred response.

"Attend me."

He heard no affirmative or denial as the com went quiet. It would be a few moments. Gathon had his private apartments several levels below and at this time of day, though the minister would normally be up and around, Pan did not doubt the elder Choya was probably napping late. Pan thrust himself to his feet and got himself cleaned and dressed, feeling as wobbly as a newborn, before a soft knock issued on the door to his suite. Gathon came in without further preamble.

"Sire. Is there a problem?"

Panshinea finished the lacings on the cuff of his shirt before looking up. He had braced one hip against the back of the divan to keep himself steady although the shower had refreshed him somewhat. He cleared his throat. "I've altered the agenda, you will want to go over it." He cast a look out his window. It was still so early the sky had barely lightened. Perhaps it would be a dull day throughout, as dull and leaden as he felt. "And I want you to find me another pair."

Gathon had paused by the desk console, his attention caught by the deletions on the appointment display, and he barely looked up. "Pair?"

"I'm spent already, I've done nothing! Go down to the tech schools in the Western quarter, you should find a handful or two of youths readying for classes. Coax them back with you."

"Panshinea," Gathon protested, scandalized. "It's impossible. What you ask is risky enough at night, but in broad daylight—"

"I don't ask. I order. I demand! I can't function like this."

Gathon drew himself up, all brittle strength and indignity, his yellowing dark hair combed hastily back from his forehead, his eyes watery from too little sleep. "I can't do this, Pan. You'll have to make do for today. I'll handle the cancellations—" He put his hand out to further adjust the schedule, and Pan grabbed him by the wrist, halting his movement in midair.

"There are some meetings I must take today, or they will sue for tacit agreement, citing the many cancellations. I won't be talked about, Gathon, as finished. I am not done, not yet." Pan flung the other's arm aside.

Gathon winced slightly. He put his chin out. "What do you wish me to do, that I am able to do?"

"You refuse to procure for me?"

"Under these circumstances, yes." Gathon looked as if he might shatter under Panshinea's glare, but he would not bend.

Pan's mouth had stayed dry, now it felt as if his lips were cracking. The momentary flare of strength had gone, leaving him feeling weaker than ever. He softened his voices. "Gathon, I can't do this without you."

"I am afraid, sire, that you will have to. If you will ignore my advice and counsel, all I can do is stand aside."

"I don't want you to stand aside! I need you with me. I need to . . ." Pan swung around. "Cho takes all I have. There has to be a way—"

Gathon said nothing, his eyes wary as he watched.

"Don't stare at me so." Panshinea found a chair and perched on it, rather than fall to the floor in front of the minister. "What would you have me do?"

"I would have you straighten your jacket, put on your boots, go downstairs and get a breakfast down your gullet, then go to the throne room and take your appointments. Do you think they're thinking of you, Pan? No, by God-in-all, they're standing down there in the waiting room, after a body search, knees knocking, wondering if their story is good enough, their evidence compelling enough, wondering about *themselves*. It's the way of the world, Emperor. We're all egocentric."

"And not one of them wonders about me."

"Perhaps one or two, but you are more than *bahdur,* we all are. Use your mind, your training, your vast experience. This is your throne. Assert yourself."

Every word drummed hollowly somewhere inside of him. Pan rubbed his brow. "Is that what you would do?"

There was a moment's pause. Gathon answered slowly, "I don't know what I would do. I thank God I don't have to."

Even breakfast sounded like a challenge Panshinea did not wish to face. There would be his staff, reports from the guard, other informal meetings that were not on the agenda, and he would have to handle them all. His stomach, however, rumbled and clenched slightly, reminding him that his body had needs he would do well to meet. He looked up and saw the bureau against the farthest wall of his suite, a drawer slightly ajar.

He remembered the boost.

He licked his chapped mouth, remembering the gritty taste of it in his wine. Even as he spoke, the intensity of his attention drew Gathon's stare to the far end of the room, to the drawer. "Perhaps all this is for nothing, Gathon. Perhaps I have an answer." He got up, bounded to the drawer, and pulled out the container Qativar had left.

"Pan, don't."

He pulled a clean wineglass out of its rack and tapped a packet into the bottom of it. "We have all the evidence that this is the restorative the House of Tezar says it is."

"We have evidence that it is addictive enough to wreck a city, a civilization! Where has your mind been the past weeks? Palaton taunts you from boost dens, daring you to act, to help your people, to outlaw boost—Pan, you cannot do this."

Pan's anger, of which he never seemed emptied, blazed. "Palaton is a bug which, once he stops scampering around long enough, I will squash."

"Palaton is *right*."

Gathon stood next to him, reaching for the ever-present decanter of Imperial Gold even as Pan grabbed for it. Their hands collided and Panshinea reacted with the fury that had been building out of his empty center. The back of his hand cracked across Gathon's face.

The elder flew back as if hit by a cannonball. Going down, the divan's ottoman acted as if it might stop the fall, carved legs meeting the back of Gathon's head with a sickening smack.

The room went deadly quiet.

Panshinea did not move for a long moment. When he did, it was to pour the wine into the goblet, swirl it around, and drain it, then pour again to catch the dregs of the powder which had not dissolved. He set the glass down and crossed to Gathon, who had not stirred.

There was very little blood, as if his aged and wiry body could not have spared anything. No breath. No blush of life or anger or betrayal in his face except for the bruise where Pan had hit him. The eyes stared, wide and sightless, at him.

Panshinea lifted the body off the small ottoman. Its wooden frame had sharp corners, had nicked his shins more than once, the cushioned center the only thing soft or comforting about it . . . and that cushioned center was now soaked with blood.

Choyan were dreadfully hard to kill by hitting them on the head. The horn crown which protected their brow and their dual brainpan ran down the back of their skull. Gathon's had grown thin and brittle with his advanced age. It had done nothing to protect him from this blow. Pan couldn't have killed him more surely if he'd picked up the furniture and purposely caved his head in. He sucked in his breath and laid Gathon gently on the floor.

He was alone now.

The warmth of the wine began to course through his stomach and his feeling. He ought to have a tear or two for Gathon. He ought to be able to find that.

Nothing answered him.

Finally, he walked away, backward, until he reached the bureau, one hip bumping its solid surface. The wineglass rocked. Pan reached out to retrieve it, and swallowed the liquid down automatically. When he could look away from the stillness that had been Gathon, he saw the empty container. He ought to do something about that. He would need more boost until he could find someone he could trust to help him as he'd trusted Jorana, and Gathon.

The com came on, startling him.

"Sire, Qativar is here, requesting a moment of your time before official audiences start. He does not have an appointment—"

"Allow him up. I'll see him privately." Panshinea began to burn with power, felt the confidence start to surge through his veins. There was a fated convenience to this visit. He would use it: Gathon was right in that he held it in his power to outlaw boost. He had the House of Tezar in the palm of his hand. Of course, a secondary market would spring up; that was inevitable if he banned the drug, but if Vihtirne and Qativar wished to build a legitimate House, they would need a solid foundation.

They would be wise to curry his favor.

He had them just where he wanted them.

Chapter 30

A thump jolted Jorana out of her cold-laced sleep. She sat up, blinking her eyes in the dim surroundings of the storeroom, saw the door shut like a beacon closing down, and realized it had been open. She cursed herself for sleep-dulled reflexes, knowing she had just missed an opportunity to escape. Her eyes adjusted to the minimal light and saw a rolled-up rug settling not far from her makeshift bed. She recognized the color and weave. It had been one of many area rugs in Panshinea's private suite. With dismay she saw a black dampness seeping from it, darker than the other shadows pooling in the room.

Worse, though, was the aura of death which rose from it like a fog. Hesitantly, Jorana crawled over on her hands and knees and peeled back a corner of the rug. She sat back with a stifled cry, as both the sight and the feel of a painful, shocking, unexpected death hit her.

"Gathon. Poor Gathon. Who did this to you?" A warm river of feeling cascaded down her face. Jorana scrubbed the tears away awkwardly. She cried too easily now, flooded with hormones she was too often at odds with. He did not need her tears now. It was too late for him.

Had it been Qativar who'd killed him? Why, when Gathon could have been removed so many other ways?

She knew she was dealing with ambitious Choyan, ruthless and driven, but this—No. Even as she thought it, she knew she was wrong. Gathon would never have left his post voluntarily. The throne of Cho had been his life, though few not intimate with the workings of the palace would have targeted him in order to usurp that throne. His death could not have been purposeful.

No. Not unless Qativar had gone to get Panshinea and dealt with Gathon instead. This rug was from Pan's quarters, after all. Hesitantly she ran her palm over Gathon's face, not touching the cooling skin, but attempting to read the aura more closely. The bruising along the jawline had not been enough to have killed him, but had driven him back, perhaps into another blow or a fall. She had seen enough postmortem wounds to recognize the bleeding pattern of the contusion. Her hand skimmed the surface of his face.

Jorana touched another's signature and snatched her fingers back, folding her hand up quickly, denying what she had felt, jolted into her consciousness. She would not have believed it if she had been told by Gathon himself.

Her training, to protect the throne at all costs, rose in her now. She could disperse the signature aura, but doubted it was necessary. Weak, it was already thinning, and even the most competent hound would have difficulty recognizing it an hour from now. Jorana worried at a tooth, then moved Gathon's face ever so gently to look at his damp and matted hair.

The deathblow had come from the rear, where the rug was most sodden, though bleeding had long since stopped, when the heart itself had stopped. She did not need more than a probing touch or two to identify bone fragments shifting, the dome crushed. She flipped the rug back into place, hiding her old friend's face.

She looked at the locked door, and crept back to the cushioned bedding where she had fashioned a nest of sorts, warmth of a kind, on the hard floor. She had thought perhaps they'd let her live; now she knew better. She would be hostage to a purpose, but when that purpose was gone, she would be disposed of, just as Qativar had decided to dispose of another of Panshinea's kills. Her life would be of no more value to anybody and, like Gathon's body, perhaps more valuable as a corpse.

She wondered if Panshinea knew of the destructive spiral he'd begun, and how far into it he'd fallen . . . and where the bottom was likely to be. He must have plunged farther than she thought, to have been so careless as to have left Gathon's body where Qativar might find it. As for Qativar's plans for herself and the emperor, she had no illusions. Perhaps they'd die together, but she realized that she was little more than a pawn in his ultimate destruction and that she would be used where Qativar needed her the most.

She tucked a corner of a blanket under her chin to stave off the chill which crept inexorably toward her, spread by the cooling body.

Poor Gathon. Poor her.

"You did *what?*" Vihtirne said, points of color high on her face. It was the first real color he'd seen appear on it.

"Stowed Gathon's body down below with Jorana, but we'll have to move him soon, get him into cryo as soon as possible. I want that body saved. Pan thinks—" and Qativar paused dramatically, "he actually thinks that this puts us in collusion with him. He threatened to have boost outlawed, to have the House of Tezars shut down, as if he still had enough power to do such a thing." Qativar put a finger to his mouth, smiling. "He discounts us—"

"And Congress," Vihtirne said coolly.

"Not to mention Congress." He paced the rooms which had been turned into their offices, skirting consoles and readouts, reversing direction before the storage closets and filing cabinets, their racks empty of the diskettes which would be laid to rest there.

"Someone will miss Gathon soon."

"Pan plans to have him be sick in his rooms for a few days, then, like Jorana, gone, abandoning his emperor. His disappearance will cause a great deal of public speculation, but there will be no real proof by then of any wrongdoing. No one would suspect Panshinea of killing Gathon. The old Choya has been his minister and father figure for decades. If anyone believes the defection story, it simply weakens Pan that much more for us to take down. As for the boost . . ." He mused, half-aware of her.

"We have a problem there."

Now Vihtirne had Qativar's full attention. "That cargo jettisoned in Chaos happened to have been our shipment. Thomas has sent word that he's pressing production but there will be a delay. We don't have adequate supplies, Q, to enslave the world."

He ignored her ironic tone. "But he does expect to make shipment."

"Shortly. It's to our advantage to synthesize this as soon as possible. Our labs are having little success with identifying it as yet. Perhaps we could persuade Ambassador Thomas to be a little more cooperative."

Qativar answered, "I haven't the time. Use your charms on him, Vih. Remind him that we know he has Rand and that hiding a criminal from trial and prosecution is a Compact offense."

"He won't like that."

"I don't care if he likes it or not! He's a drug runner in Compact eyes if they find out what he's doing here. I'll get what I want from him, when I want it from him, or he will regret it."

Vihtirne smiled briefly. "Perhaps you had better explain that to him."

Qativar paused, composing himself. He ran a hand over his brow, brushing his thick hair back into place. He looked at her. "Is this something you think you cannot handle?"

"Why, no, but—"

"Then I suggest you handle it. I will be busy with other affairs. I have to cover half a continent this morning. Leave our guests alone, I'll have arrangements made for both of them shortly."

He took some small satisfaction in her look of surprise as he left.

*   *   *

Palaton woke on cold, damp ground, his mind still fogged with dreams that he had had which were not dreams, but insistent sendings from the Prophet. She hounded him now on a nightly basis and he continued to resist though he did not know how much longer he could do so, if it only meant a full night's sleep.

Rufeen leaned over him, a mug in her hand. Its steam smelled familiar and inviting. She pushed it into his hand. "You looked like you could use a cup."

"Thanks." He struggled to sit up, *bren* to his lips and washing down his throat with a bitter, scalding welcome. "How's Hathord?"

"Up and about. We let you sleep in. You were thrashing around."

"Thanks. I needed the rest." Which he did not get, but would not admit to Rufeen. Palaton stretched. The cloud cover overhead looked thicker and denser toward Charolon, but hung thick enough even here to disguise their movements. He would have been disappointed in them if they had let him sleep the morning away. He tossed down his drink and stood, feeling its flavor infuse him with well-being.

They had decided to hit the depot in the early morning. Night would have been more favorable if they had had weapons, been sound, and had time to scope the place out, but they had not. Therefore, the gray light of dawn seemed preferable for an attack that would require coordination and wit.

Hat strolled into view, his jacket wet and nearly devoid of bloodstains, a bag full of fresh greens in his hand. "Breakfast," he announced as he shrugged out of his jacket, laying it over a rock for whatever drying it could do.

"Make it quickly."

"A simmering would be nice, but your wish is my command." Hat stooped over a pot of boiling water and dropped in the newly washed vegetables. "We're at the leading edge of another storm. It should be overcast enough for your liking before we're done eating."

"Good." Palaton eyed the overhead sky. "We're due for a break."

That wish, too, seemed to be at his command. The depot was not carrying personnel. Rufeen had a tricky moment at the gate, but then they were in. One hangar held a four-seat skimmer, reminiscent of a flight school's trainer craft. There was no runway, but that did not stop the three *tezars*. A long flat meadow or wind-cut plateau would do just as well. They were in the air, cruising in under the network of security any Choyan city held, long before the skim craft would be missed.

Palaton let Rufeen pilot. Hat was still a little sore around the flank and as for himself, he was too uneasy at the stick. His restlessness would have translated itself as the light craft rode the winds and thermal ridges of the countryside. This was just such a plane as Traskar had flown, and thinking of it worried Palaton.

He did not know how Traskar had died. He wished that he did, for then the burden of the Choya's death would not gnaw at him. He knew now that the bitter tang to the *bahdur* which had bled so furiously out of the disabled pilot was the taste of boost, that Traskar had not trusted his own abilities. Whether his attempt to cauterize the flood of power had saved Traskar, who then gave his life to shield Palaton he would never know. Had he been successful? Had Traskar died because it had been his choice, or because the power bleed, had brought him down, or because the boost had sent him into convulsions as it had the Blue Ridge cadet? There were no answers to his questions, and riding in the skimmer now only made him that much more aware of it.

He missed Rand, more than he liked to admit, and likened himself to Traskar. Rand was his missing arm, his shield arm, that which made him complete. When he used the *bahdur* they had shared, he fought the feeling that he, too, was bleeding to death, that the soulfire roared out of him like a flashflood seeking . . . Rand? On his good days, he thought perhaps it was seeking. On his bad days, he thought only that it was leaving, burning out, and he would face that ultimate day all *tezars* faced and feared.

"Deep thoughts," said Rufeen, looking back over her shoulder at him.

"How do you know?"

"You've been quiet all morning. When I missed catching that last thermal and we dropped twenty feet, you didn't twitch."

He hadn't even felt it. Palaton shook himself and moved into the front seat, next to Rufeen. Hat pulled himself in tightly to let Palaton pass, then stretched back out with a noise that was more snore than sigh.

"How much farther?"

Rufeen put a thumb down. Palaton looked out the cockpit window at the patchwork countryside. He could see the grazing samdrens, their spotted coats like shadowy clouds below. They were over the dairylands.

"Find a place to put it down."

"And hike for two days? I thought I'd wait for signs of civilization first."

They traded looks. Palaton shrugged. "If you can stay off the nets."

"Aye, sir," she responded.

He sat back in the copilot's seat. and watched their shadow race along the ground below them. They had outrun the storm's edge hours ago, and the sun gave them the outlines of a bird skimming the earth. After a marked length of time, the instrument panel began to respond, and he could see a township on the horizon.

"Rufeen," he warned, but she'd already reacted, pulling the skimmer about and under the security network, so low to the ground he worried about sudden hillocks and too tall trees. It was from a pilot's instinct he wouldn't have been worried if he'd been at the controls. He made a poor passenger, he reflected. Their instrumentation told them what they needed to know, locating a center of unusual activity and another landing strip where there shouldn't have been one. It also held a huge cradle berth, and that had to be a launch for a shuttle.

She brought them down in another meadow, taxiing to the edge of a grove where even overhead surveillance would have trouble spotting them. When they got out, Rufeen looked the craft over.

"Wish I had a cover."

A screen would have been convenient, but they hadn't had time to procure one. Palaton said, "By the time they know to look, we won't be here."

Hat had pulled their jet sleds out of the craft's slim belly. "Fuel cells are still holding a good charge," he announced. He fired them up and left them idling while Palaton told them what he expected of them.

Rufeen listened gravely, but wordlessly. Action suited her methodology. It was Hat he expected to protest, but although his friend stood, chin down and listening, he did not say a word. When they had made their plan and agreed on it, they each claimed their jet sled and made themselves comfortable. It was then Hat spoke.

"For Blue Ridge," he said.

"For Blue Ridge," they echoed.

The outbuildings of the manufacturing center were old, well-maintained but not extraordinary. If the need to produce more lactose powder to cut boost had pumped new life into the facility, it was not readily apparent. The outlying security fences relied on sonics, more for animals than Choyan, and they got through it with minimum discomfort. Once in the lee of the outbuildings, they stowed their jet sleds and circled the perimeter of the main labs.

Rufeen gave a nod to the berth, across the quad but fairly visible from where they stood. "They're preparing for incoming."

"This is no port," Palaton argued, thinking of the need for clearance.

"None needed if it's from one of the bay stations or Galern."

The bay stations in permanent orbit were for repairs of the deep space cruisers, weather monitoring, and early warning. But as for Galern . . . Palaton knew that the House of Sky had extensive mining rights on the outer moon. He did not answer Rufeen and from the grim look on her face, he knew that she thought as he did. The mining venture would successfully hide any smuggling unless investigation were called for. Even then, it was probable Vihtirne had a smoke screen set up that would make tracing the off-world pipeline difficult.

"We need to take out the berth, if nothing else."

They eyed the concrete cradle. Not only did they have an extensive amount of open space to cross to get to it, but its configuration alone made the operation formidable.

Hat offered, "I have a grenade."

"You have a what?"

He blinked at Palaton. "A grenade. I bought one last week."

"Along with tubers and greens, I suppose," remarked Rufeen dryly.

"It doesn't matter. Placed properly . . ." Palaton leaned around the corner of the building, taking in the layout of the berthing cradle. He put his hand out. "Give it to me."

Hat hesitated. "You know how to activate it?"

Rufeen frowned and opened her mouth, but Palaton interrupted her gently, saying, "I was a combat pilot, Hat. Although I prefer strafing, I have been known to lob a grenade or two under duress." Actually, truth be told, he preferred to stay in orbit and drop war planes out of the cargo hatch of a mother ship, but he could handle what he'd told Hat he could.

Hat took a carefully wrapped bundle out of his knapsack and passed it over.

"Holy mother," said Rufeen as Palaton unwrapped it. "You've been carrying that around?"

Hat looked innocently at her. "I was told it was perfectly safe until activated."

Safe was a relative term, but since Rufeen looked shocked practically wordless, Palaton decided not to argue the matter with Hat. He had wondered whether the grenade would be powerful enough if placed strategically. Now he merely wondered if he'd have time enough to get out of the way before it blew. He looked at the timer. "Actually, Hat, this is more of a bomb with a fairly unsophisticated timing device. You're lucky you didn't blow our heads off carrying it around."

Hat's look of innocence became distressed. "I didn't know—"

"That's the trouble with picking something off the street," Rufeen said. "You never know where it's been. Give it here, Boss, and I'll be back in a nanosecond."

"No. I want the two of you here and there," he pointed, "to cover me."

Her good-natured face froze. "I think you're missing the point. I'm placing that."

"No."

"I'm expendable. You're not."

"This is my flight. You're along for the ride."

They stood toe-to-toe. "This," Rufeen drawled, "is for all of Cho. Do you think I'd risk my worthless hide just because you wanted to get even with Pan?"

A thick arm moved like a wedge between them. "It's my bomb. I'll do what I want to with it."

They both looked down at him, his Earthan height less than theirs. "You're wounded," Palaton noted.

"And you haven't a clue about the timer," Rufeen added.

Hat took a step back. "All right, then. I'm with Rufeen. She should go."

"This is not up for discussion. But if it is, I'd say I should go because I've got the bomb in hand."

Rufeen looked down as his fingers wrapped white-knuckle tight around the oblong object. She met his eyes. "Okay. We stand around much longer, and we'll draw attention." She elbowed Hat. "You stay here, I'll take up the angle over there. And, Palaton—"

"Ummm?"

"You better be able to run a hell of a lot faster than you look like you can." With that parting shot, she motivated her muscular form across the quad to take up her position.

Palaton said quietly to Hat, "If anything happens, I want you to get out. Understand?"

"But—"

"No buts. You have the capability to survive all this, better than the two of us. You're valuable to Cho's future. You're a teacher, a maestro. You remember that. And see if you can help Rindalan and Jorana if they should ever need it."

Hat swallowed tightly. "All right."

"I'm going to place the bomb, but I'm also going to start a distraction when I enter staging. They'll be boiling out of there like ants out of a hill, if they have any kind of staff there at all. Keep them pinned down. I'll be climbing."

"All right," Hat said again.

"See you in a few minutes." Palaton patted him gently on the shoulder and began to make his way across the quad.

He did not have a distraction in mind, but the walk would take him six or seven minutes, even without being circumspect. He should have something figured out by the time he reached the staging area of the berth.

There had been activity aplenty on the quad earlier. He could read mixed auras, nearly faded, nothing indentifiable or remarkable, crisscrossing the area. There were transports parked at the airstrip's edge. He wondered if he were catching Trevon the Black on a busy distribution day. So much the better. He planned to make his visit as inconvenient as possible.

The massive staging doors were open. He could hear muted voices beyond and knew that the elusive work force was busy inside, perhaps loading or unloading cargo bins. He paused inside the hangar doors, gauged his quickest approach to the cradle, and decided what he would have to do.

He threw a flame, a torch of blue heat, his signature, as big as a Choya standing on the shoulder of another, to the far wall of the hangar and let it burn. As the *bahdur* left him to fill the illusion, he made it hot, hot enough to set off any fire sensors in the building—which any decent berthing would definitely have, in case of fuel spill or bad ignition or any one of a dozen other problems he could think of.

He moved in the opposite direction, toward the cradle structure, as alarms went off almost instantaneously. His analogy to Hat had been correct. Like a churned-up hill of insects, workers began pouring out of the warehouse beyond staging, through and out of the building. No notice was taken of him. He made it up into the berth itself, climbing the armature, and toward the most vulnerable part of the placement equipment for the shuttle's cradle.

He placed the bomb, checking the timer setting. Unsophisticated had not been correct. Downright primitive. Analog numbers began to flash as soon as he activated it. Palaton slid, not climbed, his way down the concrete arch. He hit the ground running, shouting, "Fire!" along with the other workers who had decided to evacuate the building rather than put out the unquenchable flame.

He was a stride outside, when the remarkable tones of voices he knew well hit him. "Deactivate the sprinkler system! The bins are waterproof. Quit running you fools! That's no fire, that's a sending!"

Palaton turned despite his instincts. He came back a stride and halted on the threshold, his tall form parting the sea of fleeing workers, and looked to see if he had indeed recognized the speaker.

Their gazes met across staging. He was dressed in black, black with a silver piping, his conceit always in clothes, his jaw tight with contempt for the Flame facing him. No doubt they had called him Trevon the Black because of his suits.

Qativar fairly shook with rage. "Get him!"

Palaton smiled, then turned and ran with the tide of exodus. Halfway across the quad, the ground to the left of him exploded with enforcer fire. A worker stumbled with a howling cry and rolled. Palaton sprinted past him and angled toward Hat as Rufeen fired back. Her shot, however, intentionally went wide of its mark.

Like an echo of her shot that grew and grew until it

swallowed the world immediately around it, the bomb blew. The force of the blast lifted Palaton off his feet. He could feel the heat, the intensity, his horn crown thundering with the sound of it as it flung his body carelessly across the open ground.

He thudded into Hat who grunted and fell back under him. For a moment they were tangled and then Palaton got up on one knee. He could see Qativar stagger back to his feet, away from staging and the berth, its face all black, billowing smoke and orange flame, debris still floating to earth about Qativar in smoldering meteorites. No shuttle would be received or launched from here in quite a while. Palaton unholstered his enforcer and put a discouraging beam into the staging doorway, adding to the confusion.

Qativar let out a hop of frustration and irritation, shouting, "Get in there and save the cargo!" He grabbed at the stunned workers near him, hauling them to their feet, shoving them back into the smoke. "Get in there! Get those bins out the back!" He turned, still howling with anger, shooting wildly across the quad.

Rufeen, seeing Palaton in the clear, had started back to join them. It caught her. She went down, arms flailing, enforcer falling from her limp hand.

Palaton watched her get back to her feet and run, but not toward them. Away from them, decoying, determined not to draw fire to them.

Hat started to bolt after her. Palaton caught him and held him tightly.

"Where's she going?"

"Away from us."

Hunched and cramped over in pain, she wove across the quad. Qativar fired twice more. The first shot clipped the ground at her booted feet. The second sheared off one of his own men, hitting her as well. One screamed, the other did not, before the momentum of their fall took them out of range.

Palaton wrestled Hat around the corner. "Go get the sleds!"

"Rufi—"

"I'll get Rufeen. You get the sleds." Patiently, as he would to a child, to Hathord who'd never been in combat, even though he was a *tezar*. "Now."

He did not wait to see if Hat comprehended. There was no way he was going to leave Rufeen for Qativar's untender mercies. Angling around the building, away from the quad, he ran, sore and bruised, as he'd run from the bomb blast. Halfway around the building, Palaton realized he still gripped his weapon in his hand.

The outbuilding must have been a storage shed. It was mercifully compact. He reached its lee side, its shadowed edge, breathing hard, and saw Rufeen's sprawled form. His pulse thundered in his neck, he knew his body was pumping *bahdur* like it was pumping adrenaline. He built an illusion of his friend, blood and all, and left it in the sunlight for Qativar to see. Then he went to her and managed to get his shoulder under her flank, pulling her up and over in a lift.

She moaned. "Don't. Be. Stupid."

"Save your breath." Palaton took a step, felt his knees wobble. He took a deep breath and filled his body with power, felt himself shimmer and burn with it. If anyone looked, they would see a blue flame striding with its burden.

He carried her the length of the building and then cut across to where they had secreted the transports. Every step was deliberate, every movement dampened by the warm blood trickling onto him. The shallow breath from her face tickled his temple, her moans nearly inaudible. She lived and died with every heartbeat, every step, he took.

Hat met them. His face went dead white as Palaton bent over and laid Rufeen upon a sled. The Earthan had hitched two together, figuring that Rufeen would be disabled. He bit his lip, hissing with shock. He looked up at Palaton.

"I don't know," Palaton answered his silent query.

"Where do we go?" Hat shuddered, put a hand to his shoulder, and brought his palm away bloody. He looked at it in surprise.

Then Palaton saw the two bodies slumped against the side of the building.

"They were here," Hat said. "I had to do something." He put a hand on his shoulder again, wincing in pain.

The *bahdur* left Palaton so suddenly it was as if everything in the world had come to a chill and crashing halt. He took a deep, quavering breath.

Rufeen was dying. Hat had been shot a second time. He'd just expended a lifetime's worth of power. He had no choice. He had to go where he knew they would be cared for, where they would be welcome and hidden. Sled to skimmer. They might make it in time.

He helped Hat onto a sled and strapped him in. "South," he answered. "To Bayalak."

"The Prophet?"

Palaton did not answer again as he mounted the jet sled and roared it into motion. Hat leaned against the steering wheel, following.

If she was any kind of prophet at all, she would know they were coming and be ready.

Chapter 31

Qativar climbed into the control tower by the emergency stairs, the main stairwell having been cracked open like an eggshell by the blast. The rest of the tower seemed operative as he pulled himself into instrumentation.

The Choya'i taking readings turned a pale face to him. "Sir?"

"Find them!" He stabbed a hand at the readings from her console.

"Who, sir?" Her head swiveled back and forth on her neck as she scanned the board, her hands moving uncertainly across.

"Pilots. They have to have an aircraft out there. They came in to sabotage us. I want them tracked!" Rage boiled through him.

She seized on his words. "I've had no incoming traffic since set-down yesterday—they must be in a skimmer." One hand went up to adjust her headset as she listened. The other hand danced over her panel now that she had some action to perform other than watching the base disintegrate into havoc around her.

"I don't care how you do it. I just want them found." His anger flowed out of him, a visible aura, but the controller, engrossed in her task, did not seem to notice.

Qativar looked out at what remained of the tower. This unit alone seemed intact. The berthing cradle and staging below smoldered in ruins, smashed open and laid bare. The shuttle had already been transported to its hangar, but it was useless without its launch. Crew scampered at the ground level, trying to put out the fire in the warehouses, but the main warehouse had gone up. Any cargo in there, binned or not, would be ruined. The last shipment from

Galern had gone up in smoke, and the last shipment from Thomas had been jettisoned in Chaos.

He only had what had already been pipelined into the various distribution centers.

He should have killed Palaton in the wreckage of Blue Ridge when he'd had the chance, but Vihtirne had stayed his hand. She had wanted the pilot to live with his humiliation and defeat. She'd convinced Qativar that it was better than death.

He should have killed him.

I'll kill him this time.

"Sir?" The controller looked up, the whites of her eyes showing.

He had spoken aloud. Qativar shifted weight, to lean over her shoulder. "What have you found?"

"I have a heat distortion one clic east—it could be a liftoff. If it is, I won't find anything more. They're staying under the net, too low for instrument reading. And they're gone."

"What do you mean gone?" His fist pounded the console. "What do you mean you can't find them?"

"They're flying too low for the net to pick up readings." The Choya'i's face, already pale, grayed with fear. He could smell it on her, like a perfume. "It's risky, takes a lot of skill. No one would do it unless it were absolutely necessary."

"And they had the skill to do it." He'd gotten one of them, badly unless he missed his guess. But not Palaton. Not the one he needed to demolish. Qativar straightened up, glaring out the control tower windows as if he could see what her instruments could not read.

Vihtirne had talked him into making a grievous error. Now he would have to expend time and cunning to correct it. He dropped a hand on the controller's shoulder. She jumped, startled by the touch, and her breath quickened. "Keep looking. Tell me if you track anything."

She gave a tremulous nod as he made his way back to the emergency stairs. He had two choices now, two courses of action, and despite what Vihtirne might say to him this time, he wouldn't be swayed. He had Jorana, and he had *ruhl.* He would use both as ruthlessly as he had originally planned. Regardless of Vihtirne's objections, he would release the *ruhl* in the water systems they had breached. The chaos, the panic, the blame would fall on Panshinea. He, Qativar, would stand as a lone figure amid the havoc, the wreckage of all that they knew. Cho would turn to him for restoration. The world would be the way he longed for it, no longer subject to the erratic surges of *bahdur*. No one would have it, until he restored it, and then only for the length of time he allowed. It would be reliable as it had never been before, and it would no longer be allowed to stratify Choyan society.

He would do this, was doing it. Soulfire had not saved those he worked against, and could not save them now.

Jorana stared at the muzzle of the enforcer, calculating her chances, as Vihtirne faced her, and her aide struggled to move the rug-wrapped body of the dead minister. Although the storage room stayed winter chill, rigor mortis had set in, and the bundle was cumbersome. She could barely stand to watch the Choya struggle. The irony that Gathon's body would betray in his death all that he had worked to protect and uphold in his life left a harsh taste in her mouth. Asten finally got the stiffened rug over his shoulder and through the threshold. Vihtirne lingered a moment longer. She looked at Jorana.

"Whose child is it?"

"I have no intention of telling you."

Vihtirne gave a brittle smile. "Fool. That, in itself, tells me. Does Palaton know?"

"No." Jorana kept her gaze steady, her heartbeat rhythmic, wondering if Vihtirne's branch of the House of Sky were extremely empathic or not.

Vihtirne responded, "Perhaps." She tilted her head. "I could take it now, if I wanted, because of Nedar."

"Then do so." Jorana kept her chin up, letting the defiance gleam in her eyes.

"There are other purposes."

"Why are you doing this?"

"Again, fool. I had not thought of you as being so naive."

"You already had power as head of Sky. I cannot believe that Qativar's perversions would have anything to offer you." Jorana watched the enforcer.

"My House was useless." Vihtirne half-turned her face

to the door, as if listening to Asten's progress with the body. "If Nedar had had half the ambition Qativar has, none of this would have come about. But he did not. All he cared for was the piloting, and bringing down Palaton. He should have been emperor! The throne was his for the taking. His weakness destroyed him."

"Qativar will destroy us all. You must know that."

"He is the means to the end."

Jorana shifted her weight. "Why don't you take the throne? We've had our share of Choya'i emperors."

A bitter shadow darkened Vihtirne's face. "I am too old now. If I had had the means, the confidence, when I was younger! But I didn't, and it all passed me by when I lost Nedar. All but Qativar. I had no choice but to take the opportunity he gave me."

"You think too little of yourself."

"As, perhaps, you do." Vihtirne stepped back swiftly, across the threshold of the imprisoning room. "I've made my choices, have my loyalties." The door began to seal, framing Vihtirne's face in a diamond for a brief moment. "We all make sacrifices."

Panshinea awoke a second time, a coppery taste in his mouth as though he had bitten his tongue in his sleep. If sleep it could be called, for though his body tired and ached, his mind had not found peace, thoughts racing endlessly about his dreams. The blankets of his bed twisted like cable, drenched with sweat. He disentangled himself and lay for a moment, assailed by crimson visions which could not be true. He got up, found himself fully dressed, and left the bedroom.

A rug was missing. He looked at the bare, tiled floor in some bewilderment. He'd dropped a wineglass on the floor, but it had not broken. It rolled about as his boot brushed it when he passed. Panshinea stooped to pick it up. For an uneasy moment, vertigo swayed him and his aura sense picked up violence and death. He stood, free hand palm down, reading the scene until his stomach sickened. He stood, fighting for balance.

The moment swept by him, unnerved and lost. Not enough sleep, too many dreams. He felt as if he had been searching for something taken out of his soul, ripped out and cast away. Listlessly, he dropped the glass onto the divan and went to the agenda, which had been left on display. Cancellations and deletions filled the screen as if an idiot had played here, decisions made senselessly.

He put in a call to Gathon's rooms. "Gathon! What is this mockery? Get up here as soon as you can.".

His head swam again, and gooseflesh crawled across his arms and the back of his neck. Panshinea put a hand there and rubbed it reflectively. The touch of his fingers chilled him further. The taste in his mouth, he decided, had not been blood but the after dregs of boost. He recalled dropping the wineglass. Pan twirled about, the room swinging around him, none of it seemingly ground in reality, waiting.

Gathon did not answer the private line. He steadied himself and impatiently put out a call on the general palace lines. After long moments, Namen answered cautiously.

"Sire."

"Where is Gathon?"

"Sire, he—he resigned this morning. You passed his resignation along to me. He's gone."

"Gone?" Panshinea drew himself up beside the com, his fingers on the speaker button as if detached from him. His head spun and then throbbed.

"He left early this morning," the head of the guard repeated. "Can I be of any assistance?"

"No. I—" Pan looked across the room, images crowding his mind like a bizarre sending, of blood and murder. He closed his eyes and took his hand off the comline.

He could not have done what he remembered.

When he opened his eyes, he saw the bare tile where a rug normally lay facing him. There was a dissonance in the pattern of the other throw rugs. In the fireplace, ashes glowed where something had recently been burned. He did not remember lighting a fire, but the impression of Qativar throwing in a bloodstained ottoman and torching it filled his vision.

"No!" He scrubbed his hand over his face. "No."

Qativar rolling a rug tightly about a chill and shattered bundle.

No. He would never have turned to Qativar, never.

Pan put a hand out to the console to steady himself, thrust it wrist-deep in packets that rustled as he touched them. He turned to look down.

Boost.

Sparks of red-gold *bahdur* fire crackled throughout as he snatched his hand away. One or two of the packets clung to his hand, fastened there by the static energy of the soulfire. He shook them off, screaming.

The raw sound of his howling reached him, and Panshinea stood, desolate, his throat torn by his fear and grief. He bolted from his apartments and ran into the corridor, calling for Gathon, unable to believe. His voices echoed obscenely off the stone, broken and desperate, all trace of sanity gone.

*   *   *

He brought the skimmer into Bayalak under full speed, winging over the swamps with a speed that boiled the water, bent the trees, sent lingering fogs swirling away. Rufeen had lapsed even from moaning, her face more pale than alabaster. Hat slouched against the fuselage wall near her, his eyes closed, his breathing harsh and shallow, but he moved from time to time, a most un-Hat-like curse issuing whenever he did.

Palaton looked for the security network over Bayalak, found it missing, and came in over the port city, the skimmer engines screaming as he unwound them, setting the plane down with brakes smoking, the light plane bouncing harshly—and then they were down. He popped the front canopy and threw himself out, catching himself feetfirst on the wing. He could swear he felt the metal skin's heat through his boot soles.

She was waiting. Conveyances pushed forward. She was on her feet, leaning on the arm of Father Chirek, the priest who had sent her unknowing into her Change and had been at her side ever since. He brought her forward as med techs opened the side doors and clambered inside, shouting orders at one another.

The Prophet smiled. "It is enough," she said.

He clenched his teeth against warring emotions a moment, then looked at her, though she could not see him. "Do you know that?"

He had meant, do you *see* that.

Dorea's expression changed slightly and she gave a small shrug. "It must be enough to have faith. I *see* very little, in the spectrum of all that has happened and will happen."

He jumped to the tarmac. "So help me God, I'll turn around and fly them out of here if you can't give me a straight answer."

Dorea reached out and touched him. "None of us has a surety on life, Palaton. None of us. But you've given her as good a chance as you could. Let that be enough."

Father Chirek added, "We've done what we can by being here, waiting."

They had, of course. Palaton looked toward the skimmer, watching the techs handing Hathord out the door and bringing a portable créche in for Rufeen. He forced himself not to watch, knowing he could not help any more than he already had. To Chirek, he said, "The network's down."

"For you. It's already back up."

That meant that Chirek and his newly Changed were in total charge of the city now. Bayalak had metamorphosed into something they had all feared once, and now must embrace.

"No one knows."

"Not yet." Chirek made a mouth. He was a mousy Choya, common in every line of his body, dressed in modest colors as befit the clerk's position he'd held in the imperial palace.

The créche rushed past, wheeled by med techs on the run, and disappeared into its conveyance. As Palaton blinked a suddenly misty view away, it surged forward and vanished across the tarmac. The second emergency vehicle followed. He caught a glimpse of Hat through the rear panel portal and raised a hand in salute. Just before it would have been impossible to see, Hat waved weakly back.

The Prophet turned her blind face to him, seeking him out. "You stand alone now."

"Not with you two here," he answered wryly.

"Good. It's time you realized that. We have a lot to talk about. Chirek."

He took her in charge again, leading the way back to the single conveyance waiting for them. As Palaton sat down, the tang of salt air reached him, accented sharply by the smell of the skimmer's engines. He sat back in the car.

"I wouldn't be here, if I hadn't been driven to it," he commented.

"We know that." Father Chirek took the wheel and steered them ably down the landing strip to the security gates.

"All that matters is that you are here." Dorea plucked at her blindfold, then dropped her hands into her lap, twisting her young and slender fingers. The light blue dress she wore looked like bird's wings. "I must talk to you about Rand."

It did not matter if she could see his face or not, he did not want to look at her. She wanted him to bring the manling back so that she could direct the *bahdur,* the Change, and Rand was no longer capable of that.

It was Palaton's power, and he knew he did not want to use it for that. He could not have, at that moment, even if he had wanted to, having spent it on saving Rufeen. But when it returned, and it would, he knew he did not believe in Changing the world the way she did. The way Father Chirek had sacrificed himself for. *Bahdur* belonged in those who had been trained for it, who could understand its dangers and its limitations. The God-blind had no concept of what would happen to them, of what they could do, and because of that, the Change was just as dangerous and insidious as boost.

The only good thing about boost, if there was one, was that it only aided those who had been ingrained with *bahdur* from birth, who had been guided and trained.

"I don't know where Rand is," Palaton said bitterly. "I don't dare move against Qativar openly as long as they have him."

"Qativar doesn't have Rand. He's on Sorrow," the Prophet told him. "And he's in deadly danger."

Chapter 32

Maeva was sleeping in the law library when the clerk of the librarian came to rouse her, disapproval wrinkling his already prunelike face.

"Attorney Polonia, you have a visitor waiting for you in the lobby."

She sat up at the table, dazed, her elbows sore from the books and printouts she'd been leaning on. Desktop screens blinked opalescence at her, the only light in a room that had dimmed into a downtime mode. She'd meant to sleep there, feeling it the only place safe enough, but she had not thought she'd actually escape into slumber. She cleared her throat and straightened her blouse.

"I'm sorry. What—what did you say?"

"You have a visitor in the outer lobby." The librarian's clerk stood shorter than she, lank brown hair thinly combed back behind his ears, and a bow tie bobbed up and down with his Adam's apple. "I believe it to be the Choyan ambassador."

"Rindalan?" She snatched her purse and stood up, the body armor pinched her tightly under one arm as she did so. "I'll be . . . I'll be right there."

The clerk sniffed. "He can wait."

"Don't touch anything," she ordered and bolted out of the private research niche.

She brushed past him, in a hurry for the restroom. Once inside, she laved and took care of her needs as quickly as possible, then straightened her clothes and her armor, trying to imagine how it was he had even found her. She'd left no word, no trace, of where she'd gone, hiding from even Thomas. The law library's research maze had seemed the only logical place to go.

Maeva looked into the bathroom mirror. Her eyes ap-

peared cloudy blue, red-rimmed with worry, and her hair
seemed like lackluster straw. She'd aged in the past few
weeks, but the character she'd hoped for in her face did
not show; only faint lines of fatigue. She grimaced. So much
for mirrors. She'd rather look at herself reflected in Rand's
face, at what she saw in his eyes.

There she saw only beauty, and appreciation, and
perhaps . . . perhaps a certain regard.

Maeva slung her purse and terminal pouch over her
shoulder and made her way out of the lavatory, then downstairs several levels to the lobby. She could see Rindalan
though he could not see her through the paneling, but then
the tall, spindly Choya turned toward her unerringly.

She went through the door.

"Madame attorney."

"Ambassador." She reached out impulsively and took his
wrist, drawing him to one side so he could sit on a bench.

"Is this area safe?"

"To talk? Yes. We're in legal. They take incredible precautions here."

"Good. I have a matter about which I need to speak
with you." He inclined his head gravely. A sparse strand
of chestnut hair fell loose from his massive horn crown. "I
would like to claim attorney/client privilege."

"To do that, I'd have to—"

"Yes. I would like to employ you as my attorney."

Unheard of. Choyan did not need to contract the services
of another species. This had to concern Rand. Perhaps he
had finally found a way to free him. She swallowed. "I
cannot take contract with you if it interferes with previous
obligations." Warningly, in spite of the fact that the lobby
should be secure against recording.

Rindalan looked at her, eyes large and warm. "I can
assure you there will be no conflict."

"Tell me why you think you need an attorney."

"I am about to commit treason most grievous against the
throne of my people."

Maeva rocked back on the bench. Rindalan looked at
her gravely.

"Treason?" she stammered.

"Against my emperor. Does that pose a conflict with
your other contracts?"

"N—no. But I have no familiarity with your civil laws—"

"It doesn't matter. If I am wrong and lose, my life is forfeit. If I am correct and win, I won't need an attorney." Rindalan gave her a tender smile. "Do we have a contract?"

His expression urged the answer out of her. "Yes." She fumbled with her back pouch, getting the terminal out, setting it on her lap and opening it up. "Let me register it. Just a basic representation contract, nothing fancy." She brought up the model contract, affixed her thumb, and asked the ambassador to do likewise.

Bemused, the ambassador took a few minutes to scan the screen before he depressed his print where indicated. He watched as Maeva sent the transmission and waited another second or two to make sure a clear sign came up, along with a registration number.

"Waiting for shock waves?"

She glanced up at Rindalan. "Well . . . I thought somebody might notice who you were." She closed her notebook, thinking that somebody somewhere might well notice later, when the day's entries were logged and reviewed.

"May we talk now?"

"May I suggest we move upstairs, to where I have a research room reserved? It's even more private and a little more comfortable." Not that she minded sitting on marble, but the lobby was chilly and her bottom had begun to feel like part of the stone.

"If I am allowed."

"As a client, you are. I can even request an interview room, if you wish. But those are recorded."

He inclined his head. "Not necessary. However, I would like you to know that time is of the essence."

Settled in the research room, she realized she thought of him as grandfatherly, his manner elegant, reserved, and yet teasing. His mane of hair even reminded her somewhat of her own grandfather, on the side of the family from which her name, Maeva, had come. Her other grandfather had been Italian, from Rhode Island, with a great nose and huge, expressive hands. Her own more delicate features and blonde coloring had come from the maternal side of the family.

He waved a hand over the disarray. "What, if I may ask, were you researching?"

"Habeas corpus," she answered, "mostly, although a lot of this is camouflage."

"Camouflage?"

"Disguise. I was hoping to find something to force Thomas to free Rand, but Thomas has him buried under protective custody, so I haven't been able to make an issue of it. And the rest . . ." Maeva felt her face warm a little in embarrassment. "I've been living and sleeping here. I wanted to make it look like I was busy."

Rindalan put his head back and began to laugh, a warm, hearty laugh. It was the kind of humor that spilled over and finally, she tucked her chin down and laughed, too, although she had been so desperately tired she hadn't thought any could be found in her.

"And now, if you could explain habeas corpus?"

"Oh. It simply means 'holding the body.' In other words, charge the prisoner and try him or free him. But Thomas has gotten around it this time by using the legal fiction of protective custody. Although," she mused, "it's not so much of a fiction."

"If by that you mean that he would be in considerable danger if wandering around, your ambassador is most correct. But that is why I am here. Madame Polonia—"

"Please," she interjected softly. "Call me Maeva."

"Maeva." Rindalan looked amenable at the interruption. "We have to free him as soon as possible."

"That's what I've been trying to do."

"I do not necessarily mean legally."

Maeva took a quick breath. "Ambassador—"

"If you would please. Call me Rindalan, or Rindy, if you like. That's what my friends call me."

"Rindalan. I realize our contract is mostly a screen, but what we're talking about is in direct conflict with my work for Thomas."

He waved about at the clutter a second time. "Yet you were already working on it."

"But not for you. For me. . . ." She paused. "And what does this have to do with a treasonous act?"

Rindalan frowned. The expression not only creased his brow heavily, it deepened his other wrinkles. "I received word this morning that Emperor Panshinea is roaming the halls of the palace in what can only be termed as a mentally depraved state. He is distraught, howling, disoriented, and he cannot be confined or sedated."

"Why not?"

"Because—" Rindalan stopped abruptly. "That is another matter. Trust me, he cannot. Neither can he be restored. Normally, in his lack of capacity, our minister would step in, but Gathon has either resigned or been removed. No sign of him can be found."

She was aware that the heir to the throne had been forced to abdicate, though his reported death had been in error. She knew Palaton was in hiding. "You've got no one running Cho."

"For the moment, yes."

"You're not thinking of putting Rand on the throne."

His face reflected abrupt horror. Then he rearranged his expression to something approximating neutrality. "No, Maeva, that would be unthinkable."

She'd already gathered that.

He shifted in the high-backed, most comfortable chair she could find for him. "Rand's return to Cho could accomplish two things: possible restoration of Panshinea, for reasons I cannot explain to you now, or convincing and enabling Palaton to take the throne; again, for reasons I cannot explain to you now."

"Attorney/client privilege only extends so far, eh."

He lifted a brow. "Even so."

"Thomas will never release Rand."

"So you communicated to me earlier, and I cannot request his release in official standing."

"So, then—"

"I need your help assisting in what your people euphemistically call a jailbreak."

Her chair shifted abruptly under her. Maeva caught herself on the table's edge. "Impossible."

"No, it's possible. To do it, I must exercise some abilities I have not used in many years, and I need your assistance."

"I don't see how I can possibly—" and she stopped, shaking her head. "We're talking the most secured levels of the embassy."

"Do you think, young one, that your embassy is the only

one on Sorrow to have been built in such a way?" Rindalan smiled. "All of us here in the Compact are here, not because we love one another, but because we know that to continue hating one another and acting upon it will destroy us all. The enemy that imprisoned the race of Sorrow is the common enemy that bonded us. Trust is another matter altogether."

"We're talking solid rock!"

"Even so."

"What do you think you can do?"

"First, I would like you to tell me anything and everything you've observed about Rand since his imprisonment here. I will assume he was brought in under cryo and diplomatic pouch as my intelligence shows that is the only activity out of the ordinary in the last few months. I would like to know anything that has occurred in his waking hours."

She was not surprised that Thomas' actions had not gone unobserved. "He's only been awake off and on. The ambassador has him under reduction much of the time."

Rindalan nodded. "That would explain part of my experience. Anything else? Any . . . talents . . . you would consider unusual?"

She thought of Rand caught in the laser fencing, the wounds, and the remarkable healing after. She told the elder Choya of the incident, and he listened carefully, his head inclined, face grave, without interrupting. When she finished, he questioned her.

"A blue network of energy sparks and tracings, you say?"

"Yes. I thought it was the lasers, but I've never seen anything like it."

"Does he remember it?"

"No. And he doesn't seem to have any explanation for the healing either."

"Neither do I." Rindalan tilted his chair back a moment. When he brought it back to the ground, he said, "But I think I have some indication of what I'm looking for. I will have to proceed based on what we know. Can you access his cell any time you like?"

"So far. Thomas could unauthorize me, but he hasn't yet. He's been busy with some other projects, and I don't think he knows what I'm trying to do."

"Then we need to go now."

"Now?"

"Yes." The ambassador stood up. "I have a ground shuttle ready to lift off and once at the bay station, we can pick up any transport we need."

"Hijack a cruiser?"

He wrinkled his nose. "If necessary. Anything you need we can acquire later."

"I'm going with you?"

"Once this goes into motion, we cannot stop."

She stood, gathering her purse and her notepad. On second thought, she lowered her terminal to the library table. She took a deep breath. "Then I'm ready."

Standing in front of the cell, she was not so sure. Rindalan had gravely instructed her on what to say to Rand, making her pronounce a Choyan word again and again until he was satisfied she was saying it properly, then leaving her to make the journey alone. She did not understand why she had to think of Rindy as being with her, as imaging him standing there in the corridor next to her, but she knotted her brow tightly as she did so, waiting for Rand to leave the refresher and meet with her. On that, she'd been lucky. He was out of reduction and up for an exercise period.

She had no idea what the word she was to say to Rand meant, nor how Rindalan thought he could carry out a jailbreak from outside the embassy. She had neither weapon nor plan to her name. Nothing but words . . . and a mental image. She frowned so tightly her head ached.

"You'll wrinkle," commented Rand softly.

She looked up. His hair was still slightly wet and slicked back from his face. He looked thinner and paler yet. He knew that she'd been able to meet with Rindalan, but not that GNask had accosted her, or that she'd eventually fled to the safety of the law library. For all he knew, their last meeting could have happened minutes ago, instead of days and days.

She massaged her forehead with her fingers. "Thanks. How are you feeling?"

"Well enough." His expression was strained, and she had the distinct feeling he was hiding something from her. She noticed he had the white noise generator. He placed it on the floor between them.

"We haven't much time," she told him. "I can't even explain to you why. Rindy says that it's urgent—"

"Rindy? You've seen him again? He's able to help?"

"I'm not sure help is the word for it. Please. You've got to listen."

His turquoise eyes mirrored her anxiety, but he closed his mouth firmly.

"Rindy says that it's urgent you believe what I'm going to tell you. He says you're exhibiting *bahdur*—"

"*What?*"

She repeated the word a second time: "*Bahdur*—God, I hope I said it right. You have *bahdur,* not Palaton's, but your own, and he's going to help you use it to escape. We can't get you out of here quickly any other way."

His mouth tightened. She could not tell whether he understood her or not. As Rindalan had instructed her, Maeva added, "Now, Rindy," and thought of him, a beam of thought, directed through the steel and stone, upward, toward the garden where he'd told her he would be waiting.

Her head ached, then her ears felt an unbearable pressure. Just before she thought she might explode, there was movement in the corridor, a sound like thunder booming, and Rindalan stood next to her. He shook off a faint dusting of blue motes.

He looked pleased. "I have not done that in a score of ages."

Maeva thought her heart would never start beating again. She stared aghast. "What?"

"Teleportation, my dear. A rare art, even among my people."

Rand protested, "Rindy, what are you doing? And in front of her?"

"It's all right, child. She's my attorney. We have privilege. She's got to keep her mouth shut." Rindalan flexed slightly.

"She knows about *bahdur?*"

Rindalan's mouth twisted a little. "Not exactly. I taught her the word, but not the essence of it."

Rand looked about the cell as if searching for a scrap of

sanity. When he looked at them again, it was with a face deeply saddened. "Get out of here while you can."

Rindy shook an age-knobbed finger at him. "We haven't time for arguments. I thought she explained that. It's belief we need. You have *bahdur,* and if you hadn't been so ingrained in self-pity since being locked up here, you'd have realized that on your own. But we have met in dreams, you and I, and I know what I know. What you shared with Palaton may have changed you, just as you are the I'falan—"

"How do you know?"

"Child," and Rindalan looked at him with infinite fondness. "I know as much about you as I possibly can."

Rand straightened. "All right. *Bahdur* does not necessarily mean teleportation."

Maeva felt as though everything were rushing past her. She fought to grasp it. "What is *bahdur?*"

Rand looked at her. "They're a psionic race, Maeva. In fact, their abilities are probably off the scale. It's how they navigate Chaos. It's what their entire society is built on, and the talent is called *bahdur.*" He squared off to Rindalan again. The laser fencing gleamed between them. "But there are different abilities with the talent, and just because you can teleport, doesn't mean I can."

"No. But you can augment me. I can get all three us out of here with a little help."

"Through solid rock."

Rindalan inclined his head.

Maeva said weakly, "That's how he got in."

Rand ignored her. "It's better than rotting here. What do I do?"

"Wait a minute—" Maeva began, but Rindalan grasped her hand.

"Sssh," he admonished. "And think only of my garden. Rand, you must think of our *bahdur,* two streams becoming one. Do not flow into me once you feel weakness, however. That would be going too far."

"I understand."

She wished she did. Maeva closed her eyes. *Oh, beam me up, Scotty,* she thought, and imagined the embassy garden.

* * *

Rand had wanted to protest, but when he saw Maeva hold onto Rindy's hand, as trusting and earnest as a child, he decided that he could not. There was something in what Rindy was hastily trying to convince him of—perhaps he had a remnant of power left in him, enough to aid in what might be his only chance to gain freedom. For that tiny hope alone, he would try.

"Think of me," Rindalan said softly to him, and as he did so, the Choya opened his mind to an image of a garden, nothing such as they had left behind in Charolon, but a small, spare unique area of its own. *Focus on that,* Rindy said to him, but there were no words. He could sense a blue stream bathing the other, cold and clear in power and purity. He reached out to join it.

There was a moment, an aching moment, when he could feel all of them mutating, lifting, changing, and he was with them. Then, like a flicker of vision where vision had gone blind, something distracted him. Something else called him. He mentally turned toward it, and was lost.

Darkness ripped. A chill like ice pierced him. He thought he heard Maeva's voiceless scream. His own heart stopped. They were gone and he was—

Imprisoned.

As in his dreams, many times over, he found himself embedded in the crystal grave of the dead of Sorrow.

Chapter 33

Open air hit Maeva in the face. She flung her eyes wide, found herself clinging to Rindalan in the midst of the tiny embassy garden. Rand was nowhere to be seen. Her throat ached. "He's gone! Oh, God, he's gone."

Rindalan hugged her closely. His two-elbowed arms made the embrace intimate and she had never felt so protected. "Hush," he said to her. "We are still between time and place. He may yet be with us."

But his voice was bleak, and she knew he did not believe it any more than she did.

Had he materialized in solid rock? She shook, despite Rindalan's hold on her, bit her lip, and waited.

rrRusk lurked in orbit around Sorrow. He had not been successful in separating a pilot from the watchful confines of his assignment, but he knew it was only a matter of time. He had left Sorrow's surface to ready the cruiser which GNask often frequented, knowing the ambassador might request flight on a moment's notice, when the salvage request came in.

Cargo, perhaps jettisoned from a recent Chaos loss, had been located. He'd given permission to attempt to recover it. They would, if it proved convenient, file a salvage request with Compact later. It might be garbage, for all rrRusk knew, and if it was, the general had no desire to wrestle Compact red tape in hauling it in. He would simply blast it and leave it where it was.

On the other hand, if it were valuable, rrRusk was of the opinion that what the Compact didn't know, it could not protest. Either way, he felt his actions justifiable.

He sat now on the bridge, eyeing the spy monitors on the various complexes dirtside. His were duplicates of what rested in the Abdrelikan embassy and he did not often take note of the various printouts, readings, and recordings.

This time he did. From within the Terran embassy came an esper reading that was like a lightning bolt, a surge of energy that set his machine to trembling. Then, as quickly, it was gone.

rrRusk sat forward in his chair, staring. He thrummed his barrellike chest with interest. What in muddy hell had that been?

He picked up a readout. Just moments before, the humankind GNask had been most interested in surveying, Maeva Polonia, had entered the embassy wing. Terran humankind were absymally low in the esper scale. Such activity was highly unusual.

He leaned forward to the comline. "Get me Ambassador GNask," he growled.

He had been imprisoned with his eyes open, Rand thought. Like dreams which he remembered only vaguely, his body had slowed almost to a cryogenic pace. If not dead yet, he would be soon, his heart stilled, his lungs slowly eking out the last of their air, his molecular body irretrievably comingled with quartz.

Yet he did not feel dead or dying, and if he was between heartbeats, he felt as though an eternity could pass before the next, before he would begin to feel the failure. He felt expanded, the world about him as thin as a snowflake, a veil of icy coldness. He thought about putting a hand up to his face to see if he could feel his breath, and a wraithlike object moved, whisking by his chin.

Yesss, mooove. . . .

Many voices, whisper-thin, a wind of nearly inaudible tones, brushing past him. Rand tried to step forward, had the sensation of leaving or stretching out of his body, and the body, shape catching up with him.

Yesss . . . come to usss. . . .

Breath as cold as death, a breeze of faint sounds, reaching him, caressing him, pulling him forward, the same attraction which had wrenched him away from Rindalan and Maeva.

What was it?

His unpumping heart leaden in his chest, his body not a

body that he had ever used before, he moved through caverns and walls of crystal. His mind continually pushed out ahead of him, his body catching up with an almost elastic snap, as though he were stretching the atomic bonds of his existence to the limit before they rebounded. He was drawn, inexorably, toward something embedded, like himself, in the quartz.

He found himself terribly afraid to go any closer. Was it his own death he was approaching? Was this his spirit self, torn free from his imprisoned body? What would happen when the two met? Would he then die, horribly, intermingled with cold earth, earth not even of his home world? Who called him? Did he summon himself?

Even as he thought that, he knew better, for the cajoling he answered was incredibly alien. If it was himself, or the *bahdur* remnant still within him, he knew he could not face it.

Feeearrr nooot . . . come to ussss. . . .

The pause between heartbeats passed, even as he moved forward, and his organ struggled horribly to contract and pump as it had been evolved to do. The pain in his chest began like a sharp prickle and grew to a heavy, hurting weight.

He was dying.

An icy veil hung before him. Beyond it he could sense his destination, a gathering of others, voices beckoning to him. He would take a deep breath and gather his strength to pass through it, but he had no breath, and his lungs had begun sharp stabbing pains, reminding him of the urgent need for air.

His chest hurt. His heart quivered as it attempted to beat. His temples began to throb.

He moved toward the veil. Into it, cold, colder than its misty substance. It passed through him, icy fingers touching every part of his being. Was it death itself?

Rand pushed.

He emerged.

The dead of Sorrow moved foward to touch him.

Maeva shuddered. She had been holding her breath, and it had seemed to stretch forever, but now she must breathe. She buried her face in Rindalan's arm.

"He's gone."

"Not yet." The alien moved, tilted his head as though listening, no ears to help him do it, but the attitude of his body told her what he was doing. "Don't give up."

She wondered if it had been a horrible death or if Rand had died instantaneously, trapped in the stone below the embassy. Or perhaps he had made it out to the open air, gone, his molecules stretched out so thin that he was part of the wind?

Rindalan released all but her hand. "Come with me."

He steered her into a walk, then into a run, across the graveled pathways of the embassy, through the barrier which gave before them as though they did not even exist. Was it true—were they somewhere between then and now? She struggled to keep up with the long-striding ambassador as he raced across the parklike grounds, between the trees, down to the river of crystal.

"Here . . ." said Rindalan, then faced downstream. "No. Down there." He fairly sprinted down the riverbank, carrying Maeva with him, she could swear her feet never touched the ground.

When he stopped, he looked down into the frozen waters. She hesitated to look, the grotesqueries of the lost people of Sorrow so distressing to her, but she did.

She gasped, lost her breath, heart thumping, went to her knees beside the quartz.

Rand. Rand, embedded in the crystal with the long dead of another world.

"Do something!" she cried to Rindalan.

The Choyan ambassador leaned forward. "I would," he answered gently. "If I only knew what."

Welcome. You hear us. You see us.

Their voices, so reedy as to be nonexistent, heard not in his ears, but in his skull. Rand put a hand out, insubstantial, not flesh, more feeling, and brushed a nearby cheek gently.

You feel us.

He faced only a grouping of dead. He knew they lay all over Sorrow, in the rivers and lakes along the cities, as if they had been herded into the water and then transformed into a quartzite base which Compact science had not fully been able to analyze. Their alien bodies were and were not a part of the mineral, and only one had ever been allowed to be excavated, but the findings on it had been undetermined.

"I feel you," he said.

We are dead.

"I am dying."

We know. You must listen. You are the first to hear us, though we have tried for . . . the words for time eluded him, but he had a sense of millennia, as only the dead could experience it.

"Who killed you?"

If anything could save him from the laws and dealings of the Compact, it would be that answer, the answer to the mystery of Sorrow. For himself, as well as for others, he felt he had to ask it.

We killed ourselves. Listen.

They filled his mind with images, mothers taking up their children and walking down to the water, fathers and sons, brothers, employers and employees, adversaries, young and old, wanted and unwanted. All. All into the water which bordered their immediate homes, into the chill water one early spring day.

And once there, a single unified flash of their minds changed the fabric of their world, killing and entombing them for eternity.

"Why? *Why?*" He was losing feeling in his own limbs, and his heart felt as though it would explode in his chest, and he reached out. They upheld him.

Listen.

They told him a story not unlike that of Cho, of a people with powers of the mind which could affect their physical world. Of intolerance of the differences of those minds. Wars. Suspicion. Regulation. Rejection. Of an enemy from without which had been repulsed, but which had shown them a mirror of what they had themselves become, and in horror, they knew they were destroying themselves. Would go on to destroy worlds about them if left unchecked.

Warned him of their mistakes.

He thought of Palaton's fear of *bahdur* spreading among the commons. It was not the *bahdur* which would kill Choyan, it was the fear and intolerance.

They patted his face, wiping away tears.

Yes.

He had to, had to remember, to tell. Had to live.

He could not move, all strength gone from him. They supported him. One of them, moving as slowly and yet surely as a glacier, uptilted his chin. Lifted his vision from the caverns of crystal toward the surface of the river and the sun.

He saw Rindalan's face looking down at him.

The aged Choya reached out.

Rand felt them extend his arm, his hand, thrust him upward. His body ached and groaned, heaved up through solids as it became inexorably solid itself. He must weigh more than whole planets.

How could dead people overcome such gravity?

Help us.

His heart gave one last, limp flutter. Rand kept his sight looking upward. What he knew would save Palaton. To save Palaton, he must save himself.

He reached up with one hand, and with his mind, reached down. Touched the *bahdur*. Felt it flare, a nova inside him, an explosion that sent him driving upward.

His hand touched flesh. Warm, living flesh. He clasped it tightly as Rindalan drew him forth from the crystal, birthing him.

Chapter 34

Bay stations surrounding Sorrow were, of necessity, neutral ground. They intercepted incoming deep space flights and ran cargoes and personnel through customs, transferring them to harmless freight shuttles, hopefully precluding open attacks on the Halls of the Compact. They succeeded, but probably only because any one species knew it would be genocide to open fire overtly on the Compact. Retribution would be swift and unrelenting. That did not mean, however, that scurrilous acts and renegades did not abound in the bay stations.

As they came into Bay 2, Rindalan explained to Rand that he hoped to find not only a willing pilot, but an available vessel to take them as quickly as possible to Cho. Rand understood what Maeva did not, that finding a pilot would not be difficult. The *tezars* understood all too keenly that their world hung in a critical balance. It should not be hard to find one who would abandon his or her current contract, House of Tezars or no, to bring them home.

Taking a vessel, on the other hand, would be a bit more difficult. Any deep space craft docked at the bay would already be under orders and unavailable. They would have to commandeer what they wanted, and that would surely draw notice from Compact authorities. They were likely to be pursued all the way to their jump-off into Chaos. And it would take a day or two to gain the acceleration needed. Like blood in the water, that would draw the attention of the Abdreliks and the Ronins. Therefore, it behooved them to be as circumspect as possible in locating a pilot. They did not want their descriptions or needs broadcast too soon after successfully commandeering a vessel.

"You keep saying commandeering," Maeva noted. "What we're doing is stealing."

"Yet another good reason for having my attorney with me," Rindy said cheerfully.

"Not if they arrest me as well."

"We'll have to make sure to stow you away before that happens," Rand told her. "Or we can throw you off with the crew when we take the ship."

"Inside or outside the air lock," she tossed back.

"Preferably inside." Rindy looked at the deck map bayside. "When you two children are done sparring, we need to make some serious plans."

"I thought you'd already made the plans." Maeva tossed her head, and a strand of her hair fell loose across her cheekbone. She stroked it back into place. "I thought you'd already made these arrangements."

Breezily, Rindy answered, "No time." He stabbed a fingernail at the deck map. "There's a way station on level three. We can find a room, get a meal, and make contacts there." He herded them into a lift, ordered "Level three," and shepherded them out.

Maeva lifted a slim eyebrow as the ambassador obtained rooms for them under a name she didn't recognize and paid in cash. Rand, if he noticed, did not react. He remained pale and drawn, and she wondered if the strain would be too much for him. He seemed to have something on his mind that he wished to discuss privately with Rindalan, and she knew as soon as they were given their rooms, she would be shunted aside. She debated with herself as to whether she would allow it, or give in to the chance to have a hot meal and a real rest without her head on a library table. Her feet ached, her shirt looked as though it had been slept in (it had), and she wondered if Rindalan had enough cash for her to buy grav boots and some sensible clothing.

Rand looked at her and said, "She needs some decent traveling gear."

Maeva started as if he'd read her mind. He gave her a slight smile, as if he had, and had known her last thought as well. He pointed at her shoes. "You walk like your feet hurt, and it won't be comfortable going through Chaos in that."

"Right."

Rindalan peeled off some plastisheet denominations.

"There should be a shop here in the way station. Don't go far."

Maeva hesitated. Both males looked at her. She said, "I know you have something to talk about, and I don't know if I want to be here or not."

Rand said, "You don't want to be here," while Rindy cleared his throat, answering, "I don't know what you're referring to."

They traded looks. Rand's expression closed. Rindalan said, "In a conspiracy, it is not wise to keep your partners in the dark. She has as much to lose as we do. Perhaps, hmm, more. She has a reputation that is still intact."

"I am considering the security of Cho."

"In that case," Rindalan dropped a hand on each of their shoulders and squired them down the corridor toward the rooms they had rented, "I suggest we find a place more suitable to discuss this."

Rand opened the larger of the two rooms, which he would share with the elder Choya, and a whiff of fresh-scented air greeted them. He cast around the room like a dog sniffing for something, and Maeva realized as she sat down that he was searching for tangible and intangible means of surveillance.

He lifted and dropped a shoulder. "I can't find anything." Rindalan stretched out on one of the beds. "That is sufficient for me. Now, what is it you wish to talk about that you do not wish Maeva to hear."

Rand, tired as he looked, would not sit. He said, "We don't need a pilot. I can do it."

"You?" Rindy's brow arched.

"You know I have the ability."

"Ability is not experience."

"I have some experience."

"Ahhh. That explains much."

"Not to me, it doesn't," interjected Maeva. "Are we talking FTL navigating here? Because I'm not too happy crossing Chaos as it is, but without a *tezar* at the helm . . ."

"You'll be sedated," answered Rand without looking at her. "You won't know anything anyway."

"I'll know it before I go under. And I've never been very good at sedation. It's hard for me to relax when I'm tense."

Rindy asked, disregarding Maeva completely, "Why would you offer to do such a thing?"

"The fewer who know what we're trying to accomplish, the better. You need to get back. You need to tell Palaton what happened on Sorrow."

"You're not intending to go back?"

Rand looked at the floor. "No. I'll get you back, and see Maeva wherever she wants to go safely, but no. There's no place for me on Cho. The message, that's what's important. Not the messenger. I'm a *tezar* but not one which Cho will ever accept. I'll go find the experience I need, see if I can expand my training to help others."

"You are the I'falan. Would you abandon that?"

Rand wet his lips and answered slowly, raising his gaze once more to Rindy's face. "I think that part of me went with Palaton. And even if it did not, Cho rejects me for that as well."

"Not all of Cho."

"Enough. I don't want to be a part of anything which could destroy your society. There will be another, someday."

Rindy took in his words. Maeva sat, her mouth slightly open, as if listening but not comprehending a word which had been said.

"I cannot agree with you on this."

Rand put his shoulders back. "Which part?"

"The part where you want to pilot," Maeva countered. They looked at her. "Even if he could, he's in no condition to."

"That," said Rindalan gravely, "I agree with. We find a pilot."

"And increase our risks."

"This entire venture is a risk, but though I applaud your courage, you have a long way to go before you can master the Patterns of Chaos. *Bahdur* alone is not enough, or I would be a *tezar*." Rindy watched him from the pillow he had made of his hands. He lay on the bed as though tired, and Maeva suddenly said, "You should rest."

"I should," he agreed. "But we have some things to settle first. You, outfitting, and Rand and I, transportation."

"Word will spread fast enough, Rindy, without us looking for a pilot. I can do it."

This time, Rindalan raised his head and held it steady, learning on his upper elbow. "As you should be more than well aware, I can search without raising or risking a great deal of attention. If, that is, the two of you will leave me alone to rest and meditate. If you are so eager to wear down the anxieties of youth, I suggest you boot up the bay records of recent dockings and find us a likely candidate to borrow."

"You won't let me do it."

Rindalan lay back down and closed his eyes. "No."

Rand paced off three rapid, angry strides, then stopped. He rubbed the back of his neck.

"He's right."

He looked at Maeva. "I know. That's why the Choyan are so infuriating. They're invariably right."

"You should be resting, too."

He shook off a quiver, as if the thought of coming to a rest bothered him. He crossed to the small desk attached to the cubicle wall. "I'll check the dockings."

"Then I guess I'll do some shopping."

Rand sat down. He eyed her. "If you need any help—"

"I'll know," Rindy put in.

Maeva leaned back in the door. "I'll be right back." The door sealed after her.

Rand twisted in the chair as if to say something to Rindalan, but the elder's lips pursed and he let out a gentle, puffing snore. Rand opened his mouth, then closed it. Rindy looked more frail than he remembered, as if the last days had taken a heavy toll. He turned back around and gave his attention to the screen.

Something exceedingly interesting came up almost immediately.

* * *

rrRusk watched his monitors, while responding to the patch-in, trying to mollify the agitation which rippled throughout GNask. "I don't know why your monitors didn't record the event. Analysis here shows that the increased activity and other functions are ninety-eight point two percent probability a real-time event."

"In other words, our central system has been masked."

"Ambassador, it happens. The question on my mind is not whether it happened or not, but why. To cloak the movements of one humankind attorney? The effort, the expenditure of the strategy—"

"I see," interrupted GNask, and rrRusk could tell from the sudden narrowing of the other's eyes and the widening of the pupils, that the ambassador did, indeed, see. The sluglike symbiont riding his shoulder turned antenna stalk eyes toward the screen as if equally focused. "What else have you observed that would interest me?"

"My records indicate that Rindalan and companions unnamed arrived by shuttle at Bay 2 just under an hour ago."

"Visuals?"

"No. But tracking from the shuttle confirms his identity."

"And we do not have further indication of movements of the humankind attorney. Do we even know if she left the embassy?"

"No, we don't." General rrRusk held his temper. It was not his systems' failure, and he knew that the rage GNask was attempting to master was not directed at him. "Her presence in the embassy has not been unreasonable, only the effort expended to cloak her entrance."

"And possible exit. But why? What does Thomas hold that he doesn't want me to know about? *What?*" GNask looked directly at rrRusk through the screen. "Check the masses on the shuttle. If we can't ID his companions by screen, perhaps we can by other means."

rrRusk nodded.

"Do we have a fix on Thomas?"

"He's off-world, Bay 4A, been there since yesterday, checking on cargo from what intelligence has been able to ascertain.

"What cargo?"

"We don't know."

"And the cargo your troops salvaged?"

"Being brought in. I don't know if we have anything of worth or not. The shipment came from nowhere, is going to nowhere."

"No dents?"

"No."

"Smuggling."

"That would be a logical assumption."

"Ummmm." GNask relaxed slightly, leaned back in his chair, musing. "Ambassador Rindalan. There's a revote tomorrow on piloting contracts. He would not dare to miss it. rrRusk, you were correct to alert me. I don't know what's happening, but I don't intend to miss it. Order me a shuttle liftoff immediately."

"Done, Ambassador." rrRusk cut the transmission, dropping his thick hand back to the rim of the console. He had not made general by ignoring his gut intuitions, nor by following outmoded or incautious strategies. He hoped he had not damaged his career by his actions in this matter. The discovery that the Abdrelikan embassy monitors had been successfully blacked out for nearly a day, however, tended to back his judgment.

Something was stirring. He could not pinpoint the whys or wherefores of the humankind involvement, but it did not matter if Cho had been drawn in. The Choyan had been a canny adversary for far too long.

Sooner or later, they had to stumble.

He caught himself staring blankly at the monitoring screens when word came in that Ambassador GNask was boarding. rrRusk shoved himself to his feet, his mind still groggy-mud balls, how he wished he had his symbiont with him, but that was impossible, with the amount of deep space voyaging he did. A *tursh* did not take to the environs of space well; losing one would be worse than leaving it at home, to be with the family line. He missed its steadying influence, however, as well as the creature's ability to clean his hide of fungus and parasites which bothered Abdreliks, even in space.

Without a *tursh,* an Abdrelik was nothing but a hulking predator. With their intelligence and guidance, imprinted slowly after hatching and reimprinted periodically throughout adulthood, an Abdrelik could do anything. His potential was limited only by the boundaries set upon him by treaty with the Compact. He puffed his chest out as GNask entered the bridge.

"Anything new?"

"The statistics on the shuttle are indeterminate. Humanoids

could have been with Rindalan. They could also have been of any one of a number of other like-massed species. Even Ronins."

GNask's eyebrows went up. He grinned hugely. "Now that would be an interesting situation, would it not? A kidnapping. I wonder if our Ronin allies have something planned which they have not shared with us?"

"They rarely stage anything without a warship within back-up distance. I have no reports of any Spiders nearby."

"Still . . ." GNask strolled past the bank of monitors, assessing what he saw. "It would spice up what is already an intriguing stew. Not that we need any more distractions. I will bow to your acumen, rrRusk. I doubt that the Ronins have made any drastic moves without us. So. What do you suggest?"

"We wait."

"Wait?"

"The Choyan ambassador is here for some reason. He will disembark or return to Sorrow."

"And we stand ready in either case."

rrRusk nodded.

"All right, then. We wait."

*   *   *

Late night surrounded the palace. Qativar saw few signs of activity as he approached. A member of the guard let him in reluctantly. He was met by a minor clerk at the staircase. Strains of a *lindar* being played—no, played was not the word, pounded—drifted through the palace in a kind of frantic, desperate up-tempo. But the notes were a coherent melody, recognizable for all its fury. Qativar knew who was playing and stepped by the clerk to go in search of the player.

"Sir, Honored Qativar, the emperor is seeing no one."

"He'll see me." Qativar brushed by and the clerk scurried to catch up with him.'

"I'm—I'm sorry, sir, but I cannot let you into the emperor's private quarters." The clerk's upper lip twitched frantically. He had invested in good, gold chain to layer under his derma, it twitched now with his expression.

"Who can?"

"M–m–minister Gathon, sir."

"Well, find him, wherever he is." Qativar stood in determined good humor, watching the clerk squirm.

"He's not about, sir."

"I know that. He's not been about for days. Panshinea will see *me*, and if you can't escort me, I'll find him myself. It shouldn't be difficult." Already, just by moving beyond the staircase, the music had grown more distinct.

"N–n–no one is allowed in the emperor's private downstairs quarters."

"Enough of this." Qativar swerved, stretched his long-legged stride past that of the trembling clerk, and began to search the vast lower halls of the palace. The clerk was winded and ashen pale when they both pulled up outside a door. The *lindar* music boomed loud enough to make the corridor echo.

"Let me in."

"You don't have access."

Qativar clenched a fist that he desired to wrap about the obstinate clerk's throat. "If he throws me out, he throws me out. But if you don't let me in, he may well have you ordered executed in the morning. Do you understand?"

Hand shaking so hard he could barely decode the threshold lock, the clerk let him in, then bolted.

Qativar stepped into the atrium music room, taking in the surroundings. He had indeed, never been there, nor he doubted had many others. The garden, visible through the arbor was a surprise in itself. The palace, for security reasons, had never been sounded or mapped, and overhead shots were strictly forbidden. Still, most Choyan had a rough idea of the layout. This garden, though, was something else. Qativar found himself quite surprised.

Panshinea sat, disheveled, at the *lindar*. His hands hammered the keyboard, flying in sleeves grown limp from the wearing. His hair was unbound and spread over his shoulders, red-gold sparks flying from it every now and then as if he smoldered while he played.

He looked up when the piece ended and rested his hands upon the top of the instrument. "They were supposed to keep you out."

"Me? Surely you don't mean that."

Panshinea turned his arms slightly, exposing his wrists,

and looked at them as if he contemplated slitting them. His veins bulged from the vigorous activity he had just completed. "I cannot rest. I cannot sleep. They tell me I am not always sane."

"That, Emperor, I hear to my sorrow." Qativar dipped his fingers inside his inner pocket and pulled out a bundle of packets. He threw them onto the seat of the nearest chair. "I brought you some additional supplies. I worry that you are abusing them."

"What have you done to me?" Pan thrust himself to his feet, voices piercing, then abruptly collapsed back to the bench.

"I would ask, what have you done to yourself?"

"I took the boost."

Hearing it gave Qativar an enormous sense of satisfaction. He had no doubt, of course, never had had, but hearing the defeat in Panshinea's voices was sweet beyond compare. "It was the only thing you could do."

Pan put a hand over his face as if he could not bear to look at Qativar. "Was it? Was it? Tell me, no one else will, where is Gathon?"

"Do you not remember?"

"Sometimes . . ." Fingers screened his expression. "Sometimes I think I do."

"You killed him, Pan. In a fight over the boost, I expect, I don't know. You called for my help. I agreed to take the body and dispose of it. You agreed to continue to allow distribution of the drug." Qativar moved toward the massive desk which dominated his corner of the room. The wood felt alive and warm, though the room itself was chill. Pan obviously did not feel the cold, his shirt was untucked and opened practically to the waist, and sweat gleamed upon his chest. He had lost more weight and had begun to look emaciated, shrinking in on himself. Qativar perched a lean hip on the desk. "Ask me more."

Pan pushed his hand so it masked his forehead, as if checking for a fever, or brushing off unruly bangs . . . or holding the weight of his horn crown. "Where is Gathon?"

"I have his body well hidden. It will never be found unless I choose for it to be found."

The emperor closed jade green eyes a long moment. "What is it you want now?"

"I came to apologize, Emperor. To tell you that boost is, sadly, not the miracle drug we thought it. Evidence suggests that it is severely addictive. In a few cases, it can cause death. In others, it is contraindicated because the *bahdur* cannot be contained or controlled. It burns, like wildfire, out of control." He smiled at Panshinea.

"You came for the throne."

"Emperor, you accuse me of treason. No. I am here only to advise you while Congress decides whether to replace you or not, while Palaton decides whether to reclaim his heirship or not, while you decide. . . ." Qativar paused dramatically. "Whether you will let him."

"Never."

"Then take my counsel."

"Never," repeated Pan, though his voices dropped to barely audible.

"I can stand by your side as Gathon did. Then, when you are prepared to move away, I will be ready to step in. Do you think I am so foolish as to believe I, or Vihtirne, or any of us could simply take your place? Perhaps, centuries ago, when all Cho needed was a warlord, but not today. The Abdreliks and the Ronins, even the two-faced Ivrians go all aflutter at the thought of our fall. I don't want to give it to them. I want Cho, you've not mistaken me or my intentions, but not until I'm set and you're ready to give it to me."

"Do you expect me to believe you?"

"I expect you to know that you must."

"And if I do not accept you?"

Qativar tilted his head and pointed his hand at the packets of boost. "You will run out, eventually. You can try to run Cho, empty. I'm sure it won't be the first time an emperor has kept the throne while past the ability to do so. You can even buy boost on the underground . . . but it'll be cut, there. Harmless, and sometimes not so harmless, fillers and additives will have been used to extend it. You will be even less sure of your *bahdur* than you are now. Or you could take what I'm offering you, because I am young, Panshinea, and I can afford to wait. I can even afford to spar with Congress, if that's what it takes, although Cho will suffer in the long run if I have to do so. Or we can deal, you and I, and both profit."

The stream of sparks which had been running from Pans-hinea's mane ceased. Without the shimmer, he looked spent, pale, as much a corpse as Qativar had left in cold storage. He looked into Qativar's eyes as if reading his thoughts and put his shoulders back.

"What do you suggest I do?"

"Coax Palaton back in and finish him this time."

"How would I do that? He's not only elusive, he must be in duplicates." Pan laughed shrilly.

"I have the bait which will bring him. I have Jorana. She carries his child."

"He would kill me if I tried to hurt Jorana."

"Indeed. That is the idea. First, we must let the people know that you are gathering imperial *bahdur*—"

"I haven't the strength."

"You know that, and I know that. But I want Palaton prepared to strike with everything he has, and the world will be expecting it. If all goes as I've planned, neither he nor Cho will be able to help themselves."

"I don't understand."

Qativar smiled again. "You will, my emperor. You will."

*   *   *

John Taylor Thomas listened as the last bulkhead door clanged and locked into place. His eyes felt gritty with lack of sleep. Vihtirne had agreed to conference with him on Galern to seal contracts. He thought ruefully that perhaps the jettisoning of the last cargo had been fortunate. They were desperate enough for the pharmaceuticals that they would give him official status and channels for the trade. That gave him enough legitimacy to keep President Mitch-ell off his back, even if it did not give him surcease in other matters.

"Prepare for bay launch."

Thomas went to his hammock. The freighter shimmied as the berthing cradle put it into position. Its metal skin echoed every winching and angle-thrust. He thought of sleep, blessed rest once they went into Chaos, sleep even he could not avoid. Perhaps he would feel human again when they landed on Galern.

Something slammed up against the ship. It shuddered

with its whole being. Thomas slipped half out of the hammock, listening.

Everything went deadly silent.

He was headed for the door to his cabin when it burst open, his Choya pilot in the hands of another.

"Your Eminence, I am sorry, but we've been commandeered." Dilarabe did not sound particularly distressed.

Thomas shook himself free of the hammock. "What's going on here? Get out or I'll have the bay authorities on your tail."

He recognized Ambassador Rindalan as the tall, chestnut-and gray-haired being moved more fully into the light.

"What is the meaning of this?" He stopped and stared as the two Choyan moved into his cabin, Rand and Maeva in their wake.

Dilarabe looked at Thomas blandly. "I believe it is called a 'jailbreak.'"

"I beg your pardon, Ambassador," Rindalan said. "But we're taking your ship. It seems most provident."

*   *   *

rrRusk caught the incoming alert. He was on his feet, and at the monitor, shouting over the com to ready the cruiser for departure.

"What is it?" GNask, still dripping with mud and ooze, climbed over the bulkhead from the spa which was kept for him.

"We have a launch from Bay 4A, sir." rrRusk stood, watching the telemetry readings and other information being transmitted. "We have Rindalan and two humanoids boarding a freight ship, a freighter bearing Ambassador Thomas, making an authorized, but very unorthodox and hasty launch."

"Do we?" GNask toweled his shoulder, gently avoiding his tursh. "I make that out to be a possible hijacking, general. If you ascertain that the boarding was forced."

"Initial readings indicate that an outer bulkhead was blown. It looks forced to me."

"Then Ambassador Thomas and Ambassador Rindalan appear to be in danger. I see it as my duty to go after the criminals. Get us launched as soon as possible. I'll inform the Compact of our action." He paused in the doorway. "And rrRusk . . ."

"Yes?"

"Do whatever you must to catch up with them."

Chapter 35

Gilat had been a hard worker all his life. As a God-blind, he could expect nothing more as his lot. He believed in the teachings of a Change to come, and of a Bringer of that Change, the I'falan, but he did not hope to see it in his lifetime. Instead, he had learned a skill among the workings of the water filtration plants and he worked hard at what he did. He kept his mate and children happy, owned a small but sturdy house, drank *bren* for breakfast and wine on special occasions and, generally, led a good life.

He would have been content if not for his mate. Oh, Bretha had been a comely Choya'i when they were young. She'd been courted by many youths, including one brash Choya who claimed he was Housed, though they all knew he couldn't have been. No one sane would sully their genetic line with a commons if he came from a Householding. That she had chosen him had filled him with joy, and his small house with children.

But she had never quite loosened her hold on the idea that she might have married into a Householding. That her children's father might have been a Choya with the power, with *bahdur,* which could breathe far vaster possibilities into all their futures. She might even have birthed a *tezar*.

They were still young, for all their family and years together, and she still had a longing for children, but refused to have any more. Not any to be born as God-blind.

Gilat knew there was nothing he could do about it, but when she had begun going to the underground sermons, he let her go. True, the religion of the Change had been banned centuries before, and once emperors had executed those who ignored the ban, but that had been long ago. He let her go because it gave her hope, and kept her from carping at his crown day in and day out. Could have done, could have been. . . .

She had, instead, filled him with stories of Father Chirek and Malahki, the latter a Choya who had been a luminary of Danbe, until that region had been forcibly Relocated, Malahki, a common Choya with enough charisma to become emperor himself. He'd even listened when word came of a Prophet. It made her happy. She still carped at him night and day, but now it was with excitement, not complaint. It seemed harmless enough.

Until she had professed that an alien had come, the I'falan. That Gilat had rejected and it still remained the one harsh note between them. When the I'falan had gone as quickly as it had come, she had lapsed into silence.

He missed, her enthusiasm, her cheerful gossip, her reports of hopeful insurrection among the underground. The glint in her eyes when she talked of being young enough to bear a babe which would have been touched by the Change.

Although Gilat had taken a kind of personal delight in the weakness spreading like wildfire among the House-holdings because of Panshinea's use of imperial *bahdur,* Bretha had said little. She had retreated into a depression over which Gilat was as powerless as he was over the other matter, and it bothered him. As he took his battered conveyance to the power plant, he reflected that she did not want Cho lowered to her level. She wanted them all to be elevated.

He didn't much care as long as equal was equal and fair was fair. Hard work and will were what counted.

As he drove, the edges of dawn cleared the mountain ridge. Light spread across the basin of Charolon and its outer regions. He liked to watch the dawn, though his shift sometimes began before and he came to work in the dark cloak of night. Better than stormy weather.

The plant hunkered on the horizon, a dull, Choya-carved mountain of its own. It would stay, even when (or if, Gilat thought morosely) Charolon relocated. He liked being beyond the outskirts of the townships, working outside the mill of traffic and manufacturing strips. Bretha did not care for the hours of his shift, but he took care not to wake her or the children when he left, and he was often home early enough to help her with dinner or afternoon games with the children.

As his conveyance puttered toward his destination, a broadcaster came on with the current weather report and some speculation that Panshinea had once again fallen into a decline. The emperor had not been the same. Perhaps, thought Gilat, he never would be. Perhaps, in his lifetime, they would see the investiture of a new emperor. Now that would be something. Minister Gathon was not available for a statement, and rumors were rife that Gathon had left Charolon, abandoning his emperor. Rumor also said that Panshinea had gone mad.

Odd. It was not in his genetics, although if the *bahdur* had burned out of him, like it did in a *tezar,* insanity could be possible. Congress, with no legitimate heir named to the throne, was pondering its actions.

Gilat found himself chewing on the corner of his lip as he considered the broadcaster's report. It would make an interesting topic at lunch break. His mind thus mulling, he only half-noticed an unfamiliar shift crew pulling out of the water plant just before him.

He changed into his waders in the locker room and went to check on main filtration. He liked the cavernous room, with its thunder of water pouring through it, though the catwalks could be slippery now and then, and last year a coworker had fallen and been towed under to his death. He usually did not tell Bretha when this chore rotated into his shift. As much as he liked water, she feared it.

Although the inspection was supposed to be done in pairs, his coworker was late again. He thought privately that Latner probably drank too much. He could not seem to cope with the rhythms of the early day shift. Gilat decided to suggest to his supervisor that Latner be moved over.

He moved over onto the main catwalk, water spray dampening him despite his coveralls and waterproof jacket. Thousands of gallons rushed under the metal gridway, sending up a fine mist, thoroughly glistening and dampening the underground chamber. His waders gripped the surface well, and he had no fear.

In the churning, foaming water, something bobbed. It caught his eye immediately. Gilat peered closer. It did not appear to have been anything organic. Some sort of inanimate object where the water poured by in whitewater rapids. Something trapped in the pounding, artificial surf against the chamber walls. Finally, he got on his stomach and crawled to the edge of the catwalk for a better look.

A container of some kind. He needed to get that up and out, before it got caught in one of the turbines or drains. It would not bob forever. If he hooked one arm around the ladder, he should just be able to reach it. . . .

There was a moment, when the metal groaned, and the sleeve of his jacket slipped, when he thought of Bretha's fears and his drowned coworker and knew there was a possibility he might join him. He tightened his first elbow, felt his sinews stretch to their utmost, his joints groaning the way the catwalk sounded. His fingers wiggled and hooked like cunning creatures with minds of their own. Then . . . he had it!

His fingers caught the rim of the container, fishing it toward him. Gilat managed a better grip and pulled himself back to safety.

Once crouched on the catwalk, he looked the object over. Definitely a container, good-sized, out of the water, nearly as big as his torso. Once full, and now empty. Its air-filled insides had kept it afloat on the rapids. There was no sign whatsoever of the container's contents or its manufacturer. Gilat opened the lid and sniffed.

Oh, but he knew that smell. Every youth had talked about it once, just as they cherished pictures of naked Choya'i and boasted of their sexual prowess. He himself had once held a vial of it in his hand, though he had never used it, because he had Bretha's love and other Choya'i were like fish to him—so you might catch one, but what would you do with it when you had?

This was *ruhl,* a pungent and potent concentrate of the aphrodisiac. More than old wives' tales, this was genuine, though rare, the stuff of legend among the young. He straightened, container balanced between his palms.

Gilat stood on the catwalk, his heavy, thick common brow furrowed with his thoughts. Empty, but it had been full. *Ruhl* muddled the senses. Drove *bahdur* out of the Houseds, or so it was said, acted as more than an aphrodisiac, though no one would be so foolish as to want to drive the Houseds insane. What would Cho be without *bahdur?*

He remembered an unfamiliar work crew leaving as he was driving in. They had been remoting a freight hover with them, though he did not recall what had been stacked on its surface. Had they left a container behind?

To what purpose would anyone wish to dose the water supply with *ruhl?*

He thought of the madness which had swept the city when it appeared that Panshinea had drained off most of the *bahdur* into himself.

Or had he?

Anyone drinking water with this great a concentration in it—

Gilat tucked the container under his arm. He did not know what had happened, and he felt almost sure his supervisor would scoff at him. Something had definitely happened here which should not go unnoticed, but he had no evidence of what, other than this empty container which stank of *ruhl*. He had no one to go to who would take him seriously and be able to ponder this quandary, to decide if there was a problem or connection here or not. He was questioning the very existence of imperial *bahdur* and Panshinea's actions, something a commons could not do lightly.

But there was always Bretha and her idol Malahki, and the underground.

They were great thinkers. Perhaps they might have an inkling as to what could be going on. Gilat, as much as he loved his work and his solitude, left his shift early.

*   *   *

"She will live," Father Chirek told him, "but she'll need time to heal."

"That means," added Dorea softly, "that she will not be able to help you through what lies ahead."

"Prophesying?" asked Palaton wearily. He sat at the edge of Rufeen's créche, watching his friend's still face, expression folded into one of unconscious pain. It had changed little after the hours of surgery and the nighttime he'd been waiting for her to wake. The Bayalak hospital had all the modern conveniences, and she was enfolded, entrusted into them, but still he did not trust.

"A little. And common sense." Dorea stood up briskly. "Nor will Hat be of any use."

Hat lay a room away, fighting to keep his shattered shoulder from being cut away forever, to keep his shoulder and arm whole, so that he could remain whole in body to be a flightmaster. In many ways, his fight was more crucial than Rufeen's. He had been lapsing in and out of consciousness, after two surgeries, and scarcely knew Palaton when he was at his side. Though Rufeen was hardly more conscious, Palaton had felt his presence more important to imprint on her.

As Father Chirek gave her his arm to guide her, Dorea turned her face back to Palaton, as if seeing him through her blindfold. "Coming?" she asked. "The battle will not be won within these walls."

She was young enough to be his daughter, but there was that in her voices which had become ageless, tones issuing from her gift rather than her experience. Palaton looked back at her, unable to deny the urgency she projected, unwilling to give his life and destiny over to her hands.

Softening, as if sensing his resolve, she added, "They will know you were here, and they will understand why you left."

Palaton looked back at Rufeen, who barely breathed within the créche unit.

"Palaton, you burn like the Flame you are. They will know." Dorea repeated herself with patience.

He sighed and got to his feet. "And you have plans for me, I suppose."

"No, but we are ready for whatever plans you have for us." She held out her other arm to him, and walked steadily between the two of them through the hospital as if she needed no guidance at all, but had foreseen what her path would be in this moment.

As, indeed, she could have. He reflected, as the conveyance carried them from the hospital complex in the new, Housed high-rise section of Bayalak back toward the weather-beaten Common and old harbor city, that he wanted to rely on what she had seen, cling to it like a guideline as to what he should do. He wanted her to have it mapped out so clearly for him that he would not have to trust himself or make another decision. He wanted that. From the few words they had exchanged since he'd brought the skimmer in, he realized that she knew less than he did.

But they still had to talk about Rand. And, as isolated, as he'd been in the critical care ward, he'd heard the rumors coming from Charolon. Panshinea ailing, Gathon gone. Soon, it would not matter whether the prophet knew his destiny or not, he would have to act.

The quarters Father Chirek had set up as the Prophet's base of operations were not terribly different from the weatherbeaten, fish-bait-and-creosote-soaked wooden hovel that Palaton had first met Dorea in. As he walked in, he realized it had probably been a storage hangar, dry dock for boats, and huge racks for mending nets were folded up against the wall. It smelled of the sea. It was nothing like the many-roomed hall which he had dreamed of, though Palaton had not expected it to look the same. There were dorms, a galley, conference rooms, one communications center brimming with equipment that looked as out of place here as he would in an Abdrelik mud pond, and a small meditation room where Dorea received callers, her lithe frame resting in a hand carved and very battered rocking chair.

She looked more at ease in the chair than Panshinea did on his throne, Palaton thought. He took a nearby divan that Father Chirek motioned him to. Chirek went to the corner and fixed them all an iced drink before he took a chair himself.

"Where is Malahki?" asked Dorea abruptly.

Palaton flinched, then realized she directed her inquiry at Chirek. The mouse-haired cleric shook his head, then said aloud, "I don't know. I thought he would be here before us. Something must have come up."

"No doubt." However, she looked unsettled as she knitted her fingers together in her lap.

The drink soothed his parched throat, but did little to quiet him. Palaton set it aside on a small table which was little more than a balanced stone, weathered by time and tide. "Tell me about Rand."

As was her usual habit, she plucked a second at her blindfold. "He is in great danger," she answered. "Although he has passed through part of it."

"On Sorrow? How did he get there? Qativar and Viht-irne took him from me. I dared not move against them as long as he was hostage—if I had known, I would have—"

"What?" demanded Chirek. "What would you have done? Attacked them openly? With what means? Panshinea would have devoured you if you had divided your attention between them. Would you have left Cho to free Rand?"

"Possibly. Who has him? The Abdreliks?"

"He is being held by his own people. Ambassador Thomas does not ever intend for him to be free."

"There's no love lost between Thomas and Rand. I can't leave him there."

"And you cannot forsake us, either. You go, and Panshinea and Qativar will split the world between them. Nor," added Dorea gently, "can you do anything alone. You need us as well."

"I would have been stronger with Rand."

"Tell me why." Dorea lifted her chin, stared at him.

Palaton had never told anybody before of his bond with his friend. "I cannot explain it."

"I think you can."

Chirek leaned forward, one elbow on his brown-clothed knee. "You risked much bringing an alien among us. It could not have been easy for him or you."

"Would you have had me do otherwise?"

Chirek smiled ruefully. "And have lost the I'falan? You know better. But what about you? What have you lost?"

Before Palaton could say, the Prophet spoke.

"He was your *durah*, soulmate. He cleansed your *bahdur*, you shared it, he knows the heart of the Choyan empire. You were his destiny."

Her words fell into the silence of the tiny room like heartbeats.

Chirek said, "You told him of *bahdur*."

"You knew that. You must have known it—what do you think made him the Bringer of Change? What do you think he carried?"

The priest said reflectively, "I did not think. I . . . experienced it."

"I met him on Arizar," Palaton recounted. He told them what they had only had hints of before: renegade Choyan colonists who had fled Cho and done what no others had done before them. Their experiments with transferring their powers to humankind for cleansing, the many failures as humankind could not cope with *bahdur,* their successes. That the colony had done what they did out of selfishness, that the humans brought to Arizar had come hoping to become pilots, that they had been blinded, muted, made passive receptacles for tainted *bahdur.* That the humankind had come as scarcely more than children, stolen from Earth, never to return. That he, desperate to avoid burnout, had been seduced by the renegades to join their College of the Brethren, to be cleansed.

"I am not proud," Palaton added.

"You have a prodigious talent. It must have been difficult to feel its first ebbings."

"You cannot possibly imagine."

Dorea prompted. "The Abdreliks attacked. You saved Rand, brought him here." ·

"I had to. He carried my power. And . . . I was responsible for him. Many died on Arizar, many more fled. He was all I could salvage . . . my pride, my faith in myself, all was at stake. What we did not know was that Alexa, one of his friends, and Bevan, another, would be tangled in the Abdreliks efforts to secure the *tezarian* drive."

"Who is Bevan?"

"Bevan is the pilot who led the Abdrelik attack on us. He carried Nedar's power. It drove him insane, destroyed him. As for Alexa . . . I can only assume that she was an agent of the Abdreliks to the very end, though she was with Nedar. She perished with him at Blue Ridge."

Chirek lifted his chin from his hand. "Rand restored your *bahdur?*"

"I took it from him," Palaton answered shortly. "When Blue Ridge was attacked."

"Then," Father Chirek concluded, "it is you who are the I'falan."

Palaton stared at Dorea. "Ask her. She knows why I would not answer her summons."

"You cannot refuse to Change our people."

"I can, and I will. Giving you the power does not give

you the wisdom and the training to use it. Look at the mess I've made of things."

"Most of our strife has come from the struggle to be equal."

Palaton got up, paced a step away from Dorea, thinking of his dreams in which he had run, to no avail. He would not run now, though he had an undeniable wish to. "Our strengths should come from accepting our differences."

"We can be diverse and still be equal." Dorea set aside the drink she had held. "*Bahdur* molds itself to each and every Choya who holds it. Like water, like air, it is always there, seen and unseen, yet always shaped differently. But to deny us the right to breathe, to drink, is wrong."

"I need your help! Don't you think I know that? But I cannot, will not, pay your price."

Malahki entered, his sable mane lying upon his shoulders like a cloak, his bulk filling the room. "You may feel differently when you hear what I have to tell you."

Chapter 36

Removing his jacket, shaking off a light dirt, Malahki added, "My pardon for the lateness, Dorea. I have been busy."

"I know."

Palaton took the look Malahki gave him and returned it, standing firm.

Chirek said, a touch of impatience in his voices, "What do you need to tell us?"

"I've been in contact with my network." Malahki's mouth twisted. To Palaton, he added, "You're a hard act to follow."

"I should have guessed it was you who spread the House of Flame all over Cho."

"It seemed a good thing to do. You must admit, it kept Pan off your heels."

"Not entirely. But it kept him thinking."

Dorea said, in a soft warning, "Malahki."

"Ah. Yes. I got some interesting information this morning by way of a water filtration plant worker outside Charolon. I've been verifying what he's told me. Our water is being dosed with *ruhl*, at some fairly incredible concentrations." Malahki scratched his temple. "We've not been able to stop it, but we've found a pattern of sabotage in a majority of the urban areas."

"*Ruhl?* By whom?"

Only Dorea did not seem surprised. "He plans to incapacitate as many of us as he can."

"Who? And why?"

"The why should be as obvious as the who. The myth of imperial *bahdur* and the toll it exacts on the people may be hiding the real problem. Pan is weak, he can only expect to dominate those who are weaker."

"Widespread loss of power creates a need for boost," Palaton remarked. "We can't be sure Pan is at the bottom of all the trouble. Qativar is capable of doing anything to further his plans."

"Or they could be working in conjunction."

"Pan knows they want the throne. I don't think he would give it to them just to forestall any threat he sees from me."

"There is more," Malahki said grimly. "Panshinea has Jorana. There's to be a public execution tomorrow."

"He means to draw me out." Palaton's expression creased in anger. "How does he justify her murder?"

"If the emperor needs any justification, she's carrying your child. The House of Flame is never to be rebuilt again."

"Palaton," Dorea murmured. "We are here with you."

"He's mad." Palaton sat down abruptly.

"She's my foster daughter," Malahki proclaimed. "I have no intention of letting him get away with it."

Father Chirek added, "Do we assume he's ordered *ruhl* into the systems with some hope of reaching Palaton? That he would annihilate the *bahdur* of an entire planet to reach one Choya?"

"Perhaps. We're secure here at Bayalak. I've left guards at the filtration plant. We can carry bottled water if we're going into Charolon for the day."

"We'll have to do more than that." Chirek rubbed the base of his horn crown, staving off a headache. "We know what it's like to be common. We're going to have to go in, try to keep the streets calm."

"No," argued Malahki. "I need every Choya I can get for backup."

"Our people will need whatever we can offer them."

"Palaton has to go in alone."

They all stopped talking, turning to look at the Choya'i. Dorea took a short breath.

"The trap is meant for him. He alone can spring it."

"I won't allow—"

Palaton cut Malahki off. "It's all right. I expected this."

Dorea put her hand up. "We will be there, Palaton. As Father Chirek wishes. Malahki will have a handful of agents he can trust to assist you. But it is you who must face Panshinea. I tell you now, as I have spoken from the first: There cannot be two emperors on Cho."

To Palaton, she added urgently, "You must face Panshinea and his shadow, and you must be prepared to do whatever you have to."

"I am."

"Even loosing the House of Flame?"

He did not answer her immediately then, understanding the depth of her question. To the others, Dorea spoke. "The House of Flame was destroyed centuries ago for reasons we do not know. It was the tree which branched all of us, but even that did not save it in the end. We do not know why its lines were cut off, what the other Houses feared, but it must have been formidable. Are you strong enough, Palaton, to face what the rest of us could not?"

*   *   *

"They're right on our tails."

"This is a freighter," Dilarabe pointed out patiently. "Not a cruiser. Not a warship. We can't hope to outrun them forever."

"I don't want forever," Rand answered. "I just want to hit Chaos ahead of them."

"I think," the *tezar* continued, his hands playing over his instrument board, "they will let us run until they're sure we're going to warp. Then they will hit us before we can make the final jump into Chaos. I am not a combat pilot. I have preferred, in my career, to be a chaperon. But they're arming. It seems logical they plan to attack us."

"Oh, God," Maeva squeaked faintly. She shut her eyes.

"Don't worry." Rand put a hand on her shoulder, squeezed it lightly. "They don't want to blast us out of space. What they really want to do is board us."

"Oh, God," she repeated.

Rindalan suggested, "Perhaps she should be sedated for the jump."

"It's a little early for that," Dilarabe told him.

"I think it might be best."

"I disagree," intoned Thomas from across the bridge, where they had him bound to a chair. "You need everybody with their full faculties, particularly if the Abdreliks try to board."

"If we make the jump without their stopping us, we may not have time to medicate."

"There are only two of us here that the reality fugue in Chaos will bother, me and Maeva. But if the Abdreliks board us, we're all at risk."

Rand wanted to say, "Don't listen to him, he has the silver tongue of the devil," but he said nothing.

"And why," prompted Rindy, "would we want to deal with the Abdreliks?"

"You may not have a choice." Thomas turned away from them and looked at the wall.

A sudden intuition prickled at Rand. "What are we carrying, Ambassador, and what were your original flight plans?"

"We're following our original flight plans," Dilarabe answered instead of Thomas.

"You were headed to Cho anyway?"

"Yes."

"Why? This is a cargo ship. We don't have active trade treaties with Cho."

"Boost," said Rindalan faintly.

Rand's and Maeva's attention swiveled to him. The elder Choya got to his feet, despite the acceleration sway of the freighter. He stabbed a hand through the air. "You're bringing the drug in."

"Of course," answered the other wearily. "You knew it was off-world. Who did you think supplied it?"

"I have not had the time to contemplate the stupidity and greed of the species who are destroying my people."

"It was never meant to destroy you. It was never meant for you, period."

Rand put his hand on Rindalan. He could feel the agitation coursing through the Choya's body, the surge of the pulse. He feared losing Rindy. "Tell me about boost."

Rindalan returned to his chair uneasily. "It restores *bahdur*."

"That can't be bad."

"It would not seem so. But it is highly addictive, occasionally toxic, and the *bahdur* which returns is often out of control. I am told that it creates a craving which even the restoration of *bahdur* cannot sate. Nothing good can come of it. Perhaps we should let the Abdreliks catch us and annihilate the ship."

Thomas shrugged within his bonds. "Before this flight is over, you may all wish you had a dose of it."

"What good would you ever expect of it!" Rindy's voices boomed in the control room.

Thomas paused a long moment before he turned fully to speak to them, and Rand was surprised to see a wetness upon the man's cheeks. "I had it developed to save my daughter."

Maeva got up to go to him, hesitated, and when she saw no visible protest from Rand, she crossed the bridge to stand by the ambassador. "Why?"

"I wanted to free her." He leaned his head back, let Maeva dab the tears from his face. "I never knew what GNask would do to her, how it would change her. She was my daughter! I loved her. But she was never mine after he took her."

"What did he do?"

Thomas stared at Rindalan. "You drove me to it. You Choyan. You took our children. They never returned. I could find no trace of them—not even any of you who would admit to it—"

"The renegades on Arizar took them."

"I know that now. I did not then. I went to the Abdreliks and offered to help them build a case against you."

Dilarabe said wryly, "They are ever looking for leverage."

"I needed them to promote us out of Class Zed status. GNask and I formed an alliance. I did nothing that I am ashamed of, except for Alexa."

Maeva smoothed his hair from his forehead. "What did they do to her?"

"It was decided she would become one of the lost children."

"Then it was Alexa who brought the Abdreliks down on Arizar." This, from Rand.

"Yes. It did not matter that she loved you, what little love she had left in her. I gave her to GNask when she was hardly more than a toddler. What he did took her away from me forever." Thomas swallowed harshly. "That symbiont they wear—"

"The *turshes*."

"Yes. It carries some of their genetic coding, from what I gather. In segments. GNask took a section of the worm and implanted it into my daughter. After that, she was his, totally. It was as though I watched an Abdrelik wearing the skin of my daughter. She tried to hide it, but I knew. The cruelty, the darkness inside of her—"

"She never let either Bevan or me get really close to her," Rand murmured. "I thought it was because she preferred him. He thought it was because she wanted me."

"She could not have lived with either of you. I know. I caught her once when she was small. The family dog was missing, a small pet . . . I found her devouring it. Like a jackal, bathed in its warm blood, she'd hunted and killed it. She fought me when I tried to take the carcass away. I don't know if she remembered that, later, but I do know she became very secretive and reserved as she grew. She knew that she had monstrous tendencies which we wouldn't accept. I didn't know what to do, how I was going to live with what I'd created, how she could live."

"How did boost come about?"

"We found neural bonding when we did extensive tests on her. Nothing we'd ever seen before. I had a research doctor who agreed to work with me. It took years. He found a way to clear the nerve pathways of the contamination. There was also something about gene tags, I'm not entirely sure—I only know that, eventually, Dr. Maren found a drug which succeeded. By then, GNask had picked up her and Nedar."

Rindy jerked, startled. "He had Nedar?"

"Yes. And imprinted him as well. That, Ambassador, is why we may all want those drugs before this is over. GNask has learned how to infiltrate our very beings. It's the only way to deny him access."

"It'll be a long, cold day in hell," Rand said, "before I would believe anything this man says."

Thomas looked at him defiantly. "It doesn't matter if you believe me or not. You'll have the proof before your eyes in hours."

As if to punctuate his words, the freighter rocked violently, and the dull echo of an explosion reached them.

Dilarabe cried, "We've been hit!"

Chapter 37

"Everything is in place," Malahki told Palaton. Evening had long since supplanted day, and even those dark hours were wearing away. He had a few to sleep, then he would be back in Charolon, weaving his way toward a public execution scheduled to take place at noon on the Emperor's Walk, in front of the steps of Congress. Malahki stood as he spoke, sweeping away a platter of crumbs and meat scraps. He moved carefully, so as not to wake Dorea, who sat at the other end of the table, her shoulders and head slumped in sleep.

"We have been at odds," Palaton began.

Malahki interrupted him. "I prefer to think of us as uneasy allies."

Palaton looked at him levelly. "I have never thought you had less than the concern of our people in your heart."

Malahki opened his mouth to respond in kind, then paused and grinned. "I wish I could say the same for you."

He muted it, but Malahki had drawn a laugh from him all the same. "I am a *tezar*. I am sorry, but that is all I have ever wanted to be."

"I know. Perhaps that is what Cho needs most on its throne, right now."

"What Cho needs on its throne now is someone like you." Palaton looked at Malahki, and his thoughts suddenly seemed crystal clear.

Malahki ducked away and would no longer meet his gaze. "It was not I who said that." He put a shoulder to the room's door and left, food platter in his hands, looking for all the world like a waiter.

Palaton sat back in his chair, muttering to himself. "No. It was I who said it." He felt weary again and rubbed his eyes.

Dorea stirred. Her mouth curved. "It appears I must wake up, so that I can be put to bed properly."

"Did you rest?"

"As much as I ever do, now. Sleeping dreams, waking dreams . . . I am always searching for portents." She gave a sigh, for once sounding like the young Choya'i she was.

"Do you wish you had never met him?"

"The I'falan? Yes. I had a handsome young Choya courting me then. Those first few hours after the Change, I frightened him away with my ranting and raving. I needed help and care. He had nothing for me."

"Chirek is devoted to you."

"Yes," and she smiled more fully, joy in it. "He is a good Choya. I only hope he realizes soon the possibilities we have together."

"Your being the Prophet blinds him, as well."

"I think so. And what about you?"

"Being blind? I would say I have my moments."

"Was Jorana one of them?"

"Is there any doubt? I only wish I could understand how my heart could be so divided. There is Jorana, and there is . . ." he hesitated.

"Rand?"

"Yes. An alien, yet my *durah*. He is the twin to my soul, the part of me which flies and hungers for truth and tries to understand the world around me. I always thought a soulmate would álso be a sexual mate. This baffles me."

"Does Jorana understand?"

"I think so. I don't know for sure."

"And Rand?"

"Of course."

"Then you have nothing to worry about, except securing their safety."

He laughed again. "You make it sound so easy."

Her face clouded. "Nothing this next day will be easy."

"I owe you and Malahki much."

"He would ask only one thing of you: the same thing I would ask."

"I am not the I'falan." He shook his head, even though she could not see him.

"It was your *bahdur* Rand carried."

"I cannot do this for you."

She looked at him, longing aching in her face. "It is the only thing I ask."

Palaton pounded a fist on the table, muted, helpless. "Dorea . . ."

"We will take care of her. Shield her. But she has done so much for us, and she was not able to get to Rand before . . ."

"One Choya'i."

"Yes." Dorea whispered, but her voices cut into Palaton as if they had been knives.

Only one. Did that damage his resolve so much, to give in for only one?

It would be like a dam giving way. Do it for one, he would have to do it for others. It would be against everything which he had decided for himself.

The door creaked ajar. Malahki held it open and let the child slip in.

She had hair the color of winter wheat, and eyes of seafoam green, and she was so young, her horn crown had just begun to scallop its edges. The sun had not yet creased her eyelids or mouth, and she stood shyly just inside the room, watching Dorea, trying not to look at Palaton. That she was common seemed obvious, no Housed children had hair naturally her color.

"My future," said Dorea and held out her hand.

Another Prophet? Would he be doing her a favor to light the fire inside her? Or did Dorea realize that coming to the art of prophecy gently, guided, would be more of a blessing? Had she *seen* this child and brought her to the I'falan, only to be denied?

Palaton parted his lips to tell them both no, when the Choya'i looked at him with those guileless seafoam eyes.

"Please."

"Do you know what you ask of me?"

"I know it is both terrible and beautiful. It is like something you dream, and forget, and fear, and want to remember all day. I think it must be like eating fire and ice, in the same mouthful."

He sighed. Could not face that look on her face. Turned to Dorea. "What is it I should do?"

Triumph leaped in the Prophet's expression, something she curbed immediately. "Touch her with *bahdur*."

"There has to be more than that." And less. If he touched her with all the fury of the *bahdur* at his command, he could knock her senseless. Even as he thought of the child, he thought of Panshinea. Suddenly, he knew what the Houses had feared of the House of Flame, what imperial *bahdur* really was, a mythic remnant of an ability which had actually existed at one time.

Two sides of the same coin. Power that healed, opened up nerves which had not been able to conduct their genetic potential for some reason, power that unsealed those conduits and allowed *bahdur* to flow. The other, lethal, side . . . *bahdur* that shut down systems as it flowed inward, killing as it touched.

Not all Flames would have had the ability to the same extent, but losing that House explained much. Explained why no Houses had healers in their lines . . . why *bahdur* was not generally lethal. Why commons existed.

He put his hand to his head, thoughts swimming.

"Palaton?"

He looked up. "I'm all right. Come here to me . . ."

"Nerala," supplied the Prophet.

"Nerala."

The Choya'i hesitated. She looked to the Prophet, studied her blindfolded face, put her hand shyly into Dorea's. "Will I have to tear my eyes out?"

"God-in-all willing, never," the Prophet said fervently.

Nerala stepped close.

Palaton summoned his power, felt it quicken in his veins, asked of it what he willed and reached out toward the child. The power leaped, arcing, blue flame without heat crossing from his hand to her forehead.

She had her eyes closed, mouth twisted tight, feet glued to the floor. She rocked back a little as he touched her, holding her breath. Palaton reined his power back as quickly as he had made contact.

After a long moment, she opened her eyes. Her lips turned down. "Nothing," she whispered fiercely. "Nothing happened?"

Dorea sprang to her feet. "It can't be." She groped toward the child with her hands.

Power speaks to power.

Palaton stretched his own hand out again. Nothing called

to him. Nerala was as empty as she had been born. As much as he had never wanted to be the I'falan, disappointment racked him. "I could not do it."

Nerala let out a sob and ran from the room. The door banged in her wake. Dorea clung to the table's edge. "I can't be wrong. I can't."

"All this means is that I have to come back. As soon as Jorana is in the clear, you have to find Rand for me. We can't wait any longer."

"There may not be enough time." Dorea looked toward him, tugging uncomfortably on her blindfold. "I have not tried to keep things from you, but you must understand, the visions are not always perfect. Sometimes early, sometimes too late. . . ."

"What is it!"

"Chaos," she cried softly. "Lost forever. Oh, Palaton . . . I did not know."

* * *

"Third hit," counted Rand grimly as the old freighter rocked again. Central lighting flickered, then came back on. "She can't take much more." Maeva, in her sling chair, looked at him in dismay.

"I can't get any more maneuvering speed out of her. The port retros are gone."

"How much longer before you hit FTL?"

"Not soon enough," Dilarabe grunted, his attention caught by the helm. The freighter shuddered again and there was a whine which carried throughout the framework, and they could all feel the sudden deceleration. The hours spent in flight had just ended.

"That's it," stated Thomas. "They'll have a tractor on us in minutes and we'll be pried open like an oyster shell."

Rindy looked across the bridge. "I am not familiar with your oysters, but I think I understand the analogy. Ambassador Thomas, I am going to release you. I trust you have the same self-interests we all do." He reached Thomas in two strides and struck open the bonds.

Thomas hissed softly through his lips as he massaged his wrists. He looked at Rand. "I would be lying if I said we did not have a score to settle, but I agree with Rindalan.

Our mutual survival has a higher priority. We have a truce for now."

"A truce does not mean trust."

Thomas examined his hand. "You are right again." He started to get up, was rocked from his feet as the entire vessel shuddered violently.

Rand grabbed for Maeva's sling to steady himself. "It'll be all right.

"Sure. If they try to implant me, I'll sue 'em." Her voice sounded braver than she felt.

"That should stop them in their tracks."

Dilarabe secured the helm. He opened a cabinet under the console. A rack of enforcers dropped into place. "Weapons, anyone?"

The ship's engine cut out, and emergency power kicked in. Metal creaked, then let out a scream which thrilled the length of the freighter.

"They're in," said Rand.

Rindy looked at the weapons thoughtfully, then shook his head. "We don't want them to think we have something worth fighting over. We have two ambassadors here. Let's see if we can get by with a little diplomacy."

GNask rocked back in the massive chair which held him. The cavernous belly of the Abdrelik ship was but one of the small service docks inside the craft which had swallowed up their freighter so effortlessly. It smelled of the Abdreliks, dank, moist, predatory. GNask had had them escorted there with little ceremony, his war general remaining a wary distance from all of them. His small, round eyes examined them with beady interest. He had been listening and questioning for many minutes and now sat silent. Even his symbiont, which rested atop his skull like a humorous hat, appeared to watch them with stalk eyes. The Abdrelik wiped the corner of his mouth. "Now let me get this straight. You," and he looked to Rindalan, "left Sorrow of your own accord, with these two humankind."

Rindy nodded solemnly.

"And you did not have your vessel commandeered, but recognized the urgency of Ambassador Rindalan's request and agreed to carry him and his passengers to Cho."

Thomas lifted a shoulder, let it drop. "That sounds about right."

"And you," the Abdrelik frowned, coarse gashes in his thick, purplish brow. "Were not being held against your will in the Terran embassy."

"You got it," Rand answered

"You realize that you alone would be held by my president's express command and returned to Sorrow for trial?"

"I think I would have to claim diplomatic immunity."

"Would you?" GNask gave a rasping laugh. "Which one of these diplomats would have you?"

"I would," both Rindalan and Thomas answered simultaneously.

The Abdrelik let out a roaring guffaw and even his tense general, rrRusk, chuckled a bit.

When GNask had composed himself, he said, "You are most humorous. Do you expect to stand here and have me believe a word of what you've told me? After chasing you from Bay 4A to the jump-off for Chaos?"

"It does not matter if you believe us or not," Rindalan answered. "It matters only if you can prove otherwise, and I doubt you can."

"Ignoring our hailing request to heave to and let us board might prove evidential."

"Do you have any record of what transpired on Sorrow or on Bay 4A or on this vessel?" Rindalan persisted. "If you haven't, I suggest you make repairs to our craft and return us to its decks."

"I doubt you expected this would be easy." GNask heaved himself onto his feet. "Recordings such as you request would be difficult to produce, given the articles of the Compact. However, whether they exist or not, I would be hard-pressed to ignore the fact that you left Bay 4A without authorization and in a tremendous hurry, carrying personnel which the Compact has long desired to question officially. I may not be able to prove what has transpired behind closed doors, but I do have records from the station and I have warrants from a Compact court for the young manling here. I did not know he was with you, but now that I have identified him, I can scarcely ignore the fact. I would be exceedingly remiss to let any of you slip through my fingers."

His eyes narrowed. "There are other possibilities. The freighter is old. You were in full flight. It could have disintegrated under the strain."

Maeva retorted, "You wouldn't dare. Two senior ambassadors and a full attorney!"

He looked at her, curled a lip off a tusk. "Oh, wouldn't I? You should have cooperated with me when you had the chance." He crooked a finger at rrRusk. "Separate the pilot from the others."

Dilarabe reached for Rindalan as if he were an anchor. Rand put himself between the approaching Abdrelik and the Choyan, heedless of the difference in height and bulk. rrRusk shook his head in disbelief.

"Move aside, little being."

"I don't think so."

rrRusk looked around the hold. "You cannot possibly think of evading me."

"I don't have to think about it, I just have to do it."

"Weapon, rrRusk," grumbled GNask.

"They are carrying nothing."

"Not true." Rand spread his hands. "I am all I need."

Maeva, who stood at his back, said, "Don't do this, Rand."

"Move toward the bulkhead," Rand told her without looking around. "Get everybody secured in the life pods in the freighter."

Thomas said suddenly to GNask, "Take me."

The Abdrelik's coal-dark eyes flicked toward him in contempt. "I no longer need you." He moved a hand, a shape filled his fingers, and fired.

Thomas went down with a cry, grabbing at his thigh where crimson blossomed. Rindy bent over and dragged him back to his feet. Blood leaked copiously from between Thomas' fingers.

"I suggest you all sit down. rrRusk, the pilot."

rrRusk moved once more toward Dilarabe.

"There are three of us," Rand suggested to Rindalan. "We risk much." Dilarabe stepped around Rand. "Too much. I will bear this burden."

Chapter 38

He let rrRusk grab him and haul him across the hold.

Rand held himself very still, but Maeva could see the tension in his body, the fury he fought to contain. GNask stepped out of the bay behind his general.

When the bulkhead had sealed behind the Abdreliks, he had only one word for Rindalan.

"Why?"

"Because," Rindy said, slowly and with great fatigue, "he offered. It is our way, Rand. It is part of being a *tezar*." He bent, letting Thomas slump to the deck.

Maeva knelt beside the ambassador. "We've got to get the bleeding stopped." She put pressure just above the wound.

Thomas put his head back, his face pale and sweating. "Whatever happens to me, you've got to get boost down your pilot. After the implant. It's the only thing you can do for him. It'll counter whatever imprinting GNask manages."

Rand swung about almost casually, pointed his fingers at the wound, and blue fire leaped from him. Maeva flinched, but the flame bypassed her and sizzled into Thomas' leg, where the flesh gaped and blood oozed. An intense smell of burning skin filled the air and she gagged with the scent of it. She took her hand away, shaking. "It's—you've closed it."

The discharged flame dissipated, but a fine shimmering continued to envelop Rand. Thomas moaned once or twice, then grew silent. His head lolled back, and she let him sag to the floor.

"It will heal," Rand pronounced, almost absently, as if unaware of what he had done. He stared at the bulkhead beyond which GNask and rrRusk had taken Dilarabe.

Rindy sat, spindly legs suddenly uncertain, watching Rand closely. "What did you do?"

Rand did not answer, but Maeva did. "He's done it before. In the holding cell, he injured himself trying to cross the laser barrier. He was burned, to the bone. I never saw such injuries. His hands, his wrists. . . ."

"I see no scarring."

"Healing began before he was even conscious. Within days I could tell there would be no scars. I've never seen or heard of anything like it."

"Rand." This time Rindalan got his attention. "Did you know you could do such a thing?"

Rand turned and came over to Thomas' limp body. He looked down at the wound which, although it smelled as if it had been cauterized, had sealed as though invisibly stitched. Healing had already started. "I can't—" he stopped. "I had the power worked up to strike rrRusk. It had to go somewhere. I had to discharge it. That seemed the most logical thing to do with it." He spread his hands, looked at them. The aura of power remained about him.

"But did you know—?"

"No, I didn't." He peered more closely at the wound. "It's far from healed."

"And it's equally far from being fatal, which it could have been the way he was losing blood." Maeva wiped her hands on her trouser. The dark navy fabric absorbed the stain. "What do we do now?"

"We wait," answered Rindalan. He had his hand on his chest, and looked slightly pale himself.

"No. We take the chance Dilarabe gave us, and we get out of here." Rand grabbed Thomas by the shoulders. "Help me get him on his feet."

"Those bulkheads are locked," Maeva protested.

"Not to me."

She appealed to Rindy. "Can *bahdur* do this?"

"Not to my knowledge. But then, he is the I'falan. He brings a whole new dimension to the heritage of my planet." Rindy forced a wry smile as he got up, and helped Maeva with Thomas' weight.

The ambassador stirred. He said thickly, "I can walk."

"With help, maybe." Maeva got her shoulder under his. Rand went to the bulkhead. The cloud of motes encircling him spread out like a blanket, covering the locked exit. He put his hands and head to it, listening.

From far away came a muffled scream. It ululated throughout the craft like a primitive howl and carried with it unutterable pain and loss. Rindy, who had Thomas' other arm, stiffened. Maeva felt tears come to her eyes as he murmured, prayerfully, "Dilarabe. God-in-all have mercy on you."

Rand did not seem to notice, his eyes narrowing in concentration. Machinery hummed and the door inched open. The bulkhead widened, slowly, reluctantly, three-quarters of the way.

He turned, strain mirrored on his face. "Go on."

Rindy and Maeva got Thomas through. Maeva leaned back through the doorway. "Come on."

"No. I'm not leaving Dilarabe behind. You take the freighter. Jettison the cargo once you blast free. The bridge is a self-contained unit. Freed of the cargo, you should get max acceleration fairly quickly. We're inside, we can't feel the Abdrelikan cruiser moving, it's a smoother ship, but I'm willing to bet we're pretty close to jumping. GNask wants us near his home base, in his pocket. Get out, hit FTL. Rindy's no pilot, but I think he has what it takes to get you through. Get the hell out of here."

"What about you?"

"I'll be right there with you if I can. Give me fifteen minutes. If not—'" He leaned toward her impulsively, and his lips brushed her face. "Sue me," he said. He pushed her gently away from the exit, took his hands from the heavy metal threshold, and let it snap shut.

GNask watched the *tezar* who had come with them so proudly writhe now in voiceless pain. He took his *tursh* up, speaking soothingly to it, gently licked the fluids off its body where it had surrendered a segment. He settled his symbiont on his shoulder. He had done the work himself, taking satisfaction in his skillful handling of the scalpel. The task had taken a blade, not a laser which might have cauterized fine cellular layers even as it cut.

As he watched Dilarabe flail, he realized what an exceptional individual Nedar had been. What discipline for that pilot to never show the agony he had felt, to never hint to

GNask that the procedure could work, had worked, upon his Choyan physiology.

He said to rrRusk, "We are making history here."

The general stood watchfully.

"Not today, perhaps, but tomorrow or the day after, all that the Choyan have hidden from us will be ours. I have done what cunning and torture have failed to do."

rrRusk lifted his eyes to GNask. "You will face Frnark."

"Eventually. Our president is still in his prime. It would be a shame to depose him now. What I hope to gain by this, my general, is to be his only competitor. To meet him one to one, and not have to claw my way up a heap first. To conserve my strength for the one and only opponent who counts. Delivering him the Choyan empire should give me that edge." He toed Dilarabe's distressed body. "Leave him. The others will try to make a run for it. I need to decide whether we will destroy them or let them destroy themselves."

Silence fell.

Dilarabe raised his head to ascertain if they had gone. His nakedness did not bother him, but he clawed his way along the floor to his discarded uniform, a long and treacherous journey on hands he had broken pounding out his agony on the deck. His blood made the journey slick. One of his elbows had dislocated. He crooned to it, trying to soothe the agony he felt.

The *thing* which was of and from the Abdreliks insinuated itself inside of him. It crawled under his skin with a ropy sliminess he could not avoid. It left a trail of black fire that made his head pound and devoured his *bahdur* until he knew all that was left of him would be emptiness and pain. And then that *thing* would take up residence, and every thought, every memory, all his heritage and all his teaching, would be given over to GNask as though they were precious gems.

As, indeed, they were.

Dilarabe stumbled on a broken tile. It poked into his rib cage, which was already raw and bruised, and if he crawled farther, he thought it would pierce him like a stake. He hugged the deck, put his face to the cold tile, to muffle the sound of his own crying. So easily defeated.

A footfall sounded next to his hand. Dilarabe looked up.

Rand hunched over his flight suit, searching the pockets. Thomas had made them all secrete packets of the drug in their clothes.

"Rand."

The manling pivoted. "Quiet. I'll have this stuff down you in a minute." He patted down the many pockets, finally found what he was looking for, what had drawn Dilarabe crawling across what had felt like a continent.

Dilarabe thought a great deal, but could only say, "Gone."

"Not without you. Here." Gently cradling his head, Rand tore open a packet and poured fuchsia powder into his mouth.

It tasted like bitter fruit, and exploded in his mouth with a static electricity. Dilarabe felt himself jerk once, twice, in reaction to it. His tongue went dry, but he tried to swallow, tried to gather enough spit to dissolve the drug in his mouth.

"They did this to you?"

Dilarabe could not answer. He tried to shake his head in the negative, because he had done it to himself, battering himself as the worm had entered his body, cleaving him from his power, bringing nothing but pain. He tried again to swallow.

A kind of relief pushed its way down his throat. He could feel it muting the black fire of the worm, the symbiont.

"Is it working?" Rand leaned over him anxiously. "I know you're hurt badly, but I've got to get you up. I can't carry you out of here."

"Working," Dilarabe managed. "It's . . . neutralizing."

The medical bay split open. GNask ranged in the gap. "Pity," he said. "I had hoped for a successful experiment. The initial results were so spectacular. Exactly what was it you did for him?"

Rand laid Dilarabe back on the deck. "I came back for him.

"Don't be as stupid as the Compact claims you are. I have the room wired. Did you think I would go and leave my subject unobserved? What did you feed him?"

rrRusk shadowed GNask. He passed the ambassador and kicked the flight suit out of their reach. A second, unopened packet went skidding across the floor toward them. The Abdrelik general picked it up.

"I would guess it was this." He handed it to GNask.

The ambassador turned it over several times with his stubby fingers. "A pharmaceutical. Herbal or synthetic?"

"I wouldn't know." Rand stood his ground. Behind him, noises suggested that Dilarabe was attempting to get up under his own power. "Thomas had it made up for Alexa."

"And how successful was he there?" GNask smiled. "Not very, I wager. She was always more my daughter than his." He looked at Dilarabe, and his cheer fled slightly. "Although there are degrees, I suppose." He opened the packet and took a cautious sniff. "It erases the neural imprinting."

"So I'm told." Rand held himself very still, watching the two Abdreliks, as though he knew instinctively that to run against predators would set off their instinct to pursue.

GNask gave the packet to rrRusk. "Take it."

The general stammered. "W-what?"

"Take it."

"It's off-world. It could be toxic. Your Eminence—"

"Take it!" GNask roared.

Rand braced himself as Dilarabe leaned against him from the rear. He could hear the Choya's labored breathing. But he could also feel the return of the power that had coursed in the tezar's body, for it called to his own. The boost had worked, as intended.

rrRusk hesitated another moment, then lifted the packet to his mouth and ate it whole. He chewed a moment and then gave a hard swallow. GNask took a step back, watching with interest.

Rand watched also. He had no experience with the drug other than what he'd just seen Dilarabe go through. The ingestion seemed to be rapid, the results dramatic. He whispered out of the corner of his mouth, "Be ready."

Dilarabe did not answer, but one of his broken hands tightened slightly on Rand's shoulder in answer.

The Abdrelik stretched his neck and flexed in his uniform jacket as if uncomfortable. He peeled it off. He wore the customary suspendered trousers under it, torso bare. His purplish skin held a sheen of sweat. He blinked rapidly several times. Then he tossed his head up and down. Rand thought of a large bull getting ready to attack.

GNask had taken another step backward. "Tell me, rrRusk, what is it you feel?"

The general shuddered, his skin flapping inordinately, an immense amphibious dog shaking off an unseen enemy. When he swung around to face Rand and Dilarabe, nothing of intelligence glittered in his piggish eyes.

"Shit," said Rand, and lunged to the side, carrying Dilarabe with him.

rrRusk bellowed, charging into the lab.

He lost the pilot as the Abdrelik barreled into him. rrRusk tore Dilarabe in two. The pilot went down with a soft cry as rrRusk launched himself into Rand. Their momentum carried them across the room and Rand slipped away a bare second before they crashed into the wall. The section shattered under the impact, buried Rand in preform shards as rrRusk bellowed again.

The Abdrelik hauled himself to his feet, searching, glaring at the debris. He began to claw it off Rand. In those seconds, Rand knew what it was to be hunted by an Abdrelik, how it must have been on their world in ancient times. The amphibian must have been a terrible king of their world, just as a T-Rex or velociraptor had been of Earth. Hot breath grazed off Rand as drool cascaded from rrRusk's panting mouth.

The Abdrelik lifted the last panel off Rand, grunting as he did so, eyes red with blood lust. He threw the partition to one side and reached to hook Rand for himself.

GNask's weapon popped. rrRusk staggered back. He clutched at his chest. The weapon popped two more times in rapid succession. The general continued to fall back, staring in amazement at the gaping holes which flowered in his chest, at the maroon blood which gushed out. Then he toppled to the floor in a massive crash.

Rand got shakily to his feet. GNask advanced halfway across the lab.

"Too bad. He was a valued employee. He knew too much though, to keep much longer. He had . . . secrets." The ambassador looked at Rand.

"Get out of here while you can."

"You'll destroy us in mid-space."

GNask gave a rumbling laugh. "I might. Might not. That's the chance you'll take. Now go."

Rand looked across at Dilarabe's body, and did not wait for a second invitation.

As the freighter neared jump-off speed, Maeva responded to an alarm on the console.

"Rand, you were right. He's targeting. What are you going to do?"

"Open the channels."

Rindy hailed the Abdrelikan vessel. GNask's unmistakable voice filled the comline.

"Should have run faster, manling, while you had the chance."

"We'll get the speed up when we jettison the cargo," Rand answered. "You don't want to hit us."

"Don't I?"

"No. We're carrying boost. That's the drug you poured down your general's gullet. Now, I think his reaction probably meant more to you than it did to me. I think that's why you killed him, to hide the evidence. But if you want that drug, you'll let us go."

"You're carrying it."

"Yes." Rand gave an indication to Thomas, who limped with a camera and panned a shot of the hold. They'd broken open several of the packaging bins.

"I see," said GNask. "And you will jettison that for me."

"I won't have much chance of making FTL without doing it."

"All right, then. Make your run, little one. I'll be seeing you around the galaxy."

Rand cut communications. He waved everyone back to their slings, and shut the bulkheads and hatches. "Okay. Prepare for jettison. When it goes, we're hitting Chaos almost immediately. Brace yourselves."

The freighter trembled and then the bridge responded with a leap as it broke free. Maeva brought visuals up. They could see the massive body of the cargo ship tumbling free.

Rand said, "NOW!" and jumped them into Chaos.

Maeva remarked, "I wonder what GNask is going to do when the cargo blows."

"He will," Rindy said, "plan a severe and devious revenge."

Rand stood at the helm, feeling the ship melt away, his body become the craft, his eyes the instruments which would pierce Chaos. There was a dizzying moment when he did not know if he were the master, or if the miasma would swallow him whole. His blood rushed through his veins, galaxies tumbled at his feet. Faintly, he could hear the voices of the others.

He knew with dismay that Rindy had been right. He could not get them home. He was not a master of these patterns, he had not the experience. Sweat beaded his forehead as he fought to navigate the ship safely through vicious eddies.

He caught a glimpse of a pattern, began to thread their way toward it. It was not Cho. He did not know where they were.

He had taken them, and lost them.

He could only pray they did not realize it. He could only pray that the webbing he sent them after would be a signpost toward a destination he could reach for them.

Or they would be lost forever.

Chapter 39

Vihtirne woke Jorana none too gently. She tried to swing her legs around, to rouse herself and stand, but her bones felt like jelly. Her head throbbed, and the child within her protested, feeling as if she had swallowed the sun itself.

"Drink this."

Meals had been scant, but water plentiful. Jorana drank it because her body craved filling, craved the drink and the food that it needed to build the babe's body, and because her throat felt like a desert. She grabbed at the glass to drain it dry, and Vihtirne twisted it away.

"Not too much!"

"Not enough."

The older Choya'i laughed. "If you only knew. Can you stand?" She tried to balance Jorana on her feet. The jellified bones gave way. Jorana sagged, feeling as helpless and foolish as some newborn herself.

Vulnerable. This was her enemy who held her. But her thoughts twirled, muddled, as if she'd drunk and been drunk, for days, now. She'd lost track of time, Jorana knew suddenly.

Vihtirne made a noise of disgust and let her drop back onto the pallet. It creaked under her as though it would collapse entirely. "You have to get dressed."

Jorana raised an arm limply, let it fall back to her side. "Am dressed."

"Oh, no. You have an appointment this afternoon, Choya'i. You must be dressed to keep it. And on your feet."

The pleasant muzziness which cocooned Jorana felt dangerous. Inside, deep, something tried to prod at her, to awaken her senses, to kindle her training and wariness. It got a sluggish response, which whirled around and around in her brain as Vihtirne left, slamming the door behind her.

She heard muffled voices, could not make sense of them. ". . . to much *ruhl!* I can't even keep her on her feet!"

"Follow the plan. Everything will work out. If we can't get her up, we'll give her a blast of boost. Now get in there and get her into these things!"

Jorana tried to listen, to concentrate, but nothing made any sense. Her head pounded and she could not hear through its knocking. She sat up on the pallet, balancing her back against the wall of the room. She could not think of anything but hunger.

Hunger and the child.

She folded her hands protectively across her stomach. Hardly showing yet. Just enough to curve her palm. Jorana closed her eyes, letting the whirlpool of confusion drag her down. If only they would feed her and let her sleep, everything would be all right. . . .

K-arack! The sting of a hand across her face jolted her across the pallet. Her teeth clicked and her head snapped on her neck. The blow flared across her skin like a firebrand. Jorana felt a stab of energy answer the attack. She sat up and shook her head, clearing her vision. Vihtirne stood over her.

"Can you dress yourself or shall I have to?"

Jorana looked dazedly at the clothes hanging from Vihtirne's outstretched arm, the moment of clarity already fading. Her captor sighed and bent down. "Never mind. If you feel sick, tell me. I don't want these soiled."

Her face rough and bruised from the blow, she complied listlessly as the other pulled garments one way and tugged them the other. Something about it struck her as funny halfway through the ordeal and she began to giggle and did not stop until Vihtirne finished with an exasperated grunt.

"Go back to sleep if you must, but sleep sitting up."

Sleep sounded like an excellent idea. The burst of laughter had exhausted her. There was only one other thing . . . "Hungry."

"Later. When you're up and on your feet. Then I'll feed you.

Jorana felt herself sag, started to roll over and curl up

on the pallet, when she remembered that she must sit up.
She righted herself and let her head lean back against the
wall. She must also remember something else. An appointment to keep. Somewhere to go. She never heard Vihtirne leave.

*   *   *

Palaton walked the back streets toward the palace center,
just as he had walked them before. This time, however, he
was not alone. Far from it. Strung throughout the quarters
were those who followed Malahki's orders and direction,
an invisible network of Choyan who worked for a common
purpose. He paused as Emperor's Walk became visible.
Crowds filled the park below it, just as they had before,
although more guardsmen than he had ever seen before
restrained them. He started off again, but Dorea had
dropped her hand onto his arm.

He turned to Chirek and the Prophet. She drew him into
a hug. When she released him, she said, "Follow your
heart, Palaton. When all else fails, follow your heart."

Father Chirek added, "We'll meet you when she is free."

He nodded. They left him, blending deftly into the flow
of Choyan who gathered to see the death of an innocent
Choya'i. He could hear them murmuring as they passed,
then gathered him into their inexorable tide.

". . . plays the *lindar* all hours of the day and night.
Howls at the moons."

". . . and no word of the minister. None, none at all!
Some say he's gone to join the renegades from Arizar."

Now that, thought Palaton, was a possibility. He had
been concerned about old Gathon. Could the minister have
left while he still had a life of his own? He quickened his
step to stay with the flow of the crowd, letting them carry
him, be his barrier, his shield, their babble of thought hiding his. They were full of boost, he could smell it on them,
high-priced boost, having given their *bahdur,* so they
thought, to Panshinea's draw.

So full now, to be so empty and aching later.

He kept his jacket collar high. Dorea had braided his
hair for him, twining her fingers deftly through the strands,
pulling it back from his horns and his brow. It was a new

look for him, one that might confuse the enemy, even if only for a moment.

A moment was all it would take. He would strike down Panshinea, once and for all, free Jorana, and be gone in the confusion which Malahki's throngs intended to create. He had only the guard to worry about, and he thought that Jorana would be able to quell them. If not, the crowd might overrun them. They would stampede, he knew, after the last incident, at the slightest sign that Pan's *bahdur* had gone amok again. He could contribute to that.

After Jorana was safe, he and Malahkhi would decide how to confront Vihtirne and Qativar. Congress might be persuaded to do the job they were supposed to, to create a government and stand firm.

"Stay back!"

Palaton stopped in surprise. Caught up in his thoughts, he had not realized that the tide had carried him to the end of the Emperor's Walk. A guard put a shield to his chest and pushed him back beyond an imaginary barrier. He went.

The sun rose high overhead, breaking through a scattering of clouds. Palaton resisted the desire to look at it, just as he did not allow his sight to wander to the area where Traskar had crashed. He kept his eyes on the walk.

Around him, various chronograms began to chime the hour, but he did not need to hear them. A figure wearing black, and wrapped in a black hood and cloak was brought out on the walk and pushed to her knees. Jorana, wearing the colors of the dead.

He could not see her face. She knelt, with her head bowed and the hood drawn over as if she could not stand to face the crowd. If he could not get to her, could not free her, he had hoped for at least one last glimpse of her face.

Perhaps it was better not so. Palaton began to make his way through the gathering, slipping sideways, moving into position. He was jostled a lot, but more than once he was guided, a voice whispering, "Malahki," at his collar, a password, and sending him closer to his destination.

"There he is!" A murmur went up as Panshinea came onto the walkway.

Palaton watched him, slow hatred simmering inside of him. The ravages of his disability showed. He had shrunken down beyond slimness, and his hair had been bound back and red and gold ribbons fastened it, making up for the glint of auburn among the gold it had once carried. He wore a hooded cloak as well, though it was translucent and Palaton could not see his face. His colors of crimson and gold seemed tawdry in the brilliant sunlight. He walked with an escort as if he needed assistance and Palaton felt bitterness burn the back of his throat that this Choya still clung to the throne. He would take them all down with him, all to the pits of the descendancy of a House in full collapse.

Palaton thought he caught a glimpse of Qativar in the escort as they stepped back. The face was gone too soon and he let it go, concentrating on saving Jorana.

A clerk was nudged onto the walk between kneeling Jorana, who had not moved, and Panshinea, who looked as though he had to balance himself to stay upright. Palaton remembered the nervous Choya. He stuttered when stressed.

"We are g–gathered here this day to w-w-witness the execution of J–jorana of Star, for crimes against the throne and s–s–sedition with the enemy, and for the execution of the child she carries, of the House of Flame, an outlawed H–House."

Someone cried out, "Innocent!" only to be shushed. The guard lowered their riot shields and looked out over the gathered Choyan, their faces solemn. Palaton wondered how many of them she had trained, handpicked for their assignments, served with night and day in the years she had been their captain. The clerk scampered out of range of any and all outrages.

He knew that this was the bait for his trap, that Panshinea had but one reason to parade her out here like this, and yet he hesitated to spring that trap. The *bahdur* burned in his gut, a firestorm roaring to be loose, and he thought of striking and killing Pan where he stood.

He could not do that. He sprang at the edge of the walk and somersaulted over, landing on his feet between Jorana and Pan. The guard scattered, dropped to their knees and drew bead on him, but they did not fire.

"You issue your own death warrant, Panshinea of Star," he cried, and his voices rolled out of him, carrying across

the vast parkway. "For abusing the throne of Cho, and
abandoning it. For dosing your people with *ruhl* and for
pandering the drug known as boost and for refusing to
leave your office when you were no longer capable of filling it."

The figure draped in red and gold looked wildly at him,
but did not step back.

"Meet me, Panshinea, for the good of Cho."

Pan did not answer, but raised a hand as if to strike the
first blow.

Palaton took a deep breath, preparing to free the power
which churned inside of him, the power of his newly risen
House. He thought of the emperor he had known, and admired, and served, a Choya who no longer existed and perhaps had never really existed as Palaton had perceived him.
At his back, the kneeling Jorana never said a word.

Upon the Emperor's Walk, he could look out over a sea
of Choyan who seemed to hold their breath as one. He
could not tell Malahki's people from Panshinea's supporters
from the merely curious.

Because we are all one. He readied himself to take Panshinea's strike and send out one of his own, but he noted
that the guardsmen were doing nothing.

He wore bodyshielding, was prepared to take a hit or
two as they defended their emperor, but they seemed to
have dropped into the same wrinkle in time that he had,
remaining motionless. Jorana would not have liked that.
She had trained them to be loyal, regardless. They had
protected him as heir, Pan before that, and now Pan
returned.

And they waited, hesitant, holding back.

Why?

He could feel a drawing of power about Panshinea, oddly
coalescing outside of him, an aura about the red and gold,
and knew that he must do what he must do.

Follow your heart, Palaton.

But his heart did not want him to strike at the figure
who stood, now swirling in crimson and gold, whose aura
had begun to blaze as bright as the sun above it. And behind him, why did not Jorana react, cry out, welcome him?
Did they have her drugged?

Palaton pivoted, and sent his *bahdur* striking into the

figure in black, the craven imposter who knelt on the Emperor's Walk as he had been told to do, told that Palaton would strike the emperor's colors. Pan let out a cry of pain and betrayal, throwing off the ebony hood, rising up and lifting his *bahdur* against Palaton.

It stank of boost. Palaton could smell it clearly now, even as Pan staggered on the walk. Palaton struck again, with *bahdur* the like of which had not been seen or experienced on Cho for centuries, because it killed as well as healed.

Pan dropped and lay quite still.

Jorana managed to throw off her stifling cloak, and dropped to her own knees. Palaton saw a movement behind her, but did not get to her in time. He threw a curtain of power out, between her and the guard. His bodyshielding took a shot which rocked him, but did not pierce the armor.

Qativar drew his weapon. He did not waste time with *bahdur*. Enforcer fire blazed into the walkway, skimming past Jorana, missing on the first shot.

Instinctively, she rolled. The second shot caught a corner of a guard's shield, and was deflected. It sprayed into the screaming onlookers.

Then, as Palaton reached Jorana to defend her, he saw the big, sable-haired Choya rearing up behind Qativar.

Malahki caught him by the neck and twisted. The resulting snap cracked through the air. Qativar went limp in Malahki's arms. Malahki held him for but a second, then cried, "No more!" He threw the body over the walkway where the frightened crowd, running from enforcer fire, trampled it into ribbons in the ground.

Jorana began to sob. Palaton drew her up. He took the ribbons from her hair, releasing its bronze glory, wondering how he could have mistaken her for Panshinea.

Over her shoulder, he saw Vihtirne. She stepped back into a brace of guardsmen, ordering them briskly about her. She put her hands up, palms out, and then disappeared into the disorder.

"Palaton."

Her tears wet his neck. He did not think he had ever seen her cry before. He held her back a little, and touched her face.

"What is this?"

"Your damn baby," she sobbed. "I cry about everything." She put her head back on his shoulder. "Thank God for adrenaline. I can think for the first time in days."

"Nearly too late." Palaton held her tightly, thinking how close he had come to doing what Qativar had wanted him to do . . . eliminating Jorana, thinking her to be Panshinea, and then destroying himself when faced with the truth. As for Pan . . . he would never have been allowed by Qativar to live much longer. Palaton did not want to think how close he had come to doing the unthinkable.

Malahki reached him. He put his hand on Jorana's hair, tilting her head back. "Daughter."

"I'm all right," she answered. "Finally."

He nodded.

Palaton and he traded looks. He started to say something, but Father Chirek and Dorea appeared at the side of the walk. Instead, he leaned down and gave them a hand up. Dorea held his hand a moment longer than necessary before dropping it.

"It is not over."

"No. Not until we have boost out of our system, and *ruhl* banned. And I must find Rand."

Dorea looked away from him. "I'm sorry. He is lost. My seeing. . . ."

Palaton stood, stunned, unwilling to accept any kind of defeat in that moment. "No."

"He took a ship into Chaos. He has the *bahdur,* Palaton . . . but he has no guide."

"No."

Jorana said, "You were always his guide."

He looked down at her. She smiled. "You are a Flame. Burn for him. Be the beacon that draws him home to Cho. He was meant to be here, to stand with us."

And Palaton knew what she was trying to tell him, what Rand had been trying to tell him. Here was a partnership which could cleanse *bahdur,* without drugs, without harm. Different perhaps than any partnership their ancestors could have imagined, but one which could withstand the House of Flame, could temper it.

He loosened his embrace on her and stood back. He spread his arms. He threw back his head, felt his hair come loose from the Prophet's bindings, wafting in a comet stream of energy motes. He *burned* as only he could, blue flame enveloping him. He was a *tezar,* a pilot, and no pathway of the heavens could elude him, not even this one, of the purest spirit, the hottest flame.

Rand stood at the helm, his eyes stinging, his heart pounding. Somehow his *bahdur* protected them all from the ills of flying through Chaos, yet now Rindalan and Thomas had lapsed into unconsciousness, the air in the tiny pod thinning, their time running out. It would scarcely matter if he knew where to go, for then he would still have had ample time to bring them to safety, but he had not been able to find their way. Maeva took his hand, her skin chilled in his, her fingers incredibly slender and delicate.

"After all this," she said, "I want you to know I could love you."

He dared not look at her, but something in his heart shifted a little. "I could, too," he whispered back, his throat hoarse. He had been talking, and she listening.

And then he saw. Arcing like a bridge through Chaos, built out of pure *bahdur,* calling to him. Calling him home. Bringing a voice out of Flame to him, a voice so alien he could never forget it, the twin of his spirit, Palaton, navigator and master of the Chaos of the soul. He stood, a blue star on the horizon, a blazing, unmistakable beacon.

Rand let out a shout of joy, and steered toward home.